MW01115759

WALK *of* SHAME

NEW YORK TIMES AND *USA TODAY* BESTSELLING AUTHOR

VICTORIA ASHLEY

Copyright

Walk of Shame: The Complete Series
Copyright © 2019 Victoria Ashley

All rights reserved. Without limiting the rights under copyright reserved above, no part of this publication may be reproduced, stored in or introduced into a retrieval system, or transmitted, in any form, or by any means such as electronic, mechanical, photocopying, recording, or otherwise without the prior written permission of the author of this book.

This is a work of fiction. Names, characters, places, brands, media, and incidents are either the product of the author's imagination or are used fictitiously. The author acknowledges the trademarked status and trademark owners of various products referenced in this work of fiction, which have been used without permission. The publication/use of these trademarks is not authorized, associated with, or sponsored by the trademark owners.

Cover by Jay Aheer
Edited by Charisse Spiers
Edited by Virginia Tesi Carey
Formatted by N. E. Henderson

SLADE

WALK OF SHAME : BOOK 1

CHAPTER ONE

SLADE

IT'S DARK.

I love it with the lights off. She insisted on teasing me this way. My arms are tied behind me, my naked body bound to a chair. Goose bumps prickle my flesh as she softly blows on my hard cock, almost breaking my willpower. Her lips are so close, yet not close enough. I insist on teasing *her* this way.

"Na ah. Not yet."

She tilts her head up, her blonde hair cascading over her shoulders as her eyes lock with mine. They're intense. Desperate even. She's silently begging me with her eyes, asking me to let her touch me already. I'm used to this. She needs to learn that when you're in my house we play by my rules. "Slade," she moans. "Come on already."

"Look down." She tilts her head back down and runs her tongue over her lips as she eagerly looks at my cock, no doubt imagining what it would taste like in her mouth. "That's it. Don't move."

I lift my hips, bringing the tip of my head to brush her lips. "You want me in your mouth?"

She nods and lets out a sound between a moan and a growl. Damn, it's such a turn on.

"How bad do you want it? I want to fucking hear it."

Her nails dig into my thighs as she growls in aggravation. "More than anything. I want it, so just give it to me. You already know how bad I want it. Every girl does."

A deep laugh rumbles in my throat as she scratches her nails down my legs in an attempt to hurt me. What she doesn't realize is that I welcome the pain. I get off on it.

"Is that all you got?" I tease. "If you want my cock, you're going to have to do better than that."

She looks angry now. Determined. Standing up, she points a finger in my chest. "You're the one tied up. This is supposed to be my game. Why do *you* have to torture me and make me wait?"

Biting my bottom lip, I nod for her to move closer to me. When she gets close to my face, I slide my tongue out and run it over her lips, causing her to tremble as I taste her. "Show me how much you want me."

Straddling me, she screams and slaps me hard across the face before yanking my head back by my hair. If I could get any harder, I would. I love it rough.

"Now, that's what I'm talking about." I press my stiff cock against her ass, showing her just how turned on I am. Then I look her in the eye. "Show me what you can do with your mouth. First impression is always the most important."

A mischievous smile spreads across her face as she slides her way off my lap and down between my legs. Gripping my thighs in her hands, she runs her tongue over the tip of my dick before suctioning it into her mouth. It hits the back of her throat, causing her to gag. She doesn't care. She just shoves it deeper, desperate for my taste.

I moan as she swirls her tongue around my shaft while sucking at the same time. It feels fucking fantastic. "I told you it was worth the wait. Just wait until I get inside you. It feels better than it tastes."

She pulls back and licks her lips. "Then why don't you show me. I've never been so wet." She stands up and bends over in front of me, exposing her wet lips. She smiles as she runs her fingers over the folds as if she's teasing me. "You like that?" she asks seductively, tempting me. "You want this tight little pussy all for yourself, you greedy little bastard?"

I nod, playing into her little game. She seems to think she's in charge. Fuck that.

"Well, come and get it." She inserts her fingers into her mouth and sucks them clean, before shoving them into her entrance, fucking me with her eyes. Her ass moves up and down in perfect rhythm as she moans. "I'm waiting." She shoves her fingers deeper. "I want to see those muscles flexing as you ram into me. I want you to–"

Well, you won't be waiting for long.

Breaking free from my restraints, I stand up, grab her hips and flip her around before slamming her back up against the wall. "What were you saying?" I growl into her ear.

I grip both of her ass cheeks and lift her as she wraps her legs around my waist, squeezing. "I'm not sure you can handle what I have to offer." I grip her face in my hand before leaning in and biting her bottom lip, roughly tugging. "You're finally about to get what you've wanted. I just hope you don't have shit to do for the next few days because this might get a little rough. Last chance to make your escape, because once I start there's no stopping until you're screaming my name loud." I search her eyes waiting to see if she's changed her mind; there's nothing but raw heat and lust. She still wants it. She's brave. So, she'll get it. I lift an eyebrow. "Okay, then."

I take wide strides across the room to my king-sized bed and toss her atop the mattress. Before she can blink, I am between her thighs, spreading them wide for me. I run my tongue up her smooth flesh, stopping at the intersection of her thighs and clean-shaven pussy. "You ready for me to make you come without even touching you?"

I begin blowing my cool breath across her swollen, wet pussy. She thrusts her hips up, no doubt wanting more and just as I'm about to show her my skills, there's a knock at the door.

Gritting my teeth, I shake my head and look toward the door. "Give me a sec." I step down from the bed and motion for Lex to cover up. When she's done, I call for Cale to come in. "Okay, man."

The door opens right as I'm reaching for my pack of cigarettes and switching the light on. My dick is still standing at full alert, but I couldn't care less. This shithead interrupted my night. If he doesn't like seeing my dick hard, then he should have known better than to come up to my room in the middle of the night.

Stepping into my room, Cale takes notice of my hard on and quickly reaches for the nearest item of clothing and tosses it on my dick. I look down to see a shirt hanging from it. I shake it off. “A little warning next time, motherfucker. I’m tired of witnessing that shit.”

Lighting my cigarette, I laugh and take a drag. “Jealous, prick?”

Ignoring me, he walks past me when he sets eyes on Lex. She’s been coming to the club for a while now and she’s sexy as hell. All the guys have been trying to get with her, but she’s wanted nothing but my cock this whole time. He raises his eyebrows and slides onto the foot of my bed. “Damn, Lex. You get sexier every time I see you.”

Gripping the sheet tighter against her body, Lex growls and kicks Cale off the bed. “Go fuck off, Cale. I don’t want your dick.”

Jumping up with a quickness, Cale reaches for my jeans and tosses them to me. “I don’t want to fuck you, Lex. I want to pleasure you. This dick is special.” He nods toward me. “Unlike Slade’s.”

“Fuck you, Cale. What the hell do you want?”

He turns to me after smirking at Lex. “The club just called. We gotta go.”

“It’s not my night to work, man. Isn’t Hemy working?” I take a long drag of my cigarette, letting the harsh smoke fill my lungs as I close my eyes. I really need to release this tension. I will fuck her in front of him if I have to. It wouldn’t be the first time I’ve fucked in front of an audience. “I’m a little busy right now.” I dangle Lex’s thong from my finger. “If you can’t tell.”

Not getting where I’m going with this, Cale pulls out his phone and starts typing something in it. “We need to go now. There’s a bachelorette party and Hemy is getting eaten alive right now.”

“Well, then I guess we better get started.” I put out the cigarette, push past Cale and slide under the sheet. I reach for the condom on the nightstand and rip the wrapper open with my teeth. “This is going to have to be a quick one,” I mumble before spitting the wrapper out and rolling the condom over my erection.

Lex looks at me questionably and nods to Cale. “You’re going to have sex with me while he watches?”

I smirk as I flip her over and shove her head down into the mattress. “If he doesn’t get out of my room, then yes, I’m going to fuck you while he watches." I peek over my shoulder at Cale, and he lifts an eyebrow, his interest now piqued. "You've got three seconds and the counting started two seconds ago."

Pointing to Lex, he starts walking backward while chewing his bottom lip. "As much as I'd love to watch you come, I'm out. This dude gets too wild, and I'll probably hurt myself just watching." Picking my wallet up from my dresser, he tosses it at my head, but misses. "Hurry your ass up. I'm changing right now and then we need to go."

Lex moans from below me as I grip her hips, pull her to me and slide inside her. She's extra wet for me, making it easy to give her a good quick fuck. "You weren't lying when you said you were craving this cock. Fuck, you're wet."

"Dude," Cale complains from a distance; although, I can still feel his eyes watching us.

"Your three seconds were up." I thrust my hips, gripping her hair in both my hands. "Fucking shit. I'll be out in a minute."

"Leave, Cale!" Lex moans while gripping the sheet. "Holy shit, Slade. You feel even better than what I've been told. So thick and oh shit . . . it's so deep."

"Damn, that's hot."

"Out!" Lex screams.

"I'm out. I'm out." Cale backs his way out, shutting the door behind him. The truth is, if it weren't for Lex kicking him out, I couldn't care less if he stayed and watched. I'm not ashamed.

Knowing I don't have a lot of time, I need to get this chick off fast. That's my rule and I don't have many. She gets off, then I get off. There is no stopping in between for me. Once I start, this is a done deal.

I can feel her wetness thickening. "You've gotten wetter. You like him watching, huh?" I yank her head back and run my tongue over her neck before whispering, "I would've let him stay; let him watch me as I fuck you. Does that turn you on?"

Before she can say anything else, I push her head back down into the mattress and slam into her while rubbing my thumb over her swollen clit.

Her hands grip the sheets as she screams out and bites down on her arm, trying to silence her orgasm.

Slapping her ass, I ball my fist in her hair and gently pull it back, so her back is pressed against my chest. “Don’t hold back. I want to hear it. Got it?” She shakes her head so I thrust into her as deep as I can go. “Show me how it feels.”

Screaming, she reaches back and grabs my hair, yanking it to the side. This makes me fuck her even harder. “Keep going! Slade, don’t stop.”

Reaching around, I grab her breast in one hand squeezing roughly and bite into her shoulder, rubbing my finger of the opposite hand faster over her slick clit. Her body starts to tremble beneath me as she clamps down hard on my cock. “Oh, shit. Stop, I can’t take it. It feels so good, Slade.”

I grip her hips and brush my lips over her ear. “You want me to stop?” I pull out slowly, teasing her. “You don’t want this cock filling your pussy?” I shove it back in, causing her head to bang into the wall. “Huh, do you want me to stop?”

She shakes her head. “No, don’t stop.”

“That’s what I thought.” I push her completely flat on her stomach, holding my body weight with one arm as I grip the back of her neck and fuck her with all my strength. I want her to remember this because it’s the only time she’ll be getting my cock and we both know it. It’s how I work.

She’s squirming below me, shaking as if she’s in the middle of another orgasm. “Slade! Oh shit!”

A few thrusts later and I’m ready to blow my load. Pulling out, I bite her ass and stroke my cock as I come.

The relief gives me a high; a fucking drug that I can’t get enough of. Nothing else makes me feel this way. Actually, nothing else makes me feel. This is it for me.

CHAPTER TWO

SLADE

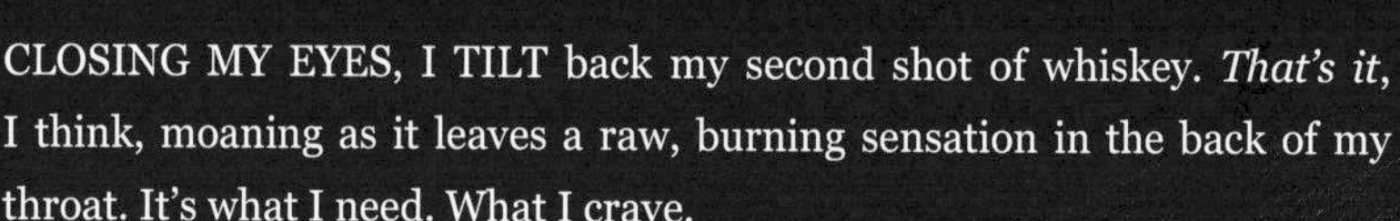

CLOSING MY EYES, I TILT back my second shot of whiskey. *That's it*, I think, moaning as it leaves a raw, burning sensation in the back of my throat. It's what I need. What I crave.

After rushing Lex out of my room and listening to Cale ramble on about one of his old friends crashing with us for the next week, I need this rush; the alcohol pumping through my veins, weakening my demons. Hell, I might even go for another one just for the numbness.

Holding up my empty shot glass, I nod at Sarah to come my way. She instantly drops what she's doing to come to me. "Give me another one."

Snatching my empty glass away, she smiles and nods over to Cale and Hemy working their shit on the girls in the back corner. "Shouldn't you be over there showing them how it's done?" She laughs while pulling out a bottle of Jack and filling a new shot glass. "They're both looking a little tired and worn down. You know how bachelorettes are; last night of freedom and all."

I turn around in my stool and look at the two idiots. Cale is standing on a couch grinding his dick in some girl's face while wiping sweat from his forehead. Hemy has some girl on the floor, rolling his body above hers, but he's moving in a rhythm slower than the music.

Tired? How the hell can they . . .

"Yeah, well give me another shot and then I'll show them what's up."

"I'm sure you will, Slade. Keep slamming these back and I might be showing you what's up later." She pushes the shot of whiskey across the bar, and I grab it. "Go ahead. Drink up." She winks.

Smirking, I hold the glass to my lips. She already knows how I work. "We've already had our night, Sarah." I tilt the glass back and run my tongue over my lips, slowly, just to remind her of how I pleasured her. This causes her to swallow hard and her breathing to pick up. "It was hot as fuck too." I slide the glass forward and stand up. "But it goes against my rules."

Her eyes linger down to the very noticeable bulge in my jeans. She smiles while running her finger over the empty glass. "Good to know I can at least still get you hard."

I toss down a twenty and start backing away. "Baby, you get every man hard." I point to the awkward looking guy that has been staring at her since I sat at the bar. "Especially that dude."

She glances at the scrawny dude with glasses and forces a smile. He smiles back and leans over the bar, awaiting conversation. "I so hate you, Slade," she growls, and I love it. Growling turns me on.

"That's all right. I'm used to it."

She tosses a straw at me, and I knock it away with my hand before turning around and making my way over to the bachelorette party.

The girls are tossing back drinks, some of them standing on tables while a few of them are watching from afar. Those are usually the married ones, the good girls. That's all right though, because I don't need to touch them to pleasure them. They'll still get off.

As I'm about to show my boys up, to my right, I notice two girls dancing and minding their own business. Instantly, my focus goes to the curvy body that is swaying back and forth, drawing my dick to instant attention.

Skintight blue jeans mold to her every curve, making me imagine what it would be like to run my tongue over that tight little ass and to taste every inch of her.

Letting my dick do the talking, I walk up to the dance floor, grab the drink out of her hand and set it down on the table beside me.

She looks pissed off, but that's all right. Pissed is sexy as hell on her. It makes me want her more. Her eyes stray from the table I just set her glass on and land on my stomach. Then my chest. Then, slowly, up to my face. She swallows and a look of lust flashes in her eyes. She wants me and I haven't even done anything yet.

Holy fuck. She is beautiful.

My eyes trail from her long blonde hair that stops just below her breasts up to her red pouty lips. I want to suck those between my lips. She's looking at me through long, thick lashes and even in the dimmed lighting, I can see that she has two different colored eyes. I can't make out the colors, but I can see the shade difference.

"Umm . . ." She smiles awkwardly and runs her hand through her hair. "Can I help you with something? We kind of have a private party going on here."

Taking a step closer, I lean in and brush my lips over her ear. "Yeah, I can help you with something," I whisper. "I can help you with a lot of things."

Her breathing picks up and I already know that I have her. It's that simple. "I'm sorry, but I don't even know you." She takes a step back, but her eyes trail down my body before coming back up to meet my face. She looks nervous. I love that. I can teach her a few things. "And I was drinking that."

I watch her with a smirk as she reaches for her drink and pretends to give me a dirty glare. It's not working on me though. I already know her body language and she's already let it slip that I do something to her. "I can give you something better than that."

Her tiny nostrils flare as her eyes rake back down my body, stopping on my crotch. If that's what she wants, then I'll give it to her. "Sorry, but I'm not interested. I'm just here for a friend's party."

She likes games. Good thing, because I like them too.

Closing the distance between our bodies, I cup her cheek in my hand. I bring my lips close to hers while looking her in the eyes. Her breath hitches as I press my body against hers and bring my gaze down to meet her lips.

"Are you sure about that?"

Her lips begin to move as if she's about to respond and I have the sudden urge to suck them into my mouth. She's breathing heavily and I can feel the heat radiating from between her thighs that are pressed against my leg while I rub my thumb over her cheekbone.

I lean in closer until my bottom lip brushes hers. "You're beautiful."

She takes in a quick burst of air and takes a step back. "That's not going to work on me. Sorry."

"Slade!" a drunken female shrieks from behind me.

Shit. I hate shriekers.

Exhaling, I turn my head, but keep my eyes glued to the beautiful blonde in front of me. For some reason, I don't want to take my eyes away.

Those lips. Fuck me, I want to fuck them. I want them wrapped around my cock.

"About time you got here." A dark-haired woman with huge breasts bounces in front of me and grabs my hand, pulling me away from the beauty in front of me. I see blondie's eyes glance down at my hand, but she quickly turns her head away and clears her throat as if embarrassed. "My favorite piece of eye candy is here." She throws her arms up and starts screaming while pulling me away. "Look everyone. It's Slade," she slurs.

Smiling to blondie as she watches me, I mouth, "You're mine later."

Her lips part, before she swallows. I have her thinking about it. It's written all over her face. Her friend starts nudging her in the side until finally she pulls her eyes away from me and smiles nervously at her friend.

Shit, I've gotta have her. I won't stop until I do.

Spinning on my heel, I pick the brunette up by her hips and sit her down on the chair in front of us. She spreads wide for me and presses her hands against my chest as I step between her legs and slowly grind my hips to the music.

Placing one hand behind my head, I grip her neck with my other as I close the space between our bodies, grinding my hips in a slow, seductive movement as if I'm slowly fucking her.

She moans from beneath me as I let her hands explore my chest and abs. The women here like to touch, and I like to give them what they want. It's my job to please them and I'm damn good at it.

"Take it off!" a few girls start screaming.

"Let us see your body. Come on!"

Pulling the brunette's chin up, I look her in the eyes as I slowly pull my shirt over my head and toss it down beside me. Most women love it when I make them feel like I'm stripping just for them. It makes them feel special.

She bites her bottom lip as her hands go straight for the muscles leading down to my cock. The girls can never get enough of it; of both.

As much as I'm enjoying getting these women off, there's one woman in particular I want to get off and I'll be damned if I'm going to let her leave here unsatisfied.

CHAPTER THREE

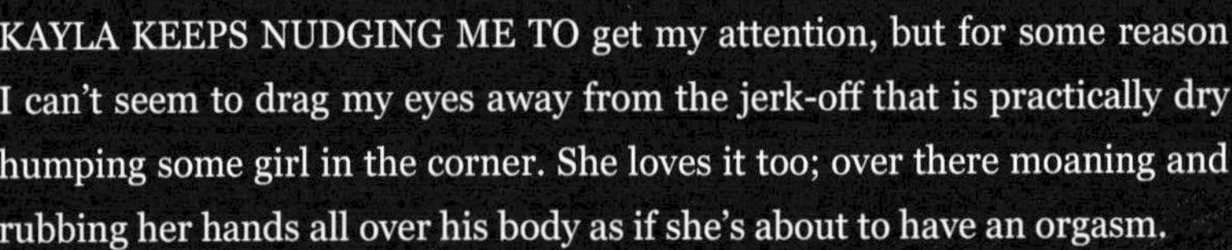

ASPEN

KAYLA KEEPS NUDGING ME TO get my attention, but for some reason I can't seem to drag my eyes away from the jerk-off that is practically dry humping some girl in the corner. She loves it too; over there moaning and rubbing her hands all over his body as if she's about to have an orgasm.

A stripper? I shake my head. *A sexy as hell one too. Who the hell does he think he is getting that close to me?*

The bad part of it is, I think he may just be the sexiest man I have ever laid eyes on. Messy black hair that falls over his deep blue eyes and the perfect five o'clock shadow that surrounds a set of full lips. Not to mention a body of pure muscle that you could easily see through that firm fitting white T-shirt he had on. Now, it's off and . . . *crap*. He has me so worked up, I can barely breathe. *That's fucked up*.

Our lips were so close I could almost taste him. For some stupid reason, I had the urge to run my tongue over those full lips. They just looked so soft and inviting; calling me to feel them against mine.

"Um . . . Aspen. Hello. Am I talking to myself? Snap out of it."

I suck in a deep breath and pull my eyes away from Mr. Sex himself. "What? I'm listening." I bring my eyes up to meet hers, but they quickly stray back over to *him* as I pretend to pay attention to her.

Brushing her burgundy locks over her shoulder, she rolls her eyes at me and grabs my hand. "Come on. Let's just get closer so you can drool over sexy stripper boy up close. There's nothing to be ashamed of. Stop being so shy. We're here to have fun."

I huff and pull my hand out of her grip. There's no way I'm going over there and giving him the pleasure of seeing me watching him. I'm only here because Paige is getting married. Hell, I'm not even watching *Cale* and I've known him for years.

"I'm good, Kayla. I'm not getting in the middle of that orgasm fest. It's pathetic." I hold my drink up and grin. "This is all the pleasure I need while I'm here. Simple as that." I take a huge gulp as my eyes once again land on him and *oh God, that ass.*

His jeans are now hanging halfway down his ass, showing his muscular ass cheeks through his white boxer briefs. The busty woman in front of him is desperately tugging on the front of his jeans, working on pulling them down his body. I don't blame her. I want to take them off with my teeth. That's a new desire for me.

Placing his hands behind her head, he pulls her face down by his crotch as he starts grinding his hips up and down in perfect rhythm to the song playing. It's a slow, seductive song that makes me think about sex. Yup, I'm definitely thinking about sex now.

Just as I think he's about to actually let this woman publicly suck his dick or something, he grips her by the hips and pulls her up to her feet. Slowly, he makes his way behind her and his eyes land on me and they stay there, locked with mine.

What the . . . why? Stop looking at me.

I tug on the collar of my white blouse and without meaning to I start fanning myself off. He smiles at this, knowing exactly what he's doing to me. He's doing this on purpose.

Cocky jerk.

Bending the girl over, he grips her hair in one hand and pulls her neck back while grinding his hips on her ass. His eyes bore into mine as he shakes himself out of his jeans and lets all his sexiness consume us. Yes, he is damn sexy and he knows it. That just pisses me off more. His legs are thick and muscular; covered with random tattoos and every muscle in his body is well sculpted.

Now that he's facing me it's easy to see his defined chest and abs flexing as he moves with the music. The muscles leading down to his briefs are staring at me, flexing with each sway of his hips; calling out to be touched. And holy hell do I want to touch.

His body is pure perfection. Plus, he has random tattoos inked across his chest, sides, lower stomach, and arms as well. Hell, he has tattoos all over and it makes him even hotter. They glisten as perspiration forms on his skin.

He's staring at me, while practically having sex with this girl with his clothes on. Still, I'm standing here watching as if it were me.

What is wrong with me?

I'm sweating now and there's a tingling sensation between my thighs as he bites his bottom lip and starts thrusting hard and deep while his eyes devour me. Well, at least I imagine it would be deep. I bet it would feel so good to have him inside you.

He must notice me sweating because he laughs a little and steps away from the girl that is still bent over with her ass in the air. Ignoring all the girls screaming for him, he starts walking with meaning. With each step, he gets closer and closer to me.

My body is heating just from his presence and my breathing picks up. I hate my body right now.

His eyes are intense; telling me he wants me as his. A part of me almost wants to give in just from that look alone.

My eyes slowly leave his eyes, searching my way down his muscular body and landing right on his hard dick.

Oh. My. God.

You can see everything through his tight briefs. The thickness of his dick and even the shape of its head. The whole package. He's so . . . hard.

Stopping in front of me, he smirks and tilts his head down toward his cock. My eyes are betraying me. They won't move away. "You know, it's against the rules, but I would let you touch it if you wanted to."

Shaking my head, I pull my eyes away and slam back the rest of my drink. This is my third one and I'm a lightweight, probably not a good thing. I take a step back as he takes a step closer. Clearing my throat, I ask, "Touch what?"

Reaching out, he grabs my hand and places it on the V of muscles that lead down to his briefs, slowly sliding it down his sweaty, slick body. "My cock," he whispers.

My body clenches from his words and I hate it. Yanking my hand away, I grab Kayla by the arm and slam my empty glass down onto the table beside me. I need to get out of here. "Thanks for the offer, playboy, but I'm here to meet a friend and like I said, I'm not interested."

Smirking, he takes a step back as Cale slaps him on the shoulder. "Dude, back away from our temporary roommate. You're freaking Aspen out."

Well, shit...

I see the smile in his eyes as if he's got me right where he wants me now and he looks like a man that always gets what he wants. Running his tongue over his bottom lip, he backs away slowly, keeping his eyes on me the whole time, until disappearing back into his crowd of fan girls.

Cale gives me a quick hug and apologizes. "Sorry about him. Just ignore him and you'll be fine." He starts backing away and smiles. "We'll catch up later, I promise."

"All right, pretty boy," I call out. "Better hurry and get back to your crazy fan girls."

Cale is the definition of pretty. Short blond hair, striking green eyes, and the sweetest dimpled smile you'll ever see. I will never understand why my sister has never hooked up with him.

Turning to Kayla, I let out a deep breath and instantly turn red with embarrassment as she starts laughing. "What!" I yell.

She smirks and pretends like she's giving a blow job.

"Stop that! You dirty bitch." I push her shoulder and she laughs. "I need another drink."

She turns toward Slade, dancing his dick off in the middle of some girls. "I would need a drink after that too. Holy shit! That is one fine piece of ass." She starts pulling me toward the bar. "Plus, you need to get your mind off a certain someone," she says to remind me. "Relax a little."

"Yeah," I breathe. "Probably so. I'm not going to let it bring me down this week."

When we reach the bar, the pretty bartender smiles at me and shakes her head.

Wondering if she's laughing at me for some reason, I take a seat on the stool in front of me and give her a hard look. Slade has me all kinds of feisty at the moment and I can't believe he's Cale's roommate. Not cool at all. "What?" I narrow my eyes at her as she reaches for an empty glass.

Scooping up some ice, she looks over my shoulder and laughs again. "Honey, no one turns Slade down. Are you insane? That is one piece of ass that you don't want to miss out on. Trust me."

Trying my best not to look behind me, I fail. I should kick my own ass. I glance over my shoulder to see Slade staring at me while using his shirt to wipe the sweat off his chest. He slowly moves it down his body as if teasing me.

I growl under my breath and ignore what she just said. Obviously, he's a manwhore. "Just give me another drink, please. Make it strong."

The bartender tilts her head and goes about her business. Thank goodness because I really don't want to think about that half naked, sexy asshole anymore.

"Right on," Kayla says happily. "It's a good thing I'm driving your ass around."

"Probably a very good thing right now," I say softly, trying to get my thoughts in check.

After setting eyes on the sexiest asshole I have ever seen, I have a feeling I'm going to need help if I'm going to be in the same house with *him* for the next week.

CHAPTER FOUR

SLADE

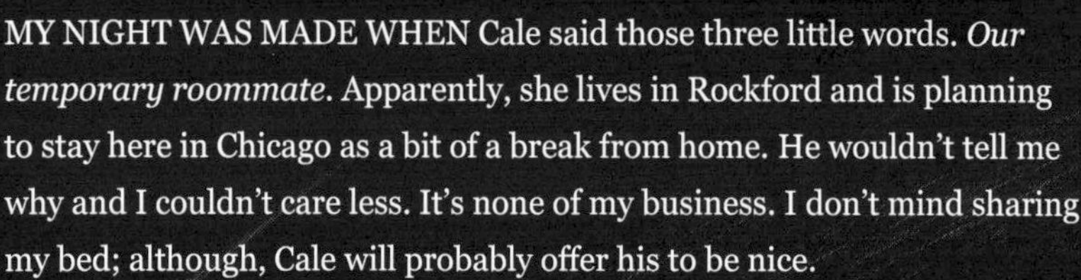

MY NIGHT WAS MADE WHEN Cale said those three little words. *Our temporary roommate.* Apparently, she lives in Rockford and is planning to stay here in Chicago as a bit of a break from home. He wouldn't tell me why and I couldn't care less. It's none of my business. I don't mind sharing my bed; although, Cale will probably offer his to be nice.

That damn pussy.

The look on Aspen's face when she realized she'll be spending the next week in the same house as me was priceless; a dead giveaway that she finds me tempting.

Pushing my cock down, I adjust my jeans and moan.

"Dude, what the shit!" Cale looks over from the driver's side and scowls. "Don't tell me you're thinking about fucking her."

Playing stupid, I cross my hands behind my head and laugh. Of course, I'm thinking about fucking her. "Who?"

Cale lets out a long huff and pulls into the driveway. "Aspen, you dipshit. She doesn't need you messing with her right now. She's dealing with some personal shit."

I push the car door open and step out before slamming it behind me. When Cale catches up to me, I laugh and lean against the door as a little red Chrysler Sebring pulls up behind my truck. Since I've had a few shots, I made Cale drive us home. I never drive after I've had a few drinks. One of my small lists of rules I never break. They were created for my own good.

"Every girl needs me messing with her. Especially that one. I'll make her forget about *everything*."

I nod toward Aspen as she steps out of the car looking sexy as shit. You don't just want this woman for dessert. You want her for breakfast, lunch, and dinner too. Any average guy would. Good thing I'm not your average guy. One night is all I need.

ASPEN

OH HELL. WOULD SOMEONE PLEASE make him stop looking at me like that? He's staring at me, burning his eyes into my body, like he's about to rip my clothes off and pound me against a wall somewhere. It's so distracting.

Taking a deep breath, I close the car door behind me, wave to Kayla and start walking to the porch of Cale's two-bedroom home. I've been here before as a guest, but it was back before Cale had a roommate. I have known Cale for years because he and my sister were best friends growing up. He's a good guy and I love him like a brother. I was excited to come here, but now . . . I'm not so sure. Maybe it was a bad idea. Just another thing to add to the list of shitty choices I've made lately.

Before I can even step onto the porch, Slade's gaze burns into mine. His eyes are so dark and broody. Is everything about this guy so intense?

I bet sex is.

Mentally slapping myself, I shake off the thought and walk over to Cale. He wraps his arms around me and squeezes me in his usual hug. "Oh man. I've missed you," I say. "Thanks for letting me crash here. You have no idea how much you are helping me out. I really needed to get away."

Shaking me roughly, he lets go and kisses my forehead. "I missed you too, gorgeous. My house is yours whenever you need it. No need to even ask. You know that."

When I turn back to Slade he's looking me up and down, branding me into the portals of his memory. He's undressing me with his eyes like he's formulating a plan of attack in his mind; the ultimate predator. I feel it; everywhere. He knows it too. He's a pro at this game.

Now that we're in the lighting of the porch, I can see a scar on his right cheekbone. He catches me staring and his jaw tightens before turning and opening the door to let us in.

I follow behind Cale, in a hurry to get this night over with. I'm so tired I can barely keep my eyes open. I want to ask where I'm sleeping, but I'm afraid Slade might have too much fun with that.

I take a glance around the house to see it looks the same as before: Black furniture, black curtains, huge TV with surround sound. Pretty much everything manly. This place really needs a woman's touch; just not mine.

"So . . ." I lift my eyebrows at Cale, hoping he gets the hint as Slade walks into the kitchen. He doesn't. He just looks at me and raises his eyebrows back in question. One of the things I've learned about Cale is he never gets the hint, ever.

"What do you want to do now?" As the words leave Cale's lips, he then glares over at Slade as he walks back into the living room, shirtless, with a bottle of whiskey pressed to his lips. "Oh boy."

Slade pulls the bottle away from his mouth and smiles a devilishly sexy smile that makes me wet. "You don't need to ask her that. She wants to come up to my room so I can bend her over my desk and fuck her."

My eyes widen in shock and anger at him being so outspoken and straightforward.

Seriously!

Taking the only thing I can think of in my outburst of anger, I toss my phone at his head. He dodges just in time and leans against the couch. The muscles in his arms and stomach flex as he holds the bottle up and takes another swig. "You're a real piece of work. Do you know that?"

"So I've been told," he says stiffly. "You haven't seen anything yet. The next time you're ready to inflict pain, you better be ready to follow through. I'll show you what a real piece of work I am, then."

"You asshole!" Bending over, I reach for my high heel and almost fall over. Cale reaches for my arm and steadies me. We'll see what he says when I stab him with my stiletto.

"Whoa, whoa." He turns to Slade and gives him the nastiest look I've ever seen on Cale's pretty face. "Dude, I told you to leave her alone. If she kicks your ass, that's on you. Then, I'll kick your ass just for making her angry."

My nostrils flare in anger as I check out Slade's sexy body. His faded jeans are fitted and hanging low on his slender waist. I swear I could kill him just for being so sexy. *That asshole.*

"All right. Your loss, Pen."

Without glancing back, he heads for the stairs, and I watch in utter shock as he holds my phone up, smiles and tosses it to me. "You're going to make hating you easy," I growl. "And don't call me Pen, manwhore."

"I've heard worse," he says calmly. "Oh and I texted your friend Kayla and asked her to join me tonight."

That prick!

Pulling my eyes from his muscular back, I turn to Cale and growl. Yes, I growled. I am so pissed, I could scream at poor Cale.

"I'm sorry. I'll get his ass in check by the morning." Leading me toward the back of the house, he rubs my shoulders and kisses the top of my head. "You can take my room. I cleaned the sheets for you last night. I'll sleep on the couch so you don't get mauled like a bear in your sleep."

Thankful, I exhale and give his muscular frame a hug. I would kiss him if it wouldn't be so weird. "Thanks. I appreciate that. I hope there's a lock on the door now." I look at him with a raised eyebrow, remembering the image of me walking in on him getting sucked off by some girl once. That was awkward.

Laughing, he pushes me into the room and starts closing the door as he takes a step back. "Don't worry, he won't come into my room. He's just being an ass because he's used to all the girls wanting him. I'll keep my eye on him." He rubs his chest and yawns. "I'm crashing."

"Goodnight," I mumble.

As soon as Cale is out of the room, I clutch my phone in my hand and scroll through my text messages. I take a deep breath and exhale when I see that he was lying about texting Kayla. For some reason that pissed me off. The thought of him having sex with her is not something I want to picture.

I strip down to my panties and bra and make a quick phone call while hopping into Cale's bed.

The phone rings a few times and just when I think it's about to go to voicemail, he picks up.

"Hello," Jay yells into the phone. I can barely hear him over the loud music. My heart sinks just knowing what he's up to.

"Jay, are you busy?" I ask with a sigh, annoyed with both myself and him.

It takes a second before he answers and all I can make out is a female giggling. "Yeah, Aspen. I'm a little busy right now."

I don't say anything for a few seconds. I just listen to his heavy breathing and the sound of her whispering and then giggling. I feel like puking, I'm so angry.

"All right. I just wanted to say goodnight." I grind my jaw, trying my best not to let my emotions consume me. I don't know why I agreed to this shit. It was stupid and I know it.

"Okay, goodnight. I'll try to talk to you tomorrow night. Right now is just bad timing. You should really be sleeping by now."

"Yeah." I sigh. "Whatever. Talk to you later."

Pulling the phone away from my ear, I hit the end button and curl myself into Cale's nice warm blankets. What I wouldn't give to be wrapped up in someone's arms right now. I make myself sick just for wanting it. I just really need an escape from myself right now.

An escape from everything.

CHAPTER FIVE

SLADE

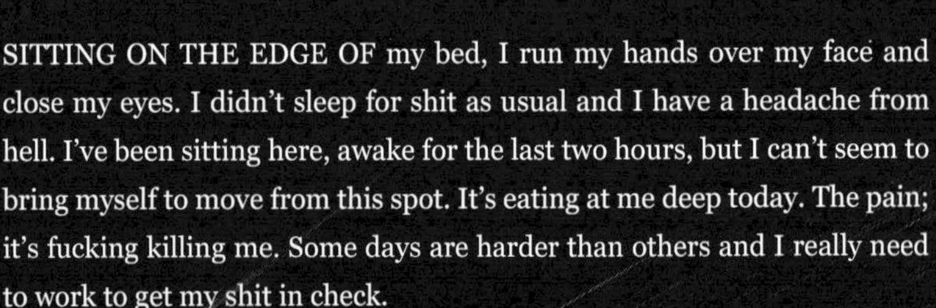

SITTING ON THE EDGE OF my bed, I run my hands over my face and close my eyes. I didn't sleep for shit as usual and I have a headache from hell. I've been sitting here, awake for the last two hours, but I can't seem to bring myself to move from this spot. It's eating at me deep today. The pain; it's fucking killing me. Some days are harder than others and I really need to work to get my shit in check.

I let out a deep breath and slip on a pair of my boxer briefs before making my way down the hallway and downstairs. The house is still dark and I can hear Cale snoring from the couch. I'm not surprised, because I'm always the first one up. Like I said, I'm not much of a sleeper. It's the one thing that comes difficult for me.

After slamming back a glass of water, I slip into the bathroom and close the door behind me. I stand here, staring at my reflection in the small, darkened room. The only light shining through is from the small beam coming from the slightly parted shades. It's just enough lighting to let my eyes fall on the scar across my cheekbone. It's not very big.

Fuck, it should be bigger.

Placing my hands in front of me, I grip the sink and lean over it. My breathing picks up as the emotions swarm through me; awakening the madness that I keep buried deep. I have an urge to put my fist through this mirror to stop the pain, but I won't. My hands are already scarred up enough. Anger and rage only douse the pain, but doesn't stop it.

I get distracted when I hear a noise coming from the hallway and then the bathroom door is pushed open. I slowly tilt my head to the side to see Aspen standing there in only a T-shirt.

Shit. She is sexy.

She takes a step back when she notices the look on my face. I would too. I'm a monster. The concern in her eyes makes my heart skip a beat and I have no idea why. She doesn't even know me, but she's looking at me as if I'm transparent, seeing straight through to my damaged soul. I don't like it one bit.

"I'm sorry." She pulls her eyes away from mine and tugs on the hem of her T-shirt, causing my eyes to trail down her legs and my grip on the sink tightens. "I didn't realize anyone was in here. It was dark and the door wasn't shut all the way."

Pushing away from the sink, I get my emotions in check and walk toward the door. If I wasn't feeling like shit, I would hit on her right now and tell her all the things I want to do to that beautiful body. I should, but I can't. I've let my inner thoughts take over and pull me down; remind me of the piece of shit that I really am. I know it, everyone else knows it and I've accepted it.

"It's cool. I was just going to take a shower, but I'll let you have it first." I wait for a response. When she doesn't say anything, I turn, now standing in front of her. I grip onto the top of the doorframe and look her in the eyes. I can't tell which one I like more; the blue one or the deep green one. They're stunning. "It's all yours if you want it."

Her eyes dart down to my chest and she swallows before shaking her head and turning away. "It's fine. I can wait. I was just going to take a quick shower and see if Cale would run me to Kayla's. It's not a big deal. He's still sleeping anyways. I'll just go and let you-"

"I'll take you," I say, stopping her mid-sentence while gripping the doorframe tighter. "I have to go to the club in a bit anyways. I'm filling in for Sarah behind the bar for a few hours."

She looks a bit surprised and not sure if she wants to take me up on the offer. That bothers me for some reason yet I don't know why. "It's fine. You don't have to. I'll just wait. You were already in here anyways."

Releasing the doorframe, I take a step closer and slowly run my hands down her sides, tracing every curve through the thin material. My hands stop amidst her hips and I squeeze, pulling her body to press against mine. My cock hardens against her stomach and she sucks in a deep breath, but doesn't pull away. A part of her wants this and the more I look at her, the more I want her; a distraction. Fucked up or not, I can't deny that I *need* this distraction, addiction, necessity, or whatever else you may want to call it. I've gotten used to the harsh judgments of my lifestyle.

"We can take a shower together." I brush my lips over her neck and whisper, "I can dirty you with my body and then clean you with my tongue."

She tilts her neck and allows me to run my tongue up it as if that's the pass code to her arousal. She likes it. I can tell by her soft moans. "Have you thought about what my cock will feel like inside you?" I suck on her earlobe and bring my hands down to cup her ass. "I want to fuck you, Aspen." I lick my lips and breathe into her ear. "And I know you want me to."

Her chest pushes out as she takes a deep breath. "I don't even know you." She places her hands on my chest and backs away. "Plus, I don't *like* you. Now, if you don't mind. *One* of us has to take a shower first. You or me? Pick one."

She presses her legs together and I can tell she's trying to hide that I have her pussy aching for my touch. She's wet and ready for me. I don't have to check; I just know. That's okay 'cause my cock wants it just as much.

Enjoying watching her squirm, I smile and lean into the doorframe. "I'm going to take care of that for you. Don't think about shit. Fuck everything else and just enjoy it."

Her eyes watch mine as I look down at her black panties that are barely peeking out from under what I assume is one of Cale's old shirts. For some reason, the thought of stripping her out of another man's shirt turns me on; gives me a rush knowing I can.

She watches me intently but doesn't say a word as I grab the bottom of the T-shirt and slowly lift it over her head and toss it behind me. She's standing there in just her thong and bra. Her breasts are plump and firm, squeezed into a tiny black bra to match her panties. My cock instantly strains to break free from the material as I imagine dropping to my knees in front of her and devouring her pussy.

Running my hand up her tight little stomach, I press her up against the wall with my hand above her head. She needs this just as much as I do. Fuck everything around us. I'll make her forget, just like I want to. "Touch yourself for me."

She's hesitant at first, but nervously licks her lips as she slides her hand down the front of her panties, her eyes never leaving mine.

"That's it. I bet you feel so fucking good." I press into her with my body as I squeeze her hip. She looks away so I grab her chin, pulling it until her gaze meets mine again. "Don't turn away. Look at me while you touch yourself." I lick my lips in satisfaction as she does what I say. "Does your pussy feel good, baby?"

She nods her head and places her bottom lip between her teeth as she starts moving her hand up and down.

"I bet. Now imagine it were my fingers fucking your tight little pussy. So thick and firm, filling you up as I pleasure you." Her hand quickens as she closes her eyes and moans. "That's it. You like the thought of me pleasuring you, don't you? Fuck yourself harder. I want to hear your pussy wet for me, Aspen."

Her breathing picks up and she begins shaking as if she's about to have an orgasm. She stops abruptly and opens her eyes, staring into mine. "What the hell am I doing?" Pulling her hand out of her panties, she places her hands against the wall behind her and looks down at my hard cock, before looking away, embarrassed. "I'm not doing this. This is beyond messed up."

Grabbing her hand, I lift it and slowly suck her wet fingers into my mouth, tasting her. I suck her fingers clean while looking her directly in the eyes. "I can fucking taste your frustration and need. Why not let me ease that frustration and show you what it's like to have me taste you. There's nothing wrong with wanting to *feel* good."

I smile against her fingers before placing my hand in the back of her hair and pulling her mouth toward mine. I won't kiss her, but I want to get a reaction out of her. And I do. She swallows, nervously, before sidestepping around me. "Don't call me baby and I shouldn't have done that. Now get out so I can take a shower."

I lick my lips one last time, tasting her on my mouth, before walking out of the bathroom.

She's trying to resist the need to have me pleasure her, but we both know as much as she hates me, she wants me. I'm going to show her it's okay to have me.

TWO HOURS LATER AND HERE I am, leaning against my motorcycle, watching with satisfaction as Aspen exits the house with a look of frustration. She looks so tense and . . . unpleased. Sickly enough, this pleases me.

Judging from her hour-long shower, I would say she couldn't please herself without my help. That only gives me more reason to want to please her. To show her how I can make her feel.

Crossing my legs in front of me I smile as she approaches and gives me a look so dirty, I might just need another shower. I don't think she understands what that look does to me. It's so sexy. "Did you have a good shower?" Tossing my helmet up, I catch it and hold it out for her to grab. "I would've finished you off and gave you the best orgasm of your life. All you had to do was ask."

"Shut up," she growls. Rolling her eyes, she exhales while looking at the helmet in my hand. "Seriously? You want me to get on that? I don't trust you enough with my life. Why not take the truck?"

That stings. But since she refuses to take the helmet, I slide it on her head and rev the engine, choosing not to get into that fucked up headspace right now. "Just get on. I don't have all day."

She shakes her head once before throwing her leg over the motorcycle and hopping on behind me. "You think this shit is funny, don't you? What you did back there."

I look over my shoulder at her sullen face and smirk. "What?"

"You know what I'm talking about. Don't play stupid, *Slade*," she growls. "You did that on purpose."

"What did I do? Tell me."

She gives me a dirty look and runs her tongue over her teeth in frustration. "Nothing. Nothing at all, okay."

"All right. Then, I apologize for doing nothing at all. Happy?"

She lets out an exasperated huff before grabbing my shoulder with her left hand and placing her other hand behind her, keeping her distance. "Let's just go. Kayla is waiting on me."

"Grab my waist," I say firmly. When she doesn't make a move to grab me, I reach for both of her arms and wrap them around my waist. She stiffens as if she doesn't know what to do. "Keep your arms around me. Got it."

Despite what she thinks, I care about her safety or else I wouldn't offer her a godman ride on my bike.

"Fine. Let's just get this over with." Locking her fingers around my waist, she tilts her head to the left. "Go down to the light and make a left. Then go to Acorn Street and make a right. All right. Be careful too."

Swallowing back my remark, I take off causing her to squeeze her arms around me for safety. I smile to myself, feeling the awkwardness in her touch. She needs to loosen up and give into her needs.

After a few minutes of riding in silence her arms finally start to relax and I can feel them inching higher, getting closer to my chest.

Every time I make a turn or pass someone, I can hear a little gasp from her as my muscles tighten from below her hands. She's trying hard to hide it, but I can tell she wants to explore. It gives me a fucking rush.

About five minutes later, we pull up to a little white house to see her friend outside waiting on her. The red car from the other night is sitting in the driveway and it makes me wonder why she didn't just ask her friend to pick her up if she hates me so much.

As soon as I stop the bike, she jumps off and takes my helmet off as fast as her fingers will allow her. She tosses it in my lap and scowls. "Thanks for the ride."

Smiling at her and her hot little friend, I slide the helmet on my head. "Anytime." I look down toward her pussy. "And thanks for the show earlier." I wink and she looks away, pissed. I can feel her eyes burning into me as I take off. Hell, I don't mind. She can undress me with her eyes anytime she wants.

When I pull up at the bar, it's completely empty. I toss my cigarette and jump off my motorcycle while looking around, preparing myself. This is a shitty shift and you don't make crap at this time. The bar opens at eleven, but really the business doesn't take off until later at night when the entertainment comes in.

I don't mind doing Sarah favors, though, because she has a young child and I want her to be able to be there for him when it's needed. That shit is very important. If anyone else asked me to cover this shift, my answer would be hell no.

Now, I'll be stuck here for the next few hours lost in my head, hoping for someone to stop in and entertain me. Not my idea of a good day. I don't need too much time to think.

Hilary has already been here and has left. I can tell as soon as I unlock the back door and walk in. The lights are all turned on and the bar is set up and ready to go.

Hilary is the owner. She's an older woman, in her early fifties. She only stops in once a day and usually it's when no one is here. She's good at what she does, though, and helps whenever she can. I really like her as a person and a manager. She treats us well. I can't complain.

A couple hours into my shift, a woman around my age, mid-twenties, finally comes into the bar and takes a seat in front of me.

I've seen her here a few times before and I have to admit that I've thought about taking her home. She's a natural redhead with a small, freckled nose, full lips, and a nice set of breasts. She looks sexy as fuck in those tight little suit skirts she always wears. She has to work in an office somewhere. I like the thought of dirtying her. She looks like she needs a good fuck to relieve some of the tension she is carrying around.

Taking a seat in front of me, she smiles and sets her purse down beside her. "I'm taking a quick break from work. Give me a drink of your choice. Anything will do." Her eyes rake over my body as I reach for a glass and come her way. There's a look saying she's looking for what I call the fuck and fly; short and hard. It's more of a business exchange between two people. I'm used to the look; prone to it. "I'm going to cut to the chase, okay. I don't have a lot of time, but I have a little time." She smirks while watching me with desperate eyes.

I'm listening . . .

Reaching for a bottle of Jack, I pour it halfway up and add a splash of Coke and a little lime juice. It may be a little strong, but she looks like she can handle it. She looks like she can handle a lot of things.

Setting the drink down in front of her, I lean over the bar as she reaches for my shirt and pulls me to her. "I've heard a lot of good things about your *dick*. I need to release some tension and I want you to *fuck* me. Can you do that? Nothing more. I'm a very busy woman."

I let my lips brush over her ear before whispering, "For the things I do, you would need a lot more than just a little time." I place my hand behind her neck and pull her closer to my lips. "I would tie you up to my bed, blindfold you and devour your pussy with my tongue. Then when I was done, I would stand you up against my wall, bind your hands above you and fuck you until you can't walk. Then I would fuck you so hard and thoroughly you will never want another cock. I don't think that is what you're looking for. Trust me, it's not easy moving on to just a quick lay after that."

A throat clears from nearby.

"I see you're still on the prowl, son."

Gritting my teeth, I pull away from the redhead and bring my eyes up to meet the one man I wish I could stay away from: my father. He's more like the devil in a suit. He's standing there as if he's so fucking perfect and can't do any wrong. It pisses me the hell off.

"What are you doing here?" I begin finding things to do, pretending to be busy. The last thing I want to do is deal with him.

Stepping up to the bar, he fixes his tie and takes a seat. "Do I need to have a reason to come see my son? We haven't spoken in over six months."

Walking over to stand in front of him, I lean down and get in his face. "We both know why too. Don't come in here acting as if it's my fault. Get out of here with that bullshit."

"Son, calm down." Pulling out his wallet he searches through it. "I'll take a Scotch on the rocks."

Rolling my neck to keep my tongue in check, I make him his drink. I set it down in front of him and lean against the register while watching him sip on it.

He makes a sour face while setting the glass back down. "I see not much has changed since the last time we've talked." I watch him with anger while he adjusts his tie as if he's better than me. "When will you realize this lifestyle isn't going to change anything? It won't make things better."

Gripping the counter, I lean over the register and turn my head away. I can't stand to look at him. "Don't even say it. I don't need to hear this shit. I'm fine with my life. Why don't you get back to yours and stop worrying about mine? Don't fucking judge me."

We both look over as the redhead slams back her drink and stands up. "I'm out, boys." She looks at me and winks. "Maybe another time."

I don't say anything. I just watch as she leaves. I'm glad, because she doesn't need to hear this.

"You don't think I'm concerned about my son? That I don't see that you've thrown your life down the drain? It makes me angry." He takes another sip and then scoots it across the bar. "You're better than this. Just because-"

"Don't you fucking say it," I growl out at him in warning and shake the counter.

"I'm just telling you that there's still meaning in your life, and you need to find that again. The pain will never go away. I get that but-"

"Fucking stop! Do you understand me?" My voice comes out firmly. "Don't you say another word about it. It's done. Over. I've moved on."

Looking me in the eyes, he stands up and picks up his glass for me to see. "This is what you call moving on? A career as a bartender that strips on the weekends and has meaningless sex with any tramp you can slip your dick into. No, son. This is not moving on. It's numbing the pain."

Grinding my jaw, I swing my hand across the counter, knocking over the bottle of Scotch along with a bunch of other items like limes, straws, and cocktail napkins. "You just don't know when to stop, do you? This is why we don't talk. This is why I stay away. You won't let me live."

Turning to leave, he stops and throws down some money. "No, I'm trying to help you live and stop being a piece of shit. Get your shit together before it's too late. You're twenty-six years old for fuck's sake. Act like it."

I hear him walking away, but I refuse to look his direction and show him just how worked up I am. He always fucking does this; acts as if he knows what I'm going through or how the fuck I feel and *should* feel. No one does.

Fighting to catch my breath and calm down, I lean over the bar and grip the front of my hair in my hands. I feel like going fucking mad right now. Today is not a good day to think about this shit.

I'm pissed. Pissed at my father and pissed at myself for knowing he's right.

Picking up a bottle of vodka, I toss it across the room at the wall. It shatters against the wall, leaving clear liquid dripping on the floor. It doesn't do shit to calm me down though. So, I just stand here and stare at the ceiling.

"Well . . . I see it's extremely busy in here today."

I look over with narrowed eyes to see Aspen walk in. She's no longer wearing her clothes from yesterday. Now, she's wearing a pair of faded jean shorts and a white tank top that shows the pink outline of her bra. She must've had her clothes in Kayla's car. She looks . . . good. This look fits her.

Exhaling, I stand up straight and gesture around me. "Yeah, really busy. I hope you're not here for a drink because I might not be able to handle making you one," I say sarcastically.

She leans against the front of the bar and starts fingering the remaining napkins. "I'm here because Kayla had to go to work and Cale isn't home. I don't have a key to get in and he didn't pick up the phone." She looks down at the mess by my feet and then looks up at me. "I suppose you could use a little company anyways."

"I guess," I mumble. "Doesn't look like I have much of a choice." I reach for a glass and scoop it full of ice. "Want a drink?"

"Just a Sprite will be fine. I only drink when I'm out at parties. It's kind of my thing. I'm a lightweight."

I watch her as she sits down in front of me and chews on her lip. "Are you nervous?" I study her reaction to the question that is making her cheeks turn red.

Shaking her head, she reaches for the glass after I finish filling it and pulls it to her lips. "Why would I be nervous? You think you make me nervous? No. You just make me mad. Those are two different things."

Nodding my head in agreement, I say, "You're not the only one."

I'm used to it. Hell, I'm pissed at myself most of the time.

She laughs under her breath and sticks the tip of the straw into her mouth. "I bet there are a lot of pissed off women running around this world due to you. I just get that vibe."

Challenging her, I lean over the bar and pull the straw out of her mouth with my tongue, being sure to get close to her mouth. "Oh yeah," I whisper. "What kind of *vibe* is it that you get from me?"

Backing away, she watches my mouth as I chew on her straw. She clears her throat and averts her eyes when she sees that I notice her staring. "A bad one," she replies.

I stand up and spit out the straw when I see Cale walk in. "Dude, what are you doing here?" For some reason the thought of him being here to pick Aspen up pisses me off.

"Sarah called and said she won't be able to make it to work at all today because her son's doctor's appointment is taking longer than she expected. Figuring you wouldn't want the full shift, I offered to come in until seven."

He walks up behind Aspen, wraps his arms around her and squeezes. "Hey, gorgeous. What are you doing here?"

She places her hands on his arms and smiles. "Hey, pretty boy," she says teasingly. "I couldn't reach you earlier, so I had Kayla drop me off here."

Looking up from behind Aspen, Cale gives me a concerned look. "Yeah, so your dad stopped by this morning, but judging from the look of this place he's already been here too," he says, looking down at the ground.

"I don't even want to hear it. Thanks for the fucking warning."

Cale releases Aspen and steps behind the bar. "I didn't say shit. He must've figured it out on his own. It's pretty simple to find your ass."

A few guys walk in and take a seat next to Aspen at the bar. I notice the preppy, clean cut one staring at her with a creepy ass smile and I have the urge to shove my fist down his throat.

He better not try to pick her up. She doesn't need a guy like that. She needs one that is going to fuck her good and please her so good that it hurts. He looks like too much of a pussy to handle her.

"Hey," he says to Aspen. "Alex."

Cale starts talking to me, but my attention stays focused on *Alex* to be sure he doesn't sign his fucking death wish.

"Aspen." She shakes his hand and then looks away uncomfortable.

Cale nudges me as he goes to approach the guys. "Get your ass out of here. I got it from here. Hemy will be coming in around four so it's all good."

"Huh," I mumble. I pull my eyes away from Aspen and look up at Cale.

"I got it, man. Aspen can hang out here while I work so she doesn't have to be at the house by herself. I'm sure you have shit to do."

Looking back toward Aspen, I notice the creepy guy has somehow gotten closer. Cale is taking their drink order and he doesn't even notice. Seriously?

"No, man. Aspen is coming with me. I don't have shit to do."

Aspen looks up and watches as I clock out.

"Come on. We're leaving."

She looks at me for a second as if she didn't hear me right.

Grabbing my helmet, I walk around to the other side of the bar and reach for her hand, pulling her up to her feet. "Let's go."

Cale and the creepy dude give me a weird look, but I couldn't care less. I'm not leaving her here with that fucking preppy douche.

Aspen looks like she's about to say something until I look her in the eyes and clench my jaw. Instead, she turns beside her to look at Cale. "I'll see you when you get home."

He gives me a warning look before turning to Aspen. "Don't let this dick get to you. If he does, let me know." He turns back to me and scowls. "And don't worry, asshole. I'll clean up your mess."

Waving him off, I walk her out of the bar. When we get to my bike, I toss her my helmet while straddling my bike. "Get on."

CHAPTER SIX

ASPEN

SITTING ON THE BACK OF Slade's motorcycle with my arms wrapped around his waist is the last thing I thought I'd be doing right now. Just earlier I wanted to rip his hair out and choke him, but I have a feeling he might like that type of thing. I might even like doing it to him. That's the sad part.

Since leaving the club, we've been riding for the last hour in dead silence. I have a feeling he needs this at the moment and hell, I do too. It's relaxing having the cool breeze hit against your skin as you ride with no worries; not knowing where you're going or where you'll end up at. The only problem is—it feels like it's about to rain.

Yup, here it comes.

Holding on tighter, I bring my body closer to his as the rain hits, pouring off the helmet and soaking my shirt. It's cool. Cooler than I expected, giving me instant chills. My nipples harden as the fabric of my now wet shirt rubs against them. Maybe it wasn't the best idea to go with lace today.

Slade tilts his head up, takes a deep breath and slowly releases it. I can feel his body tensing beneath my arms and I unintentionally squeeze tighter as he makes a quick right. He rides down a path hidden beneath the trees until finally making a stop in the middle of nowhere.

Grabbing my hand, he helps me off the bike before he quickly hops off and yanks his gray T-shirt over his head and holds it above me. He slowly backs me up until we're standing below a huge tree, hidden from the rain.

He's standing here soaked, looking at me through long, wet lashes. He has the most amazing blue eyes I have ever seen. I want to pull my gaze away, but I can't. I'm hypnotized. As much as I hate to admit it, he's so damn beautiful; dangerously beautiful. His black hair is wet and slicked back from the rain. It's thick and slightly long. I love that. The focal point is those lips. *Oh God, those lips.* The rain is falling on them, beading, and dripping down. With each drop that falls, it causes him to keep using his tongue to dry them. It's so distracting.

"Here. Use this." I pull my eyes away from his lips and take hold of his shirt, holding it above my head. "It's not an umbrella, but it will help."

He turns away and walks out into the open, but stops to stand in the pouring rain. I watch as he runs his hands over his face, the rain pouring over his head and arms while soaking his jeans. His bare chest is moving up and down as if he's trying to fight some deep emotions and with each move, his muscles flex, making me very aware of his sex appeal. It's confusing. I don't know if I want to hug him, slap him or fuck him. All I know is that I definitely want to be doing something to him.

After a few minutes of him just standing there, I walk away from the safety of the tree and struggle to hold his shirt above both of our heads. By now, it's completely drenched and not serving much of a purpose, but I don't take notice. Someone else has captured my attention. I'm standing on the tip of my toes, trying my best not to lose my balance and fall into him.

It takes him a moment, but he finally turns around. Looking me in the eyes, he reaches for his shirt and throws it down beside him. His eyes are intense; dark. "I need to finish what I started," he growls. He takes a step forward and I take a step back, but his stride is wider than mine. He leans in close to my ear and whispers, "I've been craving your pussy all fuckin' day."

He doesn't even hesitate before grabbing me by the hips and picking me up. It's as if he already knew I was going to let him do what he wants to me.

It angers me, but I have to admit it has me so turned on I don't think I could say no if I tried.

I want to say something; protest or scream no, but I don't. I should, but I won't. I'm too wrapped up in what he's about to do to me. I'm not thinking clearly. My thighs are moistening with every look at his beautiful body and every filthy word that exits his mouth.

He walks toward his black motorcycle with me wrapped around his waist. Just thinking about the way he made me feel this morning without even touching me has me so turned on that I can already feel the ache between my legs just waiting to be released. It's new to me. It's what *he* does to me.

Setting me down beside his motorcycle, he places one hand on my waist while working the button on my wet shorts with the other. I try to look at his face to see what he's feeling at the moment, but its void of any emotions. He's hard to read and it gives me an adrenaline rush; a need to figure him out.

His hands are working fast to pull my shorts down my legs and lift my feet out of them. Even with them being wet, he is a pro at stripping me out of them. He's good at getting what he wants and it makes me wonder if he's just as good when he gets it.

Standing here almost naked, my breathing picks up as he balls my thong in his hand and yanks. The thin strings rip apart, baring my pussy to him. My first thought is to cover myself up, but he lifts me up and sets me down so I'm straddling the back of his motorcycle.

My legs spread wider as he runs his hands up my thighs and licks the rain from his full lips. Sitting here like this makes me feel dirty, but a part of me really needs this right now. Maybe letting him pleasure me will be enough to take my mind off things for the moment and not worry about what a certain someone is doing back home. I probably need this more than I'd like to admit.

"Oh, fuck." He grips my thighs and bites his bottom lip. "The taste of your pussy has been on my tongue all day; teasing me and making my fucking cock hurt. You better hold on tight, Aspen. I won't be gentle. It's not in me."

Gripping my thighs, he pulls me closer to the edge of the motorcycle and runs his tongue up my thigh while grazing my flesh with his teeth. I'm already squirming on the wet bike, trying not to slip off. My heart is going wild in my chest, making it hard to breathe.

Oh. My. Goodness.

"You like that, don't you," he asks against my thigh. "I bet you're already imagining what it's going to feel like when I taste you." He bites into my thigh and pulls me closer so my legs are over his shoulders. It hurts, but feels so good at the same time. My breathing picks up as he nibbles a little harder. "You like it when it hurts, baby?" He pulls away and lets the rain fall against my swollen clit. It has me wishing his mouth was there instead, to ease my ache.

Just touch me already . . .

An aching pleasure runs throughout my body, causing me to tremble as he inches his way up to my inner thigh, right beside my pussy and bites down onto my skin. I shake my head and squirm out of his reach in an attempt to get away. I can't handle it. It's too much. He feels my pull and yanks me back down by my thighs so I reach out and yank his hair making him look up at me. "Not so rough, asshole. Don't make me regret this anymore than I already do."

"Fuck," he groans out. He closes his eyes and moans. *Oh my, that moan. So deep and rough.* "Pull my hair again and I will fuck you instead of just licking you. Got it?"

Knowing that I'm pushing my luck with him, I release his hair and grip onto the bike's handlebars behind my head. I'm already too far to turn back now. I want his tongue, but that's it. Nothing more. This is it. Just one time. Just . . .

"Oh shit," I moan out as his tongue slides up my pussy, slowly and teasingly. "This can only happen once. You know that, right?" I fight to catch my breath. "This is wrong in so many ways."

He looks up from between my thighs with a sly grin. He's a dirty little snake that has me in his grips and he knows it. "Yeah, but it feels so fucking right, doesn't it?"

I don't answer. I don't want to. All I want to do is close my eyes, lean back and let his tongue work its magic to release the tension I've had built up since this morning. When he sucked my wetness into his mouth and tasted me, I almost gave in right there and let him have me. It took every bit of strength to fight my urge to pull him into the shower and let him have his way with me; to take me just once.

His tongue works slowly at first. He's being gentle and teasing me, making me want more. His rhythm is precise and in control as if he knows the exact spot to work me up. He's slowly building me up, knowing I'll want more in the end. He's good. He's in control of his game and it makes me want to knock him down a notch; tease him a little.

I catch myself moaning as he slides his tongue down further and shoves it into my pussy as deep as it will go. He's fucking me with his tongue. The feel and the thought is enough to almost bring me to climax . . . but I fight it. I'm not ready yet and I have a feeling he won't let me get off so easily anyways.

After a few seconds he slips his tongue out and slides it up and over my clit before sucking it into his mouth. It feels so good I have to reach out and grip his hair again. I pull harder and I realize the harder I pull, the better his tongue pleases me. He gets off on this and I plan to use this to my advantage.

I yank his hair to the side and he sucks my clit so hard that I almost fall over, but he catches me. I can feel him growling against my clit and it deepens the pleasure and makes me want more as he holds me steady. "Keep going, Slade. I'm almost there."

"Fuck this shit! I want to fuck you so bad and make you scream louder while I'm pounding your tight little pussy." Standing up, he runs his tongue over his lips and places both of his hands on his bike, hovering above me. "You want me to fuck you?" He runs his tongue up my neck and stops at my ear. "Just say the word and I'll end that throbbing ache between your legs. I'll fuck you so good that my cock will be the only one you ever fucking think about again. Let me show you."

I shake my head and place my hand on his chest. "No. Dammit, Slade." I give him a shove, but against his firm body, it doesn't even make him budge. It only makes me want him more. "I don't need you to fuck me and I don't want you to. Just finish what you started."

Wiping the rain off his face, he spreads my legs wider and places his thumb over my clit and starts rubbing. "Why? Are you afraid it will feel too good? You scared that I might please you better than anyone else can?" I look at him and swallow while trying to pretend his words aren't having the effect on me that they are. "My cock will feel so good you'll never want another." Grabbing the back of my head with one hand, he shoves a finger inside me and sucks in his bottom lip. I moan and take a deep breath, feeling the thickness of his finger move in and out, making my body feel hot and tingly. "See how wet I make you."

Closing my eyes, I moan and grip onto his wet hair. I have the urge to pull it and push him even further. I want his finger deeper. I need to get off. "You're an asshole for doing this and you know it," I say between deep breaths.

"Oh yeah, baby," he breathes into my ear. "Show me how much of an asshole I am and I'll show you how good I am at pleasing you. You want me to please you; you have to fucking work for it."

What an asshole.

"Fuck you!" I scream as I dig my nails into his back, wanting to hurt him. "You're such an asshole."

He freezes and looks me dead in the eyes, clenching his jaw muscles. His eyes look fierce and I start to wonder if maybe I shouldn't have done that.

"I'm—"

"Don't finish that," he cuts me off.

Without saying another word, he lifts me up off the motorcycle and holds me up high enough for me to squeeze my thighs against his face. I can feel his lips brushing my clit and it already makes me want to lose control.

Oh shit.

Gripping my ass in his hands, he squeezes while his tongue works on catering to the aching throb between my legs. I grab onto his hair as I arch my back. My heels dig into his back as I continue to hang here while he pleasures me. He doesn't seem like this is straining him at all.

I have never felt anything so good in my life. I feel the heat surging through my body and I can tell that I'm almost there. I'm so close. "Don't stop, Slade. Faster . . ."

He grips me tighter and sucks my clit into his mouth right as my body trembles in his arms and I'm brought to climax by his tongue. *Damn, that magical tongue. I'm so damn ruined.*

"Holy shit, Slade. What did you just do to me?" I suck in a deep breath and release it. My heart is pounding so fast that I'm starting to feel dizzy. "Put me down. Put me down."

He runs his hands up my legs before grabbing my waist and helping me down to my feet. His eyes bore into mine as I take a step back and reach down for my shorts as fast as I can.

I feel like such an idiot for letting him get me off. I don't even like this guy. He's a jerk; nothing but trouble. The fucking devil in disguise, looking to taint my soul and consume my every thought. And I'm letting him.

He leans against his bike, giving me a cocky look as I quickly slip my shorts on and wipe the water off my face. "I'm ready to go. Take me back to the house."

Without saying a word, he reaches for his helmet, slips it on my head and jumps onto the bike. I grab his hand as he offers it for help. "What about your shirt?"

"Fuck it. I don't need it." His chest rumble as he laughs under his breath. "What about your panties?"

"Screw you, Slade."

He revs up the engine, makes sure I'm holding on tight and then takes off.

THE RAIN STOPPED ALMOST IMMEDIATELY after we left. The ride back was in total silence; exactly how I expected it to be. By the time we get back to the house, all I want to do is get as far away from Slade as I can. I feel so stupid for letting him work me up the way he did and catch me in a moment of weakness.

All it does is show him that he's right; he gets whatever he wants. I told myself I wouldn't let this happen, that I would be good this week and take some *me* time to figure out my life. So much for that. I've stooped as low as Jay.

I quickly hop off the motorcycle and slide the helmet off my head. Slade stays seated and watches me as I hand him the helmet. I can't help but to notice how sexy he looks shirtless on that motorcycle. Those tattoos and that perfect body. I hate it. No one should be allowed to look that sexy. "You're not coming in?" He slides the helmet on his head and adjusts the crotch of his jeans.

He turns away, takes a deep breath and reaches into his pocket. "Here's the key. I'll be back tonight."

I reach for the key and swallow. For some reason I don't want him to leave. Yeah, I wanted to get far away from him, but I wanted him to at least be in the house. "All right then," I say aggravated. "And just so you know, that is never happening again. Got it? Stay as far away from me as you can. You got to me in a moment of weakness. It won't happen again."

He grips the handles, clenches his jaw and watches as I walk away. I don't know why he even bothers waiting. I'm sure he's ready to get as far away from me as I am him. That's probably a good thing. The two of us being around each other is nothing but bad news. He's no good for me.

Letting myself in the house, I go straight for Cale's room and fall face-first onto his bed. I'm so pissed at myself that I scream. I'm twenty-three years old and I still have no control over my life. I need to stay far away from Slade before he makes everything more difficult.

I knew he was going to be trouble from the second I laid eyes on him at the club. I just knew it. Hell, even his name screams trouble. Slade Merrick. Enough said.

CHAPTER SEVEN

SLADE

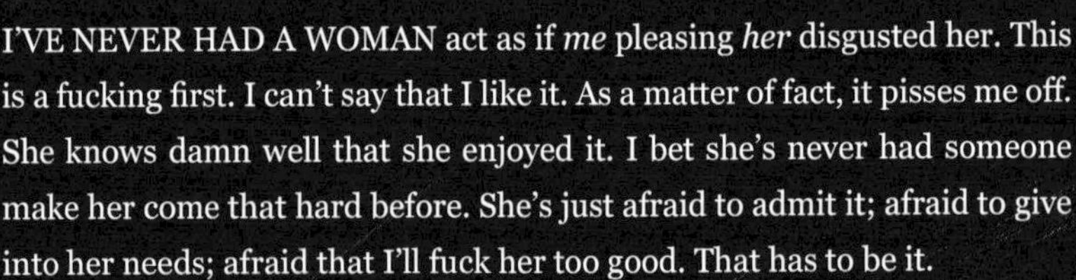

I'VE NEVER HAD A WOMAN act as if *me* pleasing *her* disgusted her. This is a fucking first. I can't say that I like it. As a matter of fact, it pisses me off. She knows damn well that she enjoyed it. I bet she's never had someone make her come that hard before. She's just afraid to admit it; afraid to give into her needs; afraid that I'll fuck her too good. That has to be it.

With the way she has me feeling at the moment, the last thing I want to do is go and exist in the same house as her just to have her avoid me and act as if she doesn't want it as much as I do. I'm not down for that shit right now. I need to get some things off my mind; cool off a bit.

Out of habit, I end up at *Walk of Shame*. Pulling my motorcycle in the back parking lot, I yank my helmet off before slamming it down on my seat and shoving my motorcycle. Cale and Hemy better be ready to keep the drinks flowing, because I have a feeling that I will be here for a while.

Stay far away from her. Yeah, I'll fucking stay far away.

I push my way through the back door, walk over to my locker and grab a shirt. I get ready to put it on, but say *fuck it* instead. I'll end up without it on by the end of the night anyways. I toss it down and make my way into the bar.

I notice that the crowd is finally starting to show up. Perfect timing. There should be plenty of entertainment to keep me busy.

As I approach the bar, I see Cale sitting on the edge of the bar talking to a group of women. They all seem to be laughing, fucking entertained.

He nods and jumps off the bar when he sees me. "Dude, why the hell do you look so pissed? I thought you were going to keep Aspen company until I get off?"

Leaning over the bar, I grab the nearest liquor bottle and reach for an empty glass. "Yeah well, she's not the easiest to entertain. I'm pretty sure she'd rather be alone right now."

Cale tilts his head back with a dirty look as he watches me pour a drink. "Yeah . . . or maybe it's just you she doesn't want to be around."

"Fuck off, Cale. I'm not in the mood today."

"Yeah, well nothing new there."

Slamming back my drink, I set the empty glass down on the bar and take a step closer to Cale so we're face to face. I want to see him when he says it. "What the hell is that supposed to mean?"

Looking away from me, he sighs and takes a step back. "You know what I mean. You're just not the same person you used to be. You're my best friend, but seriously, you need to . . ." He huffs and grips the towel over his shoulder. "Never mind. I've got work to do."

"Yeah. Me too. I have *a lot* of fucking work to do." I pour another drink and make my way over to one of the empty couches. Lucky for me, everyone seems to be in the private room with Hemy so I can get a few minutes to myself.

I set my drink down on the table next to me and lean forward with my head in my hands and my elbows resting on my knees. I just can't get over the fact that I'm so pissed off at this woman. This morning my past consumed my thoughts and now the fact that this woman angers me like nothing else has taken over and has me completely worked up. The bad part is, the more she angers me the more I want to slip between those thighs and take it out on her.

I disgust her? Nah, fuck that.

I reach for my glass and tilt it back. I need to get my mind somewhere else. The liquor won't do anything but numb it, but numbing is what I'm used to. It's what keeps me going. My cock starts to harden at the thought of a needed release. *Right on schedule.*

"What's up, dick."

I tilt my head up at the sound of Hemy's voice. He looks down at me and holds out a bottle of whiskey. I can't help but laugh a bit when I notice he's standing there wearing nothing but an American flag wrapped around his waist. He has claw marks all over his skin from the women grabbing at him. He loves it just as much as I do. He's a dirty motherfucker; like me. "What's up, man?"

"Not shit. You look like you need another one of these." He pours my glass back up to the top and leans against the arm of the couch. "You here to help me work the ladies tonight or what? It's a small crowd. A private party."

I look up at the small group of women that have started rounding up in the back room. Most of them look willing. I'm sure the thought of *me* fucking *them* doesn't disgust them. Most of them will probably be begging. How can I pass that shit up?

"Yeah." I take a gulp of my drink and watch as a few of the ladies wave over at us. "Why not. I have nothing better to do."

Hemy slaps my shoulder and stands up. "Finish that shit up and get your ass over there then. There's a certain someone that is asking for you." He starts backing away. "She has huge tits and a big fucking appetite. I'm pretty sure that's your type."

I can definitely deal with that. There's no shame in having a huge sexual appetite. I need a woman that can handle me. I like to fuck and I like to fuck dirty. The fact they get the ultimate pleasure in return is just the icing on the cake. If my cock is what does the trick, then why the fuck should I stop? It's not my fault I'm so good with it.

Taking a few more minutes to myself, I finish my drink and prep my brain by entering into fuck mode. It's what keeps my mind from going places it shouldn't while my cock is in charge. I stand and make my way over to the back room, ready to get out of my head.

Hemy has a group of women groping his ass, legs, and chest, while a few of the other women are waving money around and screaming. This is what we're used to; what we live for.

My eyes scan the room of women, until they fall on the one I'm looking for; the brunette from the other night. She's standing across the room in a tiny white dress that hugs her every curve. She's by far the most attractive woman here and the perfect distraction.

Stepping up behind her, I brush her hair behind her shoulder and whisper, "I'm here. Now what the fuck are you going to do with me?"

She turns around in my arms and bites her bottom lip when she notices I'm shirtless; less clothes for her to take off. Her eyes look hungry. "I have a few things in mind." Her eyes rake down my chest and I can tell she's been wanting me for a while. Most women do.

"You want my cock?" I run her hand down my chest and abs until it lands on my erection; always ready when I need it to be. "I'll let you have it under one condition. There are no exceptions." I wait for her to look me in the eyes to be sure she understands me. "It's yours for one night and one night only. No bullshit after. Enjoy it and move on. I need to get off and I'm pretty damn sure you do too. Are we clear?"

She lets out a soft moan and nods as her hand gropes my thick cock, moving up and down over my slightly damp jeans. The look in her eyes is pleading for me to take her right here in front of everyone. She's about to tackle me right now and ride me right here in the open. Hell yeah, it's a huge turn on.

"Even better," she whispers. "I just want one taste. I've been waiting for this opportunity for a long time." She strokes my cock through my pants. "A *very* long time."

Seeing that Hemy has the room handled, I pick the leggy brunette up and walk forward until her back is against the back wall and we have a little privacy. She moans as I slide my hand up her dress and rub my thumb over her lacy thong, teasing her through the thin fabric. "Well, it's worth the fucking wait. Trust me." Wrapping her hair around my hand, I pull her head back, exposing her neck to my mouth and graze it with my teeth as I shove my finger into her entrance. It's so wet that I can feel it dripping down my hand. "You like that, huh?"

She moans next to my ear before biting my earlobe and tugging it with her teeth. "Oh yes. I love it, Slade. Don't stop."

I move my finger in and out, slowly at first before going faster and deeper. Her legs tighten around my waist as she moans out and starts breathing heavily. "This isn't shit. Just wait until I shove my thick, hard cock in there." I bring my lips up to meet her ear. "You're going to be screaming. You like to scream?"

"Mmhmm." Grabbing my face, she attempts to pull me in for a kiss, but I turn my head out of her reach. "Come on, baby. You're not even going to kiss me? I want to taste those lips." She leans in again and I lightly pull on her hair, stopping her an inch from my face.

"No kissing." I freeze as I hold her up against the wall angry with myself. I still have the taste of Aspen on my lips and I'm being a greedy fucking bastard. I don't want to share her taste with anyone.

What. The. Fuck.

"You know what. Never mind." I release her thighs and she slides down my body, landing hard on her feet. "I'll take care of myself. I'm pretty fucking good at it."

She gives me a stunned look before fixing her dress and combing the knots out of her hair. "Are you serious, you ass?"

"Yeah. I'm fucking serious." I push away from the wall and head for the door. When I look over at Hemy, he's standing there with his hard dick swinging everywhere. We don't usually get fully nude, but on occasion if no one else is paying much attention, we end up baring it all in the VIP room. He does it the most. He has the bad ass biker look down so when women see him stripping, they go crazy over it. Shit, one of the girls is practically sucking his dick right now. They seem to love the hard steel of his piercings almost as much as his dick itself.

Heading back over to the bar, I take a seat in front of Cale and grip the bar. I really need to get my shit together. "Three shots of Jack," I say stiffly. "Actually, make it four."

Cale reaches for the shot glasses and lines them up in front of me. "I'm guessing I'll be giving you a ride home."

"Yeah. Your guess is fucking right."

Yeah, and as soon as I get home, I'll be taking a shower to wash this day away.

"So what is Aspen doing then? She didn't want to come hang out here?" He looks up from pouring the shots. "She doesn't get pissed off easily. It must be a *Slade* thing."

Not really caring to hear what he has to say, I grab the first shot and slam it back before wiping my mouth off with my arm. "How do you know this chick anyways? She's not even from around here."

Now it looks like he's battling a demon of his own. I know that look well. I wear it with pride. "I was best friends with her sister, Riley, growing up. Riley Raines. They used to live here back when we were all kids."

Okay. I've heard him mention that name before. I can't remember for shit why, though. There must be something about these sisters that make a man go nuts.

Aspen fucking Raines. What a sexy name.

CHAPTER EIGHT

ASPEN

STUPID, PIECE OF CRAP, NO good vibrator . . .

I toss what I thought was my handy dandy vibrator down beside me and roll over on my stomach, shoving my face into the pillow. I'm so frustrated, I could scream. This cannot be happening. Gripping the plush pillow, I smother my face deeper and curse my vagina.

Is it broken? Seriously. I mean my vagina. Not the vibrator. The vibrator definitely had some kicking power left in it. I think that cocky, sexy asshole broke it. Obviously, my vagina has decided it wants the best and has gone on strike until it gets it. I've never had this problem before him. Why now?

Rolling back over, I sit up and grab my panties, pulling them on with a sigh. A very frustrated sigh. After the orgasm I had yesterday, I'm ruined. No other orgasm I'll ever have will compare to it and it makes me so angry. It seems I've lost control over my vagina. I've spent the last hour just trying to have a small orgasm; any orgasm and nothing. Trust me, I've tried both ways and what were the results? Nada . . . it's completely numb now.

It's definitely time to throw in the towel. It's not happening. Maybe I just need to make some breakfast, relax, and try again later. I think I just have too much on my mind.

Yeah. That's it. I'm just mentally frustrated.

I stand from the messy confinements of the bed and grab my T-shirt from the wad of clothes on the floor, pulling it on. Exiting the room, I walk past Cale snoring on the couch and dodge my way into the kitchen. The boys didn't get in until at least two a.m. There's no way they will be waking up anytime soon. I'm surprised that I'm even up to be honest. I didn't sleep for crap. It was an endless night and a part of me wants to just crawl back in bed and force myself to sleep.

One minute I was checking my phone and the next minute I was checking the driveway. Not sure why I cared so much about when they were getting back but it seemed to drive me nuts. I haven't even gotten to spend any time with Cale and I've been here for three days. So far Slade has been my only real entertainment.

Lucky me . . .

My stomach starts growling as I begin to search through the fridge for something to cook for breakfast. Digging through the contents, I end up with a roll of sausage, a pack of bacon, and some bagels. My mouth is practically watering just anticipating the taste. At least there's *something* in this house to look forward to.

Halfway through cooking, everything starts to go horribly wrong. If I thought I was flustered before, this just confirms it. The bacon is popping grease everywhere and the stupid sausage is stuck to the bottom of the pan. The whole kitchen is full of smoke. It would be really embarrassing if the smoke detector went off right now. It's pathetic. I just can't seem to concentrate . . . on anything.

"Ow, damn!" I jump back when I get popped with bacon grease *again*. That shit really hurts.

"What the hell are you doing?"

I turn around to the sound of Slade's deep, raspy voice. He's standing there shirtless in a pair of low hanging jeans, showing off the muscles right above his . . . penis. His body is slightly damp as if he's just taken a shower, but I know he hasn't. I would've heard the water . . . I think. What is it about a wet man that is so sexy?

His eyes are dark and intense; looking at me as if he wants to either strangle me or just fuck me really hard. I can't really tell. I get a rush of excitement from both. That's really messed up.

Clearing my throat, I turn back around and start scraping the sausage off the bottom of the pan as if it's not a big deal. I just pretend I didn't mess breakfast all up. The last thing I want to do is see him standing there half naked, looking disturbingly delicious while judging my cooking skills. He looks tastier than this food. That's not what I need right now. "What does it look like I'm doing?" I ask, not bothering to hide my irritation.

When he speaks again his voice is right behind me, sending chills up my spine. His body is now pressed against mine, but not in a sexual way; in a way that makes my heart jump a little. Just a little. "Burning down the house. I hate to tell you this, but I left my fireman suit at work. I'm not prepared for this shit this early in the morning." He reaches for the spatula and hisses in my ear, "Now move out of the way."

Not budging, I reach for the spatula but he pulls it out of my reach. "I can handle it. Shouldn't you be sleeping or I don't know . . . kicking some girl out of your bed. I'm pretty sure you had a *late* night."

Giving me a stern look, he grabs me by the hips, picks me up and sets me on the counter. His lips are brushing my ear when he says, "I kicked her out last night. No girl sleeps in my bed. Ever." My heart sinks from his harsh words. He turns around and turns off the stove before throwing the spatula down. "If you needed my help then you should have asked. Is there anything you *can* do on your own?"

Narrowing my eyes at him, I get ready to jump down from the counter, but he steps right in front of me and stands between my legs blocking me. "What kind of a question is that? Is there something *else* you assume I can't do on my own?"

Running his hands up my thighs, he looks me dead in the eyes and smirks. "Yeah. Get off. I do believe you needed my help there as well."

"Fuck off, Slade. I don't need you to get off. Trust me." I place my hands on his chest and give him a little shove. Damn him; his body is pure muscle. "I can do it fine by myself. Now move."

He slides his hands up my shirt, lifts my body up and grips my ass in his hands. The skin on skin contact causes my breathing to slightly pick up. "Is that right?" Pulling me closer to him, he squeezes my ass and runs his lips up my neck. "Not from the frustrated sounds I heard coming from Cale's bedroom this morning. Those were definitely moans of frustration and not pleasure. Trust me. I know the difference." He slides his finger under the fabric of my panties and instantly I can feel the need for him to be inside me. He isn't even touching anything but the crevice between my leg and vagina.

What the hell?

Gaining my composure, I pull my neck away from him and shove him until he's out of my way. "You are so infuriating. Why are you such an ass?" I hop down from the counter and start walking away. "I'll clean this mess up later. I'm not in the mood to eat-"

"Get dressed and meet me outside in ten minutes," he says trampling over my words.

I stop when I get to the doorway and turn around to face him. "And why the hell would I do that?"

"So we can eat breakfast." He pushes the pan across the stove and picks up the spatula, tossing it in the sink. "Be ready by the time I'm dressed."

"Yeah. You're funny," I huff. "I'm good. I'm going back to bed."

"Suit yourself, but I can hear your stomach growling from over here. Stay if you want. I just want to satisfy your . . . hunger."

He walks past me and then jogs up the stairs. The muscles in his back flex and the deep scratches in his skin stand out, making me hate my body again for the reaction it gets from him.

Son of a bitch . . .

AGAINST MY BETTER JUDGMENT, I'M sitting across a booth from Slade with a piece of bacon hanging from my mouth. We both just sit here in silence eating breakfast and I'm thankful for that. I really don't feel like chatting with him. Not that he seems like the chatty type person. Actually, he's pretty far from it.

"Are you going to sit there and play with that bacon all day?" He takes a bite of his hash browns and then leans against the back of his booth. "It has to taste better than that crap you were catching on fire when I walked in."

Rolling my eyes, I point my bacon at him and start waving it as I speak. "I wasn't catching it on fire. Why are you-"

The bacon slips out of my hand and hits him on the cheek, causing me to stop and cover my mouth to keep from laughing.

Watching me stifle my laughter, he grabs the piece of bacon, smiles and takes a bite out of it. "You think that's funny, huh?"

I nod my head and laugh. "Yeah. You should have seen the way your eye twitched when it hit you. It was pretty damn hilarious."

"I bet," he replies before shoving the remainder of it in his mouth. "Now eat. I have things I have to do today."

"Yeah. Like what?"

He takes a drink of his coffee and then holds the mug under his lips. "Lots of things. Some of them include: work out, run, grocery shopping, clean the house, and then go to work tonight. The things that adults do. In between, I plan to just ride and get away. Get out of my fucking head and breathe a little. *That's* what I have to do."

I look at him a little stunned. For some crazy reason I just didn't take him as the responsible type. I expected that Cale took care of the things around the house. I have to admit, it's pretty sexy. I almost like this side of him.

"I'm done anyways." I reach for my purse and get ready to pull out my wallet, but he reaches over and snatches my purse away. "Give me my purse."

Shaking his head, he sets my purse down and pulls out his wallet. "Never expect to pay when I ask you to eat with me. I asked you because I wanted to treat you to breakfast." He pulls out two twenties and sets them on the table. "Let's go then."

He stands up right as the waitress walks over. She's a young woman, maybe in her early thirties. She looks a bit stressed out as she keeps looking back at the counter. "You guys are all set?" She picks up the money and her eyes go wide when she looks at the tab. "Sir, it's only fourteen dollars. Let me get your change."

Looking over at the counter, he watches the two kids that our waitress has been sitting with in between her running around like crazy. "No, ma'am. Keep the change." He pulls out another twenty, drops it down and grabs my hand. "Have a nice day."

I don't even get to see the woman's reaction because he pulls me out of the diner too quickly and then jumps into his truck without another word.

I keep wanting to say something, to maybe get a reaction out of him, but I can't think of what to say. I'm still stunned speechless by his generosity back at the diner. He did seem distracted while we were there. I noticed he kept looking away from the table as if something was catching his attention. Now, I know why.

"Slade," I say softly. "That was a really nice thing you did for that lady back at the diner."

He looks away from the road with a distraught look on his face. He looks like he's beating himself up over something. "Yeah, well she needed it more than me. Those kids shouldn't have to be at the diner while she works her ass off for three-dollar tips. It's not right. They don't deserve that."

I sit here and watch him as he drives. He seems a little worked up and I can't help but want to comfort him. I don't even know why. The urge just comes out of nowhere. His side profile is strikingly beautiful and the act of kindness that I just witnessed makes him even more beautiful.

Without thinking, I reach out and grip his knee, running my hand up and down his leg for comfort. He stiffens at first and glances down at my hand with a surprised look, but doesn't say a word. He just drives in silence, keeping his eyes on the road. For some reason, I keep my hand there the whole way home.

I rub and massage his leg while looking down at my small hand on his muscular thigh. It feels good under my touch; natural. It isn't until we get back to the house that I feel his muscles fully relax.

When he stops the truck and pulls the key out of the ignition, he looks over at me and then down at my hand. He's silent for a moment, his body still.

"I need to get ready to go running. I think Cale has the day planned for just the two of you." He lifts my hand off his knee and sets it on my own lap. "I'll see you later."

I nod as I watch him jump out of his truck and walk over to the door. Why is a part of me feeling down for him? Maybe it's because I feel there's something more to him than I thought. That maybe he is a real human being after all.

Hopefully Cale keeps my mind busy today. I think I need the distraction.

CHAPTER NINE

ASPEN

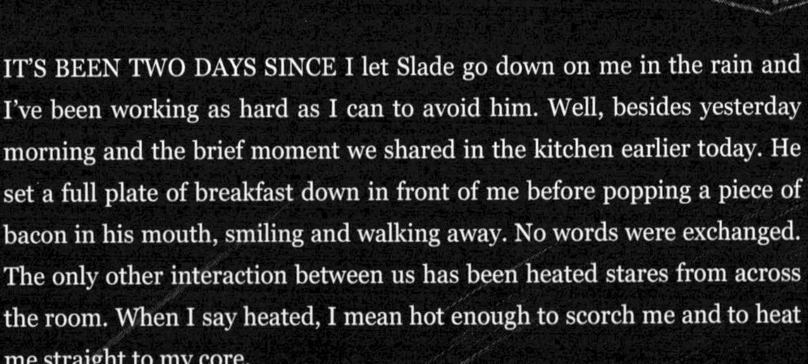

IT'S BEEN TWO DAYS SINCE I let Slade go down on me in the rain and I've been working as hard as I can to avoid him. Well, besides yesterday morning and the brief moment we shared in the kitchen earlier today. He set a full plate of breakfast down in front of me before popping a piece of bacon in his mouth, smiling and walking away. No words were exchanged. The only other interaction between us has been heated stares from across the room. When I say heated, I mean hot enough to scorch me and to heat me straight to my core.

The thought alone is almost enough for me to get off. He's so intense, I'm not sure I can handle being in the same room with him for longer than five minutes without getting wet. I'm not used to that kind of want and need. It scares me. Not to mention, I'm still a little shaken up from our diner experience. I can't quite figure him out. It's eating at me.

". . . Aspen. Hey! Are you even listening?"

"Huh?" I look up from the pile of makeup in front of me to see Kayla hovering above me. I give her a forced smile and reach for the mascara. I've never had a problem with paying attention before. "Yeah, sorry. I was just thinking."

She leans over my shoulder and grabs my red lipstick. "See. Now that's your problem. You think too much. You better not be thinking about-"

"I'm not," I cut her off. I don't even want to think about it. I've been in Chicago for four days now and haven't spoken to Jay since the first night. The only thing I'm missing back home right now is cutting people's hair and interacting with my clients. Other than that, I don't even want to think about my life back home. "I'm not worried about him. It's something else," I mutter. "Someone just makes me so angry, and I don't understand why I am letting it get to me so much."

She gives me a knowing look and yanks my hair to the side. "Tell me all about it. Did you sleep with someone? Was it Cale or that sexy hunk, Slade?" She drops down beside me and watches as I coat my lashes with mascara. "I want details before we get to the club. You've been spending a lot of time with Cale. Hell, you could melt butter off the both of them. If I was single I'd take both on at the same time."

I roll my eyes at her and push her out of my space. "Neither one. I haven't slept with anyone." I look up at her and my eye starts twitching. My nerves are getting to me and giving me away. "What?" I say as her eyes widen as if she's just figured something out.

Shit.

"You may not have had sex, but you did something sexual." She shoots to her feet and yells, "You dirty little slut. You better start talking."

I stand up and adjust my short red dress. The material is so thin, it makes me feel naked. It barely covers my breasts and hangs just a few inches below my ass. I can't even wear a bra with this dress. Kayla picked the dress out this afternoon when we went shopping. It's the first real time we've had to spend together since I've been here. Her job and family life keep her too busy. I envy her. I want that in my life.

"Maybe I did," I mumble embarrassed. "That's all you're getting because I'm not having you embarrass me tonight." I look around Cale's room until I spot my black, leather strapped stilettos. I grab them, buckle my feet in and head for the door. "Ready?"

She takes a bite of her jerky stick and grabs her purse. "More than ever. Alex is letting me cut loose tonight. Don't be surprised if you see my hands all over that biker looking stripper. Hot damn, he is fine. I swear he looks more like he belongs in a motorcycle club than a strip club. Lucky for us, he's in the strip club. Now, let's go."

I must not have paid much attention last time I was there because I don't remember seeing him. The only one that got my attention was Slade. My mind was too clouded that night and I was working hard to keep to myself. Well, not tonight. I'm out to have a little fun.

When we arrive at the club, it is jam-packed. We literally have to squeeze our way through the door and over to the bar. I've never seen such a group of crazy women before. I can't even see the guys because they're buried somewhere in the way back behind screaming women. I'm already starting to sweat just from rubbing against bodies.

As soon as we get close enough inside, I see Sarah is tending the bar along with two other women I have never seen. They all seem to be enjoying themselves, despite the crowd they have waiting on them for drinks. I admire them. I'd be freaking out right about now.

Sarah notices me when we get closer and gives me a smirk as if she remembers me from that first night. I'm surprised that out of a crowd of people, she would remember me. I'm definitely not one to stand out in a crowd. "Hey, gorgeous ladies," she says with a wink. "What can I get you girls tonight?"

"Something strong," Kayla yells out over the music. She smiles and leans over the bar. "For both of us. Especially her."

I nudge her in the side, causing her to yelp and move away from me. "Ignore her." I smile and grab my purse, pulling out some cash. "Just give me a vodka and cranberry. Easy on the vodka."

Sarah smiles and reaches for two glasses, setting them down in front of her. I hadn't noticed before, but she's actually quite beautiful. Long amber hair and big blue eyes that make you feel comfortable and at ease. I'm sort of glad she's here. "So, you ladies are back for more of the boys of *Walk of Shame*, huh. Well, I don't blame you." She scoops the glasses full of ice and starts reaching for the bottles of liquor. "I'm guessing you're here for Slade." She looks up at me and runs her tongue over her teeth as if she knows without a doubt, that she's right. "Nice choice, honey."

The more she talks, the more curious I get about Slade. She talks about him and the others as if she's had them all. I'm not sure how to feel about that. I'm not even sure I should feel *anything* about it. "So, what do you know about these boys?" She slides our drinks in front of us and waves at someone behind us.

"I know they like to fuck." She throws her towel over her shoulder and leans across the bar so that she's closer to us. "And I know they're good at what they do. You won't find any better. Trust me." She winks at me and smiles.

Sipping my drink, I look beside me to see Kayla is hanging on every word out of Sarah's mouth. I've never seen her so curious. She's practically sitting on top of the bar ready to jump on top of Sarah. "So, you've been with all of them?"

"Kayla!" I can't believe she just asked that.

"What! I'm just curious." She grins and leans closer. "So . . ."

Sarah just laughs as if the question doesn't bother her at all. She looks proud, as if her answer makes her feel good about herself. "I've been with two of them. Best experience of my life. Both at the same time and it was hot."

Okay, now I'm curious. *What! Two at the same time?*

"Details?" Kayla's mouth asks what I'm too afraid to.

Sarah raises her eyebrows and jumps up to sit on the bar in front of us. She's really enjoying this. To be honest, I'm a little nervous. "All right, you asked for it." She grins at Kayla and then over at me as I watch her with curiosity.

"Well, it was Hemy and Slade. We were at a party at Cale's house. I had been hitting on Slade all night but he was in one of his drinking binges so he wasn't really up for it. I finally gave up and was having sex with Hemy in one of the rooms. Slade walked in, drunk and looking for pussy. I've learned that look well. Hemy was laying on the bed with me riding his cock and without stopping, just looked at him.

At first I thought he was going to kick Slade out, but then he asked him if he was going to just stand there or join. I about died when Slade came stalking in and kneeled behind me on the bed, pulled his pants down, rolled a condom on and slipped inside my ass. I will never forget that feeling. Two cocks filling me at once. They never touched each other, but it was so hot.

The only bad thing is, Slade has sort of a rule. He never sleeps with the same girl twice and my one chance wasn't even alone with him. Doesn't matter, he won't budge on his stupid rule."

Why does that bother me? I'm not sure I'm liking this, but I stay and listen anyway.

Sarah makes a face as if just remembering something else. "It wasn't until later that I found out Hemy swings both ways. Talk about sexy. You haven't seen anything worth seeing until you see two sexy as hell men kissing each other. I'm telling you, it's hot. Hemy just likes to fuck. Doesn't matter if it's male or female; although, I don't think he's much for taking if you know what I mean. Being with Hemy and Slade at the same time was by far my best sexual experience, but being with Hemy and this other guy came in close second."

By the time she's done, I'm sitting here with my mouth open. Should I be turned on by this? I'm not so sure, but I definitely am... almost jealous.

"So, what about Cale?" Kayla looks over at me while taking a sip of her drink. "I bet that boy likes to get it on too."

"Kayla, I don't need to hear about Cale. That's just weird. He's like a brother to me." I look up at Sarah, hoping she's done with her story. I'm not so sure I can hear any more of this, especially right before I'm going to be seeing the boys practically naked.

Sarah shrugs her shoulders and grabs a couple glasses when she notices some girls returning back to the bar with empty ones. "He's a little tougher to take down if you know what I mean. All I know about Cale is that he doesn't sleep with women. He only pleasures them and lets them pleasure him. I don't know why. All I know is that all these women are hoping to be the lucky one that gets him to go all the way. I don't know. I would definitely take him for a ride. I heard he works wonders with his tongue. I've never experienced it firsthand, but the women around here talk. When you're a bartender, you get all the latest scoop. It's part of the reason why I love my job so much. That and those fine as fuck men. I can get off just by watching them. I can't say that about many men."

She pushes the drinks in front of the other women, then comes back to us. "All I know is that you don't come to *Walk of Shame* unless you're looking to fulfill your darkest, wildest fantasies. This place is dirty. The boys are dirty and addictive." She slaps her hand down on the bar top and laughs.

"Well, have fun, ladies. Gotta get back to work."

I swallow hard and look away from Sarah while trying to process everything that just came out of her mouth. I guess when you're hot as hell and surrounded by a sexual lifestyle, it doesn't really matter who's watching or joining in. Slade seems to like sex more than the average male and pleasures like a pro. Maybe even like an addict. Still, the sexiest man I have ever laid eyes on. He's definitely trouble and I need to keep my mind off him.

"Oh. My. God." Kayla grabs my arm and starts pulling me through the crowd. "Did you hear her? Hemy must be the other stripper I was telling you about. That's insanely hot."

"I don't know, Kayla. This place seems pretty wild. You heard her. The boys are dirty. You better be careful before you find yourself in a position you don't want to be in."

She stops and turns to me. "What? Like you?"

"I don't want to talk about it." Pulling away from her, I push through the crowd, just wanting to get away and my heart instantly stops when I lay eyes on . . . *him.* Slade is standing shirtless with a pair of leather pants hanging low on his hips, holding a water bottle above his head.

His head is tilted back as the water drips down his flawless body and his hand works its way down where it cups his dick while he practically fucks the air. He thrusts and grinds his hips while a couple of women are on their knees in front of him.

His body is slick, sexy, and hypnotizing; it's hard to breathe as I watch him move to the slow, seductive song. Kayla is standing beside me and even her breathing has picked up.

"She wasn't kidding when she said these boys are dirty and addictive," Kayla breathes while grabbing my arm and pulling me against her. "Look beside Slade." I pull my eyes away from Slade to see a very attractive guy with long dark hair. "That sexual predator there is Hemy; totally fuckable and I want to be his prey. I can't stop imagining him kissing another sexy guy now. Oh man, that would be so hot. I would pay good money to see that. I don't know why, but it has me turned on right now."

I focus my attention on Hemy in hopes it will distract me from Slade's smooth, very wet body. It helps a little. Hemy is very sexy in the mysterious, dark way. His dark hair falls just above his shoulders, and he has a beard, but not an overly long one. It's just enough to scream that he's a bad boy with dark secrets, much like Slade. His body is perfectly sculpted, and he too is covered in random tattoos. Even his neck has tattoos. He definitely screams bad and dirty.

Kayla and I watch as he moves his hips up and down, grinding in some woman's face. The woman keeps reaching out and scratching at his chest, causing Hemy to thrust her face away with his crotch. He's wearing nothing but a pair of low hanging leather pants, just like Slade. These boys are definitely killing it with those pants. They don't leave much up to the imagination since neither of them are wearing briefs underneath. I can tell from across the room. I don't even want to check on Cale. This is too dirty and sexy.

"You like looking at Hemy," a deep voice growls in my ear. "If he turns you on that much, I would let him watch as I fuck you. Maybe he could jerk off as you scream for me to let you come."

Swallowing hard, I pull away from Slade and turn around to face him. There's no humor in his eyes, just pure want and need. "Yeah. Maybe I do like watching Hemy." For some reason, I want to tease him and see what kind of reaction I can get out of him. "I can't stop imagining how hot it must be to see him kiss another sexy guy." I lick my lips and smile over at Kayla as she lifts her eyebrows, probably wondering where I'm going with this. "It's definitely got me turned on."

Slade tilts his head while wiping his hands down the front of his wet body. He's looking at me with a cocky grin that makes my legs go weak. "Does that make you wet?" He steps closer to me and without grabbing me, rubs his lips over my ear. "Does it make you think about . . . fucking?"

I nod my head and exhale. *Holy hell, he smells so good.* The sweat is only making it more tempting for me to run my tongue over his every muscle and taste him on my tongue. "Very much."

He stands up straight, sucks in his bottom lip and then turns to Hemy. "Dude, get your fucking ass over here."

Wait. What is he doing?

Hemy grabs his shirt and wipes it over his chest before running over to stand in front of us. He's even sexier up close. Full lips with a piercing off to the side, amber eyes, and a sexy smile. "What's up?" He looks over at me and a dark look takes over his eyes. It's a sexy, mysterious look that says he wants to ravish me. Maybe he really is into sex more than Slade. That's hard to believe.

Slade notices me staring at Hemy and growls, "You better fucking enjoy this." He looks to Hemy and gives him a hard look. "Don't get any fucking ideas, man."

Hemy nods his head confused. Hell, I'm confused.

Next thing I know, Slade steps up to Hemy, grips his hair and presses his lips against his. I watch as their lips move in sync with each other's. Slade even makes sure to use his tongue a little just to give me a show.

Hot damn! This is so sexy. Instant wetness.

Slade pulls away from the kiss and grabs my hand. Before I know what he's about to do with it, he presses it to Hemy's rock hard dick. It feels so thick in my hand, and I somehow forget how to breathe. "See what my tongue does to people?" He presses my hand harder against Hemy's erection and starts moving it up and down his thin pants. That's when I notice he must have a couple piercings down there as well. It makes my heart beat faster at the thought. "This is what I do to people," he growls.

I pull my hand away while fighting to catch my breath. I am so turned on right now that I can barely stand it. I'm heated to the core and if my thighs rub together I will have an orgasm right here in front of everyone.

That was sexier than I expected. Why did seeing Slade kiss another guy only make me want him more? Is it because I know he did it for me or because he wants to have me that bad?

Holy fuck.

Hemy looks at me and takes a step closer. I can't help but look down at his erection. I can't believe that Slade put my hand on his dick. I'm so embarrassed and turned on at the same time.

Slade puts his arm across Hemy's chest and stops him from getting any closer. "You can go now," he growls.

Hemy gives me one last look, smirks and walks away.

I look Slade in the eyes as he places his hand behind my neck and yanks me to him. His other hand slithers down the front of my body and stops on the inside of my thigh. "I'm not even touching your pussy and I can feel the wetness on your thighs." He bites his bottom lip and leans into my ear. "Be ready for me to take care of this later."

Then he turns and walks away. He seriously just walked away.

"Kayla," I growl out as she smiles at me. "Don't say a word. I will strangle you right now."

Kayla throws her arms up and backs away from me as she watches Hemy from across the room. "You're so damn lucky," she breathes. "That was so hot."

Yeah, lucky me.

Both men have gone back to their screaming fans, giving us all a show. A dirty, erotic, breathtaking show.

Maybe coming here was a bad idea. Yeah. Definitely a bad idea.

CHAPTER TEN

SLADE

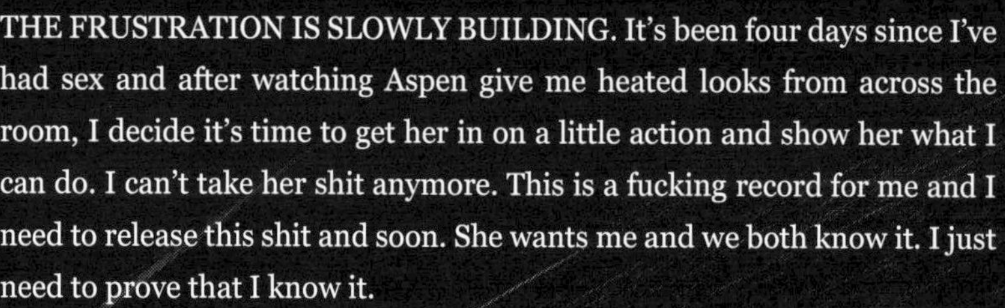

THE FRUSTRATION IS SLOWLY BUILDING. It's been four days since I've had sex and after watching Aspen give me heated looks from across the room, I decide it's time to get her in on a little action and show her what I can do. I can't take her shit anymore. This is a fucking record for me and I need to release this shit and soon. She wants me and we both know it. I just need to prove that I know it.

I walk over to her and place my hands on her hips, running my hands up her curves as her friend watches me with a huge grin. Even her friend can see what my touch does to her. She's eyeing us up, giving Aspen the nod; the one that says she's about to sit back and watch. Her own private show.

Backing her up, I nod my head to Hemy and he kicks the chair that's sitting behind Aspen closer to us. He already knows what I plan to do. I'll have to remember to thank him for looking out for me later.

I can hear the surrounding women screaming and getting excited as I guide Aspen down to the chair and place both her hands on my stomach. The women fucking love this chair and so will she. I'll fucking make sure of that.

She gives me a nervous look as I stand between her thighs and start grinding my hips to the beat of the music while slowly undoing the top of my pants. We wouldn't usually do this in such a big crowd, but I want her more than anything I've wanted in a long time. Even if that means fucking her right here, I will do it with no shame.

I pull my pants down my hips just enough so the head of my cock is exposed to her. Her eyes widen as I push her hands down further and lean down into her ear. "Like I said, it's against the rules." I suck on her earlobe as I guide her hand over my bare skin and squeeze her hand over my head. "But I want you to touch it."

Her breathing picks up as her hand starts caressing my cock through my thin pants. Each time her hand touches the head, I close my eyes and moan and so does she. It feels so fucking good that I could bend her over this chair right now, slide that dress up and fuck her. No regrets, just pure erotic sex. I don't mind giving a good show and displaying what I do best.

"That's it. You like touching my cock with everyone watching? Does it turn you on to know you're the one sitting in this chair, groping my hard cock? All these women would kill to be doing this." I grab her hand and help her to smear my pre-cum over the head of my dick. "See how bad I want you, Aspen?" I pull her hand away from my erection and bring it up to her lips. "I tasted you. Now it's your turn."

She leans her head back and closes her eyes as I brush her fingers over her lips, giving her a taste of what she does to me. It's so dark in here that I doubt anyone can see that the head of my dick is on display. She must feel the same way because she seems to be enjoying it as much as I am.

She moans and licks my taste from her lips as she rubs her hand up my erection, pulling me closer. She loves my taste. I can tell by the way she licks her lips once more, savoring the taste before opening her eyes as if she's just noticed the crazy crowd of women surrounding us. "Slade." She pulls her hands away from my body and runs them over the side of her dress, embarrassed. "I'm not doing this. Especially, right now. I told you to stay away from me," she says breathless. "I meant it."

Standing up, she pulls her dress down and pushes me out of the way.

"Go fuck yourself," she growls.

She says one thing, but her eyes say another. I think I'll listen to her eyes. They don't lie as much as her sexy mouth.

Biting my bottom lip, I bring my body against hers and pull one of her legs up to wrap around my waist. Then, I lean her back and slowly grind my hips against her aching pussy while tugging on her hair. I've been imagining this for days. It would almost be too easy for me to just pull her panties aside right now and slip right inside her. The thought causes me to moan against her lips.

Her leg tightens around me as her body starts trembling beneath my touch. I know and she knows that she's about to have an orgasm right here in front of everyone. It pleases me, knowing it's from my doing. I can get her off anywhere and she knows it.

Thrusting my hips, I move slowly to be sure she can feel the head of my cock rubbing against her clit through her thin panties. I want her to imagine just how much better it would be if it were inside of her; deep inside of her and filling her to max.

I pull her neck up and grind my hips one last time right as her body starts shaking and her breathing comes out in short quick bursts. "I told you my cock feels good, baby. It's going to feel even better inside you, claiming you."

Pulling out of my grasp, she gives me a heated but angry look before slapping me right across the face. The contact stings, making my dick even harder for her. I've done her in, and she fucking knows it. She can barely even stand right now, and it has me so turned on, I may not even make it through the rest of the night without having to release this tension. "I hate you sometimes. You're such an asshole, Slade."

The women start screaming and throwing money as she walks away and dips into the bathroom. They all want their turn, but all I want is to finish what I started. She's mad, but it's not at me. It's at herself for wanting me. It's written all over her face; enough for everyone to see.

I'M STANDING HERE WIPING MY sweat off when Hemy leans in next to me and whistles while looking across the room. "Hot dayum. She is one fine piece of ass. I think we need to tag team that shit later. You can bend her over and fuck her while she sucks my cock. I saw how worked up you got her while you were dancing for her. She needs a good fuck."

I bring my eyes up to see Aspen leaning over the bar, tugging on the back of her tight little dress. Damn, those legs are enough to hypnotize a man and almost make him forget where the fuck he's at and why he's there in the first place. Just one look at her and I can't deny that I want that all to myself.

"That, asshole, is all mine. I've already gotten a taste and I'm not sharing." I reach for the nearest shot glass and slam it back, closing my eyes as the slight burning sensation slides down my throat, giving me a temporary feeling of relief. It's nothing strong enough though. Not even enough to give me a buzz.

"Well, good luck with that shit, bro. It seems that asshole at the bar thinks otherwise." He pauses for a second as I open my eyes and look up. He points and grips my shoulder. "She doesn't seem too happy. You better take care of that shit before I do."

I growl as some drunken asshole grabs her by the hips and attempts to pull her into his lap. I can see, even from back here that she isn't into it. "Shit! I'll be right back. Start without me." I slam the shot glass down and take off toward the bar. I am so heated right now, I could break this motherfucker's jaw.

I can slightly make out what they're saying as I get closer and I am right. This asshole is definitely drunk. Not a good move on his part.

"I said no, asshole." Aspen reaches for his hand and tries prying it away from her waist while looking out in the crowd as if searching for someone. Neither one of them seem to take notice of me approaching. That's cool with me. I'm still going to fuck him up.

"Come on, babe." The guy ignores her and tightens his grip on her, pulling her down to his lap. This only pushes me further. "Look at that fine ass. I want it in my lap. We could go somewhere more private if you want."

Swinging her arm back, she elbows him in the face and stomps on his foot. "I said, let go!"

The guy stands up, pushes her and grabs his nose that is now dispersing blood. "You fucking bitch. I will-"

Anger boiling up inside me, I reach for the back of the guy's head and slam it down onto the bar beside him as hard as I can. The guy groans out in pain, obviously not expecting it as he reaches for his hair to try to release it from my tight grip.

"Fucking touch her again and I will break both your hands. Got it?" I lean in next to his ear and slam his head down onto the bar again to get my point across. Then I whisper, "Never touch what is mine again."

I look up with the guy's hair still wrapped in my hand and am not surprised to see all eyes on me as I stand here breathing heavily. It's not often fights happen in here since the majority of the population is women. My bad, but he fucking asked for it.

Aspen is looking at me with a heated look as if by hurting this prick turned her on. *Well, fuck me.* It turned me on too. I didn't know she had it in her. I like seeing her hurt someone. It's hot; especially, while she's wearing that sexy little dress.

Licking my lips, I push the asshole's head down, release his hair and walk toward Aspen. Placing one hand on her hip, I look behind her right as her friend is approaching. "Aspen won't be needing a ride." I look up at Cale as he gives me a concerned look, just now realizing what happened. "Give me the fucking keys," I growl out.

Digging in his pocket, he looks to Aspen. She doesn't take notice because she's too busy still looking at me with a very confused look on her face. She doesn't know whether to slap me or jump on me and ride me. I'll take either one. "What the fuck, man. You're not even going to finish your shift?" He tosses me the keys, already knowing my answer, and I quickly reach out and catch them.

"Nope. I have better shit to do. Take care of this asshole. Get him out of here." Grabbing Aspen's hand, I drag her past the curious crowd and out of the bar. Once outside I swing my truck door open, pick her up and set her inside.

She still hasn't said a word and I know why. She knows she's finally lost the war within herself. I'm about to fuck her and even she can't deny the sexual tension between us. It needs to be dealt with and there is only one way; to fuck and to fuck hard.

The look that she's giving me is enough to push me over the edge. I'm trying to be respectful, but I may just say fuck it and take her here and now before we can even make it back to the house.

Fuck me.

CHAPTER ELEVEN

SLADE

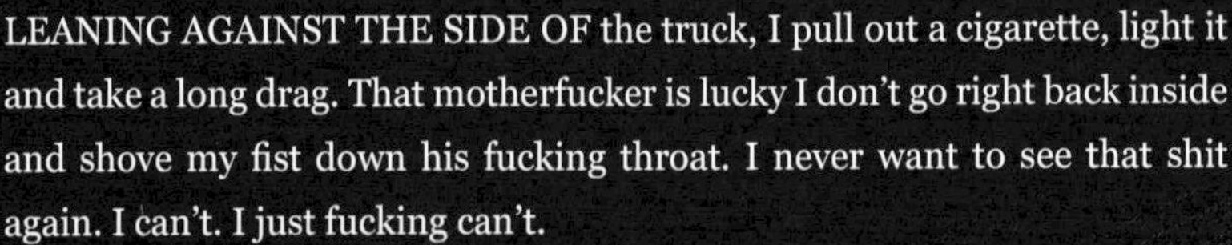

LEANING AGAINST THE SIDE OF the truck, I pull out a cigarette, light it and take a long drag. That motherfucker is lucky I don't go right back inside and shove my fist down his fucking throat. I never want to see that shit again. I can't. I just fucking can't.

I hear the sound of Aspen's heels hit the pavement beside me, but right now I'm too pissed to even look up. I'm standing here staring at my shoes, trying to keep my cool. If she opens her mouth right now, there's a huge chance I will bend her over and fuck her right now. I have way too much shit going on in my head; not to mention that asshole inside just pushed me over the edge.

"Did you enjoy that?" Her voice comes out soft, but with a hint of anger. I'm not surprised. After what I did to her in front of everyone, I'm sure she wishes it were me she elbowed in the face. "You just can't resist messing with me and pushing my buttons, can you? I don't get it."

I take another drag, close my eyes and exhale. I need another moment before I even attempt to speak. Right now, I feel like an animal released from its cage and about to pounce on its prey. The intensity of me wanting her is eating at me.

"You didn't have to save me from that idiot. Besides, it looked like you were busy over there trying to juggle a room full of women. I have a feeling you're a pro at it by now."

Okay. One more drag and I'm good to go.

I take one more drag, toss the cigarette down beside me and pin her against the side of my truck. She looks up at me with a shocked expression but doesn't say a word. Her eyes just keep jumping back and forth as I stare into them. "I did enjoy it." I lean into her ear and rub my bottom lip up her neck. "Just admit it, you did too. You think you can hide it, but I can sense it all over you." I slowly run my hand up the inside of her thigh, stopping below her panty line. "And feel it."

I am not a patient man and I've been waiting too many days for this. She better be ready. I'm about to pour all my frustration into her body because she's the reason I'm about to explode.

"You can't fucking hide it anymore and we both know it," I growl. "You want to kick my ass and fuck me at the same time. Well guess what," I whisper. "I'm fucking waiting."

I hear her breathing pick up before she places her hands to my chest and pushes as hard as she can. It only makes her angrier when her shove has no effect on me. She leans her head against my truck and exhales. "How do you know it's for you, huh?" I move my hand higher and cup her pussy in my hand, causing her to close her eyes and moan out. "It could . . ." She moans again as I start rubbing her through the thin fabric. It's getting hard for her to find her words now. I like that. "Be for someone else. How do you know," she growls questioningly.

Sliding my finger under the fabric of her panties, I shove it into her very wet pussy and grab the back of her neck. "This is how I know," I assure her. "The way your breathing picks up and your body trembles under my touch." I shove my finger deeper, causing her to raise her hips and thrust against my hand. "Do you feel that, Aspen? Your body is ready to be fucked. It needs to be fucked by me. No. One. Else."

I grab both her hands and hold them above her head while pushing my thigh between her slightly parted legs. It feels so good between her thighs. So warm and . . . wet. "You want me to fuck you?" I gently place my hand on her throat as I lean in and pull her bottom lip into my mouth and suck it, hard. She lets out a soft moan and nods her head as her lip slips from my grip. "Tell me you want me to fuck you. Say the fucking words."

Looking at me, she doesn't say a word, but the look in her eyes says it all. She lowers her hand down the front of my body, down my abs and grabs my erection in her hand. It feels so huge under her touch and I can tell by her little gasp that she feels the same way. I close my eyes and moan as she starts stroking it through the fabric as if she fucking owns it. Damn, that's such a turn on. It's all hers if she wants it.

Her hands start working on the button of my pants as she leans in and bites my nipple. She's breathing hard as she looks up at me. I'm so fucking turned on right now that I can barely contain myself. I feel like a fucking virgin about to get pussy for the first time.

What. The. Shit.

I press my body against hers and grab her legs one by one to wrap them around my waist. We both just stand here silent, looking into each other's eyes before I slam my lips against hers and claim them. I can't take it anymore. I need a fucking taste. I suck and tug, before slipping my tongue between her parted lips and sucking her tongue into my mouth. I never thought kissing could be such a turn on, but damn her lips feel so good against mine. I have to admit that I've wanted to kiss her since that day in the bathroom.

"You still haven't said it, Aspen," I groan against her lips while rubbing her hand over my hard cock. "You feel how big it is for you?" Her legs shake around me as her hand caresses my erection. "Just say the word and I will drive us back to my house and fuck you so damn thoroughly that this cock . . ." I force her to squeeze my dick as I thrust and bite her bottom lip. "Will be the only thing your body craves."

"Dammit," she hisses while pulling her hand away from my dick in a panic. "It's happening again. Put me down." She pushes at my chest and forces me to drop her to her feet. I have to catch her when she almost twists an ankle because of her high heels. "Just take me back to the house. In case you forgot." She jumps into the truck as fast as she can and slams the door closed behind her. "I'm pissed at you."

"Nothing new there," I point out.

I smirk to myself while walking over to my side of the truck and jumping in. I'm no fool. She can play hard to get if she wants, but in the end she and I both know that as soon as we get back to the house and walk in that door, I will have her riding my cock as if her life depends on it. Her body is getting desperate and so is she. Right now she hates me and is fighting against wanting me. Well, she'll hate me even more after she sees what my body can fucking do to her.

We ride in silence, but I notice her press her legs together every few minutes while glaring over at me. She can't seem to sit still and she looks as if she's about to scream. Sexual frustration is one of those bittersweet things. It claws at you until you release it and there is only one way to do so; to fuck and fuck hard. I can tell she's trying hard to keep her eyes away, but they keep scanning over my body, imagining it being on top of hers. This seems to piss her off even more.

Reaching over, I force her legs apart and slide my hand up her thigh. I slowly inch it further up her smooth skin until I feel the wetness between her legs. Then I stop. I want to see what her reaction is. I want to see how badly she needs me to release her.

She gives me a dirty look, but spreads her legs wider for me as if waiting for me to go further. I could pretend to be surprised, but I'm not. In the end, the throbbing between their legs wins out over the voice of reason in their heads. When I don't make an attempt to move, she grabs my hand and pushes it away. "You're an ass. Do you know that?" She presses her legs closed and looks out the window. "Stop screwing with me just because you think you're God's gift to women. You're gorgeous and you have a rockin' body, so what. Stop using that against my weakness. You're the only person that can piss me off this way."

She turns to look me in the eyes and her frustration is so sexy, it hurts. Yanking her legs apart, I pull her closer to me and rub my thumb over her swollen clit. I really need to get her off because by the time we get back to the house, I won't have the patience. I'm going to want to fuck her as soon as we step through the door. Her pussy has been the only thing on my mind since I tasted it for myself.

She moans as I start rubbing small circles against her body, teasing her. I start out slowly at first before moving at a faster rhythm. She starts rocking against my hand, getting more desperate the faster I go.

"Keep going." She rocks faster. "It feels so good. Why do you have to be so good at this?" She moans out in pleasure while pulling at her hair.

"It's a fucking blessing. Trust me," I groan while trying to keep my eyes on the road. "You ready to come yet?"

She nods her head and grips onto the headrest behind her. "Yes. I'm ready. I'm so ready," she breathes.

"Ask me to make you come then."

She runs her tongue over her teeth in anger before digging her nails into my arm. "Will you make me come? I want you to make me come, Slade."

I slip one of my fingers inside her while still rubbing her clit with my thumb. She moans and digs deeper into my arm, trying not to scream. "You like my finger filling you, huh? Just wait until I ram my hard cock in there." I shove another finger inside her and start moving them in and out.

"Oh damn, you're so tight, baby and so wet." I shove my fingers deeper, while moving my thumb faster. "So fucking tight. Scream for me, baby. Show me what I do to you."

I feel her body start to shake before she clamps down around my fingers. She lets go of my arm and grips the seat while screaming out her orgasm. She arches her back as I shove my fingers in one last time. "That's enough," she breathes. "Don't move. Just . . . don't. Move."

It takes her a few seconds to catch her breath. I don't blame her. That was one intense orgasm. I'll be surprised if she'll be able to walk after that shit. I slowly pull my fingers out and suck them into my mouth, tasting her as she watches me with hooded eyes. She likes it when I taste her.

Fuck me.

As soon as the house comes into view, I pull off to the side of the road and slam the truck into park. "Fuck this!" Pulling the keys out of the ignition, I hop out of the truck, slam the door behind me and rush over to her side. I can't wait any longer. I need to be inside her before I fucking explode. I won't nut until I get a feel inside her.

I yank her door open and reach inside to pull her out. Before her feet can hit the ground, I have her wrapped around my waist and I'm heading for the door. I practically bust the door down while slamming my lips against hers, both of us breathing heavily while fighting for air.

I don't even bother shutting the door behind us as I walk us over to the stairs. I set her down on the staircase and spread her legs before ripping her thin panties from her body. My eyes slowly trail from her breasts, down to her pussy as I bite my bottom lip and moan. "It's so fucking beautiful."

I force my body between her legs and press my lips against hers again. She's kissing me with such anger and frustration that it only makes me want her more. "I want to slap you so bad right now," she breathes. "I hate the way you make me want you."

"Well, I fucking love it." I grab the top of her dress and rip it open, exposing her breasts to me. I knew she wasn't wearing a bra. I could see her hard nipples even in the dim lighting of the bar earlier. She gets ready to say something; to yell at me about her dress until I suck her left nipple into my mouth, causing her to moan out instead. "You want me inside you, don't you? Just fucking admit it."

Moaning, she grabs me by the hair and yanks my head back. "I hate you so much for making me want you. Me wanting you is the last thing I need."

"Well you don't hate me enough. 'Cause if you did, then you would fuck me while punishing me. I want you to slap me, scratch me, bite me and pull my fucking hair. If you hate me, then punish me. I want to feel your fucking hate."

She yanks me up by my hair so that our faces are almost touching. Then she looks me in the eyes before pressing her lips against mine and digging her nails into my back. A burn remains in their wake, but I love the pain.

I can't fucking take it anymore. This shit is happening. I rip her dress the rest of the way off so she's lying fully naked beneath me. She looks embarrassed at first, but then relaxes as she watches me undo my pants, pull them off and reach for my cock. I stroke it for a second to see how much she likes it. Her eyes look heated as she watches me.

I stroke it a few more times before pulling a condom out of my pocket, ripping the wrapper open with my teeth and rolling it over my erection.

Not wanting to wait another second, I grip the back of her neck while sliding inside of her. We both moan as I slowly push it in all the way and stop to give her body time to adjust to my thickness.

"Fuck, you are so wet for me."

We're both panting now as I press my lips to hers and fuck her while backing her up the stairs. We get higher with each thrust until we're at the top of the stairs.

Pushing into her, I pick her up and she grabs onto the top of the doorframe while I roll my hips in and out, fucking her as hard as I can.

Her grip tightens on the doorframe as I grab her hair and yank back while pushing deep. "Fuck, you feel so damn good." I thrust into her hard and long, causing her to pull on it, almost ripping it off. "You're so tight, my cock can hardly fit inside you."

The only sound around us is the sound of our heavy breathing and our sweaty bodies slapping together as I pleasure her. It feels so fucking good, but I want to get her in my bed.

"Let go of the doorframe," I breathe in command. "Grab onto my hair, baby."

Squeezing her legs around me, she lets go of the doorframe and grips onto my hair. Her hands rub the back of my head as if she enjoys touching me and wants more. It almost makes me want more. "Slade," she moans. "I'm going to hate myself after this."

Slamming her against the wall, I thrust into her while biting her neck. "Well, until then you can fucking enjoy it."

The louder she screams, the harder I fuck her. I've been waiting for this for too long and I'm going to make sure she never forgets the way my cock makes her scream. I want her to crave my fucking cock; to never think of another one besides mine and how it fucked her so good she couldn't think straight, let alone walk. I want my cock to own her fucking pussy.

We somehow make it to my bedroom door. I hold her against it, never stopping my assault on her body while turning the knob and pushing it open as I thrust in a steady rhythm. She grips me tighter when she realizes that there's nothing behind her to support her any longer. I love having her hang on me and touch me all over. Her hands are roaming my body, taking it all in and I love it. It only proves more that she has been wanting me as long as I have wanted her.

I take a few steps inside before tossing her on my bed. I quickly jump on behind her and flip her over so her ass is up in the air, facing me. I grab her by the hips, run my tongue up her pussy, then thrust into her slow and hard.

She grips the blanket and moans as I reach around and play with her clit. "You want to come again, baby?" I rub it faster, while pushing into her, filling her to the hilt.

She nods and pushes against me with her ass.

"Show me how badly you want me to fuck you then, Aspen. Take your hate and frustration out on me. Show me and I'll make you come again."

I pull out of her and flip her over so she's looking up at me from her back. Her legs are spread wide as she takes a few deep breaths and then sits up. "You want to see my hate?" She grabs me by the hair and jumps at me so we both fall off the bed with her on top of me. "You're not the only one that has frustration to get out."

Straddling me, she slaps me across the face and then grabs my hair before sinking onto my cock and biting my ear.

Holy shit.

I'm so fucking turned on that I could bust my load right now, but I won't. This is going to last as long as I can make it. This feels too good to stop.

Grabbing her by the hips, I close my eyes and moan while she rides me. "Bite me again and I will pick you up, bind your hands behind your head and fuck you so hard that it hurts."

I don't know if she thinks I'm only messing around or if she really just wants it hard, but she bites into my ear again and tugs on my hair.

I flip her over so that I'm between her legs. Then I look her in the eyes and smirk. "You asked for it."

She lets out a little yelp as I pick her up, hold her hands above her head and slam her into the wall. "Fuck me, Slade," she moans. "I want your *big* dick deep inside of me. I want to see how long you've been wanting me. I want to know that I'm not the only one that's been suffering."

Hearing her say those words releases some kind of beast inside of me. I've never wanted to fuck someone so hard in my life. She knows just the right things to trigger me and get what she wants. She wants me to make her scream again. I can't hold back. Pleasing her turns me on more than anything.

Shit!

Thrusting back into her, I place one hand around her throat while holding her hands above her head with the other. I push in so hard and deep that she screams and scratches at my hands. She wants her hands freed to punish me and I want the same.

I release her hands and they immediately find my back and scratch long and deep as my movements pick up. I feel her starting to tremble and I know she's getting close. Our lips meet each other's, and I grab her face, forcing her to look me in the eyes as I make her come.

She moans and screams against my lips so I suck her bottom lip into my mouth and move fast and hard to finish myself off.

It only takes her kissing me hard and pulling my hair before I find myself busting my nut deep inside her still throbbing pussy. We both moan as I release myself as deep as I can. I'm not used to releasing myself inside anyone and the sensation is fucking fantastic. I usually pull out, but this felt too good to even think about it.

We stand here for several seconds, looking each other in the eyes before I pull out of her and set her back down on the floor.

I rub my hands over her face before leaning in and kissing her. She freezes at first, but then grabs the back of my head and slowly caresses her tongue with mine. It's soft, slow, and hot. The most intimate kiss I've had in years. I'm not sure how to react.

I pull away from the kiss and back away from her. She watches me with a strange look in her eyes before turning away from me and placing her hands over her face.

She sighs before speaking. "I'm going back downstairs before Cale gets home. I'm sorry. This should never have happened."

I yank the condom off my dick and toss it onto one of my old shirts. I just stand here and watch as she walks toward the door. Before I can stop myself, I say, "Wait."

She stops and waits for me to walk over to her. Stopping in front of her, I cup her face and pull it up so I can look her in the eyes. I just have to look into them and see how I make her feel; see that I pleasured her beyond belief. "Your eyes are the most beautiful fucking thing I have ever seen."

She swallows hard as her eyes dance back and forth before she closes them, as if embarrassed. "In case you're wondering, no I didn't lose a contact. I was born this way, alright? I'll save you trouble from the silly question."

"I wasn't even going to ask you that. I noticed your eyes from the very first time I laid eyes on you. They've never changed. I'm not as stupid as some people. They're beautiful. Don't let anyone else make you think any different."

She laughs and it's the most beautiful sound I have heard from her. I've never heard her laugh before and it's nice to see this side of her. "Yeah, well

I'm glad you're smarter than most. I would hate to have another reason to hate you. I already have too many to count." She pauses to push my shoulder and smile. "And thank you. Now I have one less reason to hate you. It's a start."

This makes me laugh. "Is that right?" I pick her up by her hips and set her on my desk. "I can show you a few good reasons not to hate me." I pause as I lick my lips. "Oh yeah. I already have."

She punches my chest, but this time it's playful and not out of pure hate or fuck me anger. I catch her fist and bite it to tease her. "You're such an ass. Do you know that?"

I nod and bite her harder while smiling up at her. She laughs and starts tickling me when I don't let go. "Ouch! Let go, Slade." She laughs and tickles me harder.

I didn't realize I was ticklish until now. I find myself squirming until I finally release her fist and let her jump down from the desk. She smiles at me and clears her throat. "Okay . . . I'm going now. Goodnight."

"Why not just sleep in my bed?" I grab her body from behind and pull it close to mine. I have no idea what I'm saying or doing. All I know is that it's late and I'm tired as shit. "Let Cale have his bed tonight. I'm pretty sure he's bringing some chick home. He's going to need the privacy."

She hesitates before spinning around in my arms. "You don't mind me sleeping in your bed?" Her eyes narrow as she watches for my reaction.

For some reason, at the moment, I don't. "Nah. Tomorrow you can go back to hating me from a distance. Tonight, you can hate me from my fucking bed. I promise it's a lot more comfortable than Cale's bed."

I watch her as she walks past me, smiles small and crawls into my bed. She doesn't say another word. She just looks up at me and keeps her eyes on me until I crawl in beside her and flip the lamp off. It only takes a few minutes before I crash out.

IT'S THE MIDDLE OF THE night and I try to roll over, but I can't. That's when I realize that there's a body draped over mine. My eyes shoot open and I sit up in a panic, causing Aspen to move but not wake up. I forgot she was in my bed.

I don't know what the fuck I was thinking when I asked her to sleep in my bed with me, but it's so unlike me. It must've been the adrenaline of finally getting her to have sex with me. That's my only excuse.

Stepping out of bed, I search for a cigarette in the darkened room, open the window and light it. I really need to get my shit together. My whole body is shaking and I'm covered in sweat.

I take a huge drag, close my eyes and let the harsh smoke fill my lungs before releasing it. I have to admit that she looks fucking beautiful lying there naked on my sheets and the thought of slipping back inside her is eating at me. It felt good. A lot better than I expected it to. I had never been so turned on in my life.

Fuck!

I put my cigarette out on the windowsill and take a deep breath while running my fingers through my hair, to keep from punching something. I need to get the fuck out of here. I need to go down to our gym and work this shit off. Like now.

Fucking get a grip, Slade.

CHAPTER TWELVE

ASPEN

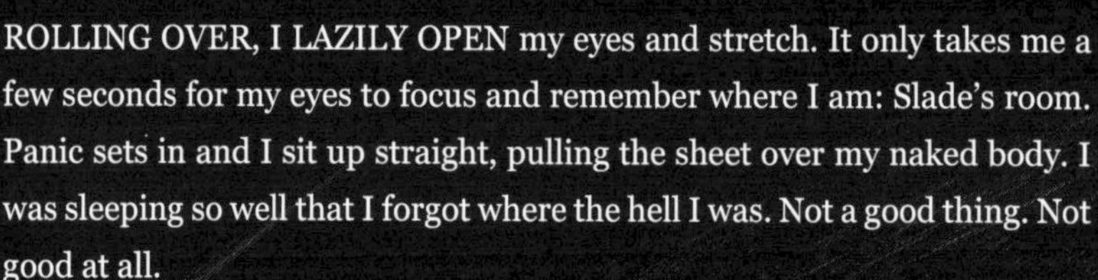

ROLLING OVER, I LAZILY OPEN my eyes and stretch. It only takes me a few seconds for my eyes to focus and remember where I am: Slade's room. Panic sets in and I sit up straight, pulling the sheet over my naked body. I was sleeping so well that I forgot where the hell I was. Not a good thing. Not good at all.

Shit! Shit! Shit!

I back up against the wall and look around to see I'm alone in the big, quiet room. Slade must have gotten up in the middle of the night and left. A part of me is glad. The last thing I want to do is face his smug ass and listen to him rub in the fact that he finally got what he wanted; not to mention that it was great. It was the best I've ever had and I can't deny it. My body already gave me away.

I tried so hard to resist. I really did, but he's too good. He's damn good at getting what he wants and he knows it. He knew I would eventually cave in and put my hate and frustration into fucking him. It's what he wanted. He likes it rough and meaningless. Well, that's exactly what he got.

While mentally cursing to myself, I jump out of his bed and look around for something to put on. I really need to get out of his room before he comes back. I don't want to see him right now. I can't.

Shit. Why did I let him rip my dress?

Cale is probably downstairs sleeping on the couch and there's no way I'm going down there naked and risking him waking up and seeing me. I really doubt he needed the bedroom like Slade said. I think Slade just wanted another thing that he could be in control of. Well, I'm sick of him being in control. I'm out of here.

I rush over to the closet, almost tripping over the sheet, but I catch myself just in time and untangle it from my legs. Reaching for the handles, I slide the doors apart and step into his very big and neat closet. I'm surprised to see how organized he is; shocked actually.

I walk all the way to the back in hopes I can find an old shirt that he will never miss. I don't know how he would react to me wearing one of his good shirts. When I get to the back my eyes land on a huge row of business suits; very expensive looking business suits.

What. The. Hell.

I run my fingers across them while counting inside my head.

Fourteen suits! Why so many?

I look up to see there are more suits stacked up on the top shelf of his closet. I don't understand what kind of stripper slash damn bartender needs so many suits. Nice ones at that. These look and feel very expensive.

Pulling my eyes away, I take a step back and look around. There are stacks of shoe boxes with expensive brand names lined up under the hanging suits. Then, to my right there is a whole rack of ties. There is definitely more to Slade than I know; more than what he shows us. I'm definitely curious.

Gripping the sheet tighter, I walk back toward the front of the closet and look up at the shelf when I notice a pile of plain black shirts stacked on top of each other. I'm pretty positive he won't miss one of these.

I reach up and try to pull the bottom one out from the stack, but am not having much luck. I'm all the way on my tiptoes and I can still barely get it in my reach.

Come on . . .

My fingers pinch the thin fabric and I tug, pulling the whole pile down with it, along with a shoe box. The shoe box lands on its side with the lid knocked off, causing a bunch of pictures and letters to fall out. I quickly struggle to gather the belongings and stuff them back inside before Slade comes back. The last thing I want him to think is that I'm snooping through his things. He definitely would not be happy about that.

After getting everything stuffed back inside, I am just about to replace the lid when a photograph catches my eye; one that has me very curious. I set the lid down beside me and reach into the box. My eyes scan the ultrasound, checking out dates, names, and any other thing that may give me a clue as to why Slade has it stacked away in his things.

Helena Valentine, December 2011.

The baby is huge. It has to be at least eight months gestation. It's from over two years ago. It makes me wonder if this child is his. I really cannot imagine him with a child. It doesn't seem like him.

Setting the photo aside, I dig a little deeper into the box to find photos of a very beautiful pregnant woman. She has long, blonde hair, sun-kissed skin, and a flawless smile. She looks happy; like the happiest woman on earth. She's holding her swollen belly, showing it off to the world as if she's the proudest woman in the world.

In a few of the photos, Slade is in the pictures with her, but he looks different; much different.

He's clean cut with short black hair, no tattoos, and the most beautiful smile I have ever seen. I also notice that the scar on his cheek isn't present in the pictures. He looks so happy; nothing like the Slade I see today. He's laughing in almost every single one of them and even kissing her belly in one. He's wearing a suit in a few of them. He looks very professional and handsome.

I hate to feel like I'm prying, but it makes me wonder where this Helena is. Where is this baby? Did he leave her and now regrets it? Is she still around, but a dark secret that he doesn't want anyone to know about? There are so many possibilities that my head is spinning. I feel lightheaded trying to piece it all together. Slade may be a lot of things, but I don't take him for reckless abandonment.

I'm sitting here just staring, in a daze, when all of a sudden I feel someone standing above me. My heart sinks to my stomach when I look up and see the hurt look in Slade's eyes. He's looking back and forth between me and the box. I instantly drop the photos and hold my breath, not knowing what to expect.

He's standing above me with his jaw steeled and his fists balled at his sides. His body is slick with sweat and his hair is dripping with water as if he's just worked out. His eyes are quick to change from hurt to pure anger and rage. I've never seen someone so angry.

"What the fuck are you doing in here?" He grips the doorframe and squeezes as hard as he can. His muscles flex so hard that his arms are shaking and his veins are popping out. "Did I say you could go through my things?"

I scramble to my feet and grip the sheet against me. "No. I wasn't trying to snoop. I was looking for a shirt to-"

"Yeah. I can fucking see that. It must have been by fucking accident then. Am I right?" His jaw clenches even harder as he reaches for my arm and pulls me to him.

He looks me in the eyes for a second and I almost see them soften; a glimpse of hope that he wants to talk to me and let me in. I can't help what comes out next. "Where are they? Did you break her heart and leave her? What about your child?"

He takes a deep breath and backs us out of the closet before slamming the doors behind me and punching the wall. "Get the fuck out!" He reaches in his dresser, grabs a shirt and tosses it to me. I catch it while trying to keep my composure. "There. That's what the fuck you were looking for. Now. Get. Out."

I clutch the shirt against my body and watch as he leans over the dresser and takes a long, deep breath. He stays in the same position for a moment before knocking everything over to the floor and then pushing his dresser over as well.

He doesn't say another word to me. He just stands there looking in the other direction, his body tight and his breathing heavy.

"I'm sorry," I stammer. "I-"

"I said get out," he says firmly. "Leave the sheet and go. I won't look at you. Just go." His voice rumbles as he grips his hair in his hands before reaching for his pack of cigarettes.

I can't stop watching him. My hands shake as I drop the sheet, quickly throw his shirt on and run out of the room, shutting the door behind me. I fall against the door and take a deep breath as I hear him breaking things and screaming from the other side. I didn't even know he was capable of feeling anything. I guess I was wrong. He's definitely feeling right now.

After a few seconds, I pull myself together enough to walk away. I don't know why, but a part of me wants to stay. A part of me wants in even though I know that will never happen. I want to see this part of him that I never even knew existed.

I quickly reach for my ripped dress and ball it up in my arms while running down the steps, past the couch and to Cale's door.

It's still dark and quiet so I doubt that he saw me. I quickly turn the knob and push the door open only to stop dead in my tracks when I set eyes on a naked Cale getting his dick sucked by some chick. He looks up while gripping her hair as if my presence doesn't even bother him.

"Holy shit!" I cover my eyes and fall against the wall. "I didn't know you were in here."

Cale lets out a soft chuckle. "Calm down, Aspen. You act as if you've never walked into this situation before." He moans before speaking again. "Your phone's been going off. It's on the dresser."

Keeping my hands over my face, I maneuver my way into the room and over to the dresser as quickly as I can. "I'll be right out. Shit!" I grab my phone and then quickly turn and rush for the door. Right as I'm about to walk out, Cale's voice stops me.

"You caved in," he says softly. "I hope you know what you're doing."

Without turning his way, I take a deep breath and exhale. There's no denying it. The proof was left on the steps. "I do. Trust me."

I step out of his room and shut the door behind me. My heart is going crazy right now and I'm in total shock and a little grossed out. I can't believe that girl didn't even stop sucking that whole time.

Seriously though!

I take a seat on the couch and look at my missed messages. My heart sinks when I see Jay's name across the screen. He called twice and sent a text message.

I touch the screen and go straight to the message.

Jay

This is a lot different than I expected it to be, Aspen. I actually miss you here. I'll see you in two days.

Swallowing hard, I drop my phone down beside me and lay down across the couch. Any other day, I would be jumping to respond to his message. Well, not today. I just don't have it in me. The need is not there.

CHAPTER THIRTEEN

SLADE

FUCK! THIS IS GOING TO be a shitty day . . .

I take a long drag off my cigarette and hold it in while leaning my body weight against the side of the building. I've been outside smoking for the last twenty minutes and I have a feeling it's going to take a lot more than just this shit before I'm able to collect myself enough to go back inside. My head is all fucked up.

I can feel my hands shake as I exhale and cross my arms over my chest to calm my breathing. My nerves are so shot today that I'm surprised I even made it out of bed to begin with. My mind hasn't stopped spinning since I kicked Aspen out of my room this morning.

What the fuck?

I toss my cigarette down, turn around to face the building and punch it repeatedly. What I wouldn't give right now for a fucking release; some kind of distraction. My mind is in such a haze I don't even notice the crackling of bones and splitting of skin. Does it hurt? Hell yeah, but physical pain I can deal with. I'm not good at dealing with *this* shit. The pain shooting through my hand does little to rest the demons inside my head. All it does is piss me off more.

I look up with guarded eyes when I hear some voices nearby. A few girls in passing; laughing and talking amongst themselves. The voices keep getting closer. I'm standing off toward the back of the building next to a dark alley that separates two buildings. It's not very often people come back this way. It's usually my safe place; a place where I can think.

"Is that you, gorgeous?"

A slim figure rounds the building and my eyes are quick to scan it out. Every single inch of it. A pair of long, slender legs lead up to firm thighs, followed by a curvy set of hips hugged by a barely there dress and a firm set of breasts. I'd know those breasts anywhere.

My eyes continue to marinate in the hot as hell female I recognize as the sexy redhead from the other day. She's no longer dressed in work attire. The perfect example of a little sugar and spice, that's for damn sure. She's in far less now.

She smiles when she notices me checking her out. She's definitely enjoying giving me a good show and I'm enjoying the view. She found a damn good time to give it too. "Sarah told me I could find you back here. You busy?" She works her lips together, smearing her red lipstick while putting her cigarette out on the bottom of her heel. "I have some *extra* time tonight and was hoping I'd find you."

Wiping my bloodied fists on the back of my pants, I step closer to the temptation in front of me and look her up and down, taking her all in. "Are you sure you have enough time for me? This may take a while."

Looking over her shoulder, she sends her friends off with a wave of her hand before turning back and flashing me a seductive smile. Her demeanor turns serious while checking out the bulge in my jeans. "I definitely have time for you."

She steps toward me, places her hands on my chest and backs me up against the building. I know exactly where she's going with this and I can't deny I need exactly that.

I pull out another cigarette and light it as she drops to her knees and starts unbuckling my belt followed by my jeans. She works fast at pulling them down my hips while rubbing my erection with her free hand. "Mmm . . . you're a big boy, aren't you?" She pulls my briefs down, letting my cock spring free from its restraints. Her eyes go wide as she licks her lips. "Definitely a big boy. I'm going to have fun with this one."

I close my eyes and take a drag as she moves in and closes her lips around my cock. She moves in a slow rhythm, swirling her tongue around while moving her hand up and down my shaft. She's a pro at this. The combination of the nicotine mixed with the suction is just what I need at the moment.

I moan as she starts moving faster. It feels fucking fantastic, but I'm not feeling the release that I should. This pisses me off.

Taking another hit, I inhale it long and deep while grabbing the back of her head and pushing it further down so my head hits the back of her throat. She grabs my ass and starts sucking faster; enjoying it.

I move my hips back and forth, fucking her mouth, matching her rhythm; looking for a release that isn't coming. Not even close.

Dammit! *I've had enough of this shit.*

Tugging her hair so she knows to stop, I pull out of her mouth, bend down and pick her up to her feet. I toss my cigarette down. "Bend over." I place my hand on her back and push her forward so her ass is in the air. Beautiful. She looks over her shoulder at me, waiting. "This isn't doing what I need it to do, sweetheart. I need to bury my cock deep in your pussy for the release I need." I bend over her and speak in her ear while pulling her dress up. "I have a lot of frustration to work out. Just a one-time release."

I turn her around so she can place both her hands on the building for support. She's going to need it. I slap the right exposed cheek, hard. She yelps and I press my front to her back. "You like that," I ask as I hook my thumbs under her panties and inch the tiny thong over her hips, letting it fall to her feet. Pushing back, I reach in my pocket for a condom.

My jaw clenches as I stare down at her slick pussy just waiting for me to ram my cock in it; to give her the same release I'm needing. For some reason, I don't feel the same rush as usual. As a matter of fact, I don't feel shit.

"Fuck!"

I toss the condom packet at the building and rub my hands over my face. I am beyond frustrated with myself at the moment. This is not fucking good.

Sex has always been my way to cope. If I don't have that, what kind of pussy am I? What the fuck am I supposed to do now?

She looks over her shoulder to see my face before she quickly stands up and pulls her dress down. She looks disappointed as fuck. "What the hell is wrong? Are we doing this or not?"

I shake my head while pulling my jeans back up and exhaling. "Not." I buckle my jeans and then turn to walk away while redoing my belt buckle. I need to get my ass busy with something. Fucking shots or something. Anything to numb this shit.

I storm my way back into the bar and over to Sarah. "Give me a fucking shot; the strongest you got . . . and quick." I sit my ass on a stool and watch as she reaches for a glass. She flashes a knowing smile while setting it down in front of me and eyeing me up and down. "What, Sarah?"

She shakes her head and pours me a shot of whiskey. "Looks like you're not the only one here to drink your mind away." She nods behind me and leans over the bar. "Look behind you by Hemy."

I grab my shot and spin around in my stool while slamming it back. The sight in front of me makes my heart race.

What the hell?

"How long has she been here?" I push the shot glass in front of Sarah and stand up. "Another one. Fast."

Sarah sighs and pours me another one. "She got here right after you went outside. She's already had three shots of vodka and a vodka and cranberry." She watches as I slam back the second shot before speaking again. "She looks like she's having some fun with Hemy. My guess is . . ." She smirks at me and grabs my empty glass out of my hand. "That you already fucked her. Women always seem to go looking for the next guy to make her feel *wanted*."

"Yeah, well we both know she isn't getting it with that motherfucker. He's worse than I am. Shit."

I can already see Hemy working his bad boy charm on Aspen and even from across the room, it looks as if it might be working. The truth is, if Hemy wants to fuck someone he will fuck them one way or another. It's how it works with him.

He's over there with his jeans unbuttoned, slowly pouring water down the front of his chest while looking her directly in the eyes and fucking the air. From my angle I can see her hands reach out to touch his stomach. I'm not sure I'm liking this shit.

Making my way across the room, I step up behind Aspen and grab her arm to turn her around. It takes her a few seconds before she even registers that she's looking at me. The drinks are clearly setting in and I'm wondering just what the hell her reasoning is for being all over Hemy. "What the fuck are you doing here?"

Aspen laughs, clearly unfazed by my tone and yanks her arm out of my reach. "I'm getting a striptease from Hemy. What does it look like?" She reaches for Hemy's jeans and pulls him closer to her. "Don't stop dancing on account of that asshole," she says with a scowl.

Hemy raises an eyebrow to me and smirks as he notices my eyes trail down toward her hands that are working their way down to his hard dick. She's clearly trying to push my buttons.

"Don't come over here and try to ruin my fun just because you're having a bad day. Clearly you have some shit to deal with." She runs her hand over Hemy's cock while looking at me. Hemy seems to fucking like this. "Maybe Hemy isn't as big of a dick as you." She laughs and looks me in the eyes. "Well, he definitely has as big of a dick as you. Maybe he knows how to use it just as good."

Okay. Now I am getting extremely fucking pissed. I don't like seeing her rub his cock one bit. It makes me want to kick the shit out of Hemy. Well, that's a fucking new feeling. "Too bad you won't be finding out. You're fucking going home. Now."

She yanks her arm away from me as I reach for it. "The hell I am. I'm having fun with Hemy. He's so damn *sexy*." She steps closer to Hemy and caresses his chest and abs. "And I bet those piercings feel . . . good. I've heard some hot, hot stories about him. Maybe I want to try him out. Have a little fun of my own for once."

Hemy goes to reach for her waist, but I place my hand to his chest and push him back. "Back the fuck up, man." My jaw steels as I look him in the eyes to let him know just how fucking serious I am. "Not a good time to fuck with me."

Hemy gives me a hard look before backing away and finding the closest chick to start grinding on. We may push each other's buttons, but we've figured out in the past just how far to push each other. We're not going that fucking route again.

"Are you serious?" Aspen reaches for her purse and starts heading for the door. "I really cannot stand you. First you fuck me and then you throw me out like trash and now you ruin my fun. What the hell goes on in your twisted mind?" She moves faster as I fall into step behind her. "Huh? Huh? What?"

"None of your business. All you need to know is that you're acting like a fucking fool. If you think Hemy will treat you any better than me, then you're fucking mistaken. He will take you home and call over a buddy while they both fuck you until you're sore. Then they will wake up and fuck you again. You will still end up alone in the end. Hemy is not going to make things any better."

She yanks the door open and rushes outside before turning around to yell at me. "So, what the hell does it matter? It seems that no one wants me. I'm not enough for anyone. Might as well just fuck them all then. I'm so tired of it. So tired of everyone treating me like I'm worth nothing but sex. What is so wrong with me?"

I watch as she turns around and stomps over to her friend's car. She struggles with unlocking the door while trying to balance on her heels. "Don't you fucking get in that car." I stride over and yank the keys from her hand. "You're not driving."

She reaches for the keys, but I hold them up high so she can't reach them. She slaps my chest and pushes me. "Give. Me. The. Keys."

I shove them in my front pocket and push up against her until her body is pinned against the car. "No. You're not driving. You're drunk." I pin her hands above her head as she struggles against me. "And you are fucking enough. We're all just fucking assholes. You need to know that."

She stops struggling against me and looks me in the eyes. I see a hint of her there but I can tell that she's pretty close to wasted. After a few seconds, she pulls one of her arms free and reaches into my pocket digging for the keys. I feel her hand brush over my cock and it instantly gets hard. "Give them to me, dammit."

I yank her hand out of my pocket and pin it back against the car while roughly pushing my body against hers. "I said you're not fucking driving. I'll call us a cab. Try reaching for those keys again and I will tie your ass up with my belt."

"Why the fuck do you care? Now you want to be the good guy?" She laughs and pushes me away with her knee. I back off and give her the space she needs. She looks hurt now. I can't deal with that. "Get off me. I'll be over here." She starts walking away. "In the bushes waiting."

I don't understand why, but I just want to get this woman home and in bed; in my fucking bed.

BY THE TIME WE GET back to the house, the full effects of the shots have kicked in. She's slurring her words and laughing at absolutely nothing at all. It almost makes me want to laugh, but I'm too fucking annoyed to enjoy this.

She laughs even harder as I pick her up and throw her over my shoulder. "My ass is showing." She starts tugging on her dress and squirming in my arms. "My thong! My thong!"

I slap her ass to stop her from moving. "No one cares. We're the only ones here and I have already seen your ass."

"Yeah. And a *whole* lot more." She begins pulling up the hem of my shirt, revealing my back. She inserts the tips of her fingers under the waistband of my jeans, lightly caressing my ass. It kind of tickles until she digs her nails into my skin and scratches upward. "I want to see more of you. Strip." She continues to scratch up my back, hard, causing me to tip her back up.

I grab her ass cheeks in my hands and she instantly wraps her legs around my waist. She bites the skin on my neck playfully as she reaches for my belt. I start walking up the stairs toward my bedroom. "Take it off, dirty stripper boy," she says teasingly. "I love your body. It's so *sexy*. I just want to lick it and taste it."

As turned on as I am by her biting me and trying to strip me, I keep my fucking cool and toss her on my bed before walking out of my room and slamming the door behind me. I can't let this shit happen for two reasons: number one, she's drunk. Number two, it's against my fucking rules.

Shit. I need a cold shower.

I take my time in the shower before quietly making my way up the stairs and to my room. When I walk in, I notice right away that she is sleeping. She's managed to strip out of her dress and heels and is now wearing one my favorite shirts. I have to admit, I like seeing her in it. She looks beautiful.

I reach for a cigarette and light it while pacing around my room and watching her sleep. She looks so fucking peaceful lying there. A part of me wants to crawl into bed next to her and hold her in my arms, but the smarter part of me is reminding me of what a horrible idea that is. So instead, I dig out my favorite picture of Helena, grab the chair and pull it next to the window and sit.

I stare at the picture until my eyes blur. I haven't looked at this in almost a year. It hurts. It hurts so fucking badly that I can't breathe . . . but there is something making it a little easier. Someone that makes me want it to be easier. That thought scares me.

I must sit there for about an hour, in the dark with my hands wrapped in my hair before I hear her mumbling and moving around. When I look up, I see that her eyes are opened and she's staring right at me.

"Talk to me, dammit," she says.

I feel an ache in my chest at the thought of talking about it. I've been holding in my emotions for so long; for too long. Maybe it's time to get it out. She'll be gone in a couple days anyways. Maybe this will help ease some shit in my head.

Here goes fucking nothing . . .

I jump to my feet, toss the picture on the bed and try to hold back the tears. "Her name *was* Helena Valentine. She was my fiancée and she was carrying my child."

CHAPTER FOURTEEN

ASPEN

OH. MY. GOD.

I feel an ache in the pit of my stomach and I feel like puking. *Was. He said was.* I blink a few times to focus my vision before reaching for the picture next to my feet and rubbing my thumb over it. It's moist and the color is smeared. It wasn't like that last time I saw it.

"I really don't want to talk about this, but it is starting to take every fucking thing in me to keep my shit together. I do everything I can to keep my mind busy. It's getting pretty fucking exhausting. I don't think I can take it anymore."

I look up at Slade and suck in a deep breath while taking in the pained look in his eyes. They're wet and I can tell it is taking everything in him to not cry. I can't even speak. I don't want to. I'm afraid to hear more. I'm scared to hear what he went through.

It's silent as he starts pacing. The silence is getting me so nervous that my stomach hurts. Not that the liquor helps any . . . but I feel totally sober now; wide awake and alert.

"I loved her with everything in me," he finally says. "I would have never left her or my child. Don't ever think that. It sends a flood of rage through my body. I may be a piece of shit now, but I wasn't always this way." He looks up toward the ceiling and rubs his hands over his face, clearly frustrated with himself. "We dated all throughout high school and I had known her since I was ten. She was my best fucking friend and I never had the courage to tell her how I felt. I went years holding it in, afraid that she would reject me and it would ruin our friendship."

He stops pacing, pulls out a cigarette and lights it before continuing. "She meant more to me than that. I couldn't lose her. I wouldn't allow it. Our freshman year I watched her date numerous assholes that always broke her heart. She always came to me for comfort and I was always there to take care of her. I promised her I always would be and I keep my fucking promises. One night after some asshole put his hands on her, I kicked the shit out of him and told her I couldn't take seeing her hurt anymore."

He takes a long drag of his cigarette and looks out the window as if trying to picture it all in his head. His voice is starting to break and I can tell this is tearing him up inside. I hate this.

"I told her I loved her; that I was *in* love with her. She was shocked as hell when I told her. I still remember the look on her face before she leaned in and kissed me harder than I had ever been kissed in my whole life. It was as if she were desperate; as desperate as I was. Come to find out, she had been in love with me the whole time and she was afraid of the same thing I was. From that day on she was mine. I took care of her." He turns to look at me. "And I never fucking hurt her. She was my life. I would have given my life for hers."

He places his hand over his face and looks down at the ground. I can't be sure, but I think I see tears falling. He puffs his cigarette and clenches his jaw. "If I could trade places with her I would, dammit. Fuck!"

He crouches down, resting his elbows on his knees with his face buried in his hands. "It should have been me. We were both in that fucking car. Not just her. Both of us, dammit!"

He starts shaking his head back and forth, hitting his head against the dresser behind him, as the tears come out steadily, dripping down his face and arms. "I didn't want to go anywhere that night. I tried so hard to get her to just stay where we were. It was New Year's Eve and all though I wasn't drinking, I knew others were. I told her. I fucking told her I didn't want to drive her home with all the crazy people that would be out that night, but she was eight months pregnant with our baby girl and she kept complaining she was uncomfortable and needed to go home to sleep. Finally, I caved in." He looks up toward the ceiling. "I'm so fucking sorry, Helena. I should have said no and put my foot down. You may have been pissed at me, but you and Hailey would be here right now. I would be taking care of you both; protecting you."

His body starts shaking as he looks back down at the ground and breaks down. He's crying so hard that I can't help the moisture building up in the corner of my eyes just from watching him. My heart aches for him. He's been holding all this pain in. That's not healthy for anyone. Not to mention the fact that he blames himself. No one should have to bear that pain.

I stand up and walk over to stand in front of him, but he doesn't look up from the ground. He just takes a quick drag and exhales. "The car killed her on impact; broke her neck. All it did was throw me around a little." He brushes his fingers over the scar on his face. "I still remember holding her until the ambulance came. It felt like forever before they got there. I knew she wasn't breathing, but I . . . I just kept on yelling at her to hold on; that her and Hailey were going to be okay, but the blood . . . it was everywhere. Her seat was soaked in it, but I never let myself believe that Hailey wouldn't be born. I refused to give up hope."

He stops and chokes back a sob before whispering, "My life ended that night, along with theirs."

Without thinking, I drop down on my knees in front of him and place my hands on his arms, but he jerks away. I grab his arms again and pull them away from his face. He looks up at me through wet lashes while dropping his cigarette and putting it out with his knee. "You can't blame yourself for that night, Slade. Please, stop blaming yourself. You did everything you could to take care of them."

His nostrils flare and his jaw muscles flex as tears roll down his blotchy face. His eyes are distant and his whole body is shaking under my touch. His pain is too much to handle. All I want to do is help ease it.

I grab his face and rub my thumb over his scar as a tear slides down my cheek. He still hasn't said another word. He just looks numb now; dead inside. He's staring at me as if he's a bit surprised by my comforting him. "It's okay for you to talk about it. It's okay to let it out and ask for help to carry some of the burden. Let me help you." He starts shaking his head as he closes his eyes, tears still falling. "I know you miss them. That is nothing to be ashamed of. Nothing at all. The world should know how much you love them. Don't let the memory of your family die out because you're too afraid to talk about it; to remember. You shouldn't live life that way."

He clears his throat and looks blankly at the wall across from him. "Every day is a struggle for me to get by. Just the thought of losing them takes the breath right from my fucking lungs. It hurts so fucking bad. I never thought a day would go by that I wouldn't have Helena by my side. We spent every day together. Even as kids. It's not easy to just move on with life after losing the biggest part of you; like losing a vital organ. After that day, I just shut down. I gave up. Every day I feel like I'm fucking dying, over and over again. I can't fucking breathe, Aspen. I can't."

Feeling my heart break for him, I wrap my arms around him and pull him to me as tightly as I can. To my surprise he doesn't push me away. Instead he snuggles his face into my neck and wraps his arms around my head, letting the tears fall. So, I sit here and hold him for a while until the tears stop. It feels like forever, but I refuse to let him go. He needs someone. All this pain has been consuming him and he's been living his life by numbing himself to the world; getting out of his own head.

Quite a bit of time passes, but finally, he pulls away from me and stands up. He doesn't even bother with wiping his face off. He just lets the last tear fall; unashamed. "You should get some rest, Aspen." He looks me in the eyes for a moment before picking me up and walking over to his bed. He stops in front of it and gently places me atop the mattress. "It's really late. Cale should be home soon. You can just crash in here."

He takes a seat at the edge of the bed and places his face back in his hands while yawning. I sit up and crawl over to him to place my hand on his shoulder. It's tense and he's still slightly shaking. "You should get some rest too. I am fine on the couch." I swallow hard while looking at his solid muscles though his snug shirt. They keep flexing as if he's struggling with something; as if he's fighting frustration. "I can stay if you need me to, though."

He turns around, wraps his arm around my waist and pulls me to him before laying back on the mattress. He gently brushes my hair away from my neck and snuggles up against me with his face against the side of my neck. His breathing is soft and warm against my flesh. It gives me goose bumps. “I need you to,” he whispers.

My heart skips a beat from his words and I find myself wrapping my arms around him for comfort and to pull him closer; as close as I can get him. For some reason, being in his arms this way is making it hard for me to breathe. I have never seen this side of him and I’m afraid the feeling is too good for me not to want more. Right now, being in his arms makes me feel special. He’s opened up to me in a way that I doubt he has with anyone else in a long time. This feeling makes me happy.

When I wake up, Slade is gone. Just like he was the last time I stayed in his room. Except this time, I know he stayed the whole night because he never let me go. He held me so tight that I could barely move. Being in his strong arms made me feel safe and at home; something I haven’t felt in a while. It confuses me.

I sit here for a while waiting for Slade to return, but he doesn’t. It’s been, I don’t know, maybe twenty minutes or more since I’ve noticed him gone. A part of me worries that he’s still suffering from the pain of last night and maybe he left to numb the pain. I’ve noticed the way he uses alcohol to numb the pain because, well, I did it last night. Pain gets the best of us all at some point.

I tiredly crawl out of bed and make my way down the stairs. When I pass the couch, I see that Cale is asleep on it. He must’ve assumed I was in his room when he got home late last night. Well, he was wrong.

When I get to the bathroom door I stop, because it is slightly cracked open, but the lights are off. Last time this happened, Slade was behind that door and I’ll never forget that look in his eyes when he saw me standing there. I’m not sure I can face that again. It made my knees weak.

Working against my nerves, I push the door open and take a step inside. Slade is standing there in a T-shirt and a pair of white boxer briefs. He’s leaning against the sink while staring up at the ceiling. He looks lost in thought.

I hesitate before speaking. I’m not sure he wants to be bothered.

“I . . . I just wanted to check and make sure that you’re okay.” I step further inside and he turns to look at me. The look in his eyes is different this time. I can’t tell exactly how, but just different. He doesn’t speak; just clenches the sink and then lets go. "Do you need anything?"

He slowly walks toward me, his eyes focused on my face. His expression is calm and relaxed. I've never seen him like this. His hands reach out and he softly caresses my cheek before bringing his eyes down to my lips. "Yeah," he whispers. "You."

"What-"

My words are cut off when he tangles his fists in the back of my hair and gently presses his lips to mine. He kisses me soft, but with a want that makes my heart speed up. My lips part enough for him to slip his tongue inside and swirl it around mine. When this man kisses like this, he doesn't just kiss you, he owns you.

His muscles flex around me as he pulls me closer to him and slowly backs me up against the wall. My hands desperately seek his body; just wanting to touch him in any way I can. Right now, we couldn't possibly get any closer, but I'm still trying; he's trying.

"I love the way your mouth tastes," he whispers against my lips. "I haven't wanted to kiss someone this much . . . in a very long time." He tugs on my bottom lip with his teeth before sucking it into his mouth and releasing it. "With you, I can't get enough of it."

Desperate for more of him, I press my lips against his and dig my nails into his strong back. He growls against my lips before he picks my legs up and walks to the right, stepping into the shower. He sets me back down on my feet while grabbing my hip and pulling me against him.

With his lips still pressed against mine, he reaches over and turns the shower on before guiding us both under the water. He continues an assault on my lips; kissing me so hard it's a little painful. The stubble from his lip scours my smooth skin, but at the moment I couldn't give a damn.

The water is cold at first, causing me to jump back, but he squeezes me tighter to him and causes a friction between our bodies. The radiation of body heat warms me up and it only makes me want him more.

His hands work slowly, pushing his T-shirt up my thighs as he works his beautiful lips against mine; teasing me in a way I have never been teased.

Every time his tongue caresses mine, I feel myself clenching my thighs to keep from going crazy. His touch and the taste of him is driving me mad; not only making my body want him but crave him. Now I see why Hemy was so hard. This man is so erotic.

Both of us are drenched; our wet clothing plastered against our bodies as we stand here trying to catch our breath. He's now looking me in the eyes as he reaches for my thong with both hands and drops to his knees, gently guiding it down my legs as if I'm delicate and he's trying not to break me.

I place my hands on his shoulders and look down at him as I lift my feet out of it. After he tosses my panties aside, he looks up at me while running his hands up my thighs, followed by his soft lips. My whole body quivers from his touch and my breathing picks up as he gets closer to the ache between my thighs.

Just when I think he's about to pleasure me, he stops and stands up while wiping the water from his face. The bathroom is still slightly dark, but I can still see the steely blue of his eyes and the intensity in them is so great that I find myself grabbing the back of his head and slamming my lips back to his for more. They can't get enough; I can't get enough.

His erection presses against my belly as he cups my ass cheeks and squeezes. He picks me up and presses me against the wall. My legs wrap around his waist on instinct. His stiffness against my pussy sends a surge of pleasure and need throughout my body, causing me to moan out against his lips.

"Why does this feel so good?" I ask breathless.

He runs his hands up my side and speaks against my lips. "Because it's with me," he breathes, "And I want you in a way I never thought I'd want anyone again. There is something about you that is different."

Pressing my body tighter against his, he rubs my pussy against his erection, making me want to scream out, even through the wet fabric. It feels so big and firm and it is still confined inside the cotton of his briefs. I've never wanted a man like this before. I want to touch him bare; undress him and pleasure him.

Loosening my legs, I slide down his front until I am standing on my two feet. I drop to my knees, my eyes level with his hard cock that is begging to be released from its cage. As I take hold of it in my hand, I picture what it felt like inside me and with that vision I lose control, having no other option than to release it from his briefs, so I do by hooking my small fingers underneath the elastic band. Pulling outward, his cock springs free, allowing me to pull them down his legs until they pile up at his feet.

His cock is standing at attention, commanding to be touched. It's the most beautiful cock I've ever seen. I run my hand up and down his shaft, brushing the tip of his penis once in a while to tease him. Each time I do this, he moans and bucks forward.

"Touching you drives me crazy," I whisper. "I want to feel you." He takes my hand and pulls me to my feet, pressing me against the wall. He touches my cheek with the tips of his finger, brushing my wet hair off my face. He lightly traces the seam of my body, stopping at my thigh and clenching it in his palm before pulling it upward to rest around his waist.

He brushes his finger of the opposite hand over my entrance, slightly dipping inside and running it up my folds before sticking it inside and slowly moving it in and out. He's good at pleasuring me and he damn well knows it. "Touch me, Slade." I run my tongue up his wet chest, then up his neck, making my way to his ear. "I love you inside me," I whisper.

Pinning me against the wall with his sculpted body, he presses deeper inside, quickening his pace at an angle like a hook. Each time he slams inside, he hits a spot and it feels amazing. I can't help but vocalize the way it makes me feel. "That's it. Don't stop. Please don't stop."

I'm beginning to zone out as the feeling of bliss takes over my body. "You like my fingers inside you, baby? Do you want my fingers to make you come or do you want my cock?"

As the last word escapes his lips, he stops as I'm on the verge of orgasm. He looks me in the eyes with those magnificent blue eyes waiting on an answer. "I want your cock, Slade. I want you to fill me completely."

I feel his chest rumble before he grabs the bottom hem of the large T-shirt, pulling it off in one quick motion. "I need you naked for this," he says in a voice that makes me want to come on the spot. Placing his palms over my ass cheeks, he trails down both of my thighs with a quickness, picking me up and pressing me against the wall, aggressively. I love this side of him.

His eyes lock with mine as he lowers me to his erection and slowly eases it inside of me. I close my eyes and moan as I feel his thickness stretching me to accommodate his girth. He holds me there for a minute, being sure that I'm okay before he slowly starts moving me up and down his cock allowing the wetness to spread. He's taking me for another ride, despite the fact it's against his rules and I'm definitely not blind to this. It gives me a rush like nothing else and is hot as hell.

We both moan with each thrust, not able to get enough of this pleasure. It's beautiful, raw, and erotic just like him.

Feeling him raw, inside of me, has my adrenaline pumping so hard that I forget how to breathe. I'm not sure if I want to. I just want to feel this moment for what it is and never forget it.

I slowly peel his shirt off him while his eyes take me in; every inch of me as if he can't get enough. His arms flex each time he enters me and his breathing picks up as he pushes himself deeper inside me. I lean my head against the wall, moaning, with each thrust.

My body becomes heated as the steam fills the shower, causing my head to become a clouded haze. Nothing else can be processed but the moment at hand. Between the water splashing against our bodies and the slow rhythm, I'm becoming hypnotized by him. It's a cruel pleasure. He's teasing me; ruining me. I can't concentrate on anything; only the sensation that is building in my body each time he pushes inside me.

He presses his lips to my neck while picking up speed and pushing harder and deeper as if he can't get enough of me. "You feel so fucking good, Aspen. This feels good." He places a hand behind my head and pulls it to him so it presses against his forehead, our lips barely brushing. "I'm about to go soon. I can't hold it in any longer. I need you to come, baby."

He presses his body weight against mine and starts thrusting into me hard and deep while swirling his thumb over my clit.

I shake in his arms and moan as I get close to climax. It feels so good, I scream out my pleasure. It's too much for me to bear internally. I fucking scream and grab onto the shower head almost pulling it off. I feel my release as I clamp down around his thick dick and squeeze my legs around his waist.

His reaction is to speed up and go even faster. He's ready to go now and for some reason I want to experience this in its fullest.

"I'm on birth control," I say out of breath.

He pauses for a second, presses his lips against mine and then fucks me so hard that I bite down onto his tongue. I suck it and he moans just before he pushes as deep as he can go and I feel him release his load inside me.

He holds me up against the wall, our lips twining as we both fight for air. Neither one of us speak. We don't need to. We just bask in our release, enjoying this moment of peace.

After a few moments, he gently sets me down, steps out of his briefs completely and we shower together with him cleaning me. With him touching me all over it's so hard to not want him back inside of me.

I can see it all over him too as he takes in my body with a look as if he's ready to back me against the wall and own me. This want is too great for me.

He leans over my shoulder and runs his lips up my neck, stopping just below my ear. "I want you to come for a ride with me after we shower. I have things I want to tell you."

I nod and close my eyes as he attends to me.

I'm not used to this kind of treatment. I mean from anyone. Is this the way he always was before his life fell apart? Is this the person he has been fighting so hard to hide?

If so . . . then I'm in deep trouble.

CHAPTER FIFTEEN

SLADE

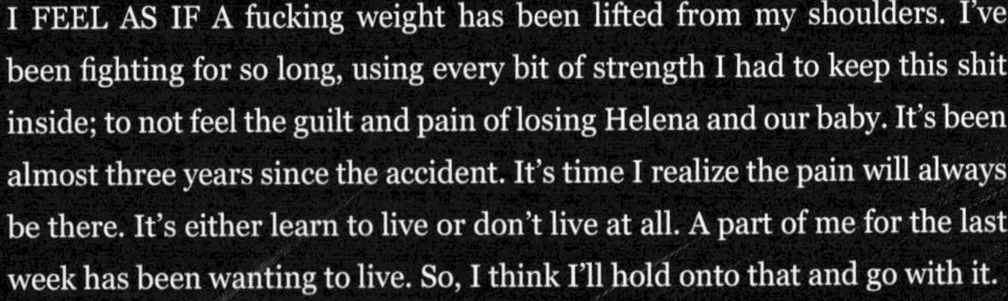

I FEEL AS IF A fucking weight has been lifted from my shoulders. I've been fighting for so long, using every bit of strength I had to keep this shit inside; to not feel the guilt and pain of losing Helena and our baby. It's been almost three years since the accident. It's time I realize the pain will always be there. It's either learn to live or don't live at all. A part of me for the last week has been wanting to live. So, I think I'll hold onto that and go with it.

I'm just throwing on my shirt, when the bedroom door opens and Cale steps inside. He looks like a hot mess as if he didn't sleep for shit. Not a pretty sight.

"Dude. What the fuck was all that noise a bit ago? You had some chick fucking screaming like mad in the shower. It woke my ass up and probably woke Aspen up too. It's too early for this shit."

I raise an eyebrow at him while slipping on my Chucks and fastening my belt. "It *was* Aspen. Don't worry, man. She's perfectly fucking fine. Trust me."

He takes a step back and scrunches his forehead up. "Whoa, man. What the fuck do you mean it was Aspen?" He takes quick steps in my direction and stops right in front of me. "That has to be a fucking joke. I know you fucked her the other night. It never happens twice with you. Are you fucking with me?"

I place my hand on his shoulder and squeeze. "Nah, man. I'm not fucking with you." I smile and slap him on the back, almost making him fall forward. "I'm taking her for a ride on my motorcycle and chilling for a bit before work." I walk toward the door and stop to look back at him. "It's a nice day out. I don't want to be cooped up inside."

"What. The. Fuck." He gives me a shocked ass look and runs his hands over his face really fast as if trying to wake himself up. "I must need to go back to sleep. I think I'm hearing things now."

"Definitely not hearing things. Now get the fuck out of my room, motherfucker." I nod my head and laugh as he walks past me, keeping his eyes on me the whole time. He's looking at me as if he's waiting on something. I don't have time for this shit. "What the hell is wrong with you?"

"Nothing. I'm just trying to wrap my head around this shit. Not only did Aspen *let* you fuck her more than once, but you *wanted* to."

"All right, man. Well I don't have time to stand here while you try to wrap your big head around this shit. I have to be at the club in three hours." I walk past him and make my way down the stairs.

Right as I reach for my keys, Aspen steps out of Cale's room wearing a pair of faded jeans, a white tank top, and some old Chucks.

All right. My kind of girl.

I grab her by the waist, pull her to me and suck her bottom lip into my mouth. She seems a little surprised at first, but eventually wraps her hands in the back of my hair and moans as I rub my hands up her sides.

I release her lip and look her up and down, taking all her raw sexiness in. "Shit, you're so fucking sexy." I press my lips against hers while backing her up against the door and cupping her ass in my hands. Right now, I just can't keep my hands off her. "Fuck, just one taste and I can't get enough. I want more of you."

"Wow. I definitely was not expecting this shit. This is way fucked up and unnatural. For the both of you."

Aspen pulls her mouth away at the sound of Cale's voice and clears her throat. She nervously looks me in the eyes and maneuvers her way out of my hold. "I'll be back in a bit. Slade is just taking me on a ride."

Cale lifts an eyebrow and leans against the couch. "You mean another one? Isn't two enough?"

"Ha. Very funny, smartass." Aspen shoots him an icy glare before reaching for the door handle and pushing me out of the way so she can walk outside.

I turn back to Cale and nod at him. "All right, man. We're out. By the way, you can stop worrying about her. I know what the fuck I'm doing."

He crosses his arms over his chest and stares at the door with a sullen expression. "Maybe it's not her I'm worried about." He turns and walks away without another word.

All fucking right . . .

When I get outside, Aspen is leaning against my motorcycle while staring down at her phone as if waiting on something. She shoves her phone in her pocket and smiles when she notices me watching her.

"You ready? Where are we going?" She's looking at me as if she doesn't know how to act around me. I don't blame her. Right now, I'm probably confusing the shit out of her. She knows my fucking rules. She knows I broke those fucking rules . . . and for her. I wouldn't know how to react either.

I walk over to my bike, grab my helmet and slip it on her head. There is something about a girl on the back of a motorcycle in jeans and a tank that is extremely sexy . . . or maybe it's just her on the back of the motorcycle. Once the strap is fastened, I straddle my bike and grab her arm, pulling her on behind me. "Hold on tight."

She wraps her arms around my waist and snuggles up close behind me. The unexplainable feeling I have with her against me doesn't go unnoticed before I fire up the engine and take off.

We ride for about an hour until we finally pull up at the same spot I took her a few days ago. The memory of her soaking wet in more ways than one instantly floods the banks of my memory. The reminder of what happened here last time already has my dick hard and ready for more. I'd always wanted to pleasure a woman out in the rain. I can't deny it was one of the hottest things I've ever done. Not to mention, I was a little surprised she let it happen. That only turned me on more.

Fuck me. Now during a summer rain, I'll never be the same.

I help Aspen off my bike. As I get off, I take notice of the bulge underneath my jeans and adjust the enlarged area of my crotch. My cock is so hard right now that my jeans are almost not loose enough to contain it. I see Aspen looking down at my dick and swallowing as I push it down. She wants me again and it gets me so fucking hot just knowing that I have her ready for more so soon.

"Get over here, babe."

She seems hesitant at first but walks over to stand in front of me. Her eyes are studying mine and she looks curious. I want to know what the hell this woman is thinking. What the hell, curiosity wins out. "Ask."

"I want to know more about your life, Slade. Why do you have all those suits in your closest? Please don't tell me they're costumes for work because I know that's not true. I saw the pictures of you wearing them. You looked . . . different. Nothing like you do today."

My eyes study her face. She's really serious about this. She wants to know about me. It may sound a little fucked up, but she's the first woman to ask me anything personal about my life. All the other women wanted was a good fuck and they knew they would get it from me. I grew used to it; got comfortable and became accustomed to it. It became my escape; my addiction. It may make me sound like shit, but when you basically fuck for a living you get used to it; crave it and then it gets hard to stop.

For some reason I want to tell her. I want her to know more about me. "All right. I'll tell you." I pick her up by the hips and set her down so she's straddling the back of my bike just like the last time we were here. I just hope she's ready for this because it's a long fucking story and one I don't usually tell.

"I used to be a lawyer." She gives me a shocked look by widening her eyes but stays quiet. I know, it's quite a fucking shocker from looking at the man you see today. "I worked for my father's law firm. It wasn't what I wanted to do. It was what I was expected to do. I didn't have a passion for it; although, I was one of the best. Everyone wanted me to handle their cases because they knew they wouldn't get any better. I was a damn good lawyer. I just didn't like it. I worked very hard; too hard. It got boring as shit and fast."

I grab her legs and yank her to me so her legs are wrapped around my waist and my hands are locked behind her back. "After the accident, I shut myself off from the world. I didn't leave my house for about a month straight. When that month was up, I couldn't force myself to go back to that life. No matter how hard my father pushed me, I just pushed back. I couldn't do it anymore. I was tired of living life the way he wanted me to. There was only one option; to quit.

"A few months later, after draining the money I had in my savings account and not doing shit but eating, showering, and sleeping, Cale asked me to come out to a party at *Walk Of Shame*. I hadn't been out of the house pretty much at all since the accident, so I agreed to go out and try to get my mind off things. Cale was dancing that night along with Hemy and somehow the women kept mistaking me for one of the dancers. They couldn't keep their hands off me. I hadn't felt anything in a long time and that night, I had such a rush that I was on some kind of high. It was the first feeling I had since the accident. I grew addicted to the rush and depended on it. It was my normalcy, so I took a job at the club and became roommates with Cale a few months later. I've just barely been getting by. First it was the dancing and the sex, then it became the tattoos and the pain I got from them. It kept me feeling something; made me feel more alive. When that didn't help me anymore, I moved on and it became the drinking. The alcohol was enough to numb it. It has gotten me by . . . until now. I want more though. I just don't know if I can have it; if I deserve it."

She scoots closer to me and reaches out to cup my face in her hands. Without thinking, I reach up to place my hands over hers as I look into her eyes. It feels nice. "Thanks for sharing that with me. I know how hard this must be for you. I also know that you don't open up very often. It means a lot to me." She leans in, hesitates, but then presses her lips against mine.

She gets ready to pull away, but I tangle my hands in the back of her hair and pull her as close to me as I can. The feeling I have right now is unexplainable. It's so fucking good that I could just kiss her all night and not give a damn about anything else. I haven't talked to anyone about my past and with her, she makes it feel so natural; so damn easy. It's like she's the medicine I've needed all along; the way to cope.

The feel of her in my arms and the taste of her in my mouth makes me feel . . . at ease. Just a little bit of peace finally; not enough to kill the pain, but enough to give me a little hope.

I pick her up off my bike and wrap her legs around my waist while kissing her long and hard. I want her to know that she's only making me want her more each and every day. At first, it was just a sexual attraction; the need to have something that I couldn't, but it's become more to me than just that. She's different than the other girls. She's more than just a fuck. She's addictive, but the right kind of addiction. I have a very addictive personality and she may be the thing I need to feed it.

A few minutes pass before she pulls away from the kiss and places her forehead against mine. We look into each other's eyes and I run my finger over her cheek.

"What?" she asks. "Tell me what you're thinking."

"I'm thinking about how beautiful you are and the way you make me want more than what I have."

She sucks in a deep breath and turns her head away from me. Right before she turned away, I caught a look in her eyes that made my chest ache. There's something she's not telling me. I can tell.

"We should get going, Slade. You have to be at work soon. Okay?" She forces a smile and taps my chest so I know to set her back down to her feet.

When her feet hit the ground, she goes straight for my motorcycle and slips my helmet on. She's ready to get away from me. I don't like that feeling. Not one fucking bit.

I stalk over to her, pull her into my arms and make her look me in the eyes. "Tell me something about your life back home other than you're a hairstylist, you're twenty-three and have a black cat named Puma. I want to know more about you than Cale can tell me."

She looks surprised that I know these things about her and tries turning her face away, but I don't let her. I need to be able to read her eyes when she talks. "I've been at the salon four years. I hate seafood. I eat ranch sauce on everything and have a passion for reading. I'm not much for the party life and would rather curl up with someone that cares about me and watch a movie instead of going out." She pauses to look down at my lips before looking back up. "There's not much else to tell."

I release her face and we both just stand here in silence. Something feels a little off about the way she's acting. Maybe it's just me. I don't blame her for not wanting to get close to me; especially, not knowing my intentions. I don't even know them myself. This is all new to me.

"Okay." I turn and walk to my bike, unsatisfied. "Let's go."

SARAH HAS BEEN GIVING ME weird looks all fucking day. I'm not really sure what's on her mind, but it's starting to get on my nerves.

"Say it," I mutter.

She sets her towel down on the bar and begins wiping it off. "Say what?"

I look up from putting the glasses in the cooler and study her face. She definitely has something on her mind. She knows I don't like playing these games. I'm not a fucking mind reader. "You have something you want to say. Since when do you hold back?"

Shaking her head, she turns away and starts working faster at wiping down the bar. "Okay, then." She drops her towel, leans against the bar and smiles. "You broke your fucking rules." Pushing away from the counter, she walks over to me and kneels down next to me. "Someone finally broke you. I'm in total awe of this woman. She's a goddess. I'm definitely jealous, Slade."

Grunting, I slam down the glass in my hand and stand up before rubbing my hands over my face. "Fucking Cale." I reach for her arm and pull her up to her feet. "I swear he gossips just like a fucking chick."

She quickly grabs for a beer and places it in front of one of her customers before rushing back over to me. "He called me this morning to see if I wanted to get off work early; said he needed some extra cash. He got on the subject of Aspen and it came out. He's just as shocked as I am. Believe me."

"Yeah. Well, you're not the only ones. Don't even ask me to explain it because I can't. I wouldn't even if I knew how so back off." I lean against the register and watch as a few girls look at me from across the bar, smiling to each other. They're both looking desperate; watching my every move as if their lives depend on it. I'm sure it won't be long before they approach me and try to pull me into the back. I've had it happen more than once while working. It used to get me all worked up. Right now, I'm not even feeling it.

"Do you need to take a break?" Sarah stands next to me and eyes the two girls before nudging me. "I can handle the bar. I don't need you."

"Nah." I push away from the register and start checking the bottles of liquor to see if any need to be replaced. I need anything to keep me busy.

"Not this time."

"Wow. Two surprises in one day," she says teasingly while walking back over to clean the bar. "I don't know how to take all this in."

"Yeah, well I can be full of fucking surprises. Trust me."

"Oh yeah. Well, here's another one. Look who's here."

I turn behind me to see that Aspen and her friend have just walked in.

Fuck me. She is fucking beautiful.

Aspen's eyes stay focused on me the whole time that her and Kayla make their way up to the bar. They both stop in front of Sarah and order a couple drinks. I see her trying hard not to look at me. I can tell it's a tough struggle for her.

After the way we left things earlier, I'm not sure how the fuck to feel about her being here. I don't get the way she was acting. I opened up to her and it feels as if she's trying to keep me out.

Fuck that. I don't need that right now.

Seconds later, Cale comes walking in and I focus my attention on him. Just the asshole I need to speak with.

The girls have taken their drinks and are heading over to one of the empty couches. Now would be a good time to give Cale a piece of my mind.

I wait for him to step behind the bar before I get straight to the fucking point. "You have a big fucking mouth."

He looks at me and then over to Sarah. "You can take off if you want. I've got it from here. I'm sure you don't want to deal with this side of Slade."

Sarah nods her head and grabs for her things. "Yeah, I'll be more than happy to get the hell out of here." She starts walking away, but then stops to look back at us. "I already closed out my tabs. You boys have fun now; just not too much without me." She winks and takes off in a hurry, waving back at Aspen and Kayla.

"My bad, man. I didn't think you'd get pissed about it. You've never been secretive about your sex life before. It just sort of came out. It's a big deal. I still can't believe it."

"Yeah well, it's a big deal for me too so let's just drop it."

"All right." He looks over at Aspen and Kayla. "You do realize she'll be leaving soon, right?"

"Yeah. So?"

"She probably won't be coming back for a long ass time. There must be something special about her for you to let her get to you the way she has for this past week. Are you sure you're willing to let her go?"

I take a deep breath and release it. I look up to see Aspen laughing at something some moron is saying to her. I feel my stomach drop as I watch her having a good time with him. "Yeah. It's not my place to have her stay. There's nothing going on between us. She'll be gone tomorrow, and things will go back to normal."

"Really?" Cale asks. "Is that why you're breathing heavy right now and your fists are clenched at your sides?" He studies me from the side. He's good as fuck at reading me. "You want to rip that guy's head off right now; especially now that he keeps getting closer to her as if he's going to take her home. You're about to freak the fuck out. Admit it."

Fucking shit, he's right.

I jump over the bar, walk up beside her and nod at the douche in front of her. He looks a bit nervous suddenly. Yeah, well he should be. "What's up?" I step in between them, pull her to me by the back of her neck and press my lips against hers, immediately wrapping my hands in the back of her hair.

I kiss her hard, spreading her lips open with my tongue before picking her up and wrapping her legs around my waist. From the corner of my eye, I see the asshole has gotten the hint and has stepped away.

Smart move, motherfucker.

She moans softly before pulling her lips away from mine and running her tongue over them. She seems a bit shaken up by my bold move. "Umm . . . wow," she breathes. "I mean. What are you doing?"

"Kissing you. Isn't it pretty fucking obvious?" I pull her face close to mine before running my lips up her neck and stopping at her ear. "You like my lips kissing yours, sucking them and owning them. Just remember that."

I set her down and walk away. I'm heated.

Cale watches me as I make my way past the bar and outside. I need a fucking cigarette right now. The thought of that guy even trying to take her home has my blood boiling. I need to relax before I break something. I'm not used to this kind of jealousy.

Inhaling the cigarette in record time, I make my way back inside and try my best to focus on anything but . . . her. I never once thought a woman could be such a fucking distraction. All I can do is think about taking her in the back and fucking her; making her scream my fucking name. It's like my body can't get enough of her. I just have to touch her and taste her. She's in for it tonight. As soon as I get her ass home, she's mine.

It's been three hours since Aspen and Cale have gotten here and it's almost time for me to get the fuck out of here. I don't care what Cale says, she is leaving with me. She doesn't need to hang out here all night while he works. Her friend Kayla left about an hour ago, said she had to leave for work. So, Aspen has been going back and forth between hanging out at the bar with me and Cale and talking to some girls she met while getting a drink earlier.

By the way she keeps looking at me, I can tell she's just as ready to get out of here as I am.

"You taking off soon?" Cale's voice causes me to look up from wiping down the bar.

"Yeah." I toss the towel in the bucket and walk over to the register to see what tabs I need to close out still. "As soon as I close out these two tabs."

I look up just in time to see Aspen waving the girls off that she's been hanging out with. She laughs at something one of the girls says and then starts making her way over to us.

Just as she's about to walk up in front of me, some guy calls her name, stopping her in her tracks.

"Aspen." The guy has light brown hair, styled in the front and is wearing a black button down shirt with dark jeans. He's a little shorter than me and almost as thick in build but is clean cut.

There is something about the look on her face that I don't like. She seems surprised and not happy at all.

She turns around slowly and rubs her hands down the side of her skirt. "Jay. What are you doing here?"

Jay as she called him, walks over to her and wraps his arms around her waist, pulling her body against his.

Without thinking, I take a step forward, about to kill this asshole for putting his hand all over her, but Cale stops me.

"Get the fuck off me, Cale." I push his hand away, but he just pushes my chest harder. "Back the fuck up. That asshole is all over her."

Cale takes a long, deep breath and then exhales. "Yeah well, that asshole is her boyfriend."

What the fuck . . .

CHAPTER SIXTEEN

ASPEN

THIS CANNOT BE HAPPENING RIGHT now . . .

Jay leans in and presses his lips against mine while lifting me in the air. Without thinking, I press my hands to his chest and push away from the kiss. This is so unlike me, but he doesn't even take notice. "Damn, babe," he moans, while looking down at my breasts and setting me back down to my feet. "You're looking sexy today. It kind of makes me regret this last week."

Kind of? Asshole...

I hear something break from behind the bar before I hear Cale calling out Slade's name. When I look behind me, Slade is leaning over the register, gripping the counter, all his veins popping out as his muscles flex. He looks like he's about to kill someone. I cringe at the thought of Slade being pissed off at me. I have no idea how I'm going to explain this all to him. It's not what it looks like; not exactly.

Jay looks over at the bar and shakes his head before slipping his hands up my skirt and cupping my ass. I instantly grab his hands and yank them away. I don't like the idea of him touching me sexually in public. When it comes from him it makes me feel dirty; always has.

"Jay. I thought you weren't coming until tomorrow. Why are you here today?" My heart races at the idea of leaving so quickly. I don't know why, but I don't feel ready; not one bit. "Why today?"

Jay flashes me his perfectly charming smile and grabs my chin, causing me to look into his brown eyes. They seem so dull compared to Slade's. "I'm here to hang out with a few of my boys. They're going out for a few drinks here soon. Figured I would come a day early and have a little fun of my own here in Chicago. Now that I see how incredibly sexy you look, I think I'll swing by later tonight, pick you up and bring you home."

"I . . . you should've at least told me. Called or sent a text. Something. What if I had plans?" I can't help my eyes from landing back on Slade. They can't seem to focus on anything but.

Jay laughs, bringing my attention back to him. It's not just a laugh, it's one of those laughs he does when he's making fun of me. I've grown to hate it. He can be such a prick at times. "What is the fun in that? You know I'm a surprise kind of guy and you have plans? I doubt it. Don't be stupid, Aspen. You know you never have plans that don't include me and that's the way it will stay." He leans in and gives me a quick kiss before backing away. "I gotta go. The guys will be meeting up soon. It's a good thing I remembered where you said Cale worked. I love surprising you. I'll text you in a bit for the address. Be ready when I get there."

He backs away while laughing as if he still can't get over the idea that I may have plans. It makes me want to scream. I hate when he makes me feel this way. Once he gets to the door, he turns around and heads outside without another word. Good thing for him. I don't even know what to say or think right now.

I look down at the ground and take a few deep breaths, in an attempt to calm my racing nerves. I can't even look up right now. I know how bad this must look to Slade and I'm not sure he'll even give me the chance to explain. It's why I got so nervous earlier when he was spilling his guts out to me. I just don't know what to do. I shouldn't have pushed him to open up to me. It's a bit hypocritical when I can't even return the favor. I shouldn't have let it get this far.

I stand here, not making an attempt to move until I see Slade's shoes come into view. I hold my breath waiting for what's to come next as I look up at him.

His expression is hard and cold; eyes so intense that it steals my breath away. "Outside. Now." His voice seethes anger and could cut like a knife.

I watch as he walks away and yanks the door open before stepping outside. I feel as if I can't move. Why do I feel so fucking guilty? Slade is the one that pushed me to this point and he just wanted me for sex; nothing more. He used me. I play tug of war with the confusion in my mind, *but . . . then why*? Why do I feel like total shit right now?

I gather myself and start heading for the door. Cale tries stopping me, but I hold my arm out to show him that I'm doing this. I need a chance to explain myself. I can't stand the thought of leaving with Slade hating me. It's just too much and would eat at me forever.

When I step outside, I look around but don't see Slade anywhere. I catch a movement in my peripheral vision and he steps around from the back of the building with a cigarette in his mouth. He's pacing back and forth, not even bothering to look up at me. I can see him shaking as he pulls the cigarette from his mouth and blows the smoke through his lips quickly. He's really worked up over this and it somewhat surprises me.

He stares off into the distance for a few minutes, before finally walking toward his truck and nods for me to follow.

I take small steps while going over a speech, trying to think of the best way to explain Jay. It's not an easy thing for me to talk about. Once I get next to his truck, he backs me up against it and places his hands on either side of me so his hands are pressed against his truck door.

He leans in close to my face; so close I can feel the warmth of his breath kissing my lips. "You have a fucking boyfriend?" His jaw steels as he looks me in the eyes. They hold nothing but pure rage. "This whole fucking time you've had a boyfriend and you couldn't have fucking said something." He slams his hands against the truck before punching it. "I opened up to you. I let you in and told you things I haven't talked about in years. I don't like cheaters. It's one thing that I hate. I know what I do isn't much better, but at least I'm always honest first. Fuck, Aspen!"

I take a deep breath and slowly exhale. I feel like bursting out in tears right now, but I won't let it happen. I won't. "It's not exactly what you think, Slade. You know nothing about what I've been through over the years with that man. You have no right to accuse me of being a shitty person without even listening to what I have to say."

"What? What do you have to say? That you just needed to get away for a bit and clear your fucking head and then I came along and you decided to just let me fuck you knowing that your boyfriend would never find out? Did you think you could just go back to living your happy fucking life with him? Is that it?"

Anger builds up inside as he looks at me accusingly. I didn't want this. I didn't ask for this. I will not be judged without him even having proper cause.

I push his chest to try to give us some distance, but he doesn't move. "Fuck you, Slade. Fuck you!" I push him again but decide to give up. He isn't budging. "It was him that didn't want me. You want to know why I'm here? I'll tell you why. It's because *he* decided he needed to fuck other women for a while. *He* needed a little space before he could give me his full attention. He expected me to be the good little girlfriend while he was back home fucking who knows what. I was supposed to be here just clearing my head and trying to deal with what I had to do to keep him mine. Then, you fucking came along and I caved into you. I broke my own rules for you. I said I wasn't going to stoop to his level because I loved him too much, but you just had to come along and make me want you, Mr. Irresistible."

I give him another shove and this time he lets me push him away enough for me to escape him. I can't look him in the eye right now. I feel too low; the only thing that makes me this way. "We've been together for five years. I was afraid of losing him. I was prepared to do anything I could to prove to him that my love for him was strong enough to handle anything. It killed me to know that I wasn't enough for him; that he needed other women to satisfy him."

Clenching his jaw, he punches the truck and leans against it. "So you were just going to let him go around fucking everyone and then come back to you like nothing ever happened?"

"Yeah, well. If you must know, I knew how he was to begin with and I let myself fall for him anyways. He was the kind of guy always out to find the next best *fuck;* staying out late at night and not coming home sometimes. All the lies. The fucking lies." I stop to wipe a tear off as it falls down my cheek.

I hate letting people see me breakdown. I hate showing what Jay does to me. "All I wanted was for a chance to make that change. I thought if I did this . . . that . . . that he would finally just be mine; that he would love me with everything in him just as I have loved him all along. I thought that I could be enough for once. All I wanted was to be enough but I was stupid. I was stupid for letting it come to this. I never should've agreed."

It's silent for a few seconds before once again, I am pushed up against his truck with his body blocking me in. He wraps his hands in the back of my hair and pulls my face close to his so our lips are almost touching. "If he doesn't see that you're enough, then he isn't fucking worth it. He's fucking blind. You deserve better." He pauses and his eyes lock with mine. "Tell me you're not going back with him."

"Yes," I whisper. "I have to."

He presses his body against mine and his arms flex as his grip on my hair tightens. "No you don't. Fuck him. He doesn't deserve you. You deserve someone better than him . . . better than the both of us, but I'm fucking stingy."

He runs his hands through my hair and brushes his lips against mine. "Stay here, Aspen." His breath softly caresses my lips as his breathing picks up. "Don't leave with him. Let me give you a reason to stay."

I sigh against his lips, fighting myself. "It's not that easy. I can't just throw five years away. We have a lot of history. We live together. He was my first. I can't just walk away. I don't know how. There's too much to figure out."

"How do you feel about me," he growls.

"It was fun, Slade," I manage to whisper.

Pushing me harder against his truck, he leans into my ear. "That wasn't the fucking question. Fuck!"

Feeling trapped, I shove his chest, hard. I don't know why. I'm just so fucking scared to answer this question; scared of knowing the answer. He always finds a way to push me.

"You like that? Did it fucking feel good?" He presses his erection against me, causing me to moan against his lips. "Harder, dammit. Right across the face this time. Slap me."

Completely lost in the moment, I slap him as hard as I can across the face. It feels good to let my frustration out. Not to mention the fact that his dick flexes from my hit. This man turns me on like no other man can. I'm completely breathless; lost to him.

Without even giving me a second to register his reaction, he picks me up and wraps my legs around his waist. "Here is your reason to stay."

His hand works fast to pull out his erection before he slips my panties to the side and pushes himself deep inside me. He stops for a moment before rocking his hips back and forth and slamming his lips against mine. My legs tighten around him as my whole body shakes from the feel of him filling me; stretching me.

"Let me make you feel this way every day." He pushes in deeper before slowly pulling out and lifting my hands above my head. I'm so turned on right now that I couldn't care less if someone catches us. "Does he make you feel this way? Does he fuck you as good as I do?"

I shake my head, but don't answer him. I can't. I can't speak.

"Say it. I want to hear the fucking truth." He leans in against my mouth while rolling his hips in and out, giving me pleasure so intense I feel as if I can't even breathe. I'm overwhelmed by this man; completely stunned. "Say it, babe."

"No," I moan out as he lifts me with his hips and starts moving a little faster. Our bodies are so close that there is no space between us. We're both desperate for this moment; our last. "No one has." I lean my head over his shoulder and dig my nails into his back as he works his hips on me.

"Then stay," he whispers. "Give me a chance to change."

I shake my head, but he presses his lips against mine, claiming my mouth with his. Once again, this man completely owns me. At this moment, I am almost willing to give him everything; not just my body, but my heart.

With one arm wrapped behind my head, he grips my hip with the other while fucking me hard; rolling his hips and slamming hard into me. He can't handle taking it slow at the moment and to be honest, neither can I.

"Slade," I moan out, as my body bounces with each thrust of his strong hips. "Fuck . . ." I grip his hair in my hands and scream out as I feel my orgasm building. The consistent thrusts of his hips and the way he pushes me against the truck with each deep shove, has me ready to explode. "I'm about to come . . . oh shit." I clamp around his dick and this only causes his movement to pick up.

The truck starts to move from behind me as he puts all his anger and frustration into fucking me. His grip on my neck tightens before he moans out and I feel his dick throb as he releases himself inside me. Breathing heavily, we both relax into each other with our eyes locked. I can't turn away from the beauty of this man in front of me; I don't want to.

It's silent with him still inside me as he leans in once more and presses his lips to mine. They're soft and sweet, making me want more of them. I always want more. He's like an addiction. Everything about him just calls out for me; my body needing him to survive. He's an addiction I'll have to break. I have no choice. Too bad, I know guys like him will never change. Jay didn't. I won't start over with another man that's just like Jay. I have a lot to figure out.

When he pulls away from the kiss, he looks me in the eyes and sighs. He can see my guilt written all over me. He could probably even taste it in our kiss. "You're still leaving, aren't you?"

I nod and turn my head away. I can't do this right now.

"Fucking shit."

He pulls out of me and gently sets me back down to my feet while pulling his jeans back up. "I don't blame you for not trusting me," he says stiffly. "I don't even trust myself. I don't know how the fuck I feel. All I know is that with you . . . I feel something and I don't want to give that up." He looks away before opening the door for me to get in. "I guess I'll have to. Me wanting to change isn't good enough and I fucking get that, but I can't make any promises. I won't make one that I know I can't keep."

I feel a burning sensation in my chest and it becomes hard to breathe. It's taking everything in me not to cry right now. As wrong as it was, we both needed that one last time. It's unfortunate that it felt even better than the last two. I will forever be fucked after leaving here. Slade isn't someone you can easily forget about. I already feel that; the pain is too strong to ignore.

I HAVEN'T SPOKEN TO SLADE since we got back to the house a couple of hours ago. I decided to lock myself up in Cale's room and hide. I can't face him at the moment, because seeing him will only make me want to change my mind about going. I can't stay though. He'll only hurt me more than Jay has. Jay made a promise to me this time. The problem is, I don't know if I want it now.

I'm sitting here on Cale's bed with my suitcase next to me, staring up at the ceiling, when my phone goes off. My hand shakes as I go to reach for it because I know my time is up. I'm not ready yet. A big part of me is holding me back and telling me to stay.

The look in Slade's eyes was almost enough to convince me he wanted me. I could see the struggle within himself while he was asking me to stay. Asking a girl to stay with him is not something he's used to. I think we both know that it wouldn't last. I couldn't commit myself to the pain of losing a man as great as him. I already feel attached and I barely know him. I can't even imagine how I could feel in a few months. I would fall hard and fast . . . right on my face.

I have to go. Home is where I need to be.

I already know that Jay is outside because I hear a car door slam. He's most likely opening the trunk for my luggage. I just hope Slade didn't hear it, because I can't face seeing the hurt in his eyes. He didn't speak to me the whole way back to the house. It killed me. I just need to slip out of here unnoticed. I can't let my heart break anymore tonight.

I grab my suitcase, stand up and drag it over to the door. When I open the door, I look around but don't see Slade anywhere. I should be happy.

Right?

I stand here for a moment, not wanting to move. I feel stuck. I allow myself a few moments of pity, suck it up and make my way outside. The first thing I notice is that Slade's motorcycle is gone. Not sure how I missed him leaving, but he's gone and the ache in my chest returns. I'll probably never see him again. The thought kills me.

Why does it hurt so much? Why do I wish he was here so I could see him one last time?

Jay stands next to the trunk but doesn't make a move to help me as I drag my suitcase across the ground. Usually, this wouldn't bother me because I'm used to him being this way, but right now, it bothers me. It bothers me a lot. Slade may be all tough and closed off, but he would help me without a second thought. I know that and I love that about him. He's more than what he shows the world. There's a really great side to him that I love and want more of.

Dammit, this is so hard.

I feel numb and closed off as I step up beside Jay and look at him. I thought I would be happy for this moment . . . but I'm not. I'm fucking miserable right now. Seeing him is doing nothing but making me angry. The feeling of wanting to kiss him has now been replaced with wanting to punch him. Unlike Slade, he wouldn't get off on it.

Fucking Slade. Why can't I stop thinking about him?

I stop and look around as if I expect Slade to just pull up on his bike, jump off and kiss me; save me from this possible mistake. The thought gives me the ultimate rush like it did when he kissed me in the bar with the assumption that guy was trying to pick me up. I loved that. It made me feel sexy and wanted. Something I've never really felt with Jay.

What the hell is wrong with me?

"Come on," he says while looking down at his phone impatiently. "I have to be to work early and it's a long drive."

I let out a soft breath and struggle with tossing my suitcase into the back. He doesn't even notice. He's too busy on his phone. I really feel a lot of hate for him right now; enough to almost stay, but staying might break me even more than leaving.

I get ready to say something, but he looks up and smiles. It's the sweet smile that I fell in love with. "Missed you, gorgeous."

I feel a little bit of my anger fade, but not enough. "I missed you too," I say while shutting the trunk and walking over to get inside the car. I feel like shit because to be honest with myself, I don't mean it; not one bit of me.

I just hope I'm not making the biggest mistake of my life.

CHAPTER SEVENTEEN

SLADE

THREE WEEKS LATER . . .

IT'S BEEN THREE WEEKS SINCE Aspen left and I still feel like the biggest ass for not fighting harder for her to stay. The one thing that made my life worth a shit I let slip through my fingers. I couldn't even face her. Instead, I left. I couldn't stand to stick around while she packed her shit to leave. I left and rode for hours just thinking back on my life and all the fucked up things I have done over the past couple of years. It took her for me to realize that I'm not proud of what I've become; not one fucking bit. In the end I may not have her, but she has helped me in more ways than she knows and I will always be thankful for that.

I owe her a lot for finally waking me up and I still think about taking my ass to Rockford and showing her how much I have changed, but I know it would be pointless. She made up her mind. I don't blame her for not wanting to give her heart to an asshole like me. I meant what I said when I told her she deserves better than me. We both knew that. That's why she left. She did what she had to do to protect her heart. She could probably see that things would turn out disastrous. She chose to stay far away from me; choosing to walk away when I couldn't.

It's a Friday night at *Walk of Shame* and I'm working the bar with Sarah. Hemy and Cale are working on training some new kid, Stone, or some shit. The kid looks like he's having a fucking blast; probably fresh out of school and dying to get his unexperienced cock wet. He's like the old version of me: dark, dirty, and out for a good fuck. Well, this kid is in for the ride of his life here.

"You okay, Slade?"

I lean against the bar next to Sarah and nudge her with my shoulder. "Don't I look it," I ask teasingly. "You've been asking me that practically every fucking day. You're starting to sound like a broken record."

She lets out a little laugh and squeezes my arm. "It's fucking weird," she says.

"What?"

"Not having you out there. How am I supposed to get used to this shit? You not taking down every woman in your path or slamming back shots and getting naked. It's a big fucking change. Are you sure you're okay? Have you talked to-"

"Don't even bring her up, Sarah." I take a deep breath and slowly exhale. "I'm cool, okay. It's just going to take a little while to get used to the changes. You can't expect me to do this forever. I just need a change of scenery."

She nods as I walk away to help a young woman waving me over with a flirtatious smile. She's beautiful; long brown hair, big blue eyes. You would think she would be enough to tempt me back into my old ways, but no. Surprisingly, she does nothing for me. I'm not sure how the fuck to feel about that. All I know . . . is that I'm feeling for the first time in years. It's a scary feeling, but I think I'm going to go along for the ride; I have to.

"What can I get you?" I ask while leaning over the bar.

The brunette looks at me long and hard while eyeing me up and down. She almost looks as if she's ready to strip down right here and jump my shit. She's desperate and it's actually turning me off. I liked having to work for it.

"Whatever you're willing to give." She smiles before leaning in and running her tongue over her lips. "You're Slade, right? I've heard *a lot* of things about you."

I stand here slightly amused, watching as she tries desperately to make herself seem willing and available.

"I've had a rough couple days and am looking for someone to take my mind off things. I've heard you're the man to do the job." Her eyes rake over my body as she tugs on the top of her dress, exposing more of her breasts to me. "I've heard you're the best."

Clearing my throat, I turn my head and point across the room to Hemy. I wait for her eyes to follow. "I'm good . . . but go take your offer to my buddy over there. He'll be sure to fuck you nice and thoroughly. He'll even throw in a friend to take you up the ass while he's deep inside you, making you scream." She looks curious and a little excited. "If you're looking for a night to remember then Hemy will give you just that. He fucks like a rock star and he's dirty as shit. He'll give you anything you want. He holds nothing back in the sack."

The brunette looks me up and down before fixing the top of her dress and nodding her head. "He'll do just fine. It's a shame you're not up for the task, though. I had my tastes set on something . . . specific."

"It *is* a fucking shame." I pour her a shot of vodka and slide it across the bar. "You're a little too late, but the shot's on me, sweetheart."

I walk away and take a deep breath; a little pissed at myself for not even being the slightest bit turned on by her offer. A couple weeks ago, I would have taken her right here in front of Sarah and then let Sarah suck her taste off my cock.

Damn. This girl really did something to me.

Sarah rushes over to me and shoves my shoulder before slapping me with a towel. "Are you serious? I would have even fucked that one. Are you sure you're not sick?"

"Sarah. Leave his ass alone."

I look up to see Cale step behind the bar, wiping down his sweaty chest with his shirt.

"How's the new kid doing?"

Cale smirks while grabbing a bottle of water. "I'm almost positive you two fuckers are related." He opens the water and pours some over his face. "Are you sure Stone isn't your long-lost brother? He's a slightly smaller version of you, but with shorter hair and less tattoos. It's a little fucking scary. It's a lot like what you looked like when you were a suit."

"Good. Then he can make up for your slack like I did."

Cale punches my arm before pouring the rest of the water over his head. "She's still eating at you, isn't she?"

I ignore his question. "Have you heard from her yet?"

He shakes his head. "Nah, man. I haven't heard shit."

To be honest, I'm still a little pissed off at Cale for not telling me Aspen had a boyfriend the whole time. That asshole knew we were fucking and he couldn't even warn me? What happened to the bro code? I find that a little fucked up and he knows that. He could've told me when he slipped other small details of her life to me. Knowing she had a boyfriend, over having a cat would've been a little more useful.

"Dude, stop looking at me like that. I told you it wasn't my place to say shit. They were sort of on a break and plus you usually only fuck them one time and move on. I didn't know you would fall for her."

My jaw clenches from his words. I don't like hearing that shit out loud. Even though she's been on my mind constantly since she left, it really pisses me off that she has this effect on me. "Yeah, well neither did I."

"Sorry, man." Cale slaps my shoulder and starts backing away. "I'm sure she'll come back as soon as that asshole hurts her again."

The thought of that asshole even touching her makes me want to rip his fucking throat out. The thought of him hurting her, makes me want to kill him. She deserves to be treated like a fucking queen. She deserves to know that she's wanted. That's why I didn't fight harder for her to stay. I was afraid I would never be able to give her that.

Seeing the person that I've become, I have begun to believe that maybe I could have been what she needs after all. Maybe a part of me knew and I was afraid I would fall too far and then fuck up and she would leave me. If she were here now, I know I would do everything in my power to make her mine. She makes me want to be a better man; makes me want to be the old me.

Once upon a time I actually cared about my image and the way I looked from another's perspective. I would have never been caught dead working in a place like this, fucking every hot female with a wet pussy waiting between her legs and drinking myself into my grave. I actually wanted to love and to be loved. I had it before but lost it and myself, but she makes me long to be that person again. She made me realize that sometimes you have to peel back the layers to discover who someone really is. Otherwise, you may miss a remarkable person.

It's almost closing time now and the only ones left in the bar besides me, Cale, and Sarah is a small group of females that can't keep their eyes off me or Cale. I recognize one of the girls, because I fucked her in the back a couple months ago. Her eyes haven't left me once since the crowd died down. It's starting to get a little on the creepy side.

"Dude, that chick is all up on your shit hardcore." Cale leans over the bar and starts wiping it down. "Are you sure you're not down? We can make a great fucking time out of this."

I look from Cale, over to the tatted-up redhead whose eyes are practically fucking me. I'm definitely not down. I just don't feel the need. "I'm good. They're all yours, man."

All I want to do is get my ass out of here. It's been a long ass day and I'm exhausted. The last thing I want to do is deal with some horny ass chick trying to get on my cock.

Just when I think the girls are finally going to get up and leave, I hear the door open and the sound of heels pounding on the marble flooring. The first thing I think is that another girl is joining the group of women that have been waiting impatiently for me and Cale to get off.

"We're closed," I say without looking up.

"I'm sorry. I was hoping to get here sooner."

My heart stops at the sound of her voice and my breath catches in my throat. I feel every muscle in my body tense as I bring my eyes up to see the woman that has been haunting me for the last few weeks. She's standing there in a little green dress with those sexy strappy heels that I love on her.

Holy shit, she steals my breath away.

She smiles shyly when her eyes lock with mine. She looks nervous. "I can wait outside," she says while pointing to the door. "It's not a big deal."

I get ready to respond, but Cale jumps up from the ground and hops over the bar to stop her before I can. "Holy shit! What are you doing back?"

Aspen looks at me for a second longer before turning her attention to Cale as he reaches in for a hug and shakes her back and forth. "Did you miss me that much?" she asks out of breath as Cale squeezes her half to death and then releases her.

"You know it." He takes a step back and I can't help but watch them.

Everything in me wants to jump over that bar and kiss her, but I'm trying my best to hold back. "So, what the hell are you doing here? Are you staying with us again?"

My heart speeds up just at the thought of her being under the same roof as us; a chance for me to show her that I've changed; a chance to let her fall for me.

"No," she says. "I'm actually here because well . . . I moved here."

Holy fucking shit. It's suddenly hard to breathe.

"I just couldn't stay with Jay anymore. As soon as we got back home I told him it was over. I started looking around for a new job and packed up all my shit." She stops to smile at Cale. "I found a job here in a salon and decided I wanted to be back home. I've missed it here and there's nothing left for me back in Rockford. Riley is moving back in a couple months, anyways."

Cale looks paler than a fucking ghost, but I ignore his reaction and focus on Aspen. I can't help the excitement that rushes through me. Every part of me is screaming to fucking kiss her and make her mine while I can. I can't hold back. I need to do this. If I don't, someone else will.

Fuck it!

I jump over the bar, grab her face and slam my lips against hers, tasting her with desperation. The feel of her lips gives me a fucking rush and I know that after this I won't be able to go on without having her as mine. I need her and I'm going to show her she needs me too.

When we're both short of breath, she pulls away and her eyes search mine. She looks scared and lost. The feeling makes my chest ache. I don't want to do that to her.

She just stares, breathing heavily, with her body trembling. Then without a word, she turns and rushes for the door. "Wait. Don't fucking run away again."

I step up behind her and grab her arm right as she's reaching for the door. She yanks it out of my grip and takes a step back as I take a step forward. It seems to be our little game. "Why? Why should I wait?"

I don't hesitate to tell her the truth this time and I don't give a shit that everyone is staring at us as if we're some kind of fucking soap opera. This time, I'm not letting her get away; I can't. "Because I love it when you touch me. It makes me feel as if I'm breathing; makes me feel . . . alive."

Her breathing picks up as I run my lips over her neck and brush her hair over her shoulder. "You make me want to be a better man. I want to take care of you. I want to make you feel wanted like you deserve." I stop to kiss her neck before gently tugging her hair to the side. "I may not be perfect all the fucking time. I'm far from it, but you make me want to be as close to it as I can be. Give me a chance to make you feel good; feel wanted. I want you to be mine. I want to be the one you snuggle with and watch a movie with at night. I want to be the one you stay home with because you don't like to go out. I don't like fucking cats, but I'll love them because you love them."

"I don't know," she whispers. "I'm scared. I can't handle being crushed by you. It will only fucking destroy me, Slade."

"I am too. Trust me. This feeling is new to me. You've done something to me and I can't stop fucking thinking about you. You've fucking ruined me. I'm not giving you up so easily."

Her lips part and it takes everything in me to not press my lips against them again and make her mine. I want her so bad, but I want her to want me just as much. I can't force her to want me this time. It will never work that way.

"You really can't stop thinking about me?" I nod my head and run my thumb over her lip. "What about all the other women, Slade? I can't be with a man like that again. I just can't." She looks around the room at the group of women watching us. She looks upset by them and a bit jealous. I don't like that look on her. "I didn't mean for my presence to distract you from your job. I just wanted to let you know you'd be seeing me around more. I didn't come looking for this."

I cup her face in my hands and step closer to her to show her I don't give a fuck about those women. "I haven't been with any other women since you. The closest I got to having sex with a woman was before you left and I was still being a horny, heartless dick. I was confused and not ready for change. I won't lie to you about that. I'll never lie to you. I haven't had sex or have even wanted to since you fucking left me that night. That's a big fucking deal for me."

A tear falls down her cheek, but she tries to hide it before I can see it. She's too late. I catch her face and rub the tear away with my thumb. She seems a bit surprised and torn. I don't blame her. I was a major dick and I don't deserve her trust. "I don't understand why, Slade. You can have anyone that you want. I do mean anyone and everyone."

"But I want you. I know I've been an asshole and I'm sorry. I don't even know how I let things go so far and let myself become an asshole . . . but when you fall it happens all too fast." I step closer to her so that my lips are brushing hers. "All I'm asking is for you to give me a chance. We can take things slow. The last thing I want to do is hurt you. I can't stop thinking about you, Aspen. No one has been able to make me feel the way you do. No one has been able to make me feel at all."

She tilts her head up and rubs her lips against mine but doesn't kiss me. "I don't know. I'm not sure it's a good idea."

"How do you feel about me?" I tilt her face up so she can look me in the eyes. The eyes always give the heart away. "Tell me how you feel. I don't want a bullshit answer this time. I'm standing here in front of everyone asking you if you feel the same way I do. It took me a week to fall in love with you, Aspen. I need you to tell me the truth."

Her eyes search mine and I can see her walls break down a bit. She cares for me, but just how much? Is it enough? I can only hope. "I haven't stopped thinking about you since the first time I laid eyes on you. I knew then that I wouldn't be able to forget you. I was right. I was hoping that I'd be able to go the whole week and force myself to hate you. It didn't happen. Every day, I fell further for you." She reaches up and wraps her hands in my hair and gently tugs it. "Then you opened up to me and I fell even more in love with you. It was unstoppable and I knew I was screwed in the best way possible. I wanted to know more. I wanted to help ease your pain. I wanted to cure you."

I pull her face to mine and suck in her bottom lip before releasing it. "You did cure me. Now give me a chance to cure you. If I fuck up you can punish me." I smirk and she lightly taps my cheek. "I mean it."

Her eyes search mine for a second and I leave them open for her. I want her to read them; to see how I truly feel and that I meant every word that I said. "We'll take things slow?" she asks. "At my pace?"

"At your pace." I smile as I bite her lip and press my body against hers. "Except for in the bedroom."

She laughs and again, it's the most beautiful sound in the fucking world. Especially when it's because of me. I never want to forget that sound. "I think I can handle that," she whispers. "Just don't hurt me, please. I can't handle it."

"I won't do that. If I hurt you, I will only be hurting myself more." I gently suck her bottom lip into my mouth before kissing her. She kisses me back with a desperation that says she's missed me as much as I've missed her before pulling away and placing her forehead to mine.

"Maybe you should stay at my house tonight. You know, come help me unpack."

"All right, guys." Cale jumps in between us and places his hand on my chest. "This is getting too fucking mushy. Slade, are you running a fucking fever?"

"Fuck you, Cale." I push him out of the way and grab my woman, throwing her over my shoulder. She giggles and slaps my ass. I like it. "Have fun closing up the bar. I'm out."

Before Cale or Sarah can respond, I'm out the door. I smack Aspen's perfect little ass, causing her to bite me as I head for the white Jeep that she points to.

Looks like I have a lot to prove before Aspen will completely trust me and give herself to me fully. I'm willing to give it my all. She deserves better than what she's had and that's what I'll be working to be. She's opened my eyes and I'm not going to fucking let them close again. I'm tired of not living and just getting by day by day, trying my best to feel less dead.

I have no idea where this will take me and if it will work out, but it's worth fighting for. That's the only thing I know at the moment.

I'm going to show this woman that I can be her man and more; show her and myself that I'm still human . . .

HEMY

WALK OF SHAME : BOOK 2

PROLOGUE

HEMY

A HAND ON MY SHOULDER roughly shakes me, causing me to groan and run my hands over my face. I'm so fucked up that I can barely even move. To be honest, this could just be my mind screwing with me again, so I choose to ignore it.

"Hemy. Get the hell up." The person shakes me again, but rougher this time. "Wake up, bro."

I try to open my eyes, but all they do is end up rolling into the back of my head and closing again. I'm in the middle of my drug-induced coma, fucked out of my mind. My eyes are so heavy I don't even bother trying to open them again. All I want to do is sleep, to not have to think. My mind is a fog, no clues as to where it's been or what it's done in the past twenty-four hours; my synthetic nirvana.

"It's time for you to get out, man. Take Rachel and go. I've got shit to do today." The voice echoes through my ears, not sticking to my mind, except for one word.

All it takes is Rachel's name for my mind to register what the hell is going on and for me to sober up enough to move. I knew I shouldn't have come here last night. All I wanted was a quick release from my hell for ten minutes. I didn't expect to get as trashed as I did, but then again, I never do until it's too late.

Sitting straight up I open my eyes and shake my head, as if that's going to take me out of the state I'm in. The room starts spinning around me, so I lean forward with my head in my hands and squeeze my eyes shut. I need to come down, but my mind is still off in the land of the thoroughly fucked up.

"Dude . . . I told you to take it easy last night, but you were unstoppable as usual. You need to get your shit together."

My brain finally starts to process, and I open my eyes again to see my good friend, Mitch, standing above me with my shirt in his hands. He looks both angry and sorry for me at the same time. That can't be good.

He throws my shirt at my face and it ends up landing on my lap, which I just now realize is covered with Rachel's face buried in the middle. Rachel groans and digs her face into my hard on, but doesn't wake up.

Fuck.

In one quick movement I push Rachel out of my lap and jump to my feet. "Ah, fuck." I rub my hands over my face and step away from the bed. "What is this shit?"

Rachel opens her eyes and smiles seductively while reaching for my pant leg. I shake her hand off and push it away. "What's wrong, baby? You seemed to be into me last night. Did I do something wrong?" She pokes her bottom lip out in a pout.

Pointing my finger in her face I take a deep breath and exhale, trying to keep my anger in check. "The fuck I was. You know damn well I don't want shit to do with you." I grab my shirt and start backing away. "I'll deal with your ass later. I told you this shit had to stop. I have to go."

I rush through the house with Mitch trailing closely at my heels. As soon as I push my way outside, I stop and take a few deep breaths to gather myself from the shitstorm I just walked out of. My head is spinning even faster now, and I have no idea how I'm going to get my ass home in this condition. I can barely even stand up straight, but I need to get to *her*.

"I have some bad news, bro." Mitch's voice is soft and full of regret coming from beside me.

I don't like the sound of this. I lean against the brick wall of the house and rub my hands over my face as fast as I can. "Just say it, man."

Mitch leans against the wall beside me. He hesitates for a short moment, meaning he doesn't want to say what it is he has to tell me. "Onyx came looking for you this morning. I tried telling her that you weren't here, but man, she isn't stupid."

I turn around and pound my fist into the brick wall as hard as I can, repetitively, angry with myself. The crackling of bone against the wall tells me how much pressure I'm exerting behind each swing. The drugs swarming through my bloodstream numb my mind from the pain I would be experiencing otherwise. "What did she see?" I ask through gritted teeth. "Why didn't you wake me up? Fuck, I could have explained everything."

"I tried waking your ass up. You were too fucked up. She walked into the bedroom and saw you shirtless with Rachel lying across your lap. She just stood there motionless for a while before turning around and walking out. She seemed pretty calm, man. I don't know. I tried explaining, but she just kept walking, mumbling something about eternal heartache. I think she's done this time."

I let out a huff and glide my fingers through my sweaty hair. "How the hell did Rachel get in there with me? When I went to that room last night I was alone. I didn't do shit with her. I never once touched her." My jaw tenses as I picture Rachel's scheming hands on me. This isn't the first time she has pulled this shit.

"I don't know, dude. I just went in there this morning to make sure your ass was still *breathing* and there she was, half-naked, and sleeping on your lap. I didn't know what the hell happened, so I just left you two alone." He throws his arms up to show me he doesn't really want to get involved. "I'm sorry, man. I think your time with Onyx is up. Everyone has a breaking point, a moment when they throw in the towel and walk away. You've screwed things up way too many times. You need to get your shit together before you end up dead and alone."

I stand here and let his words sink in as he pushes away from the wall and walks away, ending the conversation. I'm at a loss for words. I know I'm nothing but a big fuck up. I've always been worthless. Even my parents thought so.

Giving my mind a few more minutes to wake up and get with the program, I just stand here with my eyes closed, gripping the wall in front of me. I can feel the blood starting to ooze out of the torn skin, running down my fingers, but only because of the wetness and not the pain. I'm still numb from the pain, I always am. It's what I spend all my time chasing, and the reason I'm in this situation. How the hell am I going to explain this to Onyx? She'll probably be gone by the time I get there.

Dammit, I fucked up . . .

About an hour later I pull up in front of my apartment and hop off my motorcycle. It took me that *long* to be able to somewhat function normally, to leave. Even from the street I can see a couple of her suitcases on the porch, telling me what a screw up I am.

I stand here watching Onyx as she throws another bag out onto the porch, not even bothering to look my direction. It's really happening. She's really leaving and I am too fucked up to even fight for her. I am barely holding the bile down that is rising in my throat. Even I think I'm a piece of shit. How am I supposed to convince her otherwise?

Setting my helmet down on my seat, I sprint over to the porch and reach for her arm just as she sets down another bag. "It wasn't what it looked like. Let me explain."

Her scorching green eyes meet my amber ones and I feel my heart drop to my stomach. There is nothing left in her look but hatred and pain, and it hurts even more knowing where it came from. I did this to her and I've been doing it for the last six years.

"It doesn't matter, Hemy," she mutters, yanking her arm away. "You don't think I know you didn't sleep with that bitch? I know it . . . but the question is how much did she enjoy getting off on you while you were drunk, high, and passed out? How do you expect me to feel about all of this? The thought of her touching you makes me want to puke. Her hands groping your body, touching your hair; being places mine should be. I can't do it anymore, I can't continue to stay in the shadows, tormenting myself mentally over you. I just can't."

I swallow and place my hand on her chin, stepping closer to her. Her eyes dart down to my lips before she pulls her face away and takes a step back. "Don't," she whispers. "Just. Don't. Please, let me go."

It hurts having her push me away. Not being able to touch my woman is the worst pain ever, but I don't blame her. "I have no excuse. I'm a mess. I know that. I'm trying to get by the only way I know how, which is to forget sometimes."

"Well, I can't take it anymore. I just can't deal with it. I gave it everything I had, and now there is nothing left to give. Every day I'm with you I die a little more inside and lose a little more hope. I understand that you had a messed up childhood. I understand that your shitty parents left you. You were a young child, alone, and scared out in the world. I get that, and I can't tell you that your sister is still out there, or that she is even still alive. I can't take that all back, but what I can do is show you that love exists, that I'm always here for you. I have tried. I really have, but I can only take so much, Hemy. I understand your reasoning behind your behavior, but at the end of the day . . . I should be your only." Her voice is broken and it kills me.

She breaks down in tears while moving further away from me as if being close hurts too much. I have the urge to run my hands though her strawberry curls and hold her close, but I don't. I can't. I don't deserve to. "You're a lost cause, Hemy. I can't force you to change. You can't and won't. I'm only eighteen and you're only nineteen. This is all too much to handle. We're too young for this. Can't you see that?"

"I can change. I just need time. My head is not in a good place and I'm not strong enough to move on just yet. Do you know how hard it is to wake up every morning with these memories?" I point to my head, my hand shaking. "The places I have been. The people I have seen. The things I saw my parents do to Sage. It's a gaping wound on my brain. Now I don't even know where the hell she is. She was only nine at the time. I was supposed to protect her. I'm trying my best here, okay?"

"I'm sorry," she whispers. "I tried to help you. I tried, but I can't continue to immerse myself into this filth and heartache. You may not have touched her this time, but what about next time? What extent will you go to in order to get your way of forgetting? I have to get out of here before I lose myself." Her eyes meet mine and her bottom lip quivers. "I've already lost *you*, because you were never fully there to begin with. I have known you for six years; for six years, Hemy, and you have only gotten worse. Don't turn into your parents. Don't let them win."

I turn away from her, no longer able to look at the disappointment in her eyes. It hurts too much. "Can you just give me one more chance? I promise I would never hurt you on purpose. The things you've seen in the past were beyond my control. I may have flirted a little when I was high out of my mind, but I have never taken another woman to bed."

"From what you know of, Hemy," she bites out in a clipped tone. "We don't know that for sure and I'm not sticking around to find out. I have to go. I *need* to go. You've hurt me too many times and I feel as if I can't breathe anymore. It hurts so much."

She turns around and heads for the door, but then stops. "I just have one question. Have you ever loved me?"

Her words linger in the air as I try to force myself to speak. I want to say yes, but the truth is, I'm not sure I know what love truly is. "Onyx, I—"

"No. No. No. I don't want to hear any excuses. I get it." She grips the doorframe, but doesn't turn to face me. "Tell me you love me, Hemy. Give me some kind of hope, because I've lost it all."

My heart speeds up and it becomes hard to breathe. I'm not worth it and we both know it. She said it earlier when she said I was a lost cause. "I'm sorry," is all I can manage to get out. Someone of my caliber doesn't know how to love. It isn't in my genetic makeup. As bad as I want to keep her here, she deserves so much better. But I'm selfish when it comes to her.

Without turning back she lets out a soft cry and covers her mouth. "Don't bother contacting me, Hemy. I'm moving away from Chicago and I have already changed my number. There's nothing more to be said between the two of us."

"Don't say that," I whisper. "I can't fucking lose you too."

"It's too late. You already have." She bends down and reaches for one of her bags, and that's when I notice her brother outside tossing her bags into his trunk. "My family has already been instructed not to tell you where I'm going. You won't be able to change their minds, so don't try. Goodbye, Hemy. It was fun while it lasted, right?" She laughs sarcastically. "Have a nice life."

I fall against the back wall while letting her harsh words sink in. I reach up to cover my face and my heart feels as if it's been ripped from my chest. I'm no longer breathing.

The longer I stand here without her, the more it hurts. The more I feel like dying. *What the hell am I doing?*

"No, wait!" I run to the door and open it, but I'm too late. She's already gone. I quickly search for my phone, but of course I am so stupid that I must have lost it last night.

I turn around and reach for the closest thing to me, slamming it down next to my feet before punching a hole through the wall. What's a few more breaks or scratches going to hurt? Maybe the physical pain in my hands will take away from the pain that is now throbbing in my chest. Trying to catch my breath, I fall against the wall behind me and drag my back down it until I'm on the floor burying my hands in the thickness of my hair.

So this is what love truly feels like . . . and losing it hurts like a bitch.

CHAPTER ONE

HEMY

FOUR YEARS LATER . . .

THE AIR AROUND ME SMELLS of booze, sex, and drugs, my usual Saturday night scene. At one point I lived for these wild nights that consist of bodies upon bodies of people just looking to let loose, get fucked up, and fucked hard without the harsh judgments of society. It became my life. My very reason to breathe . . . until it *fucked* my life up. Then it became my ruin.

I'm leaning against the wall, casually chillin' in the shadows while slamming back a bottle of whiskey. Lurking in the darkness is the person I've become. I've been at it for the last hour. This party is piled high with willing pussy and roaming hands, yet I've let my thoughts pull me under and drown me in my own fucked up world of mistakes and regret. Tonight, I may need a bit of a challenge to get me off. I'm going to need it rough, deep, and fast.

While slamming back another drink of whiskey my eyes stray over to a petite brunette; Nico's new girl. I met Nico a few years ago at one of these parties while I was high out of my mind. We partied together and we slowly became friends. I like him because he's just as fucked up and twisted as I am.

Nico's girl is slowly swaying her hips to a seductive song while rubbing her ass all over his dick. Her eyes are glued to me, eyeing me up and down like a siren luring her next victim. Fucking perfect. I like the seductress types, because they usually like the rough and rowdy sex that I require. The more she dances the more erotic her moves become. She's working it well, because my feet move in her direction, not thinking of anything but giving her what she wants. It's a nice distraction.

Nico's lost in his own little world, grinding himself on her backside, but he stops to tilt back a drink of beer and takes notice of me approaching. He watches me with satisfaction; his eyes say it all. A cocky smirk takes over his lips as he gives me a nod and steps aside. He knows exactly what's coming, and he welcomes it. "Hey, man." He gives me a fist pound before practically pushing his woman into my arms. "Take care of Peyton for me. I know you'll treat her right." Most men don't want to share once they've claimed a woman, but Nico thrives on it. I told you he is just as fucked up as I am.

I grab his girl by the hip and pull her flush against my body. Grinding my hips in rhythm of the music, I press her against the wall and brush my tongue over her lips, causing her to moan and wrap her arms around me. Our bodies press into each other's as I lean in to whisper in her ear. "You've been watching me all night." I press my body a little closer to hers and tug her hair a little. "Are you sure you can handle me once you get me? I'm not so sure Nico has told you about me. I don't fuck like a boy, I fuck like a man. I like it wild, wet, rough, and rowdy. If you want a lover this is your chance to back out."

She sucks in her bottom lip before turning to Nico who is now standing right next to us with a smile on his face. "So this is Hemy, huh?" She gives me a look of approval before letting out a growl and leaning over to bite Nico's lip. "I can definitely get down with this, baby. Are you sure?"

Nico nods while tilting back another drink of beer.

Don't ask me why, but Nico has this weird shit of getting off to me fucking his girls. It's like it turns him on to know that I've been inside them. It could always be that he just enjoys the show. Either way, I'm not complaining.

I slide one hand up her skirt to grip her ass while running my lips up her neck. "You want me to take you upstairs and fuck you? I bet you're already wet for me." She nods her head and plays with the top button of my shirt while biting her lip with need. "Has Nico told you the filthy things I do, because I'm not one to take it easy? Once I'm inside you, it's deep and hard. There's no in between, sweetheart."

She reaches up to grip my hair as Nico pushes behind her with his body and wraps one of her legs around my waist. He grips her thigh and bites her neck. The way that he's grinding his hips is causing her pussy to rub against my erection, which makes me want to fuck right here in this crowded room. It wouldn't be the first time. "This is so hot right now," she breathes. "I'm ready for this." She lets out a satisfied moan and leans her head back and turns it to the side so that Nico can press his lips against hers.

Ignoring everyone around us, I lace my hand in the back of her hair and run my tongue over her neck as she grinds into me while kissing Nico. I pull away from her neck and run my tongue over my bottom lip. "Are you sure you can handle me giving your girl a good fuck, Nico? I have some pent-up shit to get out. I'm not playing it fucking nice tonight."

He releases the lock their lips have been in, and nods his head. Grasping the top of her head, he pulls downward, revealing her neck closer to his lips for access. "I need this tonight. We both want it and you know damn well that you do too," he says with a cocked eyebrow. "Don't back out on me, Hemy."

I smirk as Nico runs his tongue along her jugular and steps back, pushing his hair out of his face. "You know I'm down. Just giving your ass a warning."

With force, I grip Peyton's thighs and pick her up to wrap her legs around my hips. Immediately, she locks them around my waist. The lust in her eyes is thick. No matter the girl, they all have a wild side waiting to be released.

I turn back to Nico while gripping Peyton's ass and sliding one hand under her short dress. There is nothing but a thin string between her pussy and my fingers. Her wetness coats me as she moves back and forth, swaying her hips against me. "You ready to watch Peyton's pretty little pussy get fucked?"

Nico watches me as I push my way through the crowd with his girl plastered to my front. He usually gives me time alone first before he joins in. It's a little routine that he has developed since we started this.

Sucking on Peyton's bottom lip I make my way up the stairs and to the nearest empty room. Turning the knob with my free hand I push the door open with my knee and toss her down onto the bed in front of us.

With her hands gripping the blanket, she spreads out on her back, her eyes locked with mine. Her breathing is out of control with need. "I've never done anything like this before." She runs her tongue over her lips and backs up against the headboard. "I want to. I do. I'm a little nervous though."

Yanking my shirt over my head I walk over to the foot of the bed and grip her thighs while crawling onto the bed above her. Her eyes widen as they take in my build. "Don't be nervous. I want to fuck you and he wants to see it. There's no shame in that." Gripping her thighs tighter, I spread her legs wide for me and pull her up to meet my hips with a smirk. "I hope you like it long and deep, because that's all I can give you."

Before she can respond I have her dress above her head, ripping it away from her body. My eyes trail over her toned form, admiring it for a moment. "Damn, girl." I pull her up, so that she's straddling my lap as I grind my cock against her swollen clit. Her underwear is already moist, just the way I expect them to be.

Her hands reach out to grip my hair as she rocks back and forth, enjoying the feel of my body against hers. "You're so sexy," she whispers. "I can see why Nico gets off to this. It's a little different, but it's the hottest thing I've ever done."

Sitting up on my knees, I arch her back and run my lips over her stomach, stopping at her breasts. "Oh yeah? You like this?" Reaching behind her with one hand, I grip the thin fabric of her bra and rip it open. Her eyes watch me with need as I run my other hand up her stomach before pushing her bra out of the way.

My lips come down to meet her right nipple, gently at first, before I tug on it with my teeth. They are puckered, revealing just how turned on she is. A moan escapes her lips as she rocks her hips into me again, causing me to run my tongue over her soft flesh and growl. "Hemy," she breathes, "I want your cock inside me."

I strain my eyes to look up at her, but keep her nipple in my mouth, sucking the pebble gently and then hard, as I slide my hand down the front of her thong. I glide my finger up and down her wetness before burying it deep inside her pussy.

Her breathing picks up as her hands dive into my long hair, tugging and tangling with deep pants. "Oohhh, that feels so good. Don't stop." Her eyes close as I run my tongue along her smooth body, moving from one breast to the other, all while working my finger deep inside her. Her wetness starts to drip down my hand as her body shakes in my arms.

"Not yet," I demand. "Save it for Nico." I slow my movement, knowing that at any second Nico will be arriving. She's too preoccupied to take notice, but I hear the footsteps down the hallway getting closer with each passing second. I want him to watch her come under my touch. It's pleasurable for all of us. He likes being the audience and I like being the actor; she gets a good fuck out of it. Everyone wins.

I tilt my head to the side and smirk as Nico steps into the room. *Perfect timing*. Grinding my hard cock underneath her body, I shove another finger inside her and start fucking her hard and fast while gently biting her nipple.

"Shit! Oh fuck! That's it, right there. I'm so close..." Her screams come out with a moan as her orgasm takes over, her body clenching my fingers upon her release. "Hemy," she breathes. "Don't stop. I need more." I always did favor a vocal woman in the bedroom, one that tells me exactly what she wants.

I grab her face and turn it to face Nico. Her breathing picks up as he leans against the door watching us. She's starting to feel the high that Nico gets a rush on. It's easier to digest when you realize it's no different than watching a porno, only in real life. Then it doesn't seem so twisted to the outside looking in.

"Take a seat, Nico." I run my tongue up Peyton's lips while pulling my finger out of her pussy. "Things are just heating up. I hope you're ready."

Without waiting for a response I grip her panties in my hands and quickly pull them down her slender legs. I toss them toward Nico and see them land on the arm of the chair he is now sitting in.

Peyton takes turns looking between me and Nico while breathing heavily. She wants to be sure he's watching, silently awaiting his approval to continue. The thought of knowing he's there turns her on. It turns me on.

Standing up from the bed, I pull her by her ankles, aligning her ass with the edge of the bed. I grab both of Peyton's hands and place them on my belt as she sits up. "Take it off. Everything."

Her hands work fast to undo my belt before she goes for my button and zipper. Within seconds, my jeans are being pushed down my thighs and I'm quickly kicking them out of the way.

"Have you ever had a pierced cock inside of you before?" She shakes her head as her eyes look downward toward my erection. "Good. Take my briefs off, Peyton. Show Nico how hard I am for you."

She glances over at Nico before biting her bottom lip and slowly pulling my briefs down. My cock springs free from the material, getting a small gasp from Peyton. I can't tell if she's excited or terrified by its size, not to mention the two steel bars pierced through it. This girl is in for something she never saw coming.

"You like my cock, Peyton?" She nods. "Taste it." I tangle my fingers into the back of her hair while pushing her head down to my cock. The thought of her boyfriend watching her take in my thick cock only makes me harder; making me want to fuck her mouth even faster and deeper.

Her tongue darts out to swirl around the head of my cock before she suctions the top of it into her mouth. She has to open her mouth extra wide to take in its thickness.

I turn to the side and grip her hair harder while giving Nico a view of me fucking his woman's mouth. His eyes meet mine for a brief second before moving down to my length that is barely even halfway in Peyton's mouth. I thrust in and out, grinding my hips while pulling on her hair. Nico's cock grows hard through his jeans as he takes in a deep breath and exhales.

"Touch it," I demand. "Pull out your cock and stroke it while I fuck her mouth. Pretend her lips are on *your* dick, sucking it. Show her how good it makes you feel."

His eyes darken with desire as he shoves his hand down the front of his jeans and starts stroking himself with a loud moan. He's slowly working himself up to join.

"Peyton," I whisper. "Stand up."

She runs her hand up and down my shaft a few more times before pulling her mouth away and doing what she's told. Her tongue runs over her mouth, tasting me on her lips before she looks behind me at Nico.

"Grab my hair and hold the fuck on," I growl. "And you better fucking watch, Nico."

Her hands reach out and grip my hair as I lift her up so that she is sitting spread eagle on top of my shoulders, her pussy in my face. I walk over to the wall next to Nico and press Peyton's back against it, hard. I want to be sure he can see *everything* I'm about to do to her body. I look up at her. "Hold on tight and don't let go."

Once she has a good grip on my hair, I spread her pussy lips and run the tip of my tongue over her clit. I feel her body tremble from my touch, so I softly suck it into my mouth while shoving a finger inside of her, fucking her soft and slow to loosen her up for what's to fill her later.

From the corner of my eye, I see Nico undo the button of his jeans before leaning back in his chair and gripping his hair. "That's so hot. Yeah. Finger fuck her tight little pussy."

I devour her pussy even harder as I reach up with one hand and grip her breast in my hand, squeezing it until I hear her moan out. Her moans turn to screams as I suck her clit harder into my mouth in rotation with running my tongue up and down her wetness and moving my finger in and out in perfect rhythm.

I hear the sound of Nico's zipper before I see his cock break free from his boxers from my peripheral vision. He's stroking his cock with one hand while gripping the arm of the chair with his other. He's so turned on that he doesn't know what to do with himself. He can't even sit still. I don't blame him. Seeing me fuck Peyton with my tongue has to be a hot sight. I know I'm good at pleasuring anyone I get my hands on; eating pussy is my specialty.

I look up at Peyton while circling my tongue over her swollen clit. "You ready to come again? Then, when you're done, I'll bury my cock deep inside of you."

She leans her head back and tries to keep her leg from shaking. Her thighs are practically squeezing my head off, but I keep spreading them wide so Nico can see my tongue on her soft pink flesh.

"Yes." She nods her head while moaning. "Yes. This feels so good. So good."

I smile against her pussy before pulling away from the wall and kneeling on my knees, setting her down on the plush carpet close to where Nico is sitting with his cock in his hand. "Turn over and get on your knees." I rest on my knees and stroke my hard cock while waiting for her to get positioned. "Such a hot little pussy, Nico. Thanks for letting me get a taste."

I run my hand down the seam of her spine and down the crack of her ass until I reach her wet pussy. Spreading her wide, I bend forward until my tongue is aligned over her pussy, plunging it inward. I fuck her with my tongue and run the thumb of my free hand over the puckered hole above, causing her to tense; the reaction I was looking for. I like a little anal play from time to time, and the girls love the sensation mixed with filling their pussy.

Her hands grip the carpet as she moans out, "I'm about to come. I'm so close." I speed up, shoving my tongue deeper while massaging the opening to her ass above. "Yes! Right there. Ahhhh!"

Her body trembles beneath me and I have to catch her to keep her from falling over. I can hear Nico's breathing pick up as his strokes become longer and faster, desperate for more action than he's getting. He wants to get off so bad, but he's fighting it.

Slapping Peyton's ass, I reach beside me in the pocket of my jeans and pull out a condom. I rip it open with my teeth before rolling it over my dick and adjusting it over my piercings. "You ready for me to fuck you hard?" Peyton nods. "You want to see Nico get off on us? I'll make sure you both come; show him how good your pussy is."

"Mmm . . . yes. Please. Just put it in me." She reaches behind her and grips my dick while licking her lips. "It's so big. Will the piercings hurt?"

I lean my head back and moan as she works the head of my dick up and down her folds. Reflexively, she is backing her ass up closer to me. "Fuck me. It won't be the piercings that hurt. Trust me. That's the last thing you should worry about."

Pushing her head down, she frees me from her hold and places both hands flat on the floor. I position my dick at her entrance before shoving it in with one swift movement, slamming against her with force. Her hands grip the carpet as she screams out in pleasure. I still for a second, letting her adjust to my size before pulling it out and ramming back into her a second time. With each hit against her wall, she inches forward slightly, screaming out in a pleasure filled pain. I pick up my speed while yanking back on her hair to keep her still.

"Stroke your cock faster," I demand. "Get yourself off for her."

Nico looks at me with hard eyes. He spits in his open hand and closes it around his dick to give it the effect of her wet pussy, and continues stroking it hard and fast. "Fuck. Her. Harder." He starts moaning and thrusting his hips up and down, fucking his hand. "Shit. This has me so hard," he moans.

Smirking, I grab a breast in each hand for leverage to make each thrust harder and deeper. I bend forward and grind my cock each time it disappears inside her completely. Slowly pulling back, I ram it hard at the same time I bite her shoulder. She screams out and a throaty groan sounds out from Nico. "You want a fucking taste? Huh?" I look over at him while slowing my movement down. "Take your jeans off and get down here on your knees."

Nico lets out a long puff before nodding his head and squeezing his eyes shut. "Hell yes." He stands and drops his jeans down to the ground before stepping out of them and yanking his shirt over his head. He's in good shape, but not even close to my build. Still, he's a damn good catch for the ladies.

I pull out of Peyton, but continue to fuck her with my finger, one finger at first, and then two. She's so wet it's oozing out of her pussy. She's still enjoying it. I pull my hand free from her body. "Lay on your back, baby, and spread your legs wide for us."

Peyton does as she's told, baring her clean-shaven pussy to us. Nico is now on his knees next to me, eyeing her wet, glistening body as if he's never seen her this way before.

"Good. Now I want you to watch this, Peyton. You want to see how bad he wants you?" She nods her head and looks over at Nico, who is watching her with want in his eyes. "That's my girl." I stand up and grip the back of Nico's head, which gets an instant reaction from Peyton. I like reaction. It's what gets me off. "Does it make you hot to see two men together?"

She lets out something between a moan and a growl, letting us both know what she wants.

Nico runs his tongue over his lips while watching her squirm. His eyes land on Peyton as she reaches down to pull my hand over to her pussy, running it through her wetness. He watches the both of us play with her, until finally, he leans in and presses his lips against mine, tasting her sweetness on my tongue. I can feel his body reacting to mine. His body wants what it wants. No judgment here. To me, a kiss is just a kiss. I can partake in the activity without associating it with the gender of who is on the other side. Like I said, it's reaction that gets me off.

Gripping his hair with one hand, I suck his tongue into my mouth before releasing it and pulling away. He's breathing heavily while looking down at my finger buried inside of Peyton. "You like that, Peyton? Huh? You want to see more?"

She nods her head and grabs a breast in each hand, pinching her hardened nipples. She looks him in the eyes, moaning, as she lowers one hand to her clit and begins to rub it as she speaks. "Suck his dick for me, baby." She runs her tongue over her lips. "Do this for me and I'll do anything you ever ask. I promise."

Nico's nostrils flare as he looks down and takes in my size. This is a line we have never crossed, but fuck it. The way I'm feeling at the moment, I couldn't care less whose mouth is around my dick. If it gets her off, then it gets me off.

He hesitates for a moment, looking between the two of us, before leaning down and taking my cock in his mouth. He's gentle at first, clearly uncomfortable, and barely moving until he starts to get the hang of it.

I push my cock further into his mouth as I look down to see Peyton finger fucking herself while she watches him suck my dick. It's evident that she is turned on by this just as much as he is. Her pace increases in speed to match his the faster Nico takes me.

"She tastes good doesn't she?" I push my dick in further and pull on his hair, causing him to choke a little. "Suck it harder, Nico. You have to get her off by sucking my dick. I don't want to come. I want her to come. Make her come."

He stops for a second to moan before taking it out on me. He takes my dick so hard and fast that it's almost better than most girls I've had. I'm fucking impressed. "You see how much he wants you, Peyton? You see what he's willing to do to get you off? Rub yourself faster, fuck yourself harder, picturing your fingers being his dick." My filthy words coaching her, has her screaming and moaning from another orgasm.

I pull out of Nico's mouth and start stroking my cock. Peyton is crossing her legs from the aftermath of her self-induced orgasm, still playing with her breasts and licking her lips for more. "Get down on all fours. I want you to take my cock in your mouth this time." Hers eyes meet mine as she gets positioned in front of me. She plays with my cock piercings before taking it deep into her mouth and reaching down to play with her pussy. "Get behind her, Nico. Show her how turned on this shit has you."

Gipping her by the hips, Nico gets behind her and slips inside her. He lets out a little moan as he squeezes her ass and slowly starts moving in and out. "Oh shit! Yeah, baby. Suck his dick faster. Take it deep."

I wrap Peyton's hair around my fist and start thrusting my hips faster as her speed picks up. "Fuck yeah, baby. Take it at the back of your throat. I'm about to blow." I feel my orgasm building, so I pull out of Peyton's mouth, yank my condom off, and aim for her mouth.

She opens wide, taking my cock into her mouth, and swallowing every last drop like a pro. I reach over and grab the back of Nico's head, causing him to speed up. The sight of me busting my load in Peyton's mouth pushes him over the edge, and within seconds he is shaking in his own orgasm.

He pushes himself deep, burying his cum as deep as he can. "Holy shit! What the fuck! That feels so damn good." He stills for a second and pulls out before pulling Peyton's body up so that her back is pressed against his chest. He lays one arm across her breasts, cupping the farthest one and runs the opposite hand down her stomach until it's cupping her mound.

She leans her head back and I grab the back of Nico's head, pushing his mouth against hers. He almost pulls back from the taste of me in her mouth, but I reach out and grab his hand, pushing his finger into her wet pussy. She begins grinding her bare ass against him, causing him to go stiff instantly. This is enough to get him going again.

He kisses her harder and deeper while moaning, ready for another round. He watches as Peyton breaks the kiss, lies on her back, and spreads her legs wide before him. I grab his shaft and begin stroking as he watches her. "You see your cum running out of her pussy, Nico?" I increase speed, making him hard as a rock. He nods. "She can hold more . . ."

After a few more strokes, I rub Nico's cock over Peyton's wet little pussy, aligning it with the opening, causing them both to moan out. "Fill her, fuck her, and don't stop until she's filled to max capacity with your cum."

I back away from the two of them as he follows my command. I reach for a cigarette and enjoy the show before me. I deserve one after this. I should feel some kind of pride for getting them both off and for knowing that they both came here looking for it. But I still feel empty.

There's my screwed up and twisted. This is the person I've become, the life I live . . .

CHAPTER TWO

HEMY

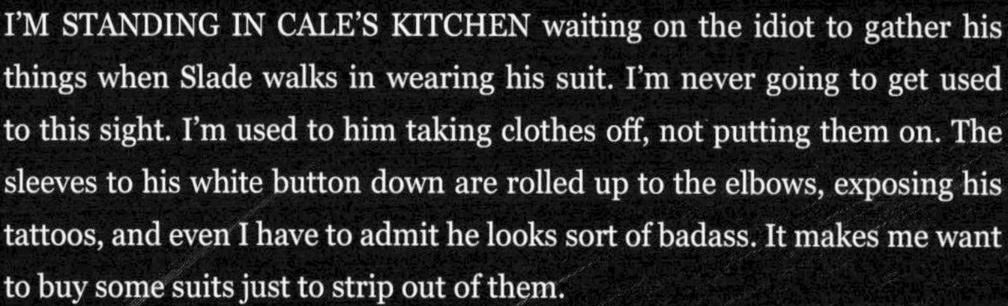

I'M STANDING IN CALE'S KITCHEN waiting on the idiot to gather his things when Slade walks in wearing his suit. I'm never going to get used to this sight. I'm used to him taking clothes off, not putting them on. The sleeves to his white button down are rolled up to the elbows, exposing his tattoos, and even I have to admit he looks sort of badass. It makes me want to buy some suits just to strip out of them.

"Dude." I grip his shoulder and shake him as he reaches in the fridge to pull out a beer. "Since when the hell do you drink beer?"

He smirks while leaning against the fridge and unbuttoning his shirt with one hand. "I told you, man. I'm done with that hard shit. I don't need it anymore." He takes a swig of his beer. "I can't be all shitfaced when I have a woman to please and a job to do. I'm not fucking shit up."

Wish I would have been that smart.

"Good shit. Where is that sexy little mama anyways? I'm sure she's missing me by now." I wink and grab his beer out of his hand. I get ready to take a drink, but he swats my dick, causing me to groan as he steals his beer back.

"My bad, motherfucker," he says with a grin. "And hell no. She doesn't miss you. Trust me. I keep my woman well above satisfied. Why do you think we never leave the bedroom?" He gives me a cocky grin.

"It would be better if I joined. You can't deny it," I tease, causing him to tense up. "She's already touched my—"

"Umm. What are you boys doing in here?"

We both look over to see Aspen leaning against the door wearing one of Slade's t-shirts. She smiles at me before turning her attention to Slade.

Slade tilts back his beer before shoving it into my chest and walking over to stand in front of Aspen. He presses his body against hers and kisses her neck before picking her up and wrapping her legs around his waist.

"Mmm . . . damn, baby. You've been here waiting for me?" Aspen nods her head while biting her bottom lip. "I've been thinking about your sexy ass all day."

She pulls Slade's bottom lip into her mouth, causing him to growl. "I want to see you strip out of that sexy suit, baby. You know, I still can't get used to seeing you in it, but it's *so, so, so* sexy." I watch as she trails her tongue along his jaw up to the lobe of his ear.

"Oh yeah. Keep on talking like that and I'll take you right here."

Pushing down on my erection, I lean against the counter and eye them both up. "Hell yes. Just don't get mad if I jerk off to you guys fucking. I'll do my best not to join." I pause as they both look over at me. "Unless you want me to. I don't mind getting you both off. My cock is irresistible, so don't complain if you get addicted."

"Fuck off, Hemy," Slade calls over his shoulder as he starts walking away with Aspen. "Save your dick for the private party tonight. I'm sure you'll be using it a lot."

Aspen smiles at me from over Slade's shoulder and I bite my bottom lip as I point at my cock in question. She laughs and shakes her head as I tilt back the bottle of beer.

Aspen and I have a little playful side, but Slade has gotten used to it. He knows I would never really fuck with his woman. Back before, I thought nothing of it, because Slade treated women just as I do now. Nothing but a good fuck to pass the time and get my head off of shit. Things are different now. Slade is a changed man. He's been seeing Aspen for a month now. I've never seen him so happy in my life. He even started taking on some cases against drunk drivers or some shit and has completely stopped stripping. He's working hard toward a happy life for them. Aspen is his Onyx. At least he's smart enough to keep her.

Cale passes the happy couple in question and pops into the kitchen. "I'm ready, man. I wanted to wear a uniform or some shit to make it more exciting tonight, but I don't have shit in my closet." Cale runs his hand through his hair while in thought. "I'm tired of just stripping out of my jeans and t-shirt. It's getting boring. Same shit different day."

"Is that right?" I think for a second while finishing off the last of the beer in my hand, before tossing the empty bottle in the trash. "Follow me. I'm sure Slade won't mind if we borrow a couple of his suits. I bet we'll look like fucking studs. If there was a way to wear an invisible sign that said guaranteed mind-blowing orgasm here, this would be it." We rush up the steps to Slade's room.

When I get to his door I hear something fall over and crash to the floor. This fucker really doesn't waste any time. I knock once on the door before pushing the door open and stepping inside.

Slade has Aspen leaned over his dresser with her hands gripping onto the sides. Her upper half is completely bare and pressed against the wood. He has each of his hands locked onto her hips, lifting her feet off the floor, and pounding into her from behind. He notices me walk in through the reflection in the mirror, so he pounds into her one last time and then stops to yell at us.

"Seriously, fuckers? Go ahead, just come on in and enjoy the show! Have some damn respect for Aspen at least. Shit."

I raise my brows at the both of them and walk over to Slade's closet. "I'm offended," I say, placing my palm over my heart. "You know damn good and well that I respect your woman. She is one fine piece of ass and she knows it," I tease and wink at her, now staring back at me in the mirror.

She smiles back at my grin, knowing it just revs his engine up more. I knew the girl had a little kinky side buried beneath that shy exterior. I'd be willing to bet she'd let me watch if he would. "Carry on as if we're not even here. Give us a few minutes and we'll be gone. We need to borrow a couple of suits for tonight." I peek over my shoulder and take in the sight of Slade moving in closer to her, as if he's trying to hide what isn't even visible. "Don't keep your lady waiting, Slade." Giving him hell is so much fun, because he's so protective of her.

"You're a real pain in the ass sometimes. You know that?" Aspen growls out trying to feign anger, but I hear the laughter in her tone she is trying to keep hidden. She has to have a sense of humor to deal with me, because I just don't give a shit. "At least Cale is decent enough to peek in from the hallway. Yeah, I see you out there."

Slade lets out a frustrated growl before standing Aspen up from the dresser and covering her nipples with the length of his arm as well as cupping her pussy with the opposite hand. He walks them over together to grab Aspen a sheet to cover up with. "Just pick out your suits and get the hell out of here. Take them all. I don't care. Just hurry the hell up. I'm putting a lock on my door tomorrow."

Cale steps into the room and laughs. "The dresser? Really?" Slade is wrapping the sheet around her and pulls out when she is covered enough we can't see her.

Slade lights up a cigarette and leans against the dresser with his cock bared for all to see. "Just because I wear a suit now doesn't mean shit. What's the fun in sex if you aren't breaking things and putting holes in the wall? Just hurry up."

"Seriously, dumbass," I jump in. "You would know that if you would actually put your dick in someone. It's fun. Give it a try sometime."

"I plan to, dick. Now let's get these suits and go before we're late." Cale shoves me into the closet and reaches for the first suit. "And women don't seem to complain when I use my tongue." He sticks his tongue out and starts waving it around.

"Gross," Aspen calls out. "I don't want to hear that, Cale."

I reach for a slick black suit and toss it over my shoulder. "Alright, man. Let's get the hell out of here."

WE ARRIVE AT THE PARTY and I kill the engine while pumping myself up. It's not very often we do parties outside of the club, but one of the girls is turning twenty-one and wanted a big blowout. To be honest, I would rather do a house party anyways. More freedom to please the women.

I see the headlights to Stone's Jeep pull up behind us and he quickly jumps out dressed all fly in his own suit. I tug on the sleeve of the white button down before reaching for the black jacket and pulling it on. It's a little tight, but I still look damn good. Cale is wearing a black suit too except his button down is more of a silver color or some shit, maybe gray, hell I don't know. It's cool though. He still looks good.

"You boys better be on your shit tonight," I say while stepping out of my truck. "Especially you, rookie." I point to Stone and shove his shoulder. "Nice fucking suit, man."

He pulls down the front of his suit as if he's all fancy and smirks. "I know." He starts grinding his hips while messing with his buttons. "Once I start grinding, this suit won't even matter." He puts one leg up against his Jeep and starts swaying his hips in a slow motion. "Oh yeah. I'm working my shit tonight."

"Take it easy, lady killer," Cale says with a smirk. "Look." He nods his head toward the small white house and lifts an eyebrow. "The ladies are spying on us."

I tilt my head to the side to look. At least six girls are shoved up to the window, watching us with open mouths while fanning themselves off. They're going to need a lot more than a hand to cool them off once we get inside.

I walk over to the door with Cale and Stone trailing closely at my heels. I don't even bother to knock. I just push the door open and step inside. A fast rhythm is playing over the speakers, so I start grinding my body to the music while pulling my tie off and wrapping it around the birthday girl.

She lets out a nervous laugh while checking me out and fixing her tiara. "Oh my . . . God." She takes a step back and I take a step forward, still grinding my hips. "Best birthday gift ever," she exclaims in a slight slur.

I wrap my hand around to grab the back of her neck before grinding my body against the front of hers and placing her hands on my chest. I don't really pay much attention to the other two, but I assume they are doing something similar from all the screaming that is piercing my ears right now.

Backing the girl up, I walk over to the stereo and change the song. A slow, seductive song comes over the speaker causing my rhythm to become slow and hypnotic. The girl's hands roam my body as I thrust my hips back and forth, close enough for my cock to hit against her stomach. I'm not wearing any briefs, allowing it to hang free. She feels it hardened against her and starts screaming in excitement.

"Oh my God!" She covers her mouth to hide her excitement as I push her against a wall and wrap one of her legs around my waist. "Is this really happening?" she squeals. "This is the best birthday ever. Thank you!"

One of the girls responds from behind me. "Anytime, Jade. Just relax and enjoy. This night is yours."

Her voice sounds a bit familiar, but in the heat of the moment I don't even bother trying to put it together. With both hands I rip my shirt open and watch the girl's eyes widen as she takes in my sculpted body thrusting in her face.

I can feel her wetness on my stomach, because she is wearing a short dress with only her panties between us, so I turn us around until she is sitting on top of a table. I run my hand across it to knock a few things out of the way before pulling my shirt and jacket completely off and throwing them aside.

I hear a few girls scream, so I look over to see Stone already down to a pair of white briefs. He has some girl in a chair and is grinding his dick in her face.

"Holy shit! Take it off! I can feel it on my face," the girl screams. "Oh my God, it's so hard."

"Bite it," another girl screams. "Take me next!"

I ignore all the noise behind me and focus on the birthday girl. She's sexy with long red hair and big blue eyes. The dress she is wearing is now pushed up above her hips and she is looking at me as if she's ready to fuck. This drives me wild, especially with everyone watching.

"Just so you know, I'll let the birthday girl touch." I lean into her ear and whisper, "Anything you want."

Her breathing picks up as she looks over my shoulder and then back at me. "I like the sound of that." She smiles and bites her bottom lip. "Dance for me. I've always loved a man in a suit."

I pull her by her thighs so her body is hanging slightly off the table. I wrap my hands into the back of her hair and press my cock against her heat, while grinding my hips. "Touch me," I whisper. "I'll even let you taste it."

Her hand reaches down in between us as she strokes my cock through the fabric. Her eyes widen as she takes in the size and piercings. "Oh. My. God." She licks her lips and closes her eyes as she strokes it faster. "I'm so horny. It's my birthday, you know." She leans in to my neck and kisses it. "No one will mind if I have a little fun. No judging tonight."

"Is that right?" I ask. "I can take you right here if you want. I'm here for entertainment and it's what I do best. I'll fuck you here, in front of your friends, and put on a good fucking show."

Reaching down with one hand I undo my pants and pull them slightly down my hips so the tip of my cock is showing. I move my hips into her and start swaying fast as the song picks up in beat. She's leaning into me, moaning, until her eyes land on the tattoo on my side. She eyes it for a few seconds before speaking. "Onyx," she whispers. "Holy shit!" She looks behind me and around for a few seconds before smiling and fingering for someone to come join us. "Look at this. One of the strippers has your name tattooed on him. That is crazy. I don't know anyone else by that name."

I turn beside me to see a woman with platinum blonde curls, tattoos, and piercing green eyes. The whole world crashes around me. It's not just any woman. It's her. It's Onyx. My Onyx. Except . . . she's different now. She's even sexier than I remember and she looks as if she's just seen a fucking ghost. I can't breathe for a moment as I take her in, trying to decide if this is really happening. It's been four years, four fucking years. She is the most beautiful woman, still, to this day.

Her eyes meet mine and her whole body stiffens, but she doesn't speak. Her eyes just take me in as if trying to figure out how I look so different.

Well, damn! I am trying to figure out the same. When did she get all of those tattoos and color her hair? She looks wild and dangerous. I love it.

She's stunning, hypnotic, and addicting . . . and I want her.

Four years I have wondered where she's at and here she is right in my damn face.

CHAPTER THREE

ONYX

MY HEART HAS LITERALLY JUST stopped in my chest. *Four years*. I have gone four years avoiding the very man that is standing next to me with his dick practically hanging out of his pants. And of course, it's for another woman. I guess some things never change.

Hemy. My Hemy?

No matter how hard I want to deny it, my traitorous heart gives me away. This man still makes my heart beat wild in my chest and steals my breath away with just one look into those amber eyes. This is going to be hard. Really hard.

It takes every bit of strength in me to pull my eyes away from his gaze. He's looking at me as if he wants to wrap his hands in my hair and pull me into his arms. The pain in his eyes is so intense that it causes an ache in my chest. It's the very look he gave me for the six years we had known each other. What started out as a friendship, turned into something passionate, wild, and painful. Very painful. I really tried healing him. I did. But a person can only take so much before they lose control themselves.

I take a step back to compose myself before bringing my eyes down to Hemy's side where sure enough, Onyx is tattooed in big black fancy letters. I feel my throat close up as tears sting my eyes. I won't do this here. I won't show my weakness. I'm different now. I've changed. I'm no longer that weak woman that just let everything slide. I'm much stronger now and no one will break me down again and let me lose myself. Not even . . . him.

"Onyx," Jade squeaks. "Do you see this?" She runs her hand over Hemy's skin causing instant jealousy that I quickly push away. I won't let myself feel. I can't.

I bring my gaze up to meet hers and put on my mask; my game face. "Yup. That is definitely my name. How strange is that?"

Hemy has finally come out of his frozen state and is now staring at me, looking me up and down. I look different. A lot different. But . . . I'm not the only one.

Holy hell!

He runs his hands through his long, dark hair and takes a step away from Jade. His hair is much longer than I remember. It's sexier, making me want to run my hands through it myself. "Onyx," he says in a painful whisper. "What the fuck?" He goes to reach for my chin, but I move away too fast for him to even make contact. "You're back and you couldn't even tell me."

I watch as he rubs his hands over his face in frustration. Of course I didn't tell him. He ruined me. Paralyzed my heart and soul. I wanted to live with him but the truth was, I was doing anything but. I was far from living. I was surviving and he was barely even doing that.

"I'm not doing this, Hemy." I turn to walk away but he grabs my arm to stop me. My heart skips a beat from his touch. "Let go," I snap. "I don't owe you anything. I told you I was leaving and I did. I had to. This is not the time or place." I give him a quick once-over, taking in his thick build, tattoos, and piercings before yanking my arm from his reach and turning away. "Just do what you're getting paid to do."

Why the hell does he have to look so delicious?

"I'm sorry, Onyx. I had no idea." Jade jumps down from the table and fixes her tiara. "I'll grab another one of the guys. It's not a big deal. You two umm . . . I'm going."

I grab her arm right before she walks away. "No. You won't. *He* is getting paid good money for tonight and he better damn well deliver. I'll be upstairs if you need me."

"Onyx, wait!"

I hold my hand out in front of me and start backing away. "Don't! Just please let my girls enjoy the night. That is all I ask. What we had was in the past. It doesn't matter now." I bite my tongue and walk away as fast as my heels will allow me. I can't let him talk. I can't let myself fall back into him.

I take the stairs two at a time and rush into the bathroom without looking back. As soon as the door closes, my back is pressed against it and I'm falling to the ground with the door supporting me. I grip my necklace as I fight to catch my breath. The necklace that Hemy gave me eight years ago. The only piece of him I took with me.

I'm not ready for this yet. I thought it would be different seeing him again. I thought I would be over us. I'm not. I'm so far from it. The truth is, if I hadn't run away when I did, then I would be wrapped up in his arms, clutching him instead of this necklace. I came back too soon.

Why do I do this to myself? Why am I still doing it?

Four years of not seeing his face or hearing his soothing voice has been damn near torture. Not a day went by that I didn't wonder where he was or what he was doing. The other problem was, I had to wonder who he was doing. I couldn't allow that to bring me down, so I found other things to occupy my time. I can almost see why he did what he did. Almost.

After a few minutes, I calm down enough to push myself back up to my feet. I need to just suck it up. I can't let him see the effect he still has on me. That will only allow him to hurt me again. I won't let that happen.

"Okay. You can do this," I whisper. "He's part of the past. He's part of the past." I try to convince myself but I suck at it. "Dammit."

I stand up tall and take a deep breath before exhaling and pulling the bathroom door open. What I see in front of me causes my breath to be taken away . . . again.

Hemy is standing there still shirtless, just staring at the door as if he had been waiting for it to open.

"Onyx," Hemy whispers. His eyes are soft and caring as they meet mine. Something in them looks different but I can't tell what that means just yet.

It's like he's looking at me with different eyes than before. It makes me want to believe he's clean but I know that's almost impossible. "We need to talk about us."

"Hemy," I breathe in frustration. I run my hands through my hair and close my eyes. "There is nothing to talk about. There hasn't been an *us* in a very long time."

I try to step around Hemy, but he places one arm against the wall, blocking me in. "There is an us. There always has been and you know it." He stops and brings his eyes down to my lips. He licks his own and slides his free hand in the back of my hair. "I've missed you, Onyx. I've tried for the last four years to find you but your family are stubborn assholes. I've ended up at their doorstep once a month for the last four years. They're dedicated. I give them that."

Hemy admitting he tried for years to find me shakes something loose inside me that I thought was long lost, but I must remain strong.

I suck in a breath as his body presses against mine. "Hemy." I place my hand to his firm chest to block him from getting any closer. "Please," I plead. "Don't do this to me. It's only going to get you hurt. I don't want to hurt you. Don't make me do it." My eyes land on his lip ring as he bites it. It's sexy. There's no denying I want to bite it too.

He takes a step back and untangles his hand from my hair before placing it against the wall so I'm completely blocked in. "You already have. You are right now, dammit. I can't believe you didn't tell me you were back. We were friends before we dated and you decided to throw that away as well. You left. You actually fucking left."

I try to concentrate on what he's saying but him being so close is making it nearly impossible. I can't think straight. Especially when I have a clear view of my name going down his side. It's not only there, but it's huge. It's definitely there for show.

"When did you get my name on you?" I ask while staring at his naked torso. "Why? Why would you do that?"

He drops his arms and takes a step back. "I got it a year after you left. Why? I got it because I couldn't get over you. And I'm still not."

My mouth opens but I can't speak. If I do then it will put me right where I don't want to be. So instead, I just walk away.

"Onyx." I keep going. "Fuck!"

I hear something crash as I walk down the stairs as calmly as I can and try to ignore the fact that Hemy is still into me. All I have to do is make it through this stupid party and then I'll just pretend I never saw him. Pretend that seeing him doesn't still take the breath straight from my lungs.

"There you are." Ash appears at the bottom of the staircase looking up at me. She brushes her brown curls behind her ear. "Why did you run off? The party is just starting. These boys are so sexy. You need a dance from Stone."

I reach for Ash's arm and pull her around the corner just as Hemy starts walking down the steps. Today is not the day for all this shit to happen. It's too soon and I can't be sure that Hemy has changed. I need to think of something fast.

I press Ash against the wall and force a smile. "Hey. I'm sorry. I was talking to Roman and he needs you to go into work. I would but I really have to be somewhere." I brush her hair behind her ear and try to calm myself. "Is that okay? Would you mind going in? It's Jade's birthday and I—"

"Onyx," she cuts in. "Of course I will go in. I could use the money anyways. No worries. I'll leave now."

She goes to walk away, but I grab her arm to stop her. "Thank you. I owe you."

She flashes me her perfectly sweet smile. "You've already done enough for me. I'll catch you later at home."

I nod and lean against the wall as she walks outside. *How the hell am I going to do this? I don't know if I can.*

Hemy appears around the corner with a frustrated scowl on his face. He looks around for a few seconds before his eyes find me. And when they do, they go soft for just a brief moment. "Don't run away again. I can't do this shit, Onyx."

My eyes rake over his gorgeous, toned body before I pull my eyes away and walk toward the door. "I have to go. Just please go take care of Jade. Tell her I had to run out."

I pull the door open and start heading for my Harley. I pull the hair tie from my wrist and wrap my hair in it before straddling my bike.

Of course that stubborn ass can't listen and I feel his presence behind me once again. Hemy walks over with wide eyes as I grip the handle and start the engine. "You ride a motorcycle," he says in disbelief. His eyes take in my ride before it finally dawns on him. "Is that my old Harley? You had it fixed up?”

I toss my helmet on and kick the stand up with my foot. “*I* fixed it.”

“Since when do you know how to work on motorcycles?”

I give him a stern look and rev the engine. “I learned from the best.” I rev the engine again and force a smile, fighting back my emotions. “Actually, I’ve learned a lot from the best.”

His jaw grinds as he watches me ride away. I don’t look back. I just ride, needing to escape.

CHAPTER FOUR

HEMY

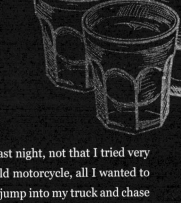

ONYX HASN'T LEFT MY MIND once since last night, not that I tried very hard to forget her. After she rode off on my old motorcycle, all I wanted to do was chase after her. I fought so hard not to jump into my truck and chase her down. I know she needs time. I'm trying to respect that, but it's been four years already. How much more time could she possibly need?

I stood outside for a good twenty minutes, just staring out at nowhere, until Cale came outside looking for me. Without a word, I followed him inside and went back to work. Nothing about it felt right. All I could think was that I was doing something wrong. How can I feel that way when we aren't even together? She practically hates me, yet I feel bad for stripping for other women. Now isn't that some shit.

"How's that engine coming along?"

I look up when Mitch snaps me out of my thoughts. He's standing on the right side of me, chewing on a sandwich. He's shirtless and equally as dirty and greasy as I am.

"Good. It's all good." I toss down my dirty rag and grab my t-shirt. "I'm going to head out so I can shower before work. I'll finish this later."

Mitch looks between me and the red Mustang I've been working on since eight this morning. He doesn't look happy. He knows something is up, but it's too soon for me to tell him. I don't feel like getting into it just yet. "What's up with you? You've been at this for the last eleven hours and now you're about to head out to *Walk Of Shame*? Don't you think you need a break? If I had known you worked tonight then I would have kicked your ass out of my shop a long time ago."

"It's nothing, man." I throw my shirt on and reach in my pocket for a cigarette. "I just wanted to get this shit done. This Mustang has been in the shop since last week and it's not even ready to go yet. I'm sure the owner is ready for his ride back." I brush the loose strand of hair out of my face that has fallen out from the rubber band before lighting my cigarette. "I'll be back after work to finish it."

"Nah, I don't think so. Not tonight. You can finish it in the morning." Mitch takes the last bite of his sandwich before shutting the hood. "This car is off-limits until you come back *after* you've gotten some sleep. I hope whatever is bothering you isn't going to make you want to—"

"It's not. Shit, Mitch." I take a long drag of my cigarette and grind my jaw. "I'm done with that shit. You don't need to worry about it." I grip Mitch's shoulder before giving it a shove and walking backward. "I'm outta here. I'll see your ass bright and early."

"Alright, man. Sorry. Just looking out for ya." He tosses his dirty rag at me and starts walking over to help a customer. "See ya."

"Yup," I mumble, while blowing out smoke. "See ya."

I ARRIVE AT *WALK OF Shame* early and with three shots of Jack and one shot of Patron in my system. The last thing I need to do is let thoughts of Onyx ruin my night. I've been doing this shit for too long to care about what someone else might think. Who gives a shit if I strip for the pleasure of women? Onyx left a long time ago. I shouldn't feel guilty. This is me now.

When I walk in, I instantly spot Sarah behind the bar. She smiles, but then gives me an *oh shit* look before reaching for a shot glass. "Jack?" She doesn't even wait for me to answer before filling up the shot glass and sliding it in front of me.

I take it and quickly toss it back with a moan. I slam the empty glass down and look around the bar. "It's slow as shit in here."

She smiles. "Because you just got here." She reaches for a glass and mixes a drink for one of her regulars. "They'll start piling in soon. I had at least ten girls ask me if you were working tonight. I told them you'd be in later ready to shake your dick. Damn vultures." She hands her regular his drink and then returns to me. "You look like shit by the way."

"Thanks for noticing." I scowl. I scoot my empty glass in front of her. "One more, Sarah. You owe me now."

"Damn you, Hemy. I swear you boys have issues. Cale is the only one that doesn't drink his dick swinging life away." She gives me a curious look and gets ready to speak.

"Just do it."

She rolls her eyes and pours another shot.

The last thing I need is her prying into my business. This is something I need to deal with on my own.

After I tilt back my fifth shot of Jack for the night, I swallow back my pride, stand up, and look back at Sarah. "Give me a bottle of whipped cream." Sarah reaches in the fridge, tosses it to me, and I catch it and walk away.

I stand in the doorway of the back room for a few minutes pushing my thoughts away, until a slow seductive song plays over the speakers. Without thinking, my body starts moving to the rhythm of the music.

I run my hands down the front of my body while grinding my hips to the beat. My jeans are sitting low on my waist and my button down shirt is rolled up at the sleeves, halfway undone. The girls take notice and instantly start screaming while waving their money around.

Stopping at the first round table I set the bottle of whipped cream down, grab the closest girl's chair, and spin her around to face me. Her eyes go wide as I straddle her lap and grab the whipped cream off the table.

I start grinding my hips to the music, pushing my erection into her as I grab her hands and place them on my chest. "Undo my shirt. Slowly."

She starts doing as told. I tilt my head back and spray whipped cream into my mouth. Reaching beside me, I grab for the sexy brunette close by and run my whipped cream covered tongue across her soft lips, slowly and teasingly. I love teasing these women. It's the perfect distraction.

When I pull away I see the brunette run her tongue over her mouth, licking off every last drop of cream. She sits back in her chair and watches me with hooded eyes, no doubt wanting to taste more.

Noticing that my shirt is now undone and hanging completely open, I yank my shirt off and wrap one of my hands in the back of the blonde's hair with one hand, while squirting whipped cream all the way down my chest, stopping at the top of my jeans.

I grind my hips against her one more time before standing up and reaching for the brunette's hand, pulling her to her feet. "On your knees," I command.

She gets down on her knees and all the women start screaming random things.

"Take it off, Hemy!"

"Grab his dick, Katy."

I block out the noise and smirk down at her. "Take my pants off."

Looking up into my eyes, she reaches for my jeans and slowly starts undoing them.

"Faster," someone screams.

That must motivate her, because she yanks my zipper down and rips my jeans down the top of my muscular thighs. I place my hand on her head and push it against the thin fabric of my white briefs.

After rolling my hips a few times, I pull away from her and smear a huge amount of whipped cream down the length of my hard cock. "You ready to get dirty?"

She nods her head as I rub my finger over the fullness of her lips, getting a feel for what's going to be wrapped around my cock. "Lick it off. All of it, from the dirtiest place first."

Running her tongue over her lips, she grabs my waist and leans in to press her tongue against my chest, rolling it in the trail of whipped cream. Her eyes watch mine as she slowly lowers her mouth, running her tongue down my abs and over my cock.

I wrap my hands in her hair and close my eyes as I slowly rock my hips into her face. I feel her teeth softly nibble my piercings and I yank her head back before stroking my hand over my cock and stepping away from her.

Ignoring the screaming women, I make my way over to the couch, and grab for the chick in a small black dress and heels that is standing up waving money at me.

Gripping her ass, I wrap her legs around my waist and start grinding my hips to the music. I move, slow and deep as if fucking her. She arches her back and wraps her hands in her own hair before sticking a wad of cash in the front of my briefs and moaning out.

I pull her back up and thrust into her one more time before setting her back down to her feet.

Just as I'm about to head over to the next table, I catch a glimpse of a woman with platinum blonde hair and tattoos. I stop dead in my tracks, my heart racing as I watch her, until she turns around to face me.

As soon as I realize it's not Onyx, my heart rate slows down and I let out a breath of frustration. A part of me wishes it were her.

"Fuck!"

I run my hands through my hair and just stand here. The screaming doesn't die down as they wait for me to continue my rounds.

A part of me doesn't want to. I knew this shit would happen. I told myself I wouldn't let myself think about her anymore. Yeah, well great fucking job.

"Hemy. Dude!"

I snap out of it enough to see Stone approaching. He grips my shoulder and pushes my chest. "What the hell is up, man? You're just standing here. You've been acting funny since last night."

I push his hand away and grind my jaw. "Nothing. I just needed a second." I pause and exhale, hating myself for what I'm about to do. "I have to go."

"What the hell? What do you mean?"

I grab my jeans and start heading for the door. "I have somewhere I have to go. It's important. I need you to take over."

Stone gives me a confused look but doesn't question me further. "Sure. Yeah. Go then."

I walk through the bar, past Sarah who gives me a confused look, and outside to my truck. I quickly hop inside and shove my keys into the ignition while tossing my jeans into the passenger seat. As stupid as I know I'm being, I know it's smarter than just letting her walk away again. I refuse to let her disappear from my life now that I've found her. There's always been something about her that draws me in, holding me to her. It's a curse as much as a craving.

I start the engine and pull out onto the dark street. Without a second thought, I head toward the house I saw her at last night. I don't give a shit what anyone thinks. I'm going to find out where she's at and I'm going to make her mine. Her and I both know that we are meant to be together. The hard part is making her see that, making her see the new me.

After about ten minutes, I pull up in front of the small white house. I kill the engine, grab for my jeans and hop out to put them on.

Just as I'm buttoning them, the front door opens and two girls walk out. I notice one of them right away: Jade.

She gives me a curious look before smiling and walking over to me.

"Look who's back," she says teasingly. "You come back for your tie?"

I lean against my truck and look over her shoulder at the door. "It's not what I forgot, it's who," I say firmly. "Where can I find Onyx?"

Jade quickly turns away and starts heading for the little black car that is sitting in the driveway. "I don't know," she calls over her shoulder. "I'll let her know you're looking for her."

I quickly catch up to her and grab her arm. "Tell me." I walk over to stand in front of her. I look into her eyes so she knows how important this is to me. "I need to know where she is. Can you just tell me where to find her?"

She lets out a breath of frustration before looking over at the other girl who nods at her. She turns back to me and rolls her eyes. "Follow us. She's at work and we're heading there now. I'm going to get in deep shit for this," she mumbles.

"Thank you, Jade." I don't waste any time jogging over to my truck and jumping inside. I've waited too long for this and she's going to listen to what I have to say.

I follow the little black car for what seems like forever. In reality it was probably a whole fifteen minutes. Still, fifteen minutes too long, and now I'm anxious as shit.

When we pull up in front of the huge black building, I sit there wondering if this is some kind of joke. There's no way that the Onyx I knew would work at a place like this.

I sit here for a few minutes until I see Jade and the other girl get out of the car. Jade looks over at me and waves her arm for me to follow. "You coming or what?"

I take a deep breath to calm myself before getting out of my truck and slamming the door behind me. Every part of me wants to scream and break something. The idea of her working here makes me sick to my stomach. "Vixens Club," I growl to myself while staring up at the neon sign.

She's a damn Vixen? A stripper . . . like me. Well fuck me.

CHAPTER FIVE

ONYX

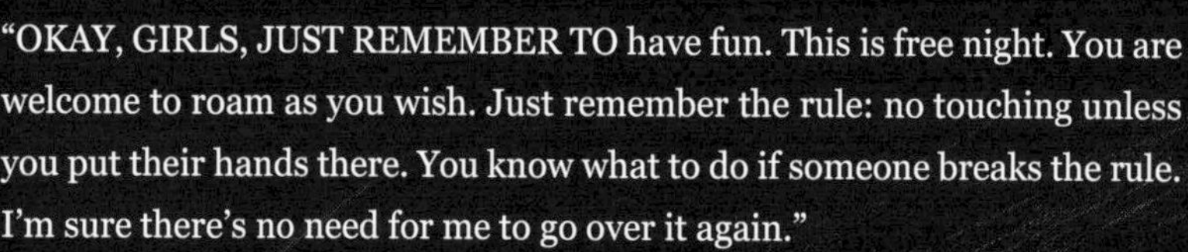

"OKAY, GIRLS, JUST REMEMBER TO have fun. This is free night. You are welcome to roam as you wish. Just remember the rule: no touching unless you put their hands there. You know what to do if someone breaks the rule. I'm sure there's no need for me to go over it again."

I get a few nods from the girls and a hell yeah from Ash.

I stand up from straddling my chair and walk in front of it, facing my group of girls. The first shift of the night is almost done, and I made sure that all my girls work together all night. I always stress their safety on free nights. I don't like the idea of not being able to keep my eye on them individually. There are quite a few creeps that come in here and I would hate to have to break a heel off in a few of their asses. That's why I have "the talk" with my girls once a week.

"Alright, ladies. Let's get ready to make some cash then." I smile and head over to my makeup vanity as the other girls head to the floor.

I've been hiding in the back for the last twenty minutes. I'm not really sure why, but my game seems to be a bit off tonight. I keep telling myself it has nothing to do with Hemy. The truth is, I'm not very convinced. I could never convince myself of anything when it came to him. I went to sleep with him on my mind and woke up with him on my mind. I guess not much has changed over the years.

"Shit. Stop thinking, Onyx." I rub my hands over my face and take a deep breath. "He'll only hurt you again. Don't do this to yourself. You finally got rid of that pathetic little girl that was nothing but a doormat for him."

I curse to myself when I feel a hand grip my shoulder. I have no idea who it is or how much of my rambling they have heard, but I suddenly feel nervous. I'm not ready to explain Hemy to anyone. I'm not sure I'll ever be.

"What's going on, Onyx?" Jade takes a seat at the vanity next to mine and starts digging through her makeup bag. "Something's been bothering you since last night. You can talk to me . . ."

"I'm fine." I force a smile and look at myself in the mirror. My blonde curls are wild tonight and my makeup is a little too dark on the eyes. I look a lot different than I did four years ago. I can't even imagine what Hemy must have thought when he saw me at the party last night. He seemed a little shocked, but couldn't seem to keep his eyes off of me. It made my heart race, making it hard for me to think straight.

I let out a little laugh and stand up, fixing my black lingerie. It's barely covering anything, yet it makes me feel more confident and alive than I have felt in years. "You know I just get a little stressed on free nights. I worry about you girls roaming around where I can't see you all. That's all."

Jade gives me a look as if she wants to say something. She almost looks nervous. She opens her mouth a few times and then shakes it off before starting in on her makeup. "Yeah. I know," she says softly. "We do fine though. You taught us all well. Stop worrying so much."

I stand here for a few seconds before I realize that Lily isn't here yet, or that I've seen. The girls usually show up together since they're roommates. "Where's Lily?"

Jade nervously clears her throat while walking over to the closet to grab her outfit. "She's here. She'll be back in a minute. She's, ah . . . showing someone around."

"Alright," I say softly. She's acting a bit strange right now and I'm not so sure that I like it. "I'll see you out there."

"Sounds good. See you in a few."

After walking through the door, it takes my eyes a couple seconds to adjust to the dim lighting. The music is playing loud and the room is filled with a light fog so I can barely make out Ash and the other girls dancing at tables for the overly eager customers.

I barely get ten feet into the room before I am called over to a table. Although I'm still feeling a bit off, I shake it off and walk over with a seductive smile.

"Hey, boys," I say sweetly.

"Mmm . . . very nice." One of the three men holds up a handful of cash as I lean over and grab his tie, winding it up in my hand. I hear him let out a little moan, so I wrap it tighter and pull myself to him, straddling his chair.

"So you like it rough, big boy?" I yank his hair back and start moving my hips to the music, grinding myself against his erection.

He bites his bottom lip and gets ready to place his hand on my ass, but I yank his hair as hard as I can, causing him to growl. "Damn, you're rough," he says with a hint of laughter. "I would love to see the things you do in bed."

"That won't be happening," a deep, rough voice growls behind me.

My heart instantly drops to my stomach as soon as the words leave his lips. It doesn't take me having to look behind me to know who it is. I've heard that voice a million times before and I'll never forget it. The only difference is, now it has a deeper edge to it.

"Excuse me," the guy below me bites out. He lets out a sarcastic laugh and places a possessive arm around my waist. "She's in my lap. Wait your turn. *If* it ever comes."

With my left hand, I choke him with his tie while yanking his head back with my right. "Don't ever touch me again."

The guy starts choking and I look back at Hemy to see his fists balled at his sides. I don't need him to protect me. He has a history of fighting and that's the last thing that I need him doing right now. He would kill this guy. This douchebag is nowhere even close to Hemy's huge build.

"Don't even think about it, Hemy." I push away from the guy and he starts fighting for air and pulling at his tie. "What the hell are you doing here?"

"Crazy bitch," the guy chokes out through breaths.

Hemy looks down at the guy with a hard look, so I place my hand across his chest and push him away.

He takes in a deep breath and exhales, his jaw flexed. I can tell he's fighting really hard right now to keep his control. "I could ask you the same," he growls. "This place isn't you."

"Ha!" I walk away from him, but he keeps following at my heels. "Like you have room to talk. You're a male stripper. Do I need to remind you of that?"

He grabs my arm to stop me from walking. "Yeah, and I'm a piece of shit. That is the difference." He turns me around to face him and backs me up against the wall with his arms and body blocking me in. "What the hell, Onyx? You could get hurt here. I would fucking kill someone for hurting you. Do you get that?"

I find an empty room in the back and push him into it. Then I turn away and fight to calm my breathing.

Neither of us speak for a few minutes.

"What are you doing here, Hemy? How did you . . ." I stop as I put the pieces together. "Damn you, Jade," I whisper.

I feel the warmth of Hemy's body as he steps up behind me. A part of me wants to lean into him, but the rational part of me moves away. "I can't stop thinking about you, Onyx. You've been on my mind every day for ten years." He wraps an arm around my waist and presses his body against mine. It feels good. So damn good. "Don't tell me I haven't been on yours," he whispers, leaning into my ear. "Tell me I've been on your mind." He pushes my hair behind my ear before brushing his lip piercing up my neck. "Say it."

I let out an unwanted moan as my eyes close to his touch. The feel is so familiar, yet it feels so much better than before. My body is reacting in a way it hasn't reacted to anyone but him. It's unstoppable. "Yes," I admit while finally pulling away and spinning around. "You have. What do you expect? You hurt me. You broke my heart."

He lets out a frustrated groan and runs a hand through his short beard. *That sexy beard.* I can't help but imagine it rubbing against my naked flesh. Everything about Hemy is sexier than I remember. He's full of tattoos, and has long, thick hair that I want to pull. Not to mention those piercings. It makes me wonder where else he might be pierced. He always was the wild one.

"I'm not the same person I was back then." My eyes land on his bare chest as he takes a step toward me. "I'm different now."

"Oh yeah?" I swallow as I reach out to trace his tattoo with my fingers before pulling away. "How so?"

He wraps his hands into the back of my hair and presses me against the wall with his body flush against mine. "I would give my last breath to be with you." He looks into my eyes with an intensity that makes my knees weak. "I will stop at nothing to make you mine, Onyx. I'm not letting you run away from me again, from us. You can hurt me all you want. You could stomp on me till I'm no longer breathing and it wouldn't make a difference. I'm. Not. Going. Anywhere."

Inside, I am going crazy. I can't think straight and my body feels like giving out on me. I can't give myself away though. As much as I wish I could, Hemy can never be trusted.

"Hemy," I say firmly. "Don't start something you're not going to like. I'm not letting myself get crushed by you again. Things are different now. You're not the only one that has changed. Do you get what you put me through?" I place my hands on his chest and push him away. "How many girls had their hands on you, how many nights I cried myself to sleep not knowing if you were even alive."

"I'll be with you every fucking night. You'll never have to worry about that again." He pounds his fist into the wall before placing both hands against it. "I'll wake up next to you and fall asleep holding you for the rest of my fucking life. Nothing else matters anymore. I've learned to let go and move on."

I suck in a burst of air and cover my face. Those are the words I longed to hear for so long in the past and they never came. Hearing those words makes my heart feel as if it's about to burst out of my chest. The ache is so strong that I have to grip my chest.

"Onyx!" Roman pokes his head into the door and looks between me and Hemy. "What are you doing? I've been looking for you." He gives me a concerned look. "Is he giving you problems?"

Hemy turns away from the wall and pops his neck. "Who the fuck are you?"

I hold my hand out and place it on Hemy's chest. "He's my boss," I snap. I turn to face Roman. "No, and he was just leaving."

Roman looks Hemy up and down one last time before turning back to me. "You have a private dance waiting in room six. Don't keep them waiting too long."

I nod my head and give Hemy a dirty look. "Okay. I'm almost done."

Hemy watches with dark eyes as Roman walks away. He looks like he's ready to kill someone. "A private dance?"

I give him a little push toward the door. "Yes. You need to go."

He walks out the door and starts looking around at the room numbers.

"What are you doing?" I bite out. "The exit is that way." I point over to the exit sign, but he ignores me and starts heading for room six. "Are you kidding me?" I follow behind him and we both stop in front of the door.

"It's my turn to see you dance." He turns to me and flashes a cocky grin. "You want to dance for me, baby?" He leans in and kisses my neck. "Because I'm not going anywhere."

"No." I lightly tug his hair back, causing him to growl. "The point of a private dance is for it to be private, Hemy. There's no way my client is going to be okay with you joining."

"Oh yeah," he says. "I wouldn't be so sure about that." He yanks the door open and walks inside. His eyes set on the handsome guy with blond hair wearing a business suit, holding a bottle of beer to his lips. He pulls out three hundred dollar bills and slaps them down in front of him. "I'm paying for the second dance." Then he pulls back a chair and sets it so he's sitting on the side of the client, but facing him. "You have a problem with that?"

The business guy looks at Hemy, a little intimidated and then down at the pile of money in front of him. "No, man. Not at all," he slurs. "Enjoy the show."

Now pissed, I slam the door behind me and yank Hemy's head back by his hair before whispering, "Just remember you did this to yourself." I push his head forward and walk over to the man in the suit.

I grab his beer from out of his hand and toss it across the room. I'm pissed. Not only at Hemy, but at this drunken idiot for agreeing to let him watch. I lift my leg, placing my heel next to him on the couch. I dig it into the leather while grabbing him by the tie and yanking his head to my breasts.

I squat so that I'm closer to his waist. I start to sway my hips to the slow rhythm while running my hands through his hair and rubbing my breasts over his lips.

I allow myself to get lost in the music playing over the speakers, doing this for a few minutes before releasing his tie, and pulling his head back by his hair. I look down at his lap and smirk. "Someone's already hard for me." Opening the top of my black bustier, I straddle his lap and start grinding myself against his erection.

The guy starts moaning while looking down at my breasts and licking his lips. "Oh yeah, baby. Keep rubbing against my dick."

I don't usually talk much with the men in private dances, but having Hemy in the room somehow makes me want to have a little fun. After all those years of me sitting by, while women touched and enjoyed him, why not give him a little taste?

"Mmm . . . you like that, big boy?" I rip his shirt open and grab onto it while arching my back and rolling my front against his. "It's so hard for me."

I grind my hips faster while moaning out and biting my bottom lip. I place my hands on my hips and roll with the beat of the music. I trail my hands upward and continue the slow hypnotic motion of the dance. I stop briefly when I reach my breasts that are peeking out of my top. I can feel his eyes on me. Hemy's too. I close my eyes and continue my path upward until I reach my long blonde hair.

The heels of my black leather knee-high boots are pressed into the leather of the sofa. I keep my balance steady as I grind against his cock. My eyes remain closed. I fist through my hair, messing it, as I seduce him with my movements.

I sit up and tease him in reverse, running my hands down my breasts, down my stomach, and in between my ass and his hard on, while looking over at Hemy.

His eyes go hard as he reaches down to adjust his cock. Seeing him hard gets me even more excited. It actually has me turned on. Our eyes lock as I grasp Mr. Professional's cock in my hand and start rubbing myself faster while stroking it through the fabric.

The guy starts moaning and gripping onto the couch.

I stand up and turn back around with my pussy in his face as he comes in his fancy slacks.

"Oh fuck," he moans while rubbing his hands over his face. "That was fast."

I look at Hemy and smirk. "That *was* fast."

Hemy runs his hand over his cock but looks pissed. I can tell he wants to get off too. Hemy's not as easy as this guy was. He needs more. "Now, it's time for round two."

"Are you sure you can handle round two?"

A rumble comes from Hemy's chest. "If I can handle losing you, I can handle anything."

Now my focus is all on wanting Hemy to come for me. As bad as it sounds, I need this. I'm wound so tight right now, and that's all I need to push me over the edge.

I pick up the three hundred dollar bills and hand them to the messy guy that couldn't hold his shit. "Leave," I say. "You should probably go clean up."

My eyes meet Hemy's and they stay there as the man quickly leaves us alone.

"Lock the door," I demand. Hemy follows him and locks the door with a smirk before he walks over to stand in front of me. "No touching," I state. "Just yourself."

Hemy grabs me by the hips and sets me on top of the table before walking away and taking a seat on the other side of the couch. The clean side.

His eyes watch me with heated desire as I open the rest of my bustier and pull it open. I reach up to rub my pierced nipples, causing Hemy to growl and adjust his cock.

"Mmm . . . you like that?" I run my hands in between my breasts until they reach the top of my panties. "I want you to come for me, Hemy. I miss seeing you lose it over me."

He watches me as I drop down on my knees and spread my legs apart. I slowly slide my hand down the front of my panties and run my finger up and down my wetness before sliding a finger inside. "Mmm . . . I'm so wet for you." I push in and out. "Can you hear it, Hemy? Remember how much you loved the sound of me being wet for you?"

"Fuck yes." He undoes his jeans before pulling down the zipper. "Fuck yourself faster and rub your nipple with your other hand." I do as he says while moaning out. "That's it, baby. Do it for me."

I position myself so that I'm sitting on my ass with my legs spread eagle in front of his face. I want to be sure he gets a good view. Then, I pull my panties to the side and bare my wet pussy to him.

"That's it, Onyx." He pulls his cock out of his jeans and I instantly notice the piercings. It has me so turned on that I have to stop all movement in fear of getting off too soon. He notices me eyeing his cock and grins. "Imagine these steel bars deep inside you as I pound into you. You know I like it deep, baby." His hand starts stroking his cock and I instantly notice the bead of pre-cum that drips off the head and onto his hand.

I bring my hand down to touch myself again and move at the same rhythm Hemy is, as he strokes himself. His eyes never stray away from my fingers shoving themselves deep inside me.

I've needed this for a long time. Ever since leaving Hemy, reaching orgasm has become almost close to impossible. Just watching him get off as I get myself off is enough to make me want to explode.

He starts stroking harder and faster while sucking on his lip ring. "I'm about to blow, baby. I wish it were inside of you."

His words set me off and I find myself shaking from the most intense orgasm I have had in years. A few seconds later, Hemy is blowing his load into his free hand, moaning out my name.

We both look at each other while coming down from our temporary high.

He reaches for a clean towel and wipes his hand off. "We still need to talk."

I cover myself back up and close my eyes. "I don't have time right now. I'm working."

Right as I'm about to close my legs, his eyes meet the inside of my right thigh.

He jumps out of his chair and grips my thigh to hold it open. "What the fuck is that?" He spreads my legs wide open and runs his hand over my tattoo while breathing heavily. "You got my name tattooed on you?"

I never meant for him to see that. It was for my own private reasons. The lettering is so small that you can barely even make out what it says unless you look extra close. "Not now, Hemy. I'm not getting into this."

He growls as I push his hands away and force my legs closed. "That was my favorite spot. I would kiss you there almost every night before bed. Is that why you did it?"

I'm not answering that. This was a horrible idea but I needed to get off.

"I don't have time for this." I climb off the table and walk toward the door with speed. I get ready to open it but get stopped by Hemy's voice.

"Come to my work when you have time." He walks past me and stops to look back at me with hurt eyes. "I'll always make time for you. I won't break anymore promises."

I stand here and watch him as he walks away. He knows damn well that he has me hanging on again. The question is . . . how tightly?

CHAPTER SIX

HEMY

IF ONYX THOUGHT FOR ONE minute I was going to back off she really doesn't remember how persistent I was when it came to her. Now that I've gotten another glimpse at what's been mine all along, there is nothing that can stop me from claiming her as mine again. I'm a lot stronger than I was back then. My head is a lot clearer. I know what I can't live without and without a doubt that is her.

Knowing that she has my name permanently inked on her skin is fucking with me so bad that I can't even think straight. She can get my name tattooed on her body, but she acts as if she doesn't want shit to do with me. It has my chest aching at just the thought.

"A fucking tattoo, man," I mumble while looking back up at Cale. "My name branding the inside of her perfect little thigh. Do you know how bad that screws with my head?"

He watches me as I take a long drag of my cigarette and slowly exhale. "I guess you both had it a lot deeper than you thought, man. She obviously loved you and missed you or else she wouldn't have gotten it. Plus, no other guy wants to see that shit, so I doubt she's seriously dated anyone since you. Think back to when you got yours. What made you do it?"

I take another drag while running my hand through my hair. I don't even need to think about this one. "I missed her so bad that the thought of her made it hard to breathe. It still does, man. It's been four years and I feel exactly the same about her. It kills me to think about all the time we have missed out on. No other girl compares to her, never will. They are simply temporary fill-ins for what I wish I still had." I toss my cigarette and pull both hands through my hair in frustration. "I'm getting her back. I don't care what it takes."

Cale nods in understanding and grips my shoulder. "Make sure she sees that. It may hurt a shit ton getting there, but it will be worth it in the end. All she has to do is see that." He watches me as I rub my hand down my short beard. "It's all good, man. You need to relax a bit. Give it some time. You remember that stupid saying we used to hear as adolescents? The one that goes, if you love something set it free and if it comes back it was meant to be?"

I look up, my interest slightly piqued. "Well, she's back, isn't she? Time, man. Just give it time."

"Yeah. Sure," I mutter. "Time . . . because four years isn't enough time." I walk past Cale and into my garage, shoving my head back under the hood of his truck.

It's been five days since I have seen Onyx and I'm starting to go insane. My patience is wearing thin and I'm not sure how much longer I can wait before I show back up at *Vixens* and take her my damn self. I'm doing my best not to push her away again. It's a lot harder than I expected, so I'm spending my time trying to occupy myself any way I can.

I'm lost in my own little messed up world, doing my best to concentrate on Cale's truck, when I hear a set of heels pounding up the driveway.

"Holy shit," Cale mumbles. "If you are Onyx then I can see why my guy is so screwed up in the head right now."

I toss down my wrench and grip the edge of the hood, trying my best to keep my cool. The thought of Onyx possibly being here gets my heart pounding. I try my hardest not to get my hopes up, but knowing that she has no clue where I even live is making it slightly difficult. It could be one of numerous girls that I have brought here in the past, but what if it's her? That means she premeditated coming here and had to find out from someone else how to get here.

"So, you've heard of me?" Onyx's voice comes out cool and calm, causing my grip on the hood to tighten. "Hemy."

I release the hood and turn around to face her, leaning my back against the truck. I look her over in her short black shorts and white tank top. I can't help but admire her stunning beauty. She always did take my breath away, even before the dark side took her, but I can't deny it looks sexy on her.

Her legs are long, slender, and well sculpted, making those shorts look as if they were made just for her. Perfection. They're hard not to stare at, and her hair that was once a strawberry blonde is now a platinum blonde, her curls falling just below her ass. The sight of her is enough to take any man's breath away.

"I'm guessing you paid Mitch a visit?" She nods. "Yeah. Figures he wouldn't tell me."

I tilt my head to Cale before reaching in my pocket for my keys. I toss them to him and he quickly catches them. "What's this for, man?"

"Take my truck. Come back after work and I'll have yours ready." I give him an impatient look as he just stands there staring. "Any day now."

Cale looks at Onyx while backing away with a smirk. "Take it easy on the guy." He winks before turning away and jogging to my truck.

Onyx walks over and stops right in front of me. Her eyes search mine for a moment before she pulls them away. "I need to ask you something and I need you to be—"

"Yeah," I answer, already knowing what her question is going to be. It's the one thing she wanted the whole time we had been together. "I'm clean. For three years now."

She looks back up and her eyes soften for a brief moment before she puts her guard back up. "How do I know you're telling the truth? That kind of life isn't easy to give up."

I take a step closer and lean down close to her face. Our lips are so close to touching that it takes all my strength to not kiss her. "I may have been a piece of shit, but did I ever lie to you?"

Hurt flashes in her eyes before she quickly shakes it off. "I don't know," she whispers. "Do you even know?"

A pain aches in my chest, knowing what she means. I was so messed up most of the time that I don't even remember a lot of shit that happened. "I would like to believe that I know." I wrap my hands in the back of her hair like I used to in the past. Her eyes close as I start to massage my fingers through it. "I've missed this."

I press my body against hers, causing her to let out a small moan. "I can't think when you touch me like this, Hemy. You should stop. Now," she says breathless.

"I can't think when I *look* at you. I never could." I turn us around and back her into the garage and against Cale's truck. I can tell how much my body against hers is breaking her willpower, and I can't help but to use it to my advantage. I press my leg between her thighs and grind into her. "You feel good in my arms, baby. You see how good this feels?"

"Hemy. I didn't come here for this."

"Answer me," I breathe. "We've always been honest with each other. Don't change that now."

She lets out a small breath and tangles her fingers in the back of my hair. "Yes," she moans. "Physically it feels great. Emotionally, it terrifies me. I'm not letting you in, Hemy. I've learned my lesson."

I run my hands down her back before cupping her ass in my hands and running my lips up her neck. "Oh, but I want in. Deep." I suck her earlobe into my mouth before whispering, "You remember what it feels like to have me inside you? The way you moaned out my name and pulled my hair. That mix between pain and intense pleasure. It can be even better now."

Her head tilts back as she falls into my touch. Her breathing picks up as I squeeze her ass tighter. "Don't make me think about sex. It brings back bad memories." She grips onto the hood with one hand as I kiss her neck. "Questions. The fear of you being with other women. All those hands groping you. How am I supposed to get over that? Maybe I want a little fun of my own."

My body stiffens from her words. As much as I hate it, she's right; because of my fuck up she had to live in fear of me being touched by other women. The thought makes me sick now. I need to somehow make it up to her. "What do you need? I'll fucking do anything for you."

"Do you realize how many women I had to see touch you while you were passed out? Every time I close my eyes I picture someone's hand down your pants. Their hands on my man. That image does a lot of damage. You'll never get that until you have to deal with it yourself. I just can't. I can't be with you like that again, Hemy. Ever."

Her grip tightens on my hair as I wrap mine in the back of hers and lean my forehead against hers. "I can arrange that," I grumble. "I'd have to fight my hardest not to kill someone, but I get where you're coming from. I would do it. I would watch it even though the thought kills me."

She looks at me in shock and laughs in disbelief. "Are you joking?" I shake my head and her face becomes serious. "And what if I want a threesome? Would you do it? With another man?"

I brush her hair over her shoulder and kiss her neck, then her chin. "If it involves me touching you or tasting you . . . then yes. I will do anything you tell me to. Even that."

She pushes away from me and turns around. "Shit, Hemy. I was joking." She grips the top of her hair and tilts her head back. "Why did you have to say that? You're supposed to make it easy to not want you in that way. I'm not supposed to want to touch you, but I do. No man turns me on like you can and it drives me mad."

I don't want to hear about other men. I just want her any way I can. "Stay with me tonight." I know her answer will be no, but I try anyway. "You don't have to let me in emotionally; not yet at least. Just let me take care of your needs."

"Hemy," she warns. "I have to work tonight, and that's a horrible idea. Do you realize what kind of shit that will start?"

"Yes," I admit. "Why do you think I asked?"

"Dammit, Hemy. I have to go." She takes off walking down the driveway as fast as she can on her tall heels. "Bye."

Without a second thought, I jog down the driveway, grab her by the waist and turn her around to face me. "Not yet. There's something I've been waiting four years to do." I grip the back of her head and roughly press my lips against hers, running my tongue over the seam of her lips for access.

All my breath leaves my body as she opens up and kisses me back, her arms snaking around my neck. It feels like the past four years disappearing between us and it feels like we are back in the past. My tongue desperately seeks hers, sucking it into my mouth as I back her up against a little blue car and cup her face in my hands.

Pressing my body against hers, I tug on her bottom lip before releasing it. Both of us stand here panting while looking into each other's eyes. I can barely catch my breath.

Standing here, looking in her eyes, I realize the distance between us still remains and I have a lot of work to do in order to close the gap. But I'm willing and in it for the long haul.

"I never want to hear bye come out of your mouth again. I'll be waiting for you. I've waited for four years. Don't think I will give up now."

I turn and walk away before she can say anything. I don't want her to. I want her to think about the last thing said between us. It gives me more confidence that she will show up at my doorstep tonight.

I hear a car door slam behind me, but I refuse to turn around. I never want to have to see her driving away from me again.

Within a few seconds, she starts the car and I hear it pull away. I walk over and stand in front of Cale's truck for a few minutes before walking inside and grabbing my phone.

I dial Nico's number and wait for him to answer.

"Yo. What's up, bro?"

I grind my jaw and take a deep breath. "I need you to do me a favor. Tonight."

Damn. I can't believe I'm doing this . . .

I PULL MY HARLEY INTO the back of *Walk Of Shame* and kill the engine. I haven't stopped thinking about my plans for tonight since Onyx drove away from my house. It's had me on edge all day.

I'm here to ease my mind a bit. Not to get plastered, but to douse the anger that is building inside at the thought of another man touching Onyx. I want to protect her, but at the same time . . . I want her back. I want to take care of her needs and ease her mind.

It may hurt like a bitch, but I deserve it. I hurt her far worse than I can ever imagine. I was her weakness. I broke down her walls while keeping mine up. I was too broken to let her in. I had lost everyone that I loved in life and I was afraid of letting myself love anyone else. I was afraid that if I lost one more person that it would push me over the edge. The day she walked out my door was the day I realized I had loved her all along. Made me realize I wasn't as damaged as I thought.

This is her payback. I need to feel her hurt, drown in my own pain and suffering. I'll do whatever it takes and you better believe I won't back down.

I see Stone as soon as I walk through the door. He nods to me with a wink while grabbing some chick's head and grinding his cock against her face.

I nod back and go to find Cale at the bar. It's a Tuesday night; it's one of our slowest days.

"What's up, man."

Cale slides a glass in front of the girl across from him before cashing her out and slipping the change into his tip jar.

"Not shit." He smiles, flashing his deep set of dimples. "Just enjoying this relaxing night. I sometimes forget how nice it can be to just bartend. No screaming girls in my ear. You know?"

"I hear ya." I pull out my wad of cash and throw him a ten. "Give me a beer."

Cale reaches below him in the fridge and slams a beer down in front of me. "You look like you need one. Things didn't go well with your girl?"

I give him a hard look and grind my jaw, trying to keep my cool. "Depends on what the hell you consider good." I tilt back my beer and look up at him. "Let's just say I arranged a little fun for her tonight and it has me a little on edge." I run my hand through my hair and tilt my head back. "I deserve it though. I have no right to be mad."

"Ouch. You just have to think of it this way. At least she wants you there for her *fun*. She could want to do whatever that is without you. It's a step, my man."

I nod while slamming back more beer. I sit here in silence for a moment and try my best to think of the positive shit this could lead to. "I suppose your ass is right. If it's one step closer to making her mine again then I'll do it and show her how far I'm willing to go for her this time."

Cale jumps up to sit on the bar and slaps my shoulder. "Right on. You know no woman can resist the Hemy charm."

I tilt my head up and give him a dirty look. "She left me, asshole. It obviously doesn't work on her."

"Yeah. And that's why you have to show her the new Hemy charm. Has any other woman been able to resist you?"

I shake my head while finishing off my beer.

"Exactly!" He jumps down from the bar and fetches me another beer. "She'll come around. Now drink that and get the hell out of here. I have shit to do."

He backs away with a smile while giving me the middle finger with both hands before turning around and helping another customer.

CHAPTER SEVEN

ONYX

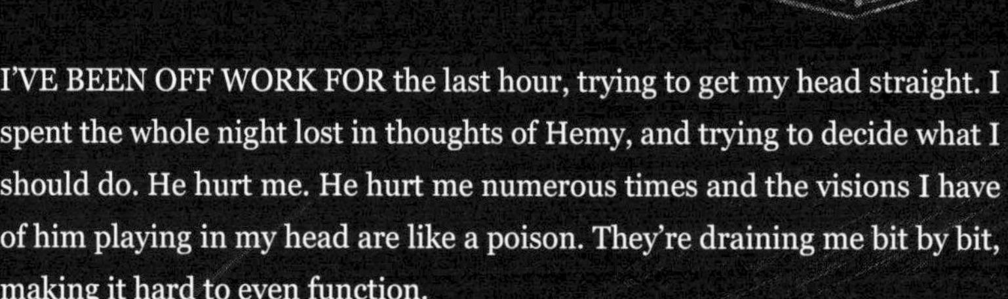

I'VE BEEN OFF WORK FOR the last hour, trying to get my head straight. I spent the whole night lost in thoughts of Hemy, and trying to decide what I should do. He hurt me. He hurt me numerous times and the visions I have of him playing in my head are like a poison. They're draining me bit by bit, making it hard to even function.

We weren't supposed to meet up like this. I was supposed to have more time to prepare. I was hoping he wouldn't recognize me at first and that I would have more time to feel him out, to see if he has changed. I have something to tell him. This is something that will change his life forever, but I need to know that he is clean, and the only way to do so is to spend time with him.

I have no idea how I'm going to be able to hang out with him without wanting him. That's why I have to be careful. I have to do whatever I can to keep him at a distance, and to keep my heart safe. The kiss that he surprised me with still has my heart beating wild and my legs trembling. It was all too familiar and reminded me of what I've been missing.

"You can do this," I whisper while looking into the mirror. "You'll just go there and feel him out." I grip the sink and close my eyes.

I need to do this. The only problem is, I have no idea what he has planned. Hemy is wild. If he thinks I want a threesome with him and another man, he'll find a way to make it happen. He has a way of getting anything that he wants. He's better at this than I am. That's why I have to push back and not give him the alone time he needs to win me back. If he wants me physically, the only way I'll be safe is by making him share me. Once he gets me alone, he wins.

I open my eyes and take a deep breath as the bathroom door pushes open to Ash peeking in. Her dark hair fall over her shoulders when she smiles. "Hey," she whispers.

I force a smile and choke back my emotions. I know I'm doing the right thing. "Hey, sweetie," I reply. "You do good on tips tonight?" I ask as a distraction.

She pushes the door open and leans against the frame. "I did great on tips." She looks me over and frowns. I guess the distraction didn't work. "What's been up with you tonight? You've been acting strange. Is everything alright?"

Not really. Not yet. "I'm good," I lie. "I'm just feeling a little off tonight." I push away from the sink and turn to walk toward the door. "There's an old friend of mine that I haven't seen in a while. It's just bringing back a lot of old memories."

She smiles in understanding and nods her head. "Memories are the last thing I want to think about. Hopefully yours are a lot better than mine."

I run my hands over my dress to dry my sweaty hands. If only she knew. "Some are good." I smile. "I'm heading out for a while. I'll be back."

She takes a step back, allowing me to walk through the door. "Onyx." I stop and turn around. "Will I get to meet this old friend?"

I swallow and nod. "Someday."

I turn and walk to the door as fast as I can.

I hope I'm strong enough to do this . . .

HEMY

NICO ARRIVED ABOUT AN HOUR ago. Of course he is always down to do whatever I ask. It's been that way since the day I met him. It's nice having someone you can rely on.

"You want another beer, man?"

I tilt my head to look at Nico. He's standing by the fridge, dressed up in a black button-down and dark jeans with his light hair styled back. He can hold his own when it comes to physical attributes. Getting girls is never a problem for him. I have no doubt that he won't please Onyx. The thought kills me, but I won't let it win and bring me down. I will smolder it on contact. She needs this. I need to give it to her, so maybe we can move on from the past. People like to say not to get even, but it's the only way to lay things to rest.

"Nah. I'm good."

My heart jumps to my throat when I see a car pull up in front of the house. I knew she would show. The question was when. It's already past three a.m. Not that it matters. She's here and that's what counts. It just gives me the confirmation that a part of her still wants me. Whether it's just physical, emotional, or both, I will find out soon enough. Time. Just a little more time.

A light knock sounds at the door, causing Nico to set his beer down and lift his eyebrows. "She's here, man."

"Yeah," I whisper to myself. "Let her in. Just remember what I said. Don't push the limits," I say firmly.

I walk to the bathroom and close the door behind me. This is going to be a lot harder than I thought. I'm already fighting the urge to crush Nico for touching her. I never was one for sharing when it comes to her. That's what makes it even harder knowing that she felt like she had to. Being sober makes it easy to feel what she must have and brings it all forth to the light. I hate myself for always keeping her in the dark.

I take a deep breath and slowly exhale as I hear their voices in the distance. I can't make out what they're saying, but I can hear the tone in Nico's voice. He's getting himself ready and easing her in for what's to come.

"Fuck." I hit the sink before leaning into it and resting my head against the mirror. "Don't be a pussy. This is for her. She deserves this," I tell myself. I need to get this over with, and fast. No putting it off. It's time to get straight to the meaning of this visit and show her I'm willing to fight for her this time. No pussying out.

Pushing the door open, I walk through the hall to meet them in the living room. Onyx instantly spots me and freezes in her tracks. She looks stunning in her little black dress and heels. It's enough to take my breath away. The ink on her skin only adds to it, giving her a sexier edge now, which is my kind of woman; although, my kind has always only been her, and always will be.

She clears her throat and looks between Nico and me. She looks slightly nervous, but quickly shakes it off. "Well, I'm here, Hemy." She runs her fingers across the wall while making her way over to the couch, seductively. She looks over her shoulder at me. "Are you sure you can handle this?" The girl I knew four years ago is forever gone. I need to keep reminding myself. We are on a different game level now.

I swallow back my anger and focus all my energy on pleasing her. I just need to remember that she needs this to move on from the world of hurt I bestowed on her. She needs me to feel what she felt. "I can handle a lot of shit. Pleasing you is one." I nod my head toward Nico. "This is Nico. He's yours to do with as you please."

"Nico." She smiles while leaning against the back of the couch. "I like that name. Come here."

Nico looks at me in hesitation before I motion for him to go. The faster, the better, cause after this is done, she's staying with me. I don't care what it takes. She'll sleep in *my* bed and wake up in *my* bed.

Already knowing the plan, Nico walks over to stand in front of Onyx. He wraps one arm around her waist while fisting her hair and kissing her neck.

Onyx lets out a little moan as her eyes connect with mine. I hold her stare and bite my bottom lip as I nod for her to go on. I'm not surprised that she's a tad hesitant.

Grabbing onto the top of Nico's shirt, Onyx pulls him into her, causing them both to fall over onto the couch. His lips instantly seek hers as he buries himself between her legs and squeezes her bare thigh.

I walk over to the leather chair and take a seat in front of them. As much as I hate the thought of someone touching her, I can't help my cock from getting hard. The plan is to watch him touch her, taste her, and arouse her for a while before I join. It's how Nico always does it with me. Sitting here now, in his seat, I'm not sure how he does it.

"Take her dress off," I command.

Nico pulls away from the kiss and they stand, before he grabs the bottom of her short, tight dress and eases it up her body, then pulls it over her head. "Fuck me," he growls out as he takes in her body.

I sit here, my eyes roaming over her body as I grab my cock and rub it through the fabric. "Don't be shy, Onyx. This is what you wanted." I bite my bottom lip in anger. "Take his clothes off. Show me how it feels to be the viewer, witnessing the ultimate betrayal from someone you trust. Hurt me like I hurt you. My heart is yours to stomp on."

She looks at me, clearly struggling on the inside. I can tell she wants to see me suffer as much as she did, but a part of her hates having to hurt me. I have to push her more, or else she may just walk away for good. I can't live with that option.

"Remember those hands on my body, Onyx. Do you still visualize all those girls touching me while I was high out of my fucking mind? How did that make you feel? Make me feel exactly how you felt."

Full of heated anger, she rips the front of Nico's shirt open and rubs her hands over his defined chest and abs with an animalistic growl.

"That's it, baby. Let it all out. Do this for you . . . do this for us." I grip the arm of the chair, biting back my anger as she goes for his jeans and tugs them off with force. He's standing there in only his briefs now.

"Touch her, Nico," I bite out. "Give her what she needs. Bend her over the couch and lick her pussy. You better fucking lick it good too."

Knowing I'm a pro at eating Onyx's pussy makes me smile to myself. There is no way she will enjoy it as much as when it's my tongue pleasuring her. Knowing that I'm here watching her will only make her realize that it can be me. All she has to do is ask.

Nico smirks while gripping Onyx's hips and pushing her down so that her hands are buried in the couch and her ass is up in the air. He squats, slowly pulling her panties down along the way, baring her pussy to both of us. My cock jumps at the sight and I have to fight the urge to run my tongue up it.

I watch as Nico positions on his knees, grips her firm ass, and runs his tongue up her pussy. I glance down at Onyx's face to see her not looking the least bit impressed. It makes me smile on the inside, although, the bigger part of me wants to yank Nico away from her. She's supposed to be mine and mine alone, but I fucked that up.

Nico gets into it, shoving his tongue deep, pulling it in and out while pulling his briefs down and stroking his cock behind her. A little moan escapes from Onyx's mouth, but nothing compared to when I pleasured her.

"Hemy," she moans out. "I need you to get naked. Take those clothes off. Now." She twists her neck to look at me in anticipation.

Smirking, I slowly unbutton my white shirt before ripping the last few buttons off and tossing my shirt aside. I stand and pull my belt through the loops, the leather sounding along the way. I unbutton my jeans, sliding down the zipper, slowly and teasingly.

Her eyes stay focused on me as I slowly pull my jeans down my body and step out of them. I'm not wearing any briefs, so I'm now standing here completely nude and hard, baring my whole body to her. I hear her suck in a breath as her eyes look me over, taking in every inch of my flesh, but mostly my hard as steel cock that gives away the effect she has on me.

Walking over to the couch, I stand beside her face, but at eye level. Her eyes follow her peripheral vision until she is staring directly at my rock hard cock before her. She licks her lips and moans as she takes me in. She always did like it rough.

"Damn, Hemy," she breathes. "I can't believe you're going through with this without killing someone. It fucking hurts, doesn't it? It killed me, Hemy. How the hell are you standing there and not choking someone?"

I grind my jaw, keeping in my anger. "Other people might not understand why I am willing to do this or why you would enjoy it, but fuck them. They never understood us in the first place and we have always been anything but normal," I whisper. "I'm doing this for you."

I stroke my cock close to her face as Nico devours her pussy from behind. "You like this, baby?" I step closer and rub the tip of my dick against her lips, causing her to tremble. "Remember how much you loved sucking my cock?"

She nods her head and lets out a little moan so I stroke it faster. I see her eyes zoned in on my piercings, letting me know she's imagining what it feels like to have them inside her. She won't be waiting for long. She'll be asking soon enough. I can see it in her eyes—all hooded

I rub the tip of my cock across her eager lips again, but this time she opens them and slowly takes my length in, moaning out as it hits the back of her throat. Looking up at me, she swirls her tongue around my shaft and slowly trails it up toward the head, focusing on the piercings. I allow her to enjoy the taste of me for a few more seconds before pulling out, causing her to groan. That should be enough to make her want more.

Nico, still stroking his cock, slaps her ass before shoving a finger inside her pussy and moving in and out while moaning in pleasure. "You want my cock," he questions. "I can fuck you good for Hemy. You want that?"

Onyx looks up into my eyes before whispering, "No. I want yours, Hemy. I want you to fuck me while he watches. You're the only one that has been able to fuck me right. God, those piercings are so hot. What are you trying to do to me?"

Now that's what I like to hear. We always did have a good time and I can't help but to gloat at the fact that no man has ever been able to pleasure her like me. I also love that she mentioned the piercings. I knew she would love them.

"Back up, Nico," I command. "Stroke your cock for her while I fuck her. Don't come until she says so."

Nico stands up with his cock in his hand before walking over and taking a seat in the chair in front of the couch. This is exactly what we were both hoping for. Nico likes to watch as I put on a show. Having Onyx as the show is not what I hoped, but if it helps her move on, then I have to do it.

Walking behind Onyx, I push her face into the cushion and hold both of her legs up, gripping her thighs. This makes it easier to pound into her from behind. Fuck, how I have missed the feeling of being deep inside her.

She may want me to go down on her first, but I'll save that for a different day since that's her favorite thing. I'm going to make this rough and deep to remind her of our wild sex life. That will only make her crave more and keep coming back until I can make love to her and make her mine again.

"No condom with me anymore, baby. I'm claiming this pussy as mine. I want to feel all of you as I pound into you." I grip onto the back of her hair with one hand and pull back. "Is this pussy mine?"

She moans and her grip on the couch tightens. "Yes. Just fuck me. Stop with the teasing. You know we've both been waiting a long time for this."

"I know," I say firmly. "Now you're going to remember what it's like to have a real man inside you. Fuck all the boys in between. This is the real thing."

I adjust my cock at her entrance and gently slide into her while wrapping my arm around her neck. I bury it deep with one thrust, causing her to moan out and dig her nails into my arm. "Fuck Hemy," she moans. "I want to feel those piercings as you pound me. Fuck me like you used to. I want it all."

Fuck! She feels so good . . . so warm and wet for me. I've never been inside her like this before and I can't help but to dwell on the fact that she didn't resist. She has to have been wanting me for as long as I have wanted her. We're both desperate for each other's touch but that's not going to be enough to stop her from guarding her heart.

"You miss screaming my name, don't you?" She nods as I pull her neck back. "You want to scream it for Nico?" I slap her ass and grip her thigh tighter. "This is just a taste of what you've been missing over the years. Hold on tight, baby."

I pull out and thrust back into her with force while holding one leg up and gripping her neck with my other hand. "Oh God," she cries out. "Yes . . ."

"Scream my name and I'll give it to you harder. I'll make both you and Nico come at the same time. As soon as you tell him to go, you're both done for."

I pound into her with deep, fast movements, causing her to scream out my name. Being inside of her has me on a temporary high. This is better than any high I used to get in the past. This is the ultimate high. She's all I need.

I continue to thrust into her, stretching her pussy to accommodate my huge size. She cries and screams with each thrust, causing Nico to stroke his cock faster.

Releasing her neck, I reach below us and rub my finger over her swollen clit while pulling her hair and pushing as deep as I can go, swaying my hips in and out in a fast rhythm.

Her screams become louder as I bite into her shoulder and moan out with her. I wish I could give her more right now, but this is what I need to do to keep her coming back and wanting more. I'll do whatever it takes. That's a fucking promise.

"Now, Nico," she cries out. "Fucking come!"

Her head tilts to the side to watch as Nico strokes his cock a few more times before he's moaning out and shooting his cum into his palm.

Right before he's done, I thrust into her one last time causing her body to convulse as she throbs around my dick, bringing me to climax along with her. I shoot my cum deep inside her pussy before pulling out, flipping her around and slamming my lips against hers.

Her lips instantly react to mine as she tangles her fingers in my hair while panting and still shaking from her release. I always did love the feel of her panting in my mouth after she came. That hasn't changed. I love it just as much.

Fisting her hair, I place my forehead against hers and rub my hand up her back. "Stay with me tonight. I want you in my bed."

She gets ready to shake her head, but I pull her closer to me and pull her bottom lip into my mouth. She always loved that in the past. "I won't take no for an answer. Just for tonight. Let me run you a bubble bath and take care of you. You need to see me for who I am now."

She lets out a little breath before relaxing in my arms. She's silent for a few moments, lost in thought, before looking up at me. "Just for tonight, Hemy. After this, I have to be careful. This is it. I have no choice. This is pushing it. I should say no."

I look over at Nico as he stands up to get dressed. "Thanks, man. You can go now."

Nico smiles while wiping his hand on his shirt and balling it up. "Not a problem, man." He grabs his shoes. "I hope you two work things out. That was some hot shit."

I turn my head away from Nico to look into Onyx's eyes. I want to see her reaction to his words. What I find is not good. She looks terrified. Being close to me scares the shit out of her. I need to change this.

And fast . . .

CHAPTER EIGHT

ONYX

I CAN'T BELIEVE I JUST let that happen. What was I thinking? Now, I'm really confused. I thought making Hemy watch me with another man would make me feel good. It didn't. It hurt. It made me feel sick to my stomach. I had to stop things before they got too far. The truth is, all I wanted was Hemy.

As much hell as Hemy put me through in the past, hurting him only hurts me more. How am I supposed to do this? How am I supposed to ever get over all the pain and suffering he put me through? I can never *be* with Hemy. All he does is hurt people. That's exactly why I need to see if he has changed before I tell him what I know. I have to be 100% positive first. I won't let him hurt anyone else like he hurt me.

I'm sitting on the couch wrapped up in Hemy's shirt when he walks out from the bathroom and runs his hand through his hair. It reminds me of how good it felt to run my hands through it and I can't help the butterflies in my stomach that are fluttering freely. "Hey," he says in a low, flat tone.

"Hey," I say back in the same voice level, not really sure what to do next. This feels so strange. Being with him again brings me back to the past, making me feel as if we were never apart.

"Come here." He reaches above him and grips the molding above him on the door. I can't help but notice all of his muscles flex as his grip tightens. It's so incredibly sexy. "Take my shirt off. I need to see all of you. Never cover up around me."

He always did hate it when I wore clothes after sex. He said he couldn't sleep afterwards unless he had my naked body pressed against his. I learned very quickly to stop getting dressed after sex, because it was pointless. If I did he would just remove them himself. Sometimes when he was out at night, I would even lie in bed naked hoping it would help me sleep better. It never did.

Standing up, I grab the bottom of his shirt and pull it over my head. I stand here in place, watching his eyes scan over my body, before walking over to stand in front of him. I want him now that I've had another taste and I hate myself for feeling this way. I'm only going to get hurt. I was devastated for far too long, and I'm finally in control of my emotions, or I was.

Biting his bottom lip, he reaches out and cups my face in his hands. His gaze meets mine, causing my heart to speed up. They look clear again. A spark of hope shoots through my body, making me want to believe it's not a coincidence that he's been clean the last few times I have seen him. I want to believe he is telling me the truth.

He must notice me focusing on his eyes, because his lips turn up into a slight smile before he tilts my chin up and looks directly into my eyes. "I wasn't lying when I said I was clean. I will never lie to you. That's a promise I made ten years ago and I'll never break it."

"Hemy . . . I—"

"I know," he breathes, cutting me off before I can finish. "It's not that simple. If you just give me the chance I will show you." He swallows hard while tracing my bottom lip with his thumb. "I will *never* hurt you again. That is a fucking promise, baby. The day you walked away changed my perspective dramatically."

Before I can respond, Hemy scoops me up in his arms and carries me into the bathroom. He steps into the huge bathtub filled with bubbles and sits down, pulling me into his lap. I instantly rest my head on his shoulder and sigh in contentment. He's never done this with me before. I'm going to soak this feeling up while I can, before I have to put my guard back up.

I should be keeping my distance, but maybe letting him in for one night won't be so bad. I mean, how much can really happen? It's just one night.

I close my eyes as Hemy wraps his arms around me, underneath my breasts. His touch is so gentle, yet possessive; as if he's telling me I am his and his alone. The thought causes my heart to pound in my chest. The thought of being his gives me a feeling of warmth and safety, even though being with him in the past was anything but that.

"I'll take care of you if you let me," he breathes into my ear. "I may have only been rough in the past, but I promise you I can be gentle with you too. Things are different . . . I'm different. If you give me another chance to love you, I promise I will make you the happiest woman in the world. I don't need other women, Onyx. None of them are you. None of them took care of me when I was a broken boy, scared, and alone in the world. None of them took me in and held me at night after my parents left me and I lost Sage. That was the most devastating time in my life. Only you were there. Not even my foster parents cared for me. They let me do as I pleased and never gave a shit, but you did."

He takes a deep breath and squeezes me tighter, resting his chin on my shoulder. His hair brushes over my neck, causing me to shiver in his strong arms. I want to give into him, but I can't. *This feels so good; too good.* "I'm sorry I couldn't be there for you like you were for me. I just . . . I had to numb myself from the world. I had a constant storm of fucked up memories in my head that consumed me. I can't change the past, but I can promise you better for the future."

I can't help the tear that runs down my face. I still remember Hemy as the broken boy I met ten years ago. He was roaming down the alley behind my house with a group of older boys—all troublemakers. He stopped when he saw me and I couldn't help but smile at him. He was the cutest boy I had ever seen and when he smiled back, a warm feeling enveloped me. After that day, I sat behind my house for at least a week waiting for him to walk by again. When he did, he walked over to me and I instantly wrapped him in a hug, surprising him. There was something about him that made me feel like he needed some tender care. I was right. He needed that and much more. After that, we were inseparable.

I let the tear roll down my cheek, being sure that it drips away from Hemy. I don't want him to know he's sparking some deep emotions inside of me. I have to be strong.

"Hemy," I whisper.

"Yeah." He pulls my hair back and holds it in a ponytail.

"I don't want to talk about us. Can we just enjoy this bubble bath without me having to hurt you? Please, I don't want to hurt you."

Letting out a small breath, he shifts so he can reach beside him and light the few candles that surround the tub. When his arms release me, a part of me feels dead inside. The feeling scares the shit out of me. I haven't even spent much time with him and I'm already dreading not being in his arms.

After lighting the candles, he grips my hips and turns me around so that I'm straddling his lap. I grip his shoulders and push away from him as he tangles his hands in my hair. "Hemy," I warn. "I need to be careful."

"There is no being careful when it comes to me," he says confidently. "I'm yours. I always have been. Nothing will ever change that."

His hands tighten in my hair and he grinds below me, digging his semi hard erection between my legs. The feel of the steel bars, poking me, make me want to jump on his cock and go for a ride.

I wrap my legs around his waist and close my eyes as he brushes his lips over my neck and shoulder. Being with him this way feels better than anything I have felt in years. I need a distraction, something to steer my thoughts in another direction.

"Do you still wonder about your sister?" I ask, stopping his kisses. "Are you still looking for her?"

His body tenses below me before he wraps his arms around my waist and pulls me closer to him. "Every fucking day. It seems no one in Wisconsin is named Sage. Wisconsin was the last place I saw her before I was adopted and my foster parents moved me here to Chicago. I still check in, hoping that maybe she will pop up. No fucking luck. I have even checked everywhere within a few hours of Wisconsin and nothing. My parents were pieces of shit and did this on purpose. They left us in different places, Onyx. They dropped me off an hour away from home and then took off with Sage. I know they dropped her off too. Then they ran. No one has seen them since. They were miserable and wanted to be sure we would be too."

I take in a gulp of air at the reminder of how Hemy was left alone at such a young age. He lost his whole family; they never even cared to begin with. Sage was the only one he truly had and he couldn't even protect her from his parents' harm.

"Do you think you would know Sage if you saw her? I mean how would you know it was her? It's been ten years and she was so young."

His eyes go hard as his jaw flexes. He has so many bad memories that I hate even asking this.

"I may not recognize her right away, but I would know if I saw the back of her neck."

I reach behind his head and wrap my fingers in his hair for comfort. "From when your father burnt her with that pan?"

"Fuck!"

I jump away from his loud outburst, but he grabs me and pulls me back to him.

"I'm sorry." He grinds his jaw and closes his eyes. "Yes. That happened like two years before I lost her. We were all in the kitchen, waiting for my mother to finish the last bit of dinner. Sage was crying. She was hungry, because we hadn't eaten in over two days. I tried to comfort her, but she just kept crying and saying *Ty, I'm hungry* over and over again. Back then I didn't go by Hemy. My father hated my mother for naming me that. He made me go by my middle name." He stops and shakes his head. "Anyways. My father got tired of her crying so he picked her up by her arm and dragged her across the kitchen and over to the stove. He grabbed for the pan my mom was cooking on and held it against the back of her neck, smiling as she screamed out in pain.

"When I ran over to help her, my dad took the pan and swung it at my face, hitting me, and causing me to fall back and hit my head on the corner of the counter. I blacked out, and all I remember is waking up to Sage crying and sitting next to me on the kitchen floor while my parents were at the table eating without us. The pan left a scar on the back of her neck. I'll always remember that mark."

I turn my head away and swipe at the tears as they begin to fall down my face. The thought of Hemy hurting kills me. Suddenly, all I want to do is go to bed and get the night over with. I can't think anymore. I want to hold him while I sleep—one last time. Just this one night.

Hemy notices me crying and instantly reaches out to dry my tears. "Don't cry for my past. It only made me stronger. I may not have been strong four years ago, but I promise you now, that I will be the strongest man you know. Taking care of you is what will make me strong; protecting what I love the most in life."

My heart takes on an odd rhythm as I watch his face. All I see is truth in his words. He's never told anyone that he loves them, except Sage and although he didn't exactly come out and say it, it's the closest thing to it for him. It makes me want to hold onto him and never let him go.

I clear my throat and pull his hands away from my face. "It's getting really late and I'm tired. Can we just go to bed now?"

He looks my face over before smiling and rubbing under my eyes one last time. "Yeah. Let me put you to bed. It's late."

He stands up and gets out of the tub. Reaching for a towel, he turns around and reaches for my hand to help me out of the water, before draping the towel over my shoulders. I stand here and watch as he blows the candles out and drains the water out of the tub.

"Next time we're in that tub, I'll be making love to you."

He grabs my hand and pulls me through the house, his body dripping wet as he guides us to his bedroom. Without turning on the light, he gets into his bed and tugs on the towel, pulling me down next to him.

"Lose this," he whispers while unwrapping me from the towel. "You know I can't sleep unless I'm wrapped up in your naked body."

I sit on my knees, naked, as Hemy takes me all in. Then, he pulls me down so that I'm lying down next to him. He leans over and presses his lips against mine, soft at first, before going rough and deep, causing us both to moan into each other's mouths. He kisses me for a few seconds longer, before moving down in between my legs, spreading them apart and kissing his name that is tattooed on the inside of my thigh.

My heart melts at the familiar feeling, making it harder to fight my emotions.

"Goodnight, baby," he whispers, while lying back down and pulling me close to him.

I close my eyes and cuddle in next to him, feeling his naked body flush against mine. It feels so good; too good.

"Goodnight," I whisper as his grip on me tightens.

Guarding my heart is going to be a lot harder than expected . . .

CHAPTER NINE

HEMY

I WAKE UP TO AN empty bed; the sheets smell of jasmine and vanilla. I always did love the scent of her hair. It always relaxed me, making me feel . . . alive. I've missed that scent almost as much as I have missed her.

Getting her to stay last night was a long shot; having her here in the morning was the impossible. I knew that from the beginning, but I learned to live with the idea and flowed with it. I just hope our night was enough to have an effect on her. If not, then I have a shit ton of work ahead of me.

Grumbling, I sit up and bury my hands in my hair. Having her next to me felt a lot better than I remembered. How can I ever live without that feeling now? She has ruined me. With her, I feel at peace. I feel like a real person. There is no way I'm giving up this fight, as much as I know she wants me to. A real man never gives up on his woman; he would die for her . . . and I would.

Sitting here, I feel empty. I don't have to work tonight so I need to find a way to keep my mind busy before I drive myself insane with thoughts of her.

"Shit! I need to do something."

I stand up, still naked and smelling of her. It instantly arouses me and I need a release. I make my way to the bathroom and run a cold shower; my thoughts stray back to her and the smooth curves of her body.

The ice-cold water should be helping with my hard on, but it's not. It's so fucking hard, it's beginning to hurt. The only way to get rid of it, is to release the pressure. Placing one hand against the shower wall, I grip my cock, close my eyes and stroke it to the images of Onyx in my head.

Picking up speed, it doesn't take long before I'm busting my load into the water, it washing down the drain.

I stand under the frigid water for a few more minutes before quickly washing up, turning off the water and reaching for a towel. The doorbell rings, just as I finish wrapping the towel around my waist.

A spark of hope surges through me at the idea that it could be Onyx. Although the rational part of me already knows that it isn't. She said so herself that she needed to keep safe. The more she's with me; she's in danger of falling for me again and getting hurt. At least in her eyes, she thinks I'll hurt her. I don't blame her for being afraid.

Securing the towel, I make my way to the living room, crack open the shade and look out. I almost feel like punching something when I realize that it's only Stone outside. What the fuck could he want?

I yank the door open and give him a hard look. I can't really be mad at him, but I can't help but to be disappointed that I was right about it not being Onyx.

"What the hell are you doing here?" I growl while pushing my wet hair away from my face.

He smirks and slaps my shoulder, walking past me and into the house. "Nice to see you too, guy." He jumps over the couch and takes a seat. "Dude, this couch smells like sex."

Slamming the door shut, I walk over to stand behind the couch. "Yeah. Your hand is in my dried up cum right now. Now what the fuck do you want?"

My attitude doesn't even phase Stone. He's so used to my mood swings that he just brushes it off. He knows I mean no harm. That's one thing I like about this kid. He may only be twenty-one and a little inexperienced, but he's a pretty decent dude and doesn't take stupid shit to heart.

Lifting an eyebrow, he shrugs off my outburst. "Let's go out tonight. It's Cale's night to work. I have a place in mind that I want to go to, but I need a partner." He pauses for a second to turn on the TV. *Sure, make yourself at home.* "There's a girl I want to see. I met her at that house we danced at last week. Her name is Ash. She's sexy as hell but I'm trying to play it cool. I know she wants me, but I'm not giving this dick up that easy."

I think about it for a second and then I realize that this Ash girl probably works with Onyx. She might not like me showing up at her work again, but I don't give a shit. I will show up there every night until she gives me a second chance. That's how stubborn I am.

"Where?" I take my towel off and run it through my hair. "I might be down."

Stone turns around to look at me right as I wrap the towel back around my waist. "*Vixens Club*. I heard from one of the other girls that she works there. I've been thinking about going to see her for a while. You down?"

"Yeah," I say stiffly. "I'm down. Meet me back here around nine."

Standing up, Stone gives me a fist pound and heads for the door. "Alright, bro. I'm out."

"Cool."

I watch as Stone walks outside, forgetting to shut the door behind him. "Idiot," I mutter before walking over to shut it.

I stand here in thinking mode for a moment. This may make me sound like a pussy, but I want to be sure to look sexy as hell for her tonight. I'm making it my mission to make her mine again.

WHEN NINE O'CLOCK ROLLS AROUND, I'm standing outside my house waiting on Stone to show up. I'm dressed in my favorite white button-down, the sleeves rolled up to the elbows and the top few buttons undone, displaying my tats. I threw on a pair of dark fitted jeans that show off my muscular thighs, black boots, and my hair is pulled back out of my face. Hell, I even trimmed my beard a bit to be sure it looks sexy for her.

Stone rolls up in his Jeep and whistles when I walk over and jump in the passenger seat. "Damn, dude. You trying to give the ladies a walking orgasm? You look studdish tonight." He reaches over and grabs the top of my collar, tugging slightly. "Damn, guy. I need to borrow that shirt sometime."

Shutting the door, I smirk slightly. "Come on, man. Stop creaming yourself over my clothes and let's go. No woman is going to want your ass if you walk in with nut stains."

"Fuck yeah, they would. Once I bust out my moves, the ladies can never resist." Stone lets out a satisfied laugh while grinding in his seat and pulling back out in the street and taking off. "No worries here."

We drive in silence for a few minutes, me lost in my own thoughts, trying to decide my best move for tonight before Stone interrupts me.

"You dressing up for someone? You never did tell me why you ran out of *Walk Of Shame* that night." He glances over at me and I grind my jaw at the thought of that night. I still can't get over what I found that night; her being in that place, rubbing all over that guy. It's just not her. Not the old her at least. "I'm guessing it's for some fine ass girl. I've never seen your ass try before. Usually the grungy Hemy look is enough, my man."

"Yeah, man, not this time. Trust me," I reply. "It's for *the* girl. Not just any fucking girl. And she works with this Ash chick so don't make a fool out of yourself around me. I need to prove to her that I'm a different person. I'm taking it easy on shots and all that hard shit. Got it?"

Nodding, he pulls up to *Vixens Club,* parks the Jeep and kills the engine. "Sure thing, man. I've been there once. Good luck is all I can say. Once a woman sees all your fuck ups, it's hard for them to see you for the good. That shit stays with them forever."

My jaw flexes from his words as I stare up at the neon sign in deep thought. It just reminds me that there's a huge chance that Onyx will never forgive me for all the crap I put her through. Doesn't matter. It won't stop me from trying.

"Come on, man. Let's go."

I jump out of the Jeep and slam the door behind me, with Stone hopping out right after. I didn't mean to close it to the point of almost breaking it, but I can't seem to control the negative thoughts swarming through my head. The thought of not having her as mine makes me want to slam my fist through something.

"Take it easy, dude." Stone flares his nostrils while looking his Jeep over for any damage. "Don't take it out on my ride. Save it for the assholes in the bar."

"My bad," I growl. "I'll buy you a new one if I fucked it up. Let's just get this over with."

We reach the door and some guy made of muscles with a bald, shiny head and long beard about six foot five comes over and asks for Stone's ID. He gets ready to ask for mine but after getting a glimpse of my face, decides against it and just waves us past.

"Seriously, dude?" Stone complains. "Is it because of my handsome baby face?" He rubs his hand over his face as if he's all smooth and shit.

I give his dumb ass a push as the bouncer gives him a blank look while crossing his arms. "Real men have beards. Grow one," I say annoyed.

After getting past the bouncer, we quickly order a couple drinks and take a seat in the far back. The club is fairly busy tonight and the thought of having all these creeps' eyes on my girl is driving me mad.

I know she hasn't danced yet because the bartender said there are a couple more girls before her. I don't really care to watch the show. Onyx is the only one I came to see. Until then, I'm invisible in the background.

Sipping back a gin and tonic, Stone pulls out his wallet and sets it on the table. "This club is nice. A hell of a lot nicer than ours." He runs his hand over the table in front of us while admiring it. "Black glass tables, red suede chairs, and look at that stage. That's a sweet ass stage. I wonder if they'll let me dance here. You know," he smirks confidently, "to help bring them some more cash in."

I tilt back my beer and block Stone out. I haven't been this fucking nervous since before I hit puberty. All I can think about is thrashing all the men in this room. I saw the way that piece of shit handled her last time I was here and it makes my blood boil that I didn't kick the shit out of him.

I look around the room, taking in all the assholes waving money around and screaming out like assholes. This must be the image Onyx has of me in her mind. I'm just like every one of these assholes. Until I can change that, that's what she sees.

Taking a long swig of my beer, almost finishing it off, I slam it down on the table and look over at Stone. He's too zoned in on the entertainment on stage to even notice me standing up. "I'll be back."

Walking away quickly, I make my way back over to the bar and call for the bartender to come over. The beautiful blonde that helped us when we walked in lifts her eyebrows and adjusts her tiny top while walking my way.

"Can I help you with something," she looks me up and down while playfully biting her lip, "big guy? You're looking awfully sexy to be here alone."

I ignore her sorry attempt to get my interest and pull out my wallet, prepared to make this shit happen my way tonight. "How much would it cost to get one of the girls to dance for me in a private room instead of on stage?"

The girl looks me up and down while leaning over the counter and reaching for my collar. "Why would you want to pay for one of these girls to dance for you when you can get *any* girl for free?"

"How much?" I growl out, pulling away from her touch. She gives me a confused look. "If you don't know then ask your manager. I need to know and quickly."

She takes a step back, her cheeks turning slightly pink with embarrassment. She clears her throat. "Umm. Well, we don't get that happening very often. If they're set to dance on stage then they usually can't do private dances until they're through. It's all on a schedule to fill the time."

Aggravation takes over as another girl enters the stage, swaying her hips wearing next to nothing. Onyx is next and I don't have time for games. I'll pay whatever the hell they want. I couldn't care less about the money.

"Tell your boss I'll pay three grand to have Onyx dance for me in private. I'm sure he wouldn't mind the extra cash. Just make it happen."

The girl holds up her finger before walking over to the phone and making a call. She comes back a minute later and points down the hall. "The room all the way to the back. It's our biggest room and it gives you some privacy in case you don't want to be seen by the dancer. Roman said he'll make it happen. I'll give Onyx the message."

I turn to walk away, but stop before taking a step. "Do me a favor and don't describe me to her."

She nods in understanding so I turn and walk away.

Hope she still likes surprises . . .

CHAPTER TEN

ONYX

HALF ASLEEP, I FIGHT TO stay awake while finishing up my makeup. As much as I don't want to be here tonight, I'm up next on stage and I really don't have much of a choice. A huge part of me wanted to call in tonight, but the other part of me knows I can't let my emotions get in the way of earning my bill money. Still, I'm just so . . . exhausted.

I crawled out of Hemy's bed around eight this morning and left while he was too deep in sleep to take notice. I knew I had to get out of there before he woke, or else he would've somehow talked me into spending the whole day with him. I couldn't let that happen. The more he brings up the past and shows me how different he is, the more I want to give in and trust him. It's too soon for that.

After I got back to my own bed, I thought I would be able to get some rest, but I couldn't shut my mind off enough to fall back asleep. I ended up spending most of the day cleaning a house that was already clean and watching TV shows, hoping they would wear me down enough to sleep. No luck there.

Tossing down my eyeliner, I look over to see if Ash is dressed and ready to go. She's up for her set on stage after me. I met Ash about a year ago, before I moved back home. We hit it off fast and after she explained how she was tired of her dull life and her parents smothering her, I thought maybe it would be nice to bring her home with me and let her live a little.

I really had no idea what the hell I was going to do for a job, but then an old friend of mine told me about *Vixens* needing a couple dancers. I mentioned it to Ash and in her rebellious state she was down for it, and ready to have a little fun. Plus, knowing that I was going to be so close to Hemy kind of made me want to rebel a bit myself. I needed a hard exterior to make me seem less vulnerable. It worked for a while.

"You still like this job, Ash?" I ask, now questioning my decision to bring her here.

Smiling, she sets down her red lipstick and uncrosses her legs. "Yeah, for now. It's not a bad place. Plus, the money is way better than waitressing at the diner I was at last year." She shrugs. "Might as well have a bit of fun while I'm still young."

I return her smile and look beside us as the door opens and Kylie rushes in. She gives me an unpleasant look and rolls her eyes. "There's been a change of plans. You're not going to be dancing on stage tonight."

Standing up, I place my hands on my hips and give her an equally disgusted look. Kylie usually seems to be friendly, but right now, I feel like slapping that smug look off her pretty little face.

"And why the hell is that?"

Mumbling under her breath, she tosses me a wad of cash and I reach out, barely catching it. "I can't believe Roman agreed to this, *but* someone paid a shit ton of money to have you do a private dance instead. Roman told me to give you a grand to do it." She turns and starts heading back for the door. "The sexy asshole is waiting in room ten. You probably shouldn't keep him waiting," she mutters and leaves the room.

I hold up the wad of cash and bite my bottom lip in thought. I feel a rush at the thought that Hemy could very well be that sexy asshole waiting on me. The problem with that is I wouldn't expect him to pay a ton of money for me to dance for him when he knows he can practically get anything he wants. He always did . . . until I left him.

Just as quickly as I let the thought consume me, I push it away and take a deep breath. I guess if anything, it's still better than being on stage. I still can't get used to dancing for a room full of men. I seem to do better one on one. Plus, it's easier to stay in command when you only have one asshole to deal with.

Handing the cash to Ash, I force a smile. "Mind putting that away for us? Looks like I have a sexy asshole waiting for a show."

We both laugh as I start backing away.

"Seems like a pretty generous asshole at least." She lifts a brow and waves the cash. "Tell him thanks from the both of us. I'll be lucky to make half that on stage."

GATHERING MY THOUGHTS, I TAKE my time walking to room ten. If this asshole was desperate enough to pay the amount of money this had to have cost, then he's desperate enough that he'll wait and still enjoy it when I get there.

Walking past the main room, I see it's almost filled to capacity now. The music is loud, the men are loud, and the flashing lights make it harder to concentrate on what's on stage. I guess the strobe effects and beat of the music make it more exciting for the men, and to make them feel they have to fight in order to see the half-naked girls swaying before them. It keeps them around longer, wanting to see more. That's what Roman thinks, at least. I think it's annoying as shit.

I make it down the hall and stop directly in front of the door, labeled with the number ten, staring for a moment before pushing the door open and stepping inside. I close the door behind me and try not to pay attention to who is in the room.

Room ten is the biggest private room we have. It's used for rich clients that want to remain discrete and don't want their faces shown to the public. Off in the back of the room, there's a huge leather chair for the client to relax in, and a light switch, giving them the option of showing their face or not. Lucky for me, this client wants to be kept a secret. It makes it easier to dance when I don't have to look into the creepy eyes that are glued to my every move.

Pushing all thoughts aside, I walk past the darkened corner, taking long, smooth steps, and swaying my hips on my way up to the stage. The music is already playing a slow, sexy song; perfect for getting aroused to.

Standing with my back against the pole, I bring one arm back to wrap around it, and slowly lower my body down the pole, while rubbing my other hand down the center of my body, over the white lace. Once I get close to the ground, I spread my knees apart and lower my hand some more, biting my bottom lip seductively.

I sway my hips to the rhythm of the music, releasing the pole, and wrapping my hands in my hair, tugging as I make my way back up the pole in a stance. I make sure to look in the direction of the darkened corner to verify to the client I'm indeed dancing for his pleasure and his alone. This usually helps me get additional tips on top of what I already get for doing the private dance.

Slowly turning around, I wrap one leg around the pole and arch my back, swinging my wild hair around, before gripping the pole and spinning around it. I spin around a few times, moving seductively to the music, before releasing the pole, walking to the edge of the small stage, and reaching for the ribbon that's holding my corset together.

Pretending as if I'm looking directly in the mysterious guy's eyes, I lower myself to the surface of the stage, down to my ass, and spread my legs wide apart, revealing the sheer lace that's in between. I slightly tug the ribbon, opening my top a little more, and rolling my hips up and down with my back pressed against the stage.

I'm lost in my own little world, hoping to get this guy off, when all of a sudden I feel two hands grip my thighs and pull me to the edge of the stage. Out of instinct, I swing one leg up and wrap it around the guy's neck, squeezing.

I expect whoever it is to let go of my thighs and apologize, but to my surprise, I get a growl and a bite on the inside of my thigh.

I recognize the growl right away, and I can't help the reaction that my body gets from it. My heart jumps to my throat and my whole body trembles with pleasure.

Another soft bite causes me to open my eyes to the sight of Hemy standing there, his hair pulled back, and his deep amber eyes set on me. His grip on my thighs tightens as I release his neck and lean my head back with my hands in my hair.

"Fucking shit, Hemy," I bite out. "You scared the shit out of me. What are you doing here? I told you—"

"Shhh . . ." he whispers against my thigh. "Don't talk. I'm not here for that. I'm here to taste my pussy and remind you of what is mine."

Before I can think of a response, my panties are pushed aside and Hemy moans out while running his thick finger over my wetness. My body instantly reacts to his touch, causing me to moan out and bite my lip.

"You miss my mouth owning your pussy? It craves my tongue, doesn't it, baby?" He runs a hand down my thigh while shoving a finger deep inside me, causing me to grip the stage. "Tell me how bad you want me to taste you," he demands.

I look up at him, now getting a bit angry at him for making me admit it first. He's doing this to see how badly I want him. It makes me want to slap him and then ride the shit out of him. He always had that effect on me.

"Maybe I don't want you to," I whisper, looking up to meet his stare. "Maybe someone else has already claimed what was once yours." I can't resist but to push him back. One of us is bound to cave first.

Pulling my body up higher, he softly blows on my clit while pushing his finger in and out. "You'll always be mine, Onyx." He squeezes my thigh and rubs his bottom lip up my heat, causing me to moan out silently. "This pussy . . . will always be mine. I claimed it years ago when I made you my girl, and nothing has changed since."

He runs his lips up my pussy again, teasing me with his lip ring. I'm fighting so hard to resist, but I can't help it. Seeing Hemy dressed up, makes me want to have an orgasm right on the spot. *Feeling* his mouth on me almost has me exploding beneath him.

I thrust my hips upward, silently begging for him to lick me. He laughs against my throbbing clit before reaching up with one hand and grabbing my left breast. His dominance has me on the verge of explosion and I want to feel this to its full extent.

"I want to feel your tongue on me," I blurt out, thrusting my hips again to meet his mouth. "Remind me of how good it feels. Now."

With a cocky smile, Hemy grips my ass with both hands and pulls my hips up to meet his face. Looking at me with pure heated desire, he runs his tongue, slowly and teasingly, up my wetness, causing me to shake uncontrollably in his arms.

He rubs circles around my clit with his tongue, before trailing it back down and pushing it into my entrance. This causes me to wrap my legs around his head and squeeze. I can't seem to get him close enough and he knows this. He knows my weakness and is using it against me to get me where he wants me. It's working and I hate him for it.

The better it feels the angrier I seem to get, until finally, I growl out and pull away from him. At least, I try to. He catches my legs and pulls me off stage so that I'm straddling his hips. With a smile, he walks us both up the stairs and up to the stage.

He stops in front of the pole, turns my back toward it, and presses me against it, breathing in my ear. "Hold on tight." With little effort, he lifts me up, causing me to reach behind me and grip onto the pole at a higher level. Before I can wonder what he's doing, he rests my thighs on his shoulders, grips my waist, and buries his face in my pussy.

His tongue works like magic, owning my pussy just like in the past. My whole body trembles from the heat of his mouth and the feel of his tongue tasting me, slowly and teasingly.

He reaches up with one hand and rubs his thumb over my clit, while working his tongue, rough and fast, speeding up to get me off. My grip on the pole tightens as he shoves his tongue back inside just in time for me to come.

I shake on his shoulders for a few seconds, high off the release of my orgasm. It feels so good I can almost cry in relief. Releasing the pole, he pulls me away from it and slowly lowers me down his body, kissing me in different places along the way. It doesn't take much for him to lower me back down to my feet and press his body into mine.

Looking into my eyes, he cups my face and runs his tongue over his lips in satisfaction. "I want you back at my place tonight." I shake my head, but he stops me by pressing his lips against mine, claiming my lips as his. The kiss is rough and possessive, and I can't help but get turned on again.

After a few moments pass, he pulls away from the kiss and turns to walk away without another word. My whole body screams to run after him, but I can't. I'm stuck in place, trying to figure out how I let him take control of me again.

Screw this. I'm letting him know that he doesn't control me. He hasn't in a long time. He has no say whether or not I go to his place and stay with him. He lost that say years ago.

Making sure that I'm covered, I rush out of the room and walk down the dark hallway. I stop when I get to the main room and look around in search of him. It doesn't take long to point him out. With Hemy looking as sexy as he is tonight, it's hard to miss him.

He's standing next to a table with another guy. I recognize him from Jade's party. He's one of the three strippers that danced that night. I recognize the black hair and tattoos. Realizing he must be here to watch one of the girls, my gut tells me to get Hemy out of here.

He might assume I'm giving into him, but I'm really just trying to preserve my secret a bit longer. He *seems* different, but I'm still scared.

Clearing my head and coming down from my temporary high, I walk over to the table, stopping in between him and the other guy. I place my hand on Hemy's chest and can't help the moan that slips out of my mouth. Just touching him has me all worked up.

"Wait for me outside. I'll go grab my things and meet you by your truck."

Biting his bottom lip, he grabs both of my hands and runs them up his chest, before pulling them up to wrap around his neck. He presses his body flush with mine and gives me a hooded look. "I don't have my truck. We'll take my motorcycle."

I smile at the memory of when the bike was his. After a while, he gave up on it and got a new one. I couldn't leave without it, because it brought back too many memories. I needed it as my safety net. I needed it to fall back on when I missed him too much, so after I packed my things and left that night, I sent my brother to pick up it up from storage. I made it mine with the memories of him.

"You mean my bike?" Smirking, I turn around in his arms and walk away, making him release me. If I know Hemy still, he'll be outside as soon as I'm out of sight.

After quickly grabbing my things and changing, I make my way outside to see Hemy leaning against my bike. Seeing him standing in front of it causes my heart to clench in pain. It brings back too many memories of us as teens, me holding on tightly as he learned how to ride it. It didn't take long and I always trusted him to keep me safe; a part of me still does.

He sees me approaching and walks over, placing the helmet on my head. "Give me the keys," he orders.

I think about it for a second and almost consider making him ride on the back, but that would just look too weird to even enjoy. Hemy is definitely too dominant for that. Alpha male is what he'll always be.

I toss him the keys without a fight, pull my helmet on, and put my backpack on. My black boots dig into the gravel as I hop on the back and watch as Hemy jumps on the front.

I don't know how much more of this I can take while guarding my heart.

I need to figure something out and fast . . .

CHAPTER ELEVEN

HEMY

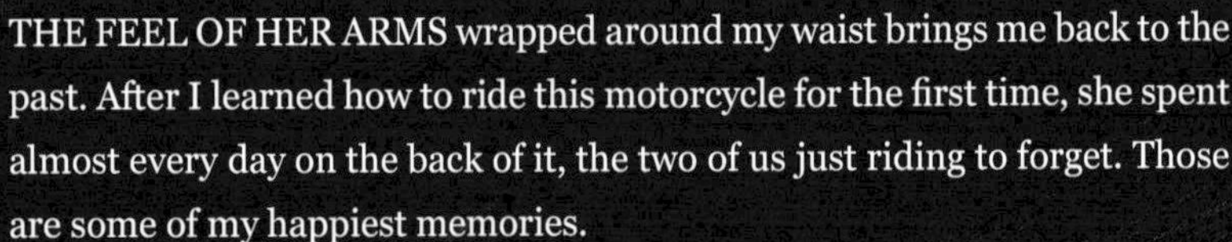

THE FEEL OF HER ARMS wrapped around my waist brings me back to the past. After I learned how to ride this motorcycle for the first time, she spent almost every day on the back of it, the two of us just riding to forget. Those are some of my happiest memories.

I can tell she's thinking about it too, because she hasn't said a word since we left the club, and not to mention that her arms are practically squeezing the life out of me. She always did that unintentionally in the past when she was deep in thought, and man does it feel good. This is exactly what I was hoping for. If I want another chance with her, then I'll have to remind her of the good stuff.

Riding past my block, I make a turn down the street that leads to Mitch's shop. Mitch's family has owned *Greenler's Mechanics* his whole life. Onyx and I spent a lot of time in it, playing and fooling around, when I was working on my motorcycle or showing off my mechanic skills to get her worked up. She always did have a thing for a dirty, hardworking man. I'm sure that hasn't changed much. At least, I can only hope.

Onyx doesn't bother looking up until we are already pulling up to the shop and parking. I can tell from her lack of smartass remarks. That, and I can feel her chin resting against my back. I don't think it's intentional, but I wouldn't dare say a word at the risk of her moving it. I feel her grip loosen as she lets out a little surprised breath. "Seriously, Hemy?" She releases my waist as I kill the engine. "Why would you bring me here? I thought we were going to your place."

Not bothering to respond, I help her off the bike and watch as she walks up to the building and stands there in silence. She probably hasn't even thought about this place in over four years. Bringing her here is sure to get the memories flowing in. It has to. I'm counting on it. Hell, I'm having a hard time just being here with her. I could do it alone over the years, but having her here makes my chest ache. It always will until she's mine again.

Grinding my jaw and pushing back my emotions, I grab Onyx's hand and pull her along with me as I walk around to the back and pull out my key. I've been meaning to work on my Harley for a while now, but I've been so busy working on other projects for Mitch that I haven't been able to touch it. It's about time I get my baby running good.

I push the door open and flip on the light. Onyx's hand squeezes mine, and then she lets go and steps inside. "I haven't thought about this place in years, Hemy." She looks around, her face void of emotions. "It looks exactly the same." She cracks a smile. "As a matter of fact, I think you guys are still working on the same vehicles too."

I let my own smile take over as I watch her laugh at her own joke. Damn, her laugh is just as beautiful as ever. I never could get enough of that sound.

I step up beside her and nudge her with my shoulder. She looks up at me. "I love that sound," I say softly.

She looks around as if listening for something. "What sound?"

"When you laugh," I say honestly. Her smile fades as I look down into her eyes and then walk away.

I keep on walking, making my way to the back where my motorcycle is parked. It doesn't take but a few seconds before Onyx is standing right behind me. She's so close that I can feel the warmth from her body. I can sense her eyes studying me as I stand here.

"Why are we here?" she finally asks.

"I need to work on my bike. Why else would we be here?"

"It's like midnight. Don't you ever sleep?"

"Not anymore. I told you, I can't sleep for shit without you naked and next to me." I walk away, unbuttoning my shirt, before pulling it off and setting it on the closest car.

I kneel down in front of my Harley and reach for my tools. Onyx watches me in silence for a few seconds before she drops her bag down beside her and takes a seat on the hood of the car next to her. "I've kind of missed this, you know." She pauses and waits for me to respond, but I don't. I want her to keep going. "You working on your bike here and me watching. Us laughing and talking. I miss you like that."

I continue to work on my bike, not looking back at Onyx. "You always made it hard to get any work done. Your smell alone was enough to arouse me, but when you would undress behind me, sitting on a car . . ." My words trail off and I smirk to myself, knowing by the sound of her breathing that she's reliving the memories.

"What," she breathes. "Don't stop there, Hemy."

"All I could think about was burying myself deep between those thighs." I stand up, drop my tools and walk over to stand between her legs. Placing my hands on her thighs, I trail my hands up them. "*My* thighs. All I wanted to do was to own your pussy and release myself so deep inside you that I would ruin you for anyone else."

Her breathing picks up as I spread her legs and step between them. "Mmm . . . and I wanted you deep inside me. I never could watch you getting dirty without wanting you to get me dirty. Funny how that works." She leans forward and runs her tongue over my mouth, her tongue lingering on my ring before sucking my lip along with it into her mouth. "You were so sexy working on your bike that my clothes practically fell off. That look you made when concentrating on your work. Oh shit, I'll never forget that look."

I tangle my fingers in the back of her hair and look down at her with a serious look of concentration, imitating what she just described. It's not all just an act. I'm taking my time and concentrating on every last inch of her beauty. I bite my lip as she closes her eyes and breathes in. I know I have her. "This one," I question, stepping in closer to press my erection between her thighs.

Her body jerks from below me as I grind my hips a little. "Yes." She opens her eyes and takes in my face, her eyes filled with lust. "That one, exactly. Why are you doing this, Hemy? You knew this would happen if you brought me here. We can't keep doing this. I can't let myself fall in love with you again."

"You falling back in love with me is the *only* thing I want." Gripping her hair tighter, I crush my lips against hers, owning her lips, breath, and taste. Everything that she is right now is mine and I intend on keeping it this way. I'm taking this moment and owning it.

Her lips instantly part, allowing me entrance just like in the past. Everything about this moment brings me back to four years ago, and it only makes me want her more. Pulling back, I breathe against her lips, my hands still tangled in her hair. "I can never get enough of this." I bring one hand down and rub my thumb over her cheek before trailing down and over her bottom lip. "Seeing you up on the hood of this car makes me want to take you right here." I kiss her neck and make my way up to her ear, stopping to whisper. "Do you want that, baby? You want to remember what it was like, me taking you here, me all dirty and sweaty?"

"No," she whispers, pushing on my chest. "That's the last reminder I need, Hemy."

Grabbing her chin, I force her to look up into my eyes. I can tell by her heavy breathing and fidgeting that she's lying. She always did have a hard time hiding her feelings from me. "Dammit, Onyx. Don't lie to me. Tell me the truth."

She nods, her breathing picking up as she reaches up to let my hair down. She looks lost in thought for a moment before she speaks. "You have no idea how sexy your hair is. Every time I look at you, all I can think about is gripping onto it as you make love to me."

My heart beats wildly in my chest, but then sinks to my stomach as she turns her head away in shame. She does that when she says something she didn't mean to. Every part of me wants her to mean those words. I may not have made love to her in the past, but things have changed. I've changed. I'm willing to give her anything she wants.

I pull her face back to mine and bring my lips down to hover over hers, our heavy breathing mingling together. "If you give me a chance," I bring my eyes up to meet hers, "I'll make love to you. I'm capable of more than you think now, Onyx."

She stares at me for a second, not saying a word, before a small smile creeps over her face. "Well, not tonight." She grips my hair and pulls on it roughly. "Tonight, I want you to fuck me like you did four years ago." She yanks my hair harder before releasing it. "Show me the old Hemy. *My* Hemy."

Her words set me off and before she can register what I'm doing, I have her back pressed against the hood of the car and her pants in my hands, yanking them down her legs. Kissing the inside of her thigh, I pull her boots off and toss them, before tossing her jeans next to them.

I spread her legs further and kiss my way up to her stomach while reaching for her white tank top. "Fuck, Onyx." I love the way she looks laying across the hood of a car. I nibble my lip ring while pulling her shirt above her head and reaching behind her to release her bra. I take a few seconds to admire her body before gripping her thong in my hand and pulling her body into mine. Nothing is standing in the way of being inside her now but my jeans and her tiny lace thong. It's exactly like it was when we first fell in love. It's just too bad she never knew it.

Twisting her panties in my hand, I rip them off, the white lace coming untied with little effort. Onyx lets out a moan and arches her back as I lace one arm beneath her and bite down into her shoulder. "Oh God, Hemy," she pants. "Hurry up and get those jeans off."

Smiling against her neck, I work on taking off my jeans with one hand, while reaching down with my other to rub circles over her clit. "Fuck, this is mine." I slide my jeans down my legs and let them drop, before spinning Onyx around and slamming her down onto the hood, grabbing the back of her hair.

"Spread your legs, baby." I lean down next to her ear and growl as she bites my arm. "Show me how bad you've missed me inside you."

She bites me harder, causing me to squeeze her left ass cheek before slapping it. She cries out with pleasure as I slap it one more time before gripping her ass with both hands and spreading her cheeks. "It's so beautiful," I whisper, while running a finger up her wetness. "Hold on, baby. I'm about to take you for a ride."

Gripping my cock, I align it with her opening, rubbing the head of it over her slickness, teasing her with my piercings before shoving it deep inside with a moan. Holding onto her hips, I pound into her hard and fast, causing her to grab onto the hood and scream. The faster I go, the more she begs for me to go harder.

Grinding my hips, I yank her hair back with one hand, pushing hard and deep. I want her to still be able to feel me inside her after we're through. I want her to know she's mine and mine alone. I may have shared her once, but that'll never happen again.

She sticks her ass up higher, gripping onto my hand as I thrust into her. I'm already as deep as I can go and she still wants me deeper. We never could get enough of each other, even when it hurt her.

A few thrusts later, I feel her clenching around my cock, so I give her one hard thrust before yanking her neck to the side and pressing my lips against hers, right as she moans. I wait for her to stop shaking before I pull out and spin her around to face me.

I crush my lips back against hers, both of us breathing heavy, as I pick her up and walk until we're pressed against the wall in our favorite corner. It was where we went to fuck when Mitch's ass wouldn't leave for the night. Even though he could still hear us, it kept us hidden pretty well in the shadows. The risk of getting caught made it more of a rush.

Pulling away from her lips, I wrap my hand around her throat and push myself inside her, causing her to shake in my arms. "Remember this spot, baby?" I pull her bottom lip into my mouth and bite into as I start thrusting hard and fast, pushing her up the wall with each movement.

I reach down and grab her hands, binding them in one hand, and raising them above her head. Both of us are breathing heavy, me holding her hands above her head while holding her up with my opposite arm supporting her waist.

"Hemy!" She pulls back on my hair as I push into her one last time, feeling my orgasm build before I release myself deep inside her.

We stand here, me holding her and her holding onto me as we fight to catch our breath. Lowering her back to her feet, I tangle my fingers in her hair and press my forehead against hers. "I fucking love you," I breathe out. "I love you so much that it hurts."

Sucking in a breath of shock, she places both her hands on my chest and shoves me away. "Damn you, Hemy!" Rushing over to her clothes, she struggles to get dressed while muttering under her breath and holding back tears.

I don't blame her for her reaction. I hurt her beyond words, and me dropping the L word like this was probably the last thing she expected . . . but I don't give a shit. I love her and she needs to know, no matter how much she hates me. I missed my chance the first time. It won't happen again. I'll never lose her again because I couldn't tell her how I felt.

I feel my heart shattering in my chest as she throws on her boots and reaches for her bag. As much as I know she needs to go, I don't want her to. She heads for the door, but then stops to turn around and throw something. Whatever it was hits the wall before she buries her face in her hands and shakes her head.

"Do you even know what pain feels like, Hemy?" Her jaw clenches as I stare at her. "Well, do you? Do you even feel pain?"

"Oh, I feel it alright. That burning sensation deep down inside that feels as if my heart is dying, being crushed." I look up from the ground and right into her eyes. "I felt it the minute you walked out my door."

She stands there, unable to say anything, before turning around and walking out the door, slamming it closed behind her. I have no one to blame but myself. I did this to her . . . to us.

It just means I need to work harder to show her the new me.

CHAPTER TWELVE

HEMY

IT'S BEEN FOUR DAYS SINCE I've seen Onyx and it's taking everything in me not to go to *Vixens* and claim her as mine. As much as it hurts, she needs time. Me forcing her to admit her feelings isn't going to do anything but make it worse on my part. I can't have that.

Taking a drag of my cigarette, I tilt my head back up to look at Slade. He's puffing on his own cigarette while texting Aspen. "You love her, man?"

Slade gives me a stern look before shoving his phone in his pocket and taking one last drag of his cigarette before tossing it. "With everything in me," he says with confidence. "There's not a thing I wouldn't do for that woman."

I can't believe I'm even doing this right now. Going to Slade for advice was the last thing I thought I'd ever do. "What would you do if you hurt her so bad in the past that she was afraid to open up and let you back in? What if you told her you loved her for the first time and she walked away?"

Taking a step closer to me, he grips my shoulder and smirks. "My guy's in love. This must be one badass chick." He shoves my shoulder before placing me in a headlock and rubbing the top of my head. "You've been holding out on me, my man."

I take one last drag of my cigarette as he releases my neck. "Yeah, she's badass. She's my first and only love, man. I fucked up bad and I'm paying for it now." I toss my cigarette and take a deep breath before quickly releasing it. "I'm trying to be patient. It's been four days and I haven't heard from her." I flex my jaw while leaning into the building and digging my fingers into it. "How much time should I give her?"

Without hesitation, he answers, "You know me, man. When I want something I go after it, sometimes a little too hard. If it's love, then you need to let her know that you're not going anywhere. Let her know you want her without pushing her away. You get me?"

I nod, getting what he means. I can still let her know I'm not going anywhere without being too pushy. My shift is almost over for the night, so as soon as I'm out, I'm going straight to *Vixens*.

"Hemy."

We both look over at the sound of Sarah's voice. "The group dance is up next. You better hurry and get your fine ass in there." She smiles at Slade before shoving his shoulder. "Your woman is at the bar waiting on you. You better hurry before someone else snags her sexy ass up."

Oh boy. She just had to go there.

Without hesitation, Slade stalks off, rushing inside to his woman. He knows he has nothing to worry about with Aspen, but he's still protective. He reminds me a lot of myself. When we find that special woman, we'll do anything for her. I just wish I wasn't too late.

"Thanks, Sarah."

"Yeah, yeah. Just hurry your ass up," she teases.

IF THERE'S ANYTHING THAT I hate, it's doing a dance routine on stage. It involves costumes and all of us men putting a dance together. That's why we only set up a dance routine once a month. It's the one thing that some of the women travel to see. It's the biggest night of every month, packed to maximum capacity.

Adjusting my tie, I laugh at Stone as he jumps up on a table and thrusts his hips while gripping onto his hat and tilting it down, over his face. "Man,

I'm such a stud in a suit."

"Is that right, asshole?" Cale asks.

"Um . . . fuck yeah," Stone replies while jumping down from the table. "Don't get mad when I get all the tips. I have this routine down pat, bros."

"Alright, *stud*." I slap the back of his head before reaching for my black hat and putting it on, tilting it a bit to the side. "This is the biggest crowd you'll see for a while, so you better show them Slade's not around anymore. A lot of them come just for that motherfucker."

"I'm the new Slade," he says with a smirk. "These women will leave screaming Stone. You feel me?" He gives both Cale and I the middle finger before jogging up the steps to the back of the stage.

This kid really has no idea what he's getting into right now. Some of these women still even scare my ass with all that shrieking.

The stage is dark when we line up next to our chairs. I can hear the screaming of hundreds of women as soon as the music starts playing. This used to get me hard at one point. Undressing for all these horny women. Now, I don't feel shit. I just want to get this over with.

Out of instinct, my body instantly reacts to the music when the lights flicker on, lighting up the stage. Placing one foot on the chair, I grab the top of my head and grind my hips to the music, the other two doing the same.

I thrust my hips slow and seductively as if I were fucking someone with deep passion. This causes the girls close by to lean over the stage and start waving a handful of cash while others toss some onto the stage.

I reach up with one hand and loosen my tie, swinging one leg over the chair to straddle it, rocking my hips a few times just before grabbing the chair and lifting it up to place at the end of the stage.

I look out into the crowd and motion with my finger for the closest girl to come up on stage. With little effort, I grab onto her arm and pull her up next to me.

Swaying my hips to the slow rhythm, I pull the knot of my tie until it transforms back into a straight piece of fabric. Grabbing each end, I slide it around her waist and pull her body up against mine, transferring the ends of the tie in one hand. I lean into her neck and grip my hat with one hand while grinding against her, causing her to scream out with excitement.

Out of the corner of my eye, I see Cale and Stone doing the exact same thing. For as little as we practice, we're completely in sync with each other. I have to admit we don't look half bad for not putting much effort into the routine.

Walking her backward, I guide her down into the chair before dropping my tie and ripping the buttons off my black button down. I grab the girl's hand and place it on my chest while standing above her lap and dancing against her.

The girl's hand goes to reach for my dick, but I grab it, stopping her before she can get there. The thought of another woman touching me there right now is not sitting well with me. It actually pisses me off.

Pushing back my anger, I tilt her chair back until I'm standing over her face, grinding my hips above her while holding the top of the chair up with one hand. My dick is directly in front of her face and all I can think about is Onyx doing something similar with some random dude in her club.

Jealousy courses through me, but I do my best to keep it in check and make it through the dance. The routine is almost over. Only one more thing left to do.

Pulling the chair back up on all fours, I run my hands down my bare chest before undoing my pants and placing the girl's hands on my waistline, allowing her to undress me. She pushes them down my legs without hesitation, leaving me standing here in my short boxer briefs, the women all screaming at us practically naked.

Picking her up and placing her to lie on her back on the stage, I slide across the floor, on my knees, while thrusting my hips until I'm above her face again. I place both hands on the ground in front of me and thrust in a fast motion, against her face with my package.

She reaches up and grabs my ass until I'm done and moving down her body, pretending to lick her body on the way down. Once I reach the bottom, I help her to her feet and smile as she shoves a handful of cash in the front of my briefs.

We do a few more short dances, filling the time, until finally the night is almost over and we're heading backstage to get dressed.

I TAKE A SEAT AND look around, swallowing the realization that none of these girls even come close to comparing to Onyx. This place isn't good enough anymore. Onyx is sexy, strong, passionate, and doesn't take shit from anyone. She has always been that way . . . except when it came to me.

I reach over to the table next to me and grab my beer. I hold it against my lips for a few seconds before pulling it away and setting it down, pissed off at myself for thinking. "Fuck me."

"Hello, sexy," a soft voice says from beside me.

Without looking over, I nod and reach for my beer again. I really don't feel like being messed with at the moment. "I'm done working for the night," I say stiffly.

"Even better." I feel the couch dip next to me, so I look over to see a sexy brunette. It's the same one that licked the whipped cream off my body that night I left to go find Onyx. She smiles victoriously as if she's been waiting for the exact moment to get me alone. "It looks like you could use some company."

She reaches over and slides her hand up my leg, gripping my thigh just below my dick. I look down at her slender hand and grab it right before she reaches for my package. "I don't want company." I set her hand on her own lap and stand up while taking a sip of my beer. "I'm good being alone."

Leaning forward, she pokes out her chest while running a finger over her half empty glass. Her lips curl up into a smile as she takes a sip and scoots closer to the edge. "I think you just need to release some tension." She licks her lips. "I'm sure I could help you with that."

"I said I'm good." I go to turn around and stop as I almost bump into someone. Not just anyone . . . Onyx.

Her nostrils flare as she stares me in the eyes, not saying a word. I can't even move. I'm frozen in place from her stare, so I just stare back, waiting for her to speak.

"Here's your chance, Hemy." She looks between me and the brunette. "Here's your chance to speak. That is, if you're not too busy."

"Hey!" The brunette sets her drink down on the table next to her and sits straight up as if ready for a fight. "Can't you see he's busy, bitch?"

Onyx runs her tongue over her top teeth before placing the heel of her boot into the girl's chest and shoving her backward, then leaning down toward her face. "I'd watch who you call a bitch. Got it, sweetheart?" She pulls her foot away and leans into her ear. "Keep your dirty little mouth away from my man or you'll be eating my heel for a late-night snack."

"Fuck me. That's hot." I set my beer down and watch as Onyx turns around to face me. "Your man, huh?"

"Shit!" She walks away from me while mumbling something under her breath.

I quickly catch up to her and grab her by the waist to stop her. "Where are you going?" I spin her around and brush a curl out of her face. "Come to my house with me."

"No." She places her hands on my chest and pushes me away as I pull her into me. "Dammit, Hemy. See what you do to me?" She lets out a breath of frustration and turns away for a second. "I didn't mean to call you that. It just sort of came out."

"It sounded damn good coming out too," I admit. "Come to my house so we can talk. I'm not taking no for an answer anymore."

"No, Hemy. We can talk here. We never talk in private and you know it."

I pull my eyes away from hers and look around to see that a lot of people have stopped to stare at us, including Sarah and one of our other bartenders, Amanda. I flex my jaw at them and they both turn away to resume minding their own business.

"Let's go," I say firmly. "We're going to my house."

"Onyx! What are you doing here?"

I look beside us to see a pretty girl with dark curls standing next to Stone. The look that crosses Onyx's face as she takes her in surprises me. She looks sick, as if she's about to pass out.

"Um . . . Ash. What are you doing here? I thought you were still at work?"

Ash looks between me and Onyx and forces a small smile. "Is this your friend?" She looks me over as if she's trying to figure something out. "The one you said I might meet someday?"

Onyx looks between the two of us, her face pained before she reaches for my arm. "Yeah, but now is not a very good time. I'm suddenly feeling like shit."

Ash steps up beside Onyx and grabs her purse. "I can take you home. I have my car outside and—"

"No," she cuts in. "You just got here. I'll be fine." She turns to face me and her eyes lock with mine. The pain in her expression confuses me. "Let's go to your house. I think we have a lot to talk about."

"Alright." I take one more look at Stone and Ash before following Onyx through the crowd and outside. As soon as Onyx gets outside, she pukes.

CHAPTER THIRTEEN

HEMY

AFTER ONYX CALMED DOWN AND the puking stopped, I took off my shirt and wiped her face off before helping her into my truck. As tough as she thinks she is now, I know she still needs a little taking care of. She deserves it and I want her to know that. I would take care of her for the rest of my life if she would just let me.

Onyx lets out a heavy breath beside me. "I can't do this, Hemy. I can't fucking do this. Stop the car."

Pulling the truck over, I grip the steering wheel before slamming my fist into it. I can't stand those words coming from her mouth. I wish she would stop trying to keep me out. "Dammit, Onyx!" I lean back in my seat and rub my hands over my face in frustration. "I've been trying to show you that I'm a different person. Can't you fucking see that? All you want to do is keep me out and push me away."

It's silent for a moment as I stare at the side of her face, taking her in. She looks so pained that it breaks my heart. I wish she would just fucking talk and put me out of my misery.

"Hemy," she breathes, breaking the silence. "I know you're trying to prove that you've changed and you can give me what I wanted back then, but you don't understand. You broke me . . . shattered me. I'm not the same girl I was, and I don't think I can love you that way again. You need to let me go. I refuse to go through that again."

Grinding my jaw, I try my best to hide my anger. "You won't even give me the chance, Onyx! I know you're not the same girl and I'm not the same guy. We are different, but that isn't a bad thing. We still belong together like we always have and always will . . ."

She holds her hand up to stop my words before tugging on her hair in frustration. "You know how easy it would be for me to give in and believe you, right? You and I, it's never been easy and I can't go down that path with you, Hemy. Please, leave me alone. Maybe we can be friends someday, but I can't handle this now."

"I can't just be your friend. I'll always want more with you, and you know you feel the same way."

She must be done listening to me, because she goes for the door handle and quickly pushes it open. "I'm just going to walk home, and please, don't come after me."

Before I can say anything, she hops out of the truck and slams the door behind her. She takes off walking as if she's trying to get as far away from me as she can. The thought crushes me and I feel as if I can't breathe. I want to be pissed at her for being scared, but I can't. It's my own doing and I need to fix this. I knew going in that there was a possibility she wouldn't take me back, but it isn't in me to give up, not this time.

Following her actions, I jump out of the truck and take off after her. I catch up to her quickly, grabbing her arm, and spinning her around to face me. She looks up at me with pained green eyes, before turning away. It's as if looking at me kills her.

"Don't walk away from me when all I've been trying to do is show you how much you mean to me." Wrapping my hands in the back of her hair, I pull her closer to me and force her to look into my eyes. "I fucking love you. Do you know how hard that is for me to say to anyone? Sage is the only other person I have ever said that to and she's fucking gone. You two are the only ones I've ever loved and I lost you both. I want us back. I can't stand to be without you."

"And you don't think I've lost the one person I ever loved? Huh?" She shoves my chest, but I don't budge an inch, which pisses her off more. "Dammit, Hemy!" She shoves me again, but I only hold her tighter, letting her know I'm not going anywhere. I'm not giving up and walking away like she did. Fuck that. I refuse. "I don't love you anymore, okay! I don't want to go back and try again. I won't let history repeat itself. There is no starting over, there is no us, and there never will be. So. Let. Me. Go."

I close my eyes and take a deep breath to calm myself. Her words sting like hell, but I don't believe her for one second. Her eyes give away the truth and that's enough to keep me going. She never was a good liar.

I drug her down into my dark, tormented world of demons and hate, slowly killing her day by day, making it hard for her to breathe. I shook the angel in her and now she's pulling me into her dark, twisted world of hate and revenge, fighting to keep me out, and forcing me to hate her. Well . . . hating her is the last thing I have in store.

"I don't believe you," I say through clenched teeth.

Picking her up, I throw her over my shoulder and hold her up by her ass. She instantly starts struggling against me as I walk her back to my truck.

"Damn you, Hemy! Why are you so hardheaded?"

I open the door and shove her inside, being careful not to hurt her. She may want to play games, but I'm going to play harder by showing her the man she fell in love with.

I lean in the window and run my hands through her hair, causing her to look up at me with a pained expression. She always loved it when I did this in the past. It calmed her down. "You can damn me all you want, but the last thing I'm doing is letting you go again."

Without a word, she swallows and looks away from me. I push back my emotions and walk over to my side of the truck to climb inside. It's time to take her home with me, where she belongs.

She's not leaving until she sees how much I love her . . .

I HATE DOING THIS. I hate trying to push him away when all I really want to do is hold him close and bury my face into his chest. It hurts more than anyone could ever imagine, lying to everyone, even yourself. It's something I have to do now. At first it was just to guard my heart, but now . . . it's because I know he's going to hate me after I tell him what I've been keeping from him for a while now. Why let myself get close and let him in when he'll be hating me soon anyways? I did it for a good reason. I had to.

Hearing him say *I love you* breaks me down, making me want to run into his arms and scream that I love him back, and that I never stopped. Shit, all that will do is guarantee for me to be crushed again. It broke my heart to lie to him and tell him I don't love him anymore. I hate it. I hate it.

Hemy doesn't waste any time driving off, heading in the direction of his street. I can see the fight in him this time. He's different: stronger, sober, and determined, all the things that I hoped for in the beginning. Now . . . it will be me to fuck things up.

I keep my face toward the window for the rest of the ride, fighting my hardest not to cry. I have been strong for four years and I refuse to let anyone see me cry now, especially Hemy. As long as I pretend that I don't have feelings, the safer from him I will be.

When we arrive at his house, Hemy turns to me and reaches out his arm. It's so inviting, making me want to crawl over to him and give into everything I'm fighting. "Come here," he whispers.

I look at him, but don't say a word. I can't or I'll cry.

"I said come here." Reaching over, he pulls me into his lap so that my knees are positioned on the outside of his thighs. "Don't be afraid of me." He wraps both hands in the back of my hair and looks me in the eyes. My heart skips a beat at the warmth of his touch. "I love you more than anything in this world. I would give my life to make you happy. Please, don't be afraid of me. It kills me."

Feeling a tear form in my eye, I try to turn away, but Hemy grabs my face to stop me, his jaw clenching as he watches me.

"Let me see you," he breathes. "I need to see that you still love me. You may not want to say it . . . but I see it. Just let me see it."

I let the tear fall freely down my face, followed by a few more that I can't seem to hold back. Hemy reaches up to wipe my tears away and that's when I lose it. My whole body shakes as I let it all go. All the pain and hurt I have been keeping inside since the day I walked out his door comes raging out.

My face is flooded with tears now. I can barely see Hemy through the mess, but I can feel him squeezing me closer, telling me to let it all out. A part of me feels relieved.

"You're so beautiful," he whispers, while pressing his forehead against mine. "I promise to show you that you're the most beautiful woman in the world to me. Do you understand?"

"Hemy," I cry out. "I need to tell you something. I—"

"Do. You. Understand?" I nod my head, while trying to catch my breath. "I don't want to talk about your doubts or anything bad tonight. I just want to be with you. Can you do that for me? Please."

Taking a deep breath, I swallow and wrap my arms around his neck, pulling him as close to me as I can. I love this man so much. He's my world and has been for ten years. This feeling I have right now, in his arms, him holding me as close as he can, is the best feeling in the world and I never want to lose it again.

Hemy places a few kisses on the top of my head before he reaches for the door and pushes it open.

"Hemy," I cry.

He places both hands on my face and looks at me with questioning eyes.

"I really have something important to tell you tomorrow. This can't wait much longer," I say nervously. "You might just hate me forever after I tell you. I'm so scared."

A small smile crosses his face before he playfully sucks in his lip ring and rubs his thumb under my eye. "Nothing could ever keep me from loving my world and you've been that for the last ten years." He helps me out of his lap and out of the truck before hopping out himself. "Let's go."

Once inside, Hemy runs a bubble bath and lights the candles while I brush my teeth, watching him in the mirror. I still can't get enough of him. I see him approaching me from behind, before I feel his arms wrap around me. I can feel the warmth of his breath kissing my neck.

I lean my neck back and moan as he teases me with his lip ring, running it up my neck and stopping under my ear. "Take your clothes off."

Turning around in his arms, I reach for the bottom of my dress and slowly lift it over my head, with Hemy's strong hands trailing up my skin behind it. His touch gives me instant goose bumps, hardening my nipples, and making my flesh tingle.

Nothing turns me on more than being naked for this man. The way he handles my body is beautiful and breathtaking. He may have a rough exterior, but once he lets you in, he's the best lover you could possibly have; although, this is the gentlest I have ever seen him. It only makes me love him more.

I toss my dress aside. Hemy reaches behind me with one hand and unclasps my bra, before kissing his way down my stomach while pushing down my panties and tossing them aside after I step out of them.

He's standing before me in just his boxer briefs, his muscles flexing as he looks me over. "Undress me, Onyx. This body is yours and yours alone. You'll never have to worry again. I promise."

His words cause me to clench at just the thought of all this beauty being mine. I hate sharing, especially when it comes to him. I never wanted to, but back then I didn't seem to have a choice.

Getting on my knees, I grip the top of his briefs in my hands and slowly peel them down his muscular body, watching as his cock springs free. Those piercings get me every time. I didn't think it was possible for Hemy to get any more beautiful, but somehow, he has. Everything about his body: his muscles, his tattoos, his piercings, even the way he moves leaves me breathless.

Once I toss his briefs aside, Hemy lifts me up and wraps my legs around his waist, me latching on as he holds me. "Remember what I said to you the last time we were in this tub?"

I nod my head and bite my bottom lip as Hemy steps into the tub and slowly lowers us into the water with me straddling his lap. I have to admit, there is nothing I want more than to have Hemy make love to me. I've wanted it for as long as I can remember and as scared as I am, I need this. I need it so bad.

Gently gripping my waist, he lifts me up before slowly setting me down on his erection, his lips pressed against my neck. We both moan as he eases into me, pushing inside of me as deep as he can fit. Our bodies are plastered together, the both of us holding on for dear life, and it feels so good, too good.

Kissing my neck, he whispers, "I love you." He pushes into me while bringing me down to meet his thrust, before whispering again, sending chills up my spine. "Let me hear you say it, Onyx."

He pushes in deeper and wraps me in his arms as tightly as he can. I hold on for dear life, wrapping my legs and arms around him, unable to get close enough. My love for this man is so strong right now that I can barely breathe. I can't hide it anymore. It hurts too much.

"I love you, Hemy." He quickens his thrusts, causing me to moan out and grip his hair. "I've never stopped. I can't. I love you so damn much."

He smiles against my lips before crushing his lips against mine and making love to me. Not the rough, crazy sex that I'm used to with him. No, him holding me tenderly and thrusting into me, our bodies both working as one. It's the most intimate moment I have ever shared with Hemy, and it breaks my heart to know that it will probably never happen again.

Tomorrow, I'm going to tear his world apart . . . and mine.

CHAPTER FOURTEEN

HEMY

WAKING UP TO ONYX IN my bed is the best thing that has happened to me in four years. Seeing her here, naked, and wrapped up in my arms is almost enough to make me forget all the bad shit in the world. Almost . . . but not quite. There is still something that's holding me down and as much as I still try to hide the pain, it's always there threatening to surface. I just hope she understands that and tries to be patient. I've grown a lot since four years ago, but I will never be one hundred percent whole.

She stirs in my arms, gripping me tighter as I kiss her on the top of the head. I've been awake for the last hour, but haven't wanted to move in fear of waking her. I'm afraid of what's to come today. She said she had something important to tell me. I have to be honest, it makes me wonder if maybe she has a child with someone that she is afraid to tell me about. I can't stand the thought of that. It kills me.

When I look back down at Onyx, she's looking up at me with a small smile. It makes my heart burst with happiness. Damn, I love this woman.

That smile is the best thing to ever happen to me.

"Morning," she whispers. "What time is it?"

I grip a handful of her hair and lean down to crush my lips against hers. She lets out a small moan before smiling against my lips. "It's noon," I respond. "I wanted to let you sleep."

She sits up with a yawn before reaching for her phone. "I should probably text Ash and let her know that I'm okay. She's probably wondering why I didn't come home last night."

Kissing her one more time, I stand up and reach for my briefs. "Alright. I'll go make us breakfast." I turn back to look at her and smile as she throws on one of my shirts. "Damn, you're sexy as hell in my shirt."

She places her hand on her hip and bites her bottom lip. "You can show me after breakfast."

"Fuck yeah," I growl, while backing away from her and turning into the hallway. Shit, that woman is going to be the death of me.

Opening the fridge, I pull out the eggs and bacon, setting them on the counter. Just as I'm about to reach in the cabinet for some pans, the front door opens. That could only be one person: fucking Stone.

"Don't you fucking knock, asswipe?" I grab the pans and set them on the stove. This idiot is just lucky that I'm in a good mood for once.

A few seconds later, Stone appears in the kitchen followed by Ash. My eyes linger on her for a moment as she gives me a worried look. There's something about the look in her eyes that seems oddly familiar.

"Is Onyx with you? I haven't heard from her since last night and I didn't know who to ask," she questions while looking around the kitchen. "I called Stone and he said she might be here. Is she?"

Pulling my eyes away, I rub my hands over my face fast and point down the hall just as Onyx appears.

"Okay, I sent her a text . . ." She looks up to see us all standing in the kitchen and freezes. Her eyes linger over to Ash and she turns ghostly white, all the color draining from her face. "Ash! What are you doing here?"

Ash walks past me and over to Onyx. "What the hell? I was worried sick about you. I'm here to make sure that you're okay."

Onyx leans her head back before turning to face the other direction and breathing heavily. "Shit! I can't do this anymore. I'm so sorry, guys. I'm so damn sorry."

My chest aches from her words. I don't understand why she's so worried about Ash coming here and why the hell she's apologizing to us. I walk toward the girls. "Talk, Onyx. What the hell is—"

I look up and my eyes meet the back of Ash's neck. My whole fucking world comes crashing down in front of me. I have to turn the other way and clench my hands together to keep from breaking something. "Fuck!" I crouch down and grip my hair in anger. This can't be happening. Please tell me Onyx has not been keeping this shit from me. "Onyx. What the fuck? You better start talking and now!"

She's hesitant for a moment, the whole room in a thick silence.

"Ash. I have something to tell you," she whispers. "I have something to tell both you and Hemy."

Taking a few deep breaths, I stand back up and turn around to face Onyx. I want to see her when she fucking crushes me and turns my world upside down. "Say it," I growl out. "Fucking say it, dammit."

She turns her head away as a tear rolls down her cheek. "God, this is so hard. I never meant to hurt anyone. I just wanted to keep you safe, Ash. Please understand that. I didn't want you to get hurt like I did. I didn't want to get your hopes up and then have your world crushed." She pauses as Ash gives her a confused look. "Back when I met you in that diner in Wisconsin and I saw that scar on the back of your neck, I had an idea of who you were."

Ash's eyes widen and her nostrils flare as she rubs a hand over the back of her neck. "What are you saying, Onyx? I don't like where this is going . . ."

Onyx looks over to face the both of us, her face wet with fresh tears. I always hated that look. It fucking hurts. "As soon as you told me you were adopted, I knew you were Hemy's sister. I knew you were Sage. I'm so damn sorry. You're probably going to hate me forever but I did it for a good reason. It's just too bad it's going to hurt us all in the end," she cries.

Ash lets out a soft breath before turning to face me. Her eyes look pained as she takes me in and shakes her head. My heart fucking hurts as I watch her; my baby sister and she's standing right in front of me.

"That makes no sense. My brother's name was Tyler. His name wasn't Hemy." She looks up at my hair. "And his hair was lighter." She swallows and looks into my eyes. "Those eyes . . ." She turns away. "Why are you messing with me? Why are you trying to hurt me? Please stop this."

Out of instinct, I step up beside Sage and touch her scar just like I used to when we were kids. Her bottom lip quivers just like in the past and she sucks in a burst of air. It's taking everything in me right now not to break down into tears. I've searched for ten years; ten fucking years, and now here she is, but on top of it Onyx knew and kept it from me. How could she keep something like this from me? Fuck!

"It's the truth, Sage. I can't believe this is happening." I pause to catch my breath and pull my hand away. "She's telling the truth. You were too young to remember, but I went by my middle name when we were growing up. Dad hated Mom for naming me Hemy so everyone started calling me Tyler. It's the only thing you knew me by. That piece of shit. Fuck!" I turn around and punch the wall. "I couldn't fucking find you. I've searched for ten years. I'm so sorry." My voice cracks as I attempt to keep my composure. It's proving to be harder than I thought and all I want to do is ruin my parents and then break down.

Sage lets out a strangled cry before falling down to her knees and covering her face. "This can't be happening. I don't . . ." She sucks in a breath. "I don't know what to say. I've wondered about you my whole life." She shakes her head and cries harder. "Tyler . . ."

Falling down on my knees next to her, I pull her into my arms and press her face into my shoulder as she cries. Holding her next to me makes me want to bawl like a baby, but I fight it. It's so damn hard. I let a few tears fall as the anger and relief floods through me. I'm relieved to have Sage in my life, but angry as hell that Onyx would do this to me when she knows how badly I've been hurting.

I look up to the sound of Stone's voice. "Holy shit. I'm going to go and give you all some time. I don't need to be here for this. Sorry, man."

I nod my head and pull Sage closer as she wraps her arms around me, her whole body a shaking mess. "I'm never letting you out of my damn sight again." She lets out something between a cry and a laugh and I can't help but smile. "I mean that, Sage. Not a day has gone by that I haven't thought about you. I love you so much."

Her grip on me tightens, but she doesn't say a word. She doesn't have to. It may take her a while to remember me as much as I remember her and that's okay. I'll give her as much time as she needs, but she's not leaving Chicago. Her home is with me, like it should have been over ten years ago.

After what seems like a lifetime, Sage pulls away and looks at my face.

She lets one last tear roll down her face before reaching for my hair. "This hair," she says with a laugh. "I think my big brother needs a haircut."

I let out a small laugh and help her up to her feet. I still can't believe she is here and standing in my house. The feeling is so surreal.

We both stand here for a moment, taking each other in with smiles before turning to find Onyx pacing around the living room. She's biting her nails and shaking as the tears pour out.

As much as I want to hold her and tell her that it's okay, it really isn't. She just made the worst mistake of her life and it's going to take a while for me to get over this. It doesn't matter what her reasoning is. She hurt me, knowing that she was, and in the worst way possible.

"I'm sorry. I'm so sorry. That's all I can say. You don't think I wanted to tell you? I did. Trust me, I did." Onyx walks over to us and looks between the both of us. "I love you both so much," she cries. "I never meant to hurt anyone, but you have to understand that Hemy is a different person than the one I knew years ago. I couldn't put you through what I had to go through. That's all I can say. I was going to tell you as soon as I knew things were different for real this time." She sucks in a breath and walks past us. "I'm sorry."

"I don't know what to fucking say," I seethe. "I trusted you."

She swallows hard and fights back more tears. "I'm going, just please don't hate me. I can't survive knowing you hate me."

Exhaling, I watch as Onyx walks down the hall and disappears into my bedroom. I'm so fucking mad right now that if I open my mouth again I will probably say something I will regret forever.

So . . . I just watch as she walks away . . . again.

CHAPTER FIFTEEN

HEMY

IT'S BEEN THREE WEEKS SINCE I found out Ash was really Sage and I watched as Onyx walked out of my life again. Not a second has gone by that I haven't thought of her and missed the shit out of her. I have wanted to call her so many times and tell her I forgive her and I understand why she did it, but the pain is still too fresh. As far as I know, she has known about Sage for over a year, over a fucking year. How am I just supposed to forget about that?

A part of me knows that she didn't find me right away because she was scared of getting hurt again and didn't know if she'd be able to handle being around me without losing control, but it hurts like hell. I could have had Sage back in my life that whole time. I just can't get over that as much as I want to.

Everything has changed in the last few weeks and besides not having Onyx in my life, things have been good. Sage has been staying with me and

I spend most of my time at Mitch's shop instead of at the club. I've told the boys I will stay on for two days a week until they can find someone else to take over. After that, I will stay and bartend. I guess I'm pulling a Slade.

It didn't take long for me and Sage to get comfortable with each other again and we have actually been spending a lot of time together talking about our childhood; only the good stuff though, I'm not reminding her of the all the fucked up shit our parents did to us. She doesn't deserve that and I won't put her through it.

I've been pacing around my living room with a beer in my hand for the last three hours, trying to drown out the noise in my head. Nothing has been working. "Shit!"

I'm just pulling out another beer when I hear the front door open, so I pull out three beers instead. Sage and Stone have been spending a lot of time together and I need to keep my eye on that slick motherfucker. I won't hesitate to hand him his ass.

"Yo!" Stone calls out while stepping into the kitchen, instantly spotting the three bottles of beer with a grin. "This is why I love you so much, man. Always looking out when a motherfucker is thirsty."

I slap him upside the back of the head as he reaches for a beer and pops the top. "Where's Sage?"

He lets out a sigh and quickly takes a drink of his beer. He's hesitant for a moment before he replies. "With Onyx. They've been talking a lot. She's meeting me here in twenty." He takes another drink of beer before setting it down and focusing his attention on me. "That girl loves you, man. I know what she did hurt you, but you have to look at it from her point of view too, man."

I take a gulp of my beer and clench my jaw. "Keep talking." Maybe I need this.

"Alright then. The truth hurts, but . . . from what I've heard, you had a lot of fucking issues. You were never really here." He points to his head and looks me in the eyes. "You can't expect her to risk hurting someone she cares about by bringing them into your sick fucked up world. I know you're not like that anymore, but for someone that experienced it every day for years, it's a little harder to convince. You ripped that girl's heart out and stomped on it and she still brought your sister back in hopes that you would be able to meet her one day. She just wanted to make sure the time was right for all of you; not just her, or you, but all three of you. You can't be mad at that, man. That's a good ass woman."

I close my eyes and run my hands through my hair, lost in thought. He's fucking right and hearing someone say it out loud really opens my eyes. She was there for me every fucking time I needed someone.

"You don't have to fucking tell me. She's the best woman I've ever known." I pause to let out a sigh. "I'll never forget that shit."

She's always done what she felt was best. This isn't any different. If I would have gotten Sage back while I was high out of my mind and always fucked up, then I would have probably lost her for good, just like everyone else; her and Onyx. Maybe I can't blame Onyx for being as cautious as she was. Maybe, I should be blaming myself and thanking Onyx. I always was the one to fuck shit up. Still am.

"I fucked up real bad, man. I'm not proud of the things I did one bit. I had a lot of shit I was dealing with and I couldn't handle it without getting out of my head." I open my eyes and grip onto the counter, realizing that I'm the one that fucked up once again. "I need to go find her. Fuck, I can't live without her. I've loved her since the day she attacked me in the alley with a hug. I fell in love with that girl and it took me what seems like an eternity to figure that out. It might be too late now. Fuck me!"

Gripping my shoulder, Stone nods in understanding. "Better late than never, asshole," he says jokingly. "Never *too late,* not when you have the kind of love you two have. I have heard it all, man. Now, I'm no mushy pussy or anything, but it's real, man. Even I can see that."

Shaking off Stone's grip, I pace around the kitchen, trying to get my thoughts in check. I really can't fuck this shit up again. At some point I'm going to be out of chances. No one gives an unlimited supply. I need to let things go and chase after what makes me happy. That has always been her. Always will be.

"I need to go." I rush past Stone and through the living room, slipping on my leather jacket. "Tell me where she lives."

He hesitates.

"Now dammit!"

"Uhh . . ." He closes his eyes in thought for a moment. "1623 Spring Drive." I open the door and get ready to walk out. "Dude, you want me to go with?" he asks.

I turn back around. "Nah. I need to do this alone." I give him a nod. "Thanks, man." Then, I turn around and rush out the door, jumping in my truck.

I'm about two blocks away from Onyx's street when it starts pouring outside. It's coming down so hard that it's making it hard to see out the window. "Fuck! Please be here." I pull up in front of the house and jump out, leaving my truck running. I don't want to waste anymore time being away from her. I can't do it.

I run up to the porch and reach for the handle, but it's locked, so I knock loudly, hoping that Onyx will answer. If it were unlocked then she wouldn't have much of a choice.

A few seconds later the door opens to Sage. She steps out, holding her car keys. "Hey. What are you doing here?" She sounds a little panicked as she looks around. "I'm sorry—"

"It's fine," I cut her off. I don't have time for this right now. "Where is she?"

She shuts the door behind her and holds her hand up in an unsuccessful attempt to block the rain. "I don't know. We were talking and then she just took off on her motorcycle like twenty minutes ago. She seemed upset and in a hurry."

Dammit! I hope she's not caught out in this downpour.

"Fuck!" I punch the porch railing and fist my hair. "I'm going to find her. Where would she be at?"

"I don't know. Maybe at *Vixens*. She didn't say . . . or maybe at Jade's."

"Alright. I have to go." I grab her head and quickly kiss her on the forehead. "Love you."

"Love you too, Hemy," she screams after me as I run over to my truck and hop in.

Riding around, I start to panic at the thought of Onyx out riding in this weather. Two wheels on slick roadways doesn't mix. I would never forgive myself if something happened to her.

I pull up to *Vixens* and drive around the whole parking lot in search of my old motorcycle. My heart sinks when I don't spot it anywhere. "Dammit, Onyx! Fuck, you better be at Jade's."

The rain doesn't let up any as I pull back out onto the street and head over to Jade's house. I pull up in front of the house that changed my life.

If it weren't for Jade's birthday party, then who knows when I would have seen Onyx again.

I notice immediately when I pull up that the motorcycle is nowhere to be seen, but I jump out anyway and run through the rain to the door. I knock as hard as I can, losing every bit of patience I have left.

As soon as the door swings open, I rush inside and look around. "Is Onyx here?"

Jade gives me a confused look. "No. What the hell is going on?" She watches me as I run my hand down the front of my face, wiping the rain off. "I haven't talked to her all day."

"Shit!" Without saying another word, I rush back outside and to my truck. Reaching in my pocket, I search for my phone, but come up empty. I must have left it on the kitchen counter at home. "Of fucking course!" I slam my fist into the horn before gripping the steering wheel and letting out an agitated breath. There's only one last place to check and this is a long shot.

Back when we dated, she would surprise me by showing up at Mitch's shop when I was working. She always loved watching me work and I loved having her watch. It was our place. We both made a lot of memories there.

Taking a chance, I head over toward Mitch's shop, looking around for signs of her out on the street, but come up empty. It's already past nine so the shop is closed. Mitch would have left at least an hour ago. That's another reason I have a feeling she's not there either, but I refuse to go home until I look.

When I pull up to the shop, I quickly park and jump out. I look around me, but don't see the bike anywhere. Jogging, I turn around the corner of the building and freeze when I see Onyx standing there in the rain, leaning against the building. She's soaked and more beautiful than if she were dolled up to perfection. The air gets sucked from my lungs at the sight of her and for this moment, I feel more alive than I have in years.

She pushes away from the building and looks at me. "I've been waiting for you," she whispers. One sentence and my heart feels like it's about to burst at the seam.

Well, she'll never have to wait again. That is a promise. . .

CHAPTER SIXTEEN

ONYX

KEEPING SAGE FROM HEMY WAS the hardest thing I've ever had to do. I just wish he would understand that I did it for Sage, because I love her like a sister myself and was only thinking of her best interests. I could never hurt her in any way. As much as I love Hemy, I had to think of Sage too. Hemy may hate me forever, but I did what I felt I had to do, even though I knew it would end up with him hating me in the end.

I just hope he'll give me a chance to explain, because I don't want to leave here without him. I never want to be without him again. I've lived day after day without him, years on end, and I can't do it anymore.

I've been here for the last half hour or so thinking about us; thinking of all the time we have missed out on and it hurts my heart so bad knowing that I left him and let him down. It kills me. I was scared and young back then. I didn't know what else to do but remove myself from the situation. I should have stuck around and tried to get him help, but I was just a kid trying to deal with something bigger than myself.

I walk closer to Hemy as he stands there in shock and relief, just looking me over as if he can't believe that I'm here. "I was hoping you would come here. I'm so sorry. I wish I could take back what I did, but I can't. You hate me and I don't blame you."

Stepping closer to me, Hemy runs his hands through my wet hair before pressing his forehead to mine, something he always did. "You're wrong," he whispers. "What if I told you I could never hate you, no matter what you do? What if I told you I have loved you since day one, but was too afraid to say it?"

I look up into his eyes and cup his face in my hands. Looking at him makes it hard for me to breathe. The pain I put him through kills me. "How could you even say that, Hemy?" I can't hold my emotions back anymore. Being here in his embrace makes me lose all composure. The tears rush out as I wrap one arm around his neck and hold on for dear life. "I hurt you. I walked out on you when you needed me the most. I never stopped loving you. I thought about you every day and not one day went by that I didn't fear for your life. I was so scared."

"I know," he breathes. He rubs both his thumbs under my eyes, wiping the smeared mascara, before cupping my face and hovering his lips above mine. "I was a fool for the way I acted and I should have done the right thing by you. I should have been the one to let you go. I hurt you so damn bad and I'll never forgive myself for what I put you through. You did the right thing. You had to for the both of us, because I was too weak. Watching you walk out of my life and waking up alone is what woke me up. I realized that you were more important than the drugs. No high is better than the high I experience when I'm with you. I'm a different person and I have you to thank for it. Don't ever question what you had to do. Do you hear me?"

His warm breath kisses my lips as he presses his body closer to mine and waits for me to nod. "Hemy," I manage to get out. "I love you so fucking much. I'll never—"

Hemy presses his lips against mine, cutting me off. My body feels weak in his arms as he pulls me as close as possible, kissing me with so much passion that the tears start falling for a whole different reason. I love this man with all my heart and after all that we have been through, I know he feels the same way.

Pulling away from the kiss, Hemy searches my eyes before kissing my tears. "I love you more than life itself. I promise to never hurt you again. All I want is to be with you. I've never wanted anything else besides having

Sage back in my life. I have Sage now," he pauses to give me a deep look, his eyes glassing over, "Let me have you. That's all I ask. I need both my girls."

Looking into his eyes makes me weak in the knees. There is so much promise behind them that I know being with him would be different this time. I'm just not sure I can get over me hurting him and Sage. It's myself that I'm angry with now, not him. I'm mad at myself for leaving.

"Are you sure you want me?" I ask, my heart pounding.

He kisses me softly before pulling away and smiling. "More than life itself."

We both stand here in the rain just looking each other in the eyes before Hemy sucks in his lip ring and smirks. "Stay here with me tonight. Do you remember those nights?"

I let out a little laugh and nod my head. "How could I forget, Hemy? I can't even count how many people's trucks we had sex in the back of."

"Twenty-three," Hemy says with a grin.

I slap his arm. "You kept count?"

He laughs and picks me up, throwing me over his shoulder. "Fuck yeah. Those were twenty-three of the best nights of my life." He bites down into my ass, making me squirm as he pulls out a key and unlocks the door. "I counted a lot of our good memories. Now, tonight will be number one that I undress you out of those wet clothes, put you in my shirt and take care of my future wife. Promise me you'll be mine, forever. Say it. Let me hear you say it."

All the breath leaves my lungs hearing those words leave his lips. I want to cry, but I don't. All I want to do is be close to Hemy and let him back in. No holding back this time.

"I'm yours. Forever," I whisper.

"I've been waiting four years to hear those words," he breathes as he walks us through the dark garage, pulls down the back of a truck bed and carefully sets me down.

He doesn't hesitate undressing himself from his jacket and shirt before pulling off my wet clothes and replacing them with his dry shirt.

He holds me close to him, whispering in my ear and rubbing the back of my head. Here, right now. I feel safe. I feel loved. This is the feeling I want for the rest of my life and can't live without.

It's him and it always has been. Tonight I'm making a promise to never let him go again.

The rest of my life starts tonight . . .

CHAPTER SEVENTEEN

HEMY

THREE WEEK LATER . . .

WE'RE ALL SITTING AROUND IN *Fortune*—a normal bar, eating dinner and having a few drinks. The whole crew is here: Slade, Aspen, Cale, Stone, Sage, Onyx, and me. It's the first time we have all gotten together since me and Onyx worked things out. I have to admit it feels good.

It took a bit of convincing, but I finally got Onyx to move in with me. I knew she would eventually cave in. The only downfall to that is that it left Sage needing a new roommate. As you can guess, Stone was quick to jump to fill that spot. I'm still keeping my eyes on that slick fucker, but he's grown on me. Plus, he seems to be crazy about her and she deserves someone to treat her the way she should have been all along.

"Dude!" I feel something hit me upside the back of my head. I pull away from kissing Onyx to look over my shoulder. Slade flicks a chicken wing at me. "Stop that shit. You're making me want to take Aspen home and fuck her. My cock does not appreciate you right now." Aspen elbows him in the side and laughs. "What?" he questions with a laugh.

"You and your dirty mouth." Aspen grins.

Slade throws his hands up. "My bad." He bends down and kisses her neck before biting it. "You can just punish me later."

"Alright, dicks," Cale says annoyed. "You all can stop your shit now. You're making me sick. I'm trying to eat."

"Shut up and go get your dick sucked," I say teasingly, causing Cale to toss a fry at my head. What's with the fucking flying food?

Onyx grips my thigh from under the table, causing me to instantly go hard. She always does it, letting me know what she wants. She knows exactly what she's doing to me and as soon as I get her alone, she's getting . . . fucked, and hard.

Aspen smiles over at Cale before taking a sip of her beer. "So . . . Riley gets home next week."

Cale turns white in the face, but quickly tries to shake it off. "Yeah? That's nice," he says, nonchalantly. "Next week, already?"

Aspen laughs and sets her beer down. "Already? It's been like six years since she moved away to Mexico."

I can't even believe how pale and nervous Cale looks. He definitely has it bad for this Riley chick. Maybe he'll man up and finally give his dick up. I knew he was holding back for a reason.

I take a bite of my steak and notice Stone getting a little cozy with my sister at the end of the table. I get ready to say something, but Onyx leans into my ear, distracting me.

"I love you, baby." She places her hand on mine and I smile down at the diamond on her left finger. Knowing that I placed it there makes me the happiest man on earth.

When I proposed to her in the hot tub last week, I about died when she broke down in tears and screamed, *yes*. I'll never forget that feeling for the rest of my life. I'm not going to lie, I shed a few tears myself. What can I say? I've waited for a lifetime to have her back in my arms and I'm never letting go. She's my everything. I love her and I love this new life with her. I can't be any happier.

I bite my lip when I realize Onyx distracted me on purpose. I know this now by her little fit of laughter. She saw me eyeing Stone and Sage down. She's good. Too good.

When I go to focus my attention on Sage and Stone again; Sage is gone and Stone is chatting with Aspen. That lucky fucker.

I feel a small arm wrap around my neck, distracting me, before Sage rests her head on the top of mine and laughs. "Stop being such a big brother." She squeezes my neck and both girls laugh as Onyx pinches my cheek. "I love you, but seriously . . . don't make me kick your ass. I know what I'm doing with Stone. Okay?"

I look over at Stone and see the look in his eyes as he focuses his attention on Sage as if she's the only woman in the room. I have to respect that. That's the same way I look at Onyx. I need to give Sage the space she needs. I keep forgetting she's a grown woman now.

"Okay," I mumble. "I trust you." She kisses my head and rushes over to sit in Stone's lap, wrapping her arms around his neck. I guess they make a nice couple.

Looking around me, I realize this is the happiest I have ever been in my life. This is where I belong. Where we all belong. This is my family. Family isn't always bound by blood. It's so much more than that. This is it, and it's what I've been missing all along.

I'm ready to spend the rest of my life making my family and future wife happy. This is my happy ending . . .

CALE

WALK OF SHAME : BOOK 3

PROLOGUE

CALE

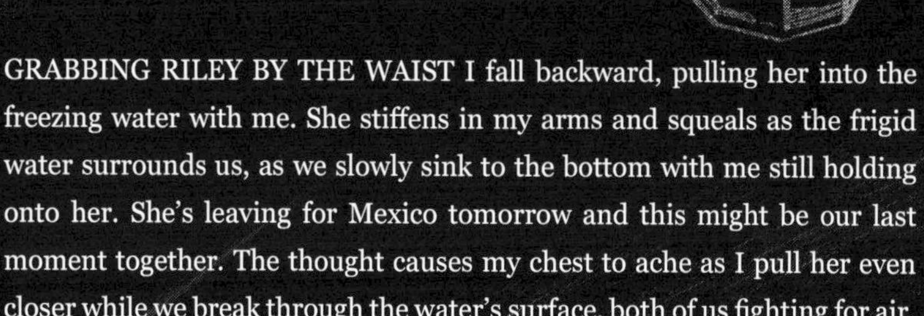

SIX YEARS AGO . . .

GRABBING RILEY BY THE WAIST I fall backward, pulling her into the freezing water with me. She stiffens in my arms and squeals as the frigid water surrounds us, as we slowly sink to the bottom with me still holding onto her. She's leaving for Mexico tomorrow and this might be our last moment together. The thought causes my chest to ache as I pull her even closer while we break through the water's surface, both of us fighting for air.

She sucks in a deep breath before releasing it and screaming, "CALE!" Turning around in my arms, she presses her hands against my chest and shoves me, while trying to keep her teeth from chattering. "The water is free... eezing."

Her body is shaking violently from the cold, so I use this as an excuse to keep her warm. I've had feelings for Riley for as long as I can remember, but timing has never seemed to be on our side. If I can't have her... then I'll wait. She means more to me than any woman ever could, and I have a plan to show her that—a promise that I made to myself. I just don't know how to tell her I want her without ruining our friendship, but I'll show her when the time is right.

Placing one arm behind her head, I pull her body against my chest and then wrap both of her legs around my waist as I back up against the wall of the pool to support her. "I've got you, Rile." I brush her wet, brown hair out of her face and smile as I reach out and touch her quivering bottom lip. I have to admit, she's adorable while freezing her ass off. I should feel bad for torturing her, but I don't. Not really. I know she loves me teasing her. "If you don't stop shaking that lip... I'm going to bite it."

I see a hint of a smile, before she punches my chest and laughs. "You can be such a dick sometimes, Cale."

"I know," I admit. "That's why you love me so much, Riley Raines."

All laughter and playfulness seems to stop as our eyes meet. It looks as if she wants to say something, but stops right as her mouth opens to speak. She looks guilty and I hate that look.

"What, Riley?" I pull her chin up as she looks away. "Say it," I whisper. "You know you can tell me anything."

She closes her eyes for a moment before shaking her head and biting her bottom lip. She looks hurt, but I have a feeling she won't give me the info I'm seeking. "It's nothing," she says softly. "It's just that... I'm going to miss you. That's all." She forces a smile and tugs on the ends of my hair playfully. "Don't look so sad, you big stud you. You'll do fine without me and forget about me in no time." She turns her head, hiding her eyes from my view.

"Not true. Don't *ever* say that." My heart is beating so hard against her chest that I wouldn't be surprised if she can tell what she does to me. She's the only girl that makes my heart race like this and hearing those words out of her mouth causes it to ache like nothing else. How can she not realize how much I'm truly going to miss the shit out of her? "It's kind of hard not to be sad."

I make my best pouty face, trying to make her feel bad. This face always seems to work on her. "I have to wait for you to come home, all alone, so I can give you my virginity."

She looks stunned for a moment before she bursts out in laughter and squirms her way out of my arms. Her laugh is so beautiful. "You jerk. You almost made me feel bad for you for a minute... and we both know you're not a virgin. Stop kidding around." She attempts to pull herself out of the pool, but I grab her waist, stopping her.

"Where are you going?"

She looks down at me, water dripping down her beautiful curvy body. I want so much to just take her right here and give her all of me, but time is not on my side at the moment; it never seems to be when it comes to Riley. "It's getting late. I told my mom I'd be home early so I can finish packing."

"Stay," I whisper, pulling her back into the pool with me. My hands cup her face and I pull her so close that our lips are almost touching. "Don't leave me here."

"What?" She shakes her head and kisses me on the cheek, her lips lingering for a moment. "I can't. My grandma needs me. I have to go, Cale. I have no choice."

I watch as she gets out of the pool and grabs my dry shirt, snuggling against it to keep warm, before pulling it over her head. I can't be sure, but it looks as if she sniffed it. I love that.

"I'm keeping this by the way." She smiles with a sad look in her eyes. "I'll be back. I promise. Time will fly by. Just watch." Her voice comes out sad and hesitant, because she and I both know that's not true. Time will definitely be a bitch while she's gone, and I'm sure it's going to feel like a lifetime without seeing her smile or hearing her beautiful laugh.

I nod my head and turn away from her as she starts walking away. I can't stand to watch her walk out of my life. It hurts more now that it's actually happening, especially knowing that there's nothing I can do to stop it, but... I need her to know one thing before she leaves. One thing that I hope will mean something to her in the future.

"I *am* still a virgin by the way," I say, wanting her to know I wasn't lying about that. I would never lie to Riley. I can't.

Her footsteps stop, before I hear a small, but painful laugh. "Yeah, me too," she says. She whispers something afterward, but I miss it, too scared to look her way. I hear her footsteps in the grass as she starts walking again and it hurts so bad that I can't breathe.

By the time I get the courage to turn around she's gone... out of my life and soon she'll be out of Chicago. She's the one and only girl I have ever loved and I never even got the chance to tell her.

CHAPTER ONE

CALE

WALK OF SHAME IS FULL of people partying and getting wasted beyond sense, but I just can't seem to get my head into being here.

My mind has been on one thing and one thing only: Riley. Ever since Aspen blurted out that Riley would be home soon, my mind has been stuck on her. I've been replaying our last moment together, before she left, and it almost feels as if it were yesterday. The ache is still there, weighing on my chest.

We haven't spoken in over two years now, and even I know that I'm not over her. I'm not sure that I ever will be, and knowing that she's coming home reminds me of the promise I kept to myself six years ago, when I was still just a stupid teen.

We kept in contact for the first four years, talking on the phone at least once a week, late into the night, until she mentioned that she'd met someone that was interested in her. It hurt like hell, but knowing that she wouldn't be back home for a while I realized that I needed to let her live while she was there. There was no way I was going to hold her back by breaking down like a pussy and telling her how much I loved her. Asking her to wait for me as I have planned on waiting for her would be selfish.

Eventually, the calls slowed down until we were at the point that we barely talked but once every few months. Then... they ended all together. I think it was necessary in order for us both to go on with our lives, because every time we talked I could hear the ache and longing in her voice. I had to make it easier for *her* to live in hopes that it would make it easier for me.

Knowing that she'll be back any day now, possibly even now, has me unable to function properly.

I've been holding back from fucking other women, only giving them oral pleasure, because to me she's more important than just a meaningless lay. I thought that after we stopped calling each other every week that I would just forget about my promise to wait, but I never did. It's always been in the back of mind, fucking with me and making it impossible for me to take a woman to bed and give myself to her. I want her to find peace in knowing that when my cock enters her that she's the only woman I've been inside of and that I plan on pleasuring her over and over again until she can no longer handle me. I won't be able to stop and I sure as hell don't have any plans to.

Standing up straight, I run my hands through my hair while letting out a frustrated breath, bringing myself back to reality. I'm not much of a drinker, but right now... I feel like downing a bottle of whiskey.

Trying to get my head back into my performance, I twist both of my arms into the chain hanging above my head and thrust to the slow rhythm, while letting my unbuttoned jeans fall lower and lower with each movement. The screaming of the crowd causes me to put on a fake smile and get into the moment as much as I will get, enough to at least finish my last performance of the night.

I'm close to the edge of the stage. Girls are reaching out to grope me as I give them a show. Sweat is rolling down my body, dripping onto the stage at my feet as I continue pretending that I'm fucking every single girl in this room.

That's what they all want. That's *all* they ever want. These girls are here because they want to feel as if I want them, so... that's what I make them believe. As fucked up as it sounds, it sends them home happy. That's what matters here at *Walk of Shame*.

"Right here! Cale!"

I open my eyes and bring them down to meet the brunette below me that is eagerly waving a wad of cash above her head. Releasing the chains, I walk to the edge of the stage, grab onto the back of her head, and grind my crotch into her face before thrusting repeatedly. In no time my jeans are on the floor and I'm standing in nothing but my white boxer briefs.

I grind slow and hard, making her reach around and shove her cash into the back of my boxer briefs, just above my ass crack. Her hands explore my ass, so I reach behind me and discretely pull them away before jumping off the stage.

The screaming of the women gets significantly louder as soon as my feet hit the main level. It's almost the end of my performance, and tonight I'm ending it with a little something special.

Making my way through the crowd I stop in front of the redhead that is hopefully going to help clear my head later. Straddling her lap, I sway my hips while running her hands up my bare chest, before pushing them down my body and stopping at the waist of my briefs.

I hear a little gasp escape her lips as I release her hands, letting her explore while I grind on her as if I were fucking her deep and hard.

Smirking, I stand up from her chair before turning the other way and doing a quick handstand so that my cock is in her face. I begin to thrust my hips, swaying them around in a circle as the music speeds up, ending my performance.

All the women go wild as I grind my hips one more time and end it with a thrust to her face, before maneuvering my way back to my feet. Looking down at the ground, I focus on catching my breath, noticing all the cash surrounding me. Even with my head fucked up and lost somewhere else, my body still knows exactly what to do.

Walking away, I head toward the back room to change, as Kash, the new kid, cleans up my stash of money. He showed up about a week ago asking for a job, so Lynx, the new owner, decided to make him our grunt for a few weeks first just to mess with him.

I'm standing here naked, just pulling a fresh pair of jeans on when I hear Kash step into the room and slap the pile of bills onto the table.

"Holy shit, dude." He slaps the money down a few more times and grins as I button my jeans and throw my white tee on. "Those girls are fucking insane. I've never seen such horny women in my life. This is a dream job. I swear my cock got grabbed at least five times just now."

Grabbing my tip money from Kash I grin and slap five twenties down into the palm of his hand. He hasn't seen shit yet. "Yeah, well you better be prepared to work that stage next week, rookie. You gotta learn to shake that cock of yours first. You've got some major shoes to fill."

He nods while stuffing the cash into his back pocket. "I already know how to work it, man. No worries."

"Alright, man." I slap his back. "I'm getting out of here. I'll see ya later."

"See ya," I hear him say right as I push my way back out into the crowd of women. It only takes me a few seconds to spot the sexy little redhead from earlier. She's watching me as if she's been waiting for me to come back out.

The cute little brunette that I was grinding on earlier is with her, sipping on her drink as they both eye fuck me all the way up to the bar.

Sarah shakes her head and slides a draft beer across the bar top. "Damn, Cale. I don't think I've ever seen you work it like that on the stage." She wipes her forehead off and waves her hand as if slinging sweat off of it. "So good tonight, baby."

I give her a half smile and reach for the frosty glass. "I have a lot on my mind tonight. I guess I was zoning out." I tip back the glass and let the refreshing liquid cool me off. I'm still sweaty from the show and all my clothes are practically plastered to my wet body, irritating me.

"Yeah, well..." She tilts her head toward the right. "Those two girls definitely liked what you had going on tonight. It looks like they're about ready to jump you before you even get a chance to finish that beer off, babe." She rolls her eyes and dries off a glass. "Lucky dick. Those ladies are hot."

A few seconds later I feel a hand on each of my shoulders, before the brunette appears on my right and the redhead on my left. I don't even bother looking at them as I speak. "Perfect timing." I guzzle back my beer and toss down some cash for Sarah. "Later, Sarah."

Sarah just waves me off as she gets called over by a small group of women. Shoving my wallet back into my jeans, I turn and walk through the crowded bar, not surprised to hear the sound of heels clicking against the floor behind me.

Yes, I could use a very long blow job right now, but to be honest, I could also do without. These two women, even combined, could never measure up to the woman that I have waited six long years for. I'm not saying that I'd turn them down, just saying that maybe I won't be seeking out tonight.

As soon as I step outside and head for my truck, I hear one of the girls call my name, stopping me. Leaning against my truck, I exhale and look up, while dangling my keys around my finger.

The redhead pushes her hand against my chest as the brunette leans in and whispers in my ear, "Let us take care of you, Cale." She runs the tip of her tongue over my earlobe before speaking again. "Just relax and enjoy."

Leaning my head back, I close my eyes and take in a small breath as my jeans get pulled to my knees, and then I feel two small hands grip around my ready cock.

A pair of soft lips wrap around my head as a hand runs up and down my shaft, and I know right away that both women are sharing right now. I'm not selfish. It's big enough for the both of them and maybe right now... this distraction... is what I need, so I let them both take turns sucking me off right here in the parking lot until I blow my load all over both of their mouths.

Licking the remainder of cum off my dick, the redhead stands up and places her arms around my neck. "Let us take you home where we can show you a *real* good time. I promise you that it will be worth it."

"More than worth it," the brunette chimes in.

That offer would usually have any man falling to his knees, but not me. I've gone twenty-four years without it and I'm damn sure I can go another few weeks.

Trying my best not to be an ass, I take turns pressing my lips to both of their temples, before saying goodnight and hopping in my truck.

Once I pull up at the house, I realize that having my dick sucked hasn't done shit to clear my head. Riley Raines is coming home and I know without a single doubt that she's going to ruin me.

CHAPTER TWO

RILEY

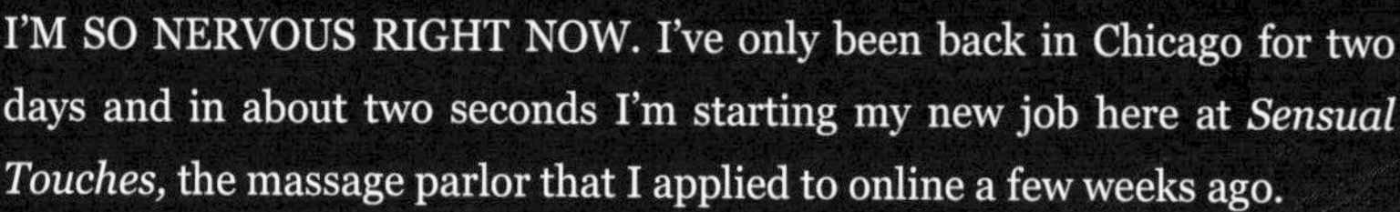

I'M SO NERVOUS RIGHT NOW. I've only been back in Chicago for two days and in about two seconds I'm starting my new job here at *Sensual Touches,* the massage parlor that I applied to online a few weeks ago.

No one knows that I'm back yet. I made sure to tell Aspen not to tell anyone until I'm ready. The only people that know are my family, and I plan on keeping it that way for a couple of weeks until things settle down and I can relax a bit. My heart is still hurting and my head is spinning out of control at the fact that Tyler and I are no longer a couple and that I have to get familiar with my surroundings again. When I made plans to move back home Tyler decided at the last minute that he didn't think he'd be up for the move... so he stayed behind.

I care about Tyler, but Chicago is where my heart is. Not to mention... it's where *he* is: Cale Kinley. As much as I've tried to convince myself seeing him again won't stir some crazy emotions inside of me, I know with everything in me that's not true. I'm not sure that I can handle seeing him while in this emotional state.

Shaking my head, I run my hands down my black, skinny jeans, wiping the sweat from my palms as I approach the door to the massage parlor. "It's no big deal, Riley. You've done this a million times before... just not here. You have magic fucking hands," I convince myself before stepping inside.

As soon as I enter the building I'm greeted by a woman that looks to be in her early twenties, with long, purple hair. She plasters on a smile and stands up from her chair, looking impatient. "Please tell me you're Riley Raines. Hailey hasn't shown up yet and we have two clients waiting. I need to get these two satisfied and hitting the road."

I nod my head as the nerves flow through me, causing butterflies to fill my stomach. "That's me," I say with a fake confidence that I don't feel at the moment. "Is there anything you need from me before I start?" I open my purse and start digging for my ID and paperwork. "Here's my—"

"No time for that, sweetness. Myles will deal with that when he gets in later. I don't get paid enough for that." She gives me an impatient look and starts shoving me down the hall. "I need you in room three. That's your room." She takes a deep breath and bites her bottom lip. "You're going to enjoy this one. *Please* put your hands all over him since I can't. Hailey is going to be pissed, but this will teach her a lesson for showing up late." She lets out a satisfied laugh while spinning on her heels. "Hurry before she gets here."

Lifting my eyebrows, I smile small and push open the door to room three, almost unable to breathe from the nerves. Without paying any attention to the waiting client, I quickly observe the room to find a chart hanging next to the door. I grab it quickly to prepare for his needs.

While searching for my supplies, I introduce myself, trying not to draw attention that I have no clue where anything is. "Sorry for the wait. My name is Riley and I'll be taking care of you today. Hailey is running a little behind and this is my first day here, so please be a little patient while I get everything ready."

Looking around the dimly lit room, I find the stereo and turn it on, letting the relaxing sounds fill the space to hide my erratic breathing as I try to stay calm. I've been at the same place for three years, and being somewhere new, with new clients, is a bit nerve-wracking; especially when you're getting rushed around by some chick that looks as if she wants to choke someone today.

After securing my apron filled with my lotions and oils, I turn to the table and my heart starts pounding like crazy in my chest as I see a body, barely covered by a small towel, just waiting to be touched by me. I swallow hard while letting my eyes roam over the stiff muscles of the tanned back on display. The top of the client's ass peeks out of the towel, displaying the roundest, firmest ass I have ever seen before... and the dimples in his back are making it hard for me to gain some much-needed confidence.

Doing a silly little shake in an attempt to shake my nerves off, I squirt some oil in my hands and slowly run my hands up the bottom of his back, being sure to make it feel as insanely good as I possibly can.

The feel of his muscled back beneath my fingers and the deep, undeniably sexy moan that escapes his throat almost has me turned on as I start to go lower, until I'm right above his ass.

"Go lower," the deep voice whispers. "Take the towel off."

I almost deny his request, when I remember that *Sensual Touches* is clothing optional. That's the *one* thing that almost kept me from applying, but comparing the pay that you get here versus the other options, I knew what my choice had to be.

"This is new to me," I whisper, before speaking up. "Let me know if you get uncomfortable and I'll replace it before you flip over on your back."

"That won't be an issue," he says huskily.

Keeping my moan to myself, I lower my hands down to his ass, removing the towel little by little as I continue to get lower. As soon as my hands reach the bottom of his ass, I remove the towel completely and hold back the gasp that fights to escape me.

Holy hotness...

Remembering that this was per his request, and that it's fully professional to be doing this here at *Sensual Touches,* I grip the back of his upper thighs and massage them while rubbing my thumbs over the bottom of his tight ass, enjoying every single moment of it.

In fact, I'm enjoying it so much that I almost feel guilty. Tyler and I have been broken up for less than a week, and here I am enjoying myself as I rub on another man's ass, listening closely for each moan that he will grace my ears with.

After spending a good, long, ten minutes on his ass itself, I focus my attention on the rest of his muscular body, mentally preparing myself for the rest of his gloriousness that I'll be seeing in the *flesh* as soon as I finish up on his backside.

Now I understand why that Hailey chick is going to be angry. Massaging this stud has to be the best part of her job here. How can you *not* enjoy this?

Pulling my hands away, I turn away to give him some privacy. "I'm ready for you to flip over, sir. Please let me know when you're ready."

"I'm always ready for you, Rile."

Fighting to catch my breath, I place my hand to my heart and slowly turn around to see that the naked stud whose ass I have been ogling over this whole time is Cale. Cale Kinley. My Cale Kinley, the one person that I've been so worried about seeing again and now here he is, naked and in front of me.

"Cale," I whisper. "Holy shit. I don't... I don't know what to say. Wow. It's you. I..."

Sitting up, he smiles and grabs my hand, pulling me closer to him as if it were old times again. "Get the hell over here, woman." Pulling me into his arms, he hugs me tightly against him, while running his nose up the side of my neck. "I've missed you so fucking bad, girl."

Feeling overwhelmed, my eyes water a little bit as I hold him as tightly as I can. A smile spreads across my face as we pull apart and check each other out. Luckily, he didn't ruin me completely and decided to cover his junk up. "You look just like you did the last time I saw you, except a hell of a lot stronger and even hotter. Holy hell, you have grown up, Cale. I didn't even recognize your voice. My Cale is a man now."

He grabs me by the hip and squeezes. "Yeah... I guess you can say I've grown quite a bit." He flexes his jaw as he checks me out, completely taking me all in. His striking green eyes almost melt me on the spot as I watch them. "All of me."

I find myself swallowing hard and slightly sweating as I try to figure out what exactly he could mean by *all of him*. I think I know the answer to that and I have to admit that it has me turned on completely.

"You look fucking beautiful, Riley." He bites his bottom lip and releases his grip on my hip, letting his hands brush over my ass, before he grips my upper thighs. "So damn beautiful."

Without even thinking, I reach out and grip the blond hair at the back of his neck. He wears it slightly shorter than he did six years ago, but still sexy as can be.

"I see you're still the same smooth talker," I say with laughter. "Good to know."

He grips my thighs tighter, pulling me closer to him. "And you're still the most beautiful woman I've ever laid eyes on."

Feeling myself come undone under his intense stare, I release his hair and reach for his hands, pulling them away from my thighs. "I've missed you, Cale." I watch him with a smile as his eyes follow my movements to my hands. I squirt a handful of oil into my palm.

His eyes take on a darkened look and he grabs my hands, placing them to his chest, and holding them there. "Why didn't you tell me you were back already?" He rubs his thumbs over my wrists, looking me dead in the eyes. "When did you get home?"

Letting out a small breath, I shake my head and begin rubbing my hands over his body while pushing him backward until he's lying flat on his back. "Only two days, Cale." I suck in a breath and try to hide the small moan as my hands explore every hard ridge of his chest and abs, attempting to continue his massage. God, this is torture right now. This is the kind of body that you only see in the movies. "I just wanted a week or so to get settled in first. No one knows that I'm back except for my family. You were going to be the next to know. I promise."

He smiles up at me and I can't help but notice the way my heart skips a beat. That smile - seeing it right now is a painful reminder of what I've been missing for the past six years. The ache in my chest almost causes me to lose my composure, wondering what all I've missed while being away.

The only thing I've heard over the years is that he works at a bar. I don't even know if he has a girlfriend. For some reason, I just couldn't allow myself to know that bit of information, so I made Aspen promise to never tell me. Well... more like I threatened to choke the life out of her through the phone.

Now standing here, touching him and seeing his beautiful smile, I can't help but want to know. Is he going home tonight to make love to some woman while she gets to put her hands on the places that I'm touching now? I don't want to know!

"Have dinner with me tonight."

A smile spreads over my face, unexpectedly from his request. It's so big that my face hurts, but I try my best to hide it. "Are you cooking me dinner, Chef Cale? If so, then I hope it's better than what I tasted the last time you attempted to cook for us," I tease, even though I'd eat dirt if it made him happy.

"Of course," he says confidently. "And it will taste damn good. I promise you the only things I'll put in your mouth are things I know will satisfy you completely and ruin you for anything else."

I swallow hard and try not to take that comment sexually, even though my body is taking it *that* way. "Alright," I agree. "I'm trusting you with my mouth, so you better not disappoint."

He lifts his eyebrows and I can't help but notice him harden beneath the towel, but I play it off as if I hadn't noticed. "You have no idea, Riley. You should be careful what you trust me with." Sitting up, he leans in and kisses me on the side of the mouth, his lips lingering for a few seconds too long. "I have an early shift at the bar today, but I'll get your number and address from Aspen."

"Alright." I smile. "I'll be here until six, but I'm free after that."

Nodding, Cale jumps up from the table, allowing his towel to drop as he reaches for his clothes to get dressed. I somehow manage to turn away before I get to see what I've been longing to see since we were in high school. I really hate myself right now.

I hear a small chuckle from Cale before his hands wrap around my waist and his lips press against my neck from behind. "Gotta go, baby. Be ready for me tonight."

Next thing I know, Cale is out the door, and I'm standing here fighting to catch my breath. "Baby..." I say softly. I have to admit I like being called that by Cale. That's definitely new.

Being back is going to be a bigger challenge than I thought...

CHAPTER THREE

CALE

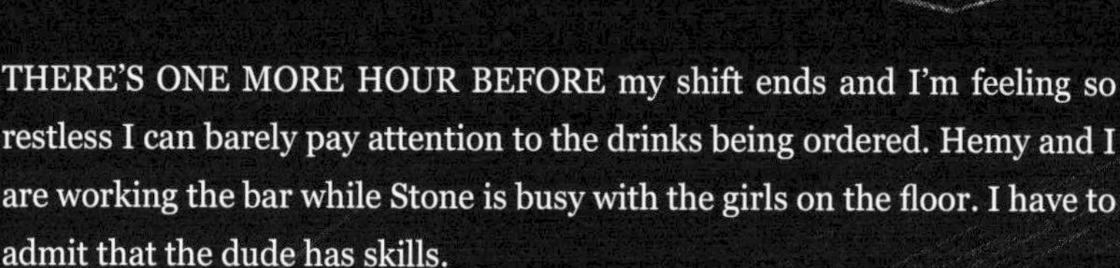

THERE'S ONE MORE HOUR BEFORE my shift ends and I'm feeling so restless I can barely pay attention to the drinks being ordered. Hemy and I are working the bar while Stone is busy with the girls on the floor. I have to admit that the dude has skills.

I wasn't sure if he'd be able to fill Slade's shoes, but I'm impressed at how crazy and out there he is with his abilities.

I look away from the crowd of crazy women, when I'm caught off guard with an elbow as it jabs me in the ribs. "What the shit?"

Turning beside me, I look up to see Hemy glaring at me. "What the fuck are you doing, staring off and shit? I'm working my dick off over here."

Ignoring his ass, I quickly snap out of it and focus on the steady flow of drinks that keep getting requested, trying my hardest to not think about Riley and how fucking fantastic it felt having her hands on my body. Truthfully, I wanted them *all* over, but I don't think she's ready for that quite yet, so I'm doing my best to respect her and take things slow. Well, as slowly as I can.

As soon as I get a free moment, I pull my phone out and send Slade a quick text, asking him to get Riley's number from Aspen. At first Slade texts back with a big FUCK YOU, before he sends another message about five minutes later, telling me he had to wrestle with Aspen to get her phone and that I owe his ass.

He's just lucky that he's my guy and that I know how much of an ass he is and still tolerate him. I have to admit that he's gotten about eighty percent better since meeting Aspen, so really, I owe *her*.

Leaning against the register, I send Riley a text, ignoring the screaming crowd for a moment. There's no way she's getting out of spending the night with me. I don't care if I have to throw her over my shoulder and handcuff her to me for the night. I've missed the shit out of her and tonight... she's mine.

Cale

Hey, baby. Where am I picking you up tonight? I hope you save room for dinner and dessert, because I'm ready to work magic with my hands...

My phone vibrates a few minutes later, causing me to turn away from the girl chatting my ear off at the bar. She's still talking as I read Riley's message.

Riley

Magic, huh? So you're that good? ;) Don't even answer that. I'll be the judge of that later. Pick me up at my mom's around seven. I'll be ready and waiting...

Damn girl... She has no idea what she's just started.

I adjust my cock and hope my boner will quickly go down. The last thing I need is something to set these women off. I barely make it through a shift as it is without getting attacked with a set of breasts in my face. I don't need anything slowing me down tonight.

"Are you free tonight?" Biting my bottom lip, I shove my phone in my pocket and shake my head at the girl in front of me, before letting her down as easily as I can.

"Sorry, beautiful, but I'm taken for the night." I slide a free drink across the bar as a look of disappointment takes over her face. "The drink is on me."

She smiles small and reaches for the drink, not doing much to hide her sour face. "Just let me know when you're free." With that, she turns and walks away, swaying her hips in the process. I know without a doubt that she's trying to lure me in, but that shit isn't working on me, especially when the woman that I've waited six years for is within my reach.

She's about to finally see how much I truly want her...

RILEY

CALE WILL BE OUTSIDE ANY minute, and for some reason that thought has me extremely nervous and sweaty. Why am I so nervous when this is the guy that I spent most of my teen years with? He's still the same guy, except... he's drop dead gorgeous and every inch of his body is covered in hard muscle that I want nothing more than to explore with my tongue.

This new desire stirs me up, making it hard for me to act normal and pretend that I don't crave to be with him. It seemed a lot easier six years ago when I saw him almost every day, but after being away from him for so long, seeing him just brings back all my old feelings on top of the ache that I felt when I could no longer spend my days with him.

I shake my head. "Doesn't matter, Riley," I whisper. "Just act normal." I rub my sweaty palms down the side of my black dress and take in a deep, calming breath. "He's still the same sweet Cale that wants nothing more than to be friends. Just friends..."

I hear a noise in the hallway that causes me to look up and walk toward my bedroom door. My parents went out to dinner after I told them that I had plans, so I've been here alone for the last thirty minutes.

"Aspen," I call out. "Is that you? I'm in my old bedroom."

I hurry into the hallway and slam into a hard body, almost causing me to stumble backward, but Cale catches me with a grin. His arm tightens around my waist as his smile broadens. "You look hot, Rile." He leans in and kisses me on the forehead, before pulling me straight up and back on my feet. "You ready to go?"

I tug on the end of my skirt, pulling it down, and then smile, as Cale looks me over with wide eyes, whistling softly. "I've missed you, Cale. You seriously have no idea." I laugh as he grabs my arm and spins me around as if checking me out. It's something he used to do to me when he would first see me for the day. I know he's doing it now to make me feel comfortable and I love him for it. It reminds me of how strong our friendship was and why I adored him so much.

"Let's go." He nods and places his hand on the small of my back, guiding me through the house. "I have dinner in the oven."

I step outside and watch him as he locks the door and closes it behind him. "Oh really?" I smile big at the thought of Cale cooking. I thought he was only kidding. "You're really cooking us dinner?"

He wraps his arm around my waist and pulls me against him as we walk to his truck. "Hell yes I am. I owe you after all those times you cooked for me while we were hanging out at your house. At my house, I will always cook you dinner, especially if it keeps you coming back for more." He winks and helps me into his truck.

He refuses to tell me what's for dinner on the way over to his house, even though I made it a point to ask him every few minutes, just to see if he'd cave. I almost forgot just how strong Cale's willpower is. He's pretty set once he makes his mind up. He's always been the strongest person that I know and I admire him for that, even though it sometimes has the power to annoy the shit out of me.

He jogs over and helps me out of his truck once we pull up to his house. "You'll be spending a lot of time here, Rile, so I hope you like it just as much as I do." I laugh and he raises a brow in question. "What? You don't believe me?"

"What makes you think that I'll like you as much as I used to?"

He pushes the door open and pushes up behind me, guiding my body with his into the house. His lips brush my ear. "I have a pretty good feeling," he whispers. "You'll like me even more..."

Walking around me, he throws his keys onto the kitchen island and walks over to the oven with a confidence that makes me melt. "Make yourself at home, because you're spending the night. We're having a movie night and I'll take you home before eight in the morning to change for work."

This time, I'm the one lifting my brows. "How do you know what time I work tomorrow, *Cale*?"

He opens the oven and pulls a pan out, setting it on the stove. "Because I asked on my way out. You didn't think I would be making all my future appointments without booking with you, did you? You're the only woman that I'll be getting a massage by from now on. I promise that."

I swallow hard and try to keep my nerves from jumping all over the place. He has no idea what his words are doing to me. He may not be trying, but they're making me extremely *hot*.

I take a seat at the table when Cale refuses to let me help with anything, and within ten minutes the table is covered with food: baked chicken alfredo, breadsticks, salad, wine for myself, and beer for Cale.

Looking at all the food makes my mouth water in anticipation. Cale cooked all this knowing that it's my favorite meal. I'll definitely owe him for this later and I'm positive he won't forget to collect. It's a good thing that I know practically all his likes and dislikes. At least... I used to.

We don't talk much until we've both eaten a good amount and we're both on the verge of being stuffed. Cale must notice me slowing down, so he leans back in his chair and smiles up at me.

"So talk to me, Rile." He takes a swig of his beer and looks at me, ready to listen.

I take another huge bite of noodles, before licking my lips and smiling up at him. "About what?" I breathe out, feeling like I'm about to pop from overeating. "About how delicious this food is? Holy crap, Cale. This is so good. I'm very impressed."

He bites his bottom lip and leans in closer to me. "Told you I'd only put tasty things in your mouth." He shakes his head with a slight smile as my face undoubtedly turns beet red. "But I want to know about you. What's been going on? Where's the boyfriend? Why are you at your parents' house? That kind of stuff."

I take a huge drink of my wine and reach for the bottle to refill it. "We broke up before I left. It's a long story that I don't feel like talking about right now. I'm only staying with my parents until I can find my own place. Aspen offered to let me stay there, but I don't want to intrude on her and Slade." I take another drink and pretend to be unaffected. "I'm sure I'll find a place soon and being back in Chicago will feel like home again. It will just take some time."

He looks me in the eyes for what feels like an eternity before he speaks. "Come stay with me."

I smile at his offer. "Thanks, but I don't know about that, Cale. My parents don't mind me staying there for a while. We haven't seen each other in six years and I don't want things to be awkward."

I stand up and get ready to clean up my mess, but Cale stops me. "I'm not worried about that mess right now. What I'm worried about is spending time with you and there's no way in hell that things could *ever* be awkward between us. I don't care if it's been twenty years, we're still Rile and Cale and I always have the time and room for that in my life." He pulls me up from my chair and grabs my glass of wine. "Pick out a movie and I'll be there in a few minutes."

"Are you sure you don't—"

"Hell no, Rile. I invited you here for dinner. There's no way I'm allowing you to clean up." He pulls me by the back of the neck, until our faces are almost touching. "Now go to my room and find a pair of my boxer briefs and a shirt. I'll meet you on the couch."

I close my eyes and nod as his smell surrounds me. He smells so good that I just want to snuggle into him and run my nose all along his chest and neck. "Okay," I say softly.

Without warning, he releases my neck and walks over to the table to start cleaning up. I watch him for a second to try and imagine what it would be like living here with Cale. Seeing him every morning when I wake up and every night before bed. I have a feeling there's no way I could handle that without wanting more. Plus, it would kill me to see him bring other girls home. Cale truly has no idea how much I care about him and I'm hoping to keep it that way.

After slipping into some of Cale's clothes, I take a seat on the floor and search through his DVDs. I instantly spot a new comedy that I've been wanting to see, so I pop it into the PS4 and curl up on the corner of the couch to wait for Cale.

A few minutes later I hear Cale approaching, so I look up. Without a care in the world he yanks his shirt over his head before stepping out of his jeans, making my heart race with every movement that he makes.

He smiles at me when he notices me watching him. "I've been waiting to get out of these clothes all fucking day." With his abs flexing, he walks toward the couch and takes a seat, practically pulling me into his lap. He reaches for the blanket on the back of the couch and drapes it over us before pressing play with the controller. "You comfortable?" he questions.

Yes... and no.

He isn't hard, but feeling his dick pressed against my ass steals my breath for a brief second. There were so many times in the past that I wanted to feel him against me, but was too afraid to get close to him, so I always found ways to avoid contact with his junk. There's no way I would have been able to withstand begging him to take me, and right now... I'm fighting that urge.

"I'm fine," I lie. "Just let me know if you want me to move and I will."

He pulls me tighter against him and smiles into my neck. "I haven't seen you in six years. There's no way in hell that I'm letting you move away from me."

My heart beats faster from his words and I have to admit to myself that those are the exact words I wanted to hear. Being with him feels like old times and I'm happy to see that Cale wants me around just as much as in the past. I was scared things would be different...

I just hope I can keep my feelings under control before I mess up everything we've had over the last ten years.

CHAPTER FOUR

CALE

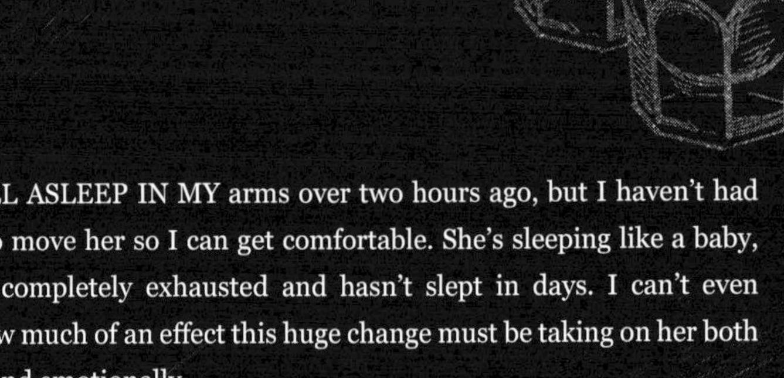

RILEY FELL ASLEEP IN MY arms over two hours ago, but I haven't had the heart to move her so I can get comfortable. She's sleeping like a baby, as if she's completely exhausted and hasn't slept in days. I can't even imagine how much of an effect this huge change must be taking on her both physically and emotionally.

Everything has changed dramatically for her in the last week. Her grandmother has gone off to a nursing home, she's packed up all her things to move from the home she has known for the last six years, and on top of that has just gotten out of a relationship that I'm guessing was not by *her* choice.

I'll sit here all night if she's content and at home for the first time since she's left Mexico. She loves her parents, but there's no way she will be able to be herself there without having them on her ass constantly, making her feel as if she's a kid again; not to mention that she must feel lonely there without someone she's close to. That's why my offer for her to stay here will always stand.

She stirs in my arms before she looks up at me with tired eyes and attempts to sit up. I pull her back into me and smile down at her as she begins to speak. "How long have I been sleeping?" she asks tiredly. "Sorry if I drooled on you."

I give her a small smile as she wipes her mouth. There's a wet circle of drool on my chest, but I couldn't care less. "You're all good, Rile. Nothing that I haven't dealt with before from you." I help her stand up before I get to my own feet. "You dozed off a couple hours ago. I figured you needed the rest so I didn't want to wake you."

"Cale." She smiles at me gratefully and pulls me in for a tight hug. "You've always been so selfless when it comes to our friendship. I think I've missed that the most about you."

I smile against her neck. "Now why don't you go crawl into my bed and fall back to sleep? I'll take the couch for the night."

She pulls away from me and looks as if she wants to say something, but doesn't. She just turns away and starts heading for my bedroom, before stopping at the door and turning back around. "Night, Cale."

I turn off the lamp and strip out of my boxers, while holding the blanket against me. "Goodnight, Rile. I'll wake you up in the morning."

Her eyes linger down to my hand that is holding the blanket, before she nervously turns away and disappears into my bedroom.

I might have forgotten to mention the little fact that I *always* sleep naked. It was a struggle for me when Aspen and Slade were staying here, but as soon as they left I went back to my nudist ways.If Riley agrees to stay here, then she's going to see me naked whether it's me running around the house or me on top of her, burying myself between those thighs of hers. I just hope that she's ready for me.

I've been more than ready for her...

THE ALARM ON MY PHONE woke me up at seven, not that I really slept much anyways. Having Riley sleeping in my bed kind of prevented that. I kept thinking about crawling into bed with her, but decided that it's probably too soon. There's no way I would've been able to lie next to her without wanting to pleasure her and make her scream until she fell asleep in my arms from exhaustion, so I spent most of the night fighting with my dick.

I quietly slip into my boxers and prepare a quick breakfast before waking Riley up. There's no way I'm sending her to work on an empty stomach.

I walk into my room to see Riley curled up in my bed, holding my spare pillow against her body for comfort. Every part of my body aches to be that comfort. It's probably been a while since she's slept alone, and seeing her having to use a pillow makes me want to show her what my body could do for her.

She looks so beautiful and peaceful, lying there in my clothes and bed, that I feel bad for having to wake her so early. A part of me just wants to crawl into my bed with her and say fuck everything else. Fuck *Sensual Touches* and fuck *Walk of Shame*. I want Cale and Riley time and you better believe that I will be getting it as soon as I get off work tonight.

Just as I'm about to lean in and brush her beautiful, brown hair out of her face, she opens her eyes as if she can sense I'm next to her.

She stretches and smiles up at me, looking sweet and innocent. It makes me wonder just how innocent her sexy little body really is; although, I have a feeling that it hasn't been as innocent over the last six years as I'd hoped.

“Morning.” Sitting up, she looks around as if trying to figure out what time it is. “Did I oversleep? Shit!” She changes position in a panic, tossing the pillow aside.

“Hell no, Rile. I wouldn't let that happen. I got you.” I reach for her hand and help her up to her feet. “Come eat so I can take you home to shower and get ready for work.”

She stops walking and gives me a funny look. “You cooked us breakfast?”

I give her a light slap on the ass to get her moving again. “No.” I laugh as her eyes light up at the food on the kitchen island. “I made *you* breakfast. I hardly eat in the morning. Plus, it's early as hell, Rile. I'm never up this early.” I lean against the fridge and cross my arms as she pulls out a stool and takes a seat. “I'm going back to sleep as soon as I drop you off. I have to work later tonight.”

She holds up a pancake, before slapping it down onto her plate. “Thank you. You really didn't have to do all of this. I could have stopped for a quick sandwich on the way to work. That's what I usually do.”

I shake my head. "You're in my house; therefore, I feed you. Now eat up."

It's silent for a few minutes while she eats, before she finally speaks up, breaking the comfortable silence. I bring a glass of orange juice to my lips. "You work at the bar tonight? Bartending, right?"

I choke a little on my orange juice, realizing that I haven't mentioned the small fact that I'm a fucking male stripper. The last time we had talked I was mostly bartending. I didn't think the stripping part was going to last.

I set my orange juice down and walk over to grab her empty plate, bringing it to the sink. "Why don't you go and change real fast and we'll talk on the way to your parents'."

She nods and sets her empty glass into the sink. "Good idea. I'm running out of time and I can't afford to lose this job if I want to find my own place soon."

I quickly dress and we both end up meeting by the front door in less than five minutes. Opening it for her, I lock the door before closing it behind us.

It feels so strange being outside at this time in the morning. It's so quiet and peaceful. I have to admit, I sort of like being up right now, and having Riley by my side makes it that much more enjoyable.

After helping her into my truck, I jog over to the driver's side, mentally preparing myself for the bomb drop. I just hope that she can handle it without thinking any less of me. I never really cared what anybody thought about it until... *now*. She's always known me as the *sweet* Cale. I'm definitely far from her sweet Cale today, especially with my body.

She smiles and faces me as I pull out of the driveway and onto the road. "So... tell me about your job, Cale. I want to know what you've been up to. I want all the details."

I grip the steering wheel and grind my jaw, preparing for her reaction. There's really no way of sugarcoating this. I just have to come out and say it and hope that she accepts it. "I'm stripping tonight."

She lets out a small laugh as if she thinks I'm joking. "Stop playing around, Cale." She grabs my knee and squeezes it. "Really, tell me."

I stop at a red light and look over at her. I give her a serious look to show her that I'm not joking. "I've been stripping at *Walk of Shame* for a while now. I only bartend a couple of nights a week now."

"Green light," she says quickly.

I turn away from her to pay attention to the road, just waiting for her to say something else. I want to know what she truly thinks about me now. I always want nothing but the truth from her and I always know that she'll give it to me straight.

"That's actually pretty cool. I bet you make a lot of money," she says, as if it's no big deal. "If you have the body, then hey... show it off. I can't imagine anyone complaining." She smiles at me and I feel a flood of relief wash through me.

"I haven't had any complaints yet."

She laughs. "Well obviously, Cale. You have the body of a God." She gives me a look that makes me want to rip her clothes off and fuck her right here. "I've always wanted to go and see male strippers. I've just never had the opportunity."

I lift an eyebrow. "You going to come and watch me one night then?"

She gently bites her bottom lip. "We'll see."

I pull into her parents' driveway and lean in to give her a kiss on the cheek. "I'll come pick you up when I get off work tonight. We still have *a lot* of time to make up for, and until then you're mine."

She huffs and glances at the house, looking as if she already wants to run away. "I'll be here, waiting. I'm off by four and I've been thinking about swinging by to see Aspen for a bit."

"Sounds good, Rile. Tell Aspen that she needs to come and see me soon. It's been too long."

"Will do." She smiles one more time before hopping out of the truck and walking away, stopping to smile back at me, before disappearing into the house.

Damn, this is going to be a long day.

CHAPTER FIVE

RILEY

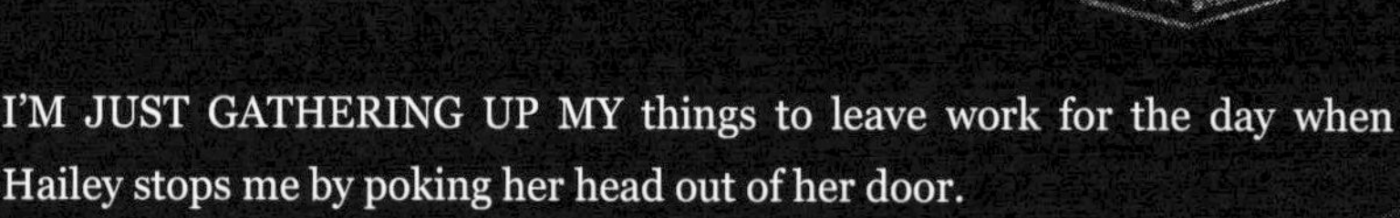

I'M JUST GATHERING UP MY things to leave work for the day when Hailey stops me by poking her head out of her door.

"Hey. Are you leaving?"

I nod and look down at the keys in my hand. "Yeah, I'm heading out right now. What's up?"

She gives me a sweet smile, obviously trying to butter me up for something. "I'm running a little behind and I have a client that's been waiting for like twenty minutes. Kylie has been on my ass and I can't handle her shit right now. Can you please take care of them so I can finish up?" She nods her head toward her door and whispers, "This guy pays a lot of money and he's not ready to leave yet. So?"

I look down at my phone in my hand to see that Aspen has finally responded to my message. Holding up my finger to Hailey, I quickly check the message to see that Aspen won't be home until at least five thirty. I really have nothing better to do anyways.

"Yeah, I can do it. I'll tell Kylie to send them to my room."

Hailey flashes me a half smile, before disappearing back into her room.

"Yeah, you're welcome," I mutter to myself.

I walk down the hall to find Kylie at her desk. She looks up from twisting her purple hair around her finger and waves me over when she hears me coming. "You better hurry up and get out of here before that bitch cons you into staying longer."

I let out a frustrated breath and lean against the desk. "Too late. Send her client to my room."

"Seriously?" she questions. "You're that easy, huh?" She grins while reaching for the phone. "I had a feeling that was going to happen so I didn't tell Hailey who her client was. You just keep getting lucky, sweets. I'll call and tell him to come back in."

"Alright," I say while walking away. "Send him on back to my room."

I'm in my room for about three minutes before the door opens and a handsome guy dressed to impress walks in. He smiles at me before reaching out to shake my hand. "Lynx," he offers. His blue eyes meet mine and capture them.

I smile back at him as he looks me up and down. "Riley," I say back. "I'll be taking care of you today. I hope you don't mind."

He offers my hand a little squeeze before releasing it. "I don't mind at all." He reaches for the top button of his black button-down and starts to undo it. "Mind if I get undressed?" He lifts a brow, waiting for my response.

I shake my head, embarrassed, and reach for the door handle. "Oh sorry. Not at all. I'll give you a few minutes."

I quickly escape to the hall and give Lynx a few minutes to get undressed and comfortable before I knock on the door in warning and push it open.

Lynx is laying on his stomach, dressed in a tight little pair of black boxer briefs clinging to his small, muscular ass.

"Oh thank goodness," I whisper to myself, glad that he didn't decide to get naked like Cale did. I'm not sure I'd be able to handle that at the moment. Cale had me about to explode from touching his body and I have to admit that I'm still worked up and sexually frustrated.

"What was that?" he asks.

I smile down at him as he twists his neck to look at me. "Oh nothing.

Sorry." I take a second to take in his body and can't help but compare him to Cale. This man is undoubtedly sexy with his dark, messy hair, and muscular, lean build, yet... he doesn't even compare to Cale.

My heart skips a beat at the thought of Cale and it's that moment that I realize I miss him already. I've been trying all day not to think about last night and the fact that I fell asleep in his arms, but seeing this gorgeous man and realizing that he *still* doesn't come close to Cale and the effect his body has on me, makes me realize just how much I truly want Cale. I guess six years hasn't done anything to make my heart forget him. It's sad that I just got out of a two-year relationship, yet it's *Cale* that's on my mind. He's always had that power over me.

ASPEN HAS BEEN TALKING ABOUT her job at the salon and other random things for the last hour, but I haven't been able to stop thinking about Cale and the fact that he's at the bar stripping right now. I didn't really think about it much earlier, but knowing that he's there now, taking his clothes off for tons of women that are probably pawing at his body, has me kind of jealous. I hate that they are there and I'm not. I really *want* to go and see what it's like.

"Let's go to *Walk of Shame*," I blurt out, cutting Aspen off.

Aspen leans back on the couch and smiles as if she's a bit surprised by my request. "Oh boy. I don't think you can handle it." She shakes her head. "As a matter of fact... I *know* you can't handle it. You don't even know the things those boys do with their bodies."

Excitement surges through me at the thought of watching Cale move his body, and now I'm anxious to hurry and get there. "I can handle it. That's where you met Slade, right? If you can survive there, then I'm sure I can too."

"Yeah," she says with a laugh. "It was a bumpy ride, that's for sure." She stands up from the couch when she hears the shower water turn off. "You should go by yourself. I think I'm going to be busy for the next couple of hours."

Standing up, I give her a surprised look as she starts ushering me toward the door. "How rude. You're just going to kick your big sister out like that?"

We both look over to the hallway when Slade appears dripping wet, his waist wrapped in a small towel that leaves little to the imagination.

"Damn," we both say in unison.

Aspen gives me a little shove as Slade smiles at us and runs a hand through his wet hair. "Hell yes I am. You have somewhere to be and I have someone to do. Goodbye."

I wave goodbye to Slade as Aspen shoves me outside and kisses me on the side of the head. "Love you too," I mumble.

"Love you, sis, but you gotta go right now." She hands me my purse. "Slade says hi and bye and hopes to see you soon. Tell Cale we love him. Buh bye."

I roll my eyes and smile when the door closes in my face. As *rude* as this was... I want that. I want to want someone like that and for him to want me just as much. I never felt that with Tyler. Yeah, I loved him and he loved me, but we were never desperate for each other and never just *had* to have each other. What I wouldn't give to have that feeling, and if I were to admit it to myself, I sort of felt that way last night when in Cale's arms. I felt this want and need to be close to him. Sort of like I do now.

I blow out a breath while walking to my car.

Walk of Shame... here I come.

I get hit with a brick of nerves as soon as I pull into the parking lot of *Walk of Shame* and see how many cars are occupying the lot. It's packed and finding parking won't be easy.

"Holy shit, these women don't play around," I mutter. Grabbing my wallet, I shove my purse under my seat and hop out of my car, pressing the lock behind me.

Just walking in the door of this place is overwhelming. My ears are instantly assaulted with the sound of screaming women and I can barely concentrate as the guy at the door checks my ID. I keep my eyes on the crowd of loud and crazy women as the guy places my ID back in my hand and greets the group of women behind me.

The crowd is pretty much shoulder to shoulder and I can barely see what's happening on the stage. That is until Cale jumps down into the crowd and starts grinding his hips to the music while bending some girl over as if he's fucking her.

He's wearing a short pair of red boxer briefs and his muscular body is covered in sweat as he continues to grind behind her, working her nice and good, before thrusting her away with his dick and dropping to the floor as if he's making love to someone below him. He's working his hips so powerfully and with such a perfect rhythm that it takes my breath away just imagining being below him. Now I know what my sister meant by not being able to handle this place. I'll never be able to look at Cale the same now, and I'm pretty positive that there's no way that man is *still* a virgin. I guess I didn't really expect him to be...

Holy. Hotness.

CHAPTER SIX

CALE

I SLOW MY RHYTHM AND close my eyes as I picture Riley below me. These women might be imagining me fucking them, but I'm imagining fucking Riley, nice and slow, and taking care of her every fucking need.

Hands grab at me and start tugging on my briefs, trying to get me naked. Someone gets my briefs down far enough in the back that my whole ass is hanging out, so I push myself back to my feet, smile at the ladies, and slowly thrust the air, giving them a view of my bare ass flexing.

Right as I'm pulling my briefs back up I look to the left and set my sights on Riley. She's looking at me with wide eyes, appearing slightly uncomfortable and out of place. My body instantly reacts to seeing her and I have to fight against my erection, knowing that these red boxer briefs will do nothing to hide what I'm thinking.

Ignoring all the women around me, I walk toward her, letting her know that I see her. The last thing I want is for Riley to feel as if she doesn't belong when she's here to see me. She's the most important woman in this room and I'm about to show her that.

When I approach Riley, I wrap my hands into the back of her hair and bury my face into the softness of her neck, pulling her as close to me as humanly possible.

She's stiff at first, but loosens up and grabs my forearms as I run my lips up her neck, grinding my hips against her. I hear her let out a little gasp as my erection presses against her stomach, and that little sound alone is enough to make me want her even more than ever.

"You came to see me," I whisper against her neck. I grab one of her legs and wrap it around my waist as I dig my hips into her. "You're the most beautiful girl in this room, Riley. I promise you that."

Reaching for her other leg, I pick her up and wrap both of her legs around my waist, thrusting my hips into her, nice and slow. I grip her ass and hold her as close to me as I can, grinding her against me.

I look up just as Stone slides a chair in front of me, giving me exactly what I need as if reading my mind. Being careful with Riley, I set her down on the chair and then straddle her lap, wrapping both of my hands into the back of her hair and forcing her to look into my eyes. I'm unsure of what she's thinking, but now is the time to show her what she could have. All she has to do is give me a clue that she wants it just like I do.

Biting my bottom lip, I reach for both of her hands, lightly lacing mine on the backs of hers, before running them slowly down my chest and abs, ensuring she feels every ridge as I grind into her. I lean into her and moan against her ear, showing her just how turned on I am without her doing anything at all.

Her body shivers and she lets out a small moan as well, confirming what I want to know, and letting me see exactly what my body is doing to her. Pleased, I pick her back up and grip her ass as she wraps her legs around me once again.

She leans her head back, getting lost in the moment as my body stills against hers and the song comes to an end.

We stand here for a few moments, holding each other, until finally she lets go and clears her throat, dropping back to her feet. "Told you I've always wanted to see male strippers." She smiles nervously and brushes her hair off her face. "You should go. The crowd is waiting."

I press my lips to her forehead and offer her a thankful smile, before turning away from her and finishing up the show.

RILEY IS OUTSIDE WAITING BY my truck when I'm done. She looks up from her phone and smiles when she sees me approaching. "Done shaking your junk for the horny women already?"

I walk up to her and kiss her on the forehead, before pulling away and laughing. "Yeah, my junk is tired from all the shaking. It's Stone's turn now."

She lets out a small laugh. "Well, you were great." Her eyes search mine before she speaks again. "Everyone loved you."

"You haven't seen anything yet, Riley." I lean against my truck, beside her. "How was your day?"

"Good," she responds. "I'm just a bit tired and sore."

I look around the parking lot in search of her car. "Did you drive here or get a ride?"

She pushes a button on her key ring, making it beep, before holding up her keys. "Drove." She yawns and leans against my truck, looking exhausted. "I was only planning on stopping in for a few minutes, but kinda got sucked in by the action," she teases.

I walk around her and open the passenger door to my truck. "Let's go. We'll get your car tomorrow."

She shakes her head while yawning. "It's fine, Cale. I'll just drive and meet you at your house."

Ignoring her request, I pick her up and set her in my truck, refusing to let her drive in her exhausted condition. "Your car will be fine. You're riding with me."

Smiling, she leans back and buckles her seatbelt. "Yes, master Cale," she quips.

"I like that," I respond with a grin. "Say it again."

Laughing, she smacks my arm and reaches for the door to close it. "Back up before your junk gets stuck in the door."

I bite my bottom lip and back away, watching her in amusement. God, I've missed this woman. Having her here reminds me of why I chose to wait in the first place.

By the time we pull up at my house Riley is practically sleeping in her seat. She slowly straightens and looks out the window while rubbing the back of her neck. "We're here already?" She unbuckles her seatbelt and turns to me as she stretches. "Sorry if I dozed off. I got stuck at work longer than expected. I guess I'm a lot more exhausted than I thought." She rubs her neck again. "And sore."

I smile at her and gently touch her bottom lip. "No worries." Hopping out of my truck, I hurry to Riley's side before she has a chance to open the door herself. "You don't have to do shit for the rest of the night. I got you, Rile."

She lets out a surprised squeal as I reach in the truck and pick her up, throwing her over my shoulder. "Cale!" She grabs onto my shirt and laughs. "What are you doing?"

I slap her ass and start walking for the door. "Stop squirming. I told you that you don't have to do shit for the rest of the night. Did you think I was joking?"

She places her hands on my ass and pushes up as I walk through the door and shut it behind us. "Well, I didn't think that included walking." She looks up at me, and smiles after I toss her on my bed. "What... are you going to undress me for the night too?"

I lift my eyebrows and look her in the eyes as I crawl onto my bed and hover above her. "Yes," I say firmly. "You've been taking care of people your whole life. Let me take care of you tonight."

She swallows as her eyes meet my lips. "Cale... you don't have to take care of me. You don't owe—"

I cut her off by pressing my lips to hers, gently but possessively, letting her know how much I want her. I've waited for far too long to kiss her, and there's no way I'm holding back. Tonight... she's going to see just how fucking good my tongue can make her feel.

She lets out a moan and grips my shoulders as I run my tongue across her lips, hinting for her to open up for me.

"Cale..." She moans again as I press my hips between her legs. "I don't know if we should do this..."

I smile against her lips and whisper, "*We* don't have to do anything." Running my hands down her sides, I kiss my way down her stomach, stopping above her jeans. "Just let *me* take care of you."

Her eyes search mine for a moment, but she doesn't say a word as I work on taking off her jeans. Slowly, I pull them down her legs, kissing the inside of her thighs on the way down, before tossing her jeans aside and gently rubbing my mouth over her thin panties.

She squirms and slams her head back while gripping the blanket in anticipation. "Cale," she breathes heavily. "I don't want to mess things up between us. You should stop..."

I slowly pull her panties down while looking her in the eyes. "Don't worry about that. Trust me, Riley. You need this... just sit back and enjoy it."

Before she can say anything else, I run my tongue over her clit, before gently sucking it into my mouth. The taste of her against my tongue is almost enough to make me bust my load.

I've wanted to taste Riley for so long now. I probably shouldn't be doing this so soon, but I can't help myself. She's just so beautiful and tense. She looks as if she hasn't been pleasured in a long time, and I want her to know how good it can feel to be taken care of, especially by me: her *sweet* Cale.

Riley's hands wrap into my hair as her hips buck upward, begging for more, so that's what I give her.

My tongue explores every last inch of her sweet pussy, tasting it as if my life depends on it. I work my tongue slow at first, teasing her and making sure that she's left wanting more. Then I speed up, fucking her with my tongue, before slipping my finger into her, pumping in and out as I move back to her clit.

Squeezing her hip, I pull her body closer to me while giving her just a small taste of my skills.

Her grip on my hair tightens as her legs begin to squeeze my face. "Oh God... Oh God... Cale..."

I suck her clit into my mouth, working my tongue and finger fucking her until she's shaking beneath me, her pussy now clenching around my finger.

I look up at her and run my tongue along her one more time, before pulling my finger out and sucking her sweet release into my mouth.

Smiling at her new, relaxed state, I crawl above her and press my lips to her forehead. "Goodnight, Riley."

Not wanting to pressure her any more than I have and make her feel uncomfortable, I help her back into her panties before heading for the door on my way to sleep on the couch.

"Goodnight," she whispers softly. "I... uh... I'll see you in the morning."

I keep my cool until I shut the door behind me. "Fuck me," I growl out.

One taste. One fucking taste and I'm ready to give her all of me. I want to bury myself between her legs so bad, but I know that moving things too fast will only ruin her.

She's too fresh out of a relationship and too concerned about ruining things between us to be able to take that step. Truthfully, I don't even know if she's going to be able to handle what I just did to her. I took it easy on her tonight. Just wait until she can see how rough I can be.

"Shit..." I strip down to the nude and lay on the couch, knowing that I won't be sleeping tonight. My dick won't either.

Closing my eyes, I grab my shaft and slowly stroke it to thoughts of Riley riding my hard cock. I want to feel her take it deep and hard, knowing that she's the first to take it.

My strokes become faster as I think back to the sexy little sounds that Riley made when she came on my tongue. "So fucking hot, Riley."

A few minutes later and I'm busting my load all over my abs, wishing that it were inside Riley's pussy instead.

Fuck me...

CHAPTER SEVEN

RILEY

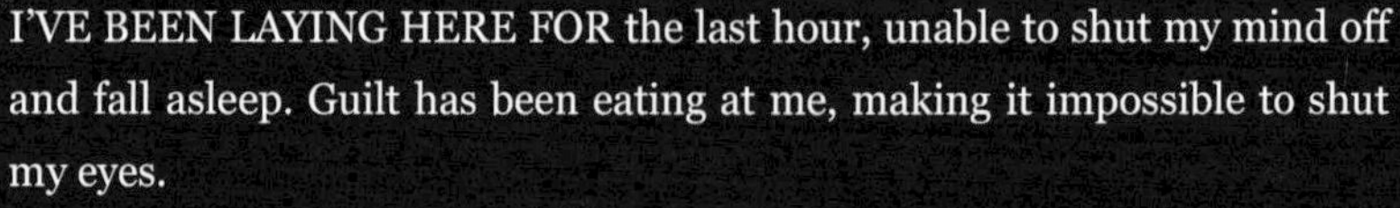

I'VE BEEN LAYING HERE FOR the last hour, unable to shut my mind off and fall asleep. Guilt has been eating at me, making it impossible to shut my eyes.

I should feel guilty for letting another man touch me so soon. I should feel guilty for kissing another man, and enjoying it, but I don't. No... I feel guilty for not feeling guilty and knowing that there is only one reason for that: Cale Kinley.

I know without a doubt that if it had been anyone other than Cale I would feel bad for letting another man touch me. Don't get me wrong; I still love Tyler. I mean... we were together for two years, so how could I not. I can't just shut my feelings off. Of course I still care about him, wonder what he's doing and how he's feeling now that I'm gone.

The part I don't understand is why when Cale's lips were on me that not one thought of Tyler crossed my mind, as if he was forgotten. Cale consumed my every thought and need, making me feel... alive, and cared for. He made me believe for just a small moment that it's possible to let everything go and let someone else take care of you. I really needed that and he could tell. He's always been able to read me.

Now I'm left with another question: how does he feel about me? I know he loves me as a friend and that he'll do anything for me, but would he really go out of his way to please me sexually if his only feelings toward me were platonic? Knowing that he's a stripper confuses me, because I'm sure he doesn't have a problem with sexual attention, and it makes me believe that he possibly does have real feelings for me. Male strippers are known for their reputations, but I hope that's not the case with Cale.

Throwing the blanket from my legs, I quietly get out of bed and walk through the living room on my way to the bathroom. I'm sure to be as quiet as possible, worried that I'll wake Cale up. He's had a long night and the last thing I want to do is take away from his sleep.

On the way back to the bedroom, I find myself wanting to see Cale one more time before falling asleep. For some reason my body aches just to get a glimpse of him.

I quietly make my way over to the couch and peek over it.

"What are you doing, Rile?"

I jump back from the sound of Cale's voice. I wasn't expecting him to be awake.

"I couldn't sleep. I just wanted to make sure you were sleeping."

He tiredly smiles at me and reaches for my arms, pulling me onto the couch with him. "I'll help you fall asleep. Come here." He lifts the blanket so that we're both underneath, before snuggling me to his chest and wrapping his arm around me.

I let out a small gasp when I feel his bare dick against the exposed skin of my belly. "You're naked, Cale?"

He just pulls me closer and starts rubbing his hand through my hair, calming me. "Just close your eyes, Rile. I got you." He kisses the top of my hair. "Go to sleep."

I'M JUST FINISHING UP WITH Lynx when I hear the door open behind me. I got a little behind because Lynx constantly wanted to talk and request that I spend extra time on his upper thighs. Every time I tried moving to the next body part, he kept saying that his muscles were still tense.

Feeling frustrated, I don't even bother turning around. "I'm almost done here. Come back in ten please. I apologize."

I hear the door close behind me, so I automatically suspect that the person left, but when Lynx opens his eyes and smiles past me, I realize that the person is still in the room.

I quickly turn around and get ready to usher the person out when my eyes set on Cale. He smiles at me before turning to Lynx. "No wonder your ass wasn't at the club."

Cale lifts an eyebrow as Lynx sits up and slowly gets dressed. "Yeah, well I was feeling a bit tense and this beautiful lady was helping me relax. What's it to you?"

I see Cale's jaw tense, but he quickly shakes it off and leans against the wall as Lynx finishes dressing.

I look between the two of them, before setting my gaze on Lynx. "So I'm guessing you're a stripper too?"

Lynx gives me a cocky grin, before walking up to Cale and squeezing his shoulder. "Nah... I'm the boss man. Right, Cale?" He winks.

Cale shrugs his shoulders and eyes him carefully as he reaches for the door handle. "When you're actually there," he says stiffly.

Lynx brushes off Cale's coldness and turns back to me. "I'll see you in a couple days, Magic hands." He winks and then disappears out into the hall.

Cale grunts to himself and quickly starts getting undressed as I clean and prepare the bed. "Is he in here a lot, Rile?"

I smooth out the new sheet and look behind me. "He's been in here a couple of times. He's pretty persistent when he wants something. I guess I can see why now."

Cale reaches out and grabs my chin, bringing my eyes up to meet his. "Has he tried anything with you? Tell me right now if he has."

I shake my head. "No, Cale. Nothing besides the extra time that he requests on his upper thighs, but I'm starting to get used to that with this job title." I let out a small laugh, but Cale still seems tense.

"Promise me that you'll let me know if he touches you. I don't like the idea of you two in here alone together. He's got quite the reputation at the club."

I place my hand on his arm and he releases my chin. "Don't worry, Cale. I'll be fine." I point down at the bed. "Now get your ass naked so I can get started." I offer him a lighthearted smile. "I'm starting to see that you do everything naked."

He pulls his jeans down and I turn my head away so he can get out of his boxers. "I'm happier when I'm naked, Rile. What can I say?"

I'm happier when you're naked too...

When I turn back around, Cale is laying on his back, looking up at the ceiling. The small towel is doing an even shittier job of hiding his junk than the last time.

Squirting some oil into my hands, I start at Cale's shoulders and slowly work my way down his chest. "You working tonight?"

He lets out a small moan when I reach his lower abdomen. "Yeah..." he breathes. "In a few hours actually."

The way that he bites his bottom lip each time my hands get lower on his abdomen makes me want to see what he'll do if I touch him sexually. Would he stop me or let me keep going? I try to push the thought aside, but each time I notice him bite his lip and growl I feel my insides jump.

He seems a little tense after seeing Lynx in here... He did do me a little favor last night. I just wouldn't be a very good friend if I let him go to work like that, now would I?

Taking a deep breath, I round the table without removing my hands to create a better angle, and then slide my hands under the towel, wrapping both of them around his thick dick, slowly stroking up and down, feeling it quickly growing in my hands.

"Oh shit... Rile." He bites his lip again, but harder this time, as he grips my waist. "Fuck... my cock is so hard for you."

As his grip on my waist gets tighter, my hands work faster and firmer, being sure to pleasure him just as much as he did me last night. His dick is now so hard and big that I need both hands to take care of him.

My heart is racing, but I don't want to stop. Touching him and knowing that I'm giving him pleasure has me more turned on than I've ever been in my entire life. I've waited a long time to touch him like this...

"Fuck yes, Rile..." He sits up and bites my shoulder, but not hard enough to hurt me. "Keep going. Ah... fuck me, Rile."

I lean my neck back as he runs his lips up the side, moaning all the way up until he stops at my ear. "You feel so fucking good, Rile." He moans. "I bet your pussy would feel even better..."

I close my eyes from his words and almost feel as if I'm on the verge of having my own orgasm. Stroking his dick, I find that both of us are now moaning, until finally he releases his load on his stomach, before pulling my bottom lip into his mouth and biting it.

As soon as he moans into my mouth once more, I surprisingly find my own release. I instantly feel embarrassed, shocked that something like that could happen without even being touched.

"Shit, Rile." He lies back on the table and runs his hands through his thick, messy hair. "I love it when you touch me."

He looks over at me and grabs my arm as I take a step back. "What's wrong?" He smiles at me and looks down at my legs that are still slightly shaking. "Did you orgasm, Rile?"

I nod, my fingertips instantly going to my mouth to create a diversion, too embarrassed to actually speak.

Cale grabs the towel and wipes himself off, before standing up and grabbing my chin after removing my hand from my mouth, forcing me to look up at him. "Well damn, Rile. That's the hottest thing I've ever heard." He smirks down at me and wets his lips. "Knowing that I can make you come without even touching you... is by far the sexiest, most satisfying thing that's ever happened to me. All it does is make me want to bend you over this massage table and fuck you until we both can't walk."

"Cale..."

He places his finger to my lips and bends down to whisper in my ear. "As soon as I know that you can handle it... you *will* be the first woman to have me inside of her. I promise that, Rile. Just wait and see."

I stand here, frozen and unable to think clearly as Cale gathers up his clothes and gets dressed.

He must be able to tell that his words have shaken me up, because the next thing I know I feel his lips on the top of my head, before I hear the door open.

"I'll see you tonight, Rile."

Shaking off my frozen state, I turn to Cale and offer him a small smile. "Yeah... I'll see you later... after work."

The door closes behind him and I instantly go into panic mode.

"He did not just say that, Riley." I walk over to the bed and start stripping it down, barely able to even function right. "You're just hearing things. There's no way in hell that Cale is still a virgin..."

I have no idea how long I've been standing here, dazed and confused, when my door opens and a woman walks in.

Pulling myself together, I smile at her and introduce myself, before walking out into the hall, giving her time to get ready.

How I'm going to be able to function for the rest of the day is beyond me. I had to have heard him wrong...

"Yeah, that's it," I try to convince myself. "I'm tired. He could have said anything."

The woman calls my name, interrupting my thoughts, so I shake off my personal thoughts and prepare to make it through the day, hoping that I'm just going crazy.

Cale... a virgin... me his first... friends... we're just friends...

CHAPTER EIGHT

CALE

MY SHIFT ENDS IN TWENTY minutes and I can't deny that I'm a little disappointed Riley didn't stop in to see me. I haven't heard from her since I left *Sensual Touches* and it's really starting to bother me.

I guess she wasn't ready to hear that I really did wait for her, and I bet that she doesn't believe me. I wouldn't believe me either if the roles were reversed. A virgin stripper.... No fucking way. Impossible right? Well, I'm the fucking exception. She is the reason that I'm the exception.

I look up from the ground when I feel a hand on my shoulder. Stone grins like a fool. "Dude... you've been standing there for ten minutes now. Just get the hell out of here. You're useless here in that state."

Shaking my head I flex my jaw. "Nah, I'm good. Just get the hell back over to your side, man. I don't want your dick over here."

Stone laughs and starts backing up. "At least I'm actually working my dick, man. That's more than you can say." Grinning like a fool he gives me the middle finger with both hands, before busting back into a dance.

I get my head back into the game for the last ten minutes, trying my best not to think about Riley and whether or not I fucked things up.

Just as I'm pushing through the crowd of women and getting ready to head into the back room, I spot Riley sitting at the bar talking to Sarah.

Sarah looks over at me and notices the stupid ass grin on my face, raising her brows as she figures it out. Hell yes it makes me happy as hell to see that Riley is here. I don't give a shit who knows.

Gathering up my things, I get dressed quickly and snatch my tips from Kash, tossing him a pile of twenties on my way out the door.

I stop dead in my tracks when I notice Lynx at the bar talking Riley up. That dick better learn his place when it comes to my woman. She may not know it yet... but she's my girl. I'm going to make that very clear, and real soon.

"Just admit that you came to see me," Lynx says with a confident grin that makes me want to choke the life out of him. "I can definitely put on a show one night if it keeps you coming back."

Riley laughs as if she finds him amusing but doesn't say anything as I approach them at the bar.

Lynx quickly turns to me as I place a kiss on Riley's head and wrap my arms around her from behind. "I didn't think you'd show up," I whisper next to her ear. I look up at Lynx as I say the next part. "I'm glad that you came to see me. I'm ready when you are."

Riley takes one last sip of her drink and slides it across the bar to Sarah. "Thank you for the drink, Sarah." She gets ready to reach for cash, but Sarah and I both stop her.

I look at Sarah. "I'll pay for it."

She shakes her head. "It's on me. A little welcome home present. Well besides what I'm sure you've given her." She winks and walks away.

Lynx stands up at the same time that Riley does. "Well, I guess I'll be seeing you tomorrow," he says stiffly. "Same time as the last." He raises his drink to me and smirks. "You did good tonight, Cale. The women got a good show. *All* of them."

I tense my jaw and bite my tongue. I know damn well what he's doing. "Let's go, Rile." I place my hand on the small of her back and guide her outside, fighting the urge to kick the shit out of that dick.

As soon as we reach my truck, I slam Riley against it and press my lips against hers, claiming them and letting her know how much I want her. Fuck Lynx. He can't have her, not now or ever.

Seeing another man wanting her only makes me want to take it out on her *sexually* and give her all that I have. I may not end up being her first, but I know that I will be her second and her *last*.

Lifting her leg, I thrust my hips into her and moan against her lips. "I want to be inside you so bad, Rile." I kiss her again, before whispering against her lips. "Let me give myself to you. I want you to be my first. I know you may not believe me, but I would never lie to you. You know that. I've done sexual shit, Rile. Lots of things, but I've never entered a woman. I promise you that."

She moans loudly and grips the back of my hair as I suck her bottom lip into my mouth. "Cale…" She moans again as I grind my hips between her legs. "You really waited all this time for me?" I roughly kiss her neck and nod, just eager to continue tasting her. "What if I told you that I'm still a virgin? Would you still want to make me your first?"

Her words cause my heart to beat erratically in my chest and I freeze mid-kiss. "What?" I pull away and run my hands through my hair. "Are you, Rile? Are you still a virgin?"

She nods and covers her face. "I just couldn't do it, Cale." She pushes me away so she can get some air. "Every single time that Tyler and I began to get sexually active I would stop him right before he could enter me." She looks up to meet my eyes. "I kept thinking about you and wondering if you really meant what you said about waiting for me. It didn't feel right so I never had sex with him. I only allowed him to touch me sexually. No wonder he didn't want to follow me to Chicago…"

"Holy fuck, Rile." I run my hands through my hair and start pacing. "You telling me that you're a virgin makes me want to fuck you right here, right now." I stop pacing and press Riley back against my truck. "But it also makes me feel like it needs to be special for you, and whenever you're ready. My virginity doesn't mean shit to me as long I lose it to you. It could be in the fucking dirt or mud for all I care."

Riley swallows hard, before standing on the tip of her toes and wrapping her arms around my neck. "Is this really happening right now?" she questions. "I thought that us waiting for each other was just some stupid fantasy that I dreamt up. I thought I was being an idiot."

"Hell no, Rile." I lean down and press my lips against hers. "You really have no idea how much I really care about you, do you?"

She shakes her head and bites her bottom lip.

"Well fuck. I'm going to show you." I open the passenger door and point. "Inside. Now."

With her eyes locked on mine, she climbs into my truck and wraps her legs around me as I step in between them. "I've missed you, Cale." She lets out a small breath. "So much. There were times when I almost ran away in the middle of the night and got on a plane. I had tickets each time, but always talked myself out of it, knowing that I couldn't leave Grams like that."

I grip the back of her hair and lightly tug. "Me too, baby. But you're here now and I'm going to make up for it." I bite her bottom lip before releasing it. "Let's go."

AS SOON AS WE PULL out of the parking lot I place her hand on my hard cock, letting her know what she's doing to me, before I slide my hand up her dress. Her pussy is so warm and wet, just waiting for me to touch it. I love that... my pussy.

We drive in silence as I gently slide my fingers in and out, loosening her up for what's to come when we get home. Knowing that no man has been inside her has me so anxious to sink deep between those beautiful thighs and take her over and over again, all night long. Now that I know how much she wants it too... it's happening.

Once we pull up at my house, I pull my fingers out of her pussy and suck them into my mouth, looking her straight in the eyes. She lets out a small moan and grips the seat. "Riley... are you sure you want this?" She nods. "You do realize that once I fuck you that it will be happening every day and there's no turning back to just being the old Rile and Cale right? I will pleasure you any and every chance that I get and there's no taking it back: giving me your first time."

"Cale..." She reaches for the door handle. "I have always wanted you to be my first. I just didn't think it would actually happen. Knowing that it can.... I'm not passing that up for anything."

My chest aches at the thought that we had to go so long without each other, waiting for this fucking moment that should have happened six years ago. "Good... because I wasn't willing to let you."

Jumping out of the truck, I run over to her side and open the door. I lean inside and wrap both of my hands into the back of her hair, before pulling her toward me and kissing her long and hard. I place one hand on her knee and slide it up her leg, shoving a finger inside of her, while biting her bottom lip and tugging.

"Fuck me... I can never get enough of kissing you, Rile. I wanted to kiss you so bad the night that you left, but I didn't have the balls to mess things up for us. If I would have kissed you then I know I would have given you so much more that night in the pool, and I couldn't make love to you and just let you leave. I knew I had to wait."

She smiles against my lips. "It's a good thing, because if you would have kissed me..." She grips my hair. "Especially like this, then there's no way I would have gotten on that plane. Just one kiss was all I needed from you."

I lean in to kiss her again but stop when her phone goes off. "Ignore it," I whisper.

"I plan to." She pulls me closer between her legs and reaches her hand down in between us to rub my cock.

I throw my head back and grip her hair tighter, so turned on by her touch. "Undo my pants, Rile."

Without hesitation she starts to undo my pants, but her phone goes off again, causing us both to freeze.

"Dammit," she mumbles. "I'm sorry. Let me turn it on silent."

I stand patiently as she pulls out her phone and unlocks the screen to silence it. The pained look on her face tells me who it is and the moment shatters on the spot.

She awkwardly clears her throat and turns her phone on vibrate. "Well that kind of kills the moment. I'm so sorry." Her whole mood has changed and now I feel as if comforting her has become my priority. Riley has a big heart and I'd be stupid not to know how this moment is affecting her.

I pull her chin up and gently kiss her lips. "It's okay, Rile." I rub my thumb over her bottom lip. "Let's go inside and I'll make us a late-night snack before bed. "Sound good?"

She nods, ashamed, and runs her hands through my hair. "Thank you.

Cale. I just want this moment to be the two of us. I don't want any hint of Tyler in the back of my mind."

I kiss her again, letting her know that I'm okay with it. "You can't just shut your feelings off, Rile; I know that and I don't expect it. This won't be our last opportunity. Trust me."

She smiles as I help her out of my truck and guide her to the front door.

I want her mind to be focused on just me once I'm burying myself between her thighs. It will happen soon.

Just not tonight... tonight she knows how much I care about her.

CHAPTER NINE

RILEY

IT'S BEEN TWO DAYS SINCE I received those missed calls from Tyler and I respect with everything in me that Cale has given me some space in case I wanted to call him back. I thought long and hard about it, and decided against it. He broke my heart when he decided just *two* days before we were to leave that he didn't want to be a part of the plans. Why should I call him back? He's the one that didn't care enough. He didn't even come to say goodbye the day I left.

Cale and I are sitting on his couch watching hilarious prank shows and snacking on popcorn, and right now... that's all that matters. He's been able to keep a smile on my face throughout the pain that I thought I'd be feeling when I got home, and he's had my back through everything. I'm here and I'm focused on the now. Tyler is no longer clouding my thoughts and I want Cale to see that.

Setting the bowl of popcorn aside, I straddle Cale's lap and gently kiss him on the lips. His lips are so soft and delicious that I unconsciously lick them before pulling away. I swear I could kiss him all day and never grow tired of those lips. I've waited too long to not take advantage now.

"Damn, Rile." Cale squeezes my hips before moving down to my thighs, while running his tongue over his lips. "What are you trying to do to me? Are you trying to get me naked, because it won't take much more of that."

I lean my head back and moan as he buries his face into my neck and roughly kisses it, pushing me down onto his lap. "See what you're doing, Rile? You feel that?" I still can't seem to get over feeling his dick against me. It's so big and hard... and I want it, every inch of it... of Cale. My Cale.

He starts grinding below me, rubbing his hardness between my legs. "Yes," I breathe. "God... yes..." Just the thought of him being inside me makes me break into a sweat. It still amazes me how turned on I get with Cale. It's overwhelming.

After not feeling him touch me for two days, I feel like I could orgasm just from the feel of his tongue alone. That's how good this man is and I have a feeling that he knows it. He may be a virgin... but the rest of his body isn't... far from it.

"I want to take you somewhere, Rile." He runs his lips up my neck and stops at my ear. "Will you come with me?"

I swallow hard from his words. He just had to use the word *come*. "Cale... it's like two in the morning. Isn't it a bit late to take me somewhere?"

He laughs against my neck and squeezes my hips, lifting me from his lap. "It's never too late, Rile." Standing up, he reaches for my hand and pulls me into his chest. His hands tangle in my hair as he runs his tongue up my lips, tasting me. "Fucking delicious, baby."

Smiling, he walks toward the door, picking up his keys on the way out. I follow behind him, curious to where it is that he wants to take me so late at night. I have no clue where he wants to go, but truthfully I'd go anywhere with Cale. I always did in the past, including late night trips... but we were just kids then. Sneaking out late at night was in. We're definitely not kids anymore and don't need to sneak out to hang out.

I'm so anxious when we get into Cale's truck that I can't stop looking out the window, trying to figure out where he's taking me. It takes me a good five minutes to figure it out.

"Cale..." I sit up straight and look out the window. "Are you taking me to your old house?"

He smirks and pulls off to the side of the road, killing the engine on his truck. "I thought a late-night dip sounded good. You know… pick up where we left off six years ago."

I sit still as Cale jumps out of the truck and jogs over to my side, opening my door. "But didn't your parents move out like five years ago?"

Laughing, he reaches into the truck and pulls me out, onto my feet. "Yeah, they did." He shuts the door behind me, and then starts pulling me through the grass, toward the back of his old house.

"What?" I look around me, nervous that someone will see us, possibly resulting in cops. "We can't just swim in some stranger's pool, Cale. What if someone catches us?"

He stops and picks me up, wrapping my legs around his waist. As soon as his lips meet mine, all worries disappear. All that exists is Cale and me. Right now I couldn't care less about the consequences.

Walking through the grass, he somehow manages to keep his lips on mine until we're both sinking into the deep water.

The water is cold at first, a shocker, but as soon as Cale pulls me into his arms… he's all that matters. My body is slightly shivering as he swims us toward the side. It reminds me of the last time we were here: the night that I left.

"Remember this?" Cale questions as he holds me up against the side of the pool.

Biting my bottom lip, I nod.

"Good…" He slides his hand behind my neck and hovers his lips above mine. They're so close I can almost taste him. "I'm about to do to you what I wanted to do six years ago."

His lips press against mine, stealing my breath away. I can barely breathe as I'm taken back to six years ago. I almost feel as if I'm getting the one moment that we missed out on, the moment that I could only dream about *after* I was gone.

"Are you on the pill, Rile?" His eyes meet mine as he pushes my hair out of my face. "Are you?"

I nod and rub my thumb over his sexy bottom lip. All I want to do is suck it into my mouth, so I do. I suck it so hard that he growls.

He leans in and kisses me again, hard and firm as he finds my aching pussy with his free hand. I moan against his lips as two of his fingers enter me. They feel so big, but I relax for him and let him loosen me up.

"So good, Rile." He pulls his fingers out and slides my shorts over to the side. He's messing around between our legs, probably pulling himself free from his black pants. He's not wearing any boxers. That was noticeable as soon as he came out of his bedroom earlier, so it doesn't take long before I feel him poking at my entrance.

I shake in Cale's hold, as he looks me in the eyes. I'm so overwhelmed with emotions that I can't even manage to speak. This man has been my best friend for ten years, and I have spent most of those years dreaming of this very moment.

"I've been waiting so long to be inside you, Rile. Are you sure you want this?" He rubs his thumb over my bottom lip as I nod. "Say it for me. Tell me that you want me inside you. I want to hear it from your lips. I've waited too long not to."

I lean my head back and moan as I feel the tip of his dick push against my opening. There's no doubt in my mind that I want this. Not having him inside me right now is torture. "I want it, Cale. I've always expected you to be my first." I lean in and whisper against his mouth, "Make love to me."

With those words, he slowly enters me, inch by inch, him holding me so tightly that I can barely breathe.

"Oh fuck," Cale whispers. "You're so tight, Rile. So fucking tight." He slowly pushes all the way in and stills, practically holding me against the wall with his dick. He's breathing so hard right now, that I can feel his chest hammering against mine.

It hurts, but feels so good to have Cale inside of me that I don't want him to stop. He can't. I dig my nails into his arms, letting him know that I need a minute. "It's so big, Cale." I let out a calming breath. "I need a second. Don't move."

Being sure not to hurt me, he reaches back and tugs his shirt off and over his head, before tossing it into the grass. He grips the edge of the pool with one hand and my waist with the other. "Can I move now?"

I wrap both of my arms around his neck and squeeze, preparing myself for him to move. "Yeah," I whisper. "I think I'm okay now."

Pressing his lips against mine, he slowly pulls out and pushes back in, both of us moaning into each other's mouths.

He does this a few more times, as gentle as he can, before his movements pick up, becoming more steady, until he's consistently thrusting inside of me, making me feel so good that it's surreal. Having Cale inside of me is so overwhelming that I can barely breathe from the emotions that are taking over me.

Gripping my thigh, he raises it and pushes in hard and deep, before stopping and grinding his hips. He's so deep that I feel as if he's about to rip me apart.

"Cale..." I dig my nails into his shoulder as he pulls out and shoves himself in deep again, stopping to kiss me on the lips.

"I want to fuck you so much harder, but I'm holding back, Rile." He lifts me up with his thrust. "Can you handle it harder?"

Hearing him ask me if I can handle it harder sets me off, and suddenly all I can think about is him fucking me so hard that I'm screaming his name. I want him so bad right now. All of him.

"Yeah," I say softly. "I can handle it."

"Alright, Rile." He wraps his hands into my hair and tugs. "Don't be afraid to scream. I don't give a shit who hears us. This is our moment... just the two of us."

I nod and almost come undone when he digs his teeth into his bottom lip and begins taking me hard and deep.

All I can hear are the sounds of the water slapping between our bodies and our heavy moans. Cale works fast, slowing down once in a while to kiss me and make me feel special... and it does. It's as if he knows exactly what he's doing and he's an expert at pleasuring women. He's almost too good to be true, and now the thought of him being inside another woman kills me.

My thoughts cause me to dig my nails into his back roughly, instigating his movements to pick up and become harder.

"This cock is yours, Rile. No one else has had it. Never fucking forget that." He pushes into me and stops. He's breathing heavily, his strong chest moving up and down. "I want to come inside of you, baby."

"Yes... do, Cale." I pull him closer to me and kiss his chest. "I want you to."

Gripping my thigh, he pushes in even deeper and rolls his hips. He does this a few more times until I'm practically moaning and shaking in his arms, about to come.

"Yeah, Rile." He pulls out before pushing in deep. "Come for me, baby. I want to feel you squeeze me."

Leaning my head into his neck, I dig my nails into his back as I feel my orgasm taking over. In that moment, Cale thrusts into me a few more times before I feel the pulsations of him filling me with his own orgasm.

Knowing that no other woman has experienced this with Cale has me on a high. He's inside of *me* right now, holding *me* and kissing *me*. A part of me is selfish and wants to keep Cale to myself. I don't want any other woman to experience this side of Cale.

We're both wet and completely satisfied, holding each other tight... in someone else's pool.

I would've never thought of my first time being like this, but it was perfect. This pool is where Cale and I spent most of our time in the summer. This pool is where I imagined giving myself to him numerous times. This pool is the last memory I had of him over the last six years.

Now this pool is where we've given ourselves to each other. It's our pool. Our memory to keep and I'll *never* forget his moment. *Ever*.

Cale smiles against my neck, before he kisses it and pulls out of me. "Holy shit." Cupping my face, he kisses me long and hard before resting his forehead to mine. "I want to take you again, right here, right now. Is that bad?"

I let out a small laugh and smile. "No," I say breathless. "It's definitely not bad."

He releases my face and pulls his pants back up. "I have a feeling we should get out of here. You were kind of loud." He smiles and I slap his chest.

"Oh... just me?"

He laughs and hops out of the pool, pulling me out behind him. He quickly grabs his shirt and picks me up, throwing me over his shoulder.

He carries me through the grass and over to his truck, the two of us soaking wet and laughing. Setting me down against his truck, he kisses me one last time before opening the door for me and giving me a boost inside.

When we arrive back at his house, he lets us both in and immediately undresses me as soon as he closes the door behind us, dropping our soaked clothes to the floor.

After we're both completely naked and standing here, he picks me up, wrapping my legs around his waist before carrying me to his bed.

He crawls in behind me and snuggles up against me, covering us up. He notices me shivering, so he pulls me closer to warm me up, just as he always has. "I got you, Rile. I'll always have you."

I smile to myself and grip his arms, feeling completely satisfied and alive, knowing that he does. *He's always had me...*

CHAPTER TEN

CALE

I'VE BEEN LAYING HERE FOR the last three hours thinking about tonight. Being inside of Riley was the best feeling in the world, and I know without a doubt that no other woman would have been able to make me feel that way. I've always known that and that's why I waited for her.

Fuck having meaningless sex just to experience a bunch of women and get off. None of that matters and I know damn well that it could never feel as good as having sex with someone you have a personal connection with. When you have that, the pleasure is intensified. You feel *everything*.

Watching Riley sleeping in my arms makes me want to bury myself between her thighs and really take her. She's seen my sweet side. I just hope she can handle my dirty side too, because she's about to experience it real soon. I'll let her sleep it off for tonight, because I'm not going to be selfish with her. Riley doesn't deserve that shit.

Pulling Riley as close as I can, I bury my face into the back of her neck and gently kiss her, wanting to show how deeply I care about her.

"Goodnight, Rile," I whisper.

SLADE, HEMY, AND STONE ARE sitting around like idiots, looking at me as if I've grown a second dick. If it doesn't stop, then I'm going to nut punch the closest one.

"What are you idiots looking at?" I shove a fry in my mouth, eyebrow raised, as I look around the table.

Slade stands up and walks over, sandwich and all, stopping in front of me. "Stand up."

I stand up.

He smirks. "I want to shake your dick and congratulate it on finally becoming a man."

I shove him backward, making him bump into Hemy. "Fuck you." I reach down and adjust my hard dick. Thoughts of Riley naked have been on my mind all morning, leaving me hard, and there's no hiding it. "Talk all you want, assholes."

Stone gets up and starts fucking the edge of the table like an idiot. "Is this how you did it?" He slows down and acts as if he's about to blow his load.

"How the fuck do you idiots even know my business?"

Hemy nods to Slade. "This asshole told me in a text. Ask him."

Slade shrugs his shoulder while biting into his steak sandwich. "Aspen, man. Your girl was on the phone with her for a good hour, talking about how *sweet* and *passionate* it was."

The guys start laughing as if it bothers me. Fuck them. I can't help it that I'm good at making love. "Laugh all you want, because I'm going to make that girl feel so fucking good that all of your women will be complaining to each other and talking shit about how all you guys care about are your own dicks. My woman will be completely satisfied. So fuck you."

"Your woman?" Slade asks with a sly grin. "It's like that already?"

"What... are you fucking surprised?" I watch as he walks around the table and takes a seat again. "I wouldn't have waited all this time for a woman if she wasn't worth it, man. Riley is more than worth it, and when she's ready... yeah... she will be *my* woman."

Stone squeezes my shoulder. "I feel ya though, guy. Sage is the one for me. Being inside her—"

"Fuck you," Hemy shouts. "Say another fucking word and see if I don't shove your dick up your ass. That's my sister, fucker."

"Yeah, I am your sister's fucker," Stone says, egging Hemy on. This dick still has some shit to learn, because that's the last thing you want to do.

Cracking his neck, Hemy stands from his chair and starts walking around me to get to Stone, but I put out my arm stopping him. "Dude, chill. All you fuckers chill and eat your food. Can't go anywhere with you dicks anymore."

Hemy's chest flexes under my arm, so I pull it away and say fuck it. I'm hungry. These two can kill each other all they want.

Stone stands up and smiles as Hemy approaches him, trying to prove he's badass. "Don't hate me, because I might be your brother-in-law someday. It'll be all good. I promise."

"Hey!" We all look away from the table when Sage comes storming in with Onyx beside her. "Sit down, Hemy! Don't you even think about it."

Hemy gets *the look* from Onyx, so like a good boy he backs off. I don't blame him. Not only does he have a spitfire for a sister, but also his woman is just as wild as her. I don't know how he handles it.

Next thing I know Hemy has his mouth pressed against Onyx's and his hands are groping all the inappropriate places. I'm pretty sure that's my cue to leave.

Standing up, I pop one last fry into my mouth before tossing some cash on the table. "I'm out. I've gotta go keep my eye on Kash and make sure he can handle his first night on the floor." Walking over, I place a kiss on the side of Onyx and Sage's cheeks, before turning back to the guys. "This kid better not make me work tonight."

I get a, "Get the hell out of here," from Hemy and an "Alright, go fuck off," from Slade, before Stone just waves and grabs his woman.

"What a great group of friends," I mutter to myself. Thank God Riley is back. I don't know how much longer I can handle these assholes.

I'VE BEEN HERE KEEPING MY eye on Kash for the last two hours, and so far I haven't had to save him. I got to give the kid some credit. The women seem to be enjoying themselves.

I have a feeling he's been watching me a lot, because right now he's got some girl on her knees and he's grinding his dick in her face. The women always seem to love that.

Pulling out my phone, I send Riley a text, hoping she's not busy. I've been thinking about her all day, reminding myself of the moment we shared in the pool. The best moment of my life.

Cale

How are you doing? Are you at home?

I get a response almost immediately.

Riley

I'm good. I'm not home at the moment.

I stare down at my phone, my stomach sinking from her stiff text. We haven't spoken all day, and I have no idea how she's feeling about last night.

Cale

Can I pick you up in an hour?

Riley

No

"Shit." Dropping my phone down onto the couch next to me, I run my hands through my hair. My jaw stiffens as I stand up and get ready to just leave and go find her.

"Because I'm already here."

I turn beside me to see Riley standing there, looking drop dead gorgeous in a little red dress. Her hair is curled and pulled over to her right shoulder, and her lips are slightly tinted pink.

"Fuck me, Rile." I grab her hand and slowly spin her around. "Are you trying to make me take you right here?"

Smiling, she wraps her arms around my neck and steps into my body. "What if I am?"

I slide my hands down her back and stop on her ass, cupping it. "Then you better be ready, because I don't think I can wait another second." I bite her neck, before pulling away. "Especially after seeing you in this dress."

Leaning her head back she laughs. "When did my Cale become so dirty?" Stepping up on her tippytoes, she sucks my bottom lip into her mouth, before releasing it and sliding her hands up the front of my shirt. "I definitely like it. A lot."

"You haven't even begun to see how dirty I can get, but you're definitely pushing me right now." Grabbing her legs, I wrap them around my waist and carry her through the darkened room and to the back corner.

Everyone is too busy paying attention to the new dick that's swinging around on stage to even notice us. Slamming her up against the wall, I slide her dress up her body. "See the things you make me want to do?" I grind my hips into her and wrap my hand in her hair. "Are you ready for this, Rile? Are you still sore?"

She doesn't say anything for a few seconds. She just plays with the ends of my hair and looks me in the eyes. "A little, but I've never been more ready for anything, Cale. I want you."

"Neither have I." Reaching down between us, I work on getting my cock out, while pressing my lips to her neck.

"Hurry, Cale." She tugs my hair. "I've been thinking about you inside me all day. I need this right now."

Hearing those words set me off. Dropping her feet to the ground, I bend down and yank her panties down her legs, before shoving them in my pocket.

Then, I pick her up and wrap her legs back around my waist, before slowly stretching her, sliding inside of her. "Oh fuck." We both moan out at the same time.

She's so wet and ready for me that it's hard to not bust my load just from the thought alone. Riley Raines... the woman I have wanted for most of my life.

I slowly slide in and out, stretching her to accommodate my size, before thrusting into her deep and hard. She lets out a small scream but muffles it against my chest.

"It's okay, baby." I pull out and thrust into her again, grinding my hips into her as deep as I can. "Let it out. I don't give a shit who hears."

Moaning, she presses her lips to mine as I push into her again. I push into her harder and harder each time, slamming her against the wall with my thrusts.

"Shit, Cale..." She digs her nails into the fabric of my shirt and buries her face into my neck. "Oh my God. Keep going.""

Speeding up, I take her as hard and fast as I can, feeling her pussy squeeze around me, bringing me to my own release.

My cock pulses inside of her, filling her with my cum. Biting her bottom lip, I hold her up with my hips and wrap both of my hands into the back of her hair. "Shit, Riley." Both of our bodies are covered in sweat. This place has never made me sweat so fucking much. "You can't dress like that anymore around me. I can't fucking handle it."

She smiles against my lips. "I was hoping for that."

"Cale, dude, what the fuck are you doing back there? Kash needs you for a minute," Lynx yells from across the room. Lazy motherfucker.

Riley's eyes widen and she throws her hand over her face. "Oh. My. God." She starts struggling to get back to her feet. "I almost forgot where we were."

I kiss her one more time and smile against her lips as I readjust myself. "Dude, I'm coming."

She slaps my chest and playfully covers my mouth. "Shh... don't say that."

"Well hurry the fuck up."

I press my forehead to hers. "Wait for me." I pull her bottom lip into my mouth. "Let me go help this dick and then we'll leave. Yeah?"

She nods and works on pulling her dress down as far as she can. "I'll wait in your truck so I can be panty-less alone."

I reach into my pocket and pull my keys out, handing them to her. "You won't be panty-less and alone for long. Trust me."

Raising a brow, I back up and start walking, before turning around to see what the hell Kash needs me for.

The faster I do the faster I can make it back out to my woman...

CHAPTER ELEVEN

RILEY

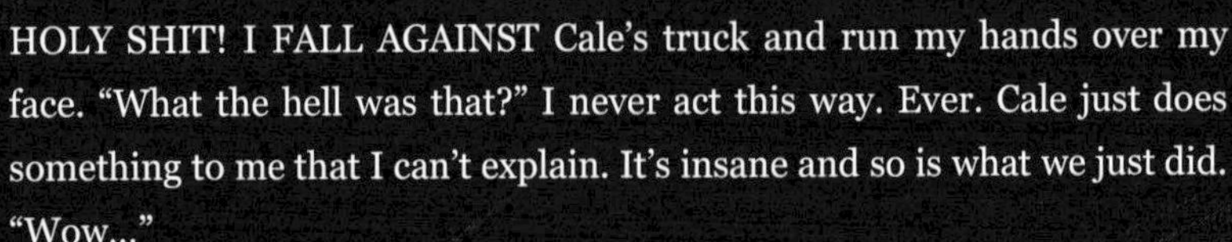

HOLY SHIT! I FALL AGAINST Cale's truck and run my hands over my face. "What the hell was that?" I never act this way. Ever. Cale just does something to me that I can't explain. It's insane and so is what we just did. "Wow..."

Anyone could've walked back there and caught us. Then what? He could've lost his job. I would've felt like a complete idiot. I need to get a grip before it's too late.

Unlocking his truck door, I jump inside and rest my head against the back of the seat. My pussy is still pulsing from my orgasm and I can't help but smile. I shouldn't be smiling after what we just did, but I can't help it. Nothing has ever felt so good in my life. Nothing.

Tyler was never able to give me orgasms. He tried multiple times and I always had to fake them just to make him happy. It always left me feeling like shit afterward. Not with Cale. With Cale I almost feel silly for having one too soon. Is that a thing? Shit… I don't know.

A few minutes later, the driver's side door opens and Cale jumps inside with a look of aggravation. "That dickhead."

I look at him and laugh. "What?"

A small smile crosses Cale's face. "He wanted me to teach him a new dance move. He actually stopped in the middle of his performance so he could ask me to teach him a new move." He shakes his head while starting the engine. "That kid needs some serious work if he wants to make it here."

I can't help but laugh. His face always cracks me up when he's aggravated. I've always found it hard to take him seriously, probably because his aggravation has never been aimed at me. Thank God.

"He seemed to be doing good to me."

Cale sits up straight and grabs my thigh. "Oh yeah?" He runs his hand higher up my thigh and stops right below my pussy. "So that's why you were so wet earlier?"

I squirm as he starts tickling me. "No…" I say in between laughs. "No… stop it!" I slap his hand until he finally stops and smiles at me.

"I didn't think so," he says confidently. "I was pretty sure it was all me." He winks and I shake my head at him.

"Confident Cale." I reach over and grab his dick, almost making him swerve off the side of the road. "You do something to me."

"Shit, Rile." He grips the steering wheel, fighting hard to keep his eyes on the road. "What did I turn you into?"

I release his dick and lean back into my seat. "A woman that likes to tease you and see you squirm. You've been doing it to me for years and just didn't know it. You and your little touches. You didn't think that I noticed how close you were to my ass and pussy sometimes? I noticed. Very much so."

Cale smirks. "Well you never said anything." He glances over at me. "I wanted to touch you so bad. That was me getting as close as I could with still being able to control myself. It was harder than you think. Trust me."

My stomach does a little happy dance as I remember the old times with Cale. It's crazy how you can want something so bad and then it happens years down the road. It almost feels as if no time has passed at all.

With Cale… I feel like we're still teenagers. He's always made me feel younger than I am. Knowing that I can finally touch him has me all worked up and extremely aroused... again.

Reaching for his jeans, I slowly undo them. I tilt my head and look up at Cale to see him watching the road with a smirk. "What are you doing?"

I bite my bottom lip as I pull his erection free, running my hand up the length. "I'm just admiring your body." I sit back in my seat and take in the image of him driving with his dick out. "I definitely like this view."

Cale glances over at me. "Oh yeah?" Keeping his eyes on the road, he grips the steering wheel with one hand and his dick with the other. "What about this?"

A small gasp escapes my lips as he slowly begins to stroke himself. "Oh. My. God." I fan myself off and crack the window some more. "Yes. The view is definitely getting better. Keep going." I whisper the last part, completely lost in him.

Leaning his head back, he quickens his strokes, letting out a small growl. "Do you have any idea how many times I have done this to thoughts of you, Rile?"

My heart jumps out of my chest from his words. "No, I don't." Completely turned on, I spread my legs a little and moan. "Tell me."

He notices me beginning to squirm in my seat so he lets out a small, amused laugh. "Too many fucking times." He slows his strokes for a second, before he releases his dick and grips my thigh, yanking me toward him. "Almost every time you left my house." He pushes my dress up, baring my lower half, and runs his fingers through my wetness. "Did you ever pleasure yourself while thinking of me... huh, Rile?"

I press my head back into the seat and grip it as his finger slips inside of me, slowly pumping in and out.

"Did you ever imagine me fucking you in your bed all those times that I slept in your room?" He shoves his finger in deep and stops. "Did you ever imagine me deep inside you, taking you and making you scream all night? Did you?" he whispers.

I jump and grip the seat tighter when he finds my spot. "Yes!" I scream. "Yes... so many times. I could never sleep," I admit. "I kept imagining how it would feel."

"Stroke me, Rile." We pull up at a stoplight, but Cale is looking at me as if he couldn't care less what others may see. "Touch me like you always wanted to."

I moan as his fingers pump into me, fast and hard. "Cale... oh my God. That feels... so... good."

"Touch me," he growls out.

Looking around, I realize just how dark it is and how high up we are in his truck. It gives me the courage that I need. Reaching over, I take him in my hand, stroking him, and imagining that we're the old Cale and Riley. I'm finally able to touch this man and it feels so good.

Leaning toward him, I take him in both hands and pump as fast as I can. Cale has me on the verge of orgasm. "Keep going," I moan. "Faster, Cale."

Turning the corner, Cale slams the truck into park and leans into me, fucking me with his fingers as fast and hard as he can, until I'm squirming in my seat, my arousal covering his fingers.

Not even a few seconds later Cale falls apart beneath my touch, releasing himself onto his shirt. "Fuck me, Rile," he says through heavy breaths. "You've got me feeling like a fucking horny teenage boy again."

I burst into laughter in between heavy breaths. "I hope that's not a bad thing."

Shaking his head, he pulls his shirt off and balls it up, before tossing it in the backseat. "Nothing you do to me can ever be bad, babe."

My heart soars as he flashes me his sweet, dimpled smile. He's the most beautiful man in the world and here I am in his truck. I'm finally able to do the things to him that I've wanted to do for most of my life, and I don't plan on stopping anytime soon.

Shifting the truck into drive, Cale reaches over, intertwining his fingers in mine. "I'm happy that you're back."

"Me too," I say with a smile. "Oh... I almost forgot." I shift in my seat so I can face him. "My parents are having a cookout tomorrow and they want you to come. They've been asking about you. Aspen and Slade will be there too. Are you up for it?"

He smiles while pulling into his driveway. "You know I'm in. I haven't had the chance to bug your parents in a long time."

I roll my eyes at just how much my mom loved Cale. I swear she had her own little crush on him. "I'm sure my mom won't mind one bit."

He points to his tight chest and abs. "I'm not sure she can handle all this new goodness that I have. Your father might have to keep her contained."

"Someone's a little cocky." I lean in and motion for him to meet me halfway. "Come here."

Smiling, he leans in and reaches his hand behind my neck. Just as he's about to kiss me, I grab his nipple and twist it. "Mmm..." he moans. "Are you trying to work me up again?"

Sucking his bottom lip into my mouth, I slap his chest, before letting my hand trail down it. "A little sleep would be nice... so..." I bite his bottom lip and pull away. "I think I'll go to bed instead."

He gives me a long, serious look, before jumping out of the truck and running over to my side.

Before I can lock it he pulls my door open and reaches inside, tossing me over his shoulder. "You should know better than to tease me, Rile. Haven't you learned anything about me over the years?"

He shuts the door and slaps my ass, before laying me down into the grass and crawling above me.

Looking into his eyes, I tangle my fingers into the back of his hair. "I don't want this to end, Cale."

He swallows and reaches down to brush my hair off of my face. "No one says it has to."

"But..." I stop to collect myself. "What if it ruins us? I can't lose you, Cale."

Pushing my thigh up, he presses himself into me and kisses me long and gentle, before pulling away. "I will never let that happen. I'll die before it does."

Rolling over, he pulls me into his chest and we both lay here, looking up at the night sky just like we used to do some nights after a late-night swim at his house. It's so calm and relaxing that I almost fall asleep, but I keep catching myself, not wanting to lose one minute I have with Cale.

"It's okay if you fall asleep," Cale whispers. "I'll carry you inside."

I shake my head and wrap my fingers in his. "I'm fine..." I yawn. "I'm not going to fall asleep."

"That's what you always say," he says softly.

Next thing I know, I'm falling asleep in his arms... just like I always did.

Cale has always been my comfort and safety...

CHAPTER TWELVE

RILEY

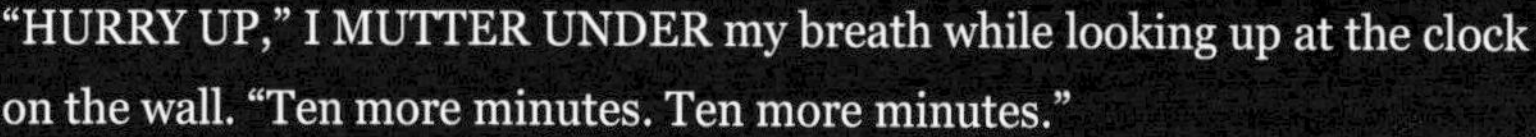

"HURRY UP," I MUTTER UNDER my breath while looking up at the clock on the wall. "Ten more minutes. Ten more minutes."

Mr. Peterson attempts to sit up, but I politely push him back down onto the table. "No more flipping over please, Mr. Peterson. We only have ten minutes left of your session."

Relaxing once again, the elderly man places his hands behind his head and lets out a long sigh. "An hour isn't enough time. What you need to do is teach my darn wife how to do that stuff you do with your hands. That's what I need."

I let out an amused laugh while firmly massaging his left calf, being sure to work out the knot as best as I can. "I'll see what I can do, Mr. Peterson." I smile down at him as he struggles to look up at me. "But then you may not need me if I do that."

"Nonsense," he growls. "You're not getting rid of me that easily. I haven't felt this young in ages. My wife..."

Mr. Peterson continues to babble on about his wife, but all I can focus on is the fact that Cale will be here any minute to pick me up. It's only been eight hours, but it feels a hell of a lot longer since I've felt his lips on mine, and it's driving me insane.

As much as I would like some alone time with him before the cookout, we're heading straight over to my parents' to please my mom. She's been asking when he's going to come visit her ever since I walked in the house a little over a week ago.

My parents haven't seen Cale in over a year, and I know without a doubt that my mom is going to freak out as soon as he walks in the door. I wouldn't be surprised if she attacks him with kisses.

She's always loved Cale, and when I had to leave to help care for my grandmother it seemed as if it hurt her that I had to leave him behind almost as much as it did me. I cried myself to sleep that night, and my mother watched me with wet eyes, telling me that Cale would still be here when I returned. She was right, even though I didn't believe it at the time.

I shake out of my thoughts in just enough time to see that our time is up.

"Alright, Mr. Peterson. We're out of time."

Grunting, he sits up and stretches as I turn on the sink to wash my hands. "Much better," he says in a raspy voice. "My wife might just be a lucky lady tonight, thanks to you."

"Glad I could help," I say, in a hurry to get him out of here. "So I'll see you the same time next week?"

I get another grunt and a, "Yes," as he stands up, letting his towel fall to the floor. I'm greeted with the sight of his baggy tightie whities, making me instantly turn my head and cover my face.

"Whoa," I say, taking this as my cue to escape. "I'll just head out and let you finish up. Tell your wife hello for me."

I hear a mutter. "Yeah. Yeah." I quickly dodge out into the hall and shut the door behind me.

"Oh, sweet freedom, how I love you," I say to myself while making my way past Hailey's door and down the short hallway.

As I get closer to the front desk I stop and instantly smile when I notice Cale is waiting inside for me. My heart goes crazy just from the sight of him, and I get this sudden urge to run and jump into his arms, but I won't do that here.

I get ready to start walking, but stop and swallow back my jealousy when I notice Kylie's hand slide across the desk and reach for Cale's arm. From afar it looks as if she's rubbing her fingertips over his muscle.

Cale looks down at her hand on his arm, but doesn't say anything as she leans over the desk in an attempt to get his attention.

Seeing another woman want him in that way feels like getting punched in the gut. Even though he doesn't seem interested, it still gives me a sick feeling in my stomach.

If it's like this here—outside of the strip club—I don't even want to begin to think about what goes on at the club when he's half-naked and shaking his goods for drunken, horny women. I've gotten a small glimpse, but I'm sure that's nothing compared to what could happen. I'm not sure what to do with that.

Sucking it up, I walk up beside Cale and get ready to greet him. Without hesitation Cale turns to me and wraps both of his hands into the back of my hair, pressing his lips to mine and pulling me as close as he possibly can.

Talk about taking someone's breath away. His lips assault mine, repeatedly sucking and tasting me in a way that almost feels desperate. He's devouring me. Pulling away, he runs his tongue over his bottom lip before biting it. "Shit, I've been waiting all day to do that."

Kylie looks us both over before rolling her eyes and sitting down in her chair, clearly aware that Cale is not interested now. "Looks like I did someone a favor last week," she says stiffly. "Better you than Hailey, I suppose."

Her words make me angry. He's been my Cale for far longer than this girl even knew he existed. Leaning over the desk, I get ready to say something, but Cale pulls me to him, cutting me off.

"Nah, actually you did me a favor." He slaps the desk, before leaning in and sucking my bottom lip into his mouth. "And it's always been her. Simple as that." With a lift of his eyebrow, he grabs my hand to get me walking. "Ready?"

Trying to fight my grin, I nod and wrap my arm around his waist as he starts walking toward the door. "So damn ready."

Just as we're about to walk out the door Hailey appears next to the desk, glaring at Kylie and complaining about something. I hear Cale's name, but choose to ignore it. I don't need anything dragging me down. Especially two girls that I can barely even stand to be around.

After hopping into Cale's truck I reach for my seatbelt and get ready to pull it down, but look up surprised when Cale reaches over me and reclines my seat back as far as it will go.

"What are you doing?" I laugh as he crawls over the seat until he's hovering over me, gripping the seat with his hand to keep balance. I can't help but notice the way his muscles flex as he stares down at me.

"Something I've always wanted to do in the past." He positions himself between my legs and presses his lips to mine... hard; so hard that it almost hurts. "I've always wanted to take you in my truck," he says against my lips.

"Cale..." I run my hands up his strong back as he sucks my bottom lip into his mouth, teasing me and turning me on completely. "There're people everywhere," I say with a small moan.

He grips my thigh and smiles against my mouth. "Then let them watch." His lips slam against mine, causing me to moan out as my eyes close. "Fuck, I can't hold back with you, Rile. I've kept my hands off of you for long enough; too damn long. Touching you everywhere is the only thing I can think about anymore."

I start reaching for the back of his shirt, getting completely lost in the moment, but jump when I look beside us to see Slade leaning against the truck, casually just chilling and enjoying the show. "Holy shit," I laugh. "Seriously?"

"What?" Cale stops kissing my neck and looks up. "Fucking idiot," he growls as soon as he sees Slade. With his jaw flexed, he rolls down the window, glaring at Slade as if he wants to kill him. "What dude? What are you doing here?"

Slade lifts an eyebrow and uncrosses his arms. "Just enjoying the show, man. Don't stop on my account. I'm curious to see just what I need to teach you. You gotta catch up with the big boys now."

Cale's grip on the seat tightens. "You're an idiot," he growls. "What do you really want?"

Slade shrugs his shoulders and grips the window. "Aspen told me you were stopping to pick up Riley on the way over. I was driving by and noticed your truck. The windows looked a little frosted and shit, so I came to hurry your ass up."

Grinning, Cale gives Slade the middle finger while rolling up the window. He leans in and kisses me quickly, breathing heavily against my lips. “Dammit! Let’s go before this dude busts a nut outside of my truck. Anything can work him up.”

I laugh and roll the window back down as Cale crawls over to his seat and adjusts the crotch of his jeans. “Hey, Slade,” I say with a small laugh.

Slade gives me a slick head nod and smiles. “Looking good, Riley.” Leaning in the truck, Slade kisses the side of my head while smiling over at Cale. “Both of you hurry your asses up.”

Cale starts the engine, gripping the wheel while glaring at Slade. “Don’t push it, fucker. We’re on the way.”

Slade winks and turns on his heels, walking over to his nice new car.

“Remind me to kill Slade later,” Cale says while pulling out of the lot.

I can’t help but laugh at the boys for acting so silly. I definitely won’t mind this kind of entertainment to get us through dinner. “Sure thing,” I say with a smile.

I try to stay cool on the way to my parents’ house, but the way Cale is rubbing my leg has me squirming in my seat and gripping the seat. The satisfied smirk on his face only shows me that he’s doing this on purpose and enjoying this much more than I am.

“You’re enjoying this, aren’t you?” I grab his hand and place it on his own lap as he pulls up in front of the house. “It’s already going to be hard enough to act normal around my parents, pretending as if nothing is going on. Please don’t make it harder.” I suck in a breath and attempt to compose myself.

He unbuckles his seatbelt and reaches over to undo mine, hovering his lips above mine. “Who said anything about acting normal?” He brushes his lips over mine, causing my heart to jump out of my chest. “You can touch me, kiss me... or fuck me for all I care. There’s plenty of rooms to choose from.” He whispers the last part before smiling and jumping out of the truck, leaving me wanting him even more.

“Damn you, Cale. You’re still a pain in my ass,” I say to myself while gripping the door handle and jumping out to catch up with him. “Well, it’s definitely going to be easy to talk to my parents now,” I tease. “So thanks for that image.”

Without bothering to knock Cale opens the screen door and lets himself in, holding the door open for me. My mom is standing in the kitchen mixing some kind of dessert when we walk in. It smells like chocolate. Cale loves chocolate.

"Oooh. Oooh." My mom cleans the chocolate off of her hands hurriedly and smiles as Cale walks over to her with open arms.

"Did you miss me?" Cale asks while squeezing my mom in a bear hug and shaking her back and forth.

She pulls away and grabs his face, looking him over. Her smile is just as big as it's always been for Cale. "You know I did. Look at you," she squeals. "Oh my goodness." She backs away and looks him up and down, taking in his large build. "You have gotten so much bigger since the last time I saw you, Cale, and more handsome too. Oh my. Come here."

She grabs my arm and pulls me next to her, while holding onto Cale's waist. "It's so good seeing you two hanging out again. It makes me feel young again. Isn't this something?"

Rolling my eyes, I kiss my mom on the cheek and laugh. "Yeah... yeah. Where's Aspen and Slade?"

My mom releases her grip on both of us and points to the back door. "They're outside with your father."

"It smells so good in here," Cale says before kissing my mom on the cheek. "I've missed your cooking. Don't be surprised if I eat all that dessert you're working on."

My mom blushes while going back to stirring her dessert. "Yeah, well what can I say? That's why I made so much. I learned my lesson eight years ago." She turns to me and winks. "The food is on the grill and should be ready to eat soon. Just hang out for a bit and keep your father company. We all know he doesn't get it very often."

"Alright, Mom. Let me know if you need help."

My mom shakes her head and motions toward the door. "Nope. Just go and enjoy yourselves. Scoot."

Cale places his hand on my lower back and guides me toward the sliding door. "Your ass looks fucking delicious in those shorts," he whispers, before sliding the door open and pulling me outside. "Can't wait to taste you later."

I break into an instant sweat from his words mixed with the heat. As soon as my dad sees us, he waves us over, holding up a beer for Cale. I just need to get away from this man before I melt into a puddle at his feet. He's the perfect distraction.

Pulling away from Cale, I rush over to Aspen and sit down in the chair next to her while Cale goes to hang out with my dad and Slade.

My dad stands up as soon as Cale approaches. Handing him a beer, he grips Cale's shoulder and greets him with a smile. I'm actually surprised to see how happy my dad looks to see him. I knew he always liked Cale. He just didn't want to admit how much.

I turn to Aspen. "This is torture," I say in a hurry.

Aspen takes a sip of her pop and looks over at the picnic table where the guys are hanging out. "Tell me about it. I'm bored already. Mom talked our ear off when we walked in the door and Dad keeps talking about his work."

I shake my head and look in Cale's direction to see his tight muscles flexing as he grips his beer and laughs along with the guys. "No, I meant Cale. All I want to do is take him up to my old room and jump on him. It's like I can't even be in the same room without touching him. You know?"

Aspen smiles at my comment and lifts a brow as she watches the guys. "I definitely know, sister. Welcome to my world."

We sit here, just watching the boys for a few minutes, before Aspen speaks up, breaking the silence. "So what *are* you and Cale anyway? Are you doing this whole 'friends with benefits' thing? Or what? That could get messy, so be careful."

I let out a frustrated breath and grab Aspen's drink, taking a sip. My mouth suddenly feels extremely dry. "I don't know, Aspen. I care about Cale a lot, you know that, but I really don't know what he wants out of this. I'm worried if I ask him that I'll mess up what we have. I can't have that. We've been friends for too long, so I'm just sitting back and enjoying the ride."

"Literally," Aspen replies.

"Shut up," I say, while punching her in the thigh. "Can you talk any louder?"

"Ouch, asshole." Aspen smiles, taking another sip of her drink. "Nothing to be ashamed of."

We both look up when my father calls us. "Girls. Get over here and eat."

We both grumble to each other before getting up and joining everyone else at the table. I take a spot next to Cale as Aspen takes her place beside Slade.

Dinner passes quickly as my parents talk to Cale about what he's been up to over the years. Leaving out the male stripper part, Cale tells them stories from his bartending experience. Now I'm just hoping they don't look up *Walk of Shame* and decide to drop in for a quick drink sometime. They are supportive like that and it might be a little awkward to explain.

After all conversation with my parents is done and everything is cleaned up, we decide to head inside for a few drinks and a game of darts. The boys talked shit to each other the whole time during dinner, betting money on who would win. Everyone was pretty surprised when my mother jumped up and threw in some money on Cale. That definitely gave him an extra confidence boost, not that he needed one.

There's fifty bucks on the line, so the boys are getting into a serious mode, trying to intimidate each other while us girls sit back and watch.

My parents are sitting in the next room watching a movie, just enjoying the fact that we're all still here. It's not very often that they have both of their girls home, and they're working to keep us here as long as they can.

I have to admit that we're all having fun, a lot more fun than I expected. It sort of feels like old times, back when Aspen and I lived at home. I like this carefree feeling right now, and I'm not ready for it to end anytime soon.

"You lucky shit," Slade spits out while yanking the darts out of the board. "That was luck not skill, so stop that smiling bullshit."

Cale tilts back his bottle of beer and grins even bigger, clearly enjoying this. "Oh trust me, that was all skill, man." He holds up his free hand, showing it off. "My hand is talented as fuck, Slade."

"Nah..." Slade throws his first dart, hitting the bull's-eye. "That's skill. Might as well give me your dick shaking tips now."

Ignoring Slade, Cale walks over to me and wraps his hands into the back of my hair, pulling me in for a kiss. His lips are soft and sweet, tasting of the chocolate dessert that he recently ate. "I can't wait to get you alone. As soon as I win this asshole's money, I'm taking you to the nearest bed and letting you have your way with me." He smiles against my lips when I grab his ass and squeeze.

"Oh, is that right?" I run my hands up his strong back and dig my nails into his shoulders. "So I can do anything that I want?"

He pulls my bottom lip into his mouth and nibbles it. "Anything," he breathes. "You're the only one with that power, so I would abuse it if I were you."

Cale clenches his jaw when one of Slade's darts comes flying at his head. "Seriously?"

Aspen wraps her arm around Slade's neck and pulls him down to her level so that she can kiss him and whisper something to him.

"You both want to play now, huh?" I grab one of Cale's darts and throw it at them. "I think us girls should get in on this game. Double it."

We're all standing here bickering, trying to decide on what to do when the doorbell rings.

A few minutes later, my mom walks in and takes one look at me in Cale's arms, before clearing her throat and looking around awkwardly. "Riley... Tyler is at the door. He said he's here to talk to you."

I just about pass out when Tyler steps into the room, looking at me as if he's waited forever to see me again.

His blond hair is cut short and slightly messy, and he's dressed in a pair of old jeans and a white shirt. I almost forgot just how cute he is, and seeing him standing here... for me... makes my heart sink.

Holy. Fucking. Shit.

CHAPTER THIRTEEN

CALE

FUCK ME... MY EYES MEET Riley's and I can see her being emotionally pulled in different directions, about to lose her composure. This is not good. Not good for me at all.

Knowing he's here to win Riley back makes me fucking sick. Now that I know what he looks like, it's easier to picture him putting his hands all over her and I don't like it. Not one bit. In fact... it makes me hate him.

"Tyler..." Riley places her hand over her mouth in shock, looking him up and down as if she doesn't know whether to slap him or run to him. "What are you doing here?"

Tyler swallows and looks around the room. Riley is standing close enough to me that I'm sure there's reason for him to question our intentions. "I miss you." He looks at me as he says the next part. "I need to talk to you, Riley. Can we talk in private?"

Everything in me is screaming for her to say no, but I know Riley. I know her more than anything, so I already know her answer before she says it.

"Uh... yeah." She looks around the room and stops when her eyes land on me. "I'm sorry. I need a few minutes."

I place my hand on her hip and give it a small squeeze, before nodding and turning away. I can't stand to watch her walk away with him. I can't fucking do it.

"Well fuck," Slade says after they walk away. "Just keep your cool, man."

I grip the pool table until my knuckles turn white. "I'm cool." I feel Aspen's hand on my shoulder. "I'm good, Aspen. I'm good."

It feels like a lifetime has passed since she's been alone with him talking. I know for a fact that me being here is making it harder for her. I hate that feeling. I hate feeling like I'm the *other* guy.

After about twenty minutes, I can't take it anymore. I feel like I'm about to burst into that room and rip his fucking head off. I keep imagining different scenarios, replaying over and over in my head, and that's when I realize that I need to get out of here before I do something I'll regret later.

"I need to leave," I grind out. Pushing away from the pool table, I turn around and give Slade and Aspen one last look. "I'm about to lose it."

Slade grips my shoulder, but I shake it off and rush out of the room before he can try to stop me. Slowing down for a quick minute, I smile when I reach the living room where Riley's parents are watching a movie. "Thank you so much for dinner."

Kay stands up and kisses my cheek. "Promise me you'll come back soon." I get ready to pull away, but she squeezes my arm, stopping me. "Promise me, Cale," she says firmly. "You know Riley more than anyone. You remember that."

Nodding my head, I pull away and give my respects to her father before hurrying out the door and to my truck. As soon as I close the door behind me, I slam my fist into the dashboard until it's covered in blood. Why the hell does this feeling kill me so much? Why do I want to kill this man?

"Fuck me," I growl.

I may give her a day to get her head on straight, but there's no way in hell I'm giving up and letting him have her back. Riley is mine. She has been from the very first day we met.

It's time that I show her that...

RILEY

WE'VE BEEN STANDING HERE FOR almost twenty minutes, yet Tyler hasn't said a word. He always does this when he's upset and trying to think of the best way to start the conversation.

"Tyler, just talk." I take a seat on the foot of my bed and look up at him. "What are you doing here? We broke up. Remember?"

He runs his hands over his face before looking at me. "I know, Riley, but damn. I've missed you so much." Looking me in the eyes, he walks over to stand in front of me and reaches out for my hands. "I've been going crazy without you. You haven't answered any of my calls and it's been killing me. Killing me, Riley."

I swallow back the guilt and pain that his words bring and try to keep in mind that *he's* the one that decided to break it off at the last minute. *He's* the one that said it would be better to just be friends.

"I'm sorry, Tyler, but I needed time. I can't allow myself to just sit around and mope over you. I have friends and family here that want to spend time with me and I needed to keep a clear head for that."

"I see that," he says stiffly. "Looks like you've been enjoying your *friend* out there quite a bit."

Looking away, I run my hands through my hair and swallow. I never meant to be intimate with someone, and especially so quickly after the breakup, but Cale is an exception. He deserves my time and attention more than anyone I know.

"Look, Tyler. Cale has been my friend for over ten years. I never meant for things to turn into something more, but..."

Tyler bends down and places his thumb to my lips, shutting me up. "I don't care about that. What I care about is making you mine again." He points down at the floor. "I'm here. I have enough bags packed to stay for a week. If we can make it work then I will fly back home and pack up all of my shit if I can't get you to come back home with me." He leans in to kiss my lips, but I turn my head. "Riley, I still love you. I've given you two years of my life."

His words cause my chest to ache. He's right. Two years means something. Maybe just throwing it away is a shitty thing to do. I'm so confused right now and all I want to do is scream.

"Do you still love me, Riley?" He grabs my chin to make me look at him when I don't respond. "Answer me, Riley. You can't tell me that you don't have any love left for me after just a short time of being apart. Tell me the truth."

I hesitate before answering him, because I don't want to give him too much hope, especially when I'm this confused. "Tyler..."

"Just give me a yes or no. I don't want an explanation of buts or maybes. Just a simple yes or no."

"Of course I do, but—"

"That's all I want to hear, and that should be good enough to at least try while I'm here." Standing up, he pulls me to my feet. "Tell me that I've got a chance, Riley. Please."

My heart is beating out of my chest as I think about Cale and what he must be thinking right now. I don't want to think about me without Cale, but Tyler flew all the way here from Mexico. That has to mean something too. I don't want to be a shitty person to the people that care about me.

I can't do this right now. I can't think straight. My breathing picks up and it's getting harder and harder to breathe. "I need time. I need to get out of here." I begin backing out of the room. "I'm sorry, Tyler."

Turning around, I rush out of the room and down the stairs, gripping the railing a little too tight. My chest feels extremely tight as I make my through the house.

My parents both look up at me as I rush to the game room. My heart stops when I poke my head inside to see only Slade and Aspen.

"He's gone," Slade says stiffly.

My throat burns when I hear those two words. "He left?" I whisper, mainly to myself. I stand here frozen for a moment, before rushing outside. Cale's truck is gone and my heart feels completely shattered.

What the hell do I do?

I want to lose control, but instead I walk. I just keep walking, needing to get away from everyone and everything. This is so messed up right now and I have no idea what I'm going to do to fix this. My heart aches for Cale, but my head is telling me that I need to at least give Tyler a chance after coming all this way. I hate this so much.

In the end... someone always gets hurt. I just hate that I have to be the one to do it.

CHAPTER FOURTEEN

CALE

IT'S BEEN TWO DAYS SINCE I've talked to Riley and I'm on the verge of losing my shit. She called me a few times the night that I left her parents' house, but I forced myself not to answer it. I want her back, but I want to give her time to get her head on straight first.

The thought that she's possibly been spending time with Tyler has been killing me, but a real man will hurt for the woman he fucking loves.

He's had two days now to prove his fucking point. Now it's my turn, and you better believe that I'm going to give her all that I have. The thought of another man pleasing her will never cross her mind. All she will be able to see is the two of us together.

I snap out of my thoughts when Hemy comes into the room shirtless, looking for me. "The show is about to start, man. You ready or what?" he asks while throwing on a fresh shirt. "Get your shit together."

I let out a frustrated breath and slam back my beer. "Yeah, man. Let's do this shit. Where are Stone and Kash?"

"They're coming out of the other room." Hemy pulls his long hair into a man bun as music starts playing from the speaker. "Fuck yeah."

He pushes the door open and dances his way out first, before I follow behind him a few seconds later, followed by Stone, and then Kash from their rooms.

All at the same time, we find a girl in the crowd and pull her chair to the center, before straddling her chair and grinding our hips.

I made sure to pick someone that I've never met so that I won't give off the wrong idea. It just so happens to be a cute brunette that reminds me of Riley with her big, beautiful eyes.

It distracts me for a moment, but I manage to not skip a beat, moving right into the next move. Tilting her chair back until her back is almost to the floor, I walk over her until my cock is in her face, before I grind my hips as if fucking her mouth nice and slow.

The girl's hands grip onto my ass and squeeze, but I don't let it distract me. I can't. I need to stay in the moment as much as I can.

Maneuvering my way off her face, I put her chair back into sitting position and make my way up to the stage, meeting the guys in the middle.

We all drop down to the ground, gripping our jeans in the front and pulling as if undressing ourselves, while thrusting in a slow, torturous rhythm. Every girl in the room starts screaming and whistling, wishing that they could be the ones below us. The simple fact that we could have *any* girl in this room used to get me hard, but not tonight, not even a slight chub.

Instead, it gives me a sick feeling in my stomach, reminding me that the one and only girl I want might be with another man right now. The thought causes me to work my hips hard and aggressively, while biting down on my lip to ease my anger.

Keeping balance with one hand, I reach behind me, pulling the back of my jeans down until my full ass is on display. Then, I replace my other hand and grind the stage, giving all the screaming women a full view of what my ass looks like while fucking.

Sweat drips down my body with each movement, but that only makes it seem more like fucking, giving the women the image that they come here for.

Standing up, we all reach for our shirts and slowly rip them off, before rubbing them over our cocks and throwing them out into the crowd. A bunch of hands fly up, fighting to get to them first. I almost die when I see Riley walk to the front of the crowd, holding my shirt in her hands.

Her eyes meet mine and pull me in, making it hard for me to concentrate on the rest of the dance. All I can think about is the fact that she's here… at *Walk of Shame*.

Running my hands down my body, I look her in the eyes, biting my bottom lip as I shove my hand down the front of my jeans and thrust the air. Watching the way she looks at me has me running my hand over my slightly hard cock, imagining it was hers instead.

I can see the lust in her eyes, making it very clear that she's been thinking about me over the last couple of days. That pleases me. That means she most likely hasn't been sexual with that prick.

The end of the song is coming, so in rhythm we all turn away from the stage and drop our jeans, cupping our packages with both hands, before turning back around and kicking our jeans off the stage.

The women go crazy, practically fighting each other to climb onto the stage. I look out into the crowd, searching for Riley as we make our way off the stage, but she's lost in the pile of screaming bodies.

Hands grab at us, groping and slapping our asses until we dodge into the back room. I go from seeing the woman of my dreams to being closed off in a room with three naked assholes.

Opening my locker, I reach for a pair of fresh jeans and a shirt and quickly get dressed, while the other guys start bickering about who did the best.

"Where the hell are you rushing off to?" Hemy asks, while pulling up a pair of jeans.

"Riley's here," I say stiffly. "I'm going to find her."

Lynx walks in with a handful of cash, but I brush past him, not giving a shit about getting paid. I just want to get to my girl before she leaves.

As soon as I walk back out into the club, a few girls walk over and start rubbing their hands on me, saying sexual things, but I don't listen to a thing they're saying. Instead, I push their hands away and look over their heads for Riley.

I spot Riley across the room, slamming back a shot by the bar. Setting her empty glass down, she tosses money in front of her before heading toward the door, dodging out as if she couldn't escape soon enough.

Rushing through the crowd, I run to the door and shove it open, trying to catch Riley before she can drive off. By the time I make it outside, she's already shutting the door to her car.

Running my hands through my hair, I let out a frustrated breath and walk over to knock on her window.

She looks up from the steering wheel, surprised to see me standing outside.

Looking me in the eyes, she rolls down her window and releases a breath. "Cale... what are you doing?"

Reaching through the window, I rub my thumb over her bottom lip. "Trying to catch you." I breathe. "Where are you going?"

She looks away for a second, before turning back to face me. "I don't know. I just... I just need to get away, Cale. I'm so lost right now. I can't stop thinking about you and what goes on here. It's driving me fucking crazy, but I also have Tyler trying to prove to me that two years isn't worth throwing away. I can't breathe, dammit."

I wrap both of my hands into the back of her hair and lean inside the window. "Here," I whisper. "Let me help you with that." Wetting my lips, I press them against hers, showing her just how much I have missed her.

I feel her breath escape her as she wraps one of her arms around my neck and breaks our kiss. "Cale..." she says while fighting to catch her breath. "Are you trying to kill me?"

Smiling, I open her car door and reach for her hand. "Come with me, Rile." She gets ready to say something, but I cut her off. "Please don't say no to me."

She looks at me for a second, before pulling her key out of the ignition and letting me help her to her feet. "You know that always works on me," she says defeated. "Not fair, jerk."

I grin, knowing that she's right. "I know. Now let's go."

About ten minutes later, we pull up in my driveway, parking in front of the garage, and she follows me outside to stand by my side of the truck. She's staring at me as if trying to figure me out.

If she wants to know what it is that I want or that I'm thinking, then I'll tell her. I'm not afraid to.

"I want to fuck you, Rile." Stepping up to her, I grip her ass in my hands and run my lips up her neck. "I want to be deep inside you right now, making you scream my name and forget about that asshole. Is that what you want to hear? I'll always tell you what's on my mind if you just ask me."

Leaning her head back, she lets out a soft moan. "I don't know if that's a good idea, Cale. I'm already confused enough as it is."

Gripping her thighs, I pick her up, wrapping her legs around my waist. "Then let me make it less confusing." I brush my lips under her ear and whisper, "Let me show you what I have to offer you. This can be yours. I can be yours. Every. Fucking. Day."

As soon as her body trembles in my arms, I know that I have her, at least for the moment, and I'm going to consume her in a way that no other man will even come close to.

Riley will see the things my body can do that no one else can...

CHAPTER FIFTEEN

RILEY

I PROBABLY SHOULDN'T BE HERE right now, but I couldn't fight it. My chest has been aching since the moment I realized that Cale walked out of the door the other night.

I went to *Walk of Shame* just to watch him from the crowd, just to get a small glimpse of him, but seeing him up there on stage and knowing that every girl in the room was most likely thinking about him fucking them was messing with my mental state even more. I couldn't make myself leave. I had to stay until the end.

I was just supposed to leave after that. I was supposed to drive home and be alone in my thoughts, but instead I'm here... with Cale. No matter what was going on in the past, just like now, I've always ended up with Cale instead of being alone. He's always been capable of drawing me to him and making me spend my time with him. The problem is, he's even better at it now.

Gripping him as tightly as I can, a moan escapes me as his soft lips brush right under my ear. There's no denying how much I want him right now, and I know he can feel it too.

"Has Tyler been inside you, Rile?" Gripping my ass, he presses me against the side of his truck, causing me to moan out.

Of course not, I want to scream out. We haven't even hung out yet, although I did promise him at least one dinner. I plan to talk to Cale about it before I leave tonight. I just hope that he will understand why I have to do it...

I shake my head. "No, but we need to talk..."

"Not right now," Cale says sternly. "We have all night. Right now... I need you."

CALE

I DON'T HESITATE BEFORE SETTING her down with her back pressed against my truck. Her dress rides up in the front, exposing her pink panties, and all I can think about is ripping them off with my teeth. This woman makes me want go fucking wild.

She watches me with lust in her eyes as I pull my t-shirt off and toss it over the truck, good and ready to have her hands all over me. I wasn't lying when I said I want her right now. I grip the bottom of her dress and wrap it in my hand, pulling her to me. I can't hold back anymore and I'm hoping she can handle it. "Fuck, Riley," I breathe against her neck. "I want to take you right here. I want to fuck you everywhere."

She lets out a gasp and reaches for the button of my jeans, clearly wanting me as much as I want her. "I really want you too, Cale. I have no idea what I'm doing right now, but I know I've been thinking about this for the last two days." Her fingers work fast on undoing my jeans, while biting her bottom lip. "It's almost crazy how much I want you right now."I look down at her, my chest heaving up and down as I grip her neck and make her look me in the eyes. "You can have me anytime and anywhere that you please. Not having you touch me is what's driving me fucking crazy." I press my erection against her stomach and she grips it with her hand, running her slim fingers along my length. "Right now I just need you to forget about him. It's just you and me, Rile."

Her breath comes out ragged as her eyes lower to land on my rock hard cock. Her eyes fill with a want that I've never seen from her, and I know for a fact that Tyler will never see that look from her. I'll make sure of it.

She swallows hard, bringing her eyes back up to meet mine. "I don't want to think about Tyler right now. I'm not. I won't. You're all I've been able to think about."

I bite into my bottom lip, before picking her up and setting her on the bed of my truck. "That's all I fucking need right now."

Her legs willfully spread as I slowly pull her dress up, exposing her delicious body that is just dying to be licked and tasted by me.

I grip her hips with force and pull her down to the edge of the truck bed, so her ass is barely hanging on the surface. Then, I bend down and run my tongue up the length of her inner thigh, stopping right by her panty line. "Mmm..." I moan against her flesh.

I can tell by the soft moan coming from her lips that my mouth being so close to her pussy is driving her mad. That only seems to make me harder. Moaning, I pull her panties aside and run my tongue over her wet pussy, causing her to grip my arms and squirm. One taste and I'm ready to take her right this second.

I close my teeth around her delicious thigh, giving it a playful bite before pulling away and working my mouth up her belly, my hands pulling her dress up on the way. When the dress reaches her head, I pull it off and throw it into the back of the truck.

With urgency, I position my face between her spread legs again, gently biting her through the thin fabric of her panties. During mid moan, I grip her thong in both hands, ripping each side open, surprising her.

Her legs tremble as she runs her hands over my chest and throws her head back. "I still can't believe we're doing this," she says softly. "People might still be awake."

A soft rumble comes from my throat as I quirk an eyebrow and grip both of her wrists in my hand, pulling her up to meet my abdomen. "Take my jeans all the way off, Rile." I grip the back of her neck and suck her bottom lip into my mouth. "Forget about everyone else."

She slides my jeans all the way down to my knees, looking me in the eyes the whole time. The look in her eyes somehow makes me want her even more. I feel like a beast about to lose control.

I yank her legs, pulling her toward me so my cock is resting above her belly. With one hand gripping her neck, I pull her hips up to meet my stiffness, gently sinking into her heat. I slowly thrust in and out a few times, loosening her up to make room, before giving her my full on thrust that is sure to make us being here known to the neighbors.

She screams out while wrapping her legs around my waist, causing me to thrust harder, rolling my hips in and out, giving her the pleasure that she deserves.

Her hold on my bicep hardens as I grip the back of her neck, wrapping my fingers in her hair and pounding into her with as much force as I can. Being inside her feels so good that I almost lose it, releasing myself inside of her right then.

Without pulling out, I grip both of her hips and flip her over so her ass is facing me. I reach down with one hand and rub my finger over her wet clit while pounding into her with fast, consistent thrusts, tugging her hair with my free hand. "Scream for me, Rile. Let it out," I demand.

She lets out a low scream as I slow my pace and wrap my arm around her waist, pulling her up so my chest is pressed against her back. "I don't want to get caught, Cale. Your neighbors..."

I bend down so my lips are hovering over her ear before I whisper, "Fuck my neighbors. It's you I want to please."

Locking my eyes with hers as she turns her head to look at me, I pound into her, causing her to scream out this time. She screams so loud that she covers her own mouth, too afraid to be seen or heard.

I quicken my pace while moving my fingers up and down her wetness, knowing that at any moment she's about to clamp around my cock and release her juices. I want to feel it surrounding me and covering me.

With one last thrust, she screams and her legs begin to shake as she struggles to not fall over. "Cale... Cale... Oh shit..."

I support her body with mine and pause for a second, allowing her body to clamp around me as she shakes. "That's it, baby." I kiss her neck and hold her until she's done shaking below me, then, I grip her hips, pull out, and slam back into her.

I do this a few more times, holding her as close to me as possible, before wrapping an arm around her neck as I release myself as deep into her still throbbing pussy as I can. We both let out a satisfied moan as I twist her neck closer and press my lips to hers. "You're so beautiful," I whisper against her lips.

She smiles and hides her blushing face as I pull out of her and clean her off with my shirt.

We're both silent as I climb into the back of my truck and lay down, pulling her onto my chest.

We lay here for what seems like hours, before I finally break the silence.

"Remember laying in the back of my truck outside your house late at night?"

She laughs and wraps her arm tighter around me. "Of course I remember. I lived for those nights, Cale. Do you realize how many times I wanted to crawl into your arms just like I am now?"

Smiling like a fool, I grip her tighter and run a hand through her hair. "I wish you would have, Rile. I definitely wouldn't have pushed you away."

"Good to know," she says with a laugh.

We go back to laying in silence, just staring at the night sky. It's so peaceful that I never want to move from this spot.

"Cale..."

I press my lips to her forehead. "What's up?"

She hesitates, clearly afraid of my reaction. I can tell by the way she's breathing so heavily.

"Say it, Rile," I say gently. "I never want you to hold back from me."

She sits up and searches for her dress, quickly pulling it back on, making sure that she's covered up. "I promised Tyler that I would let him take me out on a date." She lets out a small breath and repositions herself to get comfortable. "I had to after him coming so far. It just didn't seem right to deny him that small request." She looks up at me, focusing on my lips for a brief moment, before meeting my eyes. "Are you mad?"

Inside I feel like I'm fucking dying. The last thing I want to think about is another man taking her out on a date when I haven't even had the chance. I fucking hate it, but I'm trying my best to not be selfish when it comes to Riley. If she needs to do this, then I need to let her.

"No," I admit. "I'm not mad. I'm jealous as shit and not wanting to share you with another man." I pull her back to me and gently kiss her. "One date. I don't think I can handle more than that without wanting to kill him."

"I think I should go home for the night, Cale." She runs her fingers into the back of my hair. "I'm going out with Tyler tomorrow. It won't be right if I stay here."

I swallow back my anger as my chest tightens in pain. As much as I don't want this, I know that nothing with us will be able to move forward until he's out of the picture. Then, I'm going to make her all fucking mine and hold onto her until I take my last breath. That's a promise.

"I'll drop you off." I hop out of the truck and grab Riley's hand, helping her out and on her feet. "Let's go."

This hurts like a bitch, but there's no way I'm giving up on her. Fuck that...

CHAPTER SIXTEEN

RILEY

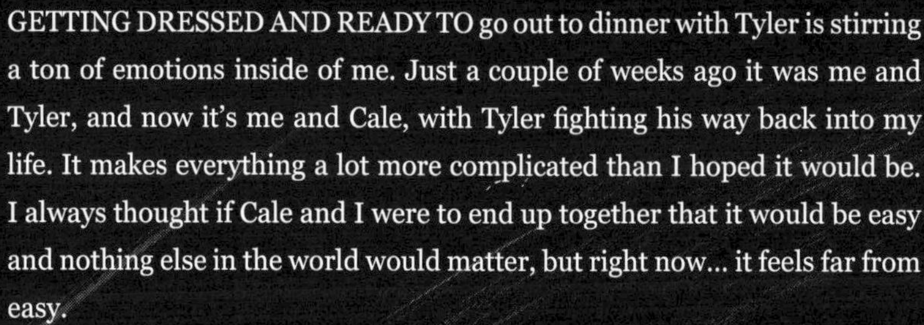

GETTING DRESSED AND READY TO go out to dinner with Tyler is stirring a ton of emotions inside of me. Just a couple of weeks ago it was me and Tyler, and now it's me and Cale, with Tyler fighting his way back into my life. It makes everything a lot more complicated than I hoped it would be. I always thought if Cale and I were to end up together that it would be easy and nothing else in the world would matter, but right now… it feels far from easy.

"Riley," my mom screams from downstairs. "Tyler's here. Are you ready?"

Sighing, I grab my purse and slip the strap over my shoulder, before making my way to the stairs. I look down at my mom and shrug my shoulders. "Yeah, I suppose so. I just want to get this dinner over with."

My mom watches me with concern as I slowly make my way down the stairs, passing her without another word. I just have so much on my mind right now that it's making it hard to think straight.

Here I am going out with Tyler while Cale is at *Walk of Shame*, taking his clothes off for a bunch of horny women. He could have any one of them. Why would he want to wait around for me... again?

"Are you okay," my dad asks, snapping me out of my thoughts.

I look up at him and smile. "I'm good. I'm fine. Just tired." *Not really, but...* "I'll be home later. I don't plan on staying out too late."

"Alright, honey," Mom says to my back as I'm walking to the door. "I'll wait up for you. I have a feeling we're going to have a lot to talk about when you get home."

I look over my shoulder at her. "I guess we'll see."

When I open the screen door I look up to see Tyler leaning against his rental car. He's too busy messing around on his phone to notice me approaching. It's probably a good thing, because right now it seems extremely hard to hide the disappointment of what I have to do tonight. One look at my face and it's a given.

I take a second to compose myself before stopping in front of him and clearing my throat.

Tyler looks up from his phone and quickly shoves it in his pocket to show me his full attention. Smiling, he says, "You look really nice." He reaches for the end of my favorite shirt and fingers it. "I've missed seeing this old thing."

I smile small, appreciative of his compliment, before pulling away a bit. "Thanks."

We both stand here in an awkward silence before Tyler holds up his keys and dangles them. "I guess we should get going. We'll discuss the restaurant on the road. Sound good?"

I nod my head and reach for the door handle. "Sounds like a plan."

As soon as I shut the door behind me, my heart starts racing at the realization that this isn't Cale's truck. This is another man's rental vehicle. My ex's to be more specific; the man that I slept next to for two years. It feels so wrong being here with him and every bit of my body is telling me this.

I sit stiffly, lost in my thoughts as Tyler hops in and shuts his door. Without any warning he reaches over and grabs my hand, pulling it into his lap like old times.

My first instinct is to pull away from him. It doesn't feel right. Not like it used to. "No," I say softly. "We're not a couple anymore, Tyler. Please no touching."

His face registers hurt, but he just nods his head and agrees. "Understandable. Sorry, it just comes so natural with you. I don't want to do anything to make you uncomfortable. No more touching unless you ask."

Relief washes through me that he understands the boundaries of this dinner. The thought of him touching me or trying to kiss me has been eating at me ever since I agreed to this dinner with him. I don't need anything else making me feel more guilty and confused than I already do.

"I know where we can eat at." I sit up and point down the street and over to the left side of the road. "I haven't been there since I was a kid."

Tyler looks over to where I'm pointing and pulls into the left lane. "I'm down."

The only reason I haven't been there since I was a kid is because Cale hates the place. We had one bad experience with some douche giving me a hard time and Cale decided that he never wanted to go back. It reminded him of that issue and always made him want to punch something.

I'd rather take Tyler here to eat dinner than a place that Cale and I enjoy together. It somehow makes me feel a little better about this whole thing.

We don't say much more as we head inside and find an empty booth to sit down in. The waitress nods at us as we take our seats, so we both just reach for a menu from the back of the table and skim over the choices while waiting.

After a few minutes, Tyler sets his menu down and stares at me. I can feel his eyes on me, distracting me from the menu.

"Just say it, Tyler.... You know I hate it when you just stare at me like that."

I set my menu down and look him in the eyes. He searches my face in silence before speaking.

"How could you do it?"

We both look up at the waitress as she walks over to take our order. We quickly give her our food and drink order as she jots it down then disappears, leaving us alone in what I'm sure is going to be an uncomfortable conversation.

"What?" I ask, feeling a bit uncomfortable. "What are you getting at?'

His facial expression changes and he suddenly looks angry. "Have sex with that Cale guy."

I suck in a deep breath and bite my tongue. I don't like him questioning me like this, and that look on his face makes me want to slap it off him.

"Why would you ask me that?" I stop talking and smile up at the waitress as she drops off our drinks, then wait for her to walk away before talking again. "I don't think this is something we should talk about, Tyler."

He reaches for his cup and takes a long, desperate drink. "Oh... it's definitely something we should talk about, and your response just confirms my suspicions. Why would you sleep with him? We were together for two years; two years, Riley, and you wouldn't let me make love to you. You've been *here* for less than three weeks and you decide to let that loser in your bed."

Sitting up, I slap the table defensively and get closer to his face, letting him see the anger in my eyes. "I don't want to *ever* hear you call Cale a loser again." I grind my jaw, trying to hold myself back from screaming. "Cale has been in my life a lot longer than you have, and he's always been there for me. You don't even know him, so don't you dare judge him."

The conversation comes to a halt again when our plates are set down in front of us. I'm so angry right now that I almost let my mouth run, not caring that someone else is listening to our conversation. No one gets to talk shit about Cale without getting an earful from me. This man has been everything to me for as long as I can remember.

The waitress smiles at us and tells us to enjoy, before walking away.

I shove my fork into my food and start eating as fast as I can. The faster I eat, the faster I can get this stupid dinner over with. I don't know what he expected to accomplish out of this dinner, but I hope he didn't expect to win me back, because this definitely isn't working.

"Calm down, Riley." Tyler reaches over the table and grabs my fork out of my hand. "Talk to me for a minute. I'm not trying to piss you off. I just want answers. You don't think this hurts me? I'm hurt right now. This hurts me."

I lean back in my seat and take a few breaths to calm myself. "I don't want to fight, okay, but if you keep running your mouth and saying things about Cale then I'm going to leave and never speak to you again. He doesn't deserve you bad-mouthing him when he has done nothing but take care of me."

Tyler's jaw flexes, as he looks me over. I can tell that he's fighting really hard not to tell me how he feels about my words.

"Let's forget about this *guy* for a minute then and talk about us. What about us? Are you really willing to just throw two years away as if it meant nothing to you?"

I sit up and let out a humorous laugh. I can't believe he's going there right now. "Oh... I don't know, Tyler. I was wondering the same thing when you decided to back out of our relationship right when we were supposed to get on a plane. Apparently our two years together didn't mean shit to you, so why should it mean anything to me now? Tell me!"

Tyler stands up and rushes over to my side of the table, scooting his way onto my booth. "I made a mistake. A huge mistake." He reaches for my face, but I turn away from him. "Riley. Please look at me. I love you. I'm in love with you. After you left, it made me realize how much of an idiot I was for not going with you. I'm here now and we can be together."

I shake my head and run my hands over my face. I don't want to be hearing this right now. I've waited for what seems like forever to hear him tell me he loves me again, and now... now here he is at the worst possible time ever and it doesn't mean anything to me.

"I don't want to hear that now, Tyler. I'm sorry, but I'm over what we had. This dinner and conversation are confirming that for me. I don't feel anything. I'm so sorry. I want to be with Cale. I always have."

Tyler stands up and starts pacing in front of the booth. "He's a fucking stripper, Riley." He narrows his eyes at me when I give him a surprised look. "Yeah, I've done my research on your little boyfriend. Is that what you really want? Huh?" He sits back down, but on his side of the table. "A man that takes off his clothes for other women and then comes home horny and ready for you? How do you know what he does at that club? What makes you think that he's not getting off on these women touching him? Open your eyes, Riley. He could have any of those women, all the ass he wants. He'll *never* be faithful to you and you're stupid if you think he will be."

My heart stops and anger that I've never felt before takes over. Standing up, I walk over to stand in front of him. "Fuck you!" Unable to stop myself, I shove my hands into his chest two times and storm out of the restaurant, needing to get away from him before I break down.

As soon as I'm about a block away from the parking lot, I break down and lose it. My chest aches and I can barely catch my breath. As much as I hate to admit it... Tyler's words had an effect on me.

I don't want to think about Cale with other women. I don't want to believe what Tyler said, but what if it's true? What if more goes on at that club than I know?

The thoughts running through my head make me just want to scream. It hurts so bad just thinking about Cale possibly wanting one of those girls. I hate it. I fucking hate it.

I hate it, but I love Cale. I've been in love with him for longer than I was willing to admit. There's no hiding it now. This man is going to ruin me...

CHAPTER SEVENTEEN

CALE

THE GIRLS HAVE BEEN EXTRA grabby tonight and I can't wait to just get the hell out of here. Here I am... with all these women pulling at me and touching me, and *all* I can think about is the fact that *my* woman is out with another man. We might not have a title, but I know without a doubt that she is mine.

No one can make her feel the way that I do for the simple fact that no other man can love her and care for her as much as I do. Actions speak louder than words, and my actions will always be to take care of Riley and *show* her how much she means to me. This Tyler guy needs to hit the fucking road and realize that she's taken. He lost his chance, and these women need to watch their damn hands before I lose it.

The song playing over the speakers slows down, so gripping my hair I roll my hips, slowing down my rhythm to match the music. "A seductive song is playing, so every girl in this room is hanging on my every move, just wanting me to fuck them to this song later. I can see it in their eyes and it makes me feel fucking guilty.

I don't know what made me think that Riley would be okay with this lifestyle, but the more I'm here, the more I worry that she will start pulling away from me when she sees just how bad it truly can get here. Tonight is one of those nights that would probably push Riley over the edge. Lynx seems to be pushing it to get as dirty as fucking possible.

Doing as Lynx instructed, I strip out of my briefs and cover as much of my cock as possible with my free hand, before replacing my hand with my boxer briefs. Dropping to the ground, I hold the thin fabric over my dick and start grinding on the ground. I feel one of the guys pour water over me, soaking me and making it even harder to cover myself with my white briefs.

Hands grab and slap at my ass as I continue to thrust in a slow rhythm, waiting for this fucking song to end. Every woman in this room now knows what my naked ass looks like while fucking. I don't feel comfortable knowing that Riley should be the only one to witness this dirty moment.

As the song comes to an end I grind my hips one more time, before making my way to my feet. A slim brunette with huge tits instantly plasters herself to the front of my body and grabs my cock. Her other hand reaches around my back side and grips my ass as she starts sliding her hand over my shaft.

"Stop," I growl out, while gripping her wrist and pulling her hand away.

Throwing herself at me, she ignores my demand and grabs at my fucking dick again. "Mmm... someone's packing," she slurs. "Show us your dick, baby, and I'll let you put it anywhere."

I grip her wrist a little tighter this time and get in her face, showing her that I'm not interested. "I'm not going to *fuck* you so just stop."

Pushing past her, I look up just in time to see Riley looking at me from across the room. Shock and hurt is on her face and all I want to do is scream for her to come to me so I can make her feel better.

She shakes her head and starts backing away as I begin making my way through the crowd. I get just a glimpse of Lynx walking her away before a group of girls walk in front of me, blocking my line of vision.

My skin heats up in anger at just the thought of Lynx being with her, so I don't think twice before brushing the group of drunken women off and pushing through them.

By the time I get to where Riley and Lynx are, over by the door, I stop dead in my fucking tracks when I see Lynx pinning her against the door in between his arms. He's whispering something in her ear, but it looks as if she just wants to leave.

Without even giving it a second thought, I grip Lynx's shoulder and spin him around, swinging my right fist into his mouth.

"What the fuck!" Lynx screams out in shock, covering his mouth. "Did you seriously just fucking hit me, you crazy asshole?"

Keeping my eyes on him, I reach down for my boxer briefs that are now on the ground and quickly slide them back on, before walking over to Riley and grabbing her chin. "Are you okay?" I grip the back of her hair and look her in the eyes. "Did he touch you?"

Someone grabs my shoulder. I turn around defensively to see that it's only Stone. "You got this, man?" he asks, while looking back and forth between me and Lynx.

"I'm good." I shake his hand off my shoulder and give Riley my full attention. "Did he touch you? Tell me."

She shakes her head and pushes me away, looking hurt and more confused than I've ever seen her. "No... but it looks as if *everyone* gets to touch you, Cale."

She pushes me away again, so I back up a bit, giving her space. I never want to make her feel uncomfortable, but I want nothing more than to touch her right now. It leaves me in a fucked up situation.

"Rile, I'm fucking sorry." I grip my hair and growl out in anger at the fact that she had to witness some other girl touch me like that. "I don't want that shit, trust me, but please don't walk out on me without talking to me. You've never just walked out on me. Don't start now."

I feel my heart fucking get ripped out of my chest when I notice that her face is wet. She's been crying. She's been fucking crying while I've been here taking off my clothes for other women and fulfilling their damn fantasies. I'm a dick.

"I'm sorry, Cale, but I can't... I just can't." She starts walking toward the door. I grab her arm to stop her, but she pulls it away and gives me a dirty look. That's how I know she needs time alone. "I need to leave right now. Please just understand that. This is so much more than I thought. So much... worse."

"I'm sorry," is all I can say. I reach out and rub my thumb over her lip, but she backs away and looks around the room as the women start screaming for Stone.

"I can't handle this, Cale. I thought I could, but I can't. I need time to think." Without another word she rushes out the door, leaving me on the verge of going crazy. I want nothing more than to go after her, but I respect her more than anyone in this world, and if she needs time then I can't take that away from her. I know that and I hate myself for it.

"Fuck!" I slam my fist into the wall repeatedly while yelling out a string of cuss words. "What did you say to her?" I bark at Lynx as his eyes size me up.

He smirks with a confidence that makes me want to fuck him up even more. "Just told her how it truly is here. How dirty all the women get. The truth. That's what."

"Fucking piece of shit." I start walking to the back to get my shit and Lynx instantly follows me, talking shit the whole way.

"You're lucky I don't fire your ass for that. I don't know who the fuck you think you are."

I ignore him, knowing that if I say anything I'm probably going to break his pretty little face.

Bursting through the door of the locker room, I start pulling out my clothes to get dressed.

"Can you fucking hear me, asshole? One more mistake and you're gone. You're lucky that you've been here for as long as you have and that you bring me money, you sorry son of a bitch, or else you'd be so done."

I take a few seconds to breathe and calm down after I pull my shirt over my head. This asshole is lucky that I have a lot of willpower.

"I'm fucking bleeding and it's all because I was talking to that bitch that wants nothing to do with either of us. That's fucked up..."

Turning around, I swing out, knocking his ass on the ground. "I fucking quit."

Stepping over him, I rush outside and to my truck. I get in, gripping the wheel. All I can think about is Riley possibly running to Tyler for comfort, and it's all I need to lose it.

"Fuck! Fuck! Fuck!"

Time... how the hell can I give her time when that's the one thing that could possibly make me lose her?

CHAPTER EIGHTEEN

CALE

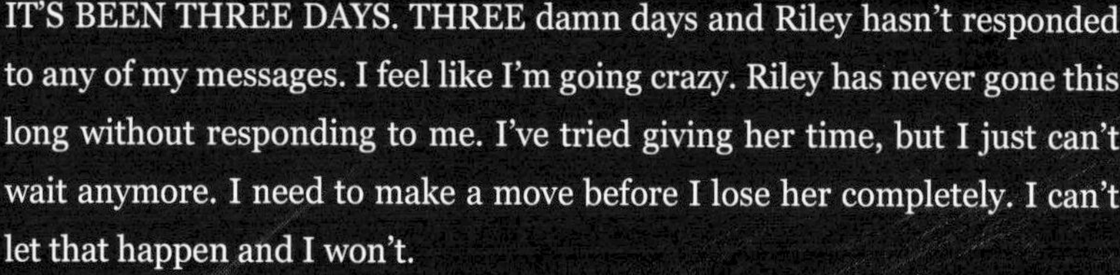

IT'S BEEN THREE DAYS. THREE damn days and Riley hasn't responded to any of my messages. I feel like I'm going crazy. Riley has never gone this long without responding to me. I've tried giving her time, but I just can't wait anymore. I need to make a move before I lose her completely. I can't let that happen and I won't.

I called her work yesterday and booked every single appointment that she had available today. I've been sitting here in the parking lot on Slade's motorcycle, waiting for them to open. I didn't want her to know I was showing up and I knew that if she noticed my truck in the parking lot that there was a chance she'd freak out and leave.

She isn't due in for another thirty minutes, but I already told Kylie that I'm waiting in her room until she gets here, and I don't give a shit what anyone says.

A few cars pull into the lot, so I look down at my phone to check the time. They opened a few minutes ago.

Hopping off of Slade's bike, I set the helmet on the seat and rush over to the door, walking inside. Kylie looks up from her desk and smiles when she notices that it's me.

"Hey, handsome," she says sweetly. "Are you sure you don't want to keep me company until *she* gets here?"

I walk past her, ignoring her completely. I don't have time for her shit. I don't want her shit. All I want is to show Riley how much I love her. She may be pissed to see me at first, but I don't care. I have to do this.

About five minutes before Riley is due to arrive, I strip out of my jeans and shirt, before getting comfortable on my back. I was in so much of a hurry that I didn't even bother throwing on any boxer briefs. It's not like I'd be wearing them for long anyways. I plan on spending most of my day, here, naked.

My heart speeds up when I hear the sound of the door opening. I've been fucking dying to be close to Riley, and knowing that she's about to be in the same room is making it very difficult to not just pull her down onto the table and take care of her.

I can hear her shuffling around and getting ready. I'm watching her, but she hasn't even bothered to look at the table yet. She's so damn beautiful that it causes my chest to ache. All I want to do is wrap my hands into that brown hair and pull her lips to mine.

"Good morning," she mumbles. "My name is Riley and..." Her words trail off when she finally looks to see who her client is. "Cale," she says in almost a whisper. "What are you doing here?"

Sitting up, I grab her arm before she can walk away. I can see the confusion and hurt written all over her face, and I know without a doubt that she wants to run away and not face me right now.

"Come here, baby." Throwing my legs off the side of the table, I pull her between my legs and wrap them around her so she will listen to me. "Just hear me out, Rile. Please."

She swallows hard and closes her eyes as I wrap my hands into the back of her hair. "Cale... I'm scared. I'm so fucking scared when it comes to you."

"Shh..." I gently kiss her neck, enjoying the sweet scent of her skin. Nothing else will ever feel this way and I know that. Now I just need to show her. "I'll never hurt you, Riley. Ever. I want you to know that. Haven't I always been good to you?"

I kiss her neck again, causing her to swallow. "Yes," she whispers. "But if you ever hurt me, it would kill me. Do you get that, Cale? That's why I can't do this. I can't get too deep and allow that to happen."

Running my lips up her neck, I stop below her ear and whisper, "I'll never let that happen, Rile." I suck her earlobe into my mouth and nibble it. "Do you know why?"

She lets out a small breath and shakes her head. "No..."

I press my lips against her ear and tug at her hair, getting as close to her as possible. "Because I'm in love with you," I whisper. "I always have been, Rile. I fucking love you."

She lets out a small gasp and presses her hand over her mouth. Pulling away, I look her in the eyes and repeat myself. "I'm in love with you. I will always put you first. I will always make you happy and think of you before anyone else. That is a promise." I pull her forehead to mine. "Do you understand that?"

She doesn't respond, so I ask her again. "Do you?"

"Cale, I can't ask you to do that. I can't..."

"You don't have to," I say honestly. "I've been doing it since we were kids. It comes natural to me now. Not doing it wouldn't feel right to me. I quit my fucking job, Rile. I'm going to focus on you." I place her hand on my chest. "This body will only be touched by you. I can promise you that on my life."

I cup her face and run my thumbs over her wet cheeks. "None of that matters to me. This is me showing you how much I love you. Words don't mean shit unless you have the actions to back it up. This is me doing my part. This is me showing you that I fucking love you."

A half laugh, half sob escapes her throat as she rubs her hand over my chest, taking me all in.

The silence in the room is making my heart work overtime. I need her to speak. I need to hear that she's willing to be mine.

"Talk to me, Rile. Please say something."

She reaches her hand up and wraps it into the back of my hair like she always does. Then, her eyes lock with mine, causing my chest to ache in anticipation. "I'm in love with you too, Cale. God, I love you so much that it hurts."

I pull her onto the table with me and crush my lips to hers, just wanting to taste her and feel her against me. "I love you, baby," I whisper against her lips. "I'm your man for as long as you will have me. Only yours."

"Show me," she says with a smirk.

I suck her bottom lip into my mouth and bite it. "Oh trust me... I plan to. All fucking day."

She laughs as if she doesn't believe me. "I do have other clients booked today, Cale."

I raise my brows and slide her hand down to my rock hard cock. "Not for the next five hours." I turn us, laying her down on the bed to hover above her. "I'm a greedy asshole today and didn't want to share you for longer than I had to." I smile against her lips. "Fuck everyone else. You're mine until then."

She grips my neck and pulls me down to kiss her, long and hard. "I fucking love you so much."

"Fuck I love hearing that," I growl. Letting my excitement take over, I yank her dress up and over her head, before pulling her panties down her legs and tossing them aside. I need to be inside my woman right now, and I need to show her how much I love her.

Laying her back down from removing her clothes, I get down, in between her legs, and allow my tongue to trail up the inside of her thigh, slowly tasting her.

Grabbing her thighs, I push her legs toward her breasts. "Fuck, I've been waiting for days to do this, Rile." I slowly trail my tongue up the wetness of her pussy, torturing her clit with the tip of my tongue, before slipping my tongue deep inside, getting a better taste. She moans and her whole body shakes with pleasure as I spread her moistness to her clit and slip a finger inside her.

I swirl my tongue around before sucking her clit into my mouth, being sure to be gentle with her. I suck and lick while moving my finger in and out in a slow, consistent motion, never losing rhythm. I know how much rhythm means to a woman's sexual needs and I will be fucked if I don't give her the greatest pleasure she's ever known. Tyler can fuck off. He's never made her come like I'm about to.

It doesn't take long before I can feel her already starting to clamp down around my finger. It doesn't surprise me though. If I'm good at one thing, it's definitely using my tongue, and I've saved my best for her. I slowly run my tongue in between her lips before sucking them into my mouth and then her clit. When I feel her starting to clamp again, I run my tongue over her thigh, before softly biting down on it. "Come for me, baby," I whisper. "Don't worry about anyone hearing you."

Her body jerks as she clamps around my finger and screams out softly,

It's so fucking tight that it squeezes my finger. It reminds me that I've been the only one to be inside of her.

Right as she's coming, I pull my finger out, replacing it with my tongue. I want to taste her when she comes. "Fuck yeah, Rile." Her breathing comes out in heavy bursts as she continues to moan below me. "Cale..." She runs her hands through her hair before biting her bottom lip and looking up to meet my eyes. "Make love to me. Please..."

Snaking my arm around her waist, I move up to press my body between her wet thighs. I kiss her, wanting to taste every fucking inch of her. Her lips are the best tasting thing in the world to me, and I swear that I will never be able to get enough.

She moans and leans her head back, pressing it into the massage table. I love seeing her come undone below me, knowing that I will be the only one. She had her chances and didn't take them. It only makes me love her more.

Gripping her thigh, I slip inside of her, causing her to moan out and dig her nails into my back. "I've missed you inside of me, Cale."

"Say it again," I whisper against her lips.

She leans up and sucks my lip into her mouth, turning me on even more. "I've missed you inside of me." She wraps her legs around my waist and squeezes me hard. "You are my best friend and the man that I love. You and only you."

Her words set me off and before I know it, I'm grinding my hips in and out of her, taking her slow and deep, deeper than I've ever taken her.

With each thrust her nails dig deeper and harder into my flesh, her moans becoming louder in my ear. Something about this moment feels so different than all of the other times we've had sex. Everything seems so much more real.

Maybe it's the fact that I know she loves me now, and this is me proving to her that I love her too. This is us making love.

My hand slips under her neck to grip her hair as I press my lips to hers and continue to make love to her, knowing that this moment is special to both of us. This is the moment that I make my best friend so much more: my woman. This moment I have been waiting on for far too fucking long.

Knowing how this feels, I would wait all over again if I had to. This is a feeling that many men aren't lucky enough to ever experience and I wouldn't give it up for anything...

AFTER TALKING AND MAKING LOVE for about the fifth time, I help Riley get dressed before getting dressed myself, then pull her into my arms and press my lips to her forehead.

"Come home tonight, baby," I whisper. "Let me take you out on a real date."

Smiling, she grabs my face and looks me in the eyes. "You making me dinner and taking care of me would be the realest that a date could ever get. If you ask me, you're the only one that has taken me on a *real* date."

My heart swells from her words and a sense of pride swarms through me. "This is why I love you so much, Rile."

Pressing my lips to hers, I kiss her long and hard, not wanting to say bye for the next three hours. I just want her home and in my bed. "Hurry home so I can make you dinner and make love to you all fucking night. I have a lot of making up to do. I'll never again lose time with you."

She smiles and pushes me away as someone knocks on the door. "Okay," she laughs. "I'll hurry back. I promise."

"Home," I say, correcting her.

She kisses me once more and smiles. "Home. I'll hurry home. Better?"

I grip her face and bite her bottom lip. "Much fucking better, baby."

The person at the door knocks again. Smiling hard, I open the door and step out.

Kylie looks up at me and then at Riley, before grunting and motioning for me to get going. "About time. Damn! Your next client is here." She turns back to me. "Move along now."

Grabbing the back of Riley's neck, I pull her to me one more time and kiss her. "Love you, baby," I say, making sure that Kylie gets the fucking hint. "See you in a bit."

Rolling her eyes, Kylie storms past us and goes back to her desk without another word.

"Love you, too." She slaps my ass and gives me a shove. "Now go, before I get fired."

I throw my hands up and start backing away. "Whoa now. Keep spanking me and I won't be going anywhere." I wink at her and then turn around to leave before I'm unable to stop myself.

Fuck me, I love this woman...

CHAPTER NINETEEN

RILEY

THREE WEEKS LATER . . .

I'M STANDING IN FRONT OF the mirror when Cale wraps his arms around me from behind. Like always when he's around, my heart starts pounding and I feel this rush. That feeling has only intensified since we have become official, and I seriously cannot get enough of him touching me.

"You look fucking beautiful, Rile." Grabbing my arm, he spins me around and whistles. "So damn beautiful."

Blushing, I wrap my arms around his neck and pull him down for a kiss. "Mmm..." I run my tongue over my lips, tasting the sweet strawberries that he just got done eating. "Save some of those for later," I say playfully. "If you keep eating them outside of the bedroom then we'll never have enough."

Grinning, he picks me up, wrapping my legs around his waist. His hands grab for my ass and squeeze. "Do we really have to go?" he questions, while pushing his erection against me. "I want to fuck my woman so bad right now that being with those assholes is the last thing on my mind. I'll call

Slade back and tell him that we're not coming."

"No!" I scream as he starts rushing into the bedroom. "Don't do it, Cale." He stops in front of the bed and I grab onto his neck tighter, holding on for dear life. "We're going. We already said we would. My sister is waiting for me."

Growling against my lips, he wraps his hands into the back of my hair. "Well shit." He kisses me and smiles. "We don't have to stay long though, right? I've waited all damn day to get you home to me." He kisses me again, his lips lingering against mine. "Fine, let's go," he grumbles in defeat.

He sets me down to my feet and kisses the top of my head, before walking away and letting me finish getting ready.

The last three weeks have been the best days of my life and there's no denying it. Cale is so much more than I ever thought he could be. If I thought he made me feel special before, the feeling is double that now. This man hasn't let me go one second without a smile on my face and I have a feeling that if it's up to him then he'll never let that happen. Cale truly is the perfect man for me.

My love for him has grown so much that my chest aches just from being away from him. It keeps me happy knowing that he's always waiting for me, just like he used to before I left. It only proves to me exactly why he waited all these years for me. When Cale loves someone, he loves them with everything in him.

I'm just lucky to say that that girl is me.

Right as I'm in the middle of throwing my hair up, Cale rushes back into the bedroom and picks me up, throwing me over his shoulder. "I told you how beautiful you looked, Rile. You don't need to change anything. Trust me. Let's go!"

"I'm not done." I playfully slap his ass, but he keeps walking, not caring. "Damn you, Cale."

He doesn't set me down until we're outside next to his truck and he's opening the door for me. "We gotta go, baby. The sooner we get there, the sooner I get to bring you home and make love to you in our bed. I don't know how long I can hold off."

I bite my bottom lip and sit back in my seat as Cale shuts the door behind me and then runs over to his side of the truck.

I swear I have to be the luckiest girl in the world to have Cale. My

Cale...

CALE

AS SOON AS WE STEP inside the bar, Stone jumps up on his chair and starts whistling for us to come over. "Dude! Over here."

I laugh as Hemy reaches over and punches him in the leg. These guys will never change, and oddly, I'm good with that. Even though they drive me insane half the time, they're like family to me. No fuck that... they *are* family to me.

Now that I have Riley back here with me, my family is complete. There's no better feeling in the world than that. Tyler has gone back to Mexico where he belongs and Riley is here with me, where she has always belonged.

Placing my hand on Riley's ass, I guide her toward the table in the back and whisper in her ear. "Remember... we're not staying long. I'm spending the night pleasuring my fucking woman."

I see her cheeks turn red from my words, but she plays it off as Aspen walks over to her and hugs her, pulling her away from me and over to where her and Sage are playing darts.

Pulling out a chair, I take a seat next to Slade, across from Hemy and Stone. "What the fuck, assholes? Stop looking at me like that."

Slade tilts back his beer and grins like an idiot. "I just can't get over it, man. Shit." He takes another drink of his beer, before sliding one over to me. "One day we will be related."

"Ah, fuck." I grab my beer and bring it to my lips. "Ain't that some shit." I smile and nudge his shoulder. "Related to the fucking man whore. I never in a million years would've thought that could be a possibility. Shit is changing, man. Things are becoming real."

Hemy slaps Onyx on the ass as she stands up, nods at me, and goes to join the other girls. "So what's the deal?" Hemy asks, before finishing his beer and pushing it aside. "Heard you punched the fuck out of Lynx and quit."

I nod and flex my jaw at just the thought of him trying to steal my woman out from under me. "Yeah, man. He had it coming."

"Hell yeah, he did," Stone agrees, tilting his beer to mine. "That asshole deserved it. Now he's all going crazy and shit, trying to find someone as good as you to take your spot. I mean Kash has been doing pretty good, but I don't know about this Styx guy. He looks scared as shit. The vultures smell fear. They may very well eat him alive."

Everyone around the table laughs. It's crazy how much things have changed over the last few months. I'm proud of every single guy at this table. I've never seen any of them happier than what they are right now, and I know for damn sure that I can now say that about myself as well.

Next week I start my management position at *The Anchor*, a bar that Riley and I can feel comfortable with me working at until I can decide what I really want to do. Slade is settling into his stiff new office job, wearing his suits and shit, Hemy has quit completely at *Walk of Shame* and is working full time at his buddy's mechanic shop. I even heard that Onyx is getting a job with Aspen at the salon and that Sage is working on writing a book or something. Everything in life is fucking good to me. My people are good and so am I.

When I look over at the girls, I catch Riley smiling and looking back over at me while talking to Onyx about something. It makes me feel so damn good seeing her getting accepted by everyone in the group. I even have a feeling that Onyx finds her attractive. As wild as that girl is sometimes, I wouldn't be surprised if she hasn't thought about being with my girl. Of course there is one wild couple out of every group. Hemy and Onyx are that for us.

Grabbing my beer, I sit back in my seat and just enjoy this moment for what it is. This is the only group that I would want to be doing this with. My *Walk of Shame* family became my real family, and I love all these fuckers to death.

This is all that a man needs to be happy. She is all a man needs to be happy. With these people, my life is fucking perfect...

STONE

WALK OF SHAME : BOOK 4

PROLOGUE

STONE

SEVEN MONTHS AGO . . .

THE EXCITEMENT OF CALE AND Riley announcing that they're having a baby kept us all out late, celebrating. As soon as I got off the stage for the night, we took off to *Fortunes* and closed the bar down with the rest of the gang.

It was a crazy night and the way that Sage had been looking at me and fucking me with her eyes, she's been making it impossible to keep my dick in control.

Sage and I made a decision last month to cool off on our messing around, before things could get too complicated, but her flirting and teasing is making it impossible to keep my hands to myself when all I want is to have them all over her beautiful body, touching her in ways that'll make her scream.

The deal when she moved in a year ago was that we'd be roommates and occasional fuckbuddies to help satisfy each other's needs.

No sleeping in the same bed.

No fucking without a condom.

No fucking twice in the same month.

No becoming attached.

No jealousy.

No commitment.

Just for fun.

With a woman as beautiful as Sage, following the rules isn't that simple. Trust me, it takes every restraint a man has. Especially when his dick is practically standing tall twenty-four-seven.

Fuck me... I want her all the time.

We've been at it for too long for her to believe that we can keep it up and just stay friends. I understand why she's afraid of commitment and I don't blame her. She's had it rough, so I'll do my best to respect that.

We're both young and have a lot of shit going on.

Maybe backing off is best for both of us.

We've just made it back to the house and Sage hasn't taken her hands off me since we left the bar. It's been weeks since the last time we've had sex and I can't deny that my cock wants nothing more than to sink into her tight little pussy, making her scream my name as I claim her body.

There's nothing I love more than my name on her lips, moaning.

Laughing, Sage straddles my lap and wraps her arms around my neck. "I've been thinking about touching you all night since seeing you on that stage. Do you realize how sexy you are and how hard you're making this strictly roommates thing?"

Smiling, I lean in and suck her bottom lip into my mouth, softly biting it, before releasing it with a growl. She loves it when I bite her and be aggressive. "I knew you were checking the goods out," I tease. Leaning into her ear, I slide her hand down my stomach and into the top of my jeans. "Touch me then. Do whatever you want."

Leaning her head back, she lets out a small moan as I gently bite her neck, trailing my mouth down her body. "I want to," she breathes. "So damn bad, but..." She lets out a small scream when I bite her harder and slaps my chest. "We need to be careful, Stone. I thought we both agreed to put an end to this for now?"

Flipping her over, I spread her legs and place my body between them. "We have been," I say against her neck, before running my tongue up it.

"Roommate fucking at its best, baby. The only strings will be when I tie you up. Now. Touch. Me."

Wrapping both of my hands in her hair, I lift my body, giving her just enough room to slip her hand where I want it.

We both want this right now and fuck me if I'm not going to just go with the flow and let it happen.

"You're so hard," she breathes, while rubbing me through my jeans. "This is going to be so hard. Why," she groans. "I don't want to follow the rules right now."

Pulling my bottom lip between my teeth, I push my jeans and boxer briefs down, freeing my erection for her. "Then don't."

Her breathing picks up as I yank my shirt over my head and toss it aside. "Stone..." She moans when I grip her thigh and press my hardness between her legs, poking her. "Stone." I poke her again to push her and work her up. "Fuck..." she moans.

Gripping her hair tighter, I slip my hand beneath her skirt, and push her panties to the side, exposing her pussy. "You wore panties this time," I point out, as I slide my finger over her wetness. "Is that your way of keeping in control when it comes to me?"

She nods her head and slides up the couch when I slip a finger inside. "Oh shit..." she moans out, while gripping the couch. "Wait."

Hearing the worry in her voice, I slide my finger out and suck it clean. "What's wrong, Sage? We've been playing by every rule since the beginning. Why are you so worried about breaking them once? One more time isn't going to make us fall in love or anything."

Breathing heavily, she places her hands on my chest to give herself more room. "Break them once and it leads to breaking them again and again." She stands up and fixes her skirt, looking regretful. "I can't take that chance with you and you know it. I should just go to bed while I'm still thinking straight." Her eyes look me over as I press down on my erection, feeling the blue balls creep in. "Stop being so sexy, asshole," she says with a small smile. "Goodnight."

Respecting her wishes, I don't say a word as I watch her go to her room, shutting the door behind her.

"Fuck me... I'm going to need a cold shower."

I've never seen her so panicked before, then again, we've never come close to breaking the rules before. We've never had sex more than once in a month and now that we've agreed to stop messing around, we almost had sex for the second time this month.

Shutting off the lights after my fight-blue balls-shower, I crawl into bed and look over to see that it's past three in the morning. We're both tired and have been drinking for most of the night.

We just need to sleep it off.

If things are meant to happen between us, they will.

With time...

CHAPTER ONE

STONE

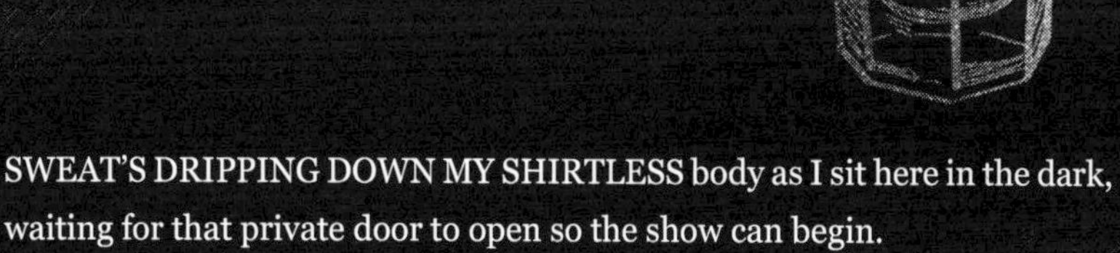

SWEAT'S DRIPPING DOWN MY SHIRTLESS body as I sit here in the dark, waiting for that private door to open so the show can begin.

It's been a long ass night and this is the last show I'm required to do, before I get my ass out of here for the night.

I've been dancing my dick off for seven hours straight, and no matter just how tired I truly am, nothing's going to stop me from showing this client a hot as fuck show.

When a client pays for a private show from me, they get the best. I put everything else behind me and dance until my body burns or my client's panties are soaking wet. Whichever comes first.

I'm not going to lie; I learned that from Slade in the beginning. Dude was a straight up beast and I knew I'd have to work hard to fill his shoes. Now with Slade, Hemy, and Cale no longer dancing, *I'm* the one that Kash and Styx have to keep up with.

I grip the chair when I hear the door creak open. It's dark enough in here that she can't see me yet, but I can see her as she nervously takes a seat on the couch below the small stage, waiting anxiously for the music to start.

When it does, the darkness on the stage dims enough for her to finally see me sitting here, half-naked, and ready to give her what she needs.

Something visual to get her off at night or maybe even here and now.

Moving my body to the slow rhythm, I slide my hand down my hard body, stopping on my cock. It's the quickest move to get her going and me out of here quickly.

Her eyes widen as I grab it and begin grinding my hips, slowly and torturously, while gripping myself as if I'm about to get off.

Hell... sometimes I do.

I don't miss it when she bites her bottom lip and lets out a small moan. It can be heard, even over the soft music.

Shit, I've barely even done anything yet, and she already looks as if she's ready to explode.

Her legs are now crossed and both of her hands are gripping the leather couch around her, her skirt riding up her legs as she grinds in her seat to get some friction.

Smirking, I stand from the chair and kick it out of the way, before sliding across the stage on my knees, until I'm sitting right in front of her.

Surprised, she throws both hands over her face, which I reach out and pull away, lowering them to the top of my jeans for her to unbutton for me.

Being this close, shows just how beautiful this woman is, but you can also see just how shy and nervous being here makes her.

A lot of women like her pay big money for these private shows. The ones that are too scared to let anyone know that they're here in the first place. Strict family. Strict job. Or hell, maybe even a significant other.

That's not my job to worry about. My only concern is making sure that they leave here satisfied and dying to come back for more. And if they get off on it, then that's a bonus.

Pulling her chin up, so I can look her in the eyes, I sway my hips as her shaky hands work slowly to undo my jeans.

Breaking eye contact, I push her face down toward my hips, while grinding the air nice and fucking slow.

This causes her to get a little too excited, yanking my jeans down my thick legs as if she suddenly can't wait to get me in as little clothing as possible.

Being that close to my cock usually does the trick with these women, letting their inner freak come out.

Standing back up to my feet, I step the rest of the way out of my jeans and kick them to the side.

She gasps as her eyes lower to my white briefs, landing on my thick erection.

"Oh. My. God," she squeals.

I might sound like a cocky jerk, but I'm used to that reaction now. Although, it never seems to get old. I fucking love it.

Smirking with confidence, I lower myself from the stage, straddling her lap.

My hands go straight for her hair, tangling up in the blonde strands as I grind against her, slow and hard, making sure that I dig into her body with each thrust.

It only takes a few seconds before her breathing picks up and I feel her jerk below me, letting out a long moan of satisfaction.

Once her orgasm stops, her eyes open back up and embarrassment crosses her pretty little features.

Taking a deep breath, she covers her face and shakes it back and forth. "I'm sorry," she says into her hands. "I'm so embarrassed."

Smiling, I remove her hands from her face. "You shouldn't be." I grab her chin. "I aim to please, baby girl."

She studies my face for a few seconds, before finally breaking into a smile. "So this happens a lot?"

Removing my other hand from her hair, I stand up and nod. "Every damn time. I have no problem being an orgasm donor. It's what my body was built for." I wink, causing her to laugh.

That's what I was going for. The last thing I want is for a client to leave, feeling bad or embarrassed because being here got them off instead of the privacy of their own home.

That's why Cale tested the private dances with me first, before letting the other guys start them. He knew with me, they'd leave here happy and satisfied. I have a way of making sure that happens.

Letting her eyes wander over my hard, sweaty body, she pulls a wad of cash from her bra and shoves it down the front of my briefs, making sure that her hand brushes the head of my dick. "Thank you. I needed that more than you know."

Looking pleased, she lets herself out of the room, leaving me alone to get dressed.

After I'm dressed and cleaned up, I stop up at the bar to grab a shot to help relax me after this long, hard night of having *everything* on my body pulled at.

Sarah smiles at me and reaches for a shot glass. "Woah there! That was a fast show. Mr. Fucking Magic Dick."

Lifting a brow, I reach for the whiskey, slamming it back. The burn feels good right now, after such a long night here with the guys. It should help blur the memory of their dicks swinging.

"Yes, ma'am." I slam the empty glass down and grab my cock. "Nickname fits me to a T. It's a curse and a blessing." I release my junk and nod my head. "One more, babe."

I look around, searching for the security guard on duty, as she pours me one last shot. "Is Kage still here?"

"Yup." She rolls her eyes. "His big ass has been in the shower for the last thirty minutes, jerking off or some shit. You can get out of here. He'll stick around for me to close down."

"You sure?" I lift a brow, while tilting the second shot of whiskey back.

"Um... yes. I said so, didn't I?"

"Just double checking."

"Hey wait." I get ready to walk away, but Sarah's voice stops me, causing me to turn back around. "You and Sage back at it yet or is she still teasing and torturing your smart aleck ass? I gave it six months and it's been seven. Just saying."

My cock instantly comes to attention at the sound of Sage's name. Damn that woman has my dick under some kind of spell.

"Apparently, my magic dick doesn't have a strong enough effect on her. She's the exception."

Winking, I walk away, with my mind stuck on Sage once again and the fact that we haven't touched each other since that night seven months ago.

You try living with a beautiful as fuck woman and keeping your hands and dick to yourself.

Impossible as shit.

As hard as I try to get through one night around her without wanting to go back to our old ways, it's becoming impossible. The woman drives me mad.

And I fucking love the torture... I'll admit it.

As soon as I walk outside, the blonde from the private dance grabs ahold of my arm, pulling me around to the side of the building.

She doesn't bother speaking, going straight for my jeans and ripping them down my thick legs.

It's been a while since I've let this happen, but I can't deny the fact that I need a little fucking action once in a while. As much as I want it with Sage... it's not going to happen.

A man has needs and I'm about to let this hot as fuck blonde satisfy them and try to not feel guilty, knowing that I really have no reason to.

Sage hasn't asked about my sex life since we stopped being physical and I haven't asked her about hers.

Leaning against the building, I close my eyes and imagine Sage's mouth on my cock as blondie takes me into her mouth, sucking me hard.

I jump a little when she gets a little too excited, scraping her teeth over my shaft.

"Sorry," she mumbles around my cock.

Letting her know it's okay, I grip the top of her hair and begin thrusting my hips into her face.

Getting a little too excited myself, I push in a little too deep, causing her to gag on my length and dig her nails into my ass.

All it does is remind me that Sage has been the only one able to fully handle me sexually. It's like the girl was made for me.

How fucked up is that?

Gripping the blonde's hair, I pull her back so she can answer my question. "Can you handle my cock if I give you all of it?"

She nods and grips my ass tighter, letting me know that she's ready to try.

"I hope so," I whisper, *because I need to get off.*

Hoping that she's right, I turn her around and pull her head back as far as it can go, before shoving my cock into her mouth and fucking it hard and deep.

For some fucked up reason, seeing the shape of my thickness in a girl's throat as I fuck her mouth, turns me on the most, usually getting the job done fast.

Within ten deep thrusts, I'm pulling out of the girl's mouth, releasing my load against the side of the building with a moan.

I feel the girl shove something into the back of my briefs. "Call me if you ever want to get together. *That* was me repaying you for the dance."

I don't even get a chance to turn around, before I hear the sound of the ground crunching as she walks away, leaving me alone to gather my shit.

She definitely wasn't as innocent as she looked, but nothing compared to Sage. No one ever is.

Fuck me...

CHAPTER TWO

SAGE

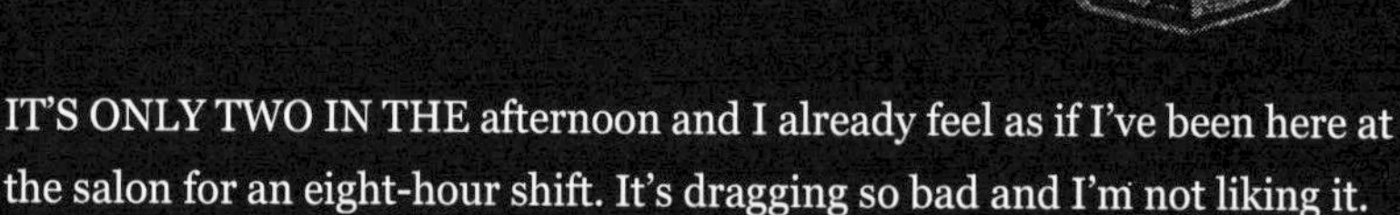

IT'S ONLY TWO IN THE afternoon and I already feel as if I've been here at the salon for an eight-hour shift. It's dragging so bad and I'm not liking it.

"Oh come on," I groan out, as I throw myself down in the chair at Onyx's station. "Is time moving slower than usual today or is it just me? It's almost physically painful."

Smiling, Onyx grips my hair, yanking me back in the chair. "Shut up and let me color your hair. I've been asking since last week to let me test something on you. You've been doing way too much griping the last few weeks. Would you just let Stone lay you already?"

"Shut up." I toss a comb at her. "If you're going to do my hair, do it in silence," I joke.

Aspen looks over at us from working on one of her clients, pointing her scissors at us as she talks. "One of you better keep your eye out for customers. We may be friends, and I love you to death, but take advantage of it and I'll kick your asses." She smiles slightly but gives us a hard enough look to let us know she means it.

Two months ago, Aspen opened up her own salon, *Raines' Salon*, and asked Onyx and me to come work for her. Business started out slow at first, until the boys of *Walk of Shame* started handing out business cards and sending the women here. Those boys ask you to do anything, you jump to it. At least these women did and not to mention that they tip well. A little something they learned from going to *Walk of Shame*.

The business picked up like crazy after a couple of weeks, barely making it possible for us to keep up, thanks to the boys. Although, I do admit, every girl that walks through that damn door, I can't help but wonder if Stone has been with since we stopped messing around.

I have to struggle between wanting to punch the girl in the face, and wanting to do my job, making her ass even prettier, when walking out that salon door.

Aspen has faith that I won't stab anyone with a stiletto, so I do my best. I just tell myself repeatedly that I'm the one who stopped us from having sex that night.

When we first started messing around, it was easy, but after a year of occasionally letting loose with him and having the *best* sex of my life... let me tell you... that man can move his body, I started to want it more and more.

I could tell he did too.

"We've got your back, sweets." Onyx winks. "I can multitask. Just ask Hemy. He has plenty of stories."

"Fucking gross," I mumble, disgusted at the thought of the crazy shit I've heard about her and my brother. "Just don't mess my hair up or I'll have to chop yours off in your sleep. I'm not sure you'd pull the bald look off so well."

"I can pull anything off, honey. Now shut it."

Closing my eyes, I try to relax and let Onyx take over. I know she'll do good, but since she's practically my older sister since marrying Hemy, I have to give her a hard time once in a while.

She's family and we treat each other that way. I'll never be able to repay her for bringing me and Hemy back together. I owe her everything and I'm willing to give it too.

I honestly don't even know at this point how I went so long without my brother in my life. We went through so much shit as children and he was always there, until he wasn't.

I don't even remember how, but we got separated and I spent years missing him and trying to find him, until Onyx found me. She found me and brought my family back together.

I love her for that.

Onyx keeps pushing my head down, making sure that I look down at my lap for the whole hour that she's messing with my hair. Luckily, only one client has come in that Onyx had to pull away from me to help and it was just a quick trim.

Now my hair is dried and curled and the torture is done. It's not easy letting her push your head around for a whole hour, without wanting to slap her.

"Holy. Shit." Onyx pulls the purple cape off me and her and Aspen look me over, making me feel nervous with their judging eyes on me. "I deserve a big tip for the miracle I worked on you, honey."

"Wow," Aspen jumps in, while playing with my hair, lifting random pieces of it to look underneath the layers. "Maybe I should have you do mine next week."

Feeling anxious to see with my own eyes, I push them both out of the way and spin the chair around to look in the mirror.

"Holy. Fuck." My eyes widen as I check out the strands of turquoise, blue, and purple, falling around my face. "This is definitely a new look. I have to give it to you... I look good," I say teasingly.

Between the new hair, lip ring, and fresh tattoos, I almost feel like a whole new woman.

A wild one... and I like it. I feel sexy and playful, ready to get out and have fun for the first time in months, after spending my nights moping and trying to get myself off as good as Stone used to.

But as much as I like it, I can't help but wonder what Stone would think, about both my new look and me wanting to go out and have fun.

It shouldn't bother me this much. I shouldn't be so worried about what he thinks. He's not my boyfriend and we both made it clear in the beginning that it was just for fun. He's just my roommate.

This is exactly what I *didn't* want us to turn into. He's grown on me big time and that's exactly why I've been avoiding anything about him that might turn me on more and change my mind. That's why I haven't even been to *Walk of Shame* in months now.

"I knew you'd like it," Onyx gloats.

I snap out of my thoughts and turn around to face my girls. "I do." I smile big and give her a quick hug, speaking next to her ear. "You're damn lucky I do. I'll admit that you had me a bit scared with how confused you looked with the colors."

"Nah... I knew what I was doing. I just wanted to mess with you a bit." She winks and starts cleaning up the mess.

Aspen is still looking me over when I turn to face her. It's as if she can't get enough of how pretty it truly turned out. "I'm digging the new look on you. It seriously looks sexy. You going to visit Stone at work and see how long it takes for him to recognize you in the crowd?" She lifts a brow, pushing. "You can't avoid the club forever."

"Don't start this." Trying to avoid discussing Stone, I rush over to the counter when a client walks in, seeing it as my way to escape. "MINE."

"Whatever," Aspen mumbles from behind me, while motioning for her client to take a seat as she walks in right afterward. "We've got three more hours to bug you. Go right ahead."

"Seriously," I mumble under my breath, while checking out the pretty brunette standing in front of me.

"The boys sent me," she says with a huge ass smile, while placing down her twenty percent off coupon.

"Awesome." I grab the coupon and quickly check out the name of who gave it to her. I'm a little relieved to see Kash's name. "Follow me, babe."

The girl decides to babble on about her experience at *Walk of Shame* over the past weekend, being sure to tell me every detail of how hot the boys were, and how sexy they moved their bodies, as if I don't already know.

That's the only *bad* and *good* thing about the boys sending them here. I feel as if there's a good chance that one of us girls would get the gossip if Stone is fucking these other women. The bad part of it is, that I hear so many stories and I can only handle so much and manage to keep my distance from there.

I hate myself for even wanting to know what goes on at the club, especially now that they have private rooms for dances.

From what I've heard, Stone's room is occupied the most and I have to say that I'm not surprised. He's very good at what he does.

By the time the salon is closed, Hemy is waiting outside for us, making sure that no one is lurking around the parking lot, even though it's only like six in the evening. It's not even dark, yet he worries so much.

Not much has changed there. He's a protector and always has been.

As soon as we walk outside, Hemy instantly pulls Onyx into his big arms and kisses her along her neck, grinding his body into hers. He's always so quick to get dirty. "Damn, baby. Ready for a ride?" Continuing to kiss her neck, he cups her ass and lifts her up.

"I missed you. It's been a long ass day and I'm more than ready for a ride," Onyx says against his lips, causing me to look over at Aspen and roll my eyes.

"Come on, guys. Seriously... you stopped in for lunch like five hours ago and fucked her in the back office. You act as if you haven't seen each other in weeks."

Releasing Onyx, Hemy walks over, draping his arm around me. From the look on his face, I know he's about to change the subject. "You going to come see dude tonight or what? Stone's somewhat of a miserable bastard without you around the club." He roughly kisses me on the side of the head. "Go watch him tonight so his pussy will stop hurting."

Grunting, I push my way out of Hemy's arms and begin digging through my purse for my keys. "Seriously? What is with it with everyone trying to get me to watch Stone dance? I'm trying to keep my thoughts in check when it comes to him. It's complicated."

"How?" he questions. "The dude is crazy over you and it's taken my ass a year to accept that shit. Now what the hell am I supposed to give him a hard time about?"

Laughing, I begin backing away. "I'm sure you'll find other things. He's Stone..." I stop when his words really sink in. "And he's not crazy about me, so don't say that again."

"Fine," Onyx cuts in. "Come to the club and watch the other boys tonight then. Hemy has to help Cale with some business crap in the office. Aspen and Riley can't make it. Don't make me sit there and drink alone. Just turn the other way when he's up."

"Maybe... we'll see. I want to write some tonight."

Saying bye to everyone, I hurry over to my truck and hop in, just ready to get home and take a short nap.

As much as I hate to admit it, I didn't sleep much last night. I ended up tossing and turning in bed, wondering what Stone was doing at work.

Maybe it's time I put on my big girl panties and go back into *Walk of Shame* again.

Then maybe it will give me the confirmation that I need, to know that he's doing fine without me around.

There's plenty of other women there that would die to get Stone's attention.

Hopefully she can do more with it than I did...

CHAPTER THREE

SAGE

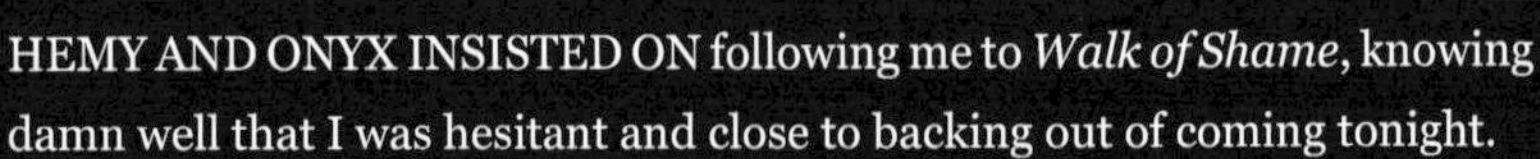

HEMY AND ONYX INSISTED ON following me to *Walk of Shame*, knowing damn well that I was hesitant and close to backing out of coming tonight.

They can't fool me; I know they're going to somehow try to get me into Stone's private room with him.

Not happening. I'm smart enough to know what will happen if he gets me alone.

I'll cave.

The jerks are teaming up on me, and I'm not so sure that I like it. Apparently, they've all grown fond of the idea of Stone and I possibly becoming a couple.

Maybe they see what we've been trying *not* to.

"Hey, Kage." I wink at the sexy security guard as he places his hand on the small of my back and guides me behind Hemy and Onyx, over to the VIP area.

"Keep winking at me and I might have to keep you to myself now that

Stone's out of the picture." He grabs a strand of my hair and smiles. "Very hot. I like my women wild looking."

"Back the fuck off, giant," Hemy growls out, while looking his six feet six frame up and down. "Don't you have a door to watch or some shit?"

Used to Hemy being a dick, Kage lifts a brow at him and smirks. "Can't help it if the *hottest* ladies in the club got my attention, man."

"And I can't help it if I rip your motherfucking dick off."

"Hemy! Enough!" Onyx grabs Hemy by the back of the shirt, pulling him back to sit next to her on the couch. "Leave his dick alone. He's gonna need it tonight." She winks at Kage. "We got your back. Thank you, sweetie."

I have to admit; being here and watching Hemy be all caveman and overprotective makes me laugh, reminding me of old times.

It used to drive me crazy when he treated Stone that way in the beginning and seeing him act this way now, shows me just how crazy his ass will be if I ever decide to go on a date.

Poor fucking guy...

"Can't take you anywhere, big brother," I tease as I take my seat. "Now get us ladies some drinks and tell Sarah hi for us, Mr. Rude."

His stripper instincts kick in, causing me to look anywhere *but* at him as he straddles Onyx's lap and grabs her face, making out with her.

When I turn back around, he stands up and licks his lips nice and slow. "I'll be right back. If any of the boys come over, tell them I said to fuck off."

"Seriously?" I scoot next to Onyx and link my arm with hers, as Hemy leaves us. "Is he ever going to give up and stop being a dick to every guy? He's so damn alpha."

Onyx shakes her head and smiles. "Nope... and I love it. Hemy will be Hemy and that's exactly why I keep his sexy ass around. That and because his..."

"No!" I yell. "I will slap you if you mention his..." I pretend to gag. "Don't make me slap you. Please."

"Girls." Styx scoots his way in between us and hands us both a drink, before throwing an arm around each of us. "I took these from Hemy's ass while he was fighting a crowd of women off." He winks. "You're welcome."

Onyx sits up straight, her eyes wandering up to the bar. She's not beyond kicking some girl's ass for groping on her man. I've seen it and trust me; it's not pretty.

"They're gone now." He laughs. "And Hemy is getting new drinks and looking around as if he wants to rip someone's head off." Smirking, he stands up and brushes a hand through his blond hair. "Don't tell his crazy ass that I'm the one that stole his drinks. I'm not trying to get my ass kicked tonight. This body has work to do. Later."

He quickly kisses us both on the cheek and rushes off to take the stage to get ready. The ladies love him with his tattoos, sexy pierced nipples, and short, blond beard. Not to mention his insanely beautiful blue eyes that are hard to not look at.

He's hot. What can I say? They all are.

Right as the music starts, Hemy heads back over from the bar, holding the replacement drinks. He growls when he looks down to see us both already holding drinks. "What the fuck? Whose ass do I need to kick? Was it Kash or Styx? Those sneaky fuckers."

We both shrug and laugh, pissing him off even more. It's fun to mess with him and see him get all worked up over the boys.

"I hate when you two team up on my ass. I give up before I get a nipple ripped off or some shit. You two are vicious." Tilting back his drink, he takes his seat on the other side of Onyx and wraps his arm around her, protectively.

We chat and drink for the next hour, making me anxious and curious about Stone.

He hasn't been seen in the whole time that we've been here. Makes me wonder if he's been giving private dances the entire time. The thought makes me sick to my stomach and I'm hating myself for it.

"You okay over there?"

"Huh?" I turn to the sound of Onyx's concerned voice. "What?"

"You've been staring off into space for the last twenty minutes, when you should be watching these boys on the stage and having some fun." She leans forward and begins looking around. "Is someone wondering about Stone? Is that it?"

I let out a fake laugh and cross my legs. "No. I was just thinking about the new book I'm working on and the asshole hero who won't stop pissing me off. Now shut up. Kash is on and his ass is looking extra sexy tonight."

Pretending to be into Kash's performance, I focus my attention on the stage and pull out some money to toss his way. He's insanely sexy, so it should be distracting me, but it's not enough to make me forget Stone and how badly I really want to watch him dance again.

Hemy disappeared twenty minutes ago to help Cale with some stuff in his office, leaving us girls here alone.

That's what he said at least, but I'm pretty sure Cale can handle it on his own.

I think he was just tired of watching the other boys strip since he can't do it himself anymore. Part of me thinks he misses it.

I definitely don't. *Vixens* was fun while it lasted, but I definitely didn't see myself there long-term.

Stripping is a big part of Hemy though. He had that when he didn't have Onyx and myself around. I think it kept him sane, while he was slowly losing himself to the darkness and pain.

My insides seem to melt and I find myself fighting to catch my breath at the sight of Stone across the room, leaning against the wall with his arms across his chest. How the hell does he manage to look so calm and cool standing there? It makes him extremely sexy and mysterious.

As much as I'm not wanting this kind of reaction, it's inevitable with Stone. He's always done this to me from the very first time I laid eyes on his painfully beautiful face.

"Fuck." I turn away and start fanning myself off in a panic. It suddenly feels extremely warm in here, knowing that he's about to work his body on stage soon.

"You okay, woman?"

As hard as I fight not to look at him, my eyes find him again in the shadows, trying to stay clear of everyone so he can clear his head. He's wearing that beanie of his, hoping that no one will spot him out until he's ready.

Well I will always be able to.

Onyx's eyes follow mine and she smiles knowingly, once she sees what I'm secretly freaking out about.

Well at least I was trying to keep it a secret freak out... isn't working so well.

"You've got it bad for that boy. Just admit it and make it easier on all of us. You guys had fun together and that's how it should be."

Both of our eyes go back toward the stage once the music stops and Kash jumps down into the crowd, getting his moment that he loves so much. Being felt up at the end is his favorite part. Figures...

"Looks like your man's up next. Think you can handle his hotness?" She lifts a brow at me, while taking a sip of her drink. "That boy's been working out some frustration or something. Damn... don't tell Hemy, but he's looking mighty fine. The last seven months have been good for his body."

We both watch as Stone walks up the side of the stage closest to us, and gets into position, waiting for his song to start.

Why the fuck does he have to be so sexy?

The room suddenly goes dark. I mean completely pitch black. I can't even see my hand in front of me.

A few women even scream, not expecting us all to be pooled in darkness. Hell, I almost screamed myself, surprised. I even spilled my drink some.

A small spotlight has us all staring at the stage as the DJ begins to play "In Chains" by Shamon's Harvest.

It's hard to make out at first, but at closer look, Stone is now down on his knees, shackled in chains.

Gripping the chains, he moves his hips in a way that is so damn sexy and hypnotizing that I accidentally bite my bottom lip too hard, while watching him move.

"Fuck me..." I breathe. "Is it hot in here?" I tug at my blouse, not removing my eyes from his every move.

"Well damn. Look what you've done to him," Onyx breathes. "So much sin in that fine as hell body."

The more he moves around, the longer the chains get, allowing him to move closer to the edge of the stage, on his knees, while flawlessly fucking the stage at the same time.

Out of nowhere, surprising us all, water sprays all over the stage, soaking him and everyone in the front as he continues to fight the chains, his muscles flexing in the best ways possible to make him look even more irresistible.

We're on the side of the stage and we even get a bit wet, and that's on top of the wetness between my legs now.

When the music speeds up, pumping us all up, he finally breaks free from the chains, causing my heart to race in excitement, as if I'm watching some intense movie or something, and the part I've been waiting for has finally just happened.

The women scream louder than I've ever heard, and wave their hands around, hoping that they'll choose them, as he walks to the edge of the stage and hops off.

I lose track of where he is, until I see a cute brunette get lifted onto the stage, followed by him jumping back up, sliding across the water on his knees to get to where she's standing.

Thrusting his hips, he slowly runs his hands down the front of his slick body, while standing up and removing his low hanging jeans.

He's wearing white boxer briefs. White! Wet and white! Dammit, Stone.

Running a hand through his dark, wet hair, he grabs the woman's hand with his free hand and runs it down his body, stopping at the top of his briefs.

I get nervous, thinking he's going to go lower, but he doesn't.

Biting his lip as the women scream, he thrusts his hips really fast, while pushing the woman down to her knees and grinding in her face.

All I can think about while his dick smacks her face, is how he used to grind his hips in my face, when giving me private dances and just how hot it made me.

Watching it happen with another woman just pisses me the fuck off.

I'm jealous. I'm actually jealous right now and this is not what I was hoping for.

Seeing this never used to bother me. Not when I was getting it at home, but now...

"I want to cut her," I mumble, surprised at my own words.

Onyx's eyes widen at my words. "Whoa there, killer. You act as if you haven't seen this a million times before."

I empty my glass and set it down. "Yeah, that was before, but I haven't seen it in a while. Maybe I'm just tired. It's been a long day."

I stand up and suck in a deep breath when Stone's eyes somehow find mine and lock on. The way he's looking at me steals my breath away. There's so much intensity behind his eyes, knowing that I haven't been here in months and now here I am. I'm pretty sure he knows that I've been avoiding watching him dance.

Fuck... that look. I can't...

“I should go.” I lean in and quickly kiss the side of her head. “Tell Hemy I said bye.”

Knowing that she’s going to try to leave with me, I push her back down when she attempts to stand. “I’m just going to bed so there’s no reason for you to come with me. I’ll see you tomorrow.”

“Sage,” she calls out when I turn to walk away. “Drive safe and call me if you need me.”

“I always do.”

I allow my eyes to land on the stage one last time, to see Stone standing still, with a small smirk on his lips. That smirk used to be my weak spot when we first met.

This pushes my ass to move faster and get myself out of here before I do something stupid, without thinking it through.

Coming here and watching him dance was a horrible idea…

CHAPTER FOUR

STONE

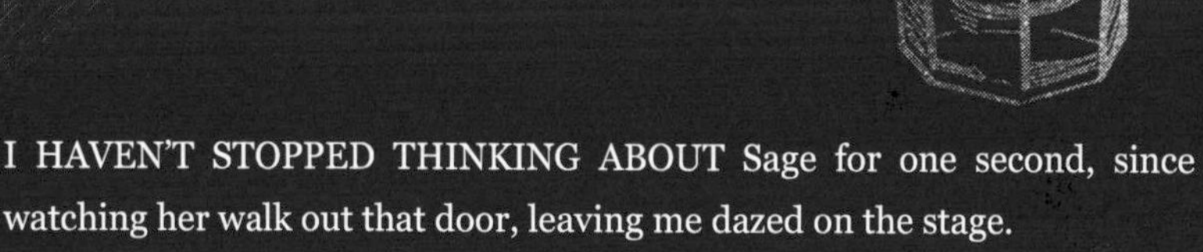

I HAVEN'T STOPPED THINKING ABOUT Sage for one second, since watching her walk out that door, leaving me dazed on the stage.

She's been avoiding coming here since we stopped messing around seven months ago and the way she was watching me so intently, reminded me of when she used to want me.

Hell maybe she still wants me to touch her just as badly as I still want to.

I barely snapped out of it, until Onyx jumped on the stage and threw her drink in my face, waking my ass up out of the trance I was in.

"You still over there thinking about Sage? Get a grip on your balls, dude," Kash teases. "Don't be mad that she stayed for my show and yours ran her out." He cocks a brow, pissing my ass off even more.

"Fuck you!" I throw my sweaty ass, soaked briefs at his face and laugh when he freaks out.

"Dude! Your balls were just in these. What the fuck."

"Next time it will *be* my balls slapping your pretty face, asshole."

"I'm out, dicks. Got a kinky ass woman waiting outside my house. If you get some pictures from me, open with caution, fuckers." Styx throws his bag over his shoulder and slaps us both upside the head, before taking off.

Asshole's lucky I don't feel like wasting my energy on his ass. Fuck, I don't feel like wasting it on anyone, but Sage. I don't need sleep. I'd spend the whole night pleasuring her if I got the chance to again.

I wanted nothing more than to run off the stage and dance for her, but I was worried she might get pissed and the last thing I want is to embarrass her by putting her on the spot.

Well fuck me...

Why was she even here tonight after so long? If it was for one of these other assholes, I won't hesitate to fuck them up. None of them are good enough for her and none of them will take care of her like I would if given the chance.

"Think Sage would let me come over tonight?" Kash teases.

"Hell no, fucker. I'm getting out of here before I kick your ass. I'm not in the mood so don't test me tonight."

Smirking, he throws his hands up and backs away to the shower. "It's all good. My hand's been good to me."

"I bet," I mumble, once I'm alone. "Mine too."

I finish gathering up my shit, before going to find Cale in his office, hoping that Hemy is still here so I can ask about Sage.

He's not.

Cale stands from his chair and starts grabbing for his things, ready to get out of here and back to his woman. "You good?" he questions.

Raking my hands through my wet hair, I let out a breath of frustration. "You saw who was here tonight," I point out. "Did Hemy tell you why?"

He walks out the door, with me following behind. "Onyx made her come, man. She didn't want to drink alone."

"Yeah," I say. "I figured she wasn't here to see me or those other dicks. Thanks, man, I'll see you later."

"Yeah... later."

BY THE TIME I GET home, the house is dark and Sage is in her room, asleep.

Unable to sleep myself, I find myself in the shower at five in the damn morning, jerking my shit to thoughts of Sage's sexy as sin body, remembering every last detail of how her body felt against mine.

It didn't help that she came into the club tonight somehow looking even sexier than usual, sporting a new hairstyle. With her wild hair, fresh tattoos, and lip ring... fuck me. She looks wild and sexy as fuck.

What I wouldn't do to suck that piercing into my mouth and nibble it. Hell... I want to feel it on my dick.

Closing my eyes, thoughts of her take control of me.

The curve of her hips.

Fuck yes.

The fullness of her beautiful breasts.

Fuck me.

The way her tight little pussy hugged my cock so perfectly.

Fuck... so damn perfect.

Gripping the shower wall, my hold on my shaft tightens and my strokes speed up, bringing me so close to losing my shit, that I almost can't handle it.

A few more long, hard strokes and I'm growling out my pleasure, while shooting my hot cum down the drain, pretending it was Sage's plump ass. How I'd love to see my release drip down her sexy little asshole.

"Oh. Fuuuuck!"

Standing in the warm shower, I close my eyes harder, while fighting to catch my breath.

That woman does something to me that I can't fight.

And it turns me on like nothing else...

AFTER MY SHOWER, I SOMEHOW managed to pass out and not wake up until close to noon.

The first thing I did when getting out of bed this afternoon, was start thinking about how Sage was at the club last night, watching me.

She looked like she was sweating from watching me. I could tell, even in the darkened room.

"Fuck this." I'm tired of this new arrangement and tired of pretending as if I don't want her.

I've stepped back for seven months now and have respected the fact that we weren't going to be physical anymore, but I want more with her and I'm tired of holding back.

I'm about to refresh her memory of me and remind her of what she's missing.

When she first moved here to Chicago, over a year ago, she couldn't stay away from me, despite her brother giving us a hard time for messing around.

We had fun. We were good with each other... for each other, until she got scared and decided we were done being friends with benefits. I wasn't ready to stop, but kept my mouth closed out of respect.

I want to show her that not everyone in her life will disappear. Not everyone will hurt her and abandon her like her parents did. Especially me.

I want to make her mine and I'm not stopping until I do. The old Stone charm is coming out to play...

CHAPTER FIVE

SAGE

THERE'S NOTHING I HATE MORE than trying to avoid Stone while being in the same house, but after going to the club last night, I haven't been able to stop thinking sexual thoughts about him.

I thought I could handle living with him and not wanting more with him, but it's becoming harder and harder with each day.

The truth is, I never wanted to stop in the first place, but I was starting to depend on him being there for me.

The feeling scared me, because after my parents abandoned us when I was a child and Hemy and I got separated, alone was all I had.

There was never anyone that I had to worry about losing, because I ended up with a family that didn't even know I existed. They were just in it for the money and couldn't give a shit whether I lived or died.

There was no one for me to lose. No one that had the power to hurt me. Hemy was already gone and he was the only person who ever mattered to me.

Then the day that Onyx found me working in that diner, she became my friend. She was the first person I had let in since losing my brother.

Stone was the second and I didn't even mean to let him in. The fucker charmed his way in and got stuck.

Distancing myself was the only thing I could do to protect myself from falling and getting hurt and the more nights we spent having fun, flirting, and having sex, the more I started to feel for him and fear him disappearing too.

I knew I shouldn't have gone to *Walk of Shame* last night. One reminder at what he could do with his body and I was completely done for. If I even give him the chance to talk to me right now, I'm utterly screwed.

It's my day off and I plan on spending it in my room, finishing up this book and keeping my mind *far* away from Stone.

Stone doesn't exist...

"Stone doesn't exist," I say out loud this time. "And neither does his humongous dick."

"Sure I do, honey and my humongous cock definitely exists as well."

Scared shitless, I practically jump out of my chair, while spinning around to the sound of Stone's voice.

"You fucker!" I suck in a deep breath at the sight of Stone gripping the doorframe. *Those muscles don't exist. That body. That bulge...* "What are you doing in here? Ever heard of knocking? Jeez, Stone."

A smirk crosses his sexy as sin face. "Since when have I ever knocked?"

Closing down my laptop, my eyes follow Stone's every move as he walks into the room and takes a seat at the edge of my desk.

I can't seem to keep my eyes off his thick, muscled thighs. I always loved that about him. So much power in them.

"Well it's always a nice gesture. I was writing."

My heart races like crazy as my eyes wander over his body, stopping on his smooth lips, waiting for him to say something. Anything.

Why does my body have to react this way to him? Why does it have to want him so badly?

"You got me thinking last night." He scoots across the desk, until he's right in front of me, pulling my chair closer, until I'm between his legs. "About how much you used to love me dancing for you."

My breath escapes me when Stone's hands come around to grip my hair and he slowly lowers his body into the armless chair and down to straddle my lap.

His warm breath tickles my ear as he leans in close, knowing what his closeness will do to me. "It's been a while, but I bet me being this close still affects you."

Letting loose for a moment, I wrap my arms around his firm body and moan when he begins grinding in my lap. "No," I breathe.

He runs his lips up my neck, stopping below my ear. "No, it doesn't still affect you?" Pulling my hand from around him, he places it on his chest and slowly starts moving it down his hard body.

"Yes," I breathe. "I mean no." Trying to keep in control, I yank my hand away from his body, before I can cave in. "Let's not do this, Stone."

"Why?" he whispers, while wrapping his hand in my hair. "Remind you of good times? Of the many ways my body made you come?"

"You know it does, jerk." I push his rock hard chest, until he finally backs away from me. "It's not like I've forgotten just because we haven't been physical in months. What's gotten into you?"

He must notice me checking his chest out, because a cocky smirk appears on his face. "Take my shirt off if you want. I'll let you lick it."

I clear my throat and stop gawking at his body, before he decides to take it as an invite back into my panties. "You're a pain in my ass," I say with a small smile. "Do you know that?"

"I want to *fuck* you," he growls out, surprising me. "This new hair. Fuck me, Sage. There's nothing you can do to make me not want you as much. You get sexier every damn time I lay eyes on you."

I can't deny the way my body gets all happy and giddy from his words. Him not being afraid to say what's on his mind always turned me the hell on.

"Stone..." I warn. "Why are you doing this?"

"I'm thinking about running my tongue over every inch of your body right now. Remember how much you loved my tongue on you?"

He runs his tongue over his bottom lip, and I instantly get wet at just the memory of how good it used to make me feel.

The boy had a magic tongue and a magic dick and I miss them both.

Shit... he needs to get out of here. Now!

"Oh I remember. Trust me, but I'm trying not to. Especially right now so I can work. Please, let's not bring up the past."

"You missed the last part of my dance last night. Come to my private room tonight at eleven and let me make up for it. Just one dance is all I'm asking." He laces his hands behind my neck like old times and leans in to press a kiss right beside my lips. "One night to be in charge and pleasure you without sex. Just give me that. You look like you need release and I want to help you with that. Nothing more."

Exhaling, I close my eyes and run my hands over my face as Stone walks out of my room and leaves.

I don't waste any time jumping out of my chair and locking the door behind him so he can't distract me anymore.

It's bad enough that my mind's been on him since last night, but now... damn him.

Now he's asking me to let him give me a private dance. Does he realize what that's going to do to me?

Yes, I got off on watching his body and yes, I do need it. He wasn't wrong about that.

But he wasn't supposed to notice.

Fuck my life...

Letting my frustration out on paper, I pull up my work in progress and end up getting in a total of six thousand words in just under three hours. Only two thousand or so more to go and it's done. My third book.

My hero somehow ended up with a lot of Stone's qualities. A cocky, smartass, sexy maniac with a magic dick.

Of course he would find a way to take over my book too. That ass.

Riley called me about an hour ago, asking me to come over and spend some time with her and her precious little baby, Haven Kinley.

She's two weeks today and so cute that I swear I could just die.

Cale's at *Walk of Shame* for the next hour so I figured it would be nice to get some girl time in and see what she has to say about my situation with Stone.

"So what should I do?"

"I'm sorry. What?" Riley looks up from baby Haven in her arms. "She's very cute and distracting," she says in a baby voice. "Repeat that please."

"Stone. He asked me to come see him tonight and..." I get distracted myself and completely lose track of what I'm saying when Haven smiles over at me. "How can something be so damn cute," I coo. "Look at you. Look at you so cute with your precious little nose and big eyes."

Riley laughs at me when I shake my head. "Told you she's distracting."

"Okay, seriously this time." I shield my face from looking at Haven, before she can work her baby voodoo on me again and mess up my thoughts. "Should I go tonight? He wants to dance for me."

Riley lifts her eyebrows suggestively. "If you want to let that boy back between your legs. Cause you know that's going to happen." She pauses to reach for Haven's bottle when she begins fussing. "There's no way that I could watch Cale strip for me without wanting him between my legs afterward. Doesn't matter if I haven't seen him in six months or a whole year. We've already tasted the goods, sweetie and we'll always want more. Those boys were trained to make us sweat."

"Tell me about it," I mutter. "That's what I'm afraid of. I thought we were done with that stuff."

"Do you want to see Stone dance? Do you miss how it made you feel? If it does, then go. Live a little."

I focus on my phone when a text comes through from Stone. Before even opening it, my heart already speeds up with excitement.

Stone

Wear that skirt I like. No fucking panties. Like old times.

My heart speeds up even more after reading it and my thoughts fill with the many times that I've worn that skirt for him, causing my pussy to clench with excitement.

I'm so hot just thinking about him and what he can do to my body, that I can barely handle it.

That's my answer.

"I guess I do. More than I should. Dammit."

Saying goodbye to Riley and the baby, I

shove my phone into my purse and jump into my truck, driving off.

I know without a doubt that by showing up tonight, I'm giving him the okay to pleasure me how he wants.

It's taken me over seven months to be okay with him not touching me anymore.

Do I really want to jump back on his sexual adventure, knowing where it will possibly lead?

I've only got three hours to figure it out and my body is begging me to say yes.

Damn you, Stone…

CHAPTER SIX

STONE

TEN MINUTES TIL' ELEVEN AND no sign of Sage yet. I almost let disappointment set in until I remind myself that I'm taking charge of tonight. It's happening whether it's here at *Walk of Shame* or back home in Sage's room.

I'm not giving up until I get her where I want her, and that's back to wanting me just as much as I want her.

I'm just getting dressed after my quick shower, when Styx walks out from the other shower, naked and dripping wet.

"Ever heard of a towel, dipshit?"

He runs a hand through his thick, wet hair and shrugs, before fingering his short beard. "Never use them. You haven't figured that shit out by now?"

I toss my dirty towel at him just to piss him off. "That's why I asked, fucker."

Standing up, I get ready to pull my shirt on, when the door opens and Kash pokes his head in. "Fuck me... when did Sage get so sexy?"

Out of instinct, I stiffen up, ready to kick his ass, but quickly remind myself that she showed up after all. "Touch her and I'll rip your dick off, pretty boy."

"Hey, man. I can't help it if I noticed how sexy she looks tonight in the skirt she's wearing. Holy fuck… my cock got hard." He steps into the room and points at his crotch. "It still hasn't gone down."

She wore the skirt like I asked. Well… hell.

"Yeah, well you better get your cock out of my way if you want to keep that shit working."

Grinning, he steps away from the door when I head toward it. "Hey. It's not my dick you have to worry about. She was with Lane when I saw her."

"Fucking shit."

I swear the damn security team here is almost worse than us strippers when it comes to the women.

I've caught Kage, Lane, and even Kass getting their fair share of blow jobs and pussy in empty rooms when Cale isn't around watching our asses.

Hell, I've been guilty of that shit too, but those fuckers are bad. Especially Lane.

By the time I fight my way through the crowd and get to Lane, Sage is gone.

"Where is she, man?"

Lane gives me a look as if I'm crazy or some shit. "Who? There's about a hundred females here tonight."

"Sage. Did she leave?"

He smiles. "I should've known she was here to see your ass." He points toward the back where the private rooms are. "She headed that way."

Feeling confident, I raise a brow. "I have a show to put on and it might take a while. Tell Kass to keep everyone away from my room. No private shows. Tell him to send them to Styx or Kash if they ask for me."

"I'm sure I can keep them busy," he says cockily. "No worries."

Not wanting to keep Sage waiting for too long, I quickly head through the private door to my room, that's just for the dancers, and slip into a suit and suspenders, remembering just how hot she got the first time I stripped out of a suit for her.

Women love my ass in a suit and tie. Add some suspenders and it's a done deal.

Getting into position on the stage, I set my eyes on Sage sitting on the couch, waiting for the music to start.

I just hope she's ready to go back to the beginning... back to when she couldn't resist my ass.

SAGE

SITTING HERE WAITING ON STONE, I can't help but wonder what I'm getting myself into.

I struggled for hours, trying to decide whether or not I should just stay home and pretend that he never barged into my room, leaving my body aching for his touch when he left.

I couldn't do it.

He's the only thing I've been able to think about since and it's been driving me crazy. As hard as I fight it, I adore everything about Stone.

"Oui" by Jeremih begins playing over the speakers, letting me know that he's now on the darkened stage, ready to do what he does best.

Getting comfortable, I lean back and cross my legs, keeping my eyes on the small stage as it lights up just enough for me to see him standing there in a suit.

Holy. Shit.

Stone in a suit has to be about the sexiest thing on this earth and he knows it.

His body begins moving to the rhythm of the music, his hands rubbing seductively down his chest, landing on his crotch as he thrusts. The way his hips move instantly gets me sweating.

Biting his bottom lip, he hops off the stage and picks me up, chair and all, and begins walking back up to the stage to set me down in the middle.

Without missing a beat, he grabs the top of my chair tilting me back until he's standing above my face. Then he begins fucking the air so damn perfectly that I bite my lip so hard that I draw blood.

Stone is good with his body. It's what drew me to him in the first place. When that music starts, there's no stopping him until you're completely fucking wet.

Placing me back upright, he stands up and his hands begin working on the buttons of his black, fitted button down.

I find myself watching in anticipation, waiting to see his body as if it were the first time. And holy shit is it exciting, especially since he's practically treating me like a stranger at the moment. It makes it feel more like the first time.

Slowly thrusting his hips, he breaks the bottom two buttons open on his shirt, pulling it off, so that he's now only in a pair of black slacks, a tie, and suspenders.

Oh my God... is he gorgeous.

His hands go up to undo his tie, before he slips it from around his neck.

Smirking cockily, he wraps it behind my neck and scoots my chair across the slippery stage, until he's straddling my lap and grinding on me.

Feeling anxious to touch him, I slide my finger under a strap of his suspenders and snap it.

With force, he captures both of my hands and pulls them behind me in the chair, before running his tongue up my neck, stopping under my ear. "No touching unless I say so."

I let out a surprised gasp as he wraps his tie around my wrists and securely ties it where he knows there's no way I'm getting out. Panic sets in a little because Stone's never been this rough before. It's new and exciting, yet I can't help but feel anxious awaiting his next move.

My insides clench as I watch him moving his body of pure tattooed muscle, while working on the straps of his suspenders.

"Oh my God," I whisper.

Stone is good. Too damn good and I'm not sure whether to love him for this hot show he's putting on or hate him for making my body crave for him once again.

Licking his hand, he runs it down his hard body and into his pants, thrusting the air three times in a way that's so seductive that I gasp for air. My eyes trail down to where his hand is moving, to see him stroking his thickness beneath the fabric.

It doesn't take much to see that he's not wearing anything beneath those suit pants and I'll admit that I want nothing more than for him to lose them.

With his free hand, he undoes the button and zipper, giving me a better view of him slowly stroking his cock. The sight has my pussy clenching and my whole body aching to touch him. Just one feel of what I used to get.

He's not going to let me. He's doing this on purpose to torture me and he's doing a damn good job at it.

Before I know it, he's done stroking himself for me and is slowly lowering me out of the chair to the ground, looking down at me and biting his lip as he walks around me.

He waits until the right moment of the song, before straddling me, working his body over mine until he's above my face.

Going with the beat of the music, he sways and grinds his hips above my face as if fucking it nice and slow. His hard cock is on display above my face and I'm fighting with everything in me not to brush my tongue along every hard inch of it and own it.

It's so insanely hot having him so close, but untouchable. I let out a small moan as he grips my hair and moves more aggressively above me, getting closer to my mouth, but still just out of reach.

Where the hell did he learn to move this way? So damn sinful.

Out of nowhere, he stands and flips me over, pulling my ass up until it's in the air and my face is pressed against the ground.

He walks around me as if admiring my form, before stopping in front of me and groping his thick erection, letting it hang out of his pants, completely.

Breathing heavily, I watch him, wanting nothing more than for him to come in front of me as he brushes his pre-cum over the head of his dick and moans.

Biting his bottom lip, he walks around me again, before dropping to his knees behind me, grabbing my hips and thrusting against my ass to the music.

I find myself gripping at the stage and moaning from release at the feel of his dick rubbing me through my thin panties. It's so damn hard and big, rubbing me in the right spot, repeatedly and in consistent thrusts.

My body jerks below him, trying to come down from its high, until he grabs my neck and pulls me back, pressing his lips below my ear, singing.

It only turns me on more.

The music stops and I find myself breathing so hard that I'm almost embarrassed that he could do this to me after so long and with me tied up.

Now that the room is silent, all I can hear is the sound of Stone's heavy breathing against my ear. "Fuck me, you wore the skirt." His hand reaches beneath my skirt to skim my panty line. "You were smart wearing these," he whispers.

"Yeah," I breathe. "I have to be around you, Stone. You're slick. I haven't forgotten."

A knock sounds at the door, causing Stone to groan into my ear and release my hair to untie my hands.

That's all it takes for me to snap out of Stoneland and gather my thoughts. "I should go so you can work. Thanks for the dance." I free myself from his hold and get back to my feet, while I still have my thoughts in check. "It was good." I smile. "Really good, but we still need to go back to how things have been. It's been working for us and I don't want to mess that up."

I make the mistake of looking back at him to see him on his knees, gripping his sweaty hair in frustration. He looks pained and disappointed.

I've never seen this kind of emotion from him. He's always the funny, carefree guy. Seeing him in this light makes my heart stop, but I try not to let it confuse me even more.

The knocking starts up again. "Give me a fucking minute," he growls out.

Standing to his feet, he walks over to me and grips the bottom of my hair. "I'm not that easy to get rid of, Sage. I have lots of things I want to do to your beautiful body. Lots of things I haven't shown you yet." He gently places a kiss beside my lips, before fixing his pants, smirking and walking out the door.

"What the hell," I breathe in a panic. "What is he doing?"

I stay in Stone's room for a good ten minutes, pulling myself back together before exiting and jumping in surprise, when Kage is waiting outside.

"Kage!" I laugh as he smiles at me. "What are you doing?"

He wraps his huge arm around me. "Stone's ass asked me to keep my eye on you. He got called back to do a short show for a bachelorette party in the back room and couldn't get out of it."

My eyes travel over to the back room when I hear a few screams of excitement. "Looks like someone has a busy night."

Kage lifts a brow. "I'm free in ten."

Smiling, I place my hand on Kage's hard stomach. "Thanks, big guy, but I have to be up early."

He winks. "Your loss."

"I'll be sure to cry myself to sleep tonight."

Pulling my hand away, I blow him a kiss and back away. "Goodnight, giant."

As soon as I get out to my truck, my mind drifts off to Stone and how badly I need to pleasure myself after what he just did to me, and I have a feeling it will be to thoughts of him and all of the things he's done to me in the past.

This is going to be a long night...

CHAPTER SEVEN

STONE

I'M SITTING OUTSIDE SLADE'S HOUSE, smiling to myself as I remember the way Sage's body reacted to me last night. Fuck me, she was so wet for me.

She may be fighting hard to keep me out, but she still wants me and last night proved it just by her showing up in the first place.

It took everything in me not to rip her wet panties off and sink so deep between her legs that she'd feel me inside her for days.

It's too soon, so I settled with getting her off the only way I knew she'd let me at that point.

Tonight is my night off and I plan to be wherever she's going to be. I haven't seen her all day since she's been working, but I plan to make tonight count.

Stone

What are you doing tonight?

A few minutes later, my phone vibrates in my hand with a response from Sage.

Sage

I have plans, big guy, and not with you.

Stone

You sure about that?

Sage

I'm pretty positive you don't have a vagina... so yes.

Stone

No... but I'd like to pound yours. Now tell me where.

Sage

Damn you, Stone... Your fucking mouth.

Stone

I'll put it anywhere you want.

Sage

... I bet you will, big guy. ;) Now bye.

She loves my mouth and I know without a doubt that she's now picturing it all over her body and remembering all of the ways I've tasted her.

That's all I need. Is to be on her mind and last night gave me the opportunity that I needed.

Jumping out of my jeep, I jog up to Slade and Aspen's door to find that it's locked, before running around to the back and letting myself in. They always keep the back door unlocked.

Stepping into the kitchen, I go to open the fridge and stop when I hear moaning and what sounds like spanking coming from the living room.

Smirking, I open a beer and toss the lid aside before going to stand in the doorway.

All I see is Slade's naked ass pounding away as if he hasn't gotten laid in weeks.

"Where's the popcorn, dude?"

Growling, Slade thrusts into Aspen one last time, before turning to look at me. "What is with you fuckers never knocking?"

Covered up, Aspen sits up from the couch and peers over the top. "Don't you guys ever get tired of walking in on us?"

I tilt back my beer and smile. "The question is... don't *you* guys get tired of us walking in on you? It's called locks, but you always leave the back door open. You enjoy it... admit it."

Slade stands up completely naked and gives me a dirty look while pulling his briefs up. "You're early, dick. I just walked in the door thirty minutes ago. Can't a guy please his wife and shower after work in peace before dealing with your ass?"

"Now that's asking a lot." I raise a brow just to annoy him more. "How are things at the office going, Suit? I bet it's exciting as shit sitting behind a desk all day."

"It's more relaxing than shaking my cock all day, fucker. How's yours now that Sage has your balls? Is it holding up on its own?"

"Nothing can keep my shit down, man." I smirk and grab my crotch. "I've got a magic dick is what I've been told."

"Yeah, well tell your magic dick to toss me a beer."

Aspen stands up, pulling the blanket with her. "I'll be upstairs showering and finishing what you interrupted so thanks for that, Stone."

I smile against my beer. "Hey, no one said you had to stop. It's not as if I've never seen it before."

Aspen's face turns red. "Well I think you've seen it enough." She walks over to kiss Slade on the neck. "I'll be waiting for you upstairs."

Growling, Slade grabs Aspen's ass through the blanket and slaps it as she walks away.

Laughing, I toss Slade a beer and he catches it, quickly popping the top off. "So how did things go last night? Sage show up?"

"Yup." I pull out a barstool and take a seat. "She's still pushing my ass away." I tilt back my beer. "But at least she came."

He smiles and takes a swig of his beer. "It's been what... six or seven months since she's watched your annoying ass dance. Good shit. So you're going all in this time? You really want more?"

"Yeah." I set my beer down and watch as he searches through the fridge. "I only held back the first time because I was respecting the fact that she wanted nothing more than to mess around. I did things her way and now I'm doing them mine. We were roommates for a whole year, messing around when she wanted to. I want more, man. I know she's scared, but I won't hurt her."

He pulls out some lunch meat and begins making a sandwich. "You sure about that?"

"Hell yeah," I say without hesitation. "I may have been pushed around and kicked in the past, but I'm not scared of love, man. Not like her."

He nods and tosses some bread my way for my own sandwich. "You better hope so. If you hurt Sage, Hemy will break your ass in two."

I think about it for a second and my answer remains the same. She's the only thing I've been able to think about since laying eyes on her. She means something to me and I want to find out just how much.

"Positive." I throw some turkey and mustard on my bread, before taking a huge bite. "I just need her to spend some time with me out of the house so she can see how much fun we used to have."

Slade watches me for a few seconds, before speaking again. "Make sure your ass is at *Fortunes* tonight then. She asked Aspen to come out with her and Jade for a few drinks around nine."

"No shit." Smiling, I stand up and look at the clock. It's a quarter to seven. "You and Aspen going?"

He shakes his head. "Nah, Aspen's had a long week. We're staying in."

"Looks like Kash's ass better prepare to come out then." I shove the last bite of sandwich in my mouth, before finishing off my beer and tossing it in the trash. "You've just made my night a hell of a lot better. I need to get my ass home and change."

"Anything to get you out of my house, fucker. My woman is waiting upstairs for me to finish what you interrupted." He tosses his empty beer in the trash. "Lock the back door on the way out."

With that, he walks away, leaving me alone in his kitchen.

I quickly clean up the mess we made and then let myself out the back, locking the door behind me.

Once back in my jeep, I send Kash a quick text, letting him know that he's coming out tonight.

He responds within a few seconds.

Kash

I'm down.

I knew he would be and I need someone to keep Jade busy so I can get close to Sage tonight.

As close as she will allow me...

CHAPTER EIGHT

SAGE

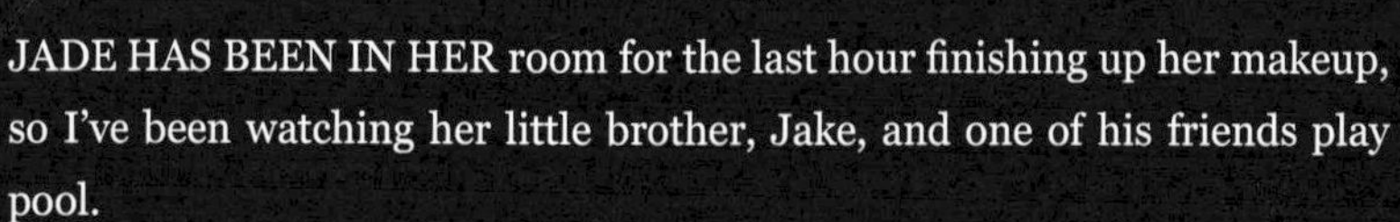

JADE HAS BEEN IN HER room for the last hour finishing up her makeup, so I've been watching her little brother, Jake, and one of his friends play pool.

Her brother just turned eighteen two days ago and seems to think that now that he's of age, that I'm going to give him a shot and let him take me home to his parents' basement.

The kid says he has huge plans for me and that his parents hardly ever come down to the basement.

Apparently, his friend seems to get a kick out of him trying and being turned down and put in his place by me, because he's been laughing his ass off for the last hour.

"You know..." Jake pauses to take his shot and misses. "I just upgraded to a queen-sized bed, baby. That means it's fit for a queen. My queen."

Laughing, I about spit my beer out. "I'm sorry, but I only lay with a king, kid. Let me know when you get your next upgrade."

"Oh damn." His friend covers his mouth with his fist and busts out in laughter.

"Really, Jake?" Jade laughs from the doorway. "You definitely got your game from uncle Frank and trust me, it's not strong, kid."

Jake rolls his eyes. "Stop calling me kid. Did you miss the part where I turned eighteen? Dammit, Jade. You're always trying to embarrass me."

Smiling, she grabs her brother's chin and starts talking in baby talk about how cute and adorable he is.

This causes him to turn red with embarrassment and toss his cue stick down. "Dude... let's get out of here, Myles, while I still have some dignity left."

"Bye, cutie," I tease. "Don't forget to call me when you get an upgrade." I wink, causing him to smirk and smooth out his shirt.

"It's the shirt, right?" He nudges his friend. "Told you she'd dig the shirt."

Jade grabs both of the boys and begins pushing them through the house. "Time to leave. Tell Mom I'll call her tomorrow."

Myles stops to check Jade out in her black skinny jeans and teal blouse. "I turn eighteen in three months." He licks his lips. "Just sayin'."

"Out!" She points. "Jake, don't forget your weird little sidekick."

We both look at each other and laugh as the boys argue their way out the front door about whose game needs the most work.

"Well... that was interesting." Jade smiles. "You ready to go out and see some *real* men now? I just heard that the after party for the MMA fights from tonight is going to be at *Fortunes*. Plenty of hard, powerful, hot men to choose from."

The thought of these MMA fighters being at the bar tonight is sort of exciting, but I can't help but think of the fact that Stone is built the same way, but even better than most of these fighters.

When I think *hard, powerful, and hot*... I think Stone.

His body is hard and powerful and he's definitely got to be the hottest guy I've ever laid eyes on.

Trying not to fall for him has been harder than I imagined. Especially when he opens his sexy mouth, telling me what he wants without holding back.

He's gone months being quiet, but I have a feeling that's about to change.

"Let's go." Shaking my head of thoughts of Stone, I follow Jade outside to her jeep.

Fortunes is already busy by the time we get there. My guess is that the fights are over and everyone is gathering around to drink with their favorite fighters.

The crowd is already rowdy from drinking and watching the fights so the bar is so loud that you have to practically scream to hear each other.

"We'll take two beers," Jade yells to the bartender, while holding up two fingers for her to see.

"Holy shit," I say next to Jade's ear as she hands me a beer. "You can't even move in this place tonight. Is it always this way after a fight?"

"Always, honey. You need to get out more," she yells.

Holding onto Jade's arm, I pull her through the crowd when I spot the last empty table in the whole bar.

It just so happens to be next to the table that a few fighters have just arrived at. The whole table is screaming and congratulating the guys on their wins, while passing cans of beer around.

"See that guy with the black shirt?" Jade asks, while pointing to the hot blond with bulging muscles. I nod my head. "That's Knight Stevens. He was the main event at the fights down the street. Looks like he won."

Within seconds, trays full of shot glasses arrive at their table, most of them being passed over to this Knight guy as he continuously slams them back, accepting them all.

I tilt back my beer while watching him. "He's a fucking trooper. Holy shit, I'd be puking my ass off by now."

"Tell me about it. I love a man that can handle his liquor." She takes a swig of her beer. "He's single too. Maybe we should go over and congratulate him."

This Knight guy must catch us looking at him and talking, because his eyes land on us and stay there as he tilts back one last shot.

Winking, he nods his head and grabs two shot glasses, before heading over to our table. He sets the shot glasses down, before eyeing us both over like he's ready to take us to his hotel room and show us a good time. "Drink up, ladies. Shots are on my table."

Jade grabs a shot and nudges me when I don't make a move to grab one.

"Thanks." She waits for me to grab mine, before clinking her glass against mine and downing it at the same time that I do mine.

Satisfied, Knight helps us both to our feet, before grabbing our table and pushing it against his. "The prettiest girls here and you guys are sitting alone. I won't have that shit. You're with me now." He winks, while getting pulled away by one of his guys.

Jade squeezes my leg and leans in. "What's wrong? Loosen up a little. You look so tense."

I pull my eyes away from Knight, who hasn't seemed to take his off me since we sat down at our now joined tables. "I'm fine." I cover my head as one of the guys at the table stands up and starts tossing cans of beers across the room to other tables, while drunkenly screaming. "These guys are just really fucking drunk and stupid. If one hits us with a beer, I'll kick them in the balls."

"You want to move? We can, but there aren't any other tables available. We're lucky we found this one."

Ducking around the crowded table, I begin looking around to see where we can possibly move to, when a beer flies right next to my head, almost hitting me.

Instinctively, my arm goes up to cover my head and anger floods through me. These dicks just really don't give a shit and I'm not about to spend the whole night dodging beers.

I stand up and grab Jade's arm, while keeping my eyes on the asshole with the beers. "We're moving."

My heart about beats out of my chest, when Stone appears out of what seems like nowhere, and grabs the drunken guy by his shirt, slamming him into the table.

"Watch where the fuck you're throwing those beers, asshole. Hit one of those girls and I'll fuck your shit up."

Knight stands up and rushes over to help his friend when he notices him in trouble, but stops when he notices Stone and Kash, as if he's seen them before and doesn't want any trouble.

Instead, he places his hand on Stone's shoulder and says something to him that has Stone releasing his grip on his asshole friend.

"He's cut off for the night, bro. No worries," Knight says loud enough for the whole table to hear. "You hear that? Tanner is done so don't send anymore shit his way."

Pulling his eyes away from Knight, Stone walks over and pulls out the chair next to me. "You alright?"

Still in shock that a fight didn't just break out, I nod my head, thankful that he's here to calm them down. "I am now," I say with a hint of a smile. "Thanks for that. I *was* about to drag Jade out of here."

Kash pulls up an empty chair next to Jade and takes a seat, instantly grabbing her attention away from any other guy at the table.

I'm a little surprised, because the way she's been looking at Knight, I expected her to go after *him*, but she's over there smiling as if he's the cutest thing she's ever seen.

Pulling my chair to face him, Stone pulls me closer until I'm between his legs. "I've dealt with these fuckers before, and I wouldn't have hesitated to fight every single one of those fuckers if you got hit with that beer."

I suck in a breath, as he reaches out and swipes his thumb over my bottom lip. "Stop making that sexy little sound when you breathe, before I bend you over in front of everyone and give you a reason to."

Holy shit...

I didn't even realize I was softly moaning, while looking him over in his fitted white t-shirt and dark jeans until now. Not to mention him standing up for me to a table full of fighters and their friends practically had me fighting for air.

This man is beyond sexy in everything he does and says and there's no denying it.

Damn him for being so fucking cute and irresistible.

"I bet you wish that I'd let you," I say next to his ear, while patting his chest.

Smirking, he grabs my wrist as I'm about to pull away, placing my hand back on his flexed chest. "I do... and you would."

I smile. I can't help it. I love this side of Stone, even though I know it will probably get me where I've been trying *not* to be. "What makes you think that?"

"Because you've always wanted to have sex in a public place and what better way to do that than with a male stripper that will make you scream until your throat's raw?"

"Oh shit!" Jade yells from beside me. "I heard that. Someone's got one dirty mouth."

Apparently, so did Knight, because he glares over at Stone, looking pissed that these male strippers have our attention and he doesn't.

A fighter is *hot*, but nothing is *hotter* than a man that can move his body in the dirty way that these *Walk of Shame* boys do.

Knight looks like he's about to say something, but gets distracted when a female throws her arms around his neck and begins whispering in his ear.

Relief washes over me, because having Stone get into a fight is the last thing I want right now, especially with some MMA fighters.

"Need another beer?" Stone questions.

I point at his empty hands. "Where's yours?"

"I'm not drinking tonight."

"Why not?"

He stands up and grabs my waist, helping me to my feet. "Someone has to keep an eye on you with all these rowdy assholes here eyeing you up."

Grabbing my hand, he pulls me through the crowd and over to the bar, holding onto me protectively.

Smiling, I watch as he orders two beers, I'm guessing one for Jade since Kash didn't look like he was drinking either.

As we're about to walk back over to the table, two girls stop Stone, acting all giddy and excited as if they've just spotted a celebrity or some shit.

"Come dance with us," one girl says.

"None of these other guys here tonight can dance. Please, Stone. Come play with us." The tall redhead smiles, but then gives me a dirty as hell look when she notices Stone holding my hand.

It pisses me off, yet makes me feel good that these other girls want him, and it's my hand that he's holding right now.

It has the feisty Sage wanting to come out and play. She better back off.

"I'd watch that face because bitch does not look good on you, honey."

Stone smiles as if he's impressed and then surprises me when he pulls me into him and runs his tongue across my lips, before biting the bottom one, causing my insides to jump with excitement. "Fuck me, Sage. You're sexy as fuck when you're feisty. Feel that?" He presses his hips into me, showing me that he's now hard. "Your mouth does this to me."

The girls give up and walk away, looking pissed that he didn't pay them any attention.

"Keep poking me with your *big* dick and I might just bite it." I smile against his ear. "Nice and hard. I don't think you want that."

I get ready to walk away with the beers, but Stone presses up behind me, wrapping his arm around my waist.

My pussy clenches as he bites my ear and possessively grips the button on my jeans as if he can rip it off any second and take me how he wants. "I'll take your mouth on my dick anyway you want. Don't think that a little pain will scare me. It will only make me fuck you harder."

Jade whistles, getting our attention as her and Kash stand up as if they're ready to move somewhere else.

"Not tonight, big guy," I manage to get out, even though my whole body is buzzing with need.

Wriggling out of his grip, I make my way over to Jade and hand her a beer, while following her over by the dartboards.

We start up a game and I try my best to not imagine Stone fucking me here in public and making me scream, but the way he keeps looking at me, makes it impossible to stop imagining.

It doesn't help any that those jeans he's wearing fit him so perfectly that any girl wouldn't be able to think straight after setting sight on his backside.

I swear my eyes have been glued to his firm ass every single time that he goes up to throw his darts.

I want to bite it.

"There's so much sexual tension between you and Stone that it's getting *my* dick hard," Kash whispers next to my ear, just as I'm about to throw my dart.

Laughing, I elbow him in the stomach, causing him to grunt and step back. "Stop trying to distract me just because I'm kicking your ass."

"Hey, I speak the truth." He wraps his arm around my neck and kisses my cheek. "Think Jade's into me? She keeps looking at my crotch and shit."

I look behind me to see Stone and Jade at the small table, talking, but her eyes keep lingering over to Kash's ass as if she can't control them.

"I'm going to take a wild guess and say yes." Smiling, I slap his chest and push him out of my space. "Now move the fuck out of my way so I can finish winning."

"Damn, baby." Kash throws his arms up and backs up. "No wonder why Stone likes you so much. I might just take you home tonight if you'll let me.

I'll take both you ladies on."

Stone continues talking to Jade, but slaps Kash upside the head, causing him to turn around in surprise.

"Watch your fucking mouth, dumbass."

Jade looks at Kash as if she likes what he just said. She winks and he pushes down on his boner, making it aware of what she does to him.

I throw my second dart and turn around to Stone standing right behind me. "I can't stop thinking about slamming you up against that wall, holding you above my head, and tasting you, Sage."

The way he draws his bottom lip into his mouth after he's done talking, has me almost panting, but I fight it.

Stay strong... don't cave in.

"Stop trying to distract me," I breathe, as he steps up behind me and presses his body to mine. "It's not going to work."

He grips my hips with both hands and softly kisses the back of my neck. "You sure about that?" His hands squeeze my hips and he slightly lifts me up to press his erection against my ass. "Take a shot then. Go ahead," he whispers.

Clearing my throat, I bump him with my ass to get him to release me. "Back up, big guy." Trying hard to focus, I throw my last dart, almost completely missing the board. "Shit."

Stone smiles in victory, before slapping my ass. "You ready to go home?" He nods his head at Kash and Jade all up close and personal with each other. "I think Kash is going to drive Jade's jeep to her house. I'll drive us."

Figuring that the game will take forever to finish, as long as it's been taking us to pay attention to our turns, I agree it's time to go.

After saying bye to Jade and Kash, Stone walks me to his jeep and opens the door for me.

He's quiet the whole way home as if he's thinking really hard about something, so I stay quiet too, not really sure what's going to happen when we get home.

I hope it's not some weird, awkward moment. We haven't really gotten any time alone since he danced for me the other night.

I'm not sure if I'll be able to tell him no after that...

CHAPTER NINE

STONE

THERE'S SOMETHING I WANT TO do to Sage as soon as I get her alone and I'm over here trying to decide if she'll kick my ass for even attempting it.

I figure the risk will be worth it. I'll take an ass whooping from her any day of the fucking week as long as it involves her hands on me.

Just the thought alone of her being rough with me makes me hard. So damn hard.

Hoping that she'll follow me, I walk around to the back of the house instead of the front, opening the gate to the pool.

I don't hesitate with yanking my shirt over my head, before dropping my jeans and kicking them to the side.

"What are you doing?" she asks, while watching my legs flex as I walk over to her.

"It's what *we're* doing."

Keeping my eyes on hers, I lower to the ground, grip the waist of her jeans and rip the button off, pulling until they're unzipped.

Surprised, she grips my hair and pulls as I yank her jeans down her legs, before lifting her up enough to pull her feet out of them.

"Stone!" she yells. "Don't throw me in that pool or I'll kick your ass. I'll hurt you, I swear."

"Is that a promise?" I question with a smirk, while lifting her up to throw her over my shoulder.

"I mean it. Don't do it," she squeals. "It's cold."

Holding on to her tightly, I walk over to the water and jump in, not releasing my grip on her, until we hit the coolness of the water.

When we come up from under the water, Sage rushes at me, slapping my chest with her hand. "What. Did. I. Say?" she questions, between each hard smack. "I'm going to... to..."

"What was that?" I cup my ear and lean in closer, when she continues to mumble, coming up with nothing to say. "If you want me to make you come, all you have to do is say so. I'm more than happy to."

Pulling her over to the shallow end, I cup her pussy with my hand and lift her up with a growl, before sliding her panties aside and slipping one finger inside.

She grips at my shoulder and moans beside my ear as I slowly begin pumping in and out, while backing her up against the wall of the pool.

"Damn you and your perfect fingers," she breathes.

"I don't have to use my fingers," I respond, while shoving a second one inside. "I can do much better."

"That wasn't an invitation," she growls out. "I think we should..." She throws her head back with a moan when I swirl my finger over her swollen clit.

"Just give your body what it wants, Sage."

Lifting her up, I position Sage so her legs are straddling my shoulders and her soaking wet panties are pressed against my face.

Squeezing my head with her thighs, she screams and pulls my hair with force. "You're pushing it, Stone. So fucking close to the edge. Put me down before I kick your ass."

"Go ahead... hurt me," I warn. "I'll make you scream with my tongue so fucking loud that the neighbors will get off on it."

Pushing me, she squeezes my face tighter. "You won't..."

"Oh I will, beautiful girl." I gently bite her pussy, causing her to yank on my hair. "You like my mouth between your legs. Admit it."

Pushing her body closer so I can tease her, I suck her clit into my mouth through her thin, wet panties, sucking so hard that she cries out with a mixture of pain and pleasure.

"Stone," she moans my name this time in desperation. "Get my fucking panties out of the way, dammit."

Licking her through the fabric, I suck her clit into my mouth once more, before releasing it. "Admit it then."

"I miss it," she breathes. "And I'm going to kill you later for making me admit it, but for now..."

She pushes my head between her legs and leans back with another moan as I rub my face in her pussy and growl against it.

I set her down on the edge of the pool so I can remove her wet panties.

Then I sink into the water in front of her, before coming back up, spreading her legs apart, and running my stiff tongue along her aching pussy.

"Take your shirt off," I growl out. "I want to see your nipples harden when I taste you. They always got so fucking hard for me."

Without hesitation, she removes her shirt, before undoing her bra and tossing it behind her. "This is as far as it goes," she attempts to say with force. "No sex. We just... just no sex."

I may not be having sex with her tonight, but her letting me pleasure her with my tongue is the only sign that I need, to know that she still aches for me just as much as I do her.

Tonight... tonight she's going to remember what it's like to have my tongue taste her so good that she's going to beg me to please her in every way possible by the end of the week.

Gripping her legs, I moan as I look over her naked body, remembering what it was like to have her above me, riding me.

"Fuck... I've missed pleasuring this beautiful body." Reaching up with one hand, I cup her left breast and bury my face between her legs.

My tongue works slowly at first to spread the moisture, being gentle and teasing her, making her want more. My rhythm is precise and in control, knowing the exact spot to work her up. I'm slowly building her up, knowing she'll want more at the end.

I catch her moaning as I slide my tongue down further and shove it into her pussy as deep as it will go. I'm fucking her with my tongue, working her up to want me back inside of her.

She rips and pulls at my hair, pushing my face further between her legs as if she wants to suffocate me with her beautiful vagina.

I'd die a happy man and ask one of the boys to inscribe it on my fucking headstone.

Pulling my tongue out, I gently suck her clit into my mouth, sucking on it, while shoving a finger inside her and pumping in and out.

This used to drive her crazy and I'm hoping it still does.

From the way that she digs into my back and squeezes my head, I'm going to take that as a *fucking hell yes*.

"Oh fuck," she moans. "Shit, Stone. Keep going." Her hands rip at my hair now. "I'm so close. I'm close... fuck!"

Her legs shake above my shoulders as her pussy clenches around my finger so hard that it's almost as if she's been deprived of orgasms since we stopped messing around months ago.

A part of me is relieved, yet the other part of me wants her to feel good all the time.

Fuck, I feel guilty for not pushing this sooner and making her cave into me pleasuring her.

I kiss the inside of her thighs, before releasing her as she slides back into the water, breathing heavily.

She doesn't look at me or speak for what seems like five fucking minutes, which has my heart completely pounding out of my chest in anticipation.

"I almost forgot how good your mouth felt," she says, still out of breath. "Your mouth has always been my weakness."

She dives into the water, swimming over to the deep end.

Smiling, I watch her as she comes up for air.

"I couldn't let you forget. I won't."

"Then are you sure we should still be roommates?" she asks with a slight grin. "This could get complicated. Do we want that?"

Biting my bottom lip, I swim over to her and wrap her legs around my waist. "The more complicated... the more satisfying that it is in the end when we both give in."

I cup her face.

"What are you doing?" she asks, sounding slightly panicked.

"Giving you a good night kiss."

Before she can say anything, I press my lips against hers, claiming them like in the past, before slowly caressing my tongue with hers as her lips part. It's soft, slow, and hot as fuck.

Our tongues instantly work together as if we've never stopped kissing to begin with. It's so fucking natural that my dick twitches, at the fact that we were made to be doing this.Stone and fucking Sage... together.

Now, I'm determined more than ever to get her into my arms for good.

Sucking her bottom lip into my mouth, I release it and pull away with a small growl. "I also couldn't let you forget my mouth on yours."

Licking her lips, she turns her face away from me. "Goodnight, Stone."

I release her from my arms, watching as she swims over to the edge of the pool and climbs out, completely naked.

Holy fuck... she's beautiful.

"Goodnight," I whisper, mostly to myself as she disappears into the house, leaving me hard as fuck in this pool.

As much as I'd love to sink into her and remind her how good I feel inside of her, I know I can't move that fast if I want to make her fall for me.

I need to remind her of the small things first.

My dick will have to wait...

CHAPTER TEN

SAGE

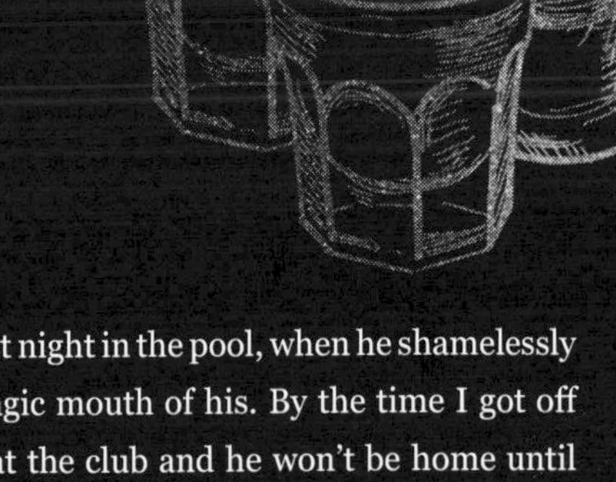

I HAVEN'T SEEN STONE SINCE last night in the pool, when he shamelessly made me come from that damn magic mouth of his. By the time I got off work this evening, he was already at the club and he won't be home until late tonight.

Why does this disappoint me?

I've been thinking about him all day and smiling to myself like an idiot. I almost feel like a teenaged girl, finding out that her crush likes her back.

So damn weird...

Lying in bed, eating chicken and rice, in my underwear and a tank top, I struggle between wanting to go to the club and telling myself that I'd be stupid to go.

If I go see him, it'll give him the impression that I want him again and that it's okay for him to do whatever he pleases with me.

As much as I want a physical relationship with him, I'm not sure I can handle that without blurring the lines, falling for him and wanting more.

I came so close in the past to losing myself to him. Too close. And I know if I let myself care for him and then lose him, I'll be devastated.

I'm not heartless. I care for Stone. I care for him very much, but after being crushed repeatedly by every person that I ever cared for or thought should've cared for me, I'm not sure I'm strong enough.

I want to be. So damn bad.

"You're staying right here in this bed," I mumble to myself, while stuffing my face with rice. "You've been strong for over seven months now. Don't cave in."

Picking up the remote, I flip through the hundreds of channels, but can't seem to concentrate on anything that's on. Not one damn thing.

All I can think about is Stone and the fact that he's got hundreds of women clawing at his half-naked ass right now, wanting him to pleasure them with his magic fucking *everything*.

Shoving the now empty container aside, I reach for my phone when it vibrates next to me. I get excited for a quick second, thinking it might be Stone, but it's not.

It's a message from Jade.

Jade

Whatcha doing? You better be awake.

Sage

Laying around and watching TV. I'm still awake, unfortunately.

Jade

Get your ass up and dressed. Kash is dancing tonight and he invited me to watch him.

Sage

Yeah... can't you go alone? I have to be up early tomorrow.

Jade

Um... no. I need you there. PLEASE!

Sage

Put your big girl panties on, Jade. I'm tired.

Jade

I can't. I need help pulling them up. PLEASE! PLEASE! PLEASE!

Sage

I hate you sometimes...

Jade

Is that a yes, gorgeous?

Sage

It's a maybe...

My phone doesn't go off for the next five minutes, so I just lay here and struggle with my damn self.

I almost think that Jade has given up on me, until it vibrates again, causing me to sit up and exhale.

Picking it up, I get ready to tell her I'll go, but the name that flashes across the screen has my stomach doing backflips and my heart beating out of my chest. Yeah... it's like *that* with him.

Stone

I can still taste you on my tongue... so distracting. Do you know how hard it is to not pop a boner every few minutes?

His text has me laughing out loud and trying hard to stop myself from smiling, but I can't. I can only picture his face right now and how he probably has that one brow lifted as he types with that cocky ass grin of his.

Sage

You could try mouthwash. Have you ever heard of it? There's a bottle in our bathroom. That might control your boner. ;)

Stone

And wash the delectable taste of your throbbing pussy out of my mouth... how else am I going to get through the night without you?

Sage

Who says you have to?

Seriously, Sage!

I mentally slap myself for allowing myself to flirt back and work him up even more than he already is, knowing where that might lead later. Last night was already pushing the friend-zone limit.

Stone

Is that an invitation? Cause' I accept with my mouth wide open.

Sage

You really are something else...

Stone

I've been told that's a good thing. By you...

He's not wrong there. His playful personality and non-filtered mouth is what made me want him in the first place. It made me feel happy and... alive.

Stone

Gotta go. See you later, roomie ;)

I jump when my bedroom door flies open to Jade coming at me with a look of disappointment.

"Why the hell isn't your ass dressed? Kash goes on in less than twenty minutes. Hurry! Get up!"

"Seriously?" Standing up, I brush past her and slip on a pair of jeans. "What made you so sure I'd even go? I never said yes."

"Because..." She smiles as I change into a cute, black shirt and quickly throw my hair up. "You didn't say no."

"I'll go." I hold up a hand, while slipping on a pair of black heels. "But only for a couple of hours. I'm gone before midnight so don't even bother with trying to get me to stay til' close."

"Deal." Her smile broadens. "You do realize that Stone will be dancing right after Kash, right? So that's within the next hour."

"I do." I lift a brow and smile to myself. "So, I'll be gone *after* he dances. If I'm going, might as well make it worth it for me too, babe."

"I won't argue there." She looks down at her phone, before grabbing my arm and pulling me through the house with her. "Ten minutes now. I don't want to miss even a second."

Surprisingly, Jade has never seen Kash dance. In fact, I think she's only been to *Walk of Shame* a few times and that was before Kash started.

It should be interesting to see her reaction when she sees just how dirty Kash can be on the stage.

He's dirty... but not as dirty as Stone or Styx.

IT'S INSANELY CROWDED HERE TONIGHT, but Lane worked his magic to find us tables right in the front row.

I have a feeling that Cale had something to do with that. He smiled at us from across the room as we were walking in, then right after that, Lane was talking into his earpiece.

God, I love that man. He's the cutest thing ever and does what he can to make sure everyone's happy.

Him taking over *Walk of Shame* has been the best thing for this place. The changes he made by adding private rooms has pretty much doubled business, making it possible for the boys to bring in a shitload of money.

Not that the boys weren't already.

"Here he comes." Jade slaps my arm, getting all giddy, when Kash appears on the darkened stage. "Is that a uniform? Please tell me he's in uniform. Oh please," she begs.

The music starts and the spotlight lands on Kash, standing there in a police uniform.

Oh shit... not tonight.

The last thing I can handle right now is Stone in uniform. I completely forgot that it was theme night, which means all of the boys will be dressed up.

Each week one of the boys chooses which theme they want and all of the boys go along with it.

I've never seen Stone in a police uniform, because I've always made it a point to stay away when I knew he'd be looking that damn sexy.

Police officers are my weakness.

I miss the first five minutes of Kash's dance, lost in my head, worrying about Stone coming out next.

"This man is the sexiest thing I've ever seen, Sage. *The* sexiest."

When I look up, Kash is already half-naked and dry humping the stage.

Jade stands up and walks up to the stage, when Kash motions for her come up.

I find myself laughing at her facial expression, as he pulls her onto the stage and forces her onto her knees and into a pair of cuffs.

Grabbing her cuffs from behind her, he begins thrusting his hips insanely fast, causing her body to bounce forward with each hard thrust.

The girls go crazy, standing up and tossing money toward the stage, loving how rough and dirty he is.

Knowing that it's about time for Stone to take the stage, I begin looking around me, in search of him standing in the shadows.

He does this *before* every show, standing back with his black beanie, trying not to stand out.

"Holy shit!" Jade breathes heavily, from beside me. "That was insane. That boy can move his body."

Pulling my eyes away from the back of the room, I turn to face Jade. She's sweaty and out of breath, fanning herself off.

"These boys are the best of the best."

Disappointment washes through me that I didn't get a glimpse of Stone before his show.

I always enjoyed seeking him out in the shadows and watching him look so mysterious in the darkened room.

"Here comes your sexy roommate," Jade says excitedly. "You ready, babe?"

My heart speeds up as the music starts. "I fucking hope so."

Holy fuck... help me now...

CHAPTER ELEVEN

SAGE

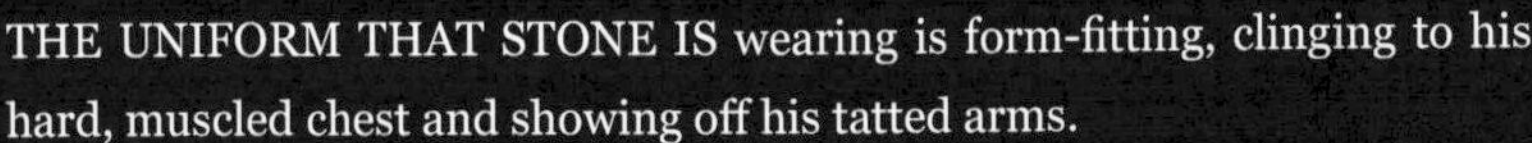

THE UNIFORM THAT STONE IS wearing is form-fitting, clinging to his hard, muscled chest and showing off his tatted arms.

I've never seen someone look so sexy in uniform until now and I have to admit that my heart is practically palpitating out of my chest, as my eyes search over his entire body.

Does this man not know just how hard he'll have the ladies clenching by the end of his performance? Me included.

It's not until the spotlight grows bigger, revealing more of the stage, that I notice there's a girl with blue hair and tattoos handcuffed to a chair.

His performances seem to be so mysterious now, compared to seven months ago and completely fucking hotter.

I don't even want to think about how that sexy chick got chosen to be a part of his performance, but I'm hoping it wasn't by him.

"Oh wow..." Jade takes a huge gulp of her drink, while eyeing the stage.

"This could get hot. Stone looks good in uniform. Really good."

Swallowing, I blindly reach beside me for my drink, not wanting to miss a thing. I have a feeling that I'm going to need a few of these after he's done.

"The man's got a body of a God, Jade. You try living with all of *that* and be able to keep any kind of self-control. It's a bitch and that uniform is doing zilch to help the situation any."

"So, then give in. I would. Especially after what all of *that* looks like in *that* uniform."

Letting Jade's words sink in, I keep my eyes glued to Stone's every move as he slowly circles around the girl, before standing in front of the chair and grabbing the back of the girl's hair, thrusting to the rhythm.

Oh. God.

The girl instantly bites her lip and watches his dick flopping through his pants, probably wishing she could take him in her mouth right now.

Hell... even I am, from the way his body's moving so hot and in perfect rhythm to the sexy song.

His dick doesn't even have to be close to my face to want it just as badly as she probably does at this very moment. It doesn't help that I've had a taste and it's the best of the best. There's no denying how delicious every inch of that man's body truly is.

Gripping the top of his shirt, Stone slowly rips it open, while rolling his body above her in the chair, before tossing the fabric aside.

Her eyes widen and she begins screaming with excitement as he climbs up on the chair, making it easier to thrust in her face.

Afterwards, he lowers himself down to straddle her lap, reaching behind her to undo her cuffs.

The woman's hands instantly find Stone's body, exploring as he grinds in her lap. Grabbing her hands to stop them from going for his dick, he stands up and turns around, before taking a seat on her lap again, but facing the crowd this time.

Taking control of the woman's hands again, Stone rubs them up the inside of his thick thighs before making her explore his abs and then his chest as he rolls his body, making the women scream out.

Keeping in his intense role as an officer, he pushes her hands away and stands up, turning around to face her again, before lowering to her lap and thrusting with force as if she's been a bad girl.

When he goes to get out of the cute girl's lap, she grips his face, pressing her lips against his with force.

My heart explodes with jealousy and anger, but I watch intently, as Stone pulls away from the kiss and backs away from her.

He looks a little thrown off, but falls back into beat with the song, smoothly picking the girl up out of the chair, doing a few small thrusts, before carrying her off stage and setting her down into an empty seat.

That's when his eyes finally seek me out for the first time. He looks excited to see me here, yet guilty or ashamed, possibly, at me seeing another woman kiss him.

I just give him a small smile and lift my drink to him, showing him that I'm not going anywhere. Someone would have to drag me out of here at this point, because I'm not taking my eyes off this sexy man until he's done.

He grins back and continues with the show, keeping his eyes on me as often as he can, while stripping down until he's down to absolutely nothing, only holding his pants over his junk.

The song is almost over now, since Stone had to waste time to walk off stage and dispose of his overzealous fan, so he does a few more quick thrusts of his hips, before dropping his pants on the stage and using both of his hands to cover up.

Keeping both of his hands covering his package, he exits the stage and walks straight for mine and Jade's table.

Whistles and screams are deafening me at this point, but I can't help but to smile as Stone's eyes look me over, before stopping to meet mine.

Leaning into my ear, he whispers, "I'm trying really fucking hard to cover how hard you have me right now. Now would be a good time to have a third hand." He lets out a deep laugh, vibrating my ear and turning me on even more. "Wait for me."

Nodding, I bite my straw and watch as he walks away, women all jumping to slap his naked, tight ass as he walks away.

STONE'S SHOW ENDED TWENTY MINUTES ago and I've been waiting impatiently for him to come back out.

I can't deny the fact that I want him sexually so bad right now, that it physically hurts. My body is screaming for him to touch me and pleasure me to the point that I almost feel desperate to have him inside of me.

Seeing that Jade is preoccupied at the bar, talking with Sarah, I make my way to the back area where the boys' locker room area is.

Kane is standing outside, guarding the door, but smiles when he sees me approaching.

"What's up, babe?" He takes a second to turn back to the girl that's practically hanging on his nuts and kissing all over his neck. "Take it easy, sugar."

"No need to stop on my account, you sexy giant." I lift a brow and flash the girl a tight smile when she looks me over, tying to size me up. "Let me in to see Stone and you can get your dick wet all you want."

Kane looks around, seeing that no one else seems to be coming back here, other than me.

"Only because it's you." He smiles big. "And because I'm afraid you'll kick my ass and I'll like it too much."

"Oh you definitely would like it, Kane. I know you." I wink and slap his chest. "Be sure not to break the poor girl in half. I've heard you fuck before." I turn to her. "I'd be scared myself."

This only seems to get the girl more excited and it somewhat makes me happy that I'm not the only one completely sexually frustrated at this second.

Plus, I need to keep him satisfied, reminding him that it was definitely worth his time to break the rules and let me in the boys' room.

Taking a deep breath, I push the door open and step inside to the steam filled room. The only thing I hear are the showers.

More than one.

The problem with this, is that you can't see shit through the thick glass doors.

I stop in front of the first one, not thinking twice, before pushing the glass door open and looking for Stone.

My face heats up when I'm greeted with the sight of Kash, naked, with soap and water running down the front of his insanely sexy body.

His eyes open and widen when they land on me watching him, following my eyes down to his partially hard dick.

"Shit! Sorry," I mouth to him. "Wrong door."

He just gives me a cocky ass smile, knowing damn well that he has nothing to be ashamed of.

Quickly closing Kash's door, I take in a deep breath, before reaching for the second door and pushing it open.

Stone is facing the shower wall, letting the water fall down his perfectly tattooed, flawless body, while running his hands over his face.

Wanting nothing more than to touch every inch of him, I step into the shower and close the door behind me, pulling my shirt over my head and tossing it to the ground.

Stone stiffens up for a second, before he slowly turns around and smirks when he sees me standing here in only my bra and jeans, looking over his body.

Swallowing, I let my eyes trail down to his very hard, pierced dick and I completely lose it.

Throwing my arms around his neck, I slam my lips against his, as he grips my thighs, picking me up to wrap my legs around his waist.

He kisses me hard and hungry, before sucking my lip into his mouth and pulling away. "Fuck me, Sage. You're in my damn shower. I hope you know this means I'm stripping you down and fucking you."

Nodding, I dig into my pocket and pull out the condom that I stole from Jade's purse when she was talking to Sarah.

Growling out, Stone gently sets me down to my feet and bends down, yanking my jeans and thong down my legs.

He gets ready to lick my pussy, but I grip his head, pushing it back. "Not this time," I breathe, heavily. "I can't. I need you inside me right now, Stone and for you to promise me one thing?"

Standing back up, he brushes my hair behind my ear and kisses under my ear. "What's that?"

Biting my bottom lip, I watch as Stone rolls the condom over his enormous, pierced dick. "Don't ever wear that uniform again. That's not fair play."

Smirking, he lifts me up and slams me against the wall that's connected to Kash's shower. "Fuck yeah it is." He bites my lip and pulls away. "Especially if gets you this worked up."

Holding me up with one arm around my waist, he grips my neck with his free hand and slams into me so hard that I scream out with a mixture of pain and pleasure.

"Fuck me," he growls against my ear, while slowly pulling out of me, before pushing back inside and freezing. "It's been so damn long. You okay?"

Gripping onto his strong shoulders, I nod and moan as the pain goes away and all I'm left with is the feel of him slowly sliding in and out of me, filling me to capacity.

"It's okay," I breathe. "You can go now."

"Are you sure?" he questions. "I'm not holding back. I've waited too long to be inside you again, Sage. I'm going to fuck you as if it'll be my last. I didn't last time and I should've. Every. Fucking. Time."

Gripping him tighter, I pull his face to mine and kiss him hard and deep, just needing him to shut up and take me like he did the very first time.

I didn't walk for two days without wanting to cry from the pain between my legs.

Moaning into my mouth, he grips my neck harder and thrusts into me over and over again as if he's letting out all of his sexual frustration from the last seven months.

It's so hard and deep that it hurts, but I don't want it to stop.

Everything about Stone is pure alpha male and having him fuck me and take me as hard and deep as he wants, turns me on more than anyone I've ever been with.

Holding onto him for dear life, I bite his mouth so hard, when he thrusts into me, that I draw blood.

This causes him to growl into my mouth and slam into me even harder, causing my head to bang into the wall behind me.

The roughness of being with Stone is worth every bump and bruise I get in the process. When this man fucks, he owns my pussy as if telling me that no other dick will feel as good as his does inside of me.

The fact that Kash is in the next shower, listening to us, must turn us both on more, making us both get louder and louder with each time he pushes inside of me.

"Stone!" I scream. "Fuck. Me..." I breathe. "Don't stop."

He slams into me and stops. "Not until your pussy is clamping down on my cock," he breathes out in response.

"Oh shit..." Comes from Kash's shower, making us both smile against each other's lips, before he pushes into me one last time, pushing me over the edge as my pussy clenches his dick so hard, that I feel his hot cum filling the condom inside of me.

Holding me up, he walks me to the middle of the shower and kisses me as the water runs over the both of us, cooling us off now that the hot water has run out.

He waits until I pull away from the kiss, before pulling out of me and setting me down.

Turning the other way, he pulls the condom off with a small moan and tosses it down, while leaning his face back into the water.

I can't help the tingles that spread throughout my body as I watch him, standing there, breathing heavily in all his naked glory, throbbing dick and all.

There's something so sexy just knowing that his heavy breathing is due to him just being inside of me.

"Shit, that was hot, Sage." He turns to look at me with a small smirk. "I might just wear my uniform around the house every fucking night if it leads you to joining me in the shower."

I can't help but laugh at the cute face he makes as he looks me over. "I'll burn it if I have to," I tease. "Don't test me."

Smiling as if he doesn't believe me, he turns the water off and walks out of the shower, before returning a few seconds later with a towel and wrapping it around me.

"Kash might've just gotten off to you screaming while I fucked you, but that asshole doesn't get to see or feel what it's like to have you naked and horny. I'll find you something to wear."

"Holy shit..." Smiling to myself, I work on drying myself off, while Stone is off finding me some clothes.

I'm pretty surprised that I actually just went through with showing up in his shower, ready to have sex, but am so happy that I did.

I've never felt so much excitement and adrenaline course through me in my entire life.

Just knowing that hundreds of people are outside that door, and that Kash was right next to us, jerking off to us fucking, has me wanting to do all sorts of crazy things with Stone.

I'm not so sure this is a feeling I'm ready to give up now. In fact... I want him sexually more now than ever.

CHAPTER TWELVE

STONE

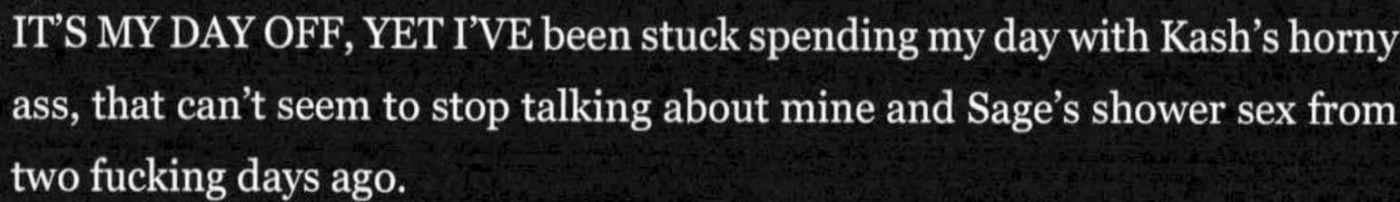

IT'S MY DAY OFF, YET I'VE been stuck spending my day with Kash's horny ass, that can't seem to stop talking about mine and Sage's shower sex from two fucking days ago.

I swear if I see his dick get hard one more time, when he mentions the fact that Sage walked in on him in the shower and checked out his shit, I'm going to throat punch his bitch ass.

"You should've saw the way her eyes grew when they landed on my love muscle, bro." He throws his last dart at the board, before walking up to retrieve them. "If I remember correctly, there may have even been a little lip biting action on her part."

"Fuck you, dumbass." I shoulder bump him on the way to the yellow line. "Her eyes grew bigger so she could find your little dangler."

Not fazed by my insult, he winks at the waitress and checks out her ass as she walks by.

"You mean the beast. Nope, she definitely got a clear view and he turned into Mr. Happy."

Choosing to ignore his ass, before I turn Mr. Happy into Mr. Fucking Sad, I throw my darts, before looking down at the time on my phone.

"I'm out of here, dick."

Kash stands up and tosses a ten on top of my twenty. "Same here, man. I've got some shit to handle. I heard Sage gets off in twenty."

I walk past him and slap him hard, upside the head. "Later, fucker."

He's right, Sage does get off in twenty and I'm hoping to get her to hang out with me.

After we left the club the other night, she went to her room to sleep, while I spent most of the night, chillin' on the balcony.

Sage worked all day yesterday and I worked all night, so by the time I got home, she was already in her bed.

She left the door cracked open and I about lost my shit when I walked by and saw what she was sleeping in.

A sheer, white shirt with no bra and a pale pink thong, displaying her perfect round ass.

The way her pierced nipples pressed against the fabric, caused my dick to instantly harden in my jeans.

I thought about waking her up, by taking her nipple into my mouth and nibbling it, but decided that might lead to me being kicked in the balls or my dick being ripped off.

That woman is feisty when it comes to her sleep. I woke her up once when I was drunk and it was not a good time for me. Trust me.

I had a shoe print on my forehead for two days from the Converse, but I guess I had it coming with my teasing.

We both laughed about it for weeks. In fact, the whole crew did.

It didn't bother me though, because seeing her laugh always made me so fucking happy. I'd let her laugh at my expense every day just to keep that woman laughing.

When I arrive at the house with pizza and wings, Sage is just walking up to the porch.

She looks exhausted, as if she didn't sleep much last night, but flashes me a thankful smile, when I hold up the food and wink.

"You read my mind, big guy." She unlocks the door and pushes it open, making room for me to carry the food through.

"I'd like to read your whole body with my tongue, but I thought I'd start with pizza first and work my way there."

She laughs and bumps me out of the way with her hip, to get to the pizza. "I really don't know what to do with you some days. Do you know that?"

"So does that mean buying you pizza won't get me in your pants tonight?" I hold up the wings and cock a brow. "What if I toss in a few wings?"

She laughs harder, almost spitting her pizza all over the counter. It takes her a few seconds to catch her breath. "You're really laying the charm on extra hard tonight, Prince Charming. You make it so hard to resist, but... I'm not that easy."

I shrug and grab a slice of pizza. "Yeah well... I am." I wink. "Just for future reference."

"Aren't all of you dirty boys."

"Abso-fuckin-lutely. Thirsty?" I ask, while walking to the fridge.

Biting into her pizza, she nods and mumbles, "Yes," around it.

Knowing that she'll probably want some white wine, I pour her a glass, before grabbing myself a beer and walking outside to the second story balcony.

I smile to myself, when I hear her following behind me, carrying the whole pizza box, and moaning whenever she takes a bite of the slice in her hand.

"You really should be careful about moaning around me. You know I see that as a challenge if it's not from my doing."

She ignores me and reaches for a second slice of pizza, while sitting on the ledge of the balcony. "I think you made me moan loud enough the other night to make up for a thousand damn moans."

My smile broadens as her eyes meet mine, before slowly trailing down my body and landing on my half-hard dick. The seductive way she licks the pizza from her lips, makes me believe that she wishes it were my cum.

Well fuck... I do too.

Clearing her throat, she quickly pulls her eyes away and finishes up her slice of pizza.

I take a swig of my beer and hand her glass of wine to her, before taking a seat beside her and watching her take a sip. "How was work?"

She shrugs. "It was okay, I guess. Onyx almost ripped some girl's tit off, but you know how that goes..."

I laugh, trying to picture that in my head. "Yeah, well she definitely doesn't take any shit from anyone. Her and Hemy were meant to fucking be."

"More than any two people I know," she replies, her eyes softening as they land on mine again. "I'm pretty tired."

"Then relax and drink your wine," I respond. "It's beautiful out tonight."

She places her lips to her glass and smiles. "It is... the problem is..."

"What's that?" I question, while licking my bottom lip. "You can't stop thinking about me bending you over this balcony and filling you with my cock?"

She crosses her legs and takes another sip of her wine, but a longer one this time. Actually, more like she downs the whole fucking glass.

"The setting is too romantic," she finally answers.

"Doesn't have to be," I reply, while bending down in front of her and spreading her thighs. "I can make it dirty. Filthy and hard is my specialty."

Pushing her dress up, I bite the inside of her thigh, causing her to scream and pull my hair with force.

"Dammit, Stone. You know I love it when you bite me." She pushes my head back. "It's too soon though."

"You sure about that?" She loosens her grip on my head, just enough for me to swipe my tongue over her pussy lips that are practically hanging out of her thong.

Her legs shake as she pushes my head back again and attempts to close her legs. "Yes," she moans. "It's been less than forty-eight hours, Stone."

Standing up, I rub my hand over the erection in my jeans and take a huge swig of my beer. "Fuck... that's going to hurt later."

Sage sucks her bottom lip into her mouth, while watching my hand press down on my insanely hard cock.

"Let me watch you," she breathes. "It's too soon to be physical with each other, but that doesn't mean I don't want to see you come."

I set my beer down and look at her. "You want me to jerk off for you?"

She sits up straight and grips the ledge. "Yeah." She swallows. "Right here in the open."

Looking around me is a reminder of just how close the houses in this neighborhood are. Getting sexual in the pool is a little different since there's a huge fence for privacy, but up here... Up here you can see *everything*.

"You want me to whip my huge, throbbing cock out and stroke it right here for you?" Biting my bottom lip, I slowly undo my pants and step closer to her. "For anyone in the neighborhood to see? Cause' they can very well be watching us right now."

She nods and finishes off her wine, before setting it aside with a playful smirk. "I'm so fucking horny right now, Stone. *You* get me so horny and wet. I'm trying to keep some kind of self-control, before I lose it all, but I can't deny that I want to see you give me a show right here."

The idea of stroking my cock for her and possibly for the neighbors to see, is really fucking turning me on for some reason. My dick is throbbing now.

"Fuck... it's so damn hard." I growl, while unzipping my jeans and pulling them down to my thighs. "I love it when you talk to me so damn hot like this."

"Good," she breathes, while keeping her eyes on my hands to see where they're going next. "Take it out and hold it in your hand. Please," she says on a small breath.

Obeying her orders, I lower my briefs, pulling my cock out and holding it in my hand. "Fuck me... this has me so horny right now."

"Me too." She grips her thigh, running her fingers over it. "Now stroke it for me."

Grabbing my length with my other hand, I work both hands over my cock, moaning at the sensation and the fact that Sage along with who knows who else, is watching me pleasure myself right now.

I start out slow, closing my eyes and picturing Sage's warm mouth wrapped around my dick.

The thought gets me so excited, that I growl out in pleasure, feeling the pressure already starting to build.

A small moan leaves Sage's mouth when I stroke it harder and faster, while biting down onto my lower lip.

Opening my eyes, I watch as Sage dips her fingers in and out of her pussy, while watching me stroke myself.

"Keep going, Stone," she moans. "Stroke it faster." She sounds desperate as her fingers speed up and she begins shaking as her orgasm rolls through her.

Hearing the wetness as she pumps in and out a few more times, is all it takes for me to lose my shit myself.

Stepping up beside her, I give her a clear view and aim my cock over the balcony, moaning out as my cum comes out in spurts, the pressure building and falling, until it finally stops completely and I can catch my breath.

I have no idea if anyone other than Sage just watched me shoot my shit over the balcony, but I can say that I just had one of the most intense orgasms of my life. At least one given from my own hand.

"Oh shit..." I breathe, while bending over and gripping the balcony. "That shot far," I tease. "Maybe even in the neighbor's yard."

Smiling, while trying to catch her breath, Sage adjusts her skirt and stands up. "You always know how to lighten the mood."

I smile as she looks me over. "Wondering how many people just watched me bust my nut for you?"

"Maybe." She grins. "Lucky them."

"I won't argue that," I respond with a cocked brow.

Clearing her throat, she reaches for her empty wine glass and walks for the door. "I think I'll have those wings now." She smiles. "Then I'm thinking we can just sit out here and talk for a bit."

I reach for my jeans and fix them, while watching her disappear inside. The excitement of what I've just done still has adrenaline pumping through my veins, making me feel wide awake now.

I'm prepared to talk her up all night, reminding her of how much fun we used to have just hanging out.

After what she just asked of me... I'm not letting her ass sleep for a while.

CHAPTER THIRTEEN

SAGE

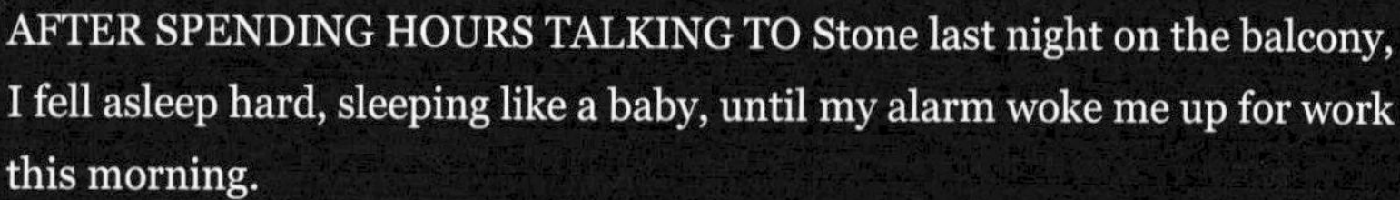

AFTER SPENDING HOURS TALKING TO Stone last night on the balcony, I fell asleep hard, sleeping like a baby, until my alarm woke me up for work this morning.

I almost forgot how fun it was to just hang out with Stone and laugh and forget about everything else. He's always had a way of relaxing me and making me feel good, as if nothing bad is in the world.

By the time I made it to my bedroom late last night, my face hurt from smiling so much and I'm pretty sure that I fell asleep, still wearing a smile because of him.

I have to admit that I've been a bit out of it this morning and even got caught napping in the breakroom earlier today by Onyx.

Apparently, I've forgotten what it's like to stay up late and get my ass up so early. It's been months since I've stayed up past two.

I've just finished cleaning off my station, when I walk up to the counter to see Onyx take a card from a pretty brunette with cowgirl boots.

Out of curiosity, my eyes wander down to the card in Onyx's hand and my heart drops, when I see Stone's name written across it.

The only thing I can seem to concentrate on now is her mouth and what's going to come out of it.

"Follow me," Onyx says with a friendly smile, before leading her over to her station, which luckily, happens to be right next to mine.

Or maybe in my case... unluckily. I'm about to find out.

"Sage," Aspen calls from the front. "Your three o'clock is here. You ready?"

"Shit," I mutter under my breath. "Send them back."

Talk about bad timing.

I smile to my client and make small talk, while getting her ready, but my mind is stuck on Onyx and her client, wanting to hear what they're talking about.

I keep leaning their way, feeling like a crazy stalker at this point. I have no idea why I even care so much. *Just friends...* I remind myself. *Roommates. Friends... with benefits?*

My client talking, while I'm off in my own little stalking world, trying to listen to a totally different conversation, is making it pretty much impossible to concentrate.

I'm doing everything I can to not mess up her beautiful, thick hair, but I'm not feeling very confident at the moment.

Get it together...

Shaking my head, I take a deep breath and give up on trying to listen to what's being said at Onyx's station. So far, Stone's name hasn't left her red, pouty lips.

I'll just have to ask Onyx about their conversation as soon as we're both done, even though it's really none of my business, but as hard as I'm trying to not care... I do.

Halfway through cutting my client's hair, she stops talking and suddenly the whole salon seems extremely quiet, as if both Aspen and Onyx can feel my stress.

Out of nowhere Onyx asks the one thing that I've been stressing over since her client walked through the door. She definitely must be able to tell just how tense I'm looking and feeling right now.

"So how was your experience at *Walk of Shame?* Did the boys treat you good? I hope so, or I'll have to kick their asses and remind them how it's done."

My body stiffens, waiting on her response and my heart is hammering in my chest. It's crazy how I feel right now.

She laughs softly. "They did," she says in a sweet southern accent. "I'm here visiting an old friend and I've never been to a male strip club before so she begged me to go. I'm glad I caved in. The boys were fantastic. Especially that Stone guy. He was so darn cute."

Aspen and Onyx stay quiet for a moment, probably worried about how I might react if she says they hooked up.

Clearing her throat, Onyx asks, "Did you get a private dance from Stone? Or..."

She laughs, embarrassed. "Oh no... no. Nothing like that. I'd be too chicken to be alone with one of those cuties. I was sweating like a pig." She smiles. "He just happened to hand me a card after his show and flashed me the most beautiful smile I've ever seen. My friend about had to pick me up off the floor."

I find myself smiling when she talks about Stone's smile and how beautiful it is. That's one of the first things I noticed about him when I first laid eyes on him and it still makes me weak.

His smile just glows and radiates this confidence, but also has this sexy sweetness to it that makes you want to melt into a puddle at his feet.

The man is extremely hard to resist and after the show he gave me last night... Oh. My. God. I want him even more. I just have to keep reminding myself in which way so the lines don't get blurred even more than they already have.

After I get off work and get home, I do a little cleaning, before checking my phone for any notifications. My heart practically jumps out of my chest with excitement when I see a missed text from Stone.

I've been contemplating sending him a message all day, but kind of wanted him to message me first.

It's kind of his thing.

Stone

My hand hurts from last night.

I had to work extra hard to put on a good show. Want to make it up to me? ;)

Sage

Ha! What's the problem? Not used to jerking off on public balconies?

Stone

No... but I kind of enjoyed it. From the sounds of your wet pussy, I'm taking it you did too.

Sage

You might just be right about that. Maybe...

Stone

I know I am and all I've been thinking about all day is making you wet again.

Shit! I can't get my cock to go down. Look what you're doing to me today.

[dick pic]

Excitement courses through me as I stare at the picture, looking at the shape of his hard dick through his jeans.

I seriously can't stop looking.

Why is it so damn big?

Stone

Surprised I could fit the whole thing in the screen? Me too.

Sage

Why did you have to send me a dick pic? Are you trying to corrupt me?

Stone

With my dick. Yes...

It's the best weapon I have.

Sage

It is kind of your best feature ;)

Although I do kind of like your mouth too. It's pretty dirty.

Stone

Kind of?

I stare at my phone with a smile, realizing just how much I want to get out of the house and see him right now.

Earlier, I was completely exhausted and ready to sleep the day away, but after texting with Stone, I'm wide awake and ready to have some fun.

Gathering something cute to wear, I jump into the shower and quickly redo my hair and makeup, before I can change my mind.

When I look down at my phone, I have two new messages from Stone, ten minutes apart.

Stone

Still hard...

Shit! Some old lady keeps looking at my junk like she wants to taste me. Would you think less of me if I admit that I'm scared? She won't stop eye raping it and I need at least one of my hands to serve drinks. I need two to cover it. Well you know that...

Laughing, I toss my phone into my purse and grab my keys, before speed walking to my truck and jumping in.

Looks like Stone might just need a bodyguard right now... Or better yet, someone to laugh at him.

CHAPTER FOURTEEN

STONE

I'VE BEEN TRYING REALLY HARD for the last twenty minutes, to pretend that Susan hasn't been sitting at the end of the bar, sucking on her straw and watching my every move as if she wants to eat me for a late-night snack.

Damn, that woman can drink fast.

And with my luck, the bar has been slow for a Monday night, so not many other women are occupying the seats to keep my ass busy.

"Over here, you cute young thing." She holds up her now empty glass, smiling as I make my way over. "My glass is empty *again*."

"You're really keeping me busy tonight."

She gives me a seductive look and does this weird little old lady dance in her seat. "Oh, I like keeping you busy and watching you work with those tight little buns."

I give her my best smile. "I'll take it," I say, while pouring her a new drink.

She leans in to get closer, her hand coming up to cover mine as I slide her glass in front of her. "Oh my." She bites her bottom lip and smiles. "Your hands are so strong." Her eyes lower back down to my jeans. "I wonder what else is strong."

A whistle from the other side of the bar has me mentally doing a victory dance and rescuing my hand from the ninja grip she now has on it.

"Hey! Over here, bartender. How about you make me that drink that I didn't get to finish last night."

A smile spreads over my face at the sound of her sweet, yet sexy voice.

"Unless you're too busy over there. You look busy. I could find someone else if you want."

Laughing, I hold my finger up to Susan and excuse myself as quickly as possible.

"You better fucking not," I say with a grin, while walking over to her. "Unless you want me to punish you with my cock later."

Her eyes widen and I think I even notice her cheeks turn a little pink. "Always using your penis as a weapon. Is that all you got?"

She's challenging me. I fucking love it.

After pouring her a drink, I lean in closer. Close enough so my lips are hovering over hers. "I've got my lips." I gently brush them against hers. "And my tongue." She lets out a soft moan as I run my tongue over her bottom lip and growl. "Want to see what I can do with my teeth next?"

Backing away, she shakes her head, while trying to hold back her smile. "What if I say no?"

I watch as she grabs her drink, taking a small sip. "Then I'd say you're lying."

"What's Stone lying about? That his dick is bigger than mine? I'll let you look again for yourself and see."

"Fuck off, Kash."

Kash is standing beside Sage, half-naked and dripping with sweat. Smiling, he turns to face her and points down at his white briefs. "Go ahead, babe. Look."

Sage smiles and reaches out as if she's going to pull out the waist of his underwear and look, but then stops and shakes her head. "I've already seen all I needed to see."

"What does that mean?" Kash asks, sounding worried. "It wasn't even hard all the way. That shit doesn't count."

I smirk. "Yeah, well she's seen mine halfway hard too, fucker."

Sage shrugs. "I'll let you boys figure that shit out on your own."

I don't need to figure shit out. I can tell by the look on Sage's face and the way that her eyes keep lowering to my dick, that she's more impressed with my bulge than his.

Kash's dick is the last thing I worry about.

"Don't you have a show to put on or some shit?"

Kash places his hand behind his head and does a little thrust for Sage, until she pulls out a five-dollar bill and shoves it into the band of his briefs.

"I'm good to go now." Winking, he backs away, almost getting away from the bar, until the older lady seeks him out and calls him over.

I watch, laughing with Sage, as she pulls out some money and motions for him to turn around so she can see his ass.

"I thought you might've needed some rescuing from your last text."

"Oh, yeah. Is that why you're here?"

She nods. "Of course. What kind of *friend* wouldn't want to see this?"

I laugh and lean over the bar. "It was the dick pic, wasn't it?" I tilt my head. "Was it the outline of the head or the thickness of the shaft that got you rushing here to see me?"

Smiling, she grips the back of my hair and leans in close to my mouth. "It was all of it." She sucks my bottom lip into her mouth, before quickly releasing it. "Now hopefully *that* will have you rushing home to see me."

With a confident grin, she stands up, shoves money down the front of my jeans and backs away to leave.

"Well fuck..." I groan, while pushing down on my erection and watching her walk away. "What time is it?"

I look up at the clock to see that I still have four more fucking hours until I get out of here tonight.

"Fuck me!"

KASH AND STYX HAVE SPENT the last hour hanging out at the bar, goofing off and having a few drinks.

"Fuck... I love it when we get a few minutes of quiet to just enjoy a few drinks, without someone tugging on our balls or dick," Styx says, while taking a swig of his third beer and chillin'.

"I agree, brother. As much as I love women, my dick needs a break once in a while." Kash tosses a straw my way, hitting me on the shoulder. "What the fuck are you doing over there? Jerking off or some shit?"

"Nah, fucker." I hold my phone out, being sure to get the whole length in the camera. It's not an easy task and that's not me being a cocky ass. It's the truth. "Just taking a selfie."

Styx bursts out laughing. "You're taking dick pics and shit over there in the corner. What the fuck. How are you even hard? There aren't even any women here."

I put my shit away and adjust it on my thigh, before walking over to join them. "The power of the mind, motherfucker. I know what's at home waiting for me and I'm horny as shit."

Kash watches me as I begin wiping down the bar, preparing for close. I'm just ready to get the hell out of here already. "So you two are at it again?" He smiles as if remembering something. "I'm going home with your ass tonight. I haven't had a good jerk since the showers."

"You fucked Sage in the showers? Damn... I missed it," Styx says, looking sincerely disappointed. "Where the hell was I?"

"Not in the next shower over," Kash answers with a cocky grin.

"Since when the hell are women allowed in the back?" Styx takes another swig of his beer. "I tried sneaking one in and Kass jumped down my throat and shit."

"They're not." I toss the dirty towel at him. He just frowns and pushes it away. "Looks like Kage was too busy working on getting pussy, than guarding the door."

"So distracting the big guys does the trick." Styx stands up and tosses some money my way for his drinks, knowing damn well I hate when one of the guys tries tipping me. "Noted."

Wadding up his cash, I toss it at the back of his head when he begins walking away. "Not picking it up," he grumbles. "See ya, dicks."

Kash looks at me and then down at the wadded up money. "Fuck you both. I'll take it then."

Finishing up my shit, I shake my head as Kash picks it up and shoves it in his pocket. "Now get the hell out of here so I can. Go find Kane and see if he's out of the shower so I can lock up. If not, tell him to hurry the hell up. I swear he takes the longest fucking showers."

"Got it."

I'm seriously going crazy to get the fuck out of here and get home to Sage. The things I've been imaging doing to her body has made being here painful as shit.

She hasn't been this playful since we stopped talking months ago and I have to admit that it makes me happy. All of me.

I'm taking this side of Sage while she's willing to give it and doing everything in my power to keep her this way.

If it takes my body to keep her for now, I'll take it and work as hard as I can to keep her emotionally later.

Damn... I hope she's still awake when I get home.

CHAPTER FIFTEEN

STONE

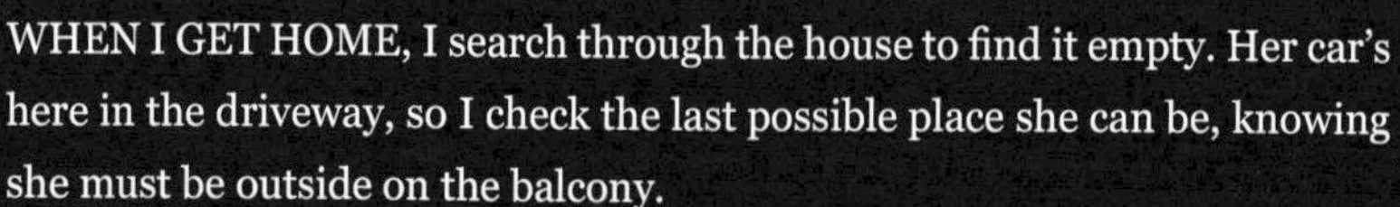

WHEN I GET HOME, I search through the house to find it empty. Her car's here in the driveway, so I check the last possible place she can be, knowing she must be outside on the balcony.

Sliding the glass door open, I smile down at her sleeping in one of the lounge chairs, with a half-empty glass of wine, sitting on the table beside her.

I find it really fucking cute that she fell asleep waiting on me to get home. Now I really need to make it worth her while.

She's usually sleeping by the time I get home, but never out here, with a glass of wine with music playing from her iPod.

Turning the music up, I smile when "Pillow Talk" from Zayn comes through the speakers. The part about pissing off the neighbors might be happening tonight.

Lowering myself to the lounge chair, I straddle her lap, brush the hair away from her ear and whisper her name, causing her to make this cute little whimpering noise.

"Stone," she says tiredly. "What time is it?"

Ignoring her question, I grab her hands and place them on my chest as I begin grinding on her lap to the music.

Her lips instantly twitch up into a smile as I begin to slowly lower her hands down my body and to my abs.

She begins fingering the dips of my muscles and reaching for the bottom of my shirt to lift it. She's still half asleep so she struggles with it.

"Take it off," she whispers. "Wake me up."

Smirking, I rip my shirt off from over my head and grab both ends of it, placing it behind her neck for support as I begin grinding harder in her lap.

Biting her bottom lip, she reaches for my belt and undoes it, before slowly ripping it from the loops of my jeans, while I move for her.

Her eyes widen when she goes for my jeans, noticing I'm not wearing anything underneath. "Jeez, Stone. Do you even own underwear anymore?"

I toss my shirt aside. "I find I don't need them much these days."

Sitting up on my knees, I lower my fitted jeans down past my hips, allowing my hard cock to plop out in front of her.

I stroke my hand up and down it a few times, before raising it up high enough for my cock to brush against her lips.

Grabbing me by the balls, she pulls me closer and swipes her tongue out to twirl it around the piercing in my dick.

She does it a few more times, before I reach for her shirt, pulling it off over her head. Her plump breasts plop out, her nipples instantly perking up for me.

Lowering myself down her body, I take her right nipple into my mouth, swirling my tongue around the piercing, just as she did to the one in my dick.

Her hands reach up to grab at my hair.

This turns me on even more. Especially when she pulls it, hard.

"Damn you..." she moans out as I kiss her stomach and slowly start lowering my mouth to beneath the waistband of her cotton shorts. "Your mouth feels good on my body. Why are you so good at this?"

I smile against her smoothly waxed pussy. "Because I take pride in making sure I can pleasure you better than anyone else can."

Trailing my tongue down her body, I slowly pull her shorts and underwear down to give me access to her wet pussy.

The moment my tongue presses against her clit, she grips my hair and moans loudly. "Holy... fuck..."

Her moaning becomes louder and louder with each flick and swirl of my tongue.

I lick and suck her for as long as I can take it, before I pull her up to her feet and bend her over the balcony.

"Hold on tight. Fuck... this is going to be rough."

I reach into my jeans for a condom, before stepping out of them and kicking them aside.

We're both out here on the balcony completely naked and turned on, not giving a shit who we might disturb.

Fuck it. Let them watch.

Roughly grabbing the back of her hair, I tangle my hand in it and pull as I slam into her.

She screams out in a mixture of pleasure and pain, while gripping even harder onto the balcony.

With my free hand, I lift her left leg up and hold it, while I continue to thrust and grind my hips, pounding into her as deeply as I can.

She moans and cries out with each hard thrust, letting me know how much she enjoys taking my cock.

I can't be gentle. Not tonight.

I want her to still feel me tomorrow. I want her to remember how hard and deep I took her tonight.

My grip on her hair tightens as I slow down and pull out, before thrusting back in, taking her breath away.

"Oh shit..." she breathes out, sounding as if she's fighting to catch her breath.

I pull out again and slam into her as hard as I can. "Let the neighbors know my name," I growl out. "I want them to know how good I feel inside of you. Show them."

Pulling her neck back so I can bite it, I pound into her fast and hard.

So fucking fast and hard that all you can hear now is the slapping of our bodies and her screaming out my name.

"Stone!" Her arm comes behind her to snake around my neck and hold me close as I bite her harder and continue to pound into her. "Oh shit... oh shit. Stone!"

She moans my name on her release and I feel her pussy tightly clamp around my dick as she comes.

There's no doubt in my mind that we've woken up at least one or two of the neighbors. But with my release... we might just wake them all.

Pushing into Sage as hard and deep as her body will allow me, I yell out, "Fuck," as loud as I can, while I release my load inside of her, filling up the condom.

Knowing that she likes it when I fuck her with my cum in the condom, I slowly thrust in and out a few more times, while reaching out to rub her clit.

It doesn't take her long, before she's shaking in my arms, gripping at her hair as she has another orgasm.

Holding her tightly, I wait for her to come down from her release, before I pull out of her and kiss the back of her neck.

"Holy fuck, we were loud." I laugh beside her ear.

She lets out a breathy laugh. "You think!" She throws her hand over her mouth and gets all embarrassed when she notices the neighbor's lights are now on next door. "Oh my God."

Laughing, I pull her into my arms and cup her face. "I'm pretty sure neighbors from two blocks over heard you screaming. Don't be ashamed. It was fucking hot."

She playfully slaps my chest and backs away to gather her things. "I should've known better than to wait for you outside. You'll fuck anywhere and in front of anyone, won't you?"

I bite my bottom lip and growl. "Do you even have to ask that?"

"No." She opens the sliding door and stops to look back at me. "Thanks."

I smile back, while pulling off the condom. "For what?"

She motions at my dick. "For having a magic dick." She winks. "Goodnight, Stone."

Feeling good about tonight, I stand back and watch her disappear into the house.

I take a few minutes to just stand outside and enjoy the fresh, night air, before making my way inside myself.

Sage stays on my mind throughout my whole twenty-minute shower, all the way up until my head hits my pillow and I pass the fuck out.

Damn... that woman is everything I want.

CHAPTER SIXTEEN

SAGE

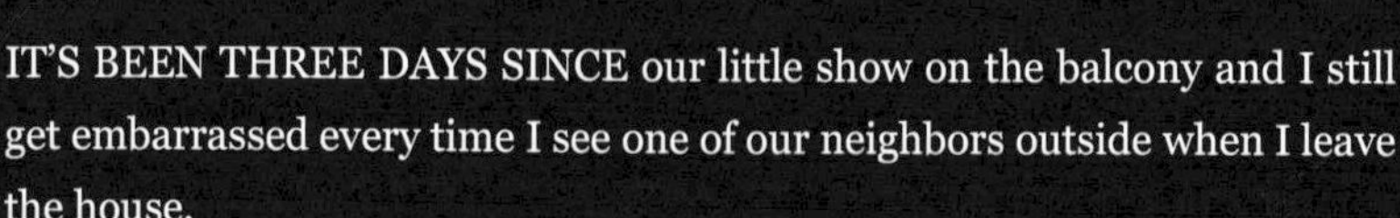

IT'S BEEN THREE DAYS SINCE our little show on the balcony and I still get embarrassed every time I see one of our neighbors outside when I leave the house.

I swear the seventeen-year-old from the house left of ours has been staring extra hard whenever he sees me now. He might've even smirked a little when we made eye contact before I left for work this morning.

If the kid's going to learn from someone, might as well be Stone, I suppose. Doesn't make it any less embarrassing though, knowing that he was probably getting his rocks off to us.

I'm in the back of the salon, finishing up my lunch, when Aspen pokes her head in the door. "There's a guy out here that wants his hair cut."

I hold up my chicken sandwich. "Alright... Why are you telling me? I'm not even on the clock. Can't Onyx take him?"

She gives me a small smile. "I don't know who the cute guy is, but he came in asking for *you* to cut his hair. Is there something I don't know about? Is that why..."

"No," I cut in. "I'm not *seeing* anyone. Trust me, if I was, I'd want a guy like Stone."

Her smile widens. "Good to hear. Hopefully you heard yourself as loud and clear as I did." She backs away. "I'll tell him you'll be out in a few."

I nod as she closes the door and then quickly finish my lunch, before checking my phone.

My stomach fills with butterflies when I see two missed texts from Stone. I don't know what he's been doing to me lately, but the idea of him excites me more than ever.

Stone

I'm off at eight tonight.
Come to Fortunes with us.

[ab pic]

The picture of Stone holding his shirt up, to flash his abs has me smiling. He's been on this kick lately of sending me random pictures of his body parts. He even sent one of his ass the other day. Or at least what he could manage to get in the pic.

Sage

Very impressive... much better than the ass pic you attempted the other day. So about tonight. Who's us?

Stone

Was my ass pic not good enough for you? I can ask Styx to take it for me this time ;)

Styx and Sarah.

I definitely can't say no to that. I never see Sarah go out, other than *Walk of Shame* and I've been dying to go out with her wild ass. She's been working with the boys for so long, that I'm pretty sure they rubbed off on her.

Sage

I'm in... and tell Styx I want that pic ;) He can send me one of his too. I wouldn't mind...

Stone

He won't be able to if his phone is broken. Mine definitely won't be though...

Tossing my wrappers in the trash, I clock back in and make my way out to the front with a laugh.

I'm surprised to see Knight sitting in my chair, waiting on me. My laughter instantly turns into confusion.

Why the hell would he be looking for me?

Onyx gives me a hard look as I walk past her to get to my station. I know how she feels about me giving Stone a chance. The last thing I need is for her to think I'm into some other guy.

Far from it.

The only guy I've been into for the last year is Stone. Who happens to be my brother's close friend and the coolest, sweetest guy I've ever met.

So basically, the last guy I want to hurt or mess up my brother's friendship with. That's why it's so hard to give him everything I know he deserves.

What if I'm just not good at loving someone? I've spent most of my life keeping everyone at a distance so they couldn't hurt me like my deadbeat parents did. They left without caring what happened to Hemy or myself. What if it's just as easy for me to leave someone that I'm supposed to love and hurt them? Or easy for them to leave me.

I have to keep that in mind when it comes to Stone. He doesn't deserve to have his heart ripped out like I have. So that's why I have to make sure he doesn't give it to me; someone that wouldn't even know what to do with it.

Knight looks up at me with a cocky grin, once he notices that I'm now standing next to him.

"I was hoping I'd catch you working today, beautiful." Sitting up straight, he runs his hands through his hair and looks in the mirror. "I need a quick trim before tonight. Ran into your friend the other day and she gave me your card. Said you're really good."

Good to fucking know... Jade.

"I try my best," I say, trying to keep the conversation light. "Are you fighting again tonight?"

His smile broadens in the mirror. "No, I was hoping to get you to come out with me and my friends tonight. I want to make up for my drunken friend acting a fool the other week."

"Thank you, but I can't." I offer him a smile in the mirror, before concentrating back on his hair. "I have plans for tonight."

He looks a little confused at me turning him down. I have a feeling hot MMA fighters don't get turned down very often. Especially ones as well-known and popular as himself.

"Maybe you can change them." He reaches out and grips my thigh, when I walk around to get the front of his hair. "I promise it'll be worth it."

His rough grip causes a small surge of excitement to rush through me, but nothing compared to Stone's touch. Knight might be sexy, strong, and highly desired with his fangirls, but he's not getting lucky with me.

Grabbing his hand, I push it away. "No, I'm good."

I let out a small yelp, surprised when he reaches out and grips my ass with both hands, pulling me between his legs in the chair. "Come on, girl. I saw the way you were checking me out that night. I'm offering you a night out with me."

Smiling, I lean in to whisper in his ear. "I don't know. I need to test something out first." Gripping his package, I squeeze as hard as I can and twist, causing him to cuss and grip the chair. "You can't handle a woman like me. Now keep your hands to yourself for the rest of your cut or I'll rip it off next time. Got it?"

When I let go, he looks me up and down, smiling as if I've only just turned him on more.

"Oh fuck." He throws his hands up. "You're tougher than some of the guys I fight. That's so hot."

Pulling at his head, I hold him still so I can get his fucking hair cut and kick him out of here, before I lose it.

"You're really just not used to being told no, are you?" I ask stiffly.

He smiles up at me in the mirror. "Fuck no. You're the first. Most girls love being handled by me. It comes with being a fighter I suppose. You're different."

"I'm not that easy, playboy and I'm definitely not one of your fighter groupies."

He bites his bottom lip and silently watches me the whole time I'm cutting his hair.

Standing up, he follows me over to the counter to pay for his cut. "Hopefully I'll see you around." He winks at me and then walks out the door.

When I turn around, both Aspen and Onyx are looking at me.

"I was so close to sticking my heel in that asshole's neck. He's lucky you handled him and not me."

I definitely agree there. Onyx is one crazy bitch when it comes to protecting her friends and family. Mess with her and there's a high possibility you could end up with a shoe sticking out of your neck. Just as she said.

"I almost kicked his ass out," Aspen joins in. "But I know how you are about not letting some asshole feel like you're weak. So I left it up to you to handle first. He won't be allowed back in though. Fuck that. He's done."

I shake my head in disbelief that he even showed up here in the first place. "I'm sure he won't be coming back anyway. He's got plenty of other girls that are too willing to jump into bed with an asshole like him."

When I make it back over to my station to clean, I notice a crisp, white business card with his info, laying in the seat.

"Wow. Seriously." I rip the card up and toss it into the trash.

"Some men," Onyx mumbles. "They're fucking idiots when it comes to women. Not Stone though."

"I agree," Aspen jumps in, smiling at me. "How's that going, by the way? Slade said you and Stone have been keeping the whole neighborhood up at night."

"What the fuck!" Onyx yells. "You guys are back to fucking and I didn't even know? Wild sex too, apparently. Sounds fun."

"Slade has a big mouth and apparently, so does Stone. I don't know what to do with these fucking men."

"Love them," Onyx says. "It's all we can do. They're a fucking handful, but they're beautiful as sin and know how to keep us satisfied."

Just then my phone vibrates in my pocket. I pull it out to see three texts from Stone.

Stone

I had to hunt Styx down for this ;)

[ass pic]

Styx's phone is broken. The fucker was going to send you a dick pic.

I agree. Stone is definitely beautiful as sin and a master at pleasing me. Too good, actually. And he knows damn well too. Damn him and that sexy ass of his...

CHAPTER SEVENTEEN

STONE

I TAKE A SHOWER AT the club and head straight for *Fortunes*, knowing that Sarah and Sage are already there, waiting on me to show up.

Styx has one more private dance before he can get away from *Walk of Shame* so I told him to just meet us after he cleans up.

The last thing I wanted to do was waste time waiting on that fucker, just so I'd get stuck seeing his ass run around the locker room naked like usual.

I've seen enough of that asshole's dick to last me a lifetime.

Plus, Sage messaged me about thirty minutes ago, letting me know they showed up early. My plan was to go home first, but there's no way I'm leaving the ladies there alone for longer than I have to, so I'm pulling into the parking lot now.

Jumping out of my jeep, I smooth out my black V-neck and adjust my dick in my jeans the best I can so it's not the first thing every woman notices when I walk by.

Apparently, I've already used all my extra boxer briefs that I had stored in my locker and there was no fucking way I was throwing my sweaty ones back on after I showered.

I'm going commando.

When I walk through the door, the waitress walking by flashes me a huge smile after looking up from my crotch.

So much for the big guy not getting noticed...

Standing in the darkened room, I search for Sage and Sarah to find them in the back corner, laughing about something.

Sarah notices me first and starts waving me over, while listening to whatever it is that Sage is focused on at the moment.

Keeping my eyes on Sage, I make my way over, smiling as she finally looks up at me, looking happy to see me standing beside her.

"Someone's looking mighty fine tonight. I've always thought black was your color." She winks, but then her eyes widen as they lower down my body, landing on the bulge in my pants. "Seriously? You can see *everything* and I do mean *everything*. You're not at the club, Stone."

Shrugging, I grab the beer they have waiting for me and take a swig of it. "Didn't have time to run home. Which might fucking suck since you look so damn hot right now. There's no way I'm going to be able to keep my dick in control."

Sarah smiles and stands up to get a look of her own. "Damn, Stone. You're really not leaving much to the imagination. I love it."

"That's because you're dirty-minded as fuck," I point out with a grin.

"True. What can I say? I've been working with you boys for too long."

Sage laughs against her drink. "Where's Styx?"

"Finishing up a private dance. He'll be here soon."

"Hopefully with underwear," she teases. "Not sure we can keep the waitresses away with you both going commando." She looks down at my jeans again, as if she can't help but look. She bites her bottom lip and reaches for her drink again. "I need to thank him for that photo you sent me earlier."

"What photo?" Sarah perks up. "Are you guys getting freaky and I don't know about it?" She holds her hand out. "Gimmie."

"You would ask too." Sage pulls out her phone with a laugh and holds it out for Sarah to look.

"Very nice ass." Sarah whistles. "Zoom in a bit. I've seen it at the club, but not up this close. Dayum."

"Hey, I made Styx look at it. Might as well let Sarah see my magnificent ass too. Zoom that shit in."

"Dude, not with your fucking ass again." Styx pulls up a seat, squeezing his way in between the girls. "You ladies are looking fucking hot tonight."

"I thought you had a private dance?" I ask while watching him place his arms around the girls as if his ass thinks he's taking one of them home tonight.

Fuck that. There's no way Sage is going anywhere near his place.

"She was a fast one. Took one look at my hard dick and came." He lifts a brow with a cocky ass grin.

"It must've been the first dick she's seen."

Grabbing the bottom of Sage's chair, I pull her over to me and away from Styx, before he can even think for one second that he has a chance.

Styx flashes me the middle finger and waves the waitress over to order the whole table a round of drinks. "What can I say… Sage can see for herself."

He winks as Sage's phone goes off on the table. Before I can snatch it up, Sarah has it in her hand with her mouth hanging open.

"Holy fuck, you're hung, Styx. Damn, your dick is perfect. Look, Sage."

"Seriously, fucker. I thought your phone was broken." I shrug as he holds his phone out for Sage to see. "That's the closest your dick's getting to her face so enjoy, asshole."

Sage's eyes widen a bit as she gives Sarah a nod of agreement. "Not bad, Styx. Definitely not bad."

"Damn straight. My dick is sexy as fuck."

After a few rounds of drinks, everyone's laughing and having a good time, but all I can think about is how hot it would be to have Sage's hand around my cock right now.

She's been trying to play it off, but every once in a while, I catch her looking down at it and biting her bottom lip.

I lean into her ear and grab her hand. "You can touch it," I whisper. "You can do anything you want to me."

Pulling her chair even closer, I place her hand on my lap and let her do the rest.

Responding to something that Sarah asked her, she smoothly glides her hand over my thigh, rubbing her hand over the shape of my dick.

It instantly gets hard under her touch, causing her to grip it hard and smile in satisfaction.

Sarah doesn't seem to notice anything going on under the table, but Styx's eyes seem to keep lowering as if he knows that Sage is playing with my cock.

"Are you playing with Stone's dick under the table?" He smirks and places Sarah's hand on his thigh. "That's not fair if I'm not getting the same treatment from Sarah over here."

Sarah punches his arm and laughs. "Not tonight, nipples. I have a date later. Wouldn't want to be thinking about you and your sexy dick if I end up getting laid."

"Why not?" Styx questions, while scooting closer to her to give her easy access. "It might help you get off harder."

Sage runs her thumb over the head of my dick, before pulling her hand away and reaching for her drink. "Yeah, well Sarah's date is actually pretty hot. She showed me a picture."

Styx lets out a huff. "I doubt that fucker's hotter than I am."

Sarah pushes her chair away from his and rests her legs in his lap. "Give me a leg rub and I'll think about taking you home one of these nights."

He smiles and grabs her legs, pushing them down so she can feel the bulge in his pants. Then he begins moving his hips. "How's this? All I have to use is my dick."

Sarah shrugs and grabs her drink. "I'll take it. Something as sexy as *that* has to be talented."

Ignoring those two goofing off, I place my hand at the back of Sage's neck and pull her in for a kiss, while placing her hand back on my dick.

Other guys keep looking her way, checking her out, but there's no way in hell I'll be letting any of them get close to her.

This is me letting them know who she belongs with. The only place she'll be going tonight, is home, to our place.

Her kiss is soft, her mouth instantly parting for me to slip my tongue inside and capture hers.

Kissing her harder, my hand tangles into the back of her hair, wanting to get as close to her as I can right now.

I'm trying really hard to not get carried away, but I can't help it when it comes to Sage.

I'm just about to pull her into my lap, when both Styx and Sarah begin whistling really loud and trying to get our attention.

"Hello! This nice waitress here is trying to offer us shots," Sarah says while sliding two shots across the table to us. "And you two are over there practically about to have sex. Break it up."

Pulling away from me, Sage reaches for the shot in front of her and slides mine closer to me, while wiping her finger over her lips to wipe her smeared lip gloss off.

Thanking the waitress, I pull out some cash and place it on her tray, before we all slam our shots back and fall into conversation.

I catch Sage's eyes keep going over to a certain part of the room, so I follow them to see what she's now looking at.

Fucking Knight Stevens.

Watching her, I can't help but notice her looking uncomfortable all of a sudden. It's almost as if she wants to get out of here.

"What's wrong?" I question, while gripping her thigh. "Did that asshole do something to you?"

"Doesn't matter." Looking flustered, she takes another sip of her drink and focuses on looking anywhere but at him. "I took care of it."

Feeling my blood boil in anger, I quickly finish my beer off, before slamming it down on the table.

That gets Knight's attention, causing him to smirk my way from his spot up at the bar now.

"That fucker's dead."

Before Sage can say anything to stop me, I'm walking across the room to where Knight is standing at the bar.

One of his friends tries to stand in my way, but I shove him into a table, letting the fucker know I'm not playing. He throws his arms up and gets out of my way.

"You fuck with my girl?"

Knight laughs, clearly drunk this time and not thinking straight. A stripper kicking his ass will be bad as shit for his reputation, but all I did growing up was fight. A lot more than I wanted to. "I think she liked it. She did grab my dick afterward."

Stepping in front of Knight, I swing my elbow out hard, connecting it with his jaw. Then I grab the back of his head, slamming it into the side of the bar.

I rotate my shoulders in anger as I look down at him, waiting for him to get up. "Get up, you piece of shit."

Standing up, he looks down at the blood on his shirt, before wiping his thumb under his nose. "You really want to do this? You do know I could probably kill your ass, right? Or are you going to hip thrust my ass like the male fucking entertainer that you claim to be."

"Fuck you."

He swings out, his fist connecting with my nose.

I wipe my nose off and tilt my head, tensing my jaw at him. Seeing red, I swing my right fist, connecting it with the fucker's jaw.

He stumbles back, but quickly regains his balance, slamming me into a nearby table, knocking all of the drinks over.

My back gets wet, but that's the last thing on my mind. This asshole did something to Sage and I'm not letting that shit past me.

I let him get his punch in a few times, before I take control, grabbing him by the neck and slamming him down to the ground.

My fists continue to swing, connecting with his face, until I'm being dragged away from the fight by someone.

It's Styx, who punches some asshole in the side of the head, that tries to push him out of the way.

"What the fuck?" he growls at me, when he releases me. "You could've warned me first."

By the time I look behind me, Knight is back to his feet, pushing and yelling at his guys that are trying to help him.

"Leave me the fuck alone!" He fixes his shirt and punches the table, pissed off that I had to be pulled from him.

"Yeah, well it couldn't wait." I make my way back over to Sage who is looking completely shocked at what I just did. I toss some money on the table, before grabbing her hand. "Let's get out of here."

Styx places his hand on Sarah's back and follows us outside to the parking lot.

Sage is the first to speak.

"I can't believe that just happened. I didn't want you to get into a fight for me, Stone."

"Doesn't matter," I say stiffly. "No one fucks with you. You couldn't have stopped me if you tried."

Sarah looks down at her watch and cusses. "I'm sorry, but my date starts soon. I need to go, but you will be explaining this shit to me later." She turns to Styx who is still fuming. "Are you good to drop me off? I don't think I should drive."

If anyone can handle their liquor, it's Styx. I'm not sure if the dude ever actually gets drunk. He cuts himself off at a buzz.

"Yeah, I'll drop you off." He turns to me. "I'm stopping by later so we can talk about what just happened. Something set you off and I don't like that shit."

Nodding, I turn away, placing my hands against the building and take a deep breath to compose myself.

Sage says her goodbyes to Sarah and Styx, before calling for a taxi.

She slides her way in between me and the building, grabbing my face and gently kissing me on the lips. "I don't like you fighting, but the fact that you did it because you care means a lot."

"I'll never let anyone hurt you, Sage," I say with honesty. "I want you to tell me if anyone ever does. Not knowing what he did to you made me see red."

Sliding my hands down from the building, I cup her face. "What did he do?"

She grabs my arms and looks up at me. "He came into the salon and tried picking me up. He grabbed my ass and I about ripped his dick off. He got the picture. At least I hoped."

The thought of him grabbing her ass, causes more anger to flood through me, but I fight it off, knowing that it will lead me back into the bar, swinging.

"Well he definitely got it now," I growl out. I look over my shoulder when I hear a car pull up. "The taxi's here." I kiss her on the forehead. "Let's get you home."

This asshole is lucky Styx was there to pull me off. Next time he won't be so lucky...

CHAPTER EIGHTEEN

SAGE

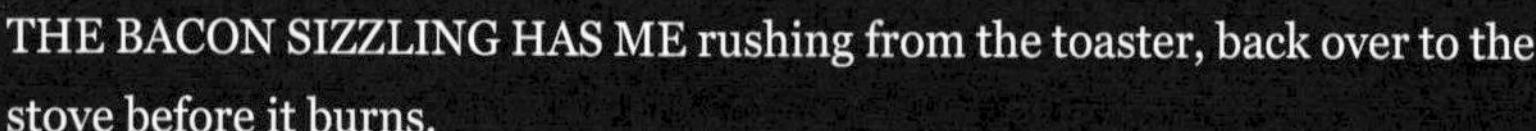

THE BACON SIZZLING HAS ME rushing from the toaster, back over to the stove before it burns.

"Owe, fuck!" *That shit hurts.*

I knew there was a reason why I stopped cooking bacon. Bacon grease hurts like a bitch when it pops you in the face.

Getting the bacon under control, I quickly whip up some eggs—over easy—like she eats them and slide them onto a plate.

It's been a while since I've cooked Sage breakfast, but after last night, all I've been able to think about are the ways that I can take care of her.

Which led me to waking my ass up at the ass crack of dawn and thawing out some bacon for breakfast.

After everything's cooked and plated up, I push her bedroom door open and walk in to see her sleeping, with the covers kicked down to her feet.

She's sleeping in a thong and that little sheer top that I love so much on her. There's only one way I can think about waking her up right now and that involves my face in her sexy, round ass.

There's a huge chance that she might kick my ass afterward, but it'll be worth the risk.

Carefully crawling into the bed behind her, I lean down and bite her ass cheek, holding her down with my hands.

She instantly begins screaming and squirming in my arms as I continue to gently bite her ass, teasing her.

"Stop!" She begins slapping at me and laughing, while trying to get away from me. "Oh my God! It tickles. It tickles. Holy shit! Stop!"

Laughing against her ass, I bite her one last time, just to work her up, before slapping her ass and releasing her, allowing her to flip around to face me.

As soon as she does, she tackles me down to the bed and straddles me, holding my arms down. "I should so kick your sexy ass right now."

Smiling, I free my arms from her hold and grip both of her ass cheeks, placing her roughly on my dick. "So you're saying you'll be aggressive with me."

I flex my dick, causing it to move beneath her. It's hard as shit now and I want nothing more than to skip breakfast and treat her to something else.

Giving me a dirty little smile, she slowly moves down my body as if she's working her face down toward my dick. Her mouth opens to bite the band of my sweats as if to pull them down with her teeth, but then she stops and sniffs the air with a playful smile. "Mmm... what's for breakfast?"

Giving my dick a hard bite through my sweats, she slaps my chest and jumps off me to run out of the room.

"Dammit," I whisper to myself.

Jumping out of her bed, I push down on my erection and make my way into the kitchen to see Sage already seated at the table, shoving bacon into her mouth.

"Soooo good," she mumbles around her food. "I almost forgot how good you are at cooking breakfast. What do I need to do to get this kind of treatment more often?"

I smile. "Sleep in that sexy little outfit and kick the blanket down at night. It might also help to keep the door open so I can creep."

"Ha! And *help* you creep. That's just too easy on your part."

"You might just wake up to a surprise." I wink.

Seeing how much she's enjoying her breakfast makes it worth the blue balls that I'll most likely have for the next hour, until I can work my shit out in the shower.

Her happiness is all I'm worried about. I'd do anything to see her smile every day and I'm hoping to show her that.

I take a seat across from her and dig into my own plate. I try to focus on my food, but I can't stop thinking about that asshole trying to fuck with Sage. "What are you doing after work? Going out?"

She looks up from her plate. "I don't know yet. Maybe writing for a bit and then hanging with Jade. Why?"

I shake my head. "Just wondering where you'll be."

"I'm not hanging out with Knight if that's what you're asking. I don't want anything to do with that asshole."

My jaw tenses at his name. "Good. That shit won't be happening as long as I'm still breathing."

"You sound like Hemy." Her mouth turns up into a small, knowing smile. "You boys and your overprotectiveness. I'll never have to worry as long as I have you both."

She gets quiet, as if she's just now realizing what she's said.

It's the fucking truth. I just hope she can see that and stop fighting it.

"Never forget that," I say firmly. "And promise me you'll call me if that asshole ever shows up at the salon again. I'll rip the fucker's throat out."

"I promise, Stone. He won't be coming back. So don't worry." She clears her throat and finishes off her orange juice, before standing. "I need to take a quick shower before work." Grabbing the back of my head, she gently kisses me on the lips, grazing me with her tongue, before she pulls away. "Thanks for breakfast."

"Welcome, babe," I whisper as she walks away. "Stop shaking your ass like that. Fuck..."

Damn... I'm going to need a long shower when she leaves.

I HAVE TWO MORE HOURS before I have to be at the club, so I go to the gym that Styx manages, knowing that he'll most likely be there until our shift starts tonight.

When he's not fucking some random chick in a back room or shaking his dick at the club, he's here working out or barking orders at people.

The dude doesn't mess around when it comes to him running the gym for his uncle. Between spending his days here and his nights at the club, I don't know how the fucker ever has any free time.

"What's up, bro." Styx runs over to me, sweaty and out of breath. "Getting some lifting in before work?"

"Nah, man. Not tonight." I pull out my headphones and toss my gym bag aside. My mind hasn't left Sage all day and running on the treadmill usually helps calm my mind. "Running off some frustration."

Styx laughs, while wiping his sweat off with his shirt. "What, jerking your shit in the shower didn't do the fucking trick?"

"Does it ever really?"

He smirks when some hot chick with pale, purple hair walks by, running her hand across his bare stomach.

"I'll be back. Maybe..."

Shaking my head, I put my headphones on and jump on the treadmill, hoping to clear my thoughts.

Every so often, I look up to see a new chick on the treadmills beside me, checking me out and giving me *the* look. Knowing that they'll never satisfy my craving for Sage, I continue to run hard, ignoring them, until they give up and leave.

Getting laid by some random chick is the last thing on my fucking mind right now.

Stepping off the treadmill, I look around to see if Styx's ass is still around. I haven't seen him since he disappeared over an hour ago.

Our shift starts in less than thirty minutes so I need to find his ass and get him out of here.

I walk around the whole gym, but don't see his ass anywhere, so I look outside for his motorcycle to see it still parked out front. I know the fucker's here somewhere.

There's only one place left he could be.

Not bothering with knocking, I push his office door open to see his naked ass as he pounds into the chick from earlier.

Holding her up against the wall, he thrusts into her hard and deep and then stops. "Fuck… your pussy feels good. Nice and wet for me."

Pulling her away from the wall, he turns around and slams her roughly against his desk, before gripping her neck, choking her.

"Shit," he growls, when he sees me. "Already?"

"Yeah, fucker. Hurry your ass up."

The hot girl tilts her head back to look at me. "Oh wow." She bites her bottom lip, while looking me over and gripping at Styx's broad shoulders, digging her nails in. "Can your friend here join?"

Styx shrugs, not giving a shit either way. As long as his dick is buried between her legs, he couldn't care less about what she does with her mouth.

"Sorry, honey." I give Styx a hard look when he begins fucking her again as if I'm not even standing here and shit. "Seriously?"

"Gotta get the job done, asshole. Just give me five minutes."

"Five minutes and you better run out the fucking door naked with your dick in your hand if you have to. We can't be late."

I back out of the office and shut the door behind me, giving him his time. All I can hear after I'm outside is the girl screaming loudly, and shit being broken. The fucker is rough as shit. Almost scary sometimes, but the women always seem to enjoy it.

Random people around the gym look my way, wanting to know what's happening in the office. I'm not lying for the asshole.

"The idiot's getting laid. I'm sure you're all used to it by now," I say, before walking away to gather my shit and wait for him outside.

I'd leave his ass, but I know damn well that Cale would ream my ass if he knew I let Styx be late on one of our busiest nights.

Fucking Styx and his dick. Always finding some way to get in trouble…

CHAPTER NINETEEN

SAGE

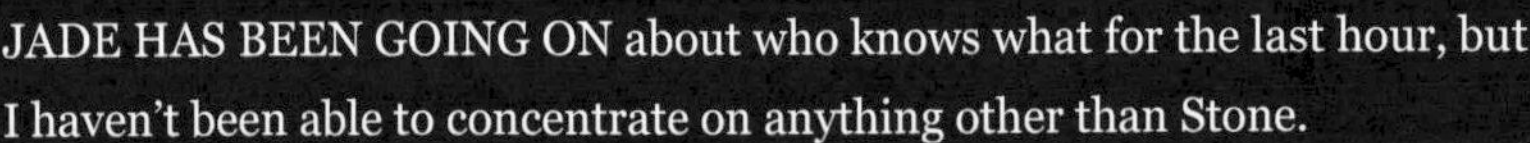

JADE HAS BEEN GOING ON about who knows what for the last hour, but I haven't been able to concentrate on anything other than Stone.

He looked stressed when I left for work this morning and I have a feeling that it was because he's worried about Knight bothering me again.

I sent him a message over an hour ago to let him know that I'm at Jade's house with her, but he hasn't responded to it. For some reason I just want to let him know that I'm safe.

It's a busy night for the club, so I doubt he'll have his phone on him at all tonight.

"...long day and I just want to get laid. Is that too much to ask? I work hard."

I only catch the end of what she says, but the get laid part is a good enough reason for her to agree to what I'm about to suggest.

"Let's go see the boys."

Jade perks up, setting her bag of bacon jerky aside. "Now that's a good idea." She jumps to her feet. "Let me throw some pants on and brush my teeth."

"Good idea." I laugh as she runs pantless into her room, looking fully awake for the first time since I walked through her door.

"You could've been nice enough to throw on pants before your guest arrived. Just saying."

"I may be nice, but not *that* nice." She grabs her purse and keys. "Let's go. I'll drive."

Jade smiles the whole way to the club.

"What are you smiling so much about?" I ask, when she parks.

She pulls her keys out of the ignition and turns to me. "We're here to watch the boys. Please do tell me what there isn't to smile about."

She has a point there.

"Gotcha."

When we get to the door, Kass is taking IDs. He gives us a wink when he notices us in the crowd. "Get up here, ladies."

A few of the girls sound their disappointment, but Kass just gives them his heart stopping smile and pulls us up to the front of the line.

"These girls are gonna love us," Jade points out. "Not that I mind one bit." She smiles sweetly. "Thanks."

"Figured you wouldn't," Kass says smoothly. "Get your asses in there."

"What would we do without you boys, Kass?" I grab his hand and wink when he reaches his out to hold mine.

"Go enjoy the show."

He gives me a pat on the butt to get me moving, before turning back to handle the line of women.

Jade grips my arm when we walk in to Styx on the stage, stripping out of a pair of leather pants and biker boots. "Holy motherfucking shit. That man is hawt. Please tell me he owns a motorcycle."

"You're not lying," I agree. "Those pants look delicious on that man's firm ass. I can see why he spends so much time in that gym he manages."

After grabbing some drinks from Sarah, we make our way over to a table and quickly look up at the stage to see what everyone is suddenly screaming about.

Styx's leather pants are hanging so low on his hips that the top of his shaft is on display for the hundreds of women in the crowd.

We all watch extra hard as he holds up a bottle of chocolate syrup and squirts it on his abs, moving his body to the slow, seductive rhythm and letting the chocolate slowly run down his body, coating his front.

Tossing the bottle aside, he fingers for some girl to enter the stage, before placing his hand on her head and dropping her down to her knees in front of him.

He thrusts his hips close to her face, before demanding her to lick the syrup from his muscles, leading her down lower to his tight abs.

When she's done, she looks up at him as if waiting for instructions on what to do next.

He grabs both of her hands and places them on the waist of his pants, before grabbing her hair and biting his bottom lip as she yanks them down his tatted, muscled legs.

His dick is exposed for a few seconds, causing the women to scream and throw money at the stage, before he covers himself with both hands and steps completely out of his boots and pants.

He's standing there completely naked now as the chosen girl licks the few last drops of chocolate from his body. And when I say from his body, I pretty much mean the base of his dick that is still exposed to us.

Suddenly, the lights go dark and everyone is left to wonder what the hell happened next. A few girls even gasp and start yelling for the lights to come back on.

I don't need to be told what is most likely going on in the dark. I know without a doubt that Styx probably dropped his hands and let the hot chick finish cleaning off every last drop of chocolate.

For all we know, he could be getting his dick sucked right here on the stage and we just can't see it. I somehow find that to be hot.

"Wow!" Jade bumps my arm and squeals with excitement. "That was really hot. What do you think Stone will do tonight?"

I grab my drink and nervously take a sip. I don't even want to know. Not if it's anything like Styx's performance. "I don't know," I whisper. "But I hope it doesn't involve chocolate."

The thought of some random girl getting to lick chocolate off Stone's body makes me sick to my stomach.

The only tongue I want on his body is mine. I'm suddenly feeling a bit selfish with him.

The lights come back on after about five minutes of complete darkness and Kash takes the stage next, also dressed in a pair of sexy leather pants.

Then Styx and Kash take the stage together, bringing two girls on stage and sharing, going back and forth.

It's been almost an hour and I haven't seen Stone at all. It reminds me that I didn't even see Stone's jeep when we pulled it. I figured it was because

I just overlooked it. But now...

"Have you seen Stone anywhere?" I ask Jade, pulling her attention away from the boys on stage.

"No... I almost forgot about him," she responds. "Maybe he's been stuck doing private shows. I'm sure he'll be out soon."

"I don't know." I sit up tall and begin looking around the darkened room, feeling a bit worried that he possibly isn't even here tonight. "I didn't see his jeep outside either."

Setting my drink aside, I pull out my phone to check for a response from him, but nothing.

I anxiously twirl my phone in my hand and begin searching the room again, somehow managing to spot Stone walking out of one of the private rooms as if he's in a hurry.

A few seconds later, three girls walk out of the same room looking completely satisfied at whatever show he just put on in there for who knows how long.

"...hey you. You want another drink or what? You've been chewing on that straw for the last ten minutes."

I look down at my empty glass. "Yeah, just a beer this time."

She smiles and holds up her wallet. "I'll be right back. Don't let none of these crazy women steal my spot. Some of the girls from the back somehow keep getting closer and closer to the stage."

I lift my eyebrows and toss my purse in her seat. "All taken care of. Just hurry!"

The stage darkens after Kash and Styx jump off the stage and get swallowed up by the heard of horny women.

"Here!" Jade shoves a beer into my hand. "Stone's up next. Sarah told me he's been caught up in private dances all night. Poor guy must be exhausted by now."

"Earned It" by The Weeknd comes through the speakers, before the stage lights up enough to see Stone standing there in a pair of leather pants with suspenders, a black tank, and a black fedora hat.

Walking out slowly, he grabs his hat and slowly moves his body to the music, while walking around the stage for the women to get a good view.

Damn... he looks fucking great in that.

Then he lowers his body and does this sexy little grind, while lifting the front of his shirt for us.

The way he's grinding his hips even has me dying for him to take it all off.

"Holy shit, Stone." I grip my beer and take a gulp of it, while keeping my eyes on his every move.

His hands move over to his suspenders, playing with the straps as he continues to move, not missing a beat.

With a sexy smirk, he yanks his suspenders to the side, letting them hang, before reaching for his shirt again.

Pulling, he rips it off and tosses it aside, before dropping to his knees and slowly fucking his way across the stage.

Once he gets to where he wants, he sits up on his knees, grabs what looks like a water bottle of some kind, and slowly pours it down the front of his body, while moving his body to the music.

He leans his head back and runs a hand over his wet chest and abs, before grabbing his dick and thrusting his hips.

The women go crazy when he throws the empty bottle into the crowd and undoes his pants to stick his hand down the front.

I scream too, joining in. I can't help it. He has me extremely excited right now.

He makes his way back to his feet, his eyes somehow finding me in the crowd. It must've been my screaming that caught his attention. I guess I was a little louder than I thought.

Giving me his sexy, confident smile, he pulls his hat off and tosses it to the ground, before making his way off the stage and coming right for me.

A few girls reach for him, but he keeps his eyes on me, not taking them off, until he's standing right in front of me.

Grabbing my chair with force, he yanks me into the middle of the aisle and straddles my lap, dancing against me.

Getting lost in the moment, I bite my bottom lip and moan under my breath when he grabs my hands, placing them to his chest and abs as he grinds on me.

Then he does something that completely and utterly surprises the shit out of me and sends my heart soaring.

Grabbing the back of my head, he crushes his lips against mine, kissing me hard and deep as if letting the whole room know that he wants me and doesn't care what they think.

I would've never in a million years expected him to kiss me during a performance, knowing that it could mess up his popularity and high demand here at the club.

But the way he's kissing me feels like more than just a kiss. It feels like he's baring his soul for the world to see. Myself included and I don't know what to do with it.

So I just kiss him back.

My heart continues to beat out of my chest the whole time that our lips mold together, our tongues desperately seeking each other's as if we're alone in the privacy of our home.

When his lips finally separate from mine, he leans in to whisper in my ear. "No one else gets this kind of treatment, babe." He tangles his hand in my hair and tugs, while breathing heavily against my ear. "The question is... what are you going to do with it?"

With that, he stands up and pushes my chair back to the table, before rushing back up to the stage to finish the last part of his routine.

Most of the girls look at me with jealousy, while some of them just look even more excited as if they expect me to just be some random, lucky chick that got a kiss from the sexiest stripper that has walked that stage.

You'd have to be blind to think it was just random. He made it extremely clear that he has feelings for me.

Not to mention that he made sure to make it clear that I need to figure out what to do with them.

That thought scares me, yet I can't move from my spot when his show is over.

"You okay?" Jade asks. "That boy cares for you. Looks like the whole room knows now too. That kiss was something deep and meaningful. You're lucky, Sage. Stone is a great guy."

"He is. He's the greatest guy I know other than my brother," I whisper, while still lost in thought.

And I want to be here for him when he gets off for the night. I'm not leaving until he does.

Maybe a small part of me does know what to do with it...

CHAPTER TWENTY

STONE

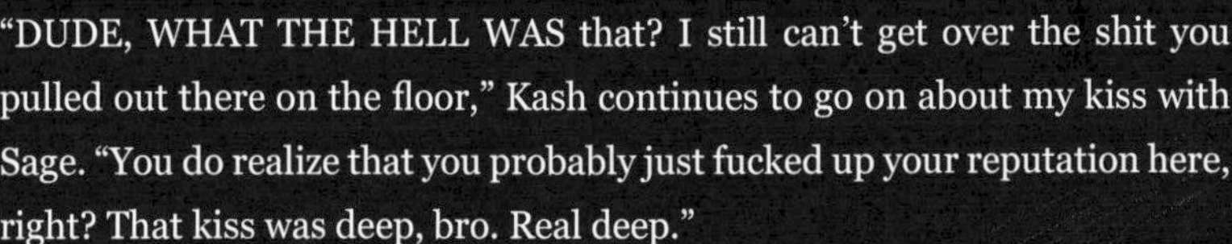

"DUDE, WHAT THE HELL WAS that? I still can't get over the shit you pulled out there on the floor," Kash continues to go on about my kiss with Sage. "You do realize that you probably just fucked up your reputation here, right? That kiss was deep, bro. Real deep."

I throw my shit into my locker and slam it closed. "Does it look like I give a shit?" I rake my hands through my wet hair in frustration.

The only thing I'm thinking about is what I whispered in her ear and how she's going to take it.

There's a huge fucking chance that I've just messed things up with Sage completely and she'll back off, wanting to go back to being strictly roommates again. I can't have it. I won't.

There's no way in hell I'll be able to live with her and not want her like I do every day. I need to see how she truly feels about me. It's been eating at me the more and more that I touch her.

"This job isn't everything, fucker. The hundreds of women that grab at me every damn night, begging to take me home to fuck them, will never keep me satisfied for longer than a night. I've been fighting to hold onto Sage for over a year. Do you get that?"

Kash nods his head in understanding and slips a clean shirt on. "I get it, man. I do. I've been there in the past. I've been hurt and I've moved on, but you still have to think about your career and what you've built here. The women want us to come off as available to them. They want to go home fantasizing that they have a chance with us. It keeps them coming back. That's all I'm saying."

"Get off his fucking ass," Styx grinds out, while stepping out of the shower, completely fucking naked as usual. "Worry about what you do and he'll worry about his own shit. I'd do it in a heartbeat for the right woman. If I ever get lucky enough to fucking find her."

"Fuck off, Styx. I'm just trying to give him some advice and get him thinking straight. I'm down for him winning Sage over as much as you two dicks are. I'm just thinking about the club too."

I throw my dirty clothes into my duffle bag and throw it over my shoulder. "I am thinking straight. I know what I want and I'm going after it at all costs. Fuck the club. Fuck what anyone thinks. She's all that matters. Later, dickheads."

Not wanting to listen to Kash and his logical fucking bullshit any longer, I hurry out of the locker room and outside toward Hemy's motorcycle.

I borrowed that shit without him knowing, while he took off to work on my jeep earlier. He told me to take his old truck, but I said fuck it and took off on his bike. He hasn't called me yet to kick my ass, but the night is still early. At least for me.

When I walk outside there are still groups of women hanging outside by the building, checking me out and going on about our performances tonight, but there's one woman in particular that catches my attention and keeps it.

No one else ever seems to exist when it comes to this woman.

Sage is leaning against Hemy's motorcycle, looking lost in thought and slightly confused. She looks torn... almost pained.

She's so deep in thought that she doesn't even notice me approaching her.

I hope like hell that it's me she's thinking so hard about right now.

Thankful that she's still here, I wrap my arms around her and pick her up, her legs instantly wrapping around my waist and squeezing.

I flash her a smile, showing her just how happy I am to see her. "Waiting on me, babe?"

She nods her head and returns my smile. "Yeah, I thought I owed it to you after that amazing kiss that you surprised me with."

"It was pretty amazing." I lift my brows and tangle both of my hands into the back of her hair. "Especially the way you kissed me back. It was sweet and hot as fuck. I haven't stopped thinking about it all night."

Her eyes catch mine and we just look at each other. Like really look at each other for the first time in a long time. Hell... maybe even ever. At least on her end.

I take this moment to look into her soul and search for any kind of feelings she might be hiding for me. She may be good at hiding her emotions, but I see something there. Even if it's just something small as hell. It's there. I just need to spark it and make it grow so she can't fight it anymore.

Breaking eye contact, Sage turns her head and clears her throat, before sliding down the front of my body and fixing her shirt. "Mind if I get a ride, big guy?"

"Depends on where you're going, beautiful girl," I tease, while grabbing the helmet and placing it on her head.

"How about for a ride," she says sweetly. "Anywhere. I don't care where. I just want to feel the wind on my face and get lost in my head. I need to get away for a bit."

"I'll take you anywhere you want." It's the honest truth. I care about this woman so much that I'll do anything she ever asks of me.

I hop on the front of her brother's bike, before grabbing her hand and helping her on the back. It feels good having her behind me. I really need to invest in one of these bikes myself.

We're both quiet as I take off and just ride for a while. I don't give a shit about where we're going or where we end up. Just as long as I'm with her and her arms are wrapped tightly around my waist as if she doesn't want to let go.

Every once in a while, I feel her press her face into my back and squeeze me tighter. My heart speeds up, wondering what she's thinking about. It's almost as if she's taking this as a free moment to hold onto me without any worries of where it might lead us.

We ride for about an hour, with her holding onto me for dear life, until I finally find an open field to park at.

I turn off the engine, but her arms stayed wrapped tightly around me. The last thing I want is for her to let go, so I spin around on the bike to face her, bringing her up to straddle my lap.

I wrap her arms back around me, before bringing my hands up to cup her face. "How do you feel right now? Don't worry about the future or what could happen. Right here. Right now. What do you feel?"

She looks me in the eyes but hesitates before responding. "It's complicated and completely confusing. I... I want to... never mind. It's just stupid."

Frustrated, she pulls her face away from my hands, but I capture it again, wanting her to look at me. I never want her to be ashamed to look at me.

"I promise you... whatever it is, it isn't fucking stupid. Tell me."

Giving up, she scoots further into my lap and wraps her arms around my neck. "I want to feel what it's like to have you make love to me. Nice. Slow. Passionate. Deep. I just want to experience it once with you and not have to worry about the future."

"Then I'll give that to you," I whisper against her neck. "Anything you want. Ask me and I'll give it to you."

Maneuvering us both off the bike, I press my lips against hers and carry her over to the grass, gently laying her down in it.

She watches me as I slowly strip out of my clothing, until I'm down to only my briefs.

"You want to do this right here? Right now?" she questions, while looking me over.

"Fuck yes," I growl out. "More than anything."

Spreading her legs, I press my body between them and capture her lips with mine again, tasting her slowly and passionately, wanting her to feel how much she truly means to me.

Moaning softly, she wraps her arms around my neck and lifts her ass up off the ground so that I can pull her jeans and panties down her slender legs. Then, she sits up, allowing me to strip her of her shirt and bra.

Lowering my body, I press kisses down her breasts and stomach, before moving back up to kiss her lips. "If I'm making love to you, I'm doing it without a condom," I say against her lips. "I want you to feel me the right way."

She nods her head. "Okay," she whispers. "I want that too."

Standing up, I pull my boxer briefs down, tossing them aside, before lowering myself back in between her spread legs.

Biting her bottom lip, I slide my hand under her neck and gently guide my hard cock into her pussy. I push into her, moaning as her tightness hugs me completely.

Her body moves with mine, her nails digging into my back as I slowly grind my hips, being sure to hit every spot of pleasure I can find. Hearing her moan and feeling her grip on me tighten, pushes me to want to pleasure her even more. I can never get deep enough when it comes to Sage.

Being inside her this way feels too good emotionally and physically, and I can't help but feel selfish and only want it to be me from now on. Hell, I'm praying that I've been the only one so far. I can't even imagine this happening with anyone else.

Bringing her legs over my shoulders, I slightly lift her hips and rock into her, biting the side of her calf as I bury myself as deep as I can, causing her to let out a small cry of pain.

"You okay?" I whisper.

She nods her head. "Yes," she moans. "Keep going."

Nearly an hour later, both of our bodies are covered in sweat. We're both breathless and completely lost in each other as I continue to thrust deep and slow for what feels like forever.

Wanting to be closer to her, I sit on my knees and bring her body up to straddle my lap. Our bodies are plastered together, not even an inch of breathing room as I kiss her flesh all over and bury myself inside of her over and over again.

I feel her nails dig into my skin and her breathing picks up next to my ear. "I've never felt anything like this before."

Holding her as close as possible, I press my lips to hers and sway my hips, pulling her body so I can get as deep as I can. I feel myself close to orgasm, so I suck her bottom lip into my mouth, moaning as she clenches around my cock.

A few seconds later, I rock into her one last time, releasing my load inside of her, being sure that she gets every last drop. I've never come so fucking hard in my life.

She drops her forehead to mine and grabs my face, looking into my eyes as we hold each other. Looking back at her, I feel an emotion rush through me that can hurt us both. Tonight everything is perfect, but what happens when we get back home and she goes back to her room and I get stuck going back to mine.

I don't want that. I want to spend the whole night, holding her in my arms, showing her that it's safe to let me.

We stay still for a while. Ten minutes. Maybe twenty. Doesn't matter. I'll stay here all night, looking at the stars with her, naked, in my lap.

Knowing that she most likely has to be up early though, I kiss her a few more times, before helping her back to her feet and helping her get dressed.

The way she watches me as I gather my own clothing, gives me hope that she wants me to spend the night in her room just as badly as I want to.

"Let's get you home, beautiful girl."

I secure her with the helmet, just like on the way here, and then help her onto the back of the bike.

Her arms come to wrap around me, holding me just as tightly as on the way here. Maybe even tighter.

Gives me more hope.

By the time we arrive back at the house, it's close to three in the morning. We're both exhausted, neither one of us jumping to speak.

We both stay quiet as I unlock the door and guide her inside and to her bedroom.

Without a word, I undress us both, before laying her on her bed and crawling in behind her, covering us up with the sheet.

Surprising me completely, she grabs both of my arms, holding me tightly as I rest my face into her neck, getting as close to her as our bodies will allow.

"Goodnight," I whisper.

She doesn't say anything back. Instead, she kisses my arm and buries her face in it.

Fuck... please tell me she won't regret this in the morning...

CHAPTER TWENTY-ONE

SAGE

FOR THE PAST WEEK, STONE has been crawling into my bed in the middle of the night and catering to my needs as if making me happy and pleasuring me is *his* only need.

It's been the best week of my life and the sex has been so intense that it's hard to breathe sometimes when he's inside of me.

The man is so good that it makes my heart ache just imagining us going back to how things were a few weeks ago. Back to just friends, when I avoided spending time with him, afraid to get too close.

It also makes my heart ache to imagine what it could be like to allow myself to keep falling deeper and deeper into his world and then have to possibly wake up without him each morning. It's easy to get too used to a good thing and then slowly die from pain and loss when it's no longer in reach.

I remember the feeling all too well, after depending on my brother for love and protection and then to have him ripped away from me without a choice.

I'm not going to lie... it scares the living shit out of me. Every day I continue to fall more and more for Stone, losing my strength to fight my feelings for him. It doesn't matter how many times I tell myself that I'm not falling in love with him.

I feel it in my heart and soul.

I find myself wanting to talk to him all day, every day. It's becoming routine to text each other every chance that we get, and I find myself waiting for his random pictures to pop up and brighten up my day.

We're beginning to feel more and more like a couple as each day passes and I have no clue how to feel about this or what to do.

"Hey, gorgeous ladies. Did ya miss me?"

My heart speeds up at the sound of Stone's voice as he enters the salon, greeting Aspen, Onyx, and myself.

"You know it. Us ladies are always happy to see you boys." Aspen smiles as he walks by, kissing her on the side of the head, before he heads over to greet Onyx.

"Hey, babe. You smell nice," Onyx quickly greets him, trying not to lose focus on her current client. "Tell me what that is later so I can make Hemy buy it."

"I'm sure his ass would love to smell like me," Stone jokes. "Is he still mad about his bike?"

Onyx laughs. "He's over it."

Smiling, he makes his way over to me, wrapping me in his strong arms and kissing me as if it's just so natural.

And it is.

Everything about us together just feels natural.

Keeping his arms around me, he picks me up and sets me on my table. "Jesus, you're damn beautiful." He steps between my legs and cups my face. "I wanted to stop in before I head to the club."

My arms instinctively wrap around his neck and pull him closer to me. I can't think when I'm around him. "Mmm..." I breathe. "You do smell nice. Sexy. I just want to eat you up."

He pulls my bottom lip into his mouth, roughly biting it, before releasing it. "Don't get my ass worked up right now, babe. It's bad enough I'll already be wanting to hurry home to see you."

I smile and slap his chest. "I'm nothing special to hurry home to."

"That's where you're wrong," he says against my lips. "You're very fucking special to me. All I can think about is being close to you. You've ruined me, Sage. Completely."

His words stop my heart and panic sets in.

Swallowing, I quickly kiss him on the lips, before jumping down to my feet. "My client just walked in." I force a smile, pretending with everything in me that his words had no effect on me. "Get your sexy ass out of here before you're late."

"I'll text you when I can." He grabs the back of my neck and firmly places a kiss on my lips. "Stop thinking too hard. Please."

I nod and watch him as he walks away. He's so beautiful and my eyes can't turn away from his muscled back and legs as he pushes the door open and steps outside.

I instantly feel a loss and my chest aches with need as he hops into his jeep and drives off.

The girls must notice my emotions going everywhere, because they both keep looking over at me with concern.

We don't get time to talk about it for another two hours, when the salon finally quiets down and we get a small break.

"I wish you wouldn't do this to yourself." Onyx walks over and grabs my face, forcing me to look up at her. "I can see your torment over Stone. You love him, don't you?"

Hearing Onyx say it out loud makes it even clearer how much I truly do love Stone. Maybe I have for a while now.

"I don't know what to do. I'm scared. You saw how I was when you found me in that diner. I was closed off and depressed. If I let Stone in and lose him... I'll be devastated."

"Honey," she says softly. "You've already let him in. And it's clear the way he feels about you. I've seen that look before." She smiles. "In Hemy's eyes every time he looks at me. I was scared too once. I left Hemy for years and it killed me. I love that man more than life itself and I spend nights thinking about everything I missed from being away from him for so long. You really just need some time to think things over."

"I agree," Aspen jumps in. "I love you and Stone together. I think you guys are truly meant to be together, but if you need time to think, take the time. Truly let your feelings work things out on their own. We're here for you if you need some time."

Onyx gives me a quick kiss and smiles at me. "I love you, woman. I haven't stopped yet. Give Stone the same faith you've given me since the beginning."

Everything they've said makes total sense. I really need to take the time to figure this all out, before we both get crushed.

Shit... Shit... Shit...

STONE

IT'S ALMOST CRAZY THE WAY that Sage hasn't left my mind once. She's fucking ruined me for anyone else and I honestly don't give two shits who knows.

I may even look like a pussy to the other *Walk of Shame* guys, but do you think that's going to stop me?

Whether that woman knows it or not, she owns me. My heart is hers to fucking break and I have a feeling that she might do just that.

I could see it in her eyes earlier when I told her how I felt.

She's scared. She's been crushed in the worst way possible in the past. Her and Hemy both.

I'm almost home now and I'm hoping with everything in me that Sage will want to spend the night in my arms, just as she has for the last week.

Everything changed that night in the field. Making love to her only made me fall deeper for her and want with everything in me to show her how much she truly means to me.

So far... things have been good. She hasn't kicked me out of her room at night and she's been texting me throughout the day.

Everything about the last week feels like we're in this together. Like we're a couple.

Fuck... I don't want this feeling to end.

I walk into the house and look around for Sage. She's not in bed and the whole house is completely dark.

"Fuck..." I growl out, while rushing to the back balcony, hoping with everything in me that she's still here.

Relief washes through me when I spot her through the glass door, holding a glass of wine.

She looks up from her chair with a small smile when I slide the door open.

"Hey," she whispers.

"Hey, babe." I take a seat at the bottom of her chair and place her legs on top of me. "You couldn't sleep?"

She shakes her head and grabs my hand. "I've been thinking all night. I'm not even tired."

Bringing her hand to my lips, I gently kiss it and then pull her into my lap. "You can talk to me, Sage. Please don't be afraid of me."

"It's so hard." She rests her cheek in my hand, when I reach up to cup it. "I'm trying so hard, but I'm scared of being hurt like I've been repeatedly. Having someone that you love abandon you is the worst feeling in the world."

A tear slides down her cheek, wetting my hand. It hurts so much to see her hurting. "Your parents didn't deserve you, Sage. Your father..." I pause, trying to figure out the best way to say the next part. "I would've killed him for the way he treated you. His fucking daughter. It's bullshit." My grip on her tightens. "And then he beat Hemy for trying to protect you. Your parents deserve to rot in hell for the shit you've both been through."

"Yeah... maybe so."

"There's no maybe about it, Sage. And your brother. He didn't leave you because he wanted to. It killed him when you two got separated. He was dead without you. Trust me. The only people who abandoned you by choice were the two people who didn't deserve you. I would *never* abandon you. I'd die before hurting you."

She wraps her arms around my neck, burying her face into my neck as the tears come out faster and harder now.

It's killing me inside right now and all I want to do is scream out to her that I love her.

"Stone..." She gently kisses my neck. "Will you come to bed with me? I just want you to hold me. Please."

I kiss the top of her head and then wipe my thumbs under her eyes to dry them. "Anything you ask."

Picking her up, I carry her inside and to my bedroom, laying her in my bed, before crawling in behind her.

I wrap my arms around her, pulling her as closely as I can possibly get her. "Did I ever tell you that my father was a drunk that abandoned me and my mother?"

She shakes her head and kisses my arm. "No. I'm sorry, Stone."

"Don't be. It was the best thing that could've happened to my family. He was an abusive piece of shit that hurt my mom every day. Sometimes the ones that don't deserve you are the ones that leave. Maybe a part of them knows that you deserve better than them. That's how I always looked at it."

"I guess that makes sense," she whispers against my arm. "I guess as a child it's just devastating when it happens. I've been trying to move on from it and let others in, but the fear is still there. The fear of being hurt like that again."

"I get it," I say honestly. As much as I hate to think that she can't trust me yet, I get why it's hard for her to let me in completely.

"Would you be okay with me staying with Jade for a few weeks?"

My heart fucking shatters at the thought of her not being here. It's almost hard to breathe.

"Yeah," I force out. "If you need time then I'll give it to you."

"Thank you." She squeezes my arm and then kisses it. "Goodnight, Stone."

"Goodnight, beautiful."

As much as I hope that her leaving for a few weeks will be enough to clear her head and really let me in, I'm also afraid that it might be enough space for her to forget me completely.

I can't let that happen...

CHAPTER TWENTY-TWO

STONE

SAGE HAS BEEN GONE FOR two weeks now and it's been eating at me that we haven't talked or spoken since that night.

I'm trying to be a man and give her the time and space that she needs, but every fucking day just gets harder and harder.

"Get out of your fucking head." Styx shoves a shot of whiskey in my face. "You need a few of these."

Wanting nothing more than to clear my thoughts for one fucking second of Sage, I slam the shot back and immediately reach for another as Sarah continues to poor them.

"Someone looks a little stressed," Sarah says with concern. "Just call her, Stone. I'm sure she's missing you just as much. Hell, she's probably waiting for you to call first. I know how women work."

"Nah." I shake my head and slam the second shot back. "Not her. She asked for space and I'm respecting that. If she missed me..." I grab another shot and slam it back, closing my eyes as the liquid slides down my throat, burning it. “She’d be back by now. Or hell… she’d at least text.”

Styx slaps my back and stands up. “She’ll be back. Drink up all you need to get that shit far from your head for now. I’ll drive your ass home when you’re ready.” He messes up my hair and laughs. “I got your back, bro.”

It’s been a long time since my ass has gotten wasted, but right now, I just need anything to make me stop thinking about Sage and trying to figure out what she’s been thinking since she’s been gone.

I’ve barely slept for shit since the night she packed up some of her shit and left. It’s like I keep thinking about how it’s going to play out when she decides to come back. Or *if* she comes back. Different shit plays out in my head every damn night.

I find myself drinking alone when Styx takes off to do his last private dance of the night.

That only makes shit worse, getting me lost in my fucked up thoughts again. Sarah’s been too busy to stay and talk to me for longer than a few minutes at a time.

Even she is beginning to look concerned with each shot I slam back as if it’s water or some shit.

“Okay…” She cleans around my half empty beer, before tossing the towel over her shoulder and meeting my eyes. “You’ve been sitting here in this same spot for the last two hours, slamming back shot after shot. You’re beginning to look like some fucking loser, Stone. That’s not you. You’re far from a loser and an asshole.”

I close my eyes and take a deep breath, slowly releasing it. I’m fully aware that I probably look like some drunken idiot at the moment, but I just can’t seem to give a shit. “I’m fine.”

“No, the fuck you aren’t.” She looks pissed when she gets called away to help a group of women. “Drink this water. Got it. Dammit!”

Feeling pissed off at my damn self, I drink the water that Sarah threw in front of me and then sit here with my head in my hands.

I stay like this for at least ten minutes, just staring down at my bottle.

“Hey, you.” I finally look up when someone sits down beside me and brushes my arm. It’s the brunette from a few weeks ago. “You’re looking a little lonely over here.”

I offer her a faint smile, not wanting to be a dick after what she did for me after her private dance that night. “I guess you can say I have a lot on my mind."

She takes a sip of her mixed drink and looks me over, checking me out. "I saw you from across the bar and thought you could use some company. I'm surprised no other women jumped to the opportunity before me."

I don't. It's the last thing that I fucking need, but I'm so drunk right now that I'm afraid I'll say something to upset her or piss her off.

So I just nod and tilt back my beer.

"You never called me," she says softly. "I was hoping you would. You just seem so different than most of the men I know. Fun and carefree. I liked that about you."

Trying to get my thoughts in check, I run my hands through my hair and release a breath. I really can't deal with this shit right now. There's too much going on in my head now. "There's a woman that I love and I've been chasing her for over a fucking year. She's the only girl I would've called. Sorry. It's nothing personal."

She looks disappointed but offers me a small understanding smile anyway. "She's one lucky girl to have *you* chasing her. Where is she?"

I run my thumb over my beer, before tilting it back again. I wish I knew more than anything right now. "I don't know."

That shit burns. Even in my drunken state.

"I'm sorry to hear that." She stands up and places her hands on my face as if to comfort me. "A man like you deserves a woman that will never want to be away from you."

I close my eyes and some fucked up part of me wants to pretend that it's Sage's hands on my face.

Maybe it's because I'm completely fucking drunk at this point and would do anything to be with her.

"I would love to spend my time with you."

Before I know it, her lips are on mine and she's pushing her way in between my legs.

Her hands tangle in the back of my hair, pulling me close to her as she runs her tongue along my bottom lip.

It takes me a few seconds to react, before I pull away from her kiss and remove her hands from my face. "I'm not available," I say stiffly. "Fuck!"

Panic sets in at the realization that another woman's lips have been on mine since Sage's. Even though I didn't want it, it feels like I've just fucking cheated.

The fucked up part is that we're not even a couple. Fuck, I don't even know if she's coming back or not.

"I'm sorry." She backs away and grabs her purse. "I didn't know. It sounded like..."

"It's not your fault." I feel guilty as fuck right now. Guilty that another woman kissed me other than Sage and guilty that I've made this woman feel like total shit. "I'm drunk and shit just isn't coming out right."

I call Sarah over. She watches me hard, as if she's waiting for what's about to come out of my mouth. I'm not taking this woman home if that's what she fucking thinks. "Please take care of her for me. Bill me later. I need to get my ass out of here and chill out."

Sarah gives me a smile as if she's proud of me or some shit. Hell, maybe she is. A lot of men in my situation *would* jump at the opportunity of taking another woman home.

That's not me. Not when I know what I truly want.

Needing to get away from all the chaos in the bar and calm down, I make my way to the locker room and pull out my phone.

Everything in me wants to text Sage and tell her how much I miss her and want her to come home.

"Fuck!" I punch the wall and then toss my phone aside.

I'm giving her a few more days. I really don't know if I can give her more.

Twenty minutes later, Styx comes in sweaty and out of breath. "Fuck, dude. You look rough as shit."

"I'm just ready to get the fuck out of here."

"I gotcha. I'll take a quick shower. Just calm your dick and relax a bit."

When Styx drops me off at home, I instantly feel the loss when stepping into the dark, empty house.

I find myself sitting outside on the back balcony until well past five in the morning, just thinking about Sage and how we used to sit out here together.

This shit is even harder than I expected...

CHAPTER TWENTY-THREE

SAGE

IT'S BEEN EXACTLY EIGHTEEN DAYS since I've seen or spoken to Stone now and it's really starting to break me down and wear at my emotions.

I thought leaving would be a good idea and it was. Not because I wanted to be away from Stone, but because a part of me needed to know how much being away from him would kill me.

Being away has shown me just how strong my need for him truly is. It's shown me that it hurts to not hear his voice or see his beautiful face every day.

Now... now I just need to figure out if I'm strong enough to give in to my feelings for him, knowing now that losing him will hurt like hell.

If it hurts this much already, I can't even imagine having him as mine and then losing him completely as a partner, roommate, and friend.

I spent the first week at Jade's house after I left, but being there just hurt. Especially since all Jade kept talking about was how she wants to go back to the club to see Kash.

Thinking about Kash or Styx only makes me think about Stone even more. I figured she would get that, but her excitement just made her overlook that little fact.

So, I've been here at Hemy's and Onyx's for the last eleven days now, hoping that spending time with family will help me feel less alone. It does, but not enough.

I threatened Hemy's big ass and made sure he promised me that he wouldn't talk about Stone or tell Stone that I'm staying with them until I'm ready.

He's been pretty good so far, although I can tell he wants talk about it. I think it's finally the time for it, because Stone seems to be the only thing I can think about lately and it's slowly killing me to not get some things off my chest.

Onyx has been asleep for the last two hours, so when the kitchen light turns on, I know that it's Hemy.

Hoping that I can handle talking to him about Stone, I make my way to the kitchen and take a seat at one of the stools.

"Hey, big brother."

Hemy gives me a tired smile and kisses the side of my head. "What are you doing awake? Don't you work in like five hours?"

I nod and watch him tilt back a bottle of water. "Yeah... I haven't been sleeping much lately."

"I've noticed and I fucking hate it. Ready to talk about it?" He takes a seat next to me and pulls my stool close to him. "I'm awake until you're good to sleep. Got it."

I take a deep breath and slowly release it. As much as I've been putting it off, I think I need Hemy's advice to move forward.

"I'm scared." I grab his arm and hug it, like how I used to do when we were kids... before we got separated. "I care about Stone so much that the thought of losing him kills me. I remember what it felt like to lose you all those years ago. I couldn't function right for years. What if the same thing happens if I lose Stone?"

He wraps his arm around me and releases a breath. "I wish I could tell you how you will feel if that ever happens, but I can't. I also wish I could tell you it would never happen, but I can't do that either. The one thing I can tell you is that I will always love you and you'll always have me to fall on for support. I will *never* leave you again. Nothing will ever separate us. No matter what happens in the future; you will never be alone, Sage. That's a fucking promise."

He stops to kiss the side of my head again. "I don't know what will happen with you and Stone, but I can tell you that he loves the shit out of you and he's hurting just as much as you are. I may give him shit, but he's a good fucking man and I know he'll treat you like you deserve. I trust him."

I find myself smiling at the fact that he just admitted what he did. Hemy doesn't trust many people. "You do?"

"Fuck yes, I do. He's one of the few, Sage. That says a lot."

"I love him," I whisper. "A lot."

"I know you do," he whispers back. "It's obvious as shit and it's killing you to be away from him. Now, you just need to let him know it."

I close my eyes and my chest instantly aches at the idea that I could possibly be too late. "It's been over two weeks, Hemy. What if he's given up and moved on already? He's a guy and I know how those fuckers work."

Hemy gives me a small squeeze. "He hasn't. Trust me."

"How do you know?"

"I talked to Sarah a few days ago..."

My heart begins to beat like crazy in my chest as I wait for him to continue.

"She said that Stone got completely fucking trashed a few days ago."

"And..." I push, my heart now beating even faster, afraid of what might come next.

"Some girl kissed him and he pushed her away. Most guys that have moved on, would not push some hot chick away. He'd be taking her ass home and fucking her. We both know it."

The thought of another girl's lips on his kills me. It stings like hell, but the fact that he pushed her away, makes my heart happy.

God, I love that man.

He really is something else. He's different.

"That fucker is something else," Hemy says, surprising me. "You should go back home and put you both out of misery. I can't stand to see you both moping around, hurting and shit."

I smile at him when he stands up and yawns. "Thank you for everything. Talking to you somehow always makes me feel better."

He smiles back at me and tiredly rubs his face. "That's what big brothers are for. Right?" He winks and then pulls me in for a tight hug, holding me there for a few minutes. "Love you, Sage."

"I love you too, my big crazy as hell brother." I laugh into his chest.

"Damn straight." He releases me and walks out of the kitchen, toward the stairs. "Goodnight. Get some sleep now."

"Goodnight," I yell back.

I spend the next hour replaying our whole conversation in my head and trying to decide what I'm going to do now.

Whatever it is that I decide needs to happen fast. I've put things off for far too long now and it's hurting the both of us.

My next move could either hurt us more or bring us together.

That scares the hell out of me...

CHAPTER TWENTY-FOUR

STONE

YESTERDAY MADE THREE WEEKS SINCE Sage took off and I spent the whole night waiting for her to come home or at least call me and tell me that she wasn't.

I barely slept for shit, because I kept checking my phone every damn hour to see if I missed anything from her.

Not a damn thing and I came close to just throwing my phone and breaking it so that I would stop.

I've decided that I'm giving her until tonight and then I'm going after her. I don't care if she gets pissed. She asked for a few weeks and I gave it to her.

She needs to know exactly how I feel about her.

"Stone! Wait up, fucker."

I look over to see Kage coming at me. "You have one more private show booked for tonight. Cale told me to have you stay and work it."

"Are you fucking serious? Shit!"

Staying here even longer than I have to is not what the fuck I want to be doing right now.

I was thirty minutes away from getting my ass out of here to go after Sage, and now having to put on a private show will add at least close to an hour to that shit.

"Sorry, man. Your private door is fucked up right now too, so Cale has someone coming in tomorrow afternoon to fix it. Go through the client's door in about ten minutes so you can beat them there."

"Alright, shit. I'm going to take a quick shower then and get this fucking sticky shit off of me. One of the girls spilled her drink down my leg when I picked her up in their chair earlier. I haven't had a free minute since."

"I hear ya, man. Go get that shit cleaned off and hurry. I'll try to hold your client off."

Frustrated as hell, I hurry into the locker room and take a quick shower, before heading into my private room.

It's completely dark and if I'm not mistaken, I see a body move from on the stage in front of what looks to be a pole.

When the fuck did my private room get a pole?

It's too dark to see, but I even smell some sweet perfume. I'm definitely not alone in here and fuck me, they smell like Sage. I'd recognize that sweet smell from anywhere.

Out of nowhere, "Close" by Nick Jonas begins playing over the speakers and the stage lights up enough for me to see Sage, standing there looking completely sexy as fuck.

Standing with her back against the pole, she brings one arm back to wrap around it, and slowly lowers her body down the pole, while rubbing her other hand down the center of her body, over the black lace. Once she gets close to the ground, she spreads her knees apart and lowers her hand some more, biting her bottom lip as she touches herself through the fabric.

My cock instantly hardens as she watches me with a seductive look in her eyes as if she wants nothing more than to make love to me right here.

Fuck, I want that more than anything right now and it's going to take everything in me not to take her right here, right now.

She sways her hips to the rhythm of the music, releasing the pole, and wrapping her hands in her hair, tugging as she makes her way back up the pole in a stance.

I can't take my fucking eyes off of her. It's been a long time since I've seen her dance. But watching her now, brings me back to the beginning when I first saw her on the stage at *Vixens* and wanted nothing more than to just taste her body.

I want to taste it now.

Slowly turning around, she wraps one leg around the pole and arches her back, swinging her long hair around, before gripping the pole and spinning around it, seductively. Her moves are so smooth and in control that you would never think that she stopped dancing over a year ago.

She spins around a few times, moving seductively to the music, before releasing the pole, walking to the edge of the small stage, and reaching for the ribbon that's holding her black corset together.

Keeping her eyes on me, she lowers herself to the surface of the stage, down to her ass, and spreads her legs wide apart, revealing the sheer, black lace that's in between.

Biting her bottom lip, she slightly tugs the ribbon, opening her top a little more, and rolling her hips up and down with her back pressed against the stage.

Out of instinct, I reach out and run my hands up her legs, pulling her to me. Breathing heavily, I lean in to her ear. "Fuck, I missed you." I brush her hair behind her ear and gently kiss up her neck. "You're so fucking beautiful, Sage. I'm glad you're here."

She grips my hair with both hands and places her forehead against mine. "I'm not going to lie. I missed you too, Stone. Not a minute went by that I didn't want to come back home and be with you."

Her words cause relief to wash through me. I've waited for what feels like forever to hear those words and I was beginning to think that I lost her completely. "I'm still waiting," I whisper. "I haven't gone anywhere."

With desperation, she presses her lips against mine and wraps her arms so tightly around my neck that it almost hurts.

It's almost as if she was afraid of losing me too.

I love the feeling. This feeling right here is so worth the last three weeks of suffering that I went through without her.

Fuck, I love her so much.

Standing up, I pick her up with me, walking over to press her back against the wall.

Holding her up with my hips, I tangle my hands in her hair and kiss her deep and hard, causing her to moan into my mouth.

"Fuck, Sage. I'm trying so hard not to be rough with you right now, but I'm fucking dying to be inside you right now."

"I never asked you to be gentle," she whispers against my lips. "Fuck me like you love me."

With force, I press my hips into her and growl against her mouth. "I do... fucking love you."

Her grip on me tightens and her eyes widen as she looks up at me. "Do you mean that? I mean... are you sure? I just left for three –"

"Hell yes, I mean it, Sage. You could leave me for a year and it wouldn't change the fact that you're the only woman I've ever loved."

"Are you sure you want to love me?" she asks with fear in her eyes.

I hate that look.

"More than anything in this fucking world," I say firmly.

With urgency, I rip her panties off, before sliding my jeans down my hips and pushing into her hard and deep.

She moans out and digs her nails into my back, hard. So hard that there's no doubt that I'm bleeding right now.

"Oh shit, Stone..." she breathes into my ear. "I've missed you inside of me. I've missed us. You have no idea."

"Oh, I do. Trust me." I slowly pull out of her, before slamming back into her and stilling. "I missed us too, baby. Everything about us. Don't ever fucking leave me again. Please."

"I won't," she breathes. "Because I love you too."

"Oh fuck..." My grip on her tightens and my body becomes desperate to take her as deeply as I can. I can't get enough of the beautiful woman right now. "Best news I've heard in my entire life. That's the truth."

I kiss her deep and hard, while continuing to thrust inside of her for what feels like hours. We're completely covered in sweat now, but there's no way I'm stopping.

Pulling away from her lips, I wrap my hand around her throat and push myself deeper inside of her, causing her to shake in my arms. "Fuck, I only want this with you." I pull her bottom lip into my mouth and bite into as I start thrusting hard and fast again, pushing her up the wall with each movement.

I reach down and grab her hands, binding them in one hand, and raising them above her head. Both of us are breathing heavy, me holding her hands above her head while holding her up with my opposite arm supporting her waist.

"Me too, Stone. Oh fuck!" She pulls back on my hair as I push into her one last time, feeling my orgasm build before I release myself deep inside her.

Not even seconds later, she's shaking in my arms, her own orgasm causing her to scream out my name and yank on my hair.

I hold her in my arms for as long as I can, before setting her down on the leather couch and dropping to my knees in front of her.

"You ready to go home now?" I kiss the side of her head, before kissing her lips. "Please fucking say yes."

I sound desperate, but I don't give a shit right now. I am desperate.

She wraps her arms around me and buries her face into my sweaty neck. "There's nowhere else I want to be. I'm miserable without your cocky ass and your dick pics."

We both smile, before bursting into laughter.

This woman truly is perfect for me and I'm taking her home where she belongs.

WE SPEND THE REST OF the night outside on the back balcony, her in my arms as we just talk about life and joke around.

When you have the *Walk of Shame* crew in your life, there's plenty of shit to talk about and laugh over.

I've never smiled so much in my life than I do when I'm with Sage. She's everything I could ask for in my life and more.

I have a feeling that we'll be spending a lot of long nights out here, looking at the stars and getting to know everything about each other.

Now that I have her heart, you're damn straight that I'll be doing everything in my power to keep it and show her how much I truly love her.

I smile when I look down to see her falling asleep in my arms. She's practically holding onto to me for dear life as if she never wants to let go.

Well, I never want her to and she'll never have to...

CHAPTER TWENTY-FIVE

SAGE

THREE WEEKS LATER . . .

STYX HAS BEEN RUNNING AROUND the backyard, fighting anyone who even dares to go close to the precious grill.

It's Stone's fucking grill and even he's not allowed to touch it, without getting Styx's wrath.

"Damn, that man's fucking crazy when he's cooking. The asshole threw a hot ass hot dog at my lip." He touches his lip as if it hurts. "Remind me not to invite his ass next time.

I can't help but to laugh as Stone takes a seat beside me and looks over at Styx manning the grill and guarding it with his life.

"Next time we'll have to tie him up so he won't be able to go near it. How about that?" I tease, while gently kissing his bottom lip.

"Hell. No." He pulls me into his lap and kisses me, harder. "He'd like it way too much being tied up. Trust me. Not happening."

Styx must be listening to our conversation, because when I look up at him, he winks and takes a bite of a kabob. He somehow makes it look extremely sexy. Must be a Walk of Shame thing.

"I think you're right." I laugh.

"Fuck yeah, he is, babe." Styx opens the grill and begins flipping the food. "But I'll still let you if you want. His ass might like to watch."

"Fuck off, asshole, before I stab your dick with that temperature fork. We'll see what the hell you can do with your dick after that."

"What the fuck?" Styx growls. "That shit isn't even cool." He covers his dick and goes back to catering to the food.

The boys continue to banter back and forth, Kash somehow finding a way to jump in and rile them up even more.

I swear I don't know what to do with them some days.

Hemy and Onyx arrive, grabbing my attention and not even ten minutes later Cale, Riley, and baby Haven show up.

Slade, Aspen, and Kash have been here since even before the food started cooking and Sarah should be arriving here soon too.

Slade and Aspen somehow managed to slip away to who knows where over twenty minutes ago, but no one has bothered to look. As long as they clean up their mess when they're done, then they're welcome to go as crazy as they want.

It's the Fourth of July so Cale and Aspen made plans to shut down their businesses for the day so that we could all be here together.

It makes my heart so happy to have us all here in one place. It never gets to happen anymore and I miss it more than I even knew.

These people are my family and the more time I spend with them, the more I love them and grow to trust them.

Especially Stone. I never thought I'd ever be able to trust a man as much as I do my brother, but Stone just continues to prove me wrong with each and every day.

The truth is, he's been showing me for over a year now. I was just too blind to see it, afraid of getting myself hurt.

We've officially been a couple for three weeks now and there's no doubt in my mind that I made the right decision by letting him in.

There's no way I'll be running off to be away from him again.

I just have to make sure that I continue to show him that.

I'm quickly learning that I love him more than I could've ever imagined...

"Are you fucking crazy? My shit never gets old. Let's go right now and have the girls judge."

When I look away from talking with the girls, Stone is standing on top of the picnic table, looking as if he's ready to strip down to his boxer briefs.

"Get your ass down," Slade complains, when he finally reappears with Aspen under his arm. "No one wants to see you shake your dick."

"Thank fucking goodness." Kash throws his empty soda can Stone's way. "We're not at the club. I want to take the night and enjoy the sight of anything *but* Stone and Styx's dicks swinging."

Stone smirks and jumps down from the table. "Alright... It's not like we need to dance to prove who's better anyway. I'll save you dicks some embarrassment."

Hemy looks away from baby Haven laying in his huge arms. She's looks like a baby doll compared to Hemy. "Come on, fuckers. There's a baby here."

Onyx slaps Hemy's leg and then leans in to bite his neck. "Yeah, so watch your mouth, big guy."

"Hey, bitches!"

Everyone looks over at the sound of Sarah's voice. She pokes her head through the fence and laughs, before walking in and guiding some chick with her.

"Hey, babe." I smile when Sarah entwines her fingers with the girl and pulls her close to her side. "Who's your friend?"

Sarah seems to have everyone's attention now.

"Stop staring and shit, jeez." Sarah grabs the girl by the back of the head and presses her lips against hers. Then she turns around to face us. "My date. Now you've seen us kiss." She points to the guys. "So don't even bother asking us to do it again and stare like idiots."

The guys seem pretty impressed with Sarah's taste and I definitely don't blame them. This chick is hot.

I guess there's a lot about Sarah that I don't know yet.

"Congrats on the book, babe." Sarah kisses my cheek and then introduces me to Kendal.

Kendal seems really nice and interested in what my books are about. I already like this chick.

Time seems to fly by after we eat and by the time eight o'clock rolls around, everyone is playing cornhole and waiting for it to get dark enough to shoot off fireworks.

I'm just about to take my turn, when Stone picks me up from behind and starts twirling me around.

"Stop!" I laugh and slap his hands, until he puts me down and kisses me. "Stop trying to make me dizzy so you and Styx win. Not cool!"

He smiles against my lips, before pressing his lips to mine and smothering me in his strong arms. "You know I don't play fair," he says against my neck.

Sarah whistles from across the yard at us. "Come on you two!"

Stone pulls away and cups my face in his hands. His face lights up as the fireworks begin shooting off above us. "I love you," he says loudly enough for me to hear.

Hearing him say those three words still makes my heart go just as crazy as it did when he said them three weeks ago.

I don't think I'll ever get tired of those words coming from his beautiful lips.

This man has become my world...

STONE

"I LOVE YOU, TOO. SO damn much and I don't plan on stopping anytime soon, Stone."

Forgetting all about the game, I pull her against me and hold her tightly, as we watch the firework display above us.

It's so fucking beautiful and having her here in my arms only makes the moment that much more perfect. I honestly couldn't ask for anything better right now.

Not to mention that our whole family is here to enjoy it with us.

It somehow just makes it feel that much more complete.

By the time the fireworks are over, everyone has pretty much forgotten about the game and any other activity everyone was involved in.

We all somehow find our way around the fire pit, roasting marshmallows and telling stories and jokes.

Styx attempts to tell a drunken story that he claims to be true, but that somehow turns into a joke too, everyone laughing and making fun of him for hours.

We don't end up making it inside until well after midnight and I have to admit that I've been dying to get Sage alone and hold her in some peace and quiet.

Sage doesn't waste any time stripping down to her sheer top that I love so much and a pair of panties, before grabbing a blanket and making her way outside on the balcony.

I strip down myself getting damn excited to finally be close to her, now that everyone's gone.

When I follow her outside, she pulls me down onto the lounge chair, between my legs and kisses my arm.

Getting comfortable, I cup her face in my hands and press my forehead to hers. "Do you have any idea how much I love you?"

She nods her head and laughs. "I have a pretty good idea, but I won't mind if you continue to keep reminding me, daily." She smiles against my lips, before kissing me, hard as if she's missed me all day. "Lay down with me. There's still random fireworks going off. I want to enjoy them with only you."

Shifting us around, so that she's positioned between my legs, I securely wrap my arms around her and just hold her.

As much as I love making love to her, holding her in moments like this means so much more at times.

It reminds me that what we have is deeper and I plan to make that last with everything in me.

This woman has my heart in her hands and I don't plan on asking for it back...

STYX

WALK OF SHAME : BOOK 5

CHAPTER ONE

STYX

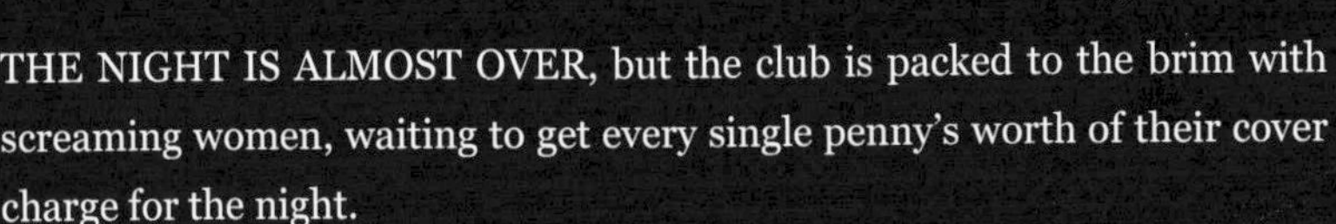

THE NIGHT IS ALMOST OVER, but the club is packed to the brim with screaming women, waiting to get every single penny's worth of their cover charge for the night.

I don't think I've ever danced so much in the whole time that I've been working at *Walk of Shame*. It's fucking insane tonight and to be honest, I can't wait to be out of here so I can think straight.

"Over here, Styx!"

"Bring your sexy ass to us and take it off!"

"Huuuurrryyy! Now!"

A group of women over in the VIP lounge, wave their money at me and whistle for me to come over to the couch as if I'm their little pet.

I've gotten used to it, but sometimes it makes me wish that I could go one night without all the screaming, whistling, and groping.

I can't even count how many times my cock has been groped and pulled on in the year that I've been here.

Lowering my jeans down my waist a bit, I straddle the lap of the closest woman in my reach and grind my hips against her, while gripping her hair, like I would if we were actually fucking.

Hands reach into my jeans, tugging in between our bodies, and fighting to shove money inside as close to my dick as they can.

One even shoves her hand in far enough to almost grab my balls.

This has me standing up from the first woman's lap and picking this new girl upside down to grind my crotch in her face.

She wants to grab my shit, then I'll pound her face with it and give her a taste of what she won't be getting tonight.

Squirming in my arms, she grabs onto my thighs and laughs as I gently bite her leg, before turning her around and setting her back on her feet.

Smiling, she places a twenty between her teeth and then bends down in front of me to shove it into the top of my jeans.

Hands grope at my ass and squeeze, my jeans immediately being ripped away, when I step out of them to get down to only my white boxer briefs.

Laughing, Sarah comes up out of nowhere and throws a pitcher of water at me, soaking myself and the women hanging on me.

This causes the crowd of women to scream and go crazy, enjoying the very visible view of my cock through the white fabric, as I fuck the air fast and hard.

Sarah lifts a brow and looks down at my dick bouncing. "You can thank my ass later, big guy."

Shaking my head, I wink at Sarah, as money comes flying from all around me, women desperate to get as good a view as they can.

I notice two women come at me at the same time, before I hear yelling and see the taller of the two girls reach for the other one's hair, yanking her down to the ground.

Kage seems to be too preoccupied with trying to get laid to notice, so I yank the taller girl away from the girl on the ground and throw her over my shoulder, stalking toward the door.

She immediately takes this as an invite to shove both her hands down the back of my wet briefs and squeeze my ass as I walk.

Lane grips my arm as I walk past him to get outside. "Another female behaving badly or is your ass trying to escape to go get laid?"

I bump him with my shoulder, too annoyed to answer his dumbass question. I need to get this woman off me so I can get this night over with. "Move," I growl, as I walk past him and into the grass.

With quickness, I pull her off me and set her back down to her feet. She just laughs and reaches for my dick as if I didn't just kick her out of the club.

She thinks this is all fun and games, but I don't take someone getting attacked around me as a fucking joke.

I yank her hands away from my dick and help her down to the ground so she won't fall over. "A cab will be called for you. Sit here and don't move."

Her eyes widen in disbelief when she realizes what just happened and that I'm about to leave her here. "Where are you going?" she yells at my back.

"Make sure she gets in a cab," I tell Lane as I walk past him and back into the loudness of the club.

Taking a second to breathe, I glance over at Kage to see him hold five fingers up. Five minutes. Five more fucking minutes and this night from stripper hell is over.

My ass is about ready to fall over from exhaustion, but these women need to leave here satisfied and ready to come back each week and it's my job to make sure that happens.

Nodding my head at Kage, I rush over to the other side of the room, where Kash is upside down on a chair, thrusting his hips in some girl's face.

Picking some random woman that catches my eye, I pull her chair away from the table and pick her up, so that her legs are wrapped around my waist.

I place her hands on my chest and run them down my body, while I move my hips against her to the music.

She covers her face with her free hand, embarrassed.

Not wanting to get mixed up in the crowd again for the night, I focus my attention on the brunette in my arms, until the last song finally ends.

I'm standing here completely drenched now, half-naked and sweating my ass off.

Kage, Kass, and Lane must notice how much tonight has kicked our asses, because they make their way through the crowd and start clearing out the room, being sure to keep the women at a distance from us.

"Holy fuck!" Kash runs past me, naked, holding a wet shirt over his junk. "This is the busiest night we've ever fucking had here. I need a few shots after this."

"No shit," I bite out. "Three different bachelorette parties this weekend and they all decided to come on the same night."

Stone emerges from the crowd, with Sage wrapped around his waist. He's soaking wet like me and Kash, but Sage couldn't care less.

She just grips onto his face, pulling him in for a kiss and letting every other girl in the room know that they can look, and maybe even touch, but she's the only one he's going home with.

They're closer than ever and I'm happy as hell for them.

After all they've been through, they deserve it.

Now to get the hell out of here before Kash tries dragging me out tonight...

AFTER THE LATE NIGHT I spent at *Walk of Shame*, shaking my dick for money, all I really want is a moment of quiet and some time to pull my thoughts together.

To be away from the screeching sounds of women screaming and hands clinging to my every muscle, desperate to touch anything of me they can.

As fun as it is to have it so fucking easy, and know that I can have any girl that I desire, I want more than that. More than a quick fuck with a woman that simply wants me because I'm a popular male entertainer with a big cock.

I may give off the impression that I'm a manwhore that takes any hot woman to bed, but there's so much more to me than that. What I'm looking for can't be found inside the walls of a male strip club.

I'm a giver and when I find that right woman, I'm giving her everything that I fucking have in me. Seeing Stone and Sage together only makes me want that more.

Until then...

A knock sounds at the door of my office, and right away, I know who is on the other side.

It's a twenty-four-hour gym, but there's only one person that ever comes between the hours of two and three a.m.

Sophie Miller.

Standing up, I rub my hands down my face and walk over to unlock the door for her.

I may be tired and stressed as all hell, but having sex with Sophie distracts my mind for a few hours, at least twice a month.

She works late nights at another club and passes the gym on the way home, usually stopping if she sees my motorcycle parked outside.

Smiling, Sophie makes her way into my office, when I open the door for her. “Rough night?” She looks me over, her eyes filled with lust and need.

“Yeah,” I breathe. “Fucking exhausted.”

Dropping to her knees in front of me, she grips the button of my jeans and looks up at me with desperate blue eyes. “Hopefully not too exhausted. I need this.”

Placing my bodyweight against the desk, I grab onto her red hair with both hands and close my eyes as she twirls her tongue around the head of my cock.

She takes me halfway in her mouth a few times, before attempting to fully take me in, but ends up choking on my length.

As much as I’m enjoying her mouth on me, I don’t have the patience or strength tonight to be here for hours.

“Stand up,” I command. “Bend over my desk and hold on tight.”

Without hesitation, Sophie stands up and bends over my desk, spreading her legs for me.

With force, I yank her jeans down, along with her panties, and slap her bare ass.

“You in a hurry tonight or something?” she questions, while squeezing the desk. “I didn’t even get to finish.”

“Yeah. It’s been a long night. I was just about to leave before you showed up.”

She reaches behind her and strokes my cock a few times. “Let’s go then.”

Pushing her head down on my desk, I pull out a condom and slip it on, before slamming into her, letting my frustration out.

With each hard thrust, she grips onto the desk, knocking things over and reaching for anything close enough for her to grab.

“Oh shit, Styx! You seem a lot more stressed than usual.”

“’Cause I am.” Gripping her throat, I choke her from behind, taking her as deep as I can, not stopping until I feel myself ready to come.

Moaning, I pull out and release myself in the condom, taking a few deep breaths, before yanking the condom off, tossing it, and pulling my jeans back up.

Now I'm not one to go quickly and especially without getting my partner off first, but I just can't find it in me to give a shit tonight.

Sophie comes to stand in front of me, once she's redressed herself. "You really need to take a week off for a vacation or something and just focus on the gym and maybe... I don't know... fucking me more than just twice a month. I'm sure we both can relieve a lot of stress then."

Fighting to catch my breath, I kiss the top of her head, because I'm not a completely heartless ass. I may not want anything emotional with her, but she's not trash.

Just not the *one* for me.

"Yeah, I'll keep that in mind." I walk her to the door. "Be careful on your way home. It's late and people are crazy. Call the gym if anyone messes with you."

She nods and smiles. "I always am. Got my mace handy at all times."

After letting Sophie out, I hang around the gym for about another hour, get a workout in and then head home for the night.

I'm off my shit tonight. Something just seems to be missing...

CHAPTER TWO

MEADOW

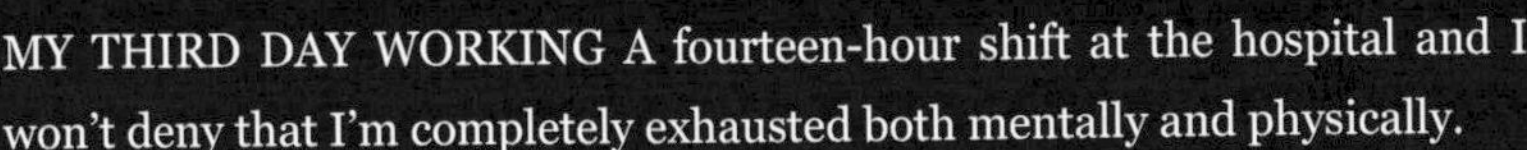

MY THIRD DAY WORKING A fourteen-hour shift at the hospital and I won't deny that I'm completely exhausted both mentally and physically.

I love my job. I do, but sometimes it can just take so much out of you. You give so much and put your heart into everything that you do here, that you honestly don't have much of a life outside of taking care of patients and worrying about how they're doing when you're not around to take care of them.

I let out a small breath, and stand to my feet, when the call light from room 316 goes off for the third time in an hour.

"I've got it," I tell Mandy. "He's only going to ask for me anyway."

She lets out a tiny laugh and continues on with her business on the computer. "He always does. I don't even bother anymore when you're here."

"I don't blame you."

Walking into Henry's room, I stop next to his bed and place my hand over his bruised one. "Anything I can help you with, Henry?"

He shakes his head and mutters at the TV mounted on the wall. "What is this garbage? It's been on all darn day."

I follow his eyes up to the TV and laugh. He always knows how to entertain the staff. "It wasn't on when I came in here about twenty minutes ago." Smiling, I hand the remote within his reach and point at the channel buttons. "You do know that this hospital has more than one channel right, Henry?"

He squeezes my hand and gives me a charming smile, although his dentures aren't in. "It makes an old guy happy when a pretty nurse is around to take care of him. It's about as much action as I can get these days."

"Oh I'm sure a guy like you can find a beautiful woman to take on a date. You'll be out in a few days, once your leg heals." I grab the remote from Henry and flip the channel to something that he might understand better and be more familiar with. "There you go. All set. Now I get off in twenty minutes, so Mandy and Kayla will be here to take care of you. Be nice to them. Don't let me hear that you're refusing your meds from them again."

He throws his arm up, waving me off. "They're not you."

Smiling, I pat his hand and start walking toward the door. "Yeah, well I can't be here twenty-four-seven. So behave yourself, old man."

"Yeah. Yeah."

Right as I'm walking out of Henry's room and closing the door just enough to give Henry some privacy, Jase winks at me and grabs my hand, pulling me around the corner and out of view.

Jase is probably about the most attractive male nurse that works here. As much as I try not to be physically attracted to one of my co-workers, you'd have to be blind not to notice him.

"Meet me in twenty by my car?" he whispers next to my ear. "I parked next to you again."

"Not tonight, Jase. I have a date with a new gym and I have *a lot* of stress to work off."

Jase looks around to make sure that no one is watching, before he slips his hand around my waist and pulls me closer to him. "I've been thinking about fucking you all day. It's been three weeks now. Take that crap out on me."

Lifting a brow, I place my hand on his firm chest and lightly push him away from me. "Yeah, well if I remember correctly, there's a few other nurses that have been keeping you quite busy. No thanks. I'm good."

Jase shakes his head and backs away from me, when Mandy walks over. He tries to play it off as if he wasn't just trying to get into my pants, but the look Mandy gives me, tells me that she picked up on it.

"What did Henry want this time?" she asks with a grin.

"For me to change the channel for him." I give Jase one last look, before walking off with Mandy and listening to her tell a story about one of the other patients.

By the time I get done cleaning everything up and saying goodbye to my patients, I'm so tired that I consider just skipping the gym and checking it out another day.

But to be honest, I need to work off some stress and Jase won't be helping with that anymore.

BY THE TIME I MAKE it to the gym, and change into my gear, it's well past midnight. There's only a few other people in the gym, one of them on the treadmill next to me and the other two, lifting weights.

The two lifting weights keep looking my way, talking loudly about my *fine ass*, but I ignore them and try my best to not give them a piece of my mind. As if they can't make it any more obvious what they want to do to me. Not happening.

After thirty minutes on the treadmill, I look around me to see that the guys are still watching me, so I give up on the treadmill and decide to move somewhere more private where I can have a moment to let my emotions out.

There's no one back there to see just how much stress and pent-up anger that I really have and if I stay here with these ogling jerkoffs then I'm going to end up taking my frustration out on them and not in a good way.

Slamming back some water, I take a few seconds to catch my breath, before shutting myself in the other room and grabbing the end of the battle ropes.

Gripping tightly onto the ropes, I start out with some power slams, before moving onto some outside circles. I move for as long as I can, until my muscles ache and lungs burn as I fight for air.

Then I toss the ends of the rope down and let out a small scream of anger and relief.

I don't even realize that I'm no longer alone, until I look up at the wall mirror and see a muscular guy with blond hair and striking blue eyes.

His arms are crossed and he's leaning against the doorframe as if he's completely comfortable just watching me.

"How long have you been there?" I question out of breath.

He lifts a brow and steps into the room when I reach for my *Swig Savvy* water bottle, just to be reminded that it's empty.

"Here." He holds out a bottle of water. "Long enough to see that you must be thirsty from working all that frustration off."

Keeping my eyes on his, I grab the water, unscrew the cap and throw it back, almost emptying it.

His eyes slowly move from my eyes, down to my lips around the top of the bottle.

"You need me?" he questions.

I pull the bottle away and laugh, while still fighting to catch my breath. "For what?"

He moves closer to me and rubs his thumb over my mouth, wiping the excess water away. "To bring you a towel..." His eyes slowly scan me over, stopping on the sweat, dripping between my cleavage. "Or to help you work out some of that frustration?"

Keeping my eyes on his cocky, but surprisingly smooth ass, I tilt the water back until it's empty, then toss the bottle back to him.

"No, thank you." I flash him a sweet smile. "After this I plan to get wet anyway and work out my frustration on my own. I don't need any help with that."

Smirking, he lifts a brow in amusement. "I like a woman that can work out her own frustration once in a while. I'm not gonna lie..." Walking past me, he grips the battle ropes in his hands and squats. "It's really fucking hot."

Swallowing, I stand back and watch his muscles flex as he does some power slams, looking as if he has just as much or more stress than me to get out.

His tattooed arms and hands have me completely hypnotized and I have to admit that he's extremely hot in that bad boy kind of way.

He looks nothing like the uptight men I have dated in the past. None of them have been able to handle me, but I have a feeling that he'd be able to do that and more.

After a few minutes, he drops the ropes and turns to face me, his body dripping with sweat as he breathes heavily.

I check him out completely, my eyes moving lower to check out his thick legs and then back up to admire his firm chest that his shirt is now plastered to. "Thanks for the water. I suppose I owe you now."

I reach for my bag and pull out my spare water bottle and toss it to him. "Anything else I can get you?"

He grins. "You really want me to answer that?"

I take a step back as he takes a few steps toward me, practically backing me up against the wall.

Trying not to let myself enjoy his closeness too much, I place my hand on his sweaty chest and push back a bit. "I don't know yet," I say honestly. "I have a feeling that it might be something that I want, but don't need."

He moves his face around my neck, to whisper in my ear. "I second that... Meadow."

I give him a surprised look as he backs away and goes back to grab the ropes. "How do you know my name? Should I be running right about now?"

He winks. "Only if you want to."

With that, he starts on the ropes again, leaving me to either stand here and watch him like a creeper again, or leave.

I smile, slightly amused, as I let myself out of the room to find something else to keep me occupied.

I'm standing here, looking around to get familiar with the gym and how it's set up, when one of the guys that was watching me earlier, steps up beside me and grips my waist. "You look a little lost." He now squeezes my hip, letting out this creepy little moan as his eyes roam over my body. "Want me and my friend to show you around?"

Disgusted, I remove his hand from my hip, but he quickly replaces it as if he has the right to touch me if he wants.

"Get your fucking hand off me before I break it off." I push his hand from my body and walk away from him, hoping he won't follow.

It does no good, because he ends up on the elliptical beside me, talking once again. "I love a girl with a little sass. My friend over here does too. It turns us on."

His friend appears next to me, watching me as he wipes his armpits off with a towel. "You single?"

"No," I bite out. "Now fuck off."

"Damn... those tits." I cringe as his eyes roam my body just as his friend's did. "And that—"

"She told you to fuck off," a voice booms, causing both the guys to look surprised and a little scared when the blue-eyed cutie appears out of nowhere, looking extremely pissed off. "Get the fuck out, before I let you out myself."

The guy on the elliptical cusses under his breath and turns off the machine. "What's up, man? Didn't realize you were still here. We were just giving the lady a little company. No harm."

Not the least bit humored by the douchebag, he grabs both of the men's gym bags and walks to the door, opening it and tossing them both outside.

He holds the door open and turns back our way. "When a lady tells you to fuck off, you fuck off. Out. Now."

I raise a brow in humor and watch as the assholes argue with each other on the way out the door, not one of them brave enough to argue with the guy kicking them out of the gym.

He lets out a long breath and then walks past me and back into the room where he came from.

Jumping off the elliptical, I make my way over to the doorway and watch as he works the ropes again.

Watching him has me completely hypnotized again, until he turns around and notices me creeping on him.

A small smirk crosses his face, before he stops for a second to breathe. "Enjoying the view?"

I ignore his question and just smile, before walking away, grabbing my bag and making my way outside to see a motorcycle parked next to my truck.

When I go to open the door, I notice what looks like a flyer on my windshield. Grabbing it, I read it over, unable to hold back the smile that takes over, mixed with slight excitement.

"Holy. Shit."

Yup. Definitely different than the men I've dated and most likely a lot more trouble...

CHAPTER THREE

STYX

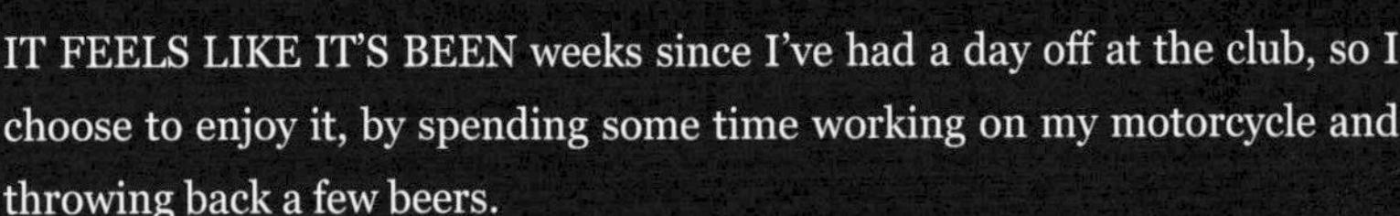

IT FEELS LIKE IT'S BEEN weeks since I've had a day off at the club, so I choose to enjoy it, by spending some time working on my motorcycle and throwing back a few beers.

I'm off in fucking La La Land, forgetting about everything else around me, until my father's shitty voice pulls me back to reality.

"Working on that old bike again. With all the money you make taking your clothes off, you think you'd purchase a new one and get rid of that junk."

Growling under my breath, I throw my torque wrench beside me and run my greasy hands over my face.

"What the fuck are you doing here?"

My father chuckles and walks further into my garage, getting comfortable, touching my damn things as if he owns the place. I don't even know what makes the piece of shit think that he's welcome in my home.

"Your mother wants you to come over for poker night. Maybe you can bet some of that G-string money you bring in. Unless you're afraid to lose it to your old man."

Standing up, I kick my toolbox out of the way and reach for a towel to clean my hands. "You're not my fucking old man." I turn to face him so he can see all my hatred for him. "You're a piece of shit that beat me up almost every day of my childhood and ruined any hope I had growing up. And my mother... well she's stupid for taking you back and thinking that she can hide the bruises. I will always have her back and I'll always protect her, but I won't be accepting any invites to *her* home, anytime soon. Got it, *old man?*"

He laughs. He actually fucking laughs.

The sound of his laughter snaps something in me, and before I know, I have him slammed against the wall with my hand wrapped around his throat.

I lean in close and give his throat a tight squeeze. "Let me see one more bruise on my mother and I will snap your neck without a second thought. Got it? I'm watching you. I'm always watching you. Don't forget."

My father's eyes widen for a split second, letting me see the fear in them, before he quickly masks it with his stupid laugh that I hate so much.

"You'll be the one breaking your mother's heart when I tell her that you won't be coming tonight." He pushes me away from him and fixes his shirt. "Your mother thinks you hate her."

"Leave," I growl. "Before I throw you out myself."

He shrugs as if being thrown out is no big deal and walks until he's standing just outside the garage door. "You've always been full of excuses, son. So your mother should be used to the disappointment."

Rotating my shoulders in anger, I hit my fist against the garage door button, and watch the door close in front of the asshole that raised me.

He ruined my childhood and took everything away from me and my mother, yet she always takes his ass back as if there's nothing else out there for her.

That's exactly why I'll only settle down when I find *the* one. I don't plan to just give my heart to anyone and when I do find her, I'll give her everything of me.

Having *him* show up unannounced has me so screwed up in the head that the last thing I can concentrate on is working on my bike.

"Well fuck."

Going inside, I take a quick shower, before I hop on my bike and head back to my uncle's gym for the second time today.

Hell, I might as well call it mine, because he's planning on me taking over soon so he can focus on his family.

I've been here more in the last week than he has in the last six months.

James, one of the personal trainers, greets me when I walk in. "Hey, man. Back again?"

I open the door to my office and toss my bag inside. "Need to work off some more steam."

He looks me over with a small grin. "Fucking shit. You're the busiest person I know, man. Between working out all day and dancing at the club, I'm surprised that you even have time to breathe."

"Me too," I say as I walk past him and hit the weights.

After spending a few hours at the gym, I shower for the third time today, and head over to the club to have a few drinks.

Sarah is working tonight, and she always finds a way to keep my mind busy and off all the bullshit.

"How's your dick?" she questions with a smirk. "Taking a break for the night?"

I raise a brow and tilt back my beer. "He's been getting more than a few breaks these days."

"I've noticed," she responds. "Good for you and your dick. I'm sure the fucker's tired."

"How about you? How's that girlfriend of yours?" I ask, making her turn red. "Never thought you'd give up the dick."

She slaps my forehead and leans in close to my face, talking against my lips. "Who says I've given it up? Having both is a lot more fun and I learn new tricks every day. You don't even know what I'm capable of these days, big guy."

I lift my beer to her and adjust my erection. "Might as well give me one more after that shit. Damn!"

She smirks and slides me another beer, jumping back in surprise as Kash jumps over the bar and reaches for the bar gun to spray his body down with water. "Ah yes. This feels so good."

"Stop moaning like that or I'll have to take you home to Kendal so we can take advantage of your sexy ass."

Kash raises a brow to Sarah. "Damn..." he moans again, just to get a reaction out of Sarah. Then he looks over to see my unamused face. "Lighten the hell up, man."

I close my eyes and growl when water hits my face and then my chest.

Both Sarah and Kash laugh, before he throws the gun down and runs back over to the small crowd of women that are yelling for him.

Sarah takes a few seconds to check me out now that my shirt is clinging to my chest, before speaking. "There's this sexy little blonde chick roaming around looking lost." She looks over my shoulder. "Looks like she's looking for someone and the boys don't seem to be it."

Setting my beer down, I turn around in my stool to see Meadow, searching the room around her.

For some strange reason, my heart starts beating fast, wondering if she could be here for me. It's not even as if she would know to look for me here.

I hope like hell that she isn't here to see Kash or one of the security dicks.

"I'll be back." Standing up, I walk up behind her and listen to her talk to herself.

"What the hell am I doing here? This is ridiculous. I'm leaving." She turns around, running straight into my chest with a grunt.

"Looking for someone?" I question, while gripping her waist to hold her steady. "Leaving because you haven't found them?"

She smiles up at me and takes a step back. "Maybe." I follow her as she makes her way to the bar and orders a drink. After Sarah brings her a beer and eye-fucks her, she turns back to face me. "So tell me again how you knew my name?"

I laugh as she eyes me over, her pale blue eyes spending an awful long time on my chest. "Is that why you're here? To find out if I'm a stalker or some shit?"

She walks away, leaving me no choice but to follow her again, as she takes a seat at a table, far away from the stage.

She lifts a brow when I sit down, as if that's her answer.

I look her up and down and pull her chair between my legs so that I can look her in the eye. "I should be asking you how you knew to find me here. Maybe *I* should be the one concerned for my safety."

Taking a swig of her beer, she gives me a look as if I'm crazy. "You left a flyer on my truck... *Styx*. I think you wanted me to find you."

Fucking Kash.

His ass thinks it's funny to come to the gym and leave flyers everywhere to make it aware to all its members that I moonlight as a male entertainer.

There's been times that I've walked in to over a hundred flyers taped to the walls.

"So you came to see me strip?" I lock the leg of her chair in place with my leg and smile when she tries scooting back. "It's my night off, but I can give you a private dance if you want. I'll even do it for free since you look so fucking beautiful right now."

She about chokes on her beer, but clears her throat and plays it off, as if what I just said didn't excite her. "You always kidnap a girl's chair so she has no choice but to hang out with you?"

"No," I answer, honestly. "This will be the first. But I like you so..."

"So..." She laughs and pulls her pale hair into a bun, making me look at her arms and take notice of her sleeve of tattoos, covering her right arm. She was wearing a V-neck long sleeved shirt the other night, keeping her arms hidden. *Damn, that's sexy*. "You decide to stalk me and then keep me captive. Good game."

I wrap the single strand of hair, that hangs in front of her face, around my finger. "I know your name, because you work out at *my* gym. There was a new member signed up by the name, Meadow, and your gorgeous body was the only one that I didn't recognize."

We sit here and just stare at each other for what feels like five minutes, before Meadow stands up and pushes her chair in. "I should go. It's been a long night."

"Where?" I question.

"Where?" she questions back, confused as to what I'm asking. "Where what?"

"Where has it been a long night?"

"The hospital. Have a good night, Styx."

She walks away, leaving me to watch the sway of her perfect ass, as she brushes right past Kash, not even stopping to take a second look.

In fact... I don't think she watched the guys dancing at all.

This has me jumping to my feet and rushing outside to catch her.

She lets out a sexy little laugh when she notices me following her. "What are you doing?"

"Walking you to your car."

She stops next to a huge truck and gives me the cutest fucking look. "Who says I drive a car? I like my rides big and fast."

Impressed, I watch her climb into her truck, before she reaches for the door. "Then you're going to love me." I smirk.

She tries to hide her smile, but completely fails as she pulls the door closed and drives away.

Holy fuck, this woman is different from the rest and I really badly want to find out in which ways...

CHAPTER FOUR

MEADOW

IT'S BEEN A FEW DAYS since I saw Styx at *Walk of Shame* and for some reason... I can't shake him from my thoughts. I keep wondering about him and wanting to know more about this man.

He's a male stripper, everything that I should run away from, yet, I want to run back to the gym or club in hopes of seeing him again.

He intrigues me. Even though he comes on a little strong, I don't feel threatened by it. It doesn't make me feel creepy and dirty like those guys at the gym did.

Styx being up front with me, makes me like his company. It's usually exhausting trying to figure men out and what they're thinking. He comes right out and just says it. No holding back.

Jase watched me for weeks, confusing me and frustrating me, before he finally hit on me and told me what he wanted to do to me.

Just like my ex, Mack. The asshole that left me right after my aunt died because he couldn't deal with my emotional state.

Although the strip club isn't my usual scene, I've talked Mandy into going with me tonight.

Yes, I want to see Styx with less clothing on… so sue me. I'm only human. The man is dangerously sexy.

"I can't believe I've let you talk me into this." Mandy shakes her head from beside me and jumps when a group of women scream in excitement when the DJ starts playing music. "Please tell me we don't have to stay here all night. My ears can't take it."

I laugh and hand her one of the Bomb Pop drinks that I ordered for us. "Just long enough to see Styx perform and then we can slip out and back to our cozy little lives."

"Let's hope he's up first then," she yells over the music, while fingering her dark hair. "This place is a little too wild for me."

We sit here for about ten minutes, before the first guy finally takes the stage. A gorgeous guy with tattoos and dark blond hair humps his way across the stage, the women going crazy and screaming out the name *Kash*.

I recognize his picture from the flyer that was on my truck the other night.

He's been on stage for all of five minutes and already owns every single girl in this room. Not one person isn't watching this hottie get down and dirty.

Once it gets close to the end of the song, Kash jumps down from the stage and dances against a few women, before bringing one up to the stage with him to dance above her face.

This is the first time that I've ever watched a male stripper, and I have to admit that it makes me feel sort of… hot.

Even though I was here a few days ago, my attention was on Styx and Styx alone. He's still the only reason I'm here now.

When I look over at Mandy, her face is red and her drink is half gone already. "You going to survive over there?" I ask with a laugh. "Breathe."

She nods, keeping her eyes glued to the stage. "I had no idea that the strippers would be this hot. Most of the online videos have men I'm not attracted to and I've seen *a lot* of videos."

I laugh at her confession. "Walk of Shame is the exception, I guess. There's got to be at least one decent male strip club out there and it looks like we're in it." I elbow her and smile, holding my straw to my lips. "Let's just enjoy the entertainment for a bit, even if Styx isn't up till last."

She nods her head in agreement. "This Kash guy is entertaining. So I'm enjoying. You couldn't get me to leave now if you dragged me out that door by my hair."

Smiling, I sit back and enjoy the show, getting excited at the idea of seeing Styx dance. If he moves anything like this Kash guy, then I have a feeling that I'm going to like it... *a lot.*

I can't help but hope that he spots me out in the crowd. For some reason, I want him to know that I'm here and to see his reaction to me showing up to watch him.

Another guy comes on next, instead of Styx, so I get up from my seat and walk over to order us a couple more drinks and two cherry bombs to waste some time.

A very tall, cute security guard walks over and offers to carry my drinks for me when he notices me struggling.

"I got it, gorgeous." He grabs the drinks and smiles down at me. "Where you headed?"

"Over there." I point to where Mandy is practically standing to get a better view of the stage. "Thanks..." I stop and search for his name.

"Kage. And not a problem. Cale would kick my ass if I didn't offer to help a beautiful woman with her drinks."

He winks and then motions for me to walk first, then he sets the drinks down for us and smiles, before walking away.

"He's good looking too," Mandy points out. "This place is full of hot guys. Why have we not come here before?"

"Because the hospital is exhausting," I point out. "Plus, I'm not sure what the hospital would think of their nurses partying it up at the strip club, waving cash at half-naked men. Then showing up for our shift, hungover and still fantasizing about the eye candy we saw the night before."

She laughs. "That does sound bad. Maybe we should keep this private. I'm not even telling Kayla about this because she has a huge mouth."

"Oh, we're keeping this between the two of us. Kayla is the last person who should find out. She'd run to that uptight bitch and have her on our asses, watching us even harder than she already does."

"Oh God. I'd have to find a new job then. Let's forget about the hospital and just enjoy before my excitement gets stomped out by thoughts of them."

We've been here for thirty minutes now and Stone is now leaving the stage.

Excitement courses through me at the idea that Styx could be next. I only saw three men on that flyer. Styx, Stone, and Kash and we've already seen the other two.

The next song comes on so I sit up straight and grab my drink, prepared to see Styx comes out, looking sexy and tempting.

I'm a little disappointed when the other two guys walk out instead and start dancing on the main floor as if the individual shows are over for the night.

"Where's this Styx guy you were talking about? Is it his night off or something?"

I let out a breath of disappointment and grab my drink, about ready to get up and drop it off at the bar to leave. "Maybe it is."

Mandy's eyes shift to behind me and go wide when a pair of hands grip my waist. "Maybe not."

Quickly, I turn around to see Styx standing behind me, dressed in a pair of ripped up, faded jeans and a white tee, hugging his firm chest. "Couldn't get enough of me?"

A smile takes over as I watch him watching me. He looks extremely amused. "Thought I would catch a show and see what you're made of." I set my drink down and grab my purse. "Guess I picked a bad night."

He smirks and grips my hip when I try to walk away. "Or maybe you picked a good one."

Before I get a chance to respond, he grabs my hand and begins pulling me through the crowd. Girls grab at him from everywhere, screaming and going crazy, but he ignores them, stopping when we get to a hallway with private rooms.

"What about Mandy? I can't just leave her out there by herself."

"Kage is keeping her busy for the next twenty minutes." He lifts a brow and smiles. "You wanted to see what I'm made of, right? Now's your chance." He leans in close to my ear, his breath hitting my skin. "Unless you think you can't handle it. It's okay if you can't. A lot of women lose it behind these doors."

I nod in response, unable to form words that won't sound stupid at the moment.

Opening the door to the private room, he guides me inside and backs me up, until I'm sitting on a couch.

I swallow and begin shifting in my seat as "Pony" by Ginuwine comes through the speakers, causing Styx to grind his hips and run his hands down his chest and abs.

Between the darkness, the hot song, and his sexy dancing, I instantly break out in a sweat, needing to fan myself off.

I can't believe that I'm watching the hot guy from the gym strip right now.

Moving to straddle my lap, he slowly grinds his hips against me, while running *my* hands down his body this time. Every dip of muscle feels so good beneath my fingers, that I find myself getting wet, just thinking about them flexing above me.

"What?" he questions with a cocky smile. "Like the way my body feels under your hands?"

Biting my bottom lip, I grab his nipple through the fabric and twist the bar a little. "I'd be lying if I said I didn't," I admit.

He leans in close to my ear and presses his lips against me. "Don't be afraid to touch me *anywhere* you want. This is your moment to live out any hot little fantasy that's running through your head right now with no judgement." He thrusts his hips against me and grips my hair so sexy that my pussy throbs. "It's just the two of us."

Pulling away from me, he sits up straight and yanks his shirt off over his head.

My eyes widen when I take in just how glorious and beautiful his body truly is. Every tattooed muscle has me wanting to trace the outline for hours.

I'd use my tongue on Styx.

He surprises me by picking me up and wrapping my legs around his waist.

Looking me in the eye, he backs me up, pressing me against the wall. Then he pins my hands above my head, thrusting me up with his hips as if he's fucking me.

I let out a little moan, lost in the moment, as he rotates his hips and slows down, looking me right in the eye. His eyes stay locked on mine as if he's daring me to look away, but I don't. I can't.

He's hard now and I can feel his thickness pushing against me.

It's so extremely hot that I can just feel myself getting wetter with each move of his hips and completely turned on by this man.

Something about the way he's dancing for me just seems so intimate and deep.

I lean my head back and close my eyes, when I feel his lips press against my neck and his hands cup my face.

It feels good so I allow it to happen for a few moments, until I feel his lips press down next to mine.

"No," I whisper, as I turn my face. "I don't know you, Styx."

He seems to like this response, because he smiles as if I've just proved something to him. "Good."

Backing me away from the wall, he places me back on the couch and steps away to strip out of his jeans.

My heart jumps out of my chest with excitement when I look down at his tight boxer briefs to see just how hard and huge that he really is.

Stepping up on the couch, he grabs my hands and places them on his abs. He looks down at me, his ice blue eyes burning into me. "The song's almost over."

I know exactly what that means.

My heart races even faster, trying to decide if it's right to do what I really want to do with his body.

No judgement.

With my heart racing, I slowly lower my hands and brush them over his large erection, being careful not to spend too much time on his dick, before gripping his thighs.

The last thing I want to do is violate him and be one of those screaming women in the next room.

He smiles down at me and climbs down from the couch, when the song ends.

"Did you feel what you expected when first coming to my room?"

I shake my head. "No. I felt so much more."

Standing up, I allow myself to check him out one more time in this no judgement room. "I wasn't expecting it to feel so... I don't know. It was good."

He laughs. "You wanted to see what I was made of..." He reaches for his jeans and slips them back on, leaving them undone. “That wasn’t all of me, yet.”

We both just stare at each other, until the door opens and what appears to be another security guard, pops his head inside. “Cale’s looking for you. He’s about to leave so you might want to hurry.”

He gives him a nod, while keeping his eyes on me. “Tell him I’ll find him in a minute, Kass.”

“Sure thing, man.”

Styx finally pulls his eyes away from me and runs his hands over his sweaty face. “I’ll see you around?”

I smile. “Maybe.”

He grabs his shirt and laughs, while backing up out the door.

I release a deep breath and smile while fighting for breath.

Seriously?

Styx is insane when it comes to dancing to turn women on. He was no disappointment.

Feeling the need to get out of this place so I can breathe again, I rush out of the private room, fighting my way through the crowd to get to Mandy.

I’m dragging her out of here, even *if* it has to be by her hair.

Seeing Kash straddling her lap, I cuss to myself, knowing that I’m about to ruin her fun if I drag her out.

I stand back for a few minutes and watch him grind against her instead.

Holy hell, this man does it extremely well too. I’m getting hot again, just picturing Styx back in my lap, grinding me like that.

As soon as Kash stands up and she shoves money into the side of his briefs, I yank her from the chair and drag her with me through the room, until we’re finally back outside where I can catch my breath.

Holy shit... Styx’s dance was the hottest moment of my life and the wet dream that I’ll be having for the next week...

CHAPTER FIVE

STYX

CALE PULLED ME ASIDE THE other night to offer me a couple days off from the club. He must've been able to tell how stressed I've been for the last week since business has exploded.

I told him that I didn't need time, but he kept pushing, telling me that the last thing he wants is to stress his guys out. He said if it came down to it that he could ask Hemy to take on a couple days to cover me.

So I agreed to the next two days off.

Pulling my motorcycle up to the second hospital that I've been to today, I kill the engine and set my helmet on the seat.

I tried just sitting at home and relaxing for once, but it didn't work out so well. Apparently, I have to always be doing something or else my mind goes places that it doesn't need to be. Relaxing is out of the fucking question for me.

Walking into the building, I step up to the information desk and smile at the lady when she looks up. "I'm looking for Meadow..."

She immediately points down the hall, toward the elevator, enthusiastically. "Ms. Jenkins is on the third floor. Just go down to the elevators and then take a right once you get to the third floor."

I flash her a grateful smile, which causes her to blush and smooth out her blouse. "Thank you, Anne."

"Anytime." She smiles back and then watches me all the way down to the elevators.

Once I get to the third floor, a couple of young nurses walk by, checking me out and whispering not so softly, about the things they'd do to me.

But the only thing I'm focused on is finding Meadow and seeing how she reacts to my ass just showing up at her work out of the blue.

She surprised the hell out of me and I figured I need to return the favor.

I walk down the long hall, peeking into the opened door rooms, until I spot Meadow changing the sheets on one of the beds, while chatting with her friend that was at the club with her last night.

Smiling, I stand back and watch her work. It's only fair after she did the same to me.

"...I'm not doing anything tonight. Going home. And going to bed. I told you."

"You're trying to tell me that you're not going back to the club tonight to look for Styx? You want to see him again. I can tell." Her friend laughs. "You've had this look on your face all day..."

Meadow's head shoots up to look at her friend. "What kind of look is that?"

"One of longing... and horniness."

Turning red, Meadow grabs a pillow and tosses it at her friend's head. "Oh shut it! You don't know what you're talking about. I'm not... you're insane."

"Is she?"

Both girls look over at the sound of my deep voice.

Meadow tries hard to hide her smile, but there's no mistaking the fact that she's happy to see me here.

"Yes," she says, while pushing her friend away. "Mandy is extremely insane. So just ignore the words that come out of her mouth."

I raise a brow and look her over in her scrubs, looking so cute. I can think of many ways that I'd like to strip her from them.

"Maybe I like the words that are coming out of her mouth. Especially the ones about you."

Mandy clears her throat and begins backing toward the door. "I'll be at the desk if you need me." She turns to me and smiles. "I'm not insane. Trust me, I know how to read my friend."

"Mandy!" Meadow looks at Mandy with wide eyes and points at the door. "Go!"

I wait for her friend to leave, before I walk into the room and greet her with a kiss on the cheek. "It's good to see you." I grab the back of her neck and look her in the eyes. "I'm not going to lie... I like what your friend was saying."

She lets out a small breath and turns her head away to hide her blush. "I'm surprised to see you here." She continues on with fixing the bed. "Was I easy to find? Or did you use some special stalker skills?"

My eyes lower down to her perfect ass when she bends over to tuck the sheet in. I'm trying really damn hard not to just walk up behind her and show her just how much she turns me on. "Doesn't matter. I had all day to search and I was on a mission."

This causes her to laugh and look up from the bed. "That bored, huh?"

She stands up straight to walk around me, but I block her with my body and slide both of my hands under her neck to look her in the eyes. She holds my stare and her breathing picks up as I lean in close to her mouth. "Spending time with you happens to excite me, Meadow. That doesn't happen very often. Not many women can stay on my mind for longer than twenty minutes. You've been on mine for days."

I pull away and watch her throat as she swallows. "What are you doing in a few hours?" she questions. "Do you have plans?"

Reaching out, I wrap a strand of her hair around my finger and then push it behind her ear, brushing my thumb over her cheek. "Picking you up from work and taking you on a ride. I want to get you alone."

"Meadow," a male voice calls out from the doorway. "Everything okay in there?" He's trying to sound concerned, but jealousy is evident in his tone.

She sucks in a surprised breath, as I wrap my arm around her waist and pull her against me. I'm not worried about what he thinks, but it somehow feels like she might be.

That tells me that she's either talking to this guy or has in the past.

"I'm fine, Jase. You can go."

I look up from Meadow, when his footsteps enter the room. "She said you can go, Jase. She's perfectly fine in my hands. She hasn't complained yet."

This pretty boy is the complete opposite of me: dark hair, dark eyes, no facial hair or tattoos from what I can see at least.

He might've been able to show her a good time in the past, but that was before I came along.

He flexes his jaw as he looks us over, looking heated. My arm is still around her waist, and she hasn't made a move to change that. "I'll be right outside if you need me."

Meadow nods and lets out a frustrated breath. "I said… I'm fine. You can go."

Jase sizes me up one more time, before he finally turns for the door and disappears.

"Sorry about that. He's just…"

"Someone that wants you as badly as I do." I release my hold on her and walk toward the door. I stop and look back at her, once I reach the door. "Looks like I'll need to step my game up. See you soon, babe." I wink and then walk off, looking Jase over as I pass him in the hall.

He might think he has a chance at this point, but when I want something, I give it my all. And right now, I'm thinking what I want is Meadow.

Eyes focus on me again as I make my way toward the elevator, the same nurses as before, watching me and trying to decide who should come talk to me.

That gets broken up when Jase walks past and tells them to get busy. One of the nurses gives him a dirty look, but they all scatter anyway and go their separate ways.

The elevator opens and I'm not surprised when Jase steps in after me.

Smiling to myself, I press the button to the lobby and wait for him to speak, because I know he has something to say. He's threatened by me.

The ride down is silent. I keep my eyes on him, letting him know that I'm waiting for him to tell me what's on his mind.

It's not until the elevator doors open that he finally speaks. "Stay away from Meadow. She's mine."

Smiling, I step out of the elevator and catch the door right as it's about to close. He looks up at me, surprised. "She won't be for long."

I turn and walk away, knowing that this asshole is full of shit.

I'm not going anywhere until Meadow tells me to and the look in her eyes whenever I'm around, tells me that it won't be anytime fucking soon…

CHAPTER SIX

STYX

THE PERSON IN FRONT OF me is driving like an asshole, slamming on their brakes every few minutes. All it's doing is pissing me off and testing my patience.

"What the fuck!" I yell out in frustration when they do it again, almost causing me to slam into them.

I'm so close to jumping off my motorcycle at the next stoplight and teaching this fucker how to drive.

They're riding the ass of the Honda in front of them and that's when I notice that the Honda is brake checking the idiot in front of me.

Frustrated as all hell, I go to switch lanes, just to have the asshole in front of me decide at the last second that they want to get over, without looking first.

The car swipes the front tire of my motorcycle, making me lose control. My helmet takes a hard hit, bouncing off the street, before I slide across the road with my motorcycle halfway on top of me.

"Fuck!" I scream out in pain once I come to a stop, and punch the road, pissed off that the asshole in front of me just hit me.

My motorcycle is further down the side of the road all banged up, causing other cars to slam on their brakes and stop to check on me.

I feel the pain radiate up into my shinbone, when I roll over and attempt to stand to my feet. I most likely have a broken ankle. I've felt this pain before. More times than I'd like to admit. I have my father to thank for that.

Fuck! I take my helmet off and slam it down, fighting to control my anger.

"Don't move!" an older guy yells when he reaches me. You hit your head pretty hard. "I called 9-1-1. Stay still, you might've hurt your back or neck."

One of the other drivers that saw what happened is arguing with the asshole that hit me and I want nothing more than to hobble over there my damn self and give him a piece of my mind, but there's two people fighting to keep me still now.

Thankful for the husband and wife who cared enough to stop and help me, I don't fight them to move. I just lay here and wait for the ambulance to arrive, telling myself that I'll find that fucker and kick his ass later.

After I get asked a few questions and hoisted into the back of the ambulance, I give them orders to take me back to Meadow's hospital. They want to take me somewhere else, but I tell them to fuck off and take me where I want them to.

I know if I complain enough that they'll do it and they do.

Once I get to the emergency room and give them a short medical history and answer some more questions, I get an x-ray that comes back as a small break to my ankle and am told that I'm stuck in this fucking walking boot for up to six weeks. I hope like hell it's a lot less time than that or else I'll be spending my time dancing in a damn chair.

I'm given some medication for the pain after a while and then moved up to the third floor, to make space in the emergency room.

Since I hit my head pretty good, they want to keep me overnight so that someone can be around to wake me up every few hours.

I keep looking for Meadow as they roll me down the hall and into my room and it isn't until right after I get into my room, that I see Meadow walk past, stopping as soon as her eyes land on me.

For as long as I've been here, it has to be about time for her shift to end by now.

I can hear her outside talking to another nurse, but can't make out what they're saying. All I know is that she sounds concerned and keeps telling the other nurse that she's fine.

Closing my eyes, I let out a small breath and run my hands through my hair, frustrated by this whole situation.

I should've been picking Meadow up on my motorcycle right about now and getting her the hell away from everyone so we could be alone.

Instead, I'm stuck here in this stupid bed and she's about to leave for the night.

A few minutes later, Meadow enters the room and places her hand on my head, softly caressing it. "Damn, Styx. What the hell happened? Are you alright? Does your ankle hurt bad?"

I smile up at her because all I can think about is pulling her into this bed with me and pleasuring her to help pass the time and make this stay enjoyable. I'm sure my lips on hers could ease a lot of this pain I'm feeling right now.

"Some asshole hit me. I still have use of my important body parts, so I'm good. Want to join me?" I pat the bed beside me.

She smiles, her cheeks slightly pink and starts messing around with the monitor, checking things. "I bet you are. I have a feeling that it takes a lot to keep a guy like you down."

"So... is that a no?" I question jokingly just to see her smile again.

"If I said yes, I'd lose my job." She turns to face me and looks me over in my gown. "I have a feeling things wouldn't be so quiet next to you. Especially when you have easy access to your dick and you look so cute in that gown." She winks and adds, "I'll be sure to keep the other nurses away."

Once I look up and realize what time it is, I raise my brows in question and watch her working as if she's in no hurry to get out of here. "Didn't your shift end ten minutes ago?"

"I decided to work a double so I can keep an eye on you and make sure that you get woken up. We're short-staffed and if I leave then you won't get the attention you need and I want to make sure that you're well cared for."

Well, fuck. She's staying for me. Is it wrong that that makes me so fucking hard?

"And you want to give me that attention?" I tease. "Looks like that ride will have to wait a bit unless you want an audience."

"You're a jokester, aren't you? A jokester and a stalker who likes to capture girl's chairs to make them stay and talk to them. Good combination." She smiles and leans down close to my face. "Get some rest. I'll be close by."

I smile and attempt to get as comfortable as I can in this shitty bed. I still wish I could get her to join me. Knowing that she'll be close by will only make me want it more. "That will keep me up all night."

"I'll be back. Just get some rest before I break your other ankle. Got it."

I close my eyes and grin as she walks away, leaving me alone to think of all the ways I can keep her as my own.

Damn this woman has just given me another reason to make me want her even more now...

I WAKE UP IN THE middle of the night to Meadow rubbing my head and bringing me some fresh water for when I wake up thirsty.

I feel her lift the blanket to check the swelling on my ankle, but I'm exhausted so I keep my eyes closed and just enjoy having the presence of someone in the room that cares.

She already woke me up an hour ago, so there's no real need for her to be in here right now. Not yet.

The guys said they'd stop by to see me, but I told them no, that I'd rather them just get some sleep and visit me when they get off work tomorrow night.

I didn't need them feeling like they *had* to waste time watching me lay in this stupid bed over a busted ankle.

Meadow thinks that I'm sleeping, but I peek over her way and watch as she takes a seat in the chair and closes her eyes.

She's exhausted and I can see it taking over her as she rubs her face and yawns repeatedly. Makes me feel guilty that she stayed to keep her eye on me.

"I'm fine," I say tiredly. "You should go home and get some sleep."

She opens her eyes and stands up. "Drink up."

I reach for the glass and slam back the water. "My head and ankle are fine and I'll be out of here in a few hours. You should go."

"Yeah, I was thinking about taking off. Jessie will be the nurse to get you out of here in the morning. I just wanted to say bye before I left, but didn't want to wake you again so soon. How are you feeling? In any pain?"

She doesn't look too happy at the idea of this other nurse caring for me, but she's already barely able to stay awake. Maybe she likes me more than she's ready to admit.

I'll just have to change that.

"It doesn't hurt much. It's nothing I haven't dealt with before."

"Ok good." She looks a little disappointed as she steps closer to me.

"I'll be back to take you on that ride. Don't worry," I tease. "I keep my word."

She laughs and adjusts my pillow, getting so close that her lips almost touch mine. I'm half tempted to close the distance between us, but I want to wait until she's awake enough to enjoy the feel of my lips capturing hers. "Maybe you will. Maybe you won't. Goodbye, Styx. Get some sleep."

All I can do is smile and watch as she walks away. This woman just sacrificed her whole night and sleep to be here for me.

That's something I'll never fucking forget and I'm more thankful than she knows. I'll make it up to her.

I lay here for a good twenty minutes or so, before I finally start falling back to sleep.

Of course, I fall sleep, while planning my return to take her on that motorcycle ride that I promised.

She may think that I'm not coming back for her, but I am. That's a promise...

CHAPTER SEVEN

STYX

I'VE SPENT THE LAST TWELVE days bartending, while sitting on this stool, waiting on my ankle to heal.

I don't mind bartending once in a while, but it's far from being easy when you have to get up and hobble around for the right bottle of liquor every five seconds.

The women seem to think it's sexy as hell and have been giving me almost more attention than I do when I'm out on the floor dancing.

Almost every drink that gets ordered comes with an offer to take me home and fuck me until my ankle doesn't hurt anymore.

It's like they like the idea of taking advantage of me and want to keep me for as long as they can.

A little too late for that shit. I've turned every offer down. The only woman I've been thinking about taking me to bed is Meadow.

She's been all I can think about since she left me in that hospital bed and I don't think I'll be able to keep my hands off her the next time I get the chance to touch her.

I just want to make it through the next couple of weeks and get this ankle healed so that I can ride my motorcycle again. I promised Meadow I'd be back for her and I still plan on it.

Cale offered me a few weeks off work to heal, but since Hemy is still a part time bartender and will be dancing to cover me, I told Cale that I'd cover for Hemy behind the bar.

Plus, sitting at home does nothing good for my head. Too much shit runs through it and going to the gym just to sit behind my desk is boring as shit. The club is the only option for me at the moment.

"Are you sure I can't take you home and get you comfortable in my bed?" The beautiful woman in front of me points to her equally attractive friend. "We can both take your pain away. We promise it will be worth it."

Sarah rushes over and leans over the counter, annoyed with everyone taking so much time to order drinks from me. "Order your drinks. There's a line behind you. You're not getting Styx's dick so move on."

I lift my brows as Sarah walks away to help her side of the bar. Damn, I love that woman sometimes.

"You heard the boss. Now, what can I get you besides my cock, ladies?"

One of the girls starts rambling on about some kind of special drink that she wants, but all I can focus on is what looks like the back of Meadow's head, walking away.

I hop off the stool on my good leg, bouncing around to try to get a better view to see if it's really her, but there are too many heads in my way to get a good look.

It's not until she's walking out the door, that I get a view of the side of her face as she says something to Lane, before disappearing outside.

"Fuck. I'll be back," I tell Sarah.

"Dammit," she says to my back as my struggling ass hops over the bar and almost falls over the other side. "Don't hurt yourself. Jeez, Styx."

I ignore her and fight my way through the crowd, getting felt up by pretty much everyone in my path.

By the time I reach the door and break free of the crowd, I get outside and look around, but don't see Meadow's truck anywhere.

Disappointment sets in as I run my hands through my hair in frustration.

I've been wanting to stop by the hospital and thank her, but I promised

I'd be back on my motorcycle to take her on that ride.

I still have at least three weeks of healing before I can make that happen and I'm making every second of it worth the wait for her.

I just hope she'll still be excited to see me by then...

CHAPTER EIGHT

MEADOW

THREE WEEKS LATER . . .

I CAN'T CONTAIN MY EXCITEMENT when I get off work to see Styx leaning against his motorcycle, waiting for me in the parking lot.

My reaction only confirms how much I've actually been looking forward to seeing him again. I've been at the gym a few times since his accident, but didn't expect him to be there since my shift has been so messed up lately. I even stopped at the bar one night, but saw him surrounded by women at the bar, so I left, knowing that I'd never get the chance to talk to him.

Now, he's here and I feel this rush that I can't contain. My heart is going crazy as I look him over.

He's dressed in a leather jacket, old faded jeans, and a pair of biker boots. He looks so sexy and badass, like he's straight from a movie that all of us women fantasize about.

Forget the motorcycle... I want to ride him.

"You ready? Told you I'd be back to take you for a ride." He grabs my bag and tosses it in my truck, before grabbing my hand and helping me onto the back of his bike.

My heart does a little jump, when he reaches for my arms and wraps them around his muscular body. He feels so good. "Hold on to me and don't let go. I tend to like to ride fast and hard."

"Your ankle?" I question in surprise at the fact that he's already back on his motorcycle. It hasn't even been six weeks yet.

"The pain is gone and I've been walking on it for days now. I'm good as new. Now hold on tight."

"Where are we going?" I question as he slides his helmet on my head.

"Somewhere I like to go to clear my head."

He takes off and I hold on as tightly as I can, leaning my face into his strong back. The scent of his cologne is one of the sexiest things I've ever smelled and it does nothing to make me want him less right now.

As if him showing up for me, looking as incredible as he does wasn't enough.

We ride for a while, just enjoying the night air, before he turns down a trail, hidden by trees. Something about him taking me to the middle of nowhere has my body buzzing with excitement and wonder.

I'm not used to men wanting to go anywhere other than the bedroom or a bar.

It's nice because I like places where I can relax and clear my head away from everyone.

Once we reach the end of the trail, he parks next to water that I didn't even know existed, hidden back here.

We sit here for a few moments, before he helps me off his bike and hops off himself, taking off his jacket and draping it over my shoulders.

"Thank you," he whispers across my lips.

"For what?" My eyes lower to his lips, before slowly moving back up to meet his eyes. "I was just doing my job."

He licks his lips and fingers a strand of my hair. "You didn't have to stay and we both knew it. You stayed because you wanted to take care of me."

I swallow and take a step back from him. The way his eyes look into me as if he can see into my soul makes me feel as if I'm coming undone for him. He's so good at making me turn away first. "You're welcome," is all I can say.

He looks me over in silence for a few seconds as if he's trying to read me, before speaking again.

"I love how quiet it is back here. No screaming, whistling or a room full of women calling out my name and telling me all the things they want and expect me to do to them. This place brings me peace... a place where I can think about what I want in life."

He grabs my hand and pulls me down closer to the water, helping me up onto a huge rock to sit. Then he climbs up himself and pulls me to sit between his legs.

"What do you want in life?" I question, quietly, as he pulls my hair back and presses his lips against my neck.

It feels so good, making me forget my own worries and stress for just a short moment.

"I want a woman to love and build a life with. I want someone to take care of and cater to. I want to prove to myself that I'm not my asshole father and I have more to give than he ever did or has. I want to be a good man that is worthy of love."

His confession has me turning in his arms and cupping his face in my hands. I knew there was something deeper to him than meets the eye. "We all have a choice to be different than our parents and choose our own path." I pause and swallow back the emotions that are coming up. "I lost my parents when I was just ten and then my aunt last year so I've had no other choice than to be myself and go my own path. I barely even remember how my parents were."

"I'm sorry," he says gently.

I smile at the genuine look on his face. There's something about the way he looks right now that is extremely beautiful and real. "It's okay. I've been pretty good at being strong and I don't plan to stop anytime soon."

"I can see that and feel that about you and I like it. A strong woman is what I need and want in my life."

I'm feeling playful, remembering our little joke from when we first met. "Is that why you continue to stalk me? Can't get enough of me, huh?"

His eyes lock with mine, before he grabs my face and runs his thumbs over my lips. "You're so fucking beautiful right now. I know you don't know me, but I have a feeling that I want you to."

Leaning in, he pulls my bottom lip into his mouth, before releasing it and breathing against my lips. "I may be acting tame as fuck around you, but truthfully, being around you makes me feel wild as hell and all I can think about is tasting every inch of you." He runs his tongue over his bottom lip. "Don't let my need to respect you make you believe that I don't want to fuck you so hard that you'll feel me for weeks. If you were any other girl, you would've been naked in the first ten minutes. That's the truth."

"Stop talking," I demand.

He's making me fucking wild inside. Something inside tells me that I should run, while the other part wants to jump on him and take him for a ride.

Jumping down from the rock, I take a few steps back, watching him as he watches me with those damn eyes that I can't get enough of.

He looks so calm and cool, watching me with a confidence that is extremely sexy to me. Even though his words shouldn't work on me, and turn me on, they have... completely.

Standing up, he silently jumps down from the rock and walks toward me, stripping his jacket from my shoulders and watching me breathe as the jacket hits the ground.

Before I can even consider what he's about to do, his lips are on mine and my legs are wrapped around his strong waist, his hands firmly gripping my ass.

His lips capture mine, completely, his lips owning me and making me forget everything around me. I don't even notice that we're walking toward the water, until we're waist deep and the cold water is creeping up my stomach, chilling me.

I grip onto him and raise my body higher to escape the water. "Why are we in the water? It's freezing!"

He presses his body into me, making it aware that he's completely hard. "Trying to make this erection go down, before I give in and fuck you like I want to."

"Oh..." I swallow and then let out a moan as he presses his erection into me again. "God, that feels so good. Don't do that. Please..."

He smiles against my lips and grinds his hips into me again, making me moan from the sensitivity. "Just because I'm trying to hold back from fucking you, doesn't mean I don't want to make you come."

Wrapping his hand in my hair, he tugs and digs his hips into me, while walking us over to the ground and laying me down, so that we're out of the water.

A small breath escapes me as he positions himself between my legs and reaches between our bodies to undo my jeans.

"Styx," I breathe.

"Don't worry," he says thickly. "I already said I'm not going to fuck you."

I lean my head into the ground as he slips his fingers into my underwear and runs his fingers through my slickness, making me even wetter.

"Fuck me... Meadow. You're so fucking wet for me."

I moan and nod as he slips a finger inside and slowly begins pumping in and out.

"Oh my God..." I moan and thrust my hips as he picks up speed and leans in to run the tip of his tongue over my lips.

The way he's working my pussy is more like a massage and he knows exactly what he needs to do to get me off.

He's not moving too fast and rough like most guys that selfishly try to get you off so they can just get the job done. No... he's working my pussy and owning it as if it's his only care and he's not stopping until my body is in full ecstasy.

Listening to his heavy breathing above me as he gets me off, has me craving to return the favor. So I rub his cock through his jeans, making him growl out and reach to undo his button with his free hand.

He moves his jeans and briefs down his waist, giving me just enough room to pull his erection out.

It feels so full and heavy in my hand, my fingers unable to reach fully around it as I stroke his length.

"Shit..." he moans. "This was supposed to be about getting you off. I was trying not to be selfish with you."

I wrap my arm around his neck and pull him down to press my lips against his. He moans into my mouth as I squeeze his cock, holding on for dear life as I come undone with his fingers inside me.

My moans escape once he releases my mouth.

"Oh... fuck... holy shit!"

Smiling down at me, he slips his fingers out and sucks them into his mouth. "You taste as sweet as you fucking look."

Every word that leaves his mouth only has my body craving for him even more, wanting to do very dirty things with him.

He roughly bites my bottom lip, before releasing it and kissing my neck. "Let's get you in my jacket and in my arms. It's cold."

I shake my head and grab his hips as he stands up and reaches his hand out. "You haven't gotten off yet."

Looking down at me, he wraps both hands into the back of my hair and watches me as I slowly swirl my tongue around the head of his dick.

I do this a few more times, causing him to moan out and pull at my hair. "I need you to stop," he growls out, while stopping me from taking him in my mouth. "Stop, Meadow."

Confused, I look up at him as he grabs my hands to help me up. "What's wrong?"

Pulling me against him, he gently yanks my head to the side and presses his lips below my ear. "Because your mouth on me is making it fucking impossible to not rip that sexy little thong off and bury myself deep inside your pussy. I only have so much restraint."

I watch him as he pulls his jeans back up and buttons them. "Should we go?" I ask as I fix myself.

He shakes his head and picks his jacket back up, draping it over my shoulders to warm me. "Not yet. Come on."

We end up back on the rock in the same position as we were before.

His arms wrapped around me.

Me between his thick thighs.

No words are exchanged.

We just sit here.

Both lost in thought.

Everything else in the world forgotten for the moment as we sit here with wet clothes and shoes, staring up at the sky.

Just two broken people enjoying each other's comfort for a short time.

I have a feeling I can get used to this...

STYX

SHE'S FALLEN ASLEEP IN MY arms, but I refuse to move and wake her up. I haven't moved a muscle in over twenty minutes now, not wanting to disturb her peace.

A hard-working woman deserves every moment of sleep and comfort she can manage to get and I'll give her every second of it tonight.

Once she's ready to go, then I'll get my sleep. But until then...

I close my eyes and breathe in the peacefulness of the night air. Being here with Meadow in my arms will probably become one of my favorite memories of this place.

I've had lots of memories here, but all alone. There hasn't been one woman before Meadow, that I've wanted to bring out here and enjoy this spot with.

My arms loosen around her, when she stirs in my arms and whispers something.

I stay quiet, unsure if she's just talking in her sleep or if she's just woken up.

"Crap, I'm sorry," she speaks up louder this time, before turning in my arms. "I'm more tired than I thought, I guess."

"No worries." I hop off the rock and pick her up, helping her down to her feet. "Let me get you home."

I grab her hand and guide her back to my motorcycle, before slipping my helmet back on her head and hopping on.

She holds on tightly, resting her head against my back the whole ride back to the hospital.

Once I pull up behind her truck, I help her off my motorcycle and grab her hand as she's about to walk away.

She gets ready to say goodnight, but I cut her off by pressing my lips against her, causing her to moan into my mouth and reach out to grip my hair.

"Holy shit," she whispers when I pull away. "Goodnight, Styx."

"I'll follow you home to make sure you get there safely. It's late."

She shakes her head and slides my helmet over my head with a cute little smile that makes me want to bite her lips. "I'll be fine. I'm house sitting for Mandy and she only lives like three minutes from here."

"I'll follow anyway," I argue. "I don't give up so easily so don't try."

"Alright. Well thank you." She backs away, keeping her eyes on me, until she's hopping into her truck.

This woman has a lot to learn about me if she thinks I won't protect her any chance that I get...

CHAPTER NINE

STYX

I'M STILL SURPRISED AS HELL with the restraint I showed with Meadow last week. It took everything in me to make myself stop her from sucking my cock and to not fuck her on the spot.

With any other woman, I would've had her screaming my name within the first ten minutes of being alone.

There's just something about Meadow that makes me want to be different with her. I've never had this feeling before, so I'm going to do everything I can to not fuck it up for as long as I can.

Now that I'm back to my long nights at the club, I haven't run into Meadow at the gym. We always seem to miss each other, and no matter how hard I've tried to get here so that I don't miss her, there's always someone at the club on my nuts, trying to hold me up.

Last night, I missed Meadow by five minutes. Five fucking minutes and it pisses me off.

I've been checking her log for the last week and she always seems to show up around twelve-thirty and leaves just before two.

Last week had been a late week for all of us at the club, but I'm making sure that I get my ass out of there early tonight. I don't care what it takes.

Logging onto the gym's membership info, I look up Meadow's information for what seems like the hundredth time in the last five days since I've seen her.

Her phone number is staring back at me, tempting me to add it to my phone so that I can reach her whenever I want.

I don't usually do this with women or members of the gym, due to their privacy, but the more I look at her number, the more I decide to say fuck the rules.

"Put your dick away and let's go," Kash says from the doorway. "Cale called and said he needs us to hurry because Stone is getting more than his ass can handle. Hemy is there and about ready to take our fucking cash if we don't get there in ten."

I look away from the computer and stare his sweaty ass down. "So let him take my spot. Tell Cale I'll be there in an hour. I have something to do first."

Kash looks stressed as hell at the idea of telling Cale that I'm not coming in early. He grips the doorframe and huffs. "Just hurry the hell up. We might even need Hemy to stay after you get there."

"I'll be there." I write down the info I need and stand up, shoving the paper into my pocket. "You fuckers will be fine until I get there. Pull Kage onto the stage if you need to. He's been dying to dry hump the floor."

Kash just nods his head and takes off, running out the door, in a hurry to get to the club. He never wastes an opportunity to make money, especially when it involves women on his dick.

Grabbing my things, I lock the office door behind me and quickly walk through the gym, making sure not to even look in the direction of any of the women here.

Every time I do, they expect me to take them back to my office and fuck them. It was fun in the beginning, but I'm over it. It was just something to pass the time and forget my worries for a while.

There would've never been anything more with any of them. Most of them came from *Walk of Shame* and got memberships here, after they found out that I ran my uncle's gym on the side.

I've seen every single one of them all over Stone's and Kash's dicks as well as mine. I'm tired of women that will jump on the opportunity of taking any one of us to bed that shows them attention first.

I want a woman that is just about me and not all over my ass because of my occupation or because they see me as a hot fuck to brag about.

That's exactly why I'm headed where I am right now. I've waited to see Meadow show up at the club just for fun, but she hasn't. Which just proves that she was only there to find me to begin with.

If she was there for the entertainment, then she would've been back by now. I know... because the women I'm used to are always back the next fucking day. Once they come to the club, they become addicted to watching us and wanting us.

Pulling my motorcycle up to the address on Meadow's profile, I kill the engine and get off my bike.

My heart fucking goes crazy at the sight of Meadow standing on the porch, watching me, when I look up.

Her little tank top has my dick twitching as I take in her breasts and tattoos.

She smiles big as I walk toward her, looking just as happy to see me as I am her. "I knew I should've put a fake address on that form," she teases. "Especially after seeing you that first night at the gym."

When I reach her, I cup her face and back her up against the door. "I would've found you anyway." Gripping her waist, I press my lips against hers, not being as gentle as the last time. I want her and I'm tired of holding back. "Trust me. When I want something as badly as I want you, I don't give up easily."

She pulls her bottom lip into her mouth as if my kiss hurt her. "Good," she whispers. "I'm tired of quitters. And men that give up because they find a new toy to play with. With all the toys you have around..." She looks up to meet my eyes. "I'm surprised you haven't already."

Her words anger me and something inside of me snaps. She thinks that she's just a fucking toy for me. She has no idea just how fucked up she's had me since day one. She's barely left my mind for longer than ten minutes. That's exactly why I'm here now. I've never gone to a woman's house because I needed to be with them as desperately as I do right now.

I grip her legs and pull them around my waist, pressing my erection against her pussy. "You really have no idea just how much I want you. If I didn't, then I wouldn't have waited until now to do what I'm about to do."

She grips the back of my hair and brushes her lips over mine. "And what is that?"

I smile against her lips. "*Fuck* you." I push the door open and begin carrying her through the house, until I find her bed. "Then I'm going to the club with you all over me because you're not just some play toy for me, dammit."

Tired of holding back, I toss her on the bed and rip her jeans down her legs, and then her panties, before flipping her over and slapping her ass, hard.

I wrap my fingers into the back of her long hair and pull as my other hand reaches around to grip her throat. I breathe heavily against her ear. "I want you." I press my cock against her ass and then pull her up so that she can feel my heart racing against her back. "Can you feel how much?"

She nods and grips the blanket. "I want you too. Really fucking bad. I'm usually never like this with men. The way you have me thinking about you at all times."

With one hand, I push my jeans down my hips and pull out my cock, before slipping a condom on and taking in the sight of her beautiful ass and pussy.

"Damn, Meadow. That only turns me on more."

My need to be rough takes over and I feel myself losing control. I growl and push her head down into the mattress, before slapping her ass again and biting it.

She moans out as my tongue slides up her pussy, slowly and teasingly, before I stop and pull away. "Are you sure?"

"Yes," she breathes.

I spread her cheeks, my tongue working her pussy slowly at first, before I speed up and then dip my tongue inside of her.

She arches her back and moans out loudly as I slide my tongue in further, fucking her with it, until I feel her shaking in my arms, close to losing it.

I lose all self-control, reaching around to grip her neck, hard, pulling her up flat against my chest. My hand squeezes, but I make sure to be gentle enough to let her know that I would never hurt her.

"Holy fuck..." I breathe. "I'll try not to be too rough, but I'm not sure that I can be gentle right now."

"Don't be." She grips the sheet and runs her tongue up my arm, before biting it. "Who says I like it gentle?"

"Fuck! I won't be then."

Sliding the tip of my dick across her entrance, I line it up just perfectly and then ease it in, before pulling out and slamming into her so hard that she bites down on my arm and screams.

She feels so good wrapped around my cock. I knew that she would, and not just physically. This is so much more to me right now.

Both of my arms wrap around her body, pulling her as closely as possible as I thrust into her repeatedly, wanting to show her just how much she gets to me.

She gets to me unlike any other woman ever has and I'm going to do everything to show her that.

I won't be stopping after tonight. She's not just a play toy for me. Fuck that shit.

"Oh fuuuuck!" I yell out, while picking her up and carrying her out of bed and over to the wall.

She grips my hair and moans out as I slam her against the wall and bury myself deep between her legs again. "Harder..." she growls against my lips. "Don't hold back, Styx. We both need this. I know you're not gentle. Let it out."

I push in deep and stop, making her scream into my arm and dig her nails in with each hard thrust after that.

I don't stop until she's shaking in my arms from her orgasm. I give her a few seconds to catch her breath. Then I walk her back over to the bed, lay her down and hold her legs over my shoulders, digging my fingers in as I fuck her deeper than I've ever fucked before.

Being inside her just doesn't feel like enough right now. I want to touch her in places that no other man ever has.

Gripping my neck, she pulls me down and presses her lips against mine, causing me to moan into her mouth as I come.

I'm so lost in the moment and this insanely beautiful woman, that I don't even bother pulling out. It's something that I always make sure to do, even though I always wear a condom.

With Meadow... I don't want to. I want her to feel what she does to me.

I pull her bottom lip into my mouth and gently suck it, before pulling away.

Then we both just lay in bed in silence, her head pressed against my chest.

I don't even know how much time passes, before my phone goes off and I come back to reality.

Groaning, I grab my phone, prepared to tell Kash to fuck off, but it's Cale instead. I can't be an asshole to him, even though I want nothing more than to stay right the fuck where I'm at.

"Fuck." I kiss her head and crawl out of bed. "I'm supposed to be at the club right now."

She looks up at me from the bed and even though she understands that I have to go, I feel guilty as shit for having to leave her.

I'm about to throw my shirt back on, but I slip it over her head instead and pulling her in for a kiss.

"I'll be back for this." I smirk. "Fuck it looks good on you."

She smiles back. "Is that your way of saying that I'll see you soon?"

I walk over to the door and stop to look back at her. "If I have it my way. Fuck yes."

"Good," she whispers.

Knowing that if I don't get out of here, that I'm going to end up saying fuck work and stay, I rush out of the house and jump on my bike.

Fuck... this woman has me. I know this now...

CHAPTER TEN

MEADOW

IT'S BEEN AN HOUR SINCE Styx left for the club, and I'm still lying here in bed, wearing his cologne-covered shirt.

This man does something to me that I just can't explain. When he showed up outside my house, unexpectedly, a rush of excitement and adrenaline coursed through me, making me feel alive with energy.

It's a feeling that I haven't gotten in a while. Something about Styx makes me believe that there's something to look forward to. I've found that hope is something that I haven't felt since losing my aunt last year so this... it surprises me.

Everything that I have loved has been lost, starting with my parents and ending with the woman that raised me since the age of ten.

That's why I've put everything I have into the patients at the hospital, almost forgetting that I have a life myself. Any attachments outside of work have been impossible for me.

That's exactly why I need to be careful when it comes to Styx. The sight of him in those perfect jeans, fitted tee, and leather jacket does things to a woman's body and mind.

I lost all sense of thought as I watched him climb off his motorcycle and walk toward me with a confidence that only Styx seems to have.

I smile when I realize I'm sniffing his shirt. "There's something about you," I whisper. "And I think I want to find out just what that is."

Making a quick decision, before I can change my mind, I jump out of bed and gather some clothes to throw on. I must look like a hot mess right now, but I don't care.

I know that Styx was just here, but I haven't seen him in days and spending the little bit of time with him that I did, just wasn't enough. It only made me want more of him.

So much more.

Within thirty minutes, I'm lining up outside *Walk of Shame*, looking around me at all the women that are waiting to get in.

There's got to be at least thirty women out here and who knows how many inside already, and almost every single one of them will be drooling over the man that I just had sex with and throwing money his way.

I've never felt anything like this before. It's exciting, yet strange at the same time, knowing that he could have any woman that he wants, but for some reason he's shown an interest in me.

I let out a flattered laugh and cross my arms, while waiting for the line to move. It seems to be taking forever and I can't tell if it's just because I'm anxious to see Styx or if it's because the line just isn't moving.

After about forty-five minutes of waiting in line, I look around me to see that the line hasn't moved much, since no one seems to want to leave to let others in.

Letting out a defeated breath, I turn around to leave, just to be stopped by strong arms encircling my waist and pulling me against a hard body.

"Miss me already?"

My heart races with that excitement that I only feel around Styx, as I turn around to look his sweaty body up and down. He's dressed in leather pants and *holy fuck* he looks dangerously sexy.

He's breathing heavily as he watches me check him out, taking in every glistening muscle. "I'm going to take that as a yes."

I laugh at his boldness and fight not to get lost in his insane blue eyes. "Maybe I was just bored," I tease.

Smirking, he steps up against me and wraps his hands into the back of my hair, before leaning in to press his lips against my ear. "I'll make sure to change that then."

Grabbing my hand, he pulls me though the crowd, nodding his head at the security guard, *Lane,* as we pass him to get inside.

The music is loud, the screaming of the women even louder than I remember it from last time.

And having everyone's eyes on me as Styx holds my hand has my body buzzing and my heart about ready to fly out of my chest with excitement.

"How did you know I was here?" I question close to his ear so that he can hear me over the noise.

"I didn't." He turns his face so that he's talking in my ear now. "I was *hoping.*"

The idea of him looking for me has me smiling so hard that it hurts. It only shows me that even with all these women around, I'm somehow still on his mind.

I get a little nervous when I realize that he's guiding me over to the VIP section where two beautiful women are sitting on the leather couch, talking and laughing.

They both look up once they notice me and Styx standing in front of them, listening to their conversation about someone named Hemy.

"Woah," the blonde with tattoos says with a smirk. "Who is this hottie?"

Styx pulls me against him and grips my hip, possessively. "She's with me. Don't let any of the other assholes get too close."

The other girl lifts a brow and looks me over, smiling, as if she approves. "The guys get a little crazy here, so don't mind his manners." She grabs my hand and pulls me down to sit next to her. "I'm Sage and that's Onyx. You're good with us."

Styx laughs when I look up at him, confused. "They're with Stone and Hemy. My family will take good care of you when I can't. Just watch out for the blonde. She gets a little frisky."

Before I can say anything, he backs away and gets lost in the crowd of screaming women.

"He'll be back for you. I know that look." Onyx looks me over with curiosity. "I never thought I'd see the day that Styx brought a woman to us. I'm impressed. You're hot, babe."

I laugh and grab the drink that Kage brings over to me. I remember him from last time and he seems to remember me since he brought me the same drink as before. "Thank you, Kage."

It looks like Kage is about to get ready to flirt, but Onyx shuts him down. "She's taken, dickhead. Go pick one of the hundreds of other women in this room."

He laughs as she waves him off. "Hey, can't blame a man for trying."

The three of us watch as he makes his way through the crowd and picks out some random blonde to try his moves on.

"These fucking men of *Walk of Shame*," Sage says with a smile. "Gotta love them all here."

My mind is still lost on what Onyx said before Kage came over.

"So should I feel special then?"

"You are," Sage says. "Styx doesn't just let *anyone* in. He seems to stick to himself."

My eyes seek him out in the crowd and lock on him once I find him grinding the stage and working it so good that even *I'm* sweating and completely turned on.

I don't even realize that I'm fanning myself off, until Sage laughs from beside me. "The boys know how to work it and they only seem to get *hotter* with each show."

Onyx grabs my hand and pulls it into her lap, while pointing across the room at a tall guy with long, dark hair, covered in tattoos. "That sexy as sin man over there is my husband Hemy. Trust me. Things only get better once they claim you as their own. What these girls get here at the club is just a glimpse into what these men can bring in the bedroom." She smiles. "Or the back of the club, pool, motorcycle, or a friend's garage... wherever they want to take you."

My eyes widen as Hemy grabs the back of some girl's head and begins fucking her face. "And you're okay with that?"

Both the girls laugh, but it's Sage that speaks.

"When these men love, they love with everything in them. I have a feeling that Styx will do just the same. What they do here in the club won't even matter once you get to feel what they bring you both emotionally and physically outside of the club."

I sip my drink and bring my eyes back to Styx just in time to see him throw his pants off the stage and slide his hands into the front of his boxer briefs.

"I've already seen what that man can do outside of the club," I say mostly to myself. "I still haven't come down from that high."

Onyx finally releases my hand and smiles as Hemy walks up the steps to where we are. "That's just the beginning, babe."

The way Hemy straddles her lap and grinds against her has my body heating up. It's as if he's fucking her right here next to me and they don't give two shits about who's watching them get off.

These men are too much to handle.

Holy fuck...

STYX

I CAN'T CONCENTRATE FOR SHIT, knowing that Meadow is here to see me. All it makes me want to do is spend all my fucking time on her.

If it weren't for the bachelorette party that Cale told me to focus on, I'd be over there right now, straddling her lap and whispering in her ear about just how beautiful she is and how I haven't stopped thinking about her since I left her house tonight.

My head has been all messed up since the moment I laid eyes on her at the gym and saw that there was something more to her than just a woman that wants to jump on my dick and take me for a test ride.

The way she looked at me, while I was buried between her thighs earlier, only confirmed that for me.

She's different than the rest.

Hands grab at me, pulling me in every direction, but I can't seem to pull my eyes away from Meadow sitting with the girls, talking and looking as if she's enjoying herself.

Every once in a while, when our eyes meet, she winks, letting me know that she's here for me.

"Fuck this," I growl out, unable to stay away anymore. My hands need to be on her fucking body.

I fight my way through the crowd of screaming women, not stopping until I have Meadow in my arms, her legs wrapping around my waist as I hold her up by her ass.

"I can't think straight with you in the same room." I run my mouth up her neck, stopping under her ear. "Do you know that? You're the only one that seems to matter when you're in the room. I would walk out right now just to spend time with you."

She grips my hair and pulls my head back to look me in the eyes. "I'll be here when you're done. I'm not going *anywhere*." Her lips curl into a smile. "I love watching you out there and I'm thinking I'd like to spend some time with you when you're done."

"Well, shit," I say with a grin. "Maybe I will just leave now. Take you back to my place and fuck you until you can't move."

I go to walk away, ready to carry Meadow out of here, but Hemy grabs my arm and stops me. "Your ass isn't going anywhere, fucker." He looks around. "Not for a long fucking time. I'd like to take my woman home and bury myself between her fucking thighs too, but we have a job to do first."

Meadow brushes her lips over mine, when I don't make a move to release her. "Go," she whispers, before pulling my bottom lip into her mouth and then releasing it. "You're worth the wait."

Her words cause my heart to pound fast in my chest and before I know it, I'm carrying her through the crowd and grabbing a chair that Kash slides my way.

Forgetting that anyone else is in the room, I lower Meadow to the chair and straddle her lap, moving my hips to the slow rhythm.

My hands reach out to wrap into her soft hair and my lips are on hers without hesitation, showing the whole room that she's with me.

Any of these other fuckers in the room even think about touching her, I'll rip their throats out. Kage has barely taken his eyes off her since she walked into the room and I sent him to bring her a drink.

I'll fuck that giant motherfucker up if he lays one finger on her.

When I break away from the kiss, and pull Meadow to her feet, Kash walks over, half-naked, and presses his body behind her, picking her up so that her legs are around my shoulders.

Then he pulls her backwards so that she's hanging from my shoulders. The women go crazy as he takes her hands and runs them down his body, stopping above his dick.

I know what he's doing, because it was our plan to treat a woman to this, but I wasn't expecting it to be Meadow.

But knowing that her hands are running down his hard, sweaty body, has my blood boiling right now. It only gets worse when he grabs the back of her head and grinds his cock in her face.

It's the first time in my life that I've known what jealously feels like and it's a shitty fucking feeling.

I feel Meadow stiffen around my neck and grip my legs as if she wants me to pull her back up, so I back away from Kash and pull her back to me.

With my heart racing, I lower to my knees and lay her on the ground, before pinning her body beneath mine.

I grip her thigh with one hand, lifting it up so that I can push myself between her legs and line my cock up with the heat between her legs.

Her eyes meet mine the whole time and it's almost as if the whole fucking room silences as I move my body against her to the slow beat.

It's not until Kash yells my name, that I come out of my head and run my hands through my wet hair.

I have no idea what the hell I'm doing right now, but I can tell that getting through the rest of this night is going to be harder than I imagined.

Grunting, I pick Meadow up, holding her close as I walk her through the crowd again and back over to the VIP section.

Both Onyx and Sage watch me with huge smiles as I lower Meadow to her feet and grab her hand, walking her over to sit back down in between them.

"Keep her safe for me. And tell Kage to keep his fucking eyes and dick in check."

Onyx grins and wraps her arm up in Meadow's. Hell, I might even have to worry about her ass trying to get close to my girl. "Oh, I'll keep her safe and comfortable next to me. No one with a dick will touch her." She winks, messing with me.

If she wasn't Hemy's girl, that fucker would kill me for even thinking it, I'd maybe even let her touch her as I watched.

'Cause I know after my cock, there's no way she'd want pussy over what I bring her in the bedroom.

But damn, if I don't want anyone touching her. Even Onyx.

Fuck... I need this night to be over.

CHAPTER ELEVEN

MEADOW

AFTER STYX GOT PULLED AWAY by Kash, he barely got another chance to come over to me.

I could see the exhaustion and need in his eyes, every time he looked over at me and all I could think about was doing something to make him feel good and let him know that I want to be close to him just as bad.

A part of me feels this need to let him know that I'm here for him and that someone else can take care of things for a while.

After the story he told me about his father, I get a feeling that he's spent a lot of his life taking care of others more than himself. He just carries so much on his shoulders and I can feel it.

"I'm going to find Styx."

Sage smiles and pulls me in close. "Check the showers. I have a feeling that you might find him in there. Just a little tip."

Onyx gives me a slap on the ass and winks at me. "Get it, girl and fuck the haters on the way."

Fixing my jeans, I walk through the crowd, holding my head up high, when I feel eyes on me from all around.

Most of the women whisper shit, giving me looks as if they're judging me because of Styx's little display of affection toward me.

Well I say... fuck it. Onyx is right.

Walking faster, I search around me, stopping to ask one of the security guards where the showers are. He's so preoccupied with some chick, that he just nods his head toward the end of the hall and goes back to sucking on her neck.

"Thanks," I say to myself with a small smile.

Pushing the door open, I walk around to the showers to see Styx, standing there completely naked, dripping with water.

He looks rushed as if he has somewhere to be.

My eyes trail down his perfect, round ass, watching the muscles in his legs flex as he pulls his jeans up.

"You should keep them off." I walk up behind him and wrap my arms around his wet body, before gripping the top of his jeans and tugging them down a bit. "They're just about as wet as I am right now."

His muscles flex beneath my fingers as he takes in a deep breath and releases it. "I wanted to catch you before you left."

I kiss his back, while gripping his jeans harder, pulling them back down his thick thighs. All I can think about right now is worshiping this beautiful as sin body. "I told you I wasn't going anywhere."

Rotating his shoulders, he cracks his neck and then slowly turns around to face me, completely naked, looking so damn beautiful and perfect that it's breathtaking.

His eyes lock on mine as he kicks his jeans away and watches me, waiting for what I'm going to do next.

Swallowing, I pull my eyes away from his and walk into the open shower stall, undressing and kicking my clothes out for Styx to see.

The water barely turns on, before Styx appears in the doorway, watching with intense eyes. "Does being here make you feel dirty?"

I shake my head and reach out for his hand, pulling him into the water. "No. I don't think you got the shower you deserved after such a hard night's work. Let me take care of you."

Closing his eyes, he leans his head back and places his hands against the shower wall as I gently run my hands over his shoulders and then down his back.

"Fuck, your hands feel perfect on me."

I press my lips against his back as I reach for the soap and trail it over his tight muscles.

I've never showered with a man before and I have to admit that I'm extremely turned on, but... I want to let Styx know that this moment is more than that.

With soap, I work my way down his body, massaging his muscled legs with my hands.

He lets out a small moan of appreciation, leaning his head down into the water and just taking a moment to relax and enjoy the feel of my hands on him.

Holy hell, I'm enjoying it just as much.

"Turn around," I say in almost a whisper.

Taking his hands away from the wall, he turns around and faces me, his eyes admiring my body as I focus on cleaning his tattooed chest, before moving down to his abdomen.

"You don't have to do this, Meadow." He grips my hair tightly as I move down to his erection, moving my soapy hands over it. "I should be doing this for you."

"I haven't spent the whole night working hard. A woman shouldn't be the only one to be catered to. Hard-working men deserve it just as much." I place my hand on his stomach and back him up against the shower wall. "Now close your eyes and enjoy."

Closing his eyes, he wraps his hands tighter into my hair, moaning as I stroke my hands over his dick, spending extra time on the head.

This man's body is so beautiful that I could spend all night doing this. He truly has no idea how easy it is to want to take care of him.

When his moans become louder, my movements pick up, knowing that he's getting close to coming.

"Come for me, Styx," I breathe, completely turned on and just as desperate for his release as he is. "All over my breasts. I want to feel you on me. Show me what I do to you."

He yanks my head back and he growls out, shooting his cum all over my breasts.

"Oh fuuuuuck." He looks down at me and massages his hands through my hair as the water washes over my breasts cleaning his release away. "Where the fuck have you been all my life? Stand up."

Pulling me up to my feet, he wraps his arms around me and holds me against him, under the water.

We stand here just letting the warm water pour down on us, not speaking for a while. We just take this moment to enjoy the feel of each other being close.

It feels good. So much better than I ever imagined and that scares me, but I don't want to leave.

After a while, he pulls away and presses his lips against mine. His lips are soft and smooth, yet his kiss is rough and firm, consuming me and making me want more of him.

Styx may be rough in bed, but he has a gentle side. A gentle side that might just make me fall harder than I hoped.

His eyes meet mine. "Now it's my turn to take care of you."

Our lips meet again and he picks me up, wrapping my legs around his strong waist. I can feel his dick rubbing against my pussy and all I want is for him to fill me with it.

Breathing hard against my lips, he backs me up against the wall for extra support, as he slides his hand in between our bodies and fills me with his tattooed fingers.

He slowly pumps in and out, causing me to moan against his lips and grind my pussy, wanting him deeper.

The water drips down my lips to Styx's. With a growl, he sticks his tongue out, catching it in his mouth, before sucking my bottom lip and moving his fingers faster and harder.

My arm snakes around his neck, my other hand digging into his back, holding on for dear life as I moan out and begin shaking in his arms from my own release.

I can't even remember a time that I've had an orgasm so quickly in my entire life, but with this man, it's impossible not to.

After a few moments, he pulls his fingers out and sucks them into his mouth, before placing his forehead to mine.

"You have no idea how badly I wished that were my cock inside you instead." He gently bites my bottom lip, before releasing it. "You make me want more than just a quick fuck though. I want to spend my time on you, worshiping every inch of that beautiful body, until you fall asleep from exhaustion."

He slowly releases me, one leg at a time, helping me down to my feet, before turning off the water and walking out to bring me a towel.

"I hope like hell that I get that night soon."

I smile and reach for the towel, wrapping it around me.

When I step out of the shower stall, Kash is standing there naked, pulling his jeans up his legs.

The same sight I got when I walked in on Styx, except Kash is facing me, his dick standing at attention.

Swallowing, I quickly turn my head away, before I can spend too much time admiring his insanely big dick and make this anymore awkward than it already is.

Styx smiles as if he's happy with how quick I was to turn away from Kash. Maybe he was expecting me to ogle over him like all the other women do.

When I turn back around, Kash is buttoning his jeans with a confident smile. "Sorry about that. I caught the end of your little shower date. Damn, that sounded hot as fuck."

My face heats up with embarrassment when I realize just how loud I was moaning while Styx was finger fucking me, just fifteen feet away from where Kash was changing.

The thought of someone possibly entering the locker room didn't even occur to me. All I could think about was taking care of Styx.

"Just hurry the fuck up, dick. You didn't have to sit around and wait for the ending," Styx snaps.

Kash looks me over in my towel, showing his appreciation. I can't deny that the way he looks at a woman heats you up in an instant. Those deep gray eyes do wonders. "No, but I wanted to." He winks at me and then grabs his shirt, walking out of the room.

Styx looks heated, his eyes watching the door as it closes behind him. "Let's get dressed so I can follow you home. It's late and I don't want you out there alone."

I reach for my clothes and quickly get dressed, before walking over to him and grabbing his face. As soon as his eyes look down to meet mine, my mind is made up. "Maybe you can stay."

The look in his eyes tells me that it's not a request that he usually even considers, but a part of him wants to right now.

"Let's go," is all he says, as he grabs my hand and walks me past some of the staff and outside.

A group of women are waiting around the door, giggling and talking loudly about how hot each and every guy was tonight.

I'm hoping like hell that they're not waiting to suck Styx into their little group, because I honestly don't know what I'd do if he left me to hang with them.

I've had it happen to me in the past a few times, proving to me that the guy I was with really wasn't who I thought or hoped he would be.

Grabbing my hand, Styx speeds up when one of the girls calls his name.

The tall brunette doesn't seem to want to give up. She calls his name a few more times, her friends joining in by whistling and yelling for him too.

My face heats up with jealousy and anger that these women won't just give the hell up. Finally, I turn around and snap.

"Don't you see that he's leaving with someone? Get some fucking class."

I can barely finish what I'm saying, before Styx yanks me to him and starts making out with me, while walking me backward into my truck.

"Get in and I'll follow you home," he says, between tugging on my bottom lip and sucking it into his mouth. "My motorcycle is across the lot."

I nod and jump inside my truck when he walks away. A few minutes later, he pulls up behind me and motions for me to drive.

I feel like an idiot the whole ride home and I have to admit that I'm disappointed in myself for even thinking a man like Styx would ever want to spend the night.

The only thing he made clear was that he was following me home. That was probably his way of letting me down gently.

After I pull up at my house, Styx parks his motorcycle behind my truck, and gets off to meet me behind my vehicle.

He's silent the whole walk to the door of my house and surprises me when he walks inside behind me and locks the door.

I don't say a word as he follows me to my bedroom, undresses me and then does the same himself, before crawling into bed beside me.

Pinning my body beneath his, he reaches over to my nightstand and grabs my bottle of lotion, squirting it on his hands and rubbing them together. "Close your eyes and relax."

His naked body, above mine, has it almost impossible to relax, but I close my eyes anyway, moaning out as his hands rub over my body, massaging me.

Oh my God. How can he be so damn good with his hands? It's like every little touch from him is pure magic. Throw in him being naked and it's like a fantasy come to life. Getting a massage from a naked Styx is heaven.

Holy hell... I want this to last all night.

After he's done rubbing lotion over every inch of my body and making sure that I feel good, he spreads my legs open with his knee and lays in between them.

The feel of his erection brushing my entrance has me wanting to thrust my hips forward and hope like hell that he accidentally pushes inside of me and continues to thrust.

"Fuck, Meadow. Don't move your hips like that. I'm trying my best not to ease inside of you right now and stay there all fucking night. I can feel the heat of your pussy tempting me. Fuck!"

The look in his eyes tells me that he's here for me. Not for sex. For me. And from what I can tell, that's new for him.

So I want the same.

I run my hands through his hair and pull him down to give him a gentle kiss on the lips, tugging on his lip as I pull away. "You make it hard to want to be good," I admit.

He moans against my neck and then rolls over beside me, pressing down on his erection. "Just wait until I get you alone again. Fuck. Come here."

The way his arms wrap around me and pull me close, says it all. I know because I feel the exact same way. Our hearts are racing and we can't seem to catch our breath in the darkness.

I want him here, but I'm scared of what can come out of it.

I'm scared of letting him in and us both getting hurt...

CHAPTER TWELVE

STYX

I WAKE UP TO AN empty bed, running my hands through my messy hair as I look around the small room.

Sleeping in a woman's bed isn't something that I do, yet I couldn't deny Meadow when she asked me to stay with her last night. Not after she stayed at the hospital to look after me.

What kind of a man would that make me?

I spent most of the night, holding her close to me and running my hands through her soft hair as she cuddled up on my chest.

Her naked body pressed against mine, her fingers tracing my chest and tattoos, it was a feeling that I welcomed and made me want to stay up even later so that I could enjoy it longer.

You better believe that I fell asleep with a boner and woke up to one, just thinking about our naked bodies being entwined.

Wanting to fuck her last night was one of the hardest cravings I've had to fight. This woman is making me fight myself and that's how I know that she's worth everything I plan to give her.

When I look beside me at the alarm clock, I see that it's past ten. Meadow's shift starts at eleven today, since she was asked to come in early, so I know that I'm alone in her house. She told me last night that she was taking on extra hours at the hospital this week.

"Well this is new..." Sitting up, I throw my legs over the side of the bed and run my hands over my face, before getting dressed and grabbing my things.

I walk through the kitchen to leave, but stop when I see a bright pink sticky note hanging from the microwave.

The smell of bacon hits my nose as I walk over and reach for the note to read it.

This is me saying thank you for last night.

-Meadow

"Well damn..." I can't help but smile as I reach into the microwave and grab the plate of food out. I've never had a woman cook me breakfast before and I love that she thought of me this morning, before she left.

I don't usually eat when I first wake up, but knowing that Meadow took the time to cook me breakfast as a thank you, there's no way I'm leaving here without eating her meal. Every last bite of it.

I'll never do anything to disrespect her or make her feel bad or unappreciated.

My mother taught me that at a young age, although she doesn't seem to look for a guy with the same qualities, because she's still with my asshole father after twenty-four years.

Trying not to think about how much I miss her talks, I quickly eat and send Meadow a text to thank her before heading home.

I'm surprised when I pull up on my motorcycle to see Kash's truck parked in my driveway. This isn't the first time.

"Well, fuck." Grunting, I slam my helmet down on the seat and walk to the door, pushing it open.

The first thing I see is Kash's naked ass, standing up on my couch, gripping some girl's hair, guiding her head up and down on his cock.

I chuck my keys at the back of his head, and he releases the girl's hair to rub the back of his head and scream. "Ouch! What the fuck!"

"Yeah exactly," I say, pissed off that he decided to have a little fuck-a-thon at my place without asking. "What the fuck are you doing here on my motherfucking couch?"

When he moves away from the girl, I see that it's Sophie, from the gym.

She smiles up at me, looking a bit embarrassed. Her dark hair is wild as shit and her eye makeup is thick and smeared across her face as if it's been a long night. "So this is where you live? I never thought I'd see it. It's nice."

Kash raises his brows and looks between the two of us as he sits down and covers his dick with his hands. "I should've known you two were pretty well-acquainted. I did meet her at your gym and all." He smirks as if it doesn't bother him.

I didn't think it would. "You have your own place, fucker. I thought I took my key away the last time I caught your naked ass on my couch."

Grunting, I walk past them and into the kitchen to grab a beer. It's too early to deal with this crap. I need something so I don't flip my shit on him.

"My roommate trashed our place. Yours was cleaner." When he enters the kitchen, he's dressed in the same pair of jeans that he left the club in last night.

"Yeah," I say, while looking him over, covered in sweat. "It *was* cleaner. Did you sleep here last night?"

He grabs a beer and pops the top. "Nah, we didn't sleep."

Sophie stands in the doorway half-dressed and looks us both over, with a look on her face, that's telling us exactly what she's imagining at the moment.

She wants to fuck us at the same time. That might've been something I'd agree to before, but it doesn't even sound appealing now.

"I've gotta go." She buttons up her blouse, trying hard to look sexy as she does. "My ride's outside and I need some sleep before tonight. Later boys. I hope."

Kash winks and watches as she walks away, swaying her ass for us.

"What made your ass so sure that I wouldn't be home last night?"

He tilts back his beer and looks at me as if I've asked a stupid question. "After that shower, I knew it was different than your usual fuck. There's no way you weren't going home with her. I was in there for at least fifteen minutes before I even heard any moaning. It's usually within less than two seconds with us. I know how we work."

I look him over, letting his words sink in. That was definitely the first shower I've had with a woman that went like that. He's not wrong about that.

"You're steam cleaning my fucking couch today before work. I'm not touching it until you do. Your ass and dick are all over it."

"You even going to be here tonight?" he questions, watching me with a cocky smirk. "If not... then you might want me to wait until tomorrow to steam clean that shit. I have another date."

I set my beer down and run my hands through my hair, while making my way to the bathroom to shower, before I get the urge to break his pretty face. "Take care of that before tonight. I'll be staying here."

He laughs around his beer and then tilts it back. "Alright, man. Chill."

After I shower and get dressed, I leave Kash to take care of the couch, while I go out to the garage to do a little more work on my bike. It's still fucked up from my accident, but I'm slowly getting it back to how it was before.

Thirty minutes in and all I can think about is Meadow and how it felt, falling asleep with her in my arms.

I already miss the feel of her body against mine and the feel of her soft breath hitting against my chest as she fought to get as close to me as possible last night. Even in her sleep. It was like she couldn't get enough of me.

The thought of her against me has me hard. I can feel it straining against my fitted jeans.

"You working with a boner and shit?" Kash steps into the garage and laughs at my frustration. "You really have it bad for this girl. It's written all over your face, man."

"Maybe I do," I say mostly to myself. "So what."

He tosses me a beer and then opens one himself. "Leaves more women for me to fuck so no complaints from me, man. Just keep it separate from the club. If the women find out that two out of three of their favorite male entertainers are taken, then they're going to come less and spend less money. You know this. You've already given the crowd a show with her. You and fucking Stone are going to mess things up for the club."

I know Kash is right. Traffic slows down at the club each time one of us seems to commit, but that's the least of my concerns. I have enough money in my savings account to get me by for five fucking years without making another dime from the club.

If Cale has to replace me, then he has to replace me. He's a smart businessman and knows what needs to be done. That's exactly why I love the guy so much.

"I gotta go." I stand up and slip my leather jacket on, once I realize that it's close to one.

Kash gives me a confused look and watches as I set the unopened beer down and toss my tools aside, before walking my bike outside of the garage. "Where you going? We don't work for another five hours."

"Somewhere I have to. Just lock up for me and I'll see you tonight."

"Alright, man. I got you."

Straddling my bike, I start it and take off down the road, my heart racing fast, just like it always does when I'm heading to this street.

So many thoughts and scenarios run through my head that I barely even remember driving there until I get to my destination and park.

Before I know it, I'm parked on the side of the road, down the street from my mother's house with my bike facing the direction that I know *he'll* be coming from.

I sit here and wait for twenty minutes, growing impatient and more on edge with each passing second that there's still no sign of my father.

He's late, which could be bad for my mother.

Finally, around one-forty he pulls into the driveway and gets out. He crosses his arms and looks my way, knowing that I'm here watching him. I always am now.

It only takes one look at my father to know whether or not he's wasted and it's usually after work that he would get fucked up and then come home to beat up on us.

That's exactly why, no matter what the fuck I'm doing, I stop and make sure that I'm here every single day when he gets off. And I will continue to do this until the day I know my mother is safe.

I want him to know that I'm watching him. He lays one finger on my mother again and his ass is mine. He may not walk again, the next time he hurts my mother.

I watch him carefully as he uncrosses his arms and then walks to the door, walking a straight line just to piss me off and show off.

He's sober. An asshole... but sober.

My eyes burn into his back, unwavering, until he's inside the house and the door is closed behind him.

Giving myself a second to cool off, I sit and just watch my mother's house to make sure there's no arguing or screaming coming from it.

When I feel safe to leave her alone with him, I start my bike and take off, heading toward my favorite burger joint.

I'm about three blocks from *Gill's Burgers* when I notice some asshole honking at cars and riding their asses as if he's in a hurry.

It only takes me a few seconds to realize that it's the asshole that hit me. I've been waiting to run into his ass again. "Oh fuck yes."

He turns down a side street so I speed up and turn down another side street, knowing that I'll meet up with him if I go fast enough.

I speed down three blocks and then turn left, blocking the road at the next stop sign, right as he comes to a stop.

Adrenaline courses through me as I jump off my bike and take wide strides over to the driver's side of the car. He looks at me with surprise as I reach into the window to turn off his car and snatch the keys out of the ignition.

The driver looks extremely worried now as he watches me grip the opened window and flex. "You're the asshole that hit me and you're still out here driving like a fucking idiot."

"Come on, man." He reaches out for his keys, but I snatch them away and shove them in my pocket. "Give me my fucking keys. Sorry, it was an accident. I didn't even see you there."

"Fuck that shit. You should learn how to drive or stay the fuck off the road, before you kill someone. Got it, asshole?"

He looks me over with a cocky smile that shows me that he doesn't give a shit about what I'm saying right now.

The asshole has to be about eighteen or nineteen at most. So I'm sure he still gets off with a lot of warnings, but fuck that. Not with me.

I reach into the window and slam his head into the steering wheel as hard as I can. "I'll be watching you, asshole."

Turning around, I chuck his keys across the street and then hop back on my bike, revving the engine as he watches me through the windshield, while holding his nose.

He's lucky I didn't break it.

I feel a bit better, grinning like a fool as I pull up at the burger joint and order for two.

I have some thanking to do myself...

CHAPTER THIRTEEN

MEADOW

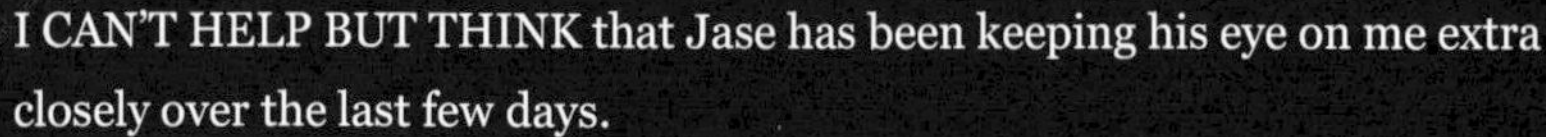

I CAN'T HELP BUT THINK that Jase has been keeping his eye on me extra closely over the last few days.

Every time I turn around, he's there asking me if I need something or if I want to go outside to his car and work off some steam. Seriously? I've worked with him for over a year and not once has he seemed so clingy until now.

At one point I might've wanted this kind of attention from him, but not anymore. Now that I'm getting it... it feels completely different than I expected.

Styx shows me attention in a way that makes me feel wanted and special. Jase has been showing me attention in a way that makes me feel smothered and annoyed as hell.

I hear something come from outside the door and immediately assume that it's Jase creeping around the corner to hit on me again. It's getting old.

"I'm busy, Jase," I huff. "I've got patients to take care of and so do you. Leave me alone, please."

I inhale a deep breath and slowly release it when I hear the door to the room close and footsteps heading my way.

Fluffing up the pillow and getting the bed as comfortable as possible for the next patient, I speak, without turning around to face him. I'm not in the mood for his games and to be honest, he's sort of pissing me off at the moment.

I might just snap if I look at him.

Styx has been the only thing on my mind all day and Jase is ruining any quiet moment that I manage to get to think about what happened last night and remember just how good it felt to wake up with him in my bed.

He looked so sexy, laying there naked, wrapped up in my sheets and I want every second that I can get to picture just that.

"No, I won't go to your car with you and no, I won't take you to my truck."

Strong arms wrap around my waist, pulling me tightly against a hard body. His scent and the way he touches me, gives him away. "Then how about my motorcycle?"

Only Styx could make my heart beat the way it is at this very moment. I've learned that very quickly.

"What are you doing here?" I ask with a grin, while grabbing his arms. "Miss me already?" I tease.

He smiles against my neck, before tilting it to the side and gently biting it with his perfect mouth. "Maybe. Or maybe I got the feeling that you missed my mouth."

His hand lowers down the front of my scrubs and in between my legs, cupping me. "And my hands."

Biting my lower lip, I close my eyes and let out a small moan as he slips a finger inside and then pulls it out. "Your pussy definitely misses me, Meadow. Not sure I'll believe your mouth if it tells me no."

He turns me around and looks me in the eye as he sucks his finger into his mouth, tasting me. "Mmmm... My mouth misses everything on this perfect little body."

"Styx..." I breathe out, as he lowers down to this knees in front of me. "We can't do this right here." I grip his hair and tug when his warm mouth lowers down the front of my body, kissing me on the way as he lowers my panties. "A patient is... Oh my God... Styx..."

As soon as his tongue swirls around my clit, I lose all train of thought, gripping onto the bed railing for support.

His strong hands grip my thighs and squeeze as his mouth consumes my mind, body, and soul, making it hard to think of the fact that we could get caught at any moment and I could possibly lose my job.

All that exists in this moment is Styx's tongue on my body, pleasuring me in a way that only Styx can.

"You took care of me at my work..." He stops to suck my clit into his mouth and swirl his tongue around it. It has me shaking above him. "Now I'm returning the favor."

Blindly, I struggle to lower the railing on the bed behind me, desperate for his mouth to keep going. "Move this..." I breathe out. "I need it gone. Now."

Styx smiles up at me, before reaching behind me and lowering the railing. Without saying a word, he grips my hips and raises me to the bed, pulling my ass to the very edge.

I lean back and grip his hair, wrapping my fingers in as he buries his face between my legs again.

With each swirl and flick of his tongue, I moan out, pulling his hair even harder. "Ohhhhh... shit... yes..."

My moans get louder, the more aggressively his mouth takes me and before I know it, I'm screaming out his name.

Styx laughs between my legs, before sitting up and covering my mouth with his hand. "Try to hold it in. I'm not here to get you fired. I'm here to thank you."

I nod, and then push his head, until he's back down in between my legs. "Don't stop again or I'll hurt you."

I'm so lost in his mouth and the pleasure that it's bringing me, that I don't even notice the door to the room opening, until I hear Jase's voice as he walks inside.

"Hey, the patient is on his..."

"Oh shit!" I sit up and push Styx's head away, just in time to see Jase stop in front of us with his mouth hanging open in shock.

Styx is quick to cover me up, making it clear that he doesn't want Jase seeing me with my pants down. "Fuuuck!"

He helps me to my feet and then runs his hands through his hair in frustration as he looks Jase over as he watches us.

“Are you fucking serious?” Jase clenches his jaw as he looks me over, clearly unhappy. “You *never* wanted to mess around in a room with me, but it’s okay when this guy wants to? Suddenly, your job doesn’t matter?”

“Jase, don’t start,” I growl out, frustrated that he had the nerve to bring *us* up.

Styx steps in between us, blocking Jase from looking at me as I quickly fix my hair and clothes, before smoothing out the bed. “Do we have a fucking problem here, Jase?”

He steps up close to his face, intimidating him. “If you even think about asking her to *your* fucking car again or to *her* fucking truck, I will hear about it and then you will hear from me. Got it? Don’t fuck with what is mine.”

My stomach fills with butterflies when I hear him say *mine* and I freeze. I don’t know if he’s just saying it to get Jase off my ass or if he really wants me as his, but holy shit, if those words didn’t make my heart about beat out of my chest.

The boys step back and out of the way as the door opens and voices fill the room as Mandy and Julie help the patient to his bed.

Mandy stops to look at the three of us, before putting her professional face back on and making sure that the patient is comfortable.

I take this as my chance to grab Styx and get us the hell out of here, before anyone can ask any questions.

I know I’ll have to explain to Mandy later, but right now, I just want an escape.

The look on Styx’s face is mixed with anger and worry as he reaches behind the empty counter and picks up a brown paper bag.

“I brought you lunch. I didn’t see anyone at the desk, so I left it here and looked for you.” He wraps his arms around me and leans in to whisper in my ear. “Thank you for breakfast...” He lets out a sexy growl, causing goosebumps to cover my whole body. “And for dessert.”

The worry on his face when he pulls away from me, causes my heart to drop. “Styx... I don’t want anything to do with Jase anymore.”

His eyes study mine, before he leans in and presses his lips against my forehead, kissing it gently. “He obviously doesn’t get the picture... yet. Maybe I need to come around more.”

He places the bag in my hand and flexes his jaw, while looking over my shoulder. “I’ll be back when you get off work.”

“Won’t you be at the club?”

His blue eyes look down to meet mine and I can see the sincerity in them. "Yeah, after I make sure you get out of here safely. The club can wait."

"Meadow," the charge nurse calls out, sounding annoyed as usual. "You're needed in room 312. Please say goodbye to your friend."

Styx grabs the bag back out of my hand and sets it behind the counter again. "I'll see you tonight." He kisses me and then turns to walk away.

My eyes trail down this strong back, landing on his firm ass and I almost forget that I'm wanted, until Dani calls me again, letting me know that she's pissed.

Giving her a fake smile, I walk past her and disappear into room 312 to catch my breath.

The patient is sleeping, so I quickly do my job and then slip out the door, hoping that I can find a second to sneak into the bathroom and go over in my head what the hell just happened in that room with Styx.

I lock myself in the empty bathroom and lean against the wall, replaying Styx's mouth on me.

Holy fuck, I can't believe I just let him do that to me. Here. At work.

I just hope like hell that Jase doesn't decide to be an asshole and get me fired.

After I have a few moments to myself, I step out of the bathroom just to have Jase waiting outside.

"What the fuck was that?" He follows beside me as I walk in an attempt to lose him. "You're fucking this guy over me? He's a male stripper. He doesn't even deserve your time, dammit."

"Fuck off, Jase." I stop abruptly and turn around to face him. "Don't you dare think that you have the right to judge Styx."

He laughs as if I just said something funny. "Styx. Real fucking nice. Sounds like a real man to me."

I shove my finger in his chest and dig it in as I look him in the eyes. "Oh he is," I say firmly. "More of a man than you'll ever be." My eyes trail down to his not so big bulge. "Styx seems to make every man other than him look small. Trust me."

"Oh come on. Don't do me like that." He follows me as I begin walking again. "Meadow... just let me take you out with me tonight. I'll show you what you've been missing. We'll have fun and you'll forget all about..."

He stops talking and lets out an angry grunt when I walk away from him to join Mandy and Dani as if he was never even talking to begin with.

This is going to be the longest day of my life...

CHAPTER FOURTEEN

STYX

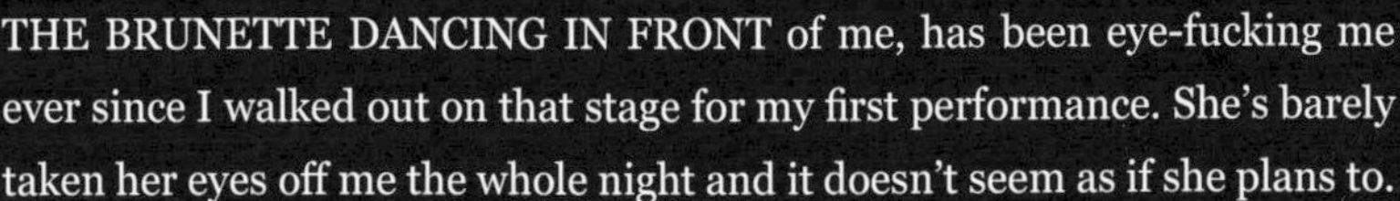

THE BRUNETTE DANCING IN FRONT of me, has been eye-fucking me ever since I walked out on that stage for my first performance. She's barely taken her eyes off me the whole night and it doesn't seem as if she plans to.

She's dressed in a short dress that barely covers her red thong and she keeps lifting it slightly in the front in an attempt to get my attention.

It's been working, but not in the way I'm sure she hopes for.

Kash appears next to me, out of breath as he watches the way she's watching me as if she wants to tear me apart with her teeth.

He slaps my back and chuckles. "You going to give her what she wants, man? She's been working all night to get your attention. I've never seen so much desperation in my life."

I reach up and wipe the sweat off my forehead, while pulling my jeans back up my hips. "No. I'm good."

Breathing heavily, I rush past the herd of women and over to the bar, grabbing the beer from Sarah as she slides it my way with a crazy smirk.

Tonight has been total insanity and I've been completely distracted with keeping my eye on the clock and trying to avoid my stalker for the night. I told Meadow I was meeting her after her shift and I plan to be there no matter what it takes.

I keep my word.

Walk of Shame will have to wait.

I've never been late when my father gets off work and I won't be for Meadow neither.

"Woah there, gorgeous. Looking a little sweaty. Your stalker wearing you out already? Want me to get the water pitcher to cool you off?" She winks and laughs as I tilt the beer back and then pour some over my head to cool off.

I'm that damn hot.

Her throwing water on us is the highlight of her night. She did it once a few months back and now it's become almost a nightly routine.

Sometimes just to fuck with us, she throws some ice in it. That's why you want to stay on her good side. Ice does not do the body good. Especially the most important part and the way she's looking at me now gives me the idea that there'd be ice in my pitcher for annoying her.

"Nope, I got it. What time is it?"

"Someone sure has been asking about the time an awful lot tonight. What... Do you think I don't have better things to do than check the time every twenty minutes for your ass?" She walks over to the register to grab her phone with a roll of her eyes. "It's a quarter to eleven. Why? It's not like—"

"Shit." I slam my empty beer down on the bar in front of her when she walks back over. "Tell Cale I'll be back in thirty. I gotta go take care of something important."

"Styx," she yells after me, when I take off through the crowd in a hurry. "What the hell. You're in the middle of a show."

"Was!" I yell back, before pushing past Lane and out the back door, shirtless with my jeans still unbuttoned.

Grabbing my helmet, I straddle my bike and rev the engine, ignoring Lane's attempts to get my attention.

I'm just about to speed off, when I feel a hand run down my bare back.

"Where you headed, Styx? I can be some pretty good company."

Growling under my breath, I let out a frustrated breath and shake my head as the tall brunette walks around me, trailing her hand along my body on the way.

This is exactly why I'm done with the girls that come to the club. They're all the same and it doesn't amuse me anymore.

"I'd love for you to take me for a ride. Ever fucked on a motorcycle?"

She lifts the front of her short dress and slides her hand inside her panties as if that's the key to getting me where she wants me.

"Yes," I say stiffly, while pulling her other hand away right as she goes to reach for my package. "But I won't be fucking *you* on *mine*."

Her face looks shocked as she scans my body over with hard eyes. "Seriously? You're saying no? To this..."

I look down at her hand as she begins pumping her finger in and out of her pussy and moaning.

That shit isn't working on me. I'm not even fucking hard.

"Fuck yes I am."

Before she can say anything else, I speed out of the parking lot and toward the hospital, not the least bit affected by her attempt to fuck me.

I've had hundreds of girls just like her throwing themselves at me since I started stripping at the club. It takes much more to hold my attention now.

Even though it's dark, I catch heads turning my way, but I ignore them all, until I'm pulling up next to Meadow's truck.

I park behind it and get off my bike to lean against her vehicle and wait. Running my fingers through my hair, I realize just how sticky I am from that beer.

Maybe I should've let Sarah pour that pitcher on me. Holy fuck this does not feel good right now, but I didn't want the ice that was sure to be in that pitcher.

I'm not even waiting for five minutes, when I look up to see Meadow watching me with surprise in her eyes.

It's as if she didn't believe I'd really be here. I hate the idea of that.

"You made it. Shirtless... but you made it." She smiles and walks toward me, stopping a few inches in front of me. Her eyes lower down to my bare chest, before raising back up to meet mine. "You really didn't have to leave work for me. All those screaming women back at the club paying to see the sexy, shirtless man in front of me and you still came to see me?" she teases. "I'm shocked you even remembered my name, Styx."

My eyes drift a few parking spots over, locking on Jase. He unlocks his Mustang, keeping his brooding eyes on me the whole time as he opens the door, making it clear that he's watching us.

"I always keep my word and I'll never forget your name," I say stiffly, to let Jase know that I plan on sticking around for a while. "What are your plans for tonight?"

I shouldn't be asking her this, but seeing the look in her eyes when she first saw me standing here, makes it impossible for me not to want to spend time with her right now.

Going back to the club to dance for other women is the last thing on my mind. I can't. So fuck it.

"My plan was to go home and watch..."

Jase pulls up behind us, rolling down his window and interrupting what Meadow was about to say.

"Everything okay out there, babe? Sure you don't want to take me up on that offer from earlier? We can pick up your car in the morning. It'll be fine here."

Instinctively, my arm wraps around Meadow's waist and I hold her close as she responds to the douchebag.

"Firstly... I'm not your babe. Don't call me that again. Secondly... I already told you to fuck off. Goodnight, Jase."

Grunting, he gives me a dirty look and speeds off, doing a burnout as if that shit is going to intimidate me.

Meadow is distracted with watching him, so I flip her around and press her against her truck.

I can't help but notice the way my heart speeds up as soon as our bodies meet. "Did he mess with you today?"

She leans her head back, resting it in my hand, as she looks up at me. "Doesn't matter. I took care of him. It's fine."

Hearing that pisses me the hell off, but there's nothing I can do now that he's gone. I'll have to deal with him later. "You've had a long night at work." I lean in and whisper in her ear. "Follow me."

I really need to take care of her right now...

CHAPTER FIFTEEN

MEADOW

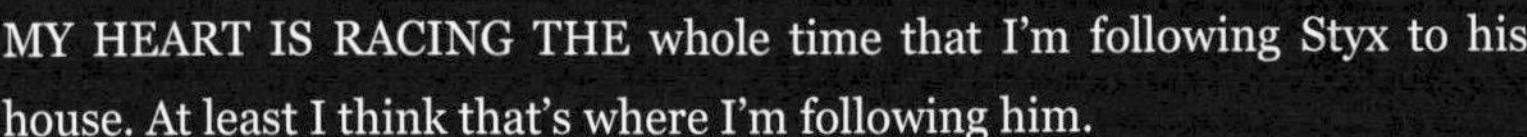

MY HEART IS RACING THE whole time that I'm following Styx to his house. At least I think that's where I'm following him.

I didn't ask any questions. I didn't feel the need to. He asked me to follow him and my entire body gave me no other choice but to listen.

He keeps surprising me and I have to admit that I love that.

I never actually expected him to leave work and show back up at the hospital like he said. I've become used to words with little action to back them up when it comes to men.

At least the one I trusted the most. He left me at my worst and I still haven't forgotten.

Styx is proving to be different and with each word that leaves his mouth, I find myself becoming more and more attracted to him and not just physically.

I feel a pull toward him that no other man has been able to make me feel since I've closed myself off ten months ago.

Not to mention that the way he looked at Jase in the parking lot was as if he wanted nothing more than to protect me from him and I have to admit that I loved it more than I expected. It made me feel safe and wanted.

A feeling that I miss with everything in me.

My heart continues to race as I pull up in the driveway beside Styx's motorcycle and unfasten my seatbelt.

I have no idea what he has in mind for us tonight, but I'm dying to find out. Spending time with him is something that I seem to look more forward to with each passing day.

Before I get a chance to even reach over and grab my purse from the passenger seat, my truck door flies open and Styx reaches in to pull me out.

The way he handles me is a complete turn on and I instantly think about sex with him, making me want him again. Once was not enough.

His blue eyes meet mine as he slams my truck door shut and lifts me up, pushing me against the side of my truck with his hips. "I've been thinking about taking care of you all night. There are so many dirty things I want to do to you right now, but I won't. You deserve so much more. You give so much to others. Let me *give* to you."

He closes his eyes and then leans in to kiss my neck, moaning against me. The vibration of his mouth against me has me moaning out loud and closing my eyes in enjoyment. "Maybe I want both sides of you, Styx. The caring and the *dirty*. Maybe I want the dirty right now. Maybe I *need* it."

He growls against my neck and then bites it, brushing my skin with his rough beard as he moves. I love the feel of his beard on me. So hot. He's not making it any easier to wait. "I won't touch you while I have other women on me, Meadow. I need to take care of you first."

He begins pulling me away from the truck, but I yank his hair, letting him know that I'm not ready to go in yet.

It's dark and quiet out here. Maybe people are awake... maybe they aren't. Doesn't matter. I want him. Right. Now.

"Wait..."

He stops walking at the sound of my voice, giving me a curious look. "Everything okay?"

I reach in between us and rub my hand over his thick erection, showing him that everything is more than okay. "I just don't want to go inside yet."

He has me completely turned on right now and it makes me want to try something that every guy I have been with before has been afraid of doing. The idea of this has always gotten me excited.

He smirks down at me once he realizes what I'm asking him to do. "Right fucking here? We'll wake the whole neighborhood."

I nod and squeeze his dick through his pants. "I don't care. Let us wake them then."

My words cause him to rush to the back of my truck and pull the tailgate down, setting me down inside.

Holy shit, this is really about to happen.

With his eyes burning into me, he grips my hips with force and pulls me down to the edge of the truck bed so my ass is barely hanging on the surface.

Keeping his intense eyes on mine, he pulls my scrubs down my legs, tossing them aside as he admires my body with a moan of appreciation.

His hands roam up my legs and thighs, giving me chills.

Before I can even register what he's doing, he has my thong in his hands, ripping them from my body with a growl.

My legs tremble with excitement and anticipation of him taking me hard, and I find myself unable to wait. I'm too turned on now.

"I need you naked, Styx. Holy shit, you're so damn sexy."

A soft rumble comes from his throat as he quirks an eyebrow and grips both of my wrists in his hands, pulling me up to meet his jeans. "You want me naked," he whispers. "Show everyone how badly. Undress me..."

Biting my bottom lip, I unbutton his jeans and yank them down with force, along with his briefs, my eyes taking in every inch of his perfection. And trust me, there's a lot of inches to take in.

I notice him struggling to reach into his jeans, before he kicks them aside and rips the wrapper of a condom open with his teeth.

My eyes are on his perfect mouth, but lower when he struggles to roll the condom over his erection.

He strokes his length a few times, watching as I yank my shirt off over my head and toss it aside, waiting for him to take me how I want him right now.

"Fuck me!" Gripping my thighs, he steps in between them and slams into me, hard.

I scream while wrapping my legs around his waist, causing him to thrust harder, rolling his hips in and out in perfect rhythm.

My grip on his bicep tightens, me wanting him harder and faster. I can't get enough of this man right now and I want him to feel this.

With each hard thrust, I scream out and dig my nails into his skin, only making him go harder and deeper, until we're both moaning out our pleasure, him coming right after I squeeze him tight.

"Fucking shit," Styx breathes against my lips. "I wanted to take care of you first. I'm dirty and sticky from the club, but I can't deny you of shit."

I laugh and suck his lip into my mouth, biting it gently, before releasing it. "I couldn't wait. I've been thinking about touching you all day."

Pulling me away from the truck, he walks us toward his opened garage, fisting my hair with his free hand as I straddle his waist and hold on tight.

The garage door closes behind us and I melt into Styx as he walks us through the house and to the bathroom.

Opening the glass door, he reaches in and turns on the shower water, before setting me down to my feet and pulling his condom off, tossing it outside of the shower. "You've had a long night at work now let me fucking take care of you."

He begins stripping my bra off and all I can think about is the fact that he should be at work, yet here he is, catering to me. He lowers down to his knees, running his hands up my legs.

"Styx..." I grab his hair and meet his gaze. "Shouldn't you be going back to the club? I don't want you losing your job over me."

He shakes his head and kisses up my thigh, stopping before he gets where I want him. "I'm not going back tonight. Forget about the club. It doesn't matter right now. I'm here with you. You matter."

Butterflies fill my stomach and a happiness that I haven't felt in a long time has me smiling so hard that I can't fight it.

What is this man doing to me?

I step under the water and close my eyes as the warmness runs over my skin, relaxing me. He's right. It's been an extremely long day at the hospital and I need this right now.

His hands rubbing soap over my skin, his lips kissing me in places that gives my whole body goosebumps. I need this.

He's gentle in the way he touches me now. The way he washes my hair. The way he massages the thick soap into my shoulders, making my whole body feel so good.

I lean into his hard body as his hands snake around the front of me, rubbing soap over my hard nipples, before disappearing between my legs.

One hand pushes my legs apart, while his other hand brushes over my sensitive pussy, making my body crave for him to take me again.

"Styx," I moan out. "I love the way you touch me. I might get too used to this if you keep being so good at it."

He stops just long enough to dip a finger inside me, before he goes back to rubbing my clit with his other fingers. "Maybe I want you to get too used it. Maybe I want you to be familiar with my touch," he whispers from behind me. "So if another man touches you, you'll crave for the familiarity of my fingers pleasing you and making you come undone."

I lean my head back and cry out as his movements speed up and his erection presses against my ass, teasing me. "Maybe I like the idea of you coming undone only for me..."

As soon as his teeth dig into my neck, I come undone under his touch, gripping onto his arm as my orgasm rides out.

"Hoooooly fuuuck..." I breathe into his arm and squeeze it. "It's like you know exactly what I need and you give it to me, but even better."

He laughs into the top of my hair. "Is that why you stalked me at the club that first night? Just one look at me and you knew I'd be good at pleasing you."

I teasingly bite his arm and laugh. "You like the idea of me stalking you so much, that you decided to stalk me back, Styx Sterling."

He holds onto me with one hand and reaches for the soap to rub down his own body now. "You like me so much that you've learned my last name." He stops and turns me around to kiss me. "Fuck, I love that," he whispers against my lips.

"Good," I whisper back, before jumping up and wrapping my legs around his waist. "You know what I love?"

"Tell me," he growls, before biting my lower lip.

"When you make me feel wanted and protected." I press my lips to his, while reaching behind him and turning off the shower water. "The way you held me the other night. The way you kiss me. The way you touch me and the way you fuck me. I could keep going on."

He grips my ass and bites my bottom lip again, but harder this time.

"Fuck, I want to keep you."

I smile against his lips. "After that delicious burger you brought to me for lunch today, I might want to keep you too. We'll see..."

He laughs and then kisses me. "Let's get you to bed. You can hardly keep your eyes open."

Holding onto him, I bury my face into his neck, taking in his sexy scent as he carries me through his house and to his bed.

If I weren't so exhausted right now, I'd ride this man all night, just to listen to him moan, while he's inside me.

Everything about Styx turns me on and makes me desperately want him right now, but a twelve-hour day dealing with sick patients has taken its toll. Once will have to be enough for tonight.

I fall asleep right when he snuggles in behind me and pulls the blanket around us.

I'm beginning to love this feeling way too much...

CHAPTER SIXTEEN

STYX

I WAKE UP TO THE sound of something vibrating from the bathroom floor. It takes about the third time, before I finally shake my sleep off enough to realize that it's my phone.

My jeans are still on the bathroom floor from when I fetched them from outside, right before crawling back into bed with Meadow.

"Fucking shit." Being careful not to wake Meadow, I slip out of my bed and rush to the bathroom, grabbing my phone right as it goes off for the fourth time.

"What the fuck, Styx." Cale's angry voice comes through the phone, making me feel instant guilt for not coming back to finish my shift like I told Sarah to tell him I would.

I've only ever heard Cale angry once. It takes a lot to piss him off and I'm an asshole for being the reason for it now.

I let out a long breath and run my hand through my hair. "Shit. I'm an asshole. I'm sorry, man. It won't happen again."

"I can't just have you leaving the club during the middle of a show like that. I understand that Sarah said it was important, but you need to talk to *me* and let *me* know that. I have no problem calling Hemy or looking for an extra dancer to fill in so you can have more time off. But fucking tell me. Got it?"

"I'm sorry, man. I planned on coming back, but then I couldn't leave her once I saw her. She's in my bed right now. Want me to come in for the last thirty minutes and do a couple songs?"

He's silent for a few seconds, before responding. "Damn, Styx." He laughs into the phone as if he's relieved. "All this time I was thinking you were in some kind of trouble with the way you've been acting lately. I should've guessed it was a woman."

"This is new to me, Cale. I'm doing my best to show her that I'm more than just a male entertainer that sleeps around for fucking fun. She's different..."

"Good. Because I'm giving you the next two nights off. Take her out on a real fucking date, Styx. Not just to the bedroom or the kitchen counter or wherever it is that you usually take her."

I smirk into the phone. "That was my plan."

"I need your head in the game on Friday when you come back. But just remember that the next time your ass leaves me hanging, I'll have to fuck you up. Better yet, I'll get Slade to do my dirty work. That fucker is always looking for a reason to slip out of his suit for a day."

We both laugh at his fake threat and then hang up.

When I walk back into the bedroom, Meadow is spread out on my bed. She smiles up at me and motions for me to come to her.

"You're so fucking sexy right now." I crawl above her and lean down to suck her bottom lip into my mouth. "I'll never get used to the way my heart jumps whenever I touch you." I suck her bottom lip into my mouth again, before releasing it. "Or my cock."

Moaning out, she bites my bottom lip and tugs, pulling me back down to her. "I want you inside me, Styx. I haven't been able to stop thinking about the truck and how good you felt. Think you have another round in you?"

I wrap her hair in my hand, before reaching over to my nightstand and grabbing inside for a condom. "After this, I don't think you'll be asking that question *ever* again."

Once I get the condom on, I stand on my knees and look down at her, while grabbing her ankles, and placing them on my shoulders. "I should be asking you if you think you can handle another round. I always have another round in me. For you, I fucking have ten if that's what you want."

I position myself between her legs and enter her in one thrust. We both moan out as I hit hard. I don't think I've ever been so deep before.

I begin to move in a slow, steady rhythm before speeding up, causing her to slam her head into the headboard. She throws her hands behind her and pushes off the bed as I continue to take her, hard and deep.

She's watching the way my body moves as if she's hypnotized by it and can't get enough of it. "I've never seen a man move his body as sexy as you do," she whispers.

I lean into her lips and whisper, "You like watching me move, baby? Does it feel as good as it looks?"

She nods her head and moans out as I slam into her and rotate my hips. "So much better. You feel better. Nothing is more real than that."

Her lips crush mine and she digs into my back as I push in deep and stop, us both breathing into each other's mouths. "You feel so good wrapped around me. I could do this all fucking night if you'd let me."

"Then do it," she growls against my mouth.

And I do.

Until we're both exhausted and our muscles are shaking.

It's been a while since I've gotten into the gym, but fuck me, this was just the workout I needed.

I'll do this every night with her if she'll let my ass.

And I have a feeling that she'll be able to keep up...

AFTER MEADOW LEFT THIS MORNING to meet up with her friend Mandy, I headed to the gym to get a workout in and meet up with my uncle Wes.

We've spent the morning signing all the necessary papers to make the gym mine and catching up since he hasn't stopped in for months.

"I can't believe that I'm giving this place up," he says with slight sadness in his voice as he looks around his old office. "It took me years to save up for this place, but family is where it's at, Styx. Never forget that shit. Your father... well he's a piece of shit and never learned the meaning."

I toss my pen aside and look across the desk at my uncle. I actually take a lot more after him than I do my father, thank fucking goodness. "Oh, you don't have to tell me that shit. I learned that at a young age. I hate that son of a bitch. Always will. He's no father. Never has been."

"Too fucking bad too. How's Lily doing? Dana hasn't heard from her in weeks. Should we be worried or are you still checking up on her every day?"

"You know I am. And I will for as long as I have to until she leaves that piece of shit."

My uncle looks at me with a smile, before standing up and gripping my shoulder. "I don't give a shit what anyone says, I'm proud of you. Fuck what your father says about you being a male entertainer. You're young still and you should live a little. But you've got your head on right and you know what's important. You just need to find it still. That's why I trust you with this gym. It's the one thing that I know you love."

I stand up and throw an arm around him, letting him know that I appreciate his words. "Thanks, man. I don't know what I would've done without you over the years."

"Well you'd be a male stripper of course." He raises a brow and smiles. "But you wouldn't have a gym."

I smile back and start cleaning my desk off. "Can't argue that. And I love your ass for it too."

He walks away to leave, but stops at the door and turns back to face me. "Love your ass too. Tell your mom hi for me and that she needs to call us once in a while. Or at least answer the phone more."

"I will. Now get out of here so you can get on the road with your family. I'll come visit when you guys get back."

"Alright, man. I'll you see you later."

"Later, Wes."

After my uncle leaves, I sit back down at my desk and look around the office, feeling proud as fuck to be the owner of this gym. I've spent the last four years practically running it and putting my time into it.

What I'm dreading is the talk with Cale, letting him know that I'm going to have to cut it down to two days a week at the club.

I want to make sure that I'm here more for my staff and members. I haven't been able to do that with the club being so busy for the last two months.

I hear a knock at my door, before Slade lets himself in and takes a seat at my desk, dressed in that fancy ass button down and slacks that he sports now that he's a lawyer again.

He grins and tosses a *Walk of Shame* flyer my way. "Shit, I don't miss going to that place and shaking my cock for hundreds of screeching women."

I get comfortable in my seat and look him over. He's gotten bigger since last time. It's been months since I've seen him. I used to see him at least two times a week, but my schedule has had me all messed up and tired.

"Fuck... your ass has gotten big. I see you've been here almost every day after work now. Everything good with Aspen?"

He laughs as if I just asked a stupid question. Hell, it was a stupid question.

"Don't ask me that shit again. Things will always be good with Aspen. How about you, dick? Cale tells me that your head hasn't been into the club lately."

I laugh. "Is this him sending you to fuck me up?"

Watching me, he begins rolling up the sleeve of his black shirt, revealing his tattoos. "Nah, I'm not trying to fuck up my new shirt." He smirks, looking confident and cool as usual. "I just wanted to check on you and make sure that you're good. I know how the stress of the club can get to you."

I take a deep breath and release it, while sitting back in my chair. "I guess I'm just tired of the same old shit. I work my ass off there and every single girl expects me to take them home and fuck them. I'm over it."

"Hell, the Styx I met over a year ago was into that. I was too in the beginning, but fucking just for the fuck of it gets old. I want to fuck because I want to hear the woman below me scream that she fucking loves me and no other man. Not because I want to pretend that love doesn't exist and fucking is just a way to forget. It took me a while to figure it out, but I did with Aspen. Leaving the club and that lifestyle behind was the best decision of my life."

I take his words in and my whole body aches to feel that with Meadow someday. For too long, I have been fucking just to forget all of the other shit in my life that sucks, and telling myself that I'll never find the right woman to change that.

But Meadow's different. I'm different with her.

"I've been thinking about leaving the club," I confess. "That place has fucked with my head for too long and I want to focus on my gym and Meadow. I can't do that when I have to spend my nights there, pleasing other women."

Slade sits up straight and gives me a questionable look, while loosening his tie. "Woah. Back the fuck up. Who the hell is Meadow?"

The sound of her name coming from his mouth has excitement coursing through me. Damn, this woman has me all fucked up over her.

"Hopefully mine soon. That's who."

"Well damn... I know that look, man. You have it bad for this woman. I know because I gave every other fucker that look when they asked me about Aspen. She was mine and I needed everyone to know." He stands up and reaches into his pocket when it starts vibrating. "I need to get back to the office for a meeting. I'm already late. Talk to Cale and tell him what you want. He'll understand. Plus, there's plenty of male entertainers banging down the door of *Walk of Shame* to get on that stage and make money. He'll be fine and so will Stone and Kash. Don't let that shit stress you out and force you into staying."

Standing up, I shake his hand and thank him, before he walks away and answers his phone.

Once he's gone, all I can think about is what he said. Maybe he's right. Maybe I need to have this talk with Cale. But that's not the only thing he's right about. I do have it bad for Meadow. Way more than I fucking know.

I pick up my phone and send Meadow a text.

Styx

I want to take you out to dinner tonight. Wear something dressy. Or hell. Anything you want.

She responds a few minutes later, causing my dick to get hard and my heart to beat fast in my chest.

Meadow

I'll wear nothing if you want me to and we can even stay in at your house. I just want to spend time with you.

"Holy fuck, this woman is perfect for me."

Now, I just want this day to hurry the hell up so I can make it to her, but I have a lot to do here first.

Just when I think I'm about to have a few minutes to myself after a long day here at the gym, James lets himself in and walks over to take a seat at my desk. He smiles and then reaches over to shake my hand. "Hell yes. Congratulations on being the owner of this badass gym. Of course, a lot of it has to do with me being here." He flashes a cocky smile as I reach out for his hand and shake it.

"You are as cocky as you fucking look, dipshit," I mutter. "What do you want?"

He stands when I do. "I need to leave early tonight. I have a date. Is that cool?"

"Yeah, man. Ben can handle it. Just let him know that you're leaving early."

"Hell yes!" He does a little dance, similar to some shit that I'd pull at the club. He's actually pretty good too.

"Did you steal that shit from me?" I joke. "Stay away from the club, fucker and don't use my moves on your date."

He winks and dances his way out of my office, shutting the door behind him.

That fucking kid is something else.

Now to give Meadow the night that she deserves...

CHAPTER SEVENTEEN

STYX

I'M SURPRISED WHEN I PULL up at my house to see my mother sitting on my porch with her head down.

Instantly, I assume the worst and thoughts of me kicking that son of a bitch's ass take over.

I barely even park my bike, before I jump off and run over to her, grabbing her face to look for bruises. "What did that asshole do now? Did he hurt you again?"

She laughs and grabs my hands, pulling them away from her face. "Sit down for a minute. Don't let yourself get so worked up, baby. I'm fine." Sternly, she points to the empty space next to her. "Sit and relax."

I release a breath and take a seat, fucking relieved that I won't have to kill that bastard today. He's lucky... for now. "Are you really okay? Don't lie to me. Don't ever lie to me to protect him. Got it?"

Smiling, she leans in close and rests her head against my shoulder. "I'm fine. I just missed my baby boy. You haven't been by to see me in almost three weeks. I wanted to make sure *you* were okay. Are you?"

I feel like shit, the instant she points out my neglect for the last few weeks, but she knows more than anyone why I haven't gone inside to see her. I'm usually sleeping or at the gym when he's gone at work and when he's there it always turns into a fight and I'm to that point where I know I won't be able to control myself when it comes to him.

"I'm fine. You're more than welcome at my house, mom and you know it. I'm always here for you, but I can't look at that piece of shit. I'll kill him if I see any more bruises on you. I can't do it anymore. We've put up with his shit for too long. I just wish you could see that. He's not worth your time and effort."

She lets out a small sigh and holds onto my arm as if she doesn't want to let go. "You're the best son any mother could ask for, but I just need you to come over once in a while and see me. We all need to move on from the past. Please… just do this for me. Your father has been going to counseling and he isn't the same he was six months ago. If we treat him like he is, then he might as well still be. Right?"

I close my eyes and pinch the top of my nose. She's asking a lot of me with this. I'll never forget or forgive the shit he's put us through. I can't.

How can you just sit in a room with a monster and pretend that he isn't the evil that ruined everything you loved growing up?

I can't answer that, but for my mother, I'll do anything, no matter how much it hurts me.

"When do you want me over? I'll do dinner, but I can't do a poker night where he's drinking all night and acting a fool. I'll be gone before that. It'll only stress me out and have me hounding his ass to make sure he doesn't get out of control."

"Tomorrow night. I'll cook your favorite meal and your father will be on his best behavior. I promise. He already knows I'm here asking you and he's promised to behave and not give you a hard time."

I sit for a few seconds, considering her offer, when my phone vibrates in my pocket. The idea that it could be Meadow, has me reaching in my pocket for it and unlocking the screen.

My mom looks down at my phone and smiles. "Who's Meadow? Do you have a girlfriend that you're keeping from me, Styx?" She playfully pushes my shoulder and laughs.

My heart speeds up with excitement as I scan over the message. I can barely hide the smile that takes over as my mother watches my face as I read the message.

It's probably been forever since my mom has seen me as happy as I feel right now with this phone in my hand.

Meadow

I wanted to let you know that I'm home and ready when you are. Can't wait to see you tonight.

I don't even realize that my mother is reading over my shoulder, until she grips my arm in excitement and squeals. "I need to meet this Meadow. Ask her to come to dinner tomorrow night for tacos. It'll be fun. I promise."

The thought of bringing her around my father has my heart sinking and my stomach twisting up in knots.

"Not a good idea." I shake my head and put the phone down on my lap. "Sorry, but I can't do that. Not with that asshole there. You'll just have to come over here and see her, Mom."

My mother's face drops into a look of disappointment and I feel my fucking heart rip apart. I hate seeing her sad.

This woman raised me and is everything good in me. She helped make me who I am today and kept me sane growing up, when I thought all hope was lost. We protected and took care of each other. I can never hurt her.

Well shit...

Swallowing, I reach for my phone and stare at it in silence for a few moments, before typing out a message.

Styx

Come to dinner with me tomorrow night to meet my mother. You're the first woman I've invited to dinner.

Looking pleased, my mother stands up and kisses me on the top of the head. "I have a lot of preparing to do. Dinner has to be perfect! These will be the best tacos of your life."

"Where are you going?" I ask as she starts walking down the porch steps. "You just got here."

"Out to lunch with Dana and then shopping for a nice outfit. It's been a while and I miss her and your uncle Wes." She winks. "I have to look good for the first woman that my son has invited to dinner. Love you, baby. Don't be late."

I smile from her excitement and stand up to watch her leave. "Love you too."

Once I'm alone, I jump in the shower and begin thinking about all the bad shit that can happen at a dinner with my father.

I hate the idea of her meeting him, but my mother deserves more from me. Like she says, he's been good for months now, so I can only hope that I won't have a reason to kill him tomorrow.

If he acts up, then Meadow will see a side of me that I'm hoping to never have to show her.

When I'm drying off, my phone vibrates with a message from Meadow. So I drop my towel and reach for it, anxious to see what she has to say.

Meadow

I definitely feel special then. I'd be happy to tell your mother stories of your stalkerish behavior. Count me in.

Styx

My mother would be proud that I've finally decided to find a beautiful as hell woman to stalk and spend more than one night with.

Meadow

Then she'll love my stories and how much I love that you want to spend more than one night with me.

Her text has me thinking, and before I know it, I'm walking around my house in the nude, thinking about how much of an ass I am for not making more time to learn things about her when we're together.

How the hell am I supposed to give her a good date, when I don't know the first thing about what she likes. I'd like to pretend that I do, but I don't.

Styx

It's occurred to me that I need to learn a lot about you. Hell, I don't even know your favorite color. So I'm going to need you to fill out this quick questionnaire.

Question #1.

Boyshorts? Bikini? Or thong?

Actually, scratch that. I already know the answer and it's hot as fuck.

Question #1, take 2.

Does size matter? 'Cause if it does, then I'm good. But does it?

Meadow

LOL. Oh no. I don't know what's going on here or if I should be scared, BUT... Yes.

Styx

Question #2.

But yes, what? That I'm good? I thought I pointed out that I already knew this.

I smirk as I type out my next question.

Styx

Question #3.

How many times a night do you fantasize about me? Be honest. Even if it is 10 times or more.

Meadow

Oh you're definitely good. And I'm going to go with at least twelve. And they're extremely HOT. Next question.

Styx

Question #4.

What's your favorite color?

Meadow

Turquoise. Did you toss this in there to throw me off?

I stop in front of my dresser and grab some clothes to throw on, unable to hold back the grin. Fuck, I love having fun with her like this.

Styx

Question #5.

A night on the town or relaxing on the couch with a movie? I can only be naked for one. Keep that in mind.

Meadow

Then definitely relaxing on the couch with a movie and then a night out under the stars with YOU. Any woman would be stupid to say otherwise.

Styx

Okay, for real now. Forget about my smartass comments. What do you truly love to do? I want to know.

Meadow

Please tell me we're not going to go out and sit across the table from each other at a stiff ass restaurant and play 21 questions. What I love is spending time with you and not needing to talk, Styx.

I love that all we need when we're together is to just be close. You're my relaxation and what I look forward to after a long day or week at work. I don't feel like words are needed when we're together.

"Holy shit. How did I get so lucky?"

I pull my jeans up and button them, while reading over her messages for a second time.

She knows just the right words to make me want her even more than I already do and suddenly I'm in an even bigger hurry than before to get to her.

Styx

Fuck. Will you marry me?

I'm not really asking of course, but damn, she's definitely wife material. I don't even know how a fucker like me got so damn lucky.

Meadow

Question #6.

I think you forgot that part ;)

Styx

Be ready for me in an hour. I'm coming for you.

Meadow

Oh... I'm always ready for you. See you soon.

My front door swings open loud and hard and then I hear the sound of Kash's annoying voice coming from the other room.

"Come on, dick. Let's get some food and beers before my shift. My ass is starving."

Grunting, I walk out to meet Kash by the couch, where he's now chillin' and watching TV.

"Can't. I'm making dinner for Meadow tonight." Walking to the fridge, I grab two beers and pop the tops. "But I'll have a couple beers so I can handle your presence before I kick you out."

He snatches the beer from me, when I hold it over the couch for him. "No shit." He takes a swig and watches me as I walk around to take a seat on the chair. "It's that serious, huh?"

Smirking, I watch his worried face as he downs half of the beer. "Calm your dick, man. And stop worrying about the club and losing business. Cale can find someone else."

"Don't fuck with me, Styx." He looks worried as he stands up and paces in front of me. "Don't tell me you're thinking about leaving *Walk of Shame*. I know that look and I don't like it."

I run my hands through my hair, but don't say anything. Kash might just take it harder than Cale will.

"Fuck, man!" I watch as he tosses his beer into the trash and then slams the lid closed. "We started this journey together. You not being there just sounds too strange for me to be able to accept that right now."

I stand up and walk over to pour the rest of my beer into the sink. "I'm not saying for sure that I want to leave, but I've been thinking about it for a while now."

"Because of Meadow?" he questions.

"Nah." I shake my head and grip the counter. "I had my fun in the beginning, but it's all just old to me now. I have a gym to run and focus on. It's time for my ass to grow up. I've been considering this before Meadow came into the picture so don't hate on her for it."

"I'm not, but shit." He grabs another beer out and drinks it in silence. "My annoying ass roommate might just squeeze his way into the club after all. He's been on Cale's ass for weeks about getting in."

"Like I said. The club will be fine if I leave. So cheer the fuck up and get out of my house. I have important shit to do and looking at your face isn't on my list."

Kash laughs and finishes off his beer. "Then you need a new list."

He gets ready to walk away, but I stop him, before he reaches the door. "Hey. Don't bring this up to Cale until I think about it some more, alright. I'll talk to him when I'm ready."

"Yeah, I got it," he grumbles. "I better go teach Colt's ass some moves. He can't dance for shit and I'm not having him embarrass me and ruin my good reputation at the club."

"Actually, I need you to grab Stone, Kage, and the other two fuckers of *Walk of Shame* and do me a favor first. Don't complain either, because I do a lot of stupid shit when you guys need it. You dicks owe me."

"Shit. What?"

I throw a wad of money his way and grin. "I need a gazebo set up in the back yard in the next forty-five minutes. The couch and the TV need be in it in and set up for movies. Got it?"

I can't help but smile as I watch him bitch his way out the door. I love the guy, but watching him sweat over shit always seems to put me in a better mood.

Probably because he's been a pain in my ass since the beginning. Just about as much of a pain as Stone's cocky ass.

I spend the next thirty minutes preparing dinner, before I rush out to my motorcycle and head toward Meadow's.

Fuck. I hope this night turns out right. This has got to be the most romantic shit I've ever done...

CHAPTER EIGHTEEN

STYX

MEADOW LOOKS EXTREMELY SEXY IN the sweats and tank top that she's wearing and I'm happy that she decided to go with the comfortable look. I'm not really into the whole fancy restaurant bullshit and I'm glad she isn't either.

My eyes wander over her body as she walks ahead of me, going straight for the front door. I'm trying to be respectful, but truthfully, I want to undress her with my teeth and skip the dinner.

I'll be her dessert. She can have me any way she wants me.

She laces her arm around my neck and smiles against my lips, when I stop her from walking into the house. "I smell something delicious. So the sexy alpha cooks." She laughs when I smile against her lips and nod. I'm not gonna lie, I'm proud of my cooking abilities. "I love a man that knows how to cook. It's so incredibly sexy. A huge turn on."

I grip her hips and brush my lips over hers, trying my best to not just take her right here on the porch. But with her back against the door and my erection pressed against her stomach, it's hard not to think of the possibilities right now. "Then get ready to fall in love. I'm a great fucking cook."

"Is that right?" I bite her bottom lip and she moans into my mouth, while running her hand down the front of my body as if admiring me. "If you're as good at cooking as you are at everything else that you do... then I believe it."

She pushes my chest with her finger and then rushes to open the front door, before I can open it for her.

I walk in after her, smiling as she tilts her head back and sniffs the air with a moan. It's so sexy. "Holy shit, Styx. It smells even better from inside. I've never had a man cook me dinner before. This is new and I love that you did this."

"I'll do a lot for you," I say, while guiding her to the kitchen table and pulling out a chair for her to sit. Surprisingly she didn't even notice that my couch and TV are gone. She's too focused on dinner. That's what I wanted. "I'm not going to lie. You're the first woman I've cooked for. You're becoming the first for a lot of things for me and it surprises the hell out of me. *You* surprise the hell out of me."

She looks up at me, speechless, before she bites her lip and turns away as if she doesn't want me to see her reaction. Too late. Hiding her face does nothing. Especially with the way she's shifting in her seat and breathing so hard that I can hear it.

My confession made her nervous.

She's falling for me just as hard as I'm beginning to fall for her and I have a feeling that it surprises her just as much.

I stuck the steak and homemade mashed potatoes in the oven, before I left to pick her up. So I pull them out and fix our plates in silence, giving her a moment to gather her thoughts.

The look on her face as I set the table for her is one of admiration and appreciation. It makes my heart speed up to see her looking at me this way. "Thank you," she says sincerely. "I want you to know that I appreciate the things you do for me. It's been a while since I've had anyone be there for me like you have just within the month that I've met you. So thank you."

My heart sinks from the sadness laced in her voice and it brings me back to the conversation we had on the rock about losing her parents when she was young and then her aunt a year ago.

Fuck, I hate the thought of her ever being alone.

It makes me want to be there for her more, but I know it's impossible right now. Not with our busy schedules. But I hope to change that soon.

I sit back and watch as she gets lost in her first few bites of steak. The way her eyes close and that sexy little moan leaves her mouth, tells me that she loves it just as much as I was hoping she would.

"Oh. My. God." When she's done chewing, she opens her eyes and smiles across the table at me. "This is *the* best steak I have ever eaten. No joke. This is insanely good."

"I'm glad to hear that." I cut a piece of my steak and lift a brow, watching as she shoves a huge chunk of hers in her mouth as if she's enjoying it a little too much. "I enjoy how much you love my meat in your mouth."

She stops chewing and throws a green bean at me, trying to hold back her laughter as it bounces off my forehead.

"I didn't mean to hit you in the face, but I have to admit that it is kind of funny." Another green bean hits my forehead, making her laugh even louder.

She's so beautiful when she laughs as if no one's watching. Well... I definitely am.

With my eyes locked on hers, I pull her chair beside mine and lock it in place with my leg just as I did that night at the club. She continues to laugh at me as I wipe my forehead off and shake my head at her.

"You're lucky you're so cute when you laugh." I lick my bottom lip, before leaning in and kissing her, right as she gets ready to speak.

Whatever she was about to say will just have to wait. My mouth needs to be all over hers right now. I can't handle not touching her.

"Oh yeah?" she questions against my lips, before tugging my bottom one with her teeth. "And you're lucky that you're the only thing I've wanted all day. Or else I'd hurt you for keeping me away from this steak."

"Yeah?" I growl, while wrapping my hands into the back of her hair and pulling her closer. "I like a dangerous woman. Go ahead. Hurt me."

She looks at me for a few seconds, her eyes soft, before she speaks. "Honestly, I don't think I could ever hurt you. Even if you wanted me to."

"Good," I whisper. "Now finish your dinner. I have something else planned for us."

I haven't been out back yet, but I hope like hell that the boys came through for me. She wants a night at home, curled up on the couch with movies and then a night out under the stars. With me, she's getting both at the same time.

By the time we're done with dinner, Meadow is looking at me with the biggest smile. She hasn't stopped smiling since we sat down to eat and that makes me happier than anything.

This night is supposed to be all about her and I'm happy that she's excited to see what comes next.

"Best dinner of my life. I'm seriously stuffed. I should've stopped eating a long time ago, but I couldn't. This... this was so good. Who taught you how to cook like that?"

I answer her while cleaning up our dirty plates and tossing them into the dishwasher. "My uncle Wes. He's the best cook that I know. So I'll make sure to keep you away from him. I don't need any competition. The fucker's handsome too."

I hear her laugh behind me, before I feel her arms wrap around my waist. "There's never any competition when it comes to you. So I wouldn't worry too much about uncle Wes."

Turning around to face her, I cup her face and lean down to kiss her with a soft moan. "I'm trying really fucking hard to be somewhat romantic so let's get you outside before I blow it and rip your clothes off right here with my damn teeth."

She stands on her tippytoes and wraps her arms around my neck, pulling me down to her with force. "Keep talking to me like that and we might not make it outside for the next part of the date."

With that, she turns and walks away, leaving me to watch her sexy ass as she heads for the back door, stopping once she reaches for the handle. "Come."

Her one-word command has me following her and kissing the back of her neck as she pulls the door open and looks around.

"Styx," she says excitedly, while shoving the screen door open. "What is this?" She walks outside to get a closer look. "Is that your couch and TV?"

"You wanted a night with movies and stars. So you're getting a night with movies and stars. You ask for something with me and I give it. That's how I work."

Grabbing my hand, she starts pulling me toward the gazebo, in a hurry to get me over to the couch. "Wow!" She looks up at the screen roof, her mouth dropping as she looks at all the stars. They're so bright tonight. "I love this! I would've never thought to do anything like this. This is amazing. You never cease to amaze me."

Taking a seat, I pull her down into my lap and wrap my arms around her, just as I did on the rock that night.

Having her in my arms feels so good and all I can think about is wanting to protect her and make her happy.

I let her control the remote, until she finds a movie that she wants to watch. The movie doesn't matter to me. It's being here with her in my arms that I've been looking forward to all day and night.

About twenty minutes into the movie, we move positions so that I'm laying behind her, with my arms wrapped tightly around her. I want her as comfortable as she can be.

Even if she falls asleep in my arms, I won't be moving. I'll sleep out here to make her happy.

"Thank you," she whispers halfway through the movie. "This is one of the best nights of my life."

"Good," I whisper back. "It's one of mine too."

She flips around to face me, wrapping her arms around my head. "You're so much different than I expected, Styx. Sweeter and more caring. One of the most caring people I've ever met. You make me feel... just... you make me feel. It's been a long time since I've cared about anything other than the hospital."

I feel an ache in my chest as I hold her as tightly as I can and place my forehead to hers. "You make me feel too. You're the first woman to make me want more in life. The first woman that I've spent my days looking forward to seeing any chance that I can get. You're special to me."

Her breathing picks up against my lips. "I go to sleep at night thinking about being with you. I miss you when you're not around. That's a big deal for me."

Leaning up, I cup her face and crush my lips against hers, wanting nothing more than to feel her against me.

This woman is everything I've been looking for and holy fuck... hearing that she misses me when I'm not around has me going fucking crazy inside.

Gently, I flip her around to her back and press my body in between her legs. "What do you miss about me?" I ask in a whisper.

"The way you make me laugh and forget about the emptiness that I've felt since losing my aunt. The way you kiss me as if you can't get enough of me. And the way you hold me in silence as if words aren't needed to describe what you're feeling for me."

Our hearts race against each other's as I trace her bottom lip with my thumb and hover my mouth above hers. "Fuck, I want you as mine."

"Then take me," she breathes. "I can be yours if you want me to."

Sitting up, I pull my shirt over my head and toss it down. Her hands slowly roam over my body, caressing my muscles as I reach for my jeans and undo them.

Her touch is gentle and caring as if she's taking the time to remember this moment forever. Like she's burning it into her brain for later.

I am too.

My heart is racing so fast and hard that I know she must feel it as I pull her up and strip her of her shirt and bra.

"You're so beautiful."

Before I know it, our naked bodies are tangled together and I'm slowly sinking into her under the stars.

Our bodies move slowly this time. Gentle as my bare cock fills her, causing her to moan into my mouth and scratch my back as if she's more lost in the moment than any other time we've had sex.

It may be gentler, but there's nothing gentle about the emotions that this is bringing out of her. Hell, out of the both of us.

"Oh fuck..." I moan out as I move inside of her, feeling her bare. It's almost too much to handle. "You're so wet for me, baby. I love feeling you this way."

Her fingers dig into my back and her legs squeeze my ass as I push in as deep as I can go and stop. "Me too," she breathes. "Oh my God you feel so good. Keep moving for me."

This must be what making love feels like. Holy fuck. It's better than any rough night of sex that I've ever had.

I'll take this every night if I can have it with her.

I'm getting close to release, so I wrap my hands into her hair and whisper against her lips. "Can I come in you?"

She nods and then kisses me so hard and deep that I know she wants me to just as badly as I want to.

I pull her up so that she's straddling my lap, my hands tugging at her hair as she rides me slow and deep, until I'm filling her with my cum.

A few seconds later, her grip on me tightens as she clenches around my cock, moaning against my mouth as her whole body shakes with pleasure.

"Holy shit, Styx." She breathes. "I honestly didn't think that sex with you could get any better... but it just did. You're amazing."

I kiss her and hold her against me, feeling our hearts beat together.

After we have both caught our breath, I clean us up and then pull the blanket from the back of the couch, covering us up with her in my arms.

Holy shit. I think I'm screwed after this. There's no way I'm letting another man ever be inside her this way...

CHAPTER NINETEEN

MEADOW

AFTER STYX SHOWED ME AN incredibly amazing night, I fell asleep in his arms, laying under the stars in the gazebo.

It was peaceful and beautiful. Nothing else mattered in that moment except my heart beating against his as he held me to his chest, making it seem that he couldn't get me close enough.

Going home this morning sucked and truthfully made me wish that we had the whole day free to just lounge around and hold each other.

But he had to go to the gym for most of the afternoon so he dropped me off at home, leaving my whole body aching for his touch, impatient to see him again tonight.

I've spent most of my morning now, trying to talk one of the other nurses into covering my shift so that I can make it to his mother's dinner tonight to repay him for everything he's done for me.

After two hours on the phone and promising Dani that I'll work a double tomorrow, I'm finally free today.

And I've spent every last second since hanging up that phone reliving last night and trying to figure out what is happening between Styx and I.

A month ago if you would've asked me if I was ready for a serious relationship, I would've said no. I was scared. Terrified of getting used to being with someone and loving them just to possibly end up alone *again*. I've lost too much and the pain is still unbearable at times.

I'm still afraid, but truthfully all I want to do is spend my time with Styx.

I get that Styx doesn't open up much to others. I get that he's not typically the romantic, serious relationship type guy, but he makes me feel that for me—he would be. And I love that. It gives me hope that things could be more than I expected.

Mandy has been watching me try on outfits for the last hour now, but I can't seem to find one that I'm completely satisfied with. What a way to spend her night off.

"The last three outfits looked good. What are you so worried about?" she asks as she watches from her seat on my bed. "He invited you home to meet his mother. From what I've heard about this guy, I doubt he cares what you're wearing. He'll just be happy to have you there."

"Yeah." I turn away from the mirror to face her. "I know. But just knowing that I'm the first woman he's invited to dinner with his mother... You get it. I just want to look nice. For her."

Mandy smiles at me. "I've never seen you like this over a man before, Meadow. It makes me happy because you deserve to feel this. You deserve someone who will give to you as much as you do to others. You're a good person."

She stands up and fixes the back of my black blouse. "I know you've lost a lot. But *please* try not to let that discourage you from getting close with Styx. I know it has in the past. But honestly... none of those men seemed to be worth it. Especially not Jase."

A tear falls from my eye and I laugh, wiping it away. No one has really mentioned that they think I give a lot. Not since my aunt has passed at least. She used to remind me that all the time when it came to guys.

"*Especially* not that ass. He was never more than just something to pass the time and I was the same to him."

"Are you sure about that?" she asks as I'm throwing my hair up.

"Why do you ask that? Of course that's all he was for me."

"I meant for him. He's been acting strange ever since you and Styx started dating. He's been very moody and almost lost in his own little world most of the time. It's weird. He hasn't even been sleeping around with the other nurses. Weird. I hate *this* Jase even more."

I sit down on the edge of my bed and slip my black heeled boots on, tucking the legs of my skinny jeans inside. "Doesn't matter. Jase is in the past. So let's not talk about him anymore. Especially when I'm about to see Styx. He'll be here any minute."

She reaches for her purse and walks past the mirror, giving herself a quick glance. "Tell me all about dinner later, okay. I want to know how it goes. Jameson is waiting for me so I should go."

Smiling, I give her a quick hug and then walk her to the door. "Have fun on your date, babe. And don't think that I won't be asking for details later. Details for details. Sounds like a fair exchange."

"You got it." She winks and jogs down the porch steps as Styx pulls up on his motorcycle. "Holy hell... he's hot on a motorcycle." Giving me the thumbs up, she turns away and walks past Styx, waving before she jumps into her car.

"Hell yeah he is," I whisper to myself, while looking him over on his bike.

I swear a man has never made a leather jacket look so good. It's my favorite thing of his that he wears.

After I quickly lock my door, I turn around and watch as he pulls his helmet off and walks toward me.

Even his walk is extremely sexy and full of confidence and the thought that this guy was inside of me without a condom last night has me fanning myself off with my purse.

I think I'm going to overheat. Especially if he keeps looking at me with those sexy blue eyes the way that he is.

As if he's about to tie me up and devour me.

"Come here," he says, while pulling me against him. "Holy fuck, I've missed you all day."

His hands grip the back of my hair and before I know it, his lips crash against mine, taking my breath away.

The way his tongue moves against mine, his soft lips all over my lips as if he owns them. This kiss is different than the rest. Deeper and more meaningful somehow.

Or maybe it's just my imagination.

He pulls away from our kiss, placing his forehead against mine. "You ready to meet my mother?"

I can tell from the look in his eyes that he's worried about bringing me to his mother's house. I'm not sure what to think about that. Maybe I was right to worry about what to wear.

"Are you sure you want me to go? I don't have to..."

He kisses me again, but harder this time, backing me up against the door and pinning me in with his body. "Fuck yes I do. Don't ever question that again. It's not you."

I look up to meet his gaze. "Tell me why you're nervous."

His eyes close and he lets out a deep breath, speaking with our foreheads still pressed together. "My asshole father will be there and there's a lot of things that you don't know about him. He's hurt both me and my mother a lot."

I reach up and cup his face, my heart breaking as I look into his eyes. "I'm sorry that he's ever hurt you or your mother. I hate hearing that with everything in me. I know you said he was an asshole..."

"He's a piece of shit. The biggest asshole that I know and honestly he doesn't even deserve to be in the same room with you, but I'm doing this for my mother."

Standing up on my tippytoes, I press my lips to his, talking against them. "He doesn't deserve a son like you. You're so far from being an asshole. You're the best person I know. So let's just go and prove to him that you're the bigger person. Let's not worry. Okay? I'm here for you."

He nods his head and breathes against my lips. "And I love you for that."

"Fuck," he whispers afterwards and turns away in a hurry, grabbing my hand to walk me down to his bike. "Let's go."

I try to focus on jumping on the back of his motorcycle and wrapping my arms around him, but all my mind is on is the fact that the word *love* just came from his lips. Even if it wasn't in the *I love you* way.

It has my heart racing and my whole body feeling weak.

This man has much more of me than I thought. He has my fucking heart. All of it and I hope like hell that he doesn't rip it from my chest.

When we pull up at his parents' house, his whole body stiffens as he stares at the empty driveway.

"Everything alright?" I ask in his ear. "Is anyone here?"

He turns off the engine but doesn't make a move to get off his bike. "Yeah, my mother's here. My father isn't."

I smile and rub his shoulders. "That's a good thing then, right? Maybe he'll miss dinner and you won't have to—"

"It's not a good thing," he growls, while helping me off the back of his bike. "Trust me. It's far from good."

Grabbing my hand, he gives me a quick kiss on the lips, before walking me to the house and pushing the door open.

"We're here, Mom."

A beautiful woman about my height comes running from the kitchen, excitedly pulling her blonde hair from her face and pinning it back. "Oh. My."

She stops in front of me and looks me over, before pulling my hand from Styx's and enclosing it in hers. "Meadow is *beautiful*." I laugh nervously as she spins me around and then hugs me. "You're perfect for my son. Just think of the beautiful babies you guys would have."

"Seriously?" Styx says, sounding embarrassed. "Let's not talk about kids when she's barely been mine for a month. Shit, Mom."

"So she is yours?" she questions, looking as if she got the information a lot easier than she expected. Grinning, she throws her arms around me and whispers, "You're the first woman he's *ever* called his. You're special to him and that makes you very special to me."

"Alright. Alright. Try not to scare Meadow away before she even makes it to the kitchen table to fucking eat. Now where's Frank?"

His mom smiles even bigger and then kisses him on the forehead. "Love you, baby," she says, ignoring his question. "Now let's go eat."

Styx grabs my hand as his mom rushes back into the kitchen as if to avoid any further talk of his father. "My mother's a little excited about tonight. So ignore some of the things she says. She's not used to me bringing women around."

I smile and squeeze his hand, excited to get to experience this. "I love her. She's so cute. I love that she's excited so let's try to forget about your father and enjoy this time with her. I want her to be happy. I want to see you both smiling tonight."

I give him a quick kiss and then head to the kitchen to help his mother.

Styx follows shortly behind, going straight to the dishes to help set the table.

"Meadow, sweetie." His mother turns to look at me, while shoving a piece of hamburger meat in her mouth. "Would you mind grabbing the cheese from the bottom drawer in the fridge? I forgot to get it out. Everything is set after that!"

"No problem," I say, returning her smile. "Thanks for having me for dinner. It smells delicious in here."

She laughs. "I learned from my son. I was a lousy cook when he was a kid and none of my food had any flavor."

I catch Styx laughing as he finishes setting up the table. "That's true. I used to go weeks skipping dinner just so I wouldn't have to eat her cooking."

"Hey!" His mother throws a taco shell at him. "That's a lie. You make it sound as if I fed you dog food as a kid." She winks. "It was cat food."

I can't help but laugh as we all sit down and start making our tacos.

I can definitely see where Styx gets his personality from.

After dinner, we spend the next hour at the table eating snacks and playing cards, listening to stories about when Styx was a teen.

A smile hasn't left our faces since we sat down and I have to admit that this is the best family dinner I've had since I was a kid.

I've forgotten what it was like to have a family. I'm glad that Styx has one and that he has the choice to still experience these moments.

There's just one thing that's been bothering me.

Every few minutes, I catch Styx looking toward the living room with a worried expression as if he's waiting for his father to show up at any minute.

I just wish I knew a way to take his worry away. But I don't and I hate it...

CHAPTER TWENTY

STYX

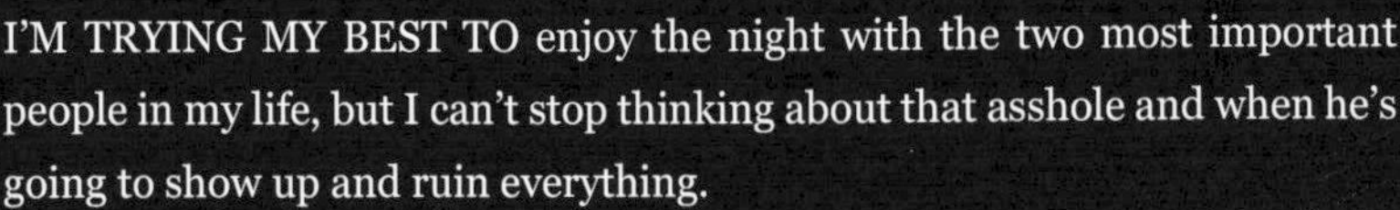

I'M TRYING MY BEST TO enjoy the night with the two most important people in my life, but I can't stop thinking about that asshole and when he's going to show up and ruin everything.

He's going to be here any second. I can feel it in my fucking bones and I will do everything in my power to protect the both of them. Nothing about this night is going to end well and I'm already hating that I've put Meadow in this position.

I stare hard. Waiting...

Come on, motherfucker and get it over with.

"Styx!" My mother laughs and tosses a card at me to get my attention. It's about the fifth time that she's had to yell at me since the game started. I'm trying hard to just be in the moment, but I can't. Fuck, it's hard to concentrate right now. "It's your turn again. Go! Don't keep us ladies waiting all night. That's rude."

"Sorry. I was just..." I pull my eyes away from the living room and get ready to toss a card down to play, when the front door bursts open, causing everyone at the table to jump in surprise. Myself included and I fucking hate my body for reacting this way.

I spent my whole childhood fearing this man, but not anymore. He will never get the pleasure of seeing fear in my eyes again. I will die before that day happens.

"Oh fuck," my mom whispers, while panicking to push all the cards into a pile.

Meadow must see the worry on her face, so she jumps to her feet and starts gathering cards too, without question. "Let me help you." She places her hands on my mother's as she continues to reach out with shaky hands. "I got it. It's okay."

Jumping to my feet, I stand straight, cracking my neck as I watch the drunken bastard enter the kitchen and stop.

Yeah, you want to stand there looking like an ass as if you didn't know we would be here. You want to play this shit so you have an excuse to be angry.

Keeping my eyes on him, I watch as he tilts back the rest of what's left of his beer and then tosses the empty bottle in the sink.

"What the fuck is this shit, Lily?" He grips the sink, before punching the counter and then turning around to face us. "You didn't tell me we'd have guests. I would've made sure to come home right after work."

My mother looks from Meadow to me and shakes her head apologetically. "I told you yesterday, remember? I mentioned going to buy stuff for tacos..."

"The fuck you did," he shouts, while picking up the closest thing to him and throwing it across the room. His jaw clenches as his eyes land on the cards that Meadow is shoving into the box. "You fucking play cards without me, Lily? Get over here. Now."

"Fuck you," I growl out, while blocking my mother from his view. He won't live to hurt her again if he makes any move to touch her. "She doesn't have to come to you. Don't ever fucking talk to her like that again. You need to leave."

"I need to leave?" He points at his chest and laughs his asshole fucking laugh that he always does. As if he's so untouchable. Not anymore. "This is *my* house. *I* pay the bills. No one tells me what to do in my own home. No even your bitch of a mother."

"Woah! Don't talk like that about her. What is your problem?" Meadow speaks up, causing my father to look at her for what must be the first time since he's walked in the door.

I instantly stiffen up at even the idea of his eyes on her. They're dark and full of whatever evil resides inside his fucked-up mind.

"Who the fuck is this little bitch in my house?" His hand slips from the counter, him nearly falling down, but he somehow manages to catch himself first. "Dammit, Lily. I'm going to beat your ass for making me look like a fool. Come. Here. Now."

In a rage, he pushes me to the side to get at my mother, but I grab him by his neck, slamming him into the sink. "You will *never* talk to my mother or girlfriend with that disrespect again. I will cut your fucking tongue from your mouth. Got it?" I look over my shoulder at Meadow, while preventing my father from moving. "I need you both outside. Now. Take my mom. Don't let her back in no matter what she says."

Meadow nods and shoots to her feet.

"Don't you dare fucking go outside, Lily. You will stay right there until I say so. This asshole won't touch me with you around to see it and as soon as he gets the fuck out of the way, you're mine. Stay," he demands.

Feeling the rage take over, I toss him down onto the kitchen floor and grab him by the throat, squeezing so hard that he starts coughing. "Let's see you try to touch her now, you piece of shit." I elbow him in the face as he attempts to push me away. "Go ahead. Hurt her! Do it motherfucker. Get past me now. Let me see you try. Put your hands on her like you have since I was ten. Make her scream and cry, balled up on the floor trying to protect herself. Go ahead!"

"Fuck you and that bitch of a mother of yours," he chokes out. "She's not good for anything but a quick fuck anyway and she won't even give that any—"

I see red and my fist connects with his face, cutting him off before he can finish his thoughts.

I will not sit here and listen to him disrespect my mother anymore.

Feeling the fire inside me build up, I lose all restraint, my fists continuing to swing over and over again.

The only sound filling my ears is my fist connecting hard with his bones.

Again. Again. And again until his face is covered in blood and I feel hands pull at me, trying to get me off him.

It takes a few seconds for me to come back to the scene around me enough to realize that my mother is crying and screaming at me to stop, while Meadow is telling me he's had enough.

They both sound worried and that's when I notice that my father isn't moving anymore or struggling to get away from me.

Releasing his throat, I fight to catch my breath while looking hard to see that he's knocked out cold. He's done for. He's had enough—she's right.

Although in my mind, it can never be enough.

Blood covers his face and my hands, but I don't feel one ounce of regret seeing him lay there helpless in his own pool of blood. I've seen my mother do the same too many times.

"What did you do?" my mom cries. "You could've killed him." She pushes at me, screaming and crying. "He wasn't going to touch me. He wasn't." She pushes me again and then drops down to her knees.

I stand up and watch as my mother grabs at his shirt and yells his name in attempt to get him to wake up.

"Frank! Get up! Open your eyes." She slaps his cheek in a panic. "Come on, dammit! Open them."

This only pisses me off more, watching her in so much agony over his pain. He deserved every hit that he took. "After everything he's put you through. Us through. You give a shit about *him* being hurt for once? After all those times he hurt you every fucking day and then beat me for trying to help you? All the broken bones I suffered as a child because of him or all the scars on the back of your head from him throwing you into anything and everything."

I grip my hair and start pacing. I want to fucking scream, but I'm trying my best not to scare Meadow anymore or give her a reason to think I'm anything like that piece of shit on the floor. "Why the fuck haven't you left him yet? Why the fuck did you put us through all that suffering after seeing how dangerous he *was*. He could've killed us both. But you stayed anyway and you still refuse to leave. Why the hell won't you walk away? Why? Tell me."

"Stop it, Styx. Dammit. Stop it," she cries out, while wiping at her face. "I love him and he hasn't hurt me in over six months. Things have been good between us and you just ruined that. He's going to hate me now." She cries harder and I can tell that it's out of fear.

I haven't forgotten that sound. I'll never forget that fucking sound.

"He hasn't hurt you in six months," I scream. "You want to know why? It's because of me. Fuck!" I point at my chest in pain. "Because I sit outside your house every fucking day when he gets off work, making sure that he can walk straight. Making sure that he hasn't been drinking so he won't feel the need to beat you for no reason. That's why he hasn't hurt you. I make sure of it. He knows I'm there every single fucking day. That's why."

I glance over at Meadow to see her watching us with her hand over her mouth and tears spilling from her eyes. She's pained by everything that she's learning about our past and it only makes me love her more.

Fuck, I hate that she has to see this, but there's no stopping this shitstorm now. There's no walking away from this situation.

This is my mother and my father. This is my life. It's been my shitty life since the day my father picked up a beer and never put one down.

My mother looks up from trying to get my father to respond to her. "You do that for me?" she questions with tears in her eyes. "Every day?"

I nod and reach for my mother's hand to pull her up to her feet. "Damn straight I do. I'd do anything for you. I'd fucking die for you. No questions asked."

My mom's arms wrap around my neck and before I know it, she's bawling into my arms, me holding her up so she won't fall to the floor. "I'm so sorry. I'm so fucking sorry. Oh my God." She holds me tighter, her whole body shaking as she cries. "I'm hurting you. It's me. I've been the one hurting you."

I glance over to see more tears roll down Meadow's face, before she wipes them away and walks over to check my father's pulse and breathing.

It hurts me so much right now that she has to be here to witness this shitty mess and check to make sure that I haven't just killed someone right in front of her eyes.

Fuck, she may hate me after this.

Once my mom calms down, I release my hold on her and walk over to throw my arms around Meadow when she steps away from Frank. "I'm so fucking sorry. I promise you that this isn't me. This pain has been building for years and I can't stand back anymore while that piece of shit hurts my mother." I kiss her cheek and whisper in her ear. "You can leave if you want. I'll understand."

She shakes her head and then cups my face, pulling me in for a kiss. She's soft and gentle, her lips still wet from the tears she's shed. "I could never leave you for having a heart and wanting to protect your family. *No one* deserves to hurt like this. I would've done it myself."

She pulls away and looks me in the eyes when the drunken bastard makes noises as if he's about to vomit and mumbles my mother's name. "I hate to say this, but your dad can't be left alone tonight. He could asphyxiate on his own vomit. He's drunk and covered in his own blood."

I see my mother looking down at that piece of shit as if she wants to help him and lessen his suffering. "I'll stay with him. Help me roll him over to his side." She looks up at me, waiting.

Rushing to her, I pull my mom away from the piece of shit and roll him over with force, just in time for him to throw up on the carpet.

"There's no way in hell I'm letting you stay here with him so he can beat the shit out of you when he gets back to his feet. No fucking way, Mom. Not happening."

I see the panic in my mother's eyes and I hate seeing her this way. It has my heart feeling like it's being ripped in two. I hate that asshole, but I love her more.

"As a nurse I can't just leave him here with the possibility of him dying, Styx. I hate what he's done just as much as you do, but someone needs to be here. I'll stay for a few hours if I have to."

"Fuck no." Frustrated, I run my hands through my hair and then grab Meadow's hand, walking her over to my mother. "I'll stay with the piece of shit so he doesn't die. You guys take the car and stay at my place."

"Styx?" Meadow questions. "Are you sure you can handle this?"

I shake my head. "No... but I'll do it for you two." I kiss the top of my mother's head and then wrap my arms around Meadow, giving her a gentle kiss. "You two take care of each other until I can, please. That's all I ask. You can leave after that if you want, but please take care of each other for tonight."

I look into my mother's exhausted eyes. They're red and puffy from crying and she looks as if she's about to fall over. "Please go with Meadow for tonight. I need you out of here. I need to know that you're safe. If anything do it for me. Fall asleep knowing that this asshole won't hurt you for once. One fucking night that you won't have to worry. I won't let that happen. He's not leaving this house."

She nods and wipes her eyes. "I'm so sorry I ruined the night. I love you so much. I don't want to hurt you anymore. I won't. You're my baby." She grabs my face. "Please. I need help to stay away from him. I can't do it alone."

"You won't have to," I point out. "You're never alone. I'm here."

Meadow jumps in and grabs my mom's hand, before wrapping an arm around her to console her. "I can get you help if you want it, Lily. We can talk about it after you rest."

Walking my mom toward the door, Meadow looks over her shoulder and whispers something that I can't quite understand.

As much as I'd love to ask her what that was, at this point, I'm just happy to see her and my mother walking out that door.

Fuck... this is going to be a long night...

CHAPTER TWENTY-ONE

MEADOW

IT WAS A ROUGH NIGHT for Lily, but she finally fell asleep just after one this morning once she promised me she'd get herself some help to stay away from Frank.

I spent most of our time together convincing her that she'll be okay without him and that a real man that loved his family wouldn't hurt them. When a real man loves his family, he does everything in his power to protect them.

Like Styx...

The son that *she* raised.

She deserves so much more than what Frank's ever given her and I'm just glad that my words made her somewhat see that.

My heart instantly ached for Styx the moment he walked through his door early this morning, looking tired and worn out, but unfortunately I couldn't stay to comfort Styx and let him know that I'm here for him.

Dani reamed my ass over the phone and only gave me fifteen minutes to make it to the hospital. I was already thirty minutes late so I don't blame her.

I practically begged to work a double today so that I could take yesterday off and now I wish with everything in me that I had today off too so I could spend time with Styx and make sure that he's okay.

I've been here for over fifteen hours now and the *only* thing that's been on my mind is Styx. I miss him like crazy.

My heart aches every time I think about him and what he had to do last night. I want to be there for him. I *should* be there for him.

As much as I want to talk to him though, I haven't messaged him because I know he's taking the day off to spend with Lily.

They need this time together and I will never get in the way of them having it. I've never seen a mother than needs her son as much as she needs Styx right now.

I'm off in an hour so if he's free then I'll let him come to me when he's ready.

For now, I'll just do my best to focus on my duties here at the hospital.

As hard as that might be...

I'VE BEEN HOME FOR ALMOST an hour, so exhausted that I can barely even stand, but that hasn't stopped my mind from worrying about Styx.

I left my phone in the bedroom when I changed so I didn't even know Styx must've been texting me, until I hear a knock at the door.

Jumping up from the couch, I rush over to open it so fast that I don't even have time to pay attention to who's standing on my porch until it's too late.

Jase pushes past my arm, letting himself inside. "We need to talk, Meadow. I can't handle this shit."

"Jase," I growl. "There's nothing to talk about so I'm going to ask you this nicely. And I will only ask nicely once. Please leave. It's late and I'm exhausted."

Shaking his head, he yanks at his hair and comes at me, grabbing my arms. "I miss you. I didn't think I cared about you as much as I do until I saw you with that asshole."

Not liking his closeness, I yank my arms away from him and start backing away. "Have you been drinking?" I point toward the opened door. "Leave. Right. Now."

He laughs and takes a step toward me, reaching out his arms. "Did you listen to anything I just said? I care about you. I want you."

I keep backing up, until I'm pressed against the wall with Jase blocking me in with his arms. This is the *last* position I want to be in with him. Especially when he's been drinking. I've already watched one drunken asshole make a fool of himself. I don't need to see another one.

"I'm sorry, Jase, but no." I place my hand on his hard chest and give him a shove, but he doesn't budge. "Get the fuck out."

He shakes his head and then grabs my wrist, hard, holding it still so he can lean in and attempt to kiss me.

I turn my head to the side and fight to get my wrist free. "Get the fuck off me, Jase!" I scream and push at him with all my might. "Don't you kiss me. Get off!"

Clenching his jaw, he picks me up and tosses me onto the couch, before throwing himself on top of me and kissing me.

He forces his mouth on mine so hard that I cut my lip on his tooth. Before I know it, his erection is pressed between my legs.

"You used to love this. Remember? Give me a chance to remind you."

"Get off!" I thrust my hips and yell, until I feel his body weight lift off me and then hear the sound of bone meeting bone.

Surprised, I sit up, fighting to catch my breath as I watch Styx, beating the shit out of Jase.

Shock takes over and for a second, I can't speak. All I can do is jump over the couch to get away from them.

The punches only seem to get harder and louder with each swing, until Jase finally throws his hands up in surrender.

Breathing hard, Styx shoves Jase's head into the floor, one last time, before jumping to his feet and rushing over to me.

His bloodied hands reach for my face, but I back away, before he can touch me.

"Are you okay? Did he hurt you?"

I close my eyes and run my hands over my face, still shocked as hell that this all just happened.

"I just need him out of here. I can't look at him. I can't." I open my eyes and look at Styx to see his reaction.

Nodding, he yanks Jase to his feet and begins pushing him toward the door. "Don't ever fucking come here again," he growls. "You're lucky I didn't kill you for putting your hands on her."

Turning away from Styx, I powerwalk to the bathroom and shut the door behind me, pacing back and forth.

My heart is racing so fast and hard right now that I can hardly catch my breath.

I don't know what to think. I'm so fucking confused. This is all too overwhelming for me.

This all has me wanting to scream. So I do.

Rushing from the bathroom, I grab Styx by the back of his jacket and turn him around, pressing my lips against his, before taking a step back and yelling. "What the fuck!" I look over his shoulder to see Jase opening the door to his car and speeding off.

"You're so much bigger than him. You could've killed him, Styx. You need to know when to stop throwing the punches. Sometimes it doesn't take twenty swings to get the message across."

Styx's eyes soften once he sees how worked up I am. "I wanted to kill him when I walked in that door to see him hurting you. He's lucky he didn't get fifty swings."

God. I love him for this, but feel like I should be mad at the same damn time.

"I understand that you were just protecting me, but I can't handle this right now. Do you understand that in less than twenty-four hours, I stood back and watched you beat the shit out of two grown men? My heart aches seeing you this way."

Pushing his hair out of his face, he walks toward me, not stopping until his body is pressed against mine. "I'm sorry I've made you watch, but I'm not sorry for hurting him. I will do everything to protect you. That's just who I am. Can you handle that?"

Closing my eyes, I nod and kiss him back, when I feel his lips on mine.

Being in his arms feels so good. Too good, but I think I need to be alone right now.

"I want to be with you tonight, Styx. I do with everything in me, but I need some alone time right now. Is that okay?"

"You want me to leave?" His body stiffens and I hate that a part of him is worried that I might not want him anymore.

"Just for tonight. I just need to draw a hot bath and relax and then go to sleep and wake up to a better day. I think we both need to sleep today off. I know it's been a rough day for you and it's been extremely rough for me too."

He presses his face into my neck, before he gently kisses it and takes a step away from me. "I need to stop by the club to talk to Cale tomorrow. So I guess I need tonight to think about what I want to say to him."

"Is everything okay?" I question.

He nods and zips up his jacket. "Yeah, it will be. Goodnight."

Standing next to the couch, I watch as he walks away and closes the door behind him.

The first thing I do is fall to my knees and cry, letting out all my frustration and pain.

I feel so alone right now, but I need to be.

After spending the whole day at the hospital looking after hurt patients, the last thing that I could take tonight was seeing another person bleeding in front of me, right on my living room floor. I've seen too much blood in the last twenty-four hours. I can't see anymore right now.

Not to mention that I've been thinking about my mother, father, and aunt since last night.

But especially my aunt since she raised me for as long as I can remember.

Spending the night with Lily reminded me what it was like to have that warm, fuzzy feeling of a parent being around to talk to.

Sometimes when I'm in moods like this, being alone is the best thing I can do. I hate letting anyone see just how broken I truly am.

I just hope that Styx will understand tomorrow...

CHAPTER TWENTY-TWO

STYX

I HAVEN'T SPOKEN TO MEADOW since last night when she asked me to leave.

I've spent the first part of my day at the gym and the second part of it at my mother's house, making sure that her locks are all properly changed now that Frank has been asked to leave.

The police escorted him out the other night and I made it clear to him that he wasn't to step foot into this house again.

I'll pay the rent for as long as my mother needs. So that piece of shit has no hold over her now. If she needs someone she can call me and I'll be there every single time. She doesn't have to be alone and she won't be.

I'm now on my way to the club to talk to Cale, even though the only thing on my mind is going to find Meadow.

I need to know that she still wants me and that I haven't scared her off. I know she said that she just needed the night, but now that she's had time to think, maybe she needs more. I don't know.

Pulling up to the club, I feel and look like shit as I hop off my motorcycle and make my way inside.

It's not extremely busy here yet, but the instant I get spotted in the crowd, half-naked girls cling to me, pulling me in different directions to get my attention.

It only reminds me more why I need to get the hell out of this place and focus on the gym more.

Having other women's hands on me makes me feel guilty as hell. The only hands that feel good on me are Meadow's.

She's the *only* person I want touching me.

Ignoring the women groping at me, I make my way up the steps to Cale's office and knock.

"It's open."

Cale stands up and walks over to shake my hand once I step inside. "Everything good, man? You look like hell."

I let out a deep laugh and take a seat in the chair across from his. "It's been a rough couple of days, man. Real fucking tough."

"Yeah, I heard." He leans back in his chair and runs a hand through his blond hair.

I feel like we've all been through a lot together here, watching each other grow and Cale is probably the best fucker I know. Quitting on him is going to be hard.

"Slade tell you?" I question.

He nods. "Yeah. But that asshole deserved it. Tell your mother hi for me and if she needs anything to get ahold of Riley or myself. We'll help in any way that we can."

My lips turn up into a thankful smile, but inside I'm feeling guilty as shit. "Appreciate that, man." I run my hands over my face and lean back in the chair, trying to get the words to come out.

"Relax," Cale says. "You might forget that I talk to Slade every day. I know what you're here for and I don't want you feeling guilty. It's not like I expect you guys to stay here forever." He laughs when I raise a brow. "Hell, I was happy as hell the day I stopped shaking my dick for money. Trust me. The time will come when Stone and Kash leave too. I'm always prepared. No worries."

"Can't tell Slade anything, apparently," I say with a grin. "That fucker."

Cale shrugs. "He wouldn't have told me if he wasn't trying to look out for you. I know Slade better than anyone else. That just means that he thinks of you as one of our family."

I stand up and shake Cale's hand. "You dicks will always be family to me. Thanks, man. But I got somewhere to be now."

He smiles and starts going through some files. "Looks like I have some auditions to set up. So get out."

I grip the back of the chair and push it to his desk, before hurrying out of his office and through the club, before some random chick can stop me.

There's only one place I want to be right now...

MEADOW

I'VE HAD THIS ACHE IN my chest all day to see Styx, but I've been fighting it, afraid of what to say to him.

He was there for me when I needed him and I had the nerve to ask him to leave so that I could be alone for the night.

I feel like the biggest asshole and there really aren't any words to explain how sorry I am.

Honestly, I felt even shittier as the night went on. All I wanted to do was curl up in bed, wrapped in his strong arms, but because of me, that didn't happen.

Pulling my truck into Styx's driveway, I sit for a few minutes, while trying to figure out how to explain to him that I have really bad days sometimes and just need to be alone.

I never meant to make him feel the way he felt when walking out my door. I'll never forget the look of hurt on his face when I asked him to leave.

"Okay, you can do this." Shaking off my nerves, I jump out of my truck and walk over to his porch, stopping at the door.

I take a few deep breaths and slowly release them before knocking.

"Please be here," I whisper. "Please."

I feel my heart crush once I realize that he isn't here. I've already driven by the gym on the way here and didn't see his motorcycle. The only other place I can think of him being is the club.

A room full of hot, horny girls screaming and groping at Styx is the last place I want to be at right now.

I honestly don't know if I'd be able to handle that. Not with all the emotions running through me right now.

Jumping back into my truck, it clicks that he might be at his mother's house. So I drive by to see that all the lights are off and his motorcycle isn't anywhere in sight.

Feeling defeated, I head home, pulling out my phone to text Styx.

I at least want him to know that I'm thinking about him.

Meadow

I want to see you so bad right now.

A few seconds later, my phone vibrates in my hand with a reply from Styx. My heart races as I open his reply.

Styx

Then get out of that truck and come to me.

Tossing my phone into the passenger seat, I hurry out of my truck to see Styx sitting on my porch, waiting for me.

I can hardly breathe as he starts toward me, dressed in that leather jacket of his and ripped up jeans that I love so much.

"Holy shit," I whisper into his arms as he pulls me into him and squeezes. "It feels so good to see you. I'm so sorry. I can explain."

His familiar scent surrounds me as his hands move up to cup my face. "You don't need to explain shit to me. You needed the night to yourself and you asked for it." He presses his forehead to mine, while running his thumb over my lip. The feel of his breath against my face brings me peace. "It feels good to see you too. Honestly, nothing fucking feels better. You have no idea."

He gently sucks my bottom lip into his mouth, before kissing me and whispering, "I hated being away from you for the last two nights. Fuck, it made my heart ache so damn bad for you."

My arms wrap around his neck and pull him closer to me, before telling him how I feel. "I barely fell asleep, because all I could think about was being wrapped in your arms and how it feels to fall asleep next to you. I've *never* had a man make me feel so safe and protected before. You're the best thing that's happened to me for as long as I can remember."

His kiss is desperate, almost knocking me off my feet as he spins us around to press me against the door. "Fuck, you have no idea how much that means to me. I want you so bad. I've never wanted to call a woman mine so much in my entire life. I want you." He whispers the last part.

His whisper has my heart going crazy for him. This man is everything I want in my life, but am afraid to keep. "Are you sure about that?" I question. "I have a lot of ugly days that I can barely even get out of bed, Styx. I get too lost in my head and need my space from the world." I close my eyes in shame and hide my face in his neck. "I try my best to be strong, but when you've felt alone for as long as I have, after you've lost *everyone* you have ever loved... giving yourself to someone else isn't the easiest. I'm so scared of being left alone again."

"Fuck," he whispers into the top of my head. "I love you. I'm not going anywhere even if you push me out the damn door. I *never* want you to be afraid with me."

I look up to meet his eyes, my heart pretty much stopping in my chest from his confession. "Did you mean what you just said?" I ask softly.

His grip around me tightens, until there's no space between us. I couldn't get away, even if I wanted to. Which I don't. I never want to get away from this man.

"With everything in me. I've been thinking it for days, but just haven't said it. I was hoping my actions were loud enough to show you. But yes. I fucking love you," he breathes across my lips.

"I love you too," leaves my lips without a second thought. "I love everything about you and us and how you make me feel. I never want to lose that. Please don't rip my heart out. I'm opening up to you, Styx. I'm giving you my all."

"Good." He smiles against my lips and then kisses me hard and deep. "Because I'm a giver when it comes to someone I love and I'm giving you every fucking thing I have in me, beginning with my damn heart."

With that, he slides his jacket off and places it over my shoulders. "Let me get you inside where it's warm."

He wraps his arms around me from behind as I reach for my keys and unlock the door.

As soon as we get inside, he picks me up and begins carrying me through the house, stopping in front of my bed.

"Now I'm spending the rest of the night making love to my woman." He reaches into his pocket and tosses his phone across the room, before laying me down on the bed. "No fucking distractions. Just the two of us."

I smile and then pull him down on top of me, capturing my lips with his.

This man is perfect and I promise to take care of him just as much as he takes care of me...

CHAPTER TWENTY-THREE

STYX

TWO WEEKS LATER . . .

TODAY IS MEADOW'S BIRTHDAY AND all she asked for was some private time for us once we're both done working for the day.

Between spending time with my mother on our days off and working at the gym whenever we both can make it in, we haven't had much of the quiet time that we both enjoy so much.

Today's been an extremely long day for both of us so I'm desperately waiting for her to make her way back into my arms so I can take care of her.

I look down at my phone to see that Meadow should be arriving any second and my heart starts racing with excitement.

This woman manages to make my heart race every day that we're together and that's a feeling that I'm not used to. That's how I know just how special she is.

The headlights of her truck shine on the rock that I'm sitting on, letting me know that she's arrived.

Smiling, I stand up and light the single candle on the cupcake, making my way to her as she steps out of her truck looking completely exhausted and worn down.

Her eyes light up the minute she sees what I'm holding. "God, you're the sweetest." She runs at me, throwing her arms around my neck.

I hold the cupcake at a safe distance from her and press my face into her hair and whisper, "Happy birthday, baby. I feel like crap that I didn't know until last week. There's a whole batch of these ugly frosted fuckers that I attempted to bake for you at home. Clearly, I need to stick to cooking and not baking."

She cries into my neck where she places a gentle kiss. "It's beautiful. This means so much to me."

When she pulls away from my neck, I dip my thumb into the frosting and then wipe it across her bottom lip. "This looks so much better on you."

I pull her frosted lip into my mouth, sucking off all the turquoise, before kissing her and then pulling off my leather jacket to drape it over her shoulders.

She laughs and then smashes the cupcake into my mouth, before tossing it aside and kissing me so hard that I almost lose my balance.

"This is one of the nicest things anyone has done for me. Why must you keep making me fall for you more and more each day?"

Picking her up, I wrap her legs around my waist and start walking back over to the rock to set her down. "Because I love you and you're worth it. I'll spend every day making sure you know that."

"I love you, Styx," she whispers. "Thank you. For everything. For just being you. It's all I'll ever need from you."

I jump onto the rock behind Meadow, just like the first night I brought her here, pulling her close to me.

My arms wrapped around her.

Her between my thighs.

No words are exchanged.

We just sit here.

Both lost in thought.

Everything else in the world forgotten for the moment as we sit here, staring up at the sky.

Just two people enjoying each other's comfort for a while.

I have a feeling that I'm never going to want to let her go...

KASH

WALK OF SHAME : BOOK 6

CHAPTER ONE

KASH

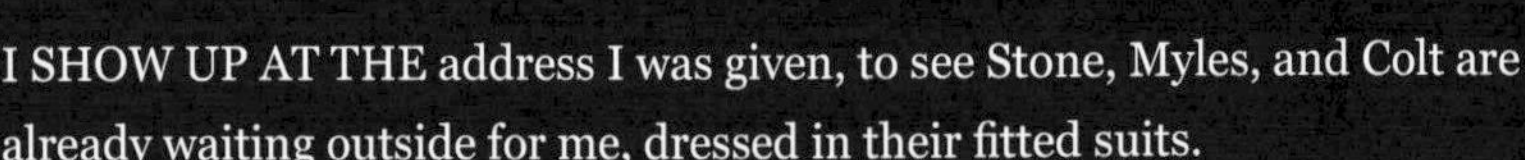

I SHOW UP AT THE address I was given, to see Stone, Myles, and Colt are already waiting outside for me, dressed in their fitted suits.

Stone tugs on his tie and checks out my hoodie and jeans as if there's something wrong with the way I look.

"Dude…" He pushes my hood back. "Where's your suit? I thought we all agreed to dress up and shit. You look like a homeless stripper."

I unzip my hoodie and walk past him with a grin, pulling it open so he can see my ripped-up t-shirt. Then I zip it back up when he flicks a rolled-up dollar bill at my head and scowls.

He knows I said no repeatedly to dressing up, but he ended the call assuming I'd listen anyway. "Nah, you three agreed on a suit. My ass got called out of bed in the middle of the night to be here so I threw on the first thing I saw."

Gotta stand out somehow when it comes to making money and I've learned women like a little mystery.

Colt looks down at his black vest, before unbuttoning it and rolling up the sleeves of his button-down. "Shit. I knew we were overdressed." He tosses his jacket at his motorcycle and scowls. "I'm making sure this shit comes off fast. I look awkward as hell."

I have to admit it's funny as shit seeing Colt dressed up. We're all used to his t-shirts, jeans, and beanies.

Just wanting to get the night over with, I ignore the idiots and walk up to the door, about ready to knock.

As I stand here with my fist in the air, I begin to think we're at the wrong house, because it's completely quiet. No signs of people talking or even a TV playing in the background.

That's extremely odd.

These kinds of parties are always filled with wild women, that can't sit still or wait for us to arrive. There's no way anyone inside that house is waiting on us.

I just hope like hell I didn't get dragged out of bed for nothing. I might just have to choke Stone then, due to the fact that I have to be up in less than six hours.

Looking around, Stone loosens his collar and stands back as if he's checking out the address. "This is it. Just walk in and start shaking your dick. They're probably waiting on us to get the party started."

I'm just about to open the door—thinking maybe they are just waiting on us—when a whistle comes from across the street, causing me to turn around.

"Over here, boys!" Some chick with long, curly blonde hair crosses her arms and leans against the closed door, watching us as we cross the street. "My friend gets confused about her address when she drinks. Either that or she just likes to screw with people. I haven't figured it out yet."

I stop in front of her and take a few moments to check her out in her tight jeans and loose-fitting shirt that hangs off one shoulder.

She looks unamused by our arrival as if she's only here because she was forced to be. The concentration on her face as she looks down at her phone and types fast, tells me there's somewhere else she'd rather be.

"Just go in and start doing whatever it is that you do. The others are eagerly awaiting your arrival. They've been talking firm bodies and tight butts all night. Said you guys are the real deal. Better prove them right."

Without looking up, she moves away from the door, allowing us access to the house.

Stone and the newest members of the club, step inside without hesitation, while I take this moment to breathe in the coolness of the night air and wake up a bit more.

Screams of excitement instantly fill the house, before music blares over the speakers, making it clear the party has started without me.

Good, let them wear the women down a little first. My ass is still half-asleep and to be honest, I'm a little intrigued by the sexy little blonde next to me.

"Why aren't you inside with the others? Groping half-naked men isn't your thing?" I question with a lifted brow.

She looks up from her phone and gives me a half smile. "Only on some nights and tonight isn't one of them."

I laugh at her response and pull out a cigarette, lighting it up and taking a long drag.

I need to be more awake before going inside and I have a feeling she's just the one to get me in the mood.

Out of the corner of my eye, I notice her checking me out, but I pretend I don't notice.

"You going to keep that hood up all night? Not quite as handsome as the other guys? Is that it?" She laughs. "Don't be shy. I'm sure you have a great body that will do the trick just fine for my friends."

I smile and take another drag off my cigarette, before slowly exhaling. As much as she doesn't want to admit it, she's desperate to see what's under this hood and probably even my jeans.

Leaning against the porch railing, I push my hood back and smirk as her eyes wander over my face, doing a double take, before finally stopping on my lips.

She swallows and then clears her throat, trying to hide the fact she's surprised by what she sees. "You better get inside with the others. Joni will notice she paid for four guys and only has three earning their pay." Her eyes gloss over, focusing on my lips, and her breathing quickens. "I need a drink," she mutters.

I lift a brow and watch as she pulls the screen door open and disappears inside.

After I finish my cigarette, I pull my hood back up and enter the house, hoping I can catch her attention once I start my routine.

Walking through the living room, I notice a lot of heads turn my way, eyes watching me as if they can't wait to see what's under this mysterious fabric.

One girl even walks away from Myles to check me out.

I walk slowly, ignoring them all, letting my eyes seek out the sassy blonde from outside.

She's in the kitchen pouring a drink, but looks over when a few of her friends grab me and pull me back into the living room.

I stand with a confident smile as they start to grab at my hoodie, unzipping it and checking me out as they rip it from my arms.

Hands grope at my chest, lifting at my shirt as I begin to move my hips to "Ride" by Chase Rice.

The sassy blonde smirks from the kitchen, watching the other girls take advantage of me as if she finds it to be funny.

This has me smiling.

She's pretending as if she's only watching for the amusement of me being attacked, but the look in her curious green eyes gives away the truth of why she hasn't turned away yet.

I'm guessing she wants to see me naked just as badly as they do. She just doesn't want to be the one to *get* me naked.

Keeping my eyes on her, I bend one of the girls over, place my hand on her lower back and grind my hips against her ass.

I grind slow and seductive, before giving her one hard thrust, almost knocking her over.

She turns back to look at me, her eyes filled with need, before she lays down on her back and waves me over with her finger, wanting more of what I've got to offer.

Standing above the brunette, I slowly pull my shirt over my head, before tossing it aside and dropping down to the ground, rolling my body above hers and rubbing my face over her neck.

Money flies at me as I place her legs over my shoulders and lift her body up, thrusting against her, while on my knees.

After a few seconds, I gently place her down to her back again, before jumping to my feet and reaching for the closest girl next to me, flipping her upside down so my cock is grinding against her face.

Slowly turning around with the girl in my arms, I glance into the kitchen to see the sexy little blonde's eyes on me. As soon as our eyes meet, she turns away and goes back to typing on her phone as if she was never watching in the first place.

Why the hell does that make me want to get to her even more?

Growling, I slap the girl's ass that's in my arms, before flipping her over and setting her back down to her feet.

Cracking my neck, I reach for the button of my jeans, causing desperate screams from all around the room. A sound I used to love, but have grown a bit tired of over the months.

But still, I'm here to do a job and that's exactly what I'll do.

I lick my bottom lip, before slipping my hand inside my jeans and running it over my erection, while slowly letting my pants fall lower with each move of my hips.

My eyes are still on the sassy blonde in the kitchen when she looks up again to see what I'm doing.

Catching her off guard, I slide across the floor on my knees, grab her ass and lift her up so her legs are wrapped around my neck.

Her hands grip at my hair for support as I stand to my feet and walk her over to the wall, pressing her back against it.

I'm not gonna lie, having her in this position has me so hard and wanting nothing more than for her body to be pressed against mine.

"Fuck it," I growl against her pussy before biting her inner thigh.

Moving to the music, I grab her legs and lower her down my body, until they're wrapped around my waist now, my dick pressed against her heat.

She says something that the music drowns out, while I hold her up with my hips, pinning her arms against the wall.

I move against her sexy body, while thrusting her up the wall with my erection pressed between her legs.

Fuck, this is extremely hot, making me wish there was nothing between our bodies.

I let out a small growl, enjoying it as she tugs on my hair and squeezes me with her thighs, moving her body perfectly against mine.

She shows enjoyment for a few short minutes, getting lost in the moment, before dropping her legs to the ground and then pushing my chest, as I release her arms.

"I'm not here for the entertainment. I'm here for my friend. Find someone else to fuck against the wall." She runs her hands through her hair, looking extremely frustrated with herself. "Shit. I need to go."

I stand in the middle of the room sweaty as fuck, trying to catch my breath as I watch her walk out the front door and leave.

My stomach drops, hating the fact that I pushed her to leave, when apparently all she wanted to do was mind her own business.

Quickly, I walk toward the door, wanting to catch her, but stop when I get blocked in by a group of screaming women, wanting a show.

One of the girls runs her hand over my arm, pulling my attention away from the door. "Don't mind her. Eden's been spending most of her time at a construction site with dirty men lately. Doesn't get out much. She forgets what *fun* is sometimes." The tall brunette grabs my hand and starts pulling me to the other side of the room where a group of women are standing in a circle. "Let's keep this party rocking and rolling, baby. I paid good money for you fine ass men to take your clothes off. I want my floor littered with items of your clothing."

I glance at the door one last time, before looking around me to see the other guys practically naked by this point. All except Stone who refuses to lose his pants at private parties now.

Usually, I'd be having the time of my life, covered in chocolate or whipped cream by now.

But damn... this party seems a lot less fun without the sassy blonde watching me.

A COUPLE HOURS LATER I'M pulling up outside my house, completely exhausted and ready for bed, again.

My roommate, Colt, won't be home for a few more hours, since he decided to stay and give Joni a private dance, now that the party has ended.

So, I'm stripping out of these sweaty clothes and my ass is crashing on the couch. My bed seems entirely too far away right now.

I'm exhausted.

At least, I think I'm crashing out. Walking up to the porch to see Sarah and her girlfriend Kendal, tells me otherwise.

Sarah instantly grabs my keys out of my hand and unlocks the door with a wicked smile. "I thought we'd never catch your ass."

I smirk as she pushes me through the door and her girlfriend follows behind. "Yeah, well I'm a busy guy. What can I say?"

Before I know it, I'm slammed against the closed door, by both Sarah and Kendal, their hands roaming over my hard body.

Closing my eyes, I lean my head back and just enjoy the feel of their mouths on me. Occasionally, Sarah and her girlfriend get an urge for dick, and they want to make sure they get it from a guy they both feel comfortable with.

Over the last few weeks, it's been me. So, I let them use my body any way they please.

Within minutes, I'm completely stripped down and Sarah is guiding Kendal's head as her mouth wraps around my cock.

It feels fucking fantastic, yet I'm still thinking about the sassy blonde from the party.

As hot as Sarah and her girlfriend are, my cock gets even harder when I imagine Eden on her knees taking me.

As fucked up as it sounds, I have a feeling it's going to be her I get off to tonight...

CHAPTER TWO

KASH

TIRED AND HALF-ASLEEP, I LEAN against the side of the warehouse, smoking a cigarette while I wait for Abe and Calvin to arrive.

They were both ordered to be here at seven A.M. sharp, yet it's already half past the hour.

My ass spends late nights dancing at the club, working my dick off. If I'm going to wake up at the ass crack of dawn to train these boys, then they better damn well be here on time and make it worth it to me.

This is the third time this week they've been late.

Pissed off, I pull out my phone and toss my cigarette on the ground, about ready to give them both hell. Just as I get ready to scroll to Calvin's name, I hear a car coming down the gravel driveway, forcing me to put my phone back into my hoodie and look up.

I stand here with narrowed eyes, watching as the red Mazda comes to a stop next to my truck.

Abe is the first one to stumble out of the car, looking half-dead and hungover as shit.

Not to mention, his clothes are wrinkled and smell like whiskey as if he just crawled out of bed, in the same clothes he passed out in.

Should've damn well known.

"About fucking time, dicks. I told you to be here at seven. I was two seconds away from going back home and getting some sleep. You're wasting my time."

Abe falls against the side of the car and pulls his hat down over his eyes to shield them from the light. "Shit. We didn't get in until four. Cut us some slack, Kash. Honestly, I think I'm still drunk. This sucks dick."

I narrow my eyes at Calvin as he smiles cockily and jumps up on the hood of the car as if it's no big deal that I woke my ass up early this morning and wasted my time, waiting on them. "We're only thirty-five minutes late. You didn't waste that much time waiting on us. It took me over an hour to get Abe's ass up. I almost came alone, but figured you'd be more pissed than if we showed up late. We're here so can we just do this?"

"Nope." I lock up the warehouse and begin walking to my truck. I'm in no mood for this shit this morning. My exhausted ass has been here since six, getting a workout in. Time and dedication is exactly what I expect from them as well. "Next time you fuckers better be on time. I'm getting some sleep before my fight tonight. Get Abe home so he can sleep that shit off."

"Oh, come on!" Calvin screams in frustration. "We won't be late again. Don't do this shit. We both want this job and you know it. Abe was just being a dick this morning. It won't happen again."

"That's what you said two days ago. If you can't take this shit seriously, then neither can I. When I open my gym, I need one hundred fucking percent from the both of you." I jump into my truck and slam the door shut, before sticking my head out the window to look at them.

They both look like hell, tired and out of it. They're not ready for what I had in store for them this morning.

"See you guys back here later for the fights still or should I call Don and tell him to replace Abe?"

"Yeah," Calvin groans. "We'll be here. Abe's fight is two ahead of yours. He'll be good by then. He's not backing out."

"Good. Go get some sleep."

Abe gives me a thumbs up and almost falls over, before crawling back into the car.

These boys might think I'm being hard on them, but I don't expect my clients to wait. If they want to be trainers at my gym once it opens, then they need to show me dedication and hard work.

I'm not getting these dicks ready to be trainers just for them to not be reliable and me have to find new guys after just a few months.

I want long term and familiarity. A family.

They better shape up and fast.

Once I get back to the house, I walk inside to see Colt in the kitchen, cooking tacos in only his boxer briefs and a black beanie.

"What the hell are you doing up this early?" I toss my keys down on the table and sit down to pull my shoes off. "And why the hell are you cooking tacos for breakfast?"

"I'm drunk, high, and hungry as shit. I'm going right back to bed after this. I feel like I'm going to die if I don't eat though."

"Whatever," I say with a laugh. "Just don't burn the house down while I'm sleeping. I'd hate to have to kill you."

I lay back on the couch and close my eyes, slowly dozing back off, until a hand runs over my chest and abs, before lowering and landing on my dick.

Grunting, I reach out and grip Harper's hand, stopping her from stroking my cock through my sweats.

"Leave him alone," Colt says from the kitchen with an amused laugh. "He's grumpy as hell this morning, babe."

"Oh, come on…" She smiles down at me and moans when I open my eyes to look at her. "But he looks so *tempting* just lying there in that mysterious hoodie of his. I want to strip it off with my teeth and run my hands all over what's beneath it."

Ignoring Colt, Harper leans in attempting to kiss me and work me up, but I bite her bottom lip, causing her to jump away from me with a squeal.

Her lips might work on other men, but not me.

"I don't do kisses," I growl out. "And I'm not in the mood to join in on your games. It's too early for this and I have a long night ahead of me."

"What did I tell you, babe?" Colt joins us in the living room, tossing a bottle of water to me, before grabbing his girl and tossing her over his shoulder. "We don't need him to have fun. I have plenty of fun tricks up my sleeve. Let's eat first though."

Letting out an annoyed breath, I sit up and open the water, emptying the whole bottle in one drink, before tossing the empty plastic across the room, hitting Colt in the back of the head as he walks through the kitchen.

He just ignores me and slips his hand into Harper's panties, not caring that her pussy is on display for me.

Seriously? These two are crazy.

Tiredly, I make my way through the house, slamming my bedroom door shut and locking it behind me.

If I don't, then I know Harper will end up half-naked in my bed again, groping me until I give in and join them.

It's been happening more frequently lately and surprisingly Colt is so chill and high most of the time he just goes with the flow.

Hell, sometimes he just sits back and smokes a blunt, watching all the ways I can make his girl moan out and beg.

Apparently, my body was built for pleasure since everyone seems to be using it lately.

There's only one person who seems to want nothing to do with it and for some reason I'm lying here, thinking about her once again...

CHAPTER THREE

EDEN

BY THE TIME KNIGHT SHOWS up at my door and lets himself in, as if he owns the place, I'm already running twenty minutes behind schedule.

It's infuriating.

He knew damn well ahead of time that I was starting back at the massage parlor this morning now that my father is back to take over his crew, yet he decided to take his precious time getting here as if it was the least important thing on his schedule today.

It doesn't surprise me one bit.

"You told me you were on the way over an hour ago. What the hell, Knight. This is not acceptable. Be here on time or see your son when I get *off* work. I can't be late again because of you."

He flashes me a cocky grin and leans against the door, crossing his huge arms. "Oh, calm down, Eden. If you lose your job at the parlor, you know damn well that daddy dearest will give you a job on one of his crews. Now, where's my son? I want to at least see him for a few minutes before you kick me out."

I let out a frustrated breath and point down the hall, fighting with everything in me not to lose my cool and scream at him. "He's in his room grabbing his backpack to go to the babysitter's. You have five minutes to say hi and don't you ever give me that crap again about me working for my father because *you* couldn't be here on time. If I wanted to work with my father, I would've chosen to do so years ago. So be on time from now on because I won't wait next time."

"Damn, baby. Chill. You know I have a fight tonight. I was training late last night and had a hard time getting up. Now is the only time I can visit him today. Why the fuck are you always so uptight?"

"Because of you," I whisper yell, while pointing at his firm chest. "And watch your mouth. Alec can hear you. You don't think your deep voice carries in this house? You will show respect when you're in *my* home or you won't step foot inside again."

"Daddy! Daddy!" We both look over just in time to see Alec rush down the hall and jump into Knight's arms. "I didn't think you were coming to see me. Mommy said we were about to leave."

"Of course, I was coming to see you, bud." Knight bends down to set Alec back down to his feet, before giving him a frowny face and messing up his blond hair. "But we have to make it fast because your mommy is rushing us. Says we only have a minute. You know how she gets."

Ugh. You son of a bitch.

He always finds some way to put the blame on me. Never fails, but I refuse to have this discussion in front of my son.

"But I want to spend time with you, Daddy," Alec whines, while tugging on Knight's jacket. "Can't I just stay with you today? I'll be good. I promise. I have games and stuff in my bag."

Knight shakes his head and reaches out to grab Alec's chin to look him in the eyes. "Sorry, buddy. Not today. Daddy's busy."

I can practically see Alec's five-year-old little heart shatter into a thousand pieces when he grabs the straps of his backpack and looks down at the ground, defeated.

"Busy," I mutter. "Just like every other time your son asks to spend the day with you. You need to get your priorities straight. You only see him once a week for twenty minutes if he's lucky."

My heart aches as I walk over and wrap my arms around Alec to comfort him. I hate seeing the disappointment on his face over and over again, each week. It never stops when it comes to his shitty father and it only makes me loathe Knight more. "It's okay, sweetie. Hannah is excited for you to come see her today. I promise you'll have lots of fun with her. You always do."

"I know, Mommy," Alec mutters against my stomach, while wiping his wet eyes. "I guess. But I never get to see Daddy. It's no fair. I want to see him."

"I know, baby." I kiss the top of his head, before rubbing it and forcing a smile. "Why don't you give your daddy a hug and then go put your bag in the Jeep. I'll be out in a second. Okay, baby boy?"

Without a word, Alec walks over and wraps his arms around Knight, holding onto him as if he never wants to let go. "Bye, Daddy. I miss you today."

"Bye, little guy." He rubs the top of Alec's head, before brushing his thumb under his eye to wipe his tear away. "Daddy loves you and will see you soon. Don't cry. You're a big boy now."

"Okay. Love you too, Daddy," he whispers, before walking away.

I wait until Alec is outside, before I lose it on Knight.

"The way you treat your son is bullshit!" I slam my keys down onto the counter and run my hands down my face in frustration. "You can treat me like shit all you want. You have for the last seven years, but you will not do the same to *my* son. He depends on you. Be a fucking father for once. Put him before everything else, like a real man should. Show him you love him." I stop and release a long breath, my chest aching. "Dammit, Knight. You're breaking him down, little by little and soon he's going to stop trusting people. He barely lets people in as it is. He needs you and you know it. Show him you need him too."

"Shut the fuck up, Eden," he growls out, before punching the wall. "I don't have to listen to this bullshit anymore. Your fucking mouth is only a reminder of why I was never happy with you. You wanna know why I cheated repeatedly? Why I never came home after a fight? Well, listen to your mouth and there's your answer."

"Oh yeah," I yell out. "How's my mouth for you now? Get the fuck out." I point at the door with a shaky hand, fighting like hell not to burst into tears of hate and anger. "Leave the child support money and go. Now."

My whole body is shaking in anger at this point. I've never met someone in my entire life that can piss me off as much as Knight can. I wouldn't even care about the child support money if it hasn't been over six months since he's paid any.

"I'll have it for you in two weeks when I win my big fight. If you want it..." He steps into my breathing space and gives me a hard look as if to intimidate me. It has me taking a step back and sucking in a breath as his strong hands grip my waist when he speaks. "Then you can fucking come get it. I'm not being a little bitch and bringing it to you."

With that, he walks out the door and jumps into his car, making a huge scene as he pulls out of the driveway.

My heart is racing as I stand here and grip the counter. I will not fucking cry anymore. Not even out of anger will I allow that piece of shit to have my tears.

I take a few seconds to calm down and get myself back together, before I join Alec in the Jeep.

He's sitting in the back, playing on his Nintendo 3DS as if he's already gotten over his father letting him down for the hundredth time this week.

I don't know how Knight does it. I feel guilty every single time I leave my son when it's for my own pleasure. Which is exactly why last night was so uncomfortable for me.

If it wasn't for Joni begging me to come, until I said yes, then I would've never went to some party to ogle over some male entertainers. That's just not what's important in my life right now. My son has top priority and always will.

I thought spending the whole night texting Hannah to check in on Alec would make me feel less guilty about leaving him, but it didn't.

All it took was a few seconds of enjoyment as one of the strippers practically fucked me against a wall, to make me lose my shit and run out of there, feeling like shit.

Made me feel like Knight.

That's the last thing I'll do to my son.

"Ready, Mommy? Hannah is waiting for me. I want to show her my new game." He starts bouncing around, making all kinds of sound effects for his game. "I did it! I did it! I beat him."

I nod my head and smile at him through the rearview mirror. "Good job, baby. Let's go before Mommy is really late."

I wish like hell I could be as strong as that kid. I try like heck to protect him, but sometimes I wish there was someone who could protect me and make me believe that everything in the world is going to be A-Okay.

Someone who could make us both believe, but I have my doubts of that ever happening.

Especially with Knight in my life.

As soon as we pull up in front of Hannah's house, Alec jumps out, dragging his backpack behind him in excitement.

Hannah is already sitting outside on the front porch, waiting on him like she said she'd be.

She flashes us both a huge smile and bends down to talk to Alec once he reaches the top step. "I've got a great day planned for us, kid. But you have to let me beat you in your new game first. Deal?"

Alec smiles and shakes his head. "I can't do that! I'm really good! I don't think I can lose."

I stand back and watch as Alec begins looking around as if he's searching for someone.

"Is he here? Is he here?"

Hannah laughs and stands up. "Not today, buddy. It's not Monday."

"It isn't?" He tilts his head. "What day is it?"

"Saturday. You'll see him the next time you're here. I promise. Now give your mommy hugs and kisses so she can go to work and we can play this new game of yours." She pats his butt. "Hurry! Hurry!"

Laughing, Alec runs at me, throwing his little arms around my neck, squeezing. "Love you, Mommy! I gotta go!"

I kiss his nose and smile. "Love you too, baby. Be good for Hannah, you hear me?"

He nods his head. "Yup! I'm always good. Promise. Come on, Hannah!"

"Who's he talking about?" I question with a smile once Alec runs through the front door in excitement. "He has a friend that comes over?"

"No, just my older brother Hunter I told you about," Hannah says with a smile. "He still brings Alec pancakes every Monday morning. They've become fast friends, which surprises me since it took so long for him to warm up to me. That's my brother though. Everyone loves him. They have fun together."

"That's nice of your brother to bring him pancakes still after all this time. They *are* his favorite." I find myself smiling at the idea that her brother is nice enough to do something like that. But I also find myself a little sad at the knowledge that this guy does something Knight isn't even capable of doing for his own child.

The last thing I want is for him to get attached to another man in his life that someday won't be there anymore.

"But don't worry. He never stays longer than an hour each week. It's usually just me here. He's a busy guy."

"I trust you, Hannah. You take good care of him and he cares about you. I'm not worried."

"Hannah! Hurry! Come on!"

"I gotta go." She holds the door open and winks. "The kid's calling and I've got to make sure I beat him. Losing is getting pretty embarrassing."

"Good luck. He's already beat me ten times this week, even though I'm not even sure we're actually playing against each other." I laugh and pull out my phone, my stomach dropping when I see it's my work calling. "Shit, I've gotta run. Thank you!"

I cuss under my breath all the way to my Jeep as I jump inside and quickly answer my phone, out of breath.

"I'm on my way. I'm so sorry. I had to wait for that asshole son of a bitch. He showed up right when I was about to leave..."

"You're fine," Riley says with a laugh. "Just wanted to make sure you'll be here in time for your first appointment. I have you booked at eight. If not I was going to call them and try to set it back a bit for you."

"Yes," I say quickly. "I'll be there in twelve minutes. Thank you so much. I owe you. I promise I'll make up for it."

Relief washes over me as I hang up the phone and take a few seconds to calm down and catch my breath.

If it weren't for Riley being my boss, I don't know what I'd do. She's been lenient on me far too many times in the past, but taking advantage of her kindness is the last thing I want to do.

And Knight keeps pushing me to do that, making me feel like total crap.

So I'll do everything in my power to prove to her over and over again just how much I appreciate this job.

Showing appreciation is very important to me. It's something Knight has never shown me over the years, yet I was stupid enough to let him in anyway. It only makes it more important that I show it to others.

I promise to be better than him in every possible way I can. Especially when it comes to my son.

And when I'm ready to let another man in mine and Alec's lives, you better believe, I'll make sure he's better than Knight in every way too...

CHAPTER FOUR

KASH

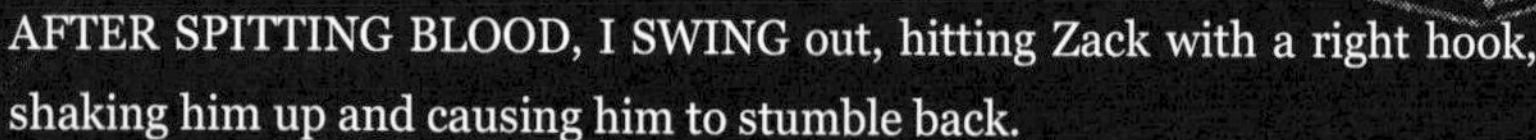

AFTER SPITTING BLOOD, I SWING out, hitting Zack with a right hook, shaking him up and causing him to stumble back.

I stand still as he circles around me, looking for his opportunity to strike. I'm giving him one chance and then I'm taking his ass out. This has gone on for too long.

These people came for a show and that's what I give them, even if it means me taking it easy in the beginning, giving my opponent a chance to get a few hits in.

Fighting to catch his breath, Zack swipes his left foot out, but I lift my leg upright as he tries kicking it out from under me. This must give him a reason to try harder, because before I know it, he swings out with his elbow and connects it to my right cheekbone before following up with a right hook.

I falter back a few steps, but I'm able to catch myself and connect my right fist to his jaw, sending him back against the ropes.

Blood splatters across his face, causing him to spit red onto his chest, before he comes at me, knocking me against the ropes.

He punches me in the ribs a few times, cornering me in, before I plow my knee into his gut and swing out with my elbow, hitting him in the nose.

He's worn out now, completely out of stamina and I know what I have to do. There's no way he's going to give up before it's over, no matter how exhausted he is.

I need to put him down.

Standing straight, I flex my shoulders and wipe the blood from my lip, before swinging out one last time, my fist connecting hard with Zack's already swollen jaw.

Cheers of excitement fill the warehouse as he drops to the mat, knocked out cold.

Adrenaline courses through me as I throw my arms up and look around at all the people here to see me tonight. This warehouse isn't the biggest, but it's jam-packed and I've come to recognize some of the faces over the months.

As much as I enjoy it though, I don't allow myself to get swallowed up by it and let it consume me like some fighters do. Fighting isn't really what I *want* to do.

Training and helping others is my main goal.

I don't even give myself a few seconds to catch my breath, before I make my way over to Zack to check on him.

One of his guys is standing over him and squirting water over his face to help him wake up, so I give him a few minutes to gather himself before reaching down and helping him up to his feet.

"Good fight, man." I throw one of my arms around him as I hold him up and encourage him to keep fighting. I've known this kid for years and the feeling sucks knowing that I probably broke his nose during this fight. "You've got a lot of heart and that's exactly why you deserve to be in that ring. Got it?"

He nods his head, showing appreciation as I check on his nose. It's definitely broken. "Appreciate it, man." He stops a second to catch his breath, before speaking again. "There was a slim chance in hell I'd beat you tonight, but I wasn't going down without a fight. Your father taught me well and once you take over this place and get all set up, I'm hoping you'll train me too."

"Of course, man." Mention of my father has me fighting back my emotions. It's moments like this that made me stop fighting after he passed just after my twentieth birthday.

It's been three years now, but I still struggle with his absence. He was a huge part of my life and every little reminder that he's no longer here kills me.

But it's time for me to man up.

Every win brings me closer to the money necessary to get my training gym up and running. It's been a dream of mine ever since I was a kid and I used to watch my dad train his men.

I always thought we'd open a gym together in the future, but that dream was crushed when he got sick and passed away.

I took a break from fighting shortly after that and just picked it back up in hopes of finally living that dream and making him proud.

Stripping became my biggest income toward making that happen a while back, but these fights are only going to make the process move faster. It's the *only* reason I'm fighting.

Not for the after parties where everyone gets shitfaced or the pleasure of dominating someone in the ring. For the money.

By the end of my second fight, I'm completely drenched in sweat and every inch of my body aches with every single move I make.

Not only from the fights, but from the training and dancing I've been doing this whole week, leading up to tonight.

And these fights are nothing compared to the fight I'll be training to take on in a couple of weeks. It's going to take a lot more preparation and dedication than what I've been doing for the last six months since I've come back.

Fighting in the warehouse is just a warm up to the big guys, I've been working my ass off to fight.

That's where the real prize money sits.

"Good fights, man." Abe appears next to me, his face swollen and bruised from his fight earlier. I can tell with one look in his eyes that he's ashamed he messed up his chance of winning tonight. "These other guys didn't stand a chance against you. Even they knew it. Congrats."

I smile and nod my head, before patting his back. "You'll get your win next time, man. Just let my ass know if you want to set up more training sessions. I'll make time for you, but you've gotta show me you want it. Got it?"

He nods and forces a smile. "I might need that. I need to get back on track. No more late- night partying for my dumb ass. Especially before a fight night."

"Alright, man." I throw the strap of my bag over my shoulder, ready to get out of here before I can get stopped again. "I have an appointment to set up. I'll see you Monday morning for training."

I'm just on my way out the door, when Callie rushes over and throws her arms around me, stopping me from walking.

"Congratulations on your wins tonight! Watching you fight is even better than watching you dance. I'm impressed, Kash."

Callie's been at *Walk of Shame* more than enough times for me to recognize her by face now. Not to mention, she's been spending a lot of money on private dances from me over the last two weeks.

Her coming here tonight was just her way of trying to get me alone without the craziness of the hundreds of women at the club. More of a chance for her to get what she wants.

Which is me, naked, and on top of her.

"Thanks, Callie." I offer her a smile, while taking my shirt and running it over my sweaty chest, watching as she practically salivates at the sight of my hard body. "Appreciate you coming."

Not wanting to deal with her groping me and trying to work her way into my bed, I begin walking again in hopes she'll take off with her friends and forget about me.

"Kash! Wait..."

Releasing a slow breath, I stop and turn around to face her, looking her over in her tight jeans and her very sexy V neck top with a laced-up front. Her huge breasts are spilling out everywhere. Cleary, she's dressed to get attention tonight.

As tempting as she may look, I'm not looking for meaningless fun tonight. I've had enough *fun* over the years and it's time to take shit more seriously. I'm a different man than I was when I first started dancing at *Walk of Shame*. I'm slowly beginning to see that.

"Me and my friends are going to the after party. Will I see you there?" Her eyes scan me over from head to toe, taking in my sweaty body, as she waits for my answer.

Unfortunately, she's not going to get the one she's looking for tonight.

I shake my head. "Not tonight. You ladies have fun without me."

Disappointment washes over her eager face as her girls walk over to join her. "You sure? It'll be fun. I'll make sure of it."

"Yeah," one of her friends joins in. "We're a fun group. We'll keep you entertained. Maybe you can invite a few of your friends, too."

I let out a small laugh, feeling a bit teamed up on now. Double teaming might've worked in the past for me, but not now. "Sorry, ladies. I have somewhere to be. Not gonna happen."

Before they can attempt to entice me anymore, I rush outside and jump into my lifted truck, checking the time.

"Shit."

Pulling out of the parking lot, I dial Riley's number in hopes she's still at work.

I'm surprised when she answers it before the second ring.

"Did you win?" she asks immediately. "I've been staring at this darn phone waiting to hear news. Spill it."

I smile into the phone. "Hi to you too, Riley."

"Oh, please. I've known you long enough that I shouldn't have to say hello anymore. Now, answer my question, Kash."

"Yes." I pull out into traffic and head toward *Sensual Touches*, hoping like hell she says yes to what I'm about to ask. "Think you can fit me in tonight for a quick rubdown with one of your massage therapists? I feel like I've been hit by a semi."

"Better hurry up. I'm only saying yes since you won tonight and I think you deserve it." I hear her laugh into the phone before she continues. "One of my ladies is looking for some extra cash. I'm sure she won't mind staying back for a bit and fitting you in for the night."

"Thank you, babe. Be there in five."

Hanging up, I speed up, taking the side roads in hopes there won't be any traffic to slow me down.

The place closes in less than twenty-five minutes and I'm in desperate need of this relaxation *tonight*. I don't care if it takes me dropping to my knees and begging this woman Riley mentioned.

I barely park my truck, before I'm jumping out and rushing for the door as if my life depends on it.

The woman leaving the parlor spins around to check me out as I hold the door open for her to pass me.

"Maybe I need to get a job here," she says with a smile of admiration. "Thanks."

"For what?" I question with a small laugh.

"Just for being so handsome." Her face turns red as she waves and turns around to leave. "Damn, I wish I was single."

Riley is standing right inside the door, grinning from ear to ear when I walk inside. "Couldn't wear a shirt, huh? As if you don't distract my clients enough already."

"You don't want me wearing that sweaty ass thing in here. Trust me." I lean against the counter and wait for Riley to tell me which room. "I pretty much used it as a towel after my fight and tossed it in the truck."

"And you're telling me some girl didn't steal it to take home and sleep in it? Surprising..." Riley looks away from the computer and smiles down at her phone when it rings. "Room four. Hurry up. Eden's just grabbing some supplies from the back so do her a favor and be ready."

"Eden?" My heart skips a beat at the mention of her name. It's not a very common one.

"Hey, handsome. Hang on a sec," she says into the phone, before answering me. "Yeah. She's one of my girls that's been away for a bit. You haven't met her yet. She's good though. I promise."

A huge ass smile takes over my face as I picture the Eden I met the other night. "Sassy blonde?"

"Yeah, that's her." She looks surprised. "How'd you know? Did you come in when I was gone one day?"

I begin backing up, even more eager for this massage now. "Later, Riley. Tell Cale about my fights since I don't have time."

I ignore her question and hurry down the hall, wanting to get to Eden's room, before she does.

Hopefully this will give me a chance to get to know the woman behind the sass...

CHAPTER FIVE

EDEN

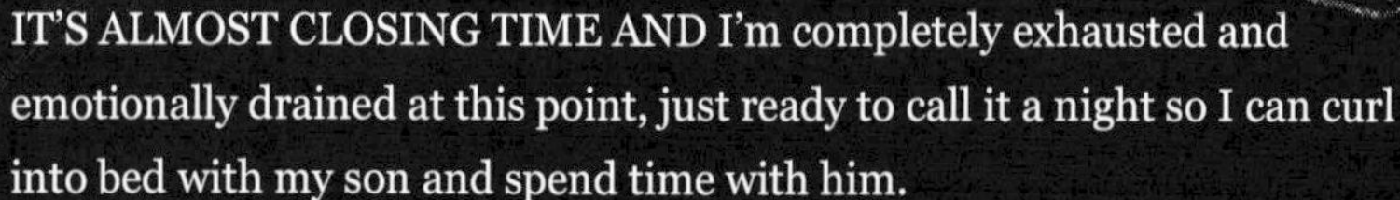

IT'S ALMOST CLOSING TIME AND I'm completely exhausted and emotionally drained at this point, just ready to call it a night so I can curl into bed with my son and spend time with him.

I can tell by the tone of his voice that he's missing me and it makes my heart ache that I can't be there for him. He doesn't deserve to have to miss two parents at the same time. He should *always* have one of us there.

"Mommy will be there soon, Alec. I promise. Can you be good for Hannah for just a bit longer? It won't be long. I promise."

"Yes, Mommy. I can do that. I be good for Hannah," he says with a yawn. "Love you, Mommy. Byyye."

"Love you, too, baby. Thank you."

I can hear Hannah in the background asking for the phone back, before she reassures me it's fine if I'm a little late tonight.

As much as I hate being away from Alec longer than I have to—I need the money.

Knight isn't doing his part and there's no way I'm relying on anyone else to take care of my family for me. That's not who I am or who I ever want to be, no matter how hard my father tries pushing money on me.

It's up to *me* to give him the life he deserves, even if that means me taking on extra shifts once or twice a week or staying later here and there. I'll do whatever it takes.

Shoving my phone into my small apron, I grab for some more oil, lotion, and a few candles, before heading back to my room to stock up.

According to Riley, my last client of the night should already be here by now and most likely set up in my room and ready for me to start.

I'm counting on that so I can get the job done and out of here as quickly as possible.

Stopping in front of the door, I knock and wait for whoever is on the other side to let me know it's okay to come in.

"I'm decent," a deep voice calls out.

A lot of the guys that come here take this as an opportunity to show me the *goods,* by tricking me to believe they're ready, but they're standing in my room completely naked on display for me to see.

I've grown to expect it at this point, but today has been exceptionally bad. My eyes can only handle so much in one day.

Please be covered up. Please no more dong and balls tonight...

Upon stepping into my room, relief washes over me as my eyes immediately land on a firm body, covering the massage table.

The client is facing down, the bottom half of his body covered by a sheet, only giving me a view of his muscular back, arms, and legs.

"Well, congratulations. You're my first honest client tonight. I'm slightly impressed." I smile as the guy laughs into the pillow. "So, thank you for not showing me your balls. I've seen more than my fair share tonight."

"Most women don't thank me for that, but you're welcome, I think." His back muscles flex as he adjusts himself to get more comfortable. "You did me a huge favor by fitting me in at the last minute tonight. The least I can do is not show you my balls... unless you ask of course. Then I guess I would owe you."

His sense of humor has me laughing as I wash my hands and dry them off. Maybe sticking around to fit this guy in will be entertaining at least. That usually helps the time to pass. Plus, I could use a laugh after such a stressful day.

"I appreciate that, but I'm one hundred and ten percent positive I won't be asking to see them..." I pause, searching for a name as I empty the lotion and candles from my apron. "What should I call you? Bob? George? Kenneth?"

"Kash," he says, sounding amused. "Those names are fucking horrible, by the way. I hope like hell I don't look as bad as those names sound."

"I hope not too," I joke. "I'd have to charge extra then."

"And fuck. I'd pay it too," he says with a laugh.

Once I get closer to the bed, I find myself swallowing as I look his body over, taking in the perfection, while I blindly reach for my oil and open the new bottle.

He definitely doesn't look as bad as those names sound.

Being this close really displays how beautiful and sculpted this man's body is. A woman's eyes can appreciate the sight I have in front of me right now.

Just hopefully my hands don't appreciate it *too* much.

I can honestly say over touching has never been an issue with any of my clients, but this body is a dirty temptation.

Take a deep breath and relax... deep breath and relax.

The music is already playing and Kash looks to be completely comfortable and ready for me to start, so I take another deep breath, like I've coached myself and say my usual lines.

"My name is Eden, by the way." I walk around to the top of the bed and squirt some oil into my hands, preparing to rub them down his muscular body. "I'm going to start at your shoulders and work my way down. Let me know if there's a certain spot you'd like me to focus on."

He lets out a sexy little growl, the moment my hands rub the first tense spot, digging in deep. I might've let out a little growl myself, feeling his firm body under my touch, but I'm hoping he didn't notice.

"I'll take whatever you can give me within the next thirty minutes," he says, his voice deep and sexy. "Honestly, I would've been down for begging you at this point and I don't beg very often. Fuuuck me, keep going, Eden. I like it hard and rough. Don't fucking take it easy on me."

The way he says *fuck* has my heart beating fast in my chest, feeling a bit excited. I didn't know that word could sound so sexy coming out of someone's mouth, until now.

"Is that you begging?" I tease.

"You'd know if I was begging, Eden," he growls out, his hard muscles flexing beneath my hands. "It'd be pleasurable for the both of us and there's no doubt I'd get what I want in the end. Trust me... I'm as honest as they come and it would most definitely end with you coming..."

If my heart wasn't beating out of my chest before, it is now. I've never had a man on my table before that had the power to make me as hot and bothered as I am at this very moment.

His words have me sweating, but there's no way I'm giving him the pleasure of letting him know he's getting to me.

Without speaking, I begin working my way further down his back side, being careful not to focus my eyes on his firm ass for too long.

I feel like such a pervert right now, but there's no denying his body feels fantastic beneath my fingertips and I like it.

It's when I work my way back up his thick legs that he speaks again, really making me think dirty. "You don't have to be careful not to get my ass, Eden. My whole back side needs attention." Before I can say anything, he reaches behind him and yanks the sheet off, revealing his muscular ass to me. "Work it nice and good."

"Really?!" I pull my hands from his legs and squirt more oil in my palm. "Out of all the places I can focus on, you choose your ass?"

"Have you ever had an ass massage, Eden?"

"No," I admit, while rubbing my hands together. "I've never really had much of any kind of a massage, to be honest."

"Then, you have no idea what you're missing out on." He places his hands on the side of the table and pushes up when he speaks. "Maybe we should switch places. Every woman deserves to be rubbed and taken care of by a man."

"As tempting as that sounds, I'm going to have to pass." I shake my head, fighting my smile. "Now lay back down so I can do my job. Time is almost up."

Thinking he's going to listen, I get ready to get back to work, but before my hands can touch his glorious ass, he's hopping off the table, and picking me up to take his place.

My breath gets sucked right out of me as he sets me on the edge of the table, his naked body pressing between my legs.

"Oh my God! What are you doing?" I try my best not to look at his naked body, as he backs away from me and throws a fresh sheet over the pillow, but I can't help but to peek between my fingers.

Just a quick glimpse of his dick is enough to let me know this guy is packing where it counts.

Oh holy hell...

"Giving you a massage," he says casually, as if this is somehow normal, when this is anything but. "Don't worry, you can keep your clothes on." Grabbing my waist with force, he flips me over and pushes my head down into the pillow, causing me to move my hands from my face.

He has me thinking dirty things—like how he might handle a woman in bed. I bet he's rough and very thorough, making sure to hit every spot.

Dammit, Eden. Don't go there...

"You do realize it's *my* job to massage you, right?" I try to ask calmly. "I work here. This is weird and could possibly get me fired."

"It won't get you fired and this is not weird," he says with a hint of laughter. "I never find a man taking care of a woman to be weird. Now lay down and relax because I'm not leaving without giving you a taste."

I suck in a breath and close my eyes to the feel of his strong hands on my shoulders, taking charge. "Can you at least put a towel on so you're not massaging me naked? Now that *is* weird."

"If that's what you really want."

"I do," I answer quickly, even though I can barely even convince myself I'm telling the truth.

I feel his warm breath hit my ear, before he speaks against it, causing chills to run over my flesh. "Are you sure? I massage better in the *nude*. It's a proven fact."

A moan escapes me as his strong hands work down my back to grab the bottom of my shirt, lifting it up over my bra. As soon as his big hands meet my bare skin, I feel my body heat up from his touch and instantly melt into him.

I barely even notice him undo my bra and at this point, I don't care, because his hands feel fantastic.

"Yes," I groan as he begins to rub harder, going deeper, almost distracting me from the fact that he still hasn't put a towel on. "Please put a towel on.

This is already unusual for me. It's not every day I allow a client to put their hands on me. Just please..."

His hands leave me for a few seconds, my body immediately missing the feel of his hands touching me and taking care of me. I've definitely been missing out over the years, always being on the giving end and not the receiving end.

Holy shit... this man's hands are pure magic.

My body melts again, the second his hands return and I find myself relaxing and just letting him take charge as he lifts my shirt higher and moves his way up my body, touching me so good.

I'm so used to overseeing everything, that it feels fantastic just letting go for a few moments and leaving things in the hands of someone else.

Even if it is a half-naked stranger with a body like a Greek God.

As soon as his hands find their way down to my thighs to spread them, I suck in a breath and grip the bottom of the table.

"Relax, Eden." He lets out a deep laugh and lifts my leg higher, sliding his hands up my shorts a little, causing my body to react from his closeness.

It feels so sexual, but so relaxing at the same time. I'm not sure if I should be turned on from this, but I totally am. No wonder why these men show up naked and pop boners from my hands rubbing them.

This is a lot more erotic than I ever knew. Truthfully, I tried to block any ideas of my job being sexy in any way. Was the only way to handle it.

But thanks to Kash...

"I'm not going to massage your pussy. *That* kind of massage, I make sure I'm naked for and you've already forced me to cover up. So, you're out of luck."

There he goes again being sexy and humorous at the same time. The perfect balance.

"Don't talk," I moan out and bite my lip as he switches to my right thigh now, getting extremely close to my vagina, but being respectful enough to keep a safe distance. His grip on my thigh is tight. Honestly, this feels too good to make him stop, so I'm going to just go with the flow for once. "Just rub... yes... right there. Oh wow..."

It's completely quiet for a few minutes, him taking the time to take care of me, before he speaks again, his voice sounding a bit breathy.

"We're going to have to set up a time for me to give you a *real* massage,

Eden. You're too fucking tense and ten minutes isn't even close to enough time for me to take care of you the right way. Your body needs dedication."

Releasing my thigh, he moves his way up my body to clasp my bra and pull my shirt back down.

The way his fingertips graze my flesh on the way down, causes goosebumps to cover my body and heat me up at the same time.

"Yeah well, I don't have a lot of time to take care of myself these days. I'm not what's most important in my life. I haven't been for a while now."

"Then you should be that for someone else," he says as I flip over and sit up to see him facing the wall and pulling his sweats up. "Just another reason for you to let me make you important even if it's only for thirty minutes out of your day. It doesn't sound like other men have done that for you. They were fucking idiots and obviously didn't know how to take care of a woman."

I watch his back muscles flex as he reaches for the door handle and pauses. "Get my number from Riley. And by the way..." He turns around and faces me, showing his face for the first time tonight.

My mouth drops open, me immediately recognizing him from last night. "It was nice seeing you again, Eden."

My gaze wanders over his firm body, taking in every dip and muscle, before lowering down to his very noticeable erection.

It's so thick and well... on display for me. He doesn't even attempt to hide it.

Holy hell.

With a small smirk, he exits the room, leaving me to sit here in surprise with my hands over my face.

Kash is the stripper that almost completely made me come undone last night from his body. I should've known there was something familiar about this guy.

He had the ability to work me up just as he did last night, before I rushed out the door, needing to get away.

Who would've thought a male stripper could have a sweet and caring side to go with his filthy mouth?

I have a feeling that could be a very bad combination for me if I agree to taking his number.

But I have to admit that the opportunity is more than tempting and temptation is something I haven't felt in a long time.

And I've already felt it twice with Kash.

With my mind racing, I quickly clean up and head out front to clock out.

"Everything okay?" Riley asks with a small smile, while flipping off the lights.

I nod my head and grip the strap of my purse. "I'm fine," I lie. "Why?"

She stops to look me over with amusement. "Your entire body is flushed." She raises a brow as I walk with her to the door. "Your last appointment go well?"

"Went fine," I say quickly. A little too quickly. "Just anxious to get home."

"Good." Riley gives me a quick nod and heads for her new car. "See you later, babe. Let me know if there's *anything* you might need."

I wait until she jumps into her car, before I throw my hand over my face in embarrassment. By *anything*, she meant Kash's number. I know that without a doubt.

So much for pretending Kash didn't get to me tonight. Even my boss can see it...

CHAPTER SIX

KASH

AFTER I PULL UP BEHIND of *Walk of Shame*, I park my truck and jump out, before pulling the tailgate down and jumping onto it.

The cool night air feels good against my face, giving me a moment to relax and think for the first time in days.

Taking my time, I lay back and place my arms behind my head, getting lost in thought.

Between working at the club, training for my upcoming fights, and helping my guys out, I haven't had a moment to breathe and actually enjoy it in who knows how long.

My shift begins in ten minutes, so you better fucking believe, I'm taking every second I can get, before I have to go in there and get groped by a ton of crazy women that will most likely try to take me home tonight.

Closing my eyes, I take in a deep breath, before slowly releasing it and reaching into my hoodie for a cigarette.

As the smoke fills my lungs, I allow myself a few moments to think about

Eden for the first time in the three days since I've seen her.

It's not that I haven't wanted to think about her, because trust me, I've wanted to. But every time my thoughts stray her way, I get distracted by someone interrupting me or my ass is just too exhausted to make sense of anything that happened that night at *Sensual Touches*.

After her running out on me at her friend's party last week, I wanted to take advantage of the time I had her stuck in a room with me, even if it was only for thirty minutes.

I wanted a chance for her to see me as something other than just a male fucking stripper that knows how to make a whole room of women *hot* and *wet*.

I'm so much more than that.

I'm a man that shows dedication to my woman and fights with everything in me to keep her feeling safe and cared for in every single way.

I hated hearing that Eden hasn't experienced that kind of dedication from a man before. If she had, then she would know what a massage feels like.

Only makes me want to take care of her more.

"What the hell..." I run my hand over my face and think about how it felt to have her soft body beneath my fingers.

As soon as I slid my hands up her little shorts, feeling the heat from between her legs, I got hard and I know without a doubt that she noticed on my way out. Her wide eyes as she looked me over, said it all.

But how the hell could I *not* get hard from touching her? She's so beautiful.

How could any man in his right mind not want to feel that day in and day out? I was completely exhausted and sore, but rubbing her and taking care of her overpowered any of that shit and made me forget about myself.

I would've spent the entire night on her body if that's what she allowed me to do. Hell, I even offered to take care of her another night, but I have a feeling I won't hear from her.

Most women would've called me as soon as they got off work, but Eden isn't like most women. I can already see that and it has me completely intrigued by her, wanting to know more.

I just hope I get that chance. I can tell there's something holding her back. I just need to find out what or *who*.

"You're late."

Taking one more drag off my cigarette, I toss it and sit up to see Stone looking down at me. He's completely covered in sweat, looking beat. A typical night here at the club for all of us, no matter how big or small the crowd is.

It takes a lot out of you physically and emotionally working at a place like this.

"It's slow in there. They'll manage without me for a few minutes." I hope.

"True. Sarah can hold the shit down at the bar for a while. Just thought I'd let your ass know because you seemed lost in your own little world over here, hiding in that hideous hoodie of yours." He pulls out his phone and smiles as if he's the happiest man alive. "My future wife is telling me to hurry my ass home to her. Fuck, I love saying that. Not sure I'll ever get used to it."

It's been six months since Stone and Sage made things official with them and just a few weeks ago, he got down on one knee and asked her to marry him.

"I still can't believe she agreed to marry your crazy ass," I tease, just to work him up. "She's so much hotter and smarter than you. Pretty much better in every way."

"What can I say?" He begins backing away in a hurry. "She sees the best in me. I got lucky and hopefully one day some hot chick will find the best in you. But I doubt it." His mouth curves into a smirk.

Laughing, I jump down from my truck and grab my gym bag. "I won't argue that. You got lucky. Tell the wifey I miss her."

"Fuck no. She's mine." He gives me the middle finger with both hands, before spinning around and waving his hand back at me. "See ya, asshole. The crazies are out tonight so have fun with that shit."

"See ya, dick." Still laughing, I shake my head and toss my bag over my shoulder, before making my way through the back entrance of the club.

The first thing my eyes land on is Kage standing outside of the locker room, keeping two drunk girls busy that keep trying to sneak past him. They're most likely trying to get to Myles who should've just gotten off stage a few minutes ago.

Stone wasn't wrong. Shit.

"Back up, ladies. You're not allowed back here." Kage shakes his head and gives me an amused look when he sees me leaning against the wall, watching him struggle. "Enjoying the show, dickhead?"

I lift a brow and push away from the wall, drawing the girls' attention my way. "I always enjoy a good show. You know this, Kage."

"Me too. A hell of a lot. So have fun with these two. They haven't given up once tonight." With a smirk, he backs away from the girls and watches as they come at me, pulling at my hoodie as if they want to see what's under it.

"Who's this hottie?" the blonde asks, while pushing my hood back and touching my facial hair. "Please tell me you're one of the strippers. We need this thing off. Like right now."

I feel her friend come up behind me, pressing her body against mine as she reaches around to grab my chest and grope me. "Nice and firm just how we like it. We need this thing off." She runs her hands down my abs, stopping when I grab them before they get to where they're headed. "Rough and mysterious. I like it. Very hot."

The blonde must take this as a good opportunity to jump back in, because before I know it, she's grabbing my cock and running her hands over my jeans, while her friend has me distracted.

With a growl, I grab her hand and lean in to whisper in her ear. "Don't touch what you can't handle. I'm rough all around. Really fucking rough."

With that, the girls back away, looking me over with heated eyes, while giggling to each other. "We were about to head out for the night, but I think we've changed our minds. See you out there, hoodie."

I turn to Kage when he laughs. "Some kind of security you are, asshole." I shake my head and shove him away from the door, before disappearing into the locker room.

I'm not sure if I should be surprised that the back door didn't do shit to keep the women off me. I'm not even on the clock yet and my dick's already been groped.

Might as well start a count for the night.

Hell, the highest I got in one night was fifty-two times and I was only here for four hours. That shit still surprises me.

Myles is just stepping out of the shower, walking naked to get to his locker when I make my way over to mine.

"Those crazy chicks still out there?" He laughs in disbelief and pulls his jeans on, without even bothering to dry off. "They followed me back here over twenty minutes ago." He rubs a red spot on his chest. "Hell, I think one of them even bit me. That shit did not feel good."

I set my bag down and dig inside for some jeans and a black shirt. "They just walked away *after* groping my ass. Well, actually my damn dick, I should say. But I'll take that over being bitten. I only like that shit in the bedroom."

"Ha! Well, good luck getting rid of them now," he says with a lopsided grin. "They won't be going anywhere tonight. Especially if they've gotten a feel of your man meat."

"Yeah..." I slip my jeans on and button them. "Well, I'm not stripping tonight. I'm working the bar. It's all Colt for the next five hours. So, good luck to that motherfucker."

Myles laughs, while running his hand through his wet, dark hair. "I'll be sure to wish him luck on the way out the door. It might not be a packed house tonight, but apparently, it's a night for all the crazies to be here."

"So I heard... and witnessed."

This only makes me thankful I'm working the bar tonight and not the floor. I seriously don't think I could handle all that shit tonight.

Not that the bar is much better, but it's less demanding and keeps your dick from being fondled every two seconds by strange women.

After I toss my bag into my locker, I make my way over to the bar, stopping when I see Cale trying to make his way through the crowd of women.

He can barely walk around this place without women swooning over him and begging him to go back to his stripper days.

I grip his shoulder. "Hey, man. I needed a few minutes to myself tonight before coming inside. Just wanted to let you know I'm late with clocking in."

Cale gives me the same understanding smile he's given me since I first walked in that door almost two years ago. "You've been here long enough to know when it's okay to not be here right on time. I trust you boys. You haven't let me down yet. I'll let you know when you do."

"Thanks, man." I slap his back and quickly make my way behind the bar to clock in, before Sarah can strangle me for leaving her hanging.

Sarah immediately greets me with a sad smile, while looking my face over. She hasn't seen me since my fight the other night. "That pretty face is all bruised up and I hate it. I heard you kicked ass though. That's hot."

I shake my head and laugh. "My face will heal. This is nothing compared to what's to come in a couple of weeks. I might even be lucky if you recognize me after that one."

"I have faith you'll kick ass then, too." She winks and then walks away to help a few girls, giving me time to slip my hoodie back on and get comfortable.

After being here for two hours, I lean over the bar top to take a moment, while it's slow on drink orders and look over to see Colt is looking completely exhausted and worn down.

He's trying to work his body to "Anywhere" by 112, but from the looks of it, his ass can hardly even dance at this point.

So, I jump up onto the bar and decide to help his tired ass out and give him a quick break.

Slowly, I make my way across the bar top, grabbing at the bottom of my hoodie as I stop and grind my hips, drawing the attention of the women my way.

Biting my bottom lip, I move the hoodie up slightly with each move I make, hoping to tease them and make them want more.

This must get their attention, because before I know it, there's a shit ton of women rushing over to throw their money my way.

Winding my fists up in the fabric, I thrust my hips, slowly and move the hoodie higher, until I'm pulling it over my head and tossing it aside.

Once I'm down to my shirt and jeans, I run my hands down my chest, moving them seductively down my body, stopping once I reach my cock.

I run my hand over it a few times, keeping my eyes closed as I thrust my hips and get lost in the music.

This has whoever's sitting in the stool in front of me, letting out a small gasp as if she's turned on by me touching myself.

Satisfied, I drop to my knees, flex my chest and pull my shirt over my head and toss it aside, before I grind my hips slowly, as if I'm fucking the person below me.

It's then that I look down to see *her* sitting on the stool, watching me with curiosity.

I have no idea when she got in the room, but I'm guessing it was right when I decided to draw all the attention my way.

I'm just glad that I have *her* attention along with the rest of the room since last time she saw me dance, she pretended not to enjoy it.

Well that was before she got the chance to get to know me. I don't see her looking away now and it has my body reacting.

Her green eyes land on mine and she looks nervous as if she's just been caught doing something she wasn't meant to, but she doesn't turn away.

Her eyes stay on me, taking me in as if she wishes it were her *hands* on me instead.

Well, damn. I wasn't expecting to see her here, but I'll take this any day over just a phone call...

CHAPTER SEVEN

EDEN

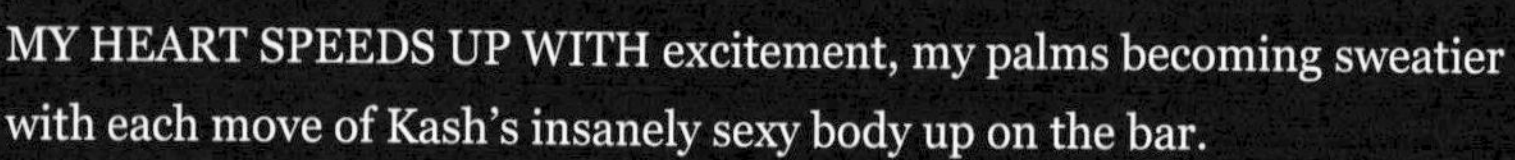

MY HEART SPEEDS UP WITH excitement, my palms becoming sweatier with each move of Kash's insanely sexy body up on the bar.

I can barely handle looking at him right now, without remembering the glimpse I got of his naked body last week at *Sensual Touches*, when I lost my battle at *not* peeking between my fingers.

There's no denying the fact that he's absolutely beautiful and I've spent some time since then, pleasuring myself to that image, wondering what it would be like to experience the real thing.

Knight is the only man I've been with sexually and if I have to be honest, he never took the time to take care of me and make sure I felt good. It was always about him and what he needed.

He was a selfish man in more ways than one.

Kash on the other hand, gives off the impression that he's all about taking care of a woman and making her feel good in every way. He showed that by giving up his massage to give me one, instead. It's a desirable quality in a man that seems to be extremely rare.

But as much as I enjoy looking at and fantasizing about Kash, and all the things he can do to me, I need to be careful when it comes to men and letting them in. My son still comes first over my needs, and I made a promise to myself the day he was born that I would never be selfish and put him in a situation that might hurt him in the end.

The only reason I'm even here in the first place tonight is to give Kash back the hundred dollar tip he left me a few nights ago. I don't deserve it and after thinking it over for the last few days, I've come to the conclusion that I need to give it back.

It's the right thing to do and I'm not leaving here without him accepting it.

He was barely even in my room for thirty minutes and ten of those minutes were spent on him massaging *me.*

I can't accept the tip. I'd feel too guilty keeping it, even though I could use the extra money right now.

Plus, I have to admit there was a small part of me that wanted to see him again, no matter how hard I tried to convince myself otherwise.

There was something about the way Kash talked to me during our time together that had me completely intrigued, wanting to know more about him and what kind of guy he truly is.

Not just the male entertainer I got a glimpse of that first night. The real him.

I was hoping to maybe get a few minutes to do that tonight, but from the looks of things, I'm not so sure now.

When Riley told me he was bartending tonight, instead of dancing, I figured it'd be the best night to stop in and give him his money back, *without* having a crazy group of women surrounding him.

I was completely wrong. These women are going crazy over him and inside, I might be just a little bit too.

'Cause holy hell...

That night I met him at Joni's party doesn't do him any justice as to how he's moving his body right now on that bar. Sort of makes me wish I would've stayed longer to see him dance.

The way his strong hands move over his hard body as he grinds his hips with perfect rhythm is completely seductive and hypnotizing.

Seeming to ignore all the women around him, Kash leans over and grabs my hands, placing them on his hard chest as he continues moving his body in front of me.

The way he looks at me is almost enough to make me believe we're the only two people in the room.

How he can manage to do that, when the room is full of beautiful women, wanting to get to him, is beyond crazy.

Some of them are even practically climbing on top of me right now, wanting a taste of this man.

But I can't help but to let him draw me in anyway, getting lost in this moment with him as if no one else is around.

Sitting up straight, he slowly runs my hands lower, with each thrust of his hips, stopping before they can reach the very visible bulge in his pants.

My heart is beating out of my chest at this point, wondering what it would feel like to go lower. To just give in for two seconds and be selfish for once in my life.

I feel like such a pervert right now. Kash has a way of doing that to me.

Leaving my hands on his body, he moves in closer to wrap his hands into the back of my hair and hold me in place as if to tell me he's dancing for me and only me.

Keeping his eyes on me and only me, he jumps down from the bar and picks me up, wrapping my legs around his waist, before he buries his face into my neck as he dances.

The way he does it is so sensual and personal, giving off a whole new vibe than that first night when all it did was make me feel dirty.

I feel anything *but* right now.

His hands move from my hips down to cup my ass as his mouth brushes up my neck. Without even thinking about it, I lean my head back exposing myself for him.

He sucks and nips at my neck, moaning as his hands grip me tighter, showing me how much he's enjoying me.

This has butterflies filling my stomach and my mind racing all over the place, wondering what in the hell I'm doing.

Before I can get too lost in him, I work my way out of his arms and toss the money down on the bar, before backing away through the crowd.

I don't make it far, before I feel a firm grip on my waist, as Kash's body slides in behind me.

Why the hell does this have to feel so good?

"I don't want your money, Eden," he whispers against my ear.

"It's not." I stop walking and close my eyes when I feel his hands brush my hair away from my ear. "It's yours. I can't accept your tip. I didn't even earn it. I'm giving it back."

I feel him smile against my ear, causing me to swallow. "Yes, you did. You took the time out of your night to help me out when I needed it. You could've said no to sticking around that night for me."

"No, I couldn't." I shake my head and remove his hand from my waist, before turning around to face him. I'm sure this will be enough to scare him off. "I have a son to take care of, Kash. It was you that was helping me out, but I can't accept money I didn't earn. I should go."

He looks me over for a quick second, before catching my arm when I try to leave. "How old is your son?"

I give him a small smile, not expecting him to care enough to ask me any questions. Most guys would be running the other way at just the mention of me having a kid. "He's five. I should really get back to him. He's with the babysitter and..."

His face lights up as he listens to me talk. "He's one lucky little guy to have you." His eyes stay on mine as he speaks again. "Let me take you out on a date, Eden. Let me take care of you for a night and show you what it feels like to go out with a real man."

I don't say anything. Honestly, I'm not sure what to say. All I know is that I could get myself into deep trouble with this man if I don't get out of here soon.

So, I just smile and back up through the crowd, before he can try to stop me again.

As soon as I make it past the security guard and outside, I walk straight over to my Jeep and fall against it with a huge smile.

Something about the look in Kash's eyes when I mentioned my son and he asked me to go out with him, tells me he's genuinely interested in me and not just getting laid.

I've been asked out on a few dates in the six months since I've been single and every single one ended up being disastrous, with the asshole assuming he was going to take me to bed at the end of the night and satisfy his own needs.

They never once asked me about my son or what's important in my life. It was obvious they weren't looking for anything deeper than a one-night stand.

That's not my style. I need a selfless and caring man that is serious about a relationship and willing to put my child before even my own needs.

I know without a doubt that it won't be easy to find and I'm not sure if

Kash can be that guy or not.

Right as I get ready to get into my Jeep to head home, I hear heavy footsteps coming up behind me, before I feel a hand grip my arm and pull me back with force.

"What the hell are you doing here, Eden?" Knight's angry voice booms beside my ear as he turns me around and presses my back against my vehicle. "I went to the house to see *my* son to find out you were at a fucking male strip club. What gives you the right to go out and leave Alec with someone else?"

"Let go of me, Knight," I growl out, while yanking my arm out of his reach and tensing my whole body. "I've been gone for exactly thirty-five minutes. You're gone every fucking day and night. Don't you come at me thinking you have the right to tell me what I can or cannot do. *My* son was already asleep before I even thought about stepping out that door. So, back off."

"Tell me what the fuck you're doing here!" His nostrils flare out in rage as he backs me against the Jeep again and closes me in so I can't move. "Who were you with?"

I attempt to push him away, but it doesn't even budge him. "Let me go, Knight."

He pushes me harder, his body hurting mine. "Answer me! Who the fuck were you with?"

"Me."

We both look over to the sound of Kash's deep voice as he comes stalking toward us, looking pissed and ready to strike.

"Don't touch her like that. Take your fucking hands off her before I remove them my damn self."

Knight lets out a small laugh as if he's amused by Kash barking orders at him. It's not something he's used to. "You're telling *me* what to do with the mother of my child?"

"Damn straight I am." With that Kash pulls him away from me and roughly slams him against the vehicle next to mine, holding him down by his neck. "You never fucking handle a woman like that, motherfucker. Got it?"

"Get the fuck off me." Knight pushes Kash away just enough to take a swing at him, but misses.

This has Kash swinging out, knocking Knight right back against the vehicle and holding him down by his neck again.

Before Knight can manage to attempt to fight back again, two security guards are pulling them apart, wrestling with them to hold them back from each other.

"Calm down, Kash," one of them says, while blocking him with his huge frame. "This is not the time or place for this to happen. Settle it somewhere else."

Kash runs his hands over his face and backs away from the security guard, before turning to face me. "You left this on the bar." He walks up to me and gently grabs the back of my neck, while slipping the tip money into my front pocket. "Riley gave you my number. Promise me you'll call me if that asshole *ever* handles you that way again. Got it?"

Looking him in the eyes, I nod my head, while fighting to calm my racing heart.

Then before I know it, Kash has us turned around so that he's blocking me from Knight as if he's still trying to protect me, even though there's no way he's getting to me again.

Knight is in the background struggling to get past the security guards, his face covered in blood from when Kash punched him in the nose.

I've never seen anyone stand up to Knight like that in the seven years I've known him.

I have no idea what could've happened, but I'm relieved it got stopped before it could go any further.

Both men are powerhouses.

"Go home and lock the door. Lane and Kass won't let your asshole ex leave until you're safe in your Jeep and have enough time to get home." His hand comes down to gently run over the red spot Knight was gripping. "Actually, fuck that. I'm driving you home myself."

"You don't have to do that. I'm fine. He won't bother me anymore tonight."

"I want to be positive. I won't stop worrying until I know for sure." He turns away from me to yell over to the security guards who are keeping Knight at a far distance. "Tell Cale I'll be back. I have something important to do real fast."

With that, he gently grips my waist and guides me over to the passenger seat of my Jeep, before jumping into the driver's seat.

"Give me your keys."

This man really knows how to make a woman's heart beat right out of her damn chest.

He's dependable, caring, and protective. Everything Knight isn't...

CHAPTER EIGHT

KASH

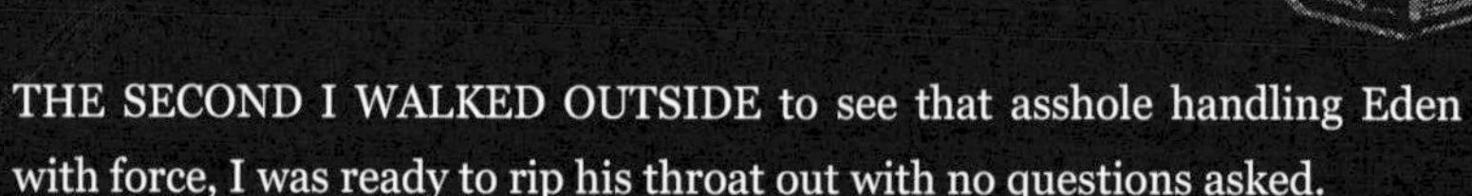

THE SECOND I WALKED OUTSIDE to see that asshole handling Eden with force, I was ready to rip his throat out with no questions asked.

That kind of shit works me up and pushes me past my boiling point like nothing else.

I will not stand for that shit and my heart is still racing from rage, everything in me wanting to kill that son of a bitch for touching her.

He's lucky she's safe in the car with me and that Kass and Lane were there to pull my ass off. There's no telling how far it would've gotten and I would've hated Eden having to witness the violence.

Without hesitation, I reach over and grab Eden's hand, pulling it into my lap, this need to comfort her taking over.

I feel a slight tug from her as if she's not sure she wants me holding her hand, but the moment I rub my thumb over her hand, it relaxes in my lap.

"Has he ever put his hands on your son?" I ask the question, not giving a shit if it's crossing the line.

I need to know this in case I see that fucker again. I have no problem sending him a bigger message than I did tonight.

"No," she says quickly. "Of course not. I'd kill that son of a bitch myself if that ever happened and he knows it. He'd never be allowed near either of us for as long as he's breathing."

I relax a bit. "And what about you? Has he ever hit you? Please, don't lie to me either. I know how men like him are. He didn't give a shit about holding you against your will back there."

It's quiet as she lets out a small breath and leans her head back into the seat. "If you mean swinging at me, then no. If you mean him holding me against the wall or dragging me into him and holding me there, then I can't say no about that. He's a possessive man and he's used to getting what he wants."

"Fucking piece of shit." Anger boils up in me, causing me to squeeze her hand and pull it further into my lap as if to protect her, even though he's not around. "And he still wants you?" That thought for some reason pisses me the hell off.

"In some ways... yes. We were together for seven years. He had it in his crazy mind that I'd never leave him. That I would stick around and put up with him cheating on me and never being home to help me take care of our child." She pauses for a second and then turns to face me, her hand squeezing mine this time as if she's the one getting angry now. "He expects me to still have sex with him and only him even though we're not together. He's a delusional asshole and we were never meant to date. I was young and stupid. Knight Stevens is a prick."

I thought that asshole looked familiar. I've seen him fight before. Should've known it was him as soon as I heard Eden call him Knight. It's not a very common name, but Stevens is what I know him by.

And she's not wrong. He's a fucking prick.

"So, let me get this shit straight?" I flex my jaw and fight to keep my cool before she really sees how angry this son of a bitch has me. "He goes around fucking any woman he wants and expects you to sit around and wait for him to come take you however and whenever he wants as if he owns you?"

"Like the asshole that he is. You would think Knight would know by now that I won't play his games. I'm not that girl and never have been." She pulls her hand from mine and points out the window. "Turn left at the next block and go five houses down and it's on the right side."

I grip the steering wheel and do as she says, stopping in front of a small brick house.

I'm so worked up right now, that I just sit here in silence, gripping the steering wheel and flexing my jaw as she looks me over.

I hope like hell now that I get to fight him in a couple weeks, come the big fight.

"Thank you for driving me home, Kash. That was really nice of you." She smiles when I reach over and undo her seatbelt. "Want to take my Jeep back to the club and I'll get a ride to pick it up tomorrow?"

I shake my head and turn my gaze to meet her eyes. They're so beautiful and full of passion and I have no doubt I'll be picturing them and wondering about her after I leave. "No. I need to get some air."

With that, I jump out of the Jeep and walk over to her side, opening the door right as she attempts to.

She gives me a surprised look and smiles as I close the door behind her. "I really appreciate you caring enough to stick up for me. There's not a lot of guys out there like you."

I smile slightly and gently grip the back of her neck, before I lean in close to her ear. "I know... and I'll never be like the asshole you're used to. I'm different, Eden. I'm not afraid to show you that."

My breath against her ear has her shivering in my arms, before she finally grabs her keys and pulls away, taking a step back.

We both just stand here looking at each other, until I finally speak again. "You have my number. Text me so I have yours."

She nods and begins backing away to her house. I can sense the hesitation, as if she wants to ask me in, but knows she shouldn't. "I think I can do that. Especially after what you just did for me."

"Was hoping you'd say that." Taking a chance, I grab her face and press my lips close to hers, hoping like hell it gives her something more to want later. The way she trembles slightly as I pull away shows me she likes my mouth so close to hers. "Goodnight."

Smiling, she clears her throat and begins backing up. "Goodnight, Kash."

I stay here, leaning against her Jeep as I watch her disappear into the house and close the door.

After about fifteen minutes, I take off jogging, making my way back to the club.

If that asshole was going to show up and cause trouble tonight, he would've done it by now, wanting to hand me my ass for attacking him.

Maybe that means he's smart enough not to cause trouble near his child.

That's the only thing I can admire about this piece of shit.

Everything else I've heard about him makes me want to teach his ass what it's like to be a real man.

By the time I make it back to the club, Kass is standing at the front by himself, smiling as he watches me fight to catch my breath.

"Your ass ran back to the club? How far does she live?"

I push past him. "About six miles."

"Well fuck. That's a good guy there. Got your hero pants on and shit."

I laugh a little and keep on walking, making my way inside and back behind the bar.

"Thanks for deciding to join us again. I'm sweating my ass off back here. Where have you..." Sarah jumps down my throat but quickly laughs at me once she sees me covered in sweat. "Alright then. Should I ask you what happened?"

I shake my head and quickly jump back into taking orders to give Sarah a break. "I'd rather you don't. Not unless you want me breaking bottles against the wall by the end of the night."

"Gotcha. Won't ask."

If I even think about that asshole handling her like that again, I'll lose it all over again and not be able to function the rest of the night.

This run was exactly what I needed to cool off some.

The only thing that will make me cool off even more is if I get a text from Eden, taking me up on that date.

Or hell. Even to just let me know that asshole doesn't show up at her place tonight.

I just hope like hell she uses my number...

CHAPTER NINE

EDEN

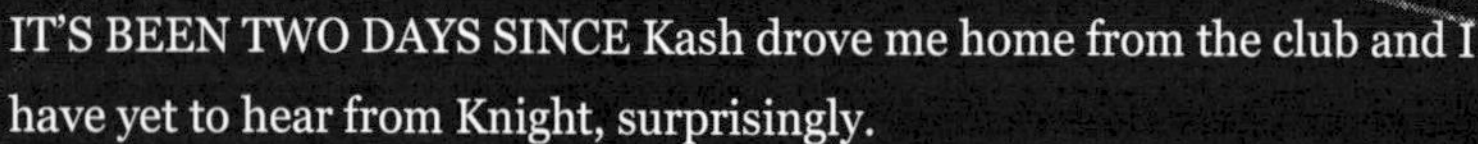

IT'S BEEN TWO DAYS SINCE Kash drove me home from the club and I have yet to hear from Knight, surprisingly.

Not that it's unusual to go days without him calling to speak to our son, but after what happened in the parking lot, I expected Knight to show up at my door and jump down my throat about Kash.

There's a huge chance he's embarrassed and that doesn't happen very often. There's not one person I know that is brave enough to attack Knight.

As much as I hate violence, I have to admit that Kash being brave enough to stick up for me was a complete turn-on and has only left me thinking about him more.

The way he rubbed me. The way he held my hand. But most of all, the way he kissed me.

His lips so close to mine and so soft and tempting. I'd be lying if I said it didn't make me weak in the knees.

I've been so close to calling him, but every time I get ready to hit that button, I think about Alec and how complicated it could get having another man in my life.

"Mommy." Alec's tired voice has me looking over the couch to see him standing there in his Star Wars underwear with his hair standing up all over the place.

"Come here, baby." I wrap my arm around him as he jumps onto the couch and cuddles against my side. "What are you doing up so late?"

He shrugs and wraps his little arm around my mine. "I don't know. My eyes opened up. I couldn't stop them. Now I'm not sleeping."

I laugh a little and look down at him. "Why are you so handsome?"

He yawns. "Because I am."

It's the same response I get every time and it never fails to make me smile.

"Close your eyes. It's late. I'll wake you up when it's time to go to Hannah's."

By the time I look down again, he's already sleeping hard against me as if he was never awake in the first place.

My heart swells as I run my hands through his thick hair and watch him sleep.

This little boy will always be the best part of me. Alec is my life. I just wish his father felt the same about him.

The longer I'm awake flipping through channels, the stronger the urge to text Kash gets.

He's most likely at the club and even that isn't enough to weaken my urge to talk to him. Usually, I would never even consider giving a guy with his job choice a shot, especially after dealing with Knight and his late nights out with the crazy women that crowded his fights.

But I can't get over this feeling that is haunting me and telling me he's different. This feeling that I need to get to know him.

"It can't hurt anything," I finally tell myself. "What's one text? Just one little text?"

Reaching beside me for my phone. I scroll to Kash's number and type out a short message.

Eden

I just want to thank you again for what you did for me. I really appreciate it.

Once I hit send, I set my phone down again, not expecting an instant response. So when I get one, I'm surprised.

My heart speeds up with excitement as I open the message and read it.

I wasn't expecting this kind of reaction out of myself just from receiving a text back from Kash, but clearly, I like him more than I admit to myself.

Kash

I'd do it again in a heartbeat, Eden. How's your son?

His response has my stomach filling with butterflies and me smiling so hard that it hurts. Kash is proving to be different than I expected.

Eden

He's a hyper little guy, full of energy and life. I guess you can say he's great. He always is...

Kash

Sounds like me when I was a kid. Hell, my ass is still hyper and full of energy. The kid like to play ball?

Eden

More than you know. That and video games. His two favorite things.

Kash

Sounds like my kind of kid.

What about you? Are you doing good?

I'm still available for that massage if you're in need of relaxing... I promise to behave as long as you want me to.

I lay back and smile as I read over his texts. He knows exactly what to say to get to my heart and make me laugh at the same time.

There's a huge chance I may begin to enjoy these texts with Kash a little too much.

Eden

Yes, I'm fine. And are you sure about that?

Kash

About what?

Eden

That you'd behave if I want you to.

Kash

I'd do anything you want me to, Eden.

If my heart wasn't racing like crazy, it for sure is now. I'm not sure if texting him was a good idea or if what I'm about to agree to is, but I can't help but want this right now.

This man has a way of making me want things and I kind of like it. No... I do like it.

Eden

My father wants to take Alec tomorrow night for a sleepover...

Kash

I'll get off work early then. Expect me around nine.

What about Knight? Did he come over after I left?

Eden

Nope. All is good.

Kash

That's what I was hoping to hear.

Grinning like a teenaged girl, I set my phone down and close my eyes, getting comfortable on the couch.

I have to be up for work in five hours and I have a feeling it's going to be close to impossible to fall asleep now.

As much as I may try to downplay my excitement about tomorrow, there's no denying that Kash has me feeling all kinds of giddy right now.

I haven't felt this excited since high school and I love it...

CHAPTER TEN

KASH

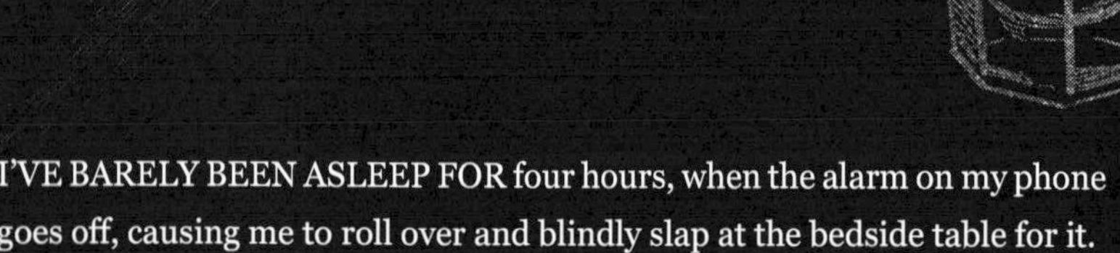

I'VE BARELY BEEN ASLEEP FOR four hours, when the alarm on my phone goes off, causing me to roll over and blindly slap at the bedside table for it.

By the time I get my phone in my hand, I hear Colt throwing things at his bedroom wall, yelling at me to shut the thing up before he chokes me.

I get pleasure in his misery, so I lay back and smirk, allowing my alarm to go off in my hand a few more times, before finally shutting it off.

He's part of the reason I couldn't fall asleep last night, thanks to him coming home drunk and horny, fucking Harper against every surface in this damn house.

The other reason was that I couldn't stop thinking about tonight and seeing Eden, but shit, Colt made it worse.

He knows more than anyone that I have a schedule in the morning I've been keeping up with for the last six months. Every Monday and sometimes on Friday.

I haven't broken it yet and I don't plan to now, not even if I didn't sleep for dick and my whole body aches from my performance last night.

"You have no idea how much I hate your ass right now." Colt appears in my doorway, half-naked, running a hand over his sleepy face. "It's like seven. Don't you ever sleep? Shit."

I jump up and reach for the closest pair of jeans and slip them on with a smile. "Nah, I have somewhere to be. Someone's depending on me. Sleep can wait."

Colt closes his eyes and falls against the wall with a grunt. "I don't know how the fuck you do it, man," he says through a yawn. "I'm going back to bed. I don't plan on waking up before seven *tonight* so have fun doing whatever the fuck it is you do this early."

"Good. You're going to need the energy tonight because I'm getting off early. It'll just be you and Myles for the last half of the night."

"Whatever. More money for my ass. Myles can't keep up for shit."

"Better teach his ass to then. He needs to prove himself before Cale replaces him."

"Yeah. Yeah. I'll work with him."

"Better work hard because if he has to bring Styx back, he'll be enough to replace you both. I don't think you want that."

"Hell no I don't. I'm not losing my job over Myles. I got him in so I'll do what I have to do to keep him in."

After Colt disappears, I throw on a t-shirt and my favorite hoodie, before rushing out the door and jumping into my truck.

I'm already five minutes behind schedule at this point, so I take the fastest route to the diner and place my usual order, before rushing out the door.

A satisfied smile takes over as I pull into my sister's driveway five minutes before eight and throw my truck into park.

"Shit, I'm getting good at this little routine."

Jogging up to the front door, I hold the plastic bags with one hand and reach for my sister's key, pushing the door open.

It's quiet, so I walk in and set the bags down on the counter, pulling out the Styrofoam containers and letting the smell of breakfast wake them up.

Just as expected, Alec comes rushing into the kitchen jumping with excitement when he sees me fixing him a plate of blueberry pancakes and fruit. "You brought me pancakes again! I must be good. I know I been. Hannah and my mommy says so."

"Good job." I laugh and walk over to the fridge to pour him a glass of milk. "I can't miss bringing you pancakes, lil man? Plus, I heard you have a new video game to show me so I got here as quickly as I could. Didn't want to wait until Monday."

He nods his head with excitement and quickly pulls out a chair at the table, pumped up as he bounces in his seat. "I do! I'll eat really fast so we can play. It's so cool!"

His eagerness to show me has me lighting up as I set his food down in front of him and start the pot of coffee for my little sister.

"Where's Hannah? Is she still being a sleepyhead?"

Alec throws his head back and laughs. "Yes. She's a big sleepyhead. Sleepyhead Hannah."

"She always has been but you know what?" I say softly, bending down close to him.

"What," he questions in a loud whisper, while sitting up straight.

"I bet if I ate her pancakes that she'd wake right up and tackle me."

Making as much noise as possible, I dig into the second plastic bag and pull out my sister's food.

Alec's laughter only makes it that much louder. I have no doubt, she'll appear in the kitchen in three, two...

"Don't you dare touch my food, Hunter Kash Knight," Hannah grumbles, while making her way over to get some coffee. "I only just fell back asleep after Alec getting dropped off. I'm not sure if I should hug you or strangle you on this lovely Friday morning."

"If I told you I brought you corned beef hash, would you settle for hugging me? I'm still a little sore. You might be able to take me right now."

Her eyes get wide with excitement as she rushes over to the table and reaches to open her food. "You brought me corned beef hash? Oh how I love my big brother."

I shake my head. "Nah, they were out."

"Jerk." She opens the Styrofoam and looks around before pushing my shoulder. "Not cool."

"I'm the only jerk that'll bring you pancakes every week though. Remember that, little sister."

She rolls her eyes. "And I suppose I love you for it. Still tired and annoyed but I guess you're pretty awesome."

"I know," I say with a smirk, before looking over to see Alec's plate almost completely empty. "Whoa, little guy. Take it easy before you give yourself a stomachache like last week."

He shoves the last bite of pancake into his mouth and jumps up with a quickness, his face a sticky mess. "I'm done! I'm done, Hunter! Come on so we can play! Hurry..."

Before I can respond, he's grabbing my hand and dragging me into the living room to play his new video game.

Although Alec usually plays on his DS, Hannah told me she bought a Wii U to make it easier for them to play together.

"Whoa, LEGO Star Wars. I've been wanting to try this game, buddy. You any good?"

He nods his head and jumps down in front of the couch, gripping the controller.

The excitement in his little green eyes has me smiling so big that it hurts. I'm not gonna lie, this little guy can make any shit day seem better. Makes me wish I could stop in and hang out with him every morning.

Since my sister's been babysitting him, I've watched myself change a lot. Alec makes me want a family of my own and that's something that hadn't crossed my mind until he started coming around.

Makes my life seem so incomplete.

After an hour of playing with Alec, I set the controller down and stand up, knowing I need to hurry and get to the warehouse to meet the guys. "It's time for me to go, lil' man. I have work to do this morning and I'm already late."

"Do you have to?"

"Yeah, it's part of being a grownup. Adulting isn't any fun, so stay a kid as long as you can. Okay?"

He nods his head and laughs. "Okay. I'll do my best."

"Sounds like a plan, lil' man." I nod my head toward the door. "Come on. I can be a few more minutes late. Only for my best little bud though so don't go telling Hannah."

"I won't! I promise."

Just like every visit, Alec rushes past me to get outside and to my truck.

He loves sitting in it, so I always let him pretend to drive me around for a few minutes before I leave.

Once I get outside, he's already standing by my huge truck, waiting on me. I boost him up into the driver's seat and close the door, before jogging over to the passenger side and getting in.

"Don't drive too fast, bud." I laugh as he turns the wheel to the left, making loud sound effects. "Whoa! Watch out."

"Don't worry," he says. "I turned just in time."

I almost lose track of time, until Hannah comes out and opens the driver's side door. "Alright, buddy. Let's get you cleaned up and dressed."

"Oh man..." He throws out his bottom lip. "I want to drive some more. Can I?"

"Sorry." I rub his little head, messing up his hair, before jumping out of the truck to lift him out. "I've gotta get going." Kneeling down in front of him, I pull a baseball out of my hoodie and hand it to him. "How about next week we play a little ball? It's been a while."

"You got me a new baseball?" He smiles, while looking it over with big eyes. "I like it!"

"I knew you would. Now why don't you run in and get cleaned up for Hannah. You gotta do that first before you play your game again. Okay?"

He nods. "Okay! I'll get nice and cleaned up for Hannah."

Hannah smiles as Alec rushes off into the house in a hurry to get cleaned up. "One day, you're going to make a good as shit dad."

I smile, while jumping into my truck, and closing the door behind me. "That's my goal, Hannah Lou Knight."

"Ugh! Don't ever call me by my full name again. I still have no idea what our parents were thinking when they named us."

"Hey, speak for yourself. My name is pretty badass."

"Yeah, alright *Kash*." She rolls her eyes. "Don't you have someplace to be?" A small cocky smile forms on her lips. "Tell Abe hi for me."

I shift the truck into reverse and laugh. "His ass still whines and cries over you dumping him last year. Maybe you should *stop* having me say hi for you. Yeah?"

"That's what he gets for being a dumbass. So no, I won't stop saying hi. I'll say hi every single day just to remind him what he lost. Let him suffer. Keeps me sane."

I shake my head, amused by my little sister as usual. "I'm out of here. Call me if you need anything."

"Yup! Will do, big brother."

By the time I make it to the warehouse for training, Abe and Calvin are sitting outside the door, looking wide awake and ready to work.

I can't help but smile at the fact that the guys are taking this shit more seriously now.

Too bad I have to ruin poor Abe's day with this...

"Hannah says hi."

"Oh come on," Abe whines, while tossing down his cigarette and stomping it out. "Why does your sister insist on ripping my heart out every damn day? It's been like seven months now and that shit still kills me."

Calvin laughs and slaps his back. "Because you were the dumbass that forced her to break up with you because you weren't *ready* for a commitment. Sucks being an immature guy that doesn't know what he wants, until it's gone doesn't it?"

"Hell yeah, it does."

We all laugh at Abe's misfortune as we make our way inside and begin setting up for the day.

There's no denying the fact that it's going to be a long ass day and night, between training and dancing, but luckily, it's starting out good so far.

I just hope like hell it can stay this way until my time with Eden is over tonight.

We're here for about two hours when my phone goes off in my pocket, distracting me.

Closing my eyes, I take a few deep breaths and release them before swinging at the heavy bag in front of me one last time, then walking away to grab my water.

After I catch my breath, I lean against the wall and pull out my phone, happy as hell when I see Eden's name across the screen.

Eden

I don't know what it is but ever since you came into my room that night, no one has been showing me their balls. Do I have you to thank?

I laugh at our conversation from that night. One of the first things she did was thank me for not showing her my balls. You won't get that from many women.

Kash

I might've asked Riley to pass on a message to anyone working the front desk. There's now a 'no balls' rule. Any guy that comes in has to sign a form.

Eden

I guess I should admit how great you are? Thanks for making my day. My eyes have never been happier.

Kash

Admitting how great I am would make my day. Then we can be even...

Eden

You're amazing! Gotta go.

I stand here and stare at my phone, smiling like a dumbass, until Abe pulls me out of it.

"Stop daydreaming little a girl and let's train."

I barely know this woman and she's already got me all wrapped up in her. Now, I need to work on getting her all wrapped up in me...

CHAPTER ELEVEN

EDEN

MY DAD PICKED UP ALEC thirty minutes ago, and I've been running around the house like a crazy person in an attempt to clean it up ever since.

Not that I intend to invite Kash in—it's definitely too soon for that—but it's the first time in weeks that I've had a few moments to get some work done, without Alec zooming around the house like a madman, wanting me to play with him.

I love that kid with everything in me, he's the very reason I breathe, but I've never met a messier or more energetic child in my life.

He takes after his father when it comes to both of those qualities and needless to say, it's exhausting sometimes.

I have to admit that the idea of Kash taking me out tonight—and wanting to take care of me—sounds like a dream come true right now.

I'm so used to taking care of everyone in my life, and putting myself last, that maybe he's right. I deserve just *one* night to have someone else take care of me for once.

Maybe I just want a chance to know what that feels like and I have a feeling that Kash is the perfect guy for just that.

I'm lost in my thoughts, just getting ready to bend down and pick up a stray sock, when the living room door opens to someone letting themselves inside.

My chest immediately tightens with stress, because I know without a doubt that it's Knight letting himself inside, without permission, as usual.

Out of all the nights he chooses to randomly stop in and most likely cause trouble, why tonight?

Damn you, Knight for ruining everything.

"Alec," he yells, while walking through the living room. "Come here, buddy. I got you something."

Shaking my head, I step into the living room and watch as he drops his jacket on the couch. "He's not here. And can you please start knocking? You don't live here anymore. Remember?"

Just as I think he's about to yell at me for Alec not being here, he tosses a small package onto the couch and pulls some flowers out from behind his back.

My stomach instantly twists into knots as his sad eyes meet mine. I automatically know where this is headed. He's good at playing people and making them feel bad for him.

Well not me. Not anymore.

"What are you doing?" Not wanting to deal with the little breakdown that I know is coming, I back up and run my hands over my face. "I can't do this again. Not tonight, Knight. Please don't."

He flashes me that smile that I once found charming and holds the flower arrangement out to me. "Come on, Eden. Don't you stand there and fucking tell me you don't miss me, baby? We both know that's a big lie."

When I still refuse to grab the flowers, he finally sets them down on the counter himself, before walking over to stand behind me.

My body stiffens from the feel of his arms wrapping around me from behind. Nothing about this feels right or good. "I didn't like seeing you with another man, Eden," he whispers against my ear. "You've been mine since high school. You're still mine. Never forget that."

"No... No, I'm not." With force, I break my way out of his arms and point at the door. "I'm not doing this with you. Leave. Please, just leave."

"Come on..." Not giving up, he comes back at me, pulling me into his huge arms again. The feel of his lips against my neck has me feeling sick. Who knows how many women those lips have been on. "Alec isn't here. It's just the two of us so stop putting on that tough show and pretending you don't still think about me."

"Knight..." I grip his arm and pull it down as he reaches up to grip my breasts. I *hate* the feeling of him touching me sexually. Makes me want to throw up. "It's not a show, asshole. I don't want you anymore so stop."

"What the fuck!" he screams, while pushing me away from him. "Who was that guy at the club then? Are you fucking him? Don't fucking lie to me either because you know I'll find out the truth."

"He hasn't been around Alec and that's *all* you need to know. The rest isn't your business." I point at the door again, making it as clear as I can that I want him gone. "Now go. Now."

"Have you fucked him?" he questions again. "I'm not leaving until you answer my damn question and we both know it."

"No! I'm not sleeping with anyone. Now go."

"Fine." He smirks, going back to the cocky asshole I've learned to hate so much. "I have shit to do anyway, but don't think for one second that I won't be back for you and Alec. You're still *my* family. This new guy has another thing coming if he thinks he can steal you guys from me."

"Just go," I growl out. "Right now. Get out."

Relief washes through me as he turns around and leaves, without further argument.

With him, you never know what to expect.

If he's in a certain mood, then nothing you can say or do can get him to go away, but luckily, he probably has one of his sluts waiting on him.

I mean, what is Knight without his group of desperate women up his ass, looking to get laid by a *somewhat* known fighter?

This is not the night to deal with this mess.

Knight is the last person I want around tonight, before seeing Kash. Not to mention that he should be here any second now for our date and they could've bumped into each other.

Having them here at the same time would've been bad news for sure.

After seeing what they're both capable of, with no one here to stop them, who knows what could've went down.

Just as I get a second to catch my breath and recover from Knight's little unexpected visit, the sound of Kash pulling into the driveway has my stomach filling up with butterflies.

I need this date more than ever now. Anything to get the bad taste of Knight out of my mouth and to forget about him touching me.

I find myself smiling as I look through the screen door to see Kash running up to the porch, tossing a baseball up and down in his hand.

He's looking so damn handsome tonight, dressed in a pair of dark jeans and a fitted button down shirt with the sleeves rolled up to just below his elbows.

The sexy smile on his face and the way his eyes look me over with admiration has my heart going crazy with excitement.

"Are we playing ball tonight?" I nod at the ball in his hand. "It's been a while since I've played with someone over the age of five."

"Me too." He smirks and tosses the ball up once more, before catching it and holding it out to me as I step outside. "I brought it for your son, but I'd be down to play anything you want, Eden. Just as long as I get to take care of you afterward."

"Is that so?" I take the ball from his hand with a smile. "Happen to have an extra ball in that truck of yours?"

He laughs as if it's a silly question. "Oh of course. Never leave home without some."

"I think I might like you even more now." I toss the ball up and catch it, feeling damn enthusiastic about playing ball with Kash. It's a beautiful night to be outside. "I'll put this inside for Alec."

Kash's eyes widen, but quickly go back to normal as if I was just imagining it.

Who knows... maybe I was. It's been a long day.

"That's a good name." He smiles. "So much better than Bob, George, or Kenneth. For a bit there, I was worried for your son's reputation."

Laughing, I push his chest, my eyes widening when it doesn't even cause him to budge. He's rock solid. Even harder than Knight. "Someone spend a lot of time at the gym or is that just from all that erotic dancing and stage humping you do?"

"Both." He flashes me the sexiest grin and reaches behind me to open the screen door. "Toss that inside so I can have fun with you."

Keeping my eyes on him, I toss the ball inside and watch as he locks the door and closes it for me.

"Where are we going?"

He opens the door to his huge truck and boosts me up by my ass, making my heart jump from the firmness of his touch. "To play baseball, of course. And if you're lucky... to get a naked massage from me later."

His face stays serious as he leans across me to buckle my seatbelt.

"What makes you think I want a naked massage from you?"

He's still leaning across me, his minty breath hitting my lips as he speaks. "Are you saying you don't?"

He smirks when I don't respond, as if he already knew what the answer would be. "I thought so."

With that, he closes the door and hops into the driver's side, a satisfied smile on his face as he drives off.

Oddly enough, that has me smiling too.

I like Kash. I really, really do...

CHAPTER TWELVE

KASH

AS MUCH AS I TRY not to think too hard about the fact that Eden's son's name is Alec, I know without a doubt that it's the same Alec I've been spending time with at my sister's house for the last six months.

It has me feeling extremely nervous, but I'm doing everything I can right now not to ruin this night for Eden and give her a reason to back out of our date.

Hannah told me when she first started babysitting that it was for a single mother, but I had so much shit going on at the gym and the club that her name slipped my mind.

I feel like a complete idiot now.

But to be honest, the idea of Alec being her son only makes me feel more connected to her, drawing me even closer to her and giving me more reason to want to get to know her.

It sure as shit doesn't scare me away. I'm not like most men who run at the idea of taking care of another man's child and knowing that it's a child I care about; there's no way in hell I'm backing down from her now.

But I know without a doubt that she'd push me away if she knew I've been spending time with her son and becoming close with him.

Eden is extremely protective of Alec, afraid he'll get hurt again. Just like his asshole father hurt him and I don't blame her.

It's easy to see how much she cares about the little guy. I don't need her telling me she's afraid to let another man in to know.

That's exactly why I'm taking it slow when it comes to learning about her son, not wanting to push it and make her feel uncomfortable.

The last thing I want to do is scare her off before I even get a chance to show her the real me.

When the time is right, I'll bring it up.

"Everything okay over there?" she asks in a soft voice.

I reach over and grab her hand, pulling it into my lap. "It's perfect since you agreed to spend time with me. Was hoping you wouldn't run from me for a third time."

I catch her smile from the corner of my eye, her face turning bright red. "Who says hanging with me is even enjoyable? I could be extremely boring and doing you a favor by running. Never know."

"Nothing about you is boring, Eden." I laugh and pull her closer to me, wanting her to feel how excited I am to be with her. "Trust me."

Her eyes widen, her face turning a deeper shade of red when she gets a feel of my hardness just an inch away from her hand. I know she can feel my pants bulging out, but I don't want to put her hand there until I know she's ready.

I'm down for having fun and showing Eden a good time, but damn if I want her to want it just as bad.

"Maybe I still have a little fun in me after all." Her voice is soft and a little breathless. "Shit, Kash. If you're trying to work me up... it's working."

"Have you been with anyone other than your ex?" I have to ask, because it seems as if she hasn't touched anyone other than him. I can tell by the sound of her breathing at just being so close to my dick.

"No," she answers, quickly. "He was my first... there hasn't been anyone since."

"Fuck Eden..." I squeeze her hand in mine, just thinking about being the only other guy to be inside of her other than the father of her child.

I have no idea why that turns me on even more, but fucking shit, I want to be her next.

I want a chance to show her how a real man takes care of a woman and gives her everything she needs and craves.

"What?" She squeezes my thigh, causing my cock to jerk. "Does that make you want me even more? Knight never did it for me."

I nod my head and grip the steering wheel with both hands, fighting so hard to control myself. "You have no idea the things that makes me want to do to you. To give to you." I place my hand over hers again and squeeze. "Especially knowing he never gave you what you deserved. A woman's needs should always come before a man's."

The rest of the drive to the baseball field is spent with me trying my damned hardest to keep some kind of restraint.

It's not easy, especially with her hand gripping my thigh, but I need to do it.

A real man knows when a woman's ready and when that time is right; I'll let go of all restraint, holding nothing back.

"Oh look, there's no one here," she says, while jumping out of my truck and shutting the door behind her.

I quickly jump out after her and reach into the bed of my truck for some balls, a bat, and a couple mitts.

"You know..." She spins around and faces me, while walking backwards. "I've gotten pretty good over the months, while playing with my son. Just a warning."

I believe it. Alec is good at playing ball. I know because I taught him.

"I guess we'll see just how good. But I should warn you..."

"Let me guess..." she says teasingly, while looking me over. "You play better in the nude."

I laugh and hand her the bat. "I do *everything* better in the nude. Again... a proven fact." I arch a brow and grab a ball, tossing it up, before catching it. "But, I was gonna say I hit pretty far. Not sure it'll be a fair game."

She keeps her eyes on me, trying her best to look intimating as she strips her light jacket off and tosses it at the fence with a cocked brow.

Her confidence is sexy right now.

"Oh yeah. Let's play a different kind of game them, Mr. Cocky. Show me how good you are when there's a little distraction."

"Okay." I laugh, dying inside to hear what she's about to come up with. "Your rules. Like I said... I'll do anything you want."

She lifts a brow and steps around the fence, up to the batter box. "Whoever hits the furthest out of three balls, gets to choose an item of clothing for the other person to take off. The first person down to their underwear, loses."

I smirk while stretching, letting her know I'm not taking it easy on her. "You do know I strip for a living, remember? Getting me out of my clothes is pretty fucking easy."

"Yes. But a challenge is sort of fun... don't you agree?" She's the one looking cocky now, as if she expects she won't have to take much off.

"More than you know." I undo the top few buttons of my shirt to give me some more wiggle room and walk over to stand at the pitcher's mound. "Game fucking on."

Placing the bat between her legs, she holds up a finger. "One sec..." I watch as she messes around behind her back as if she's either loosening or undoing her bra. "You're not the only one who needs a little more wiggle room," she admits with a grin.

"Hey... I don't have a problem with that. It's the only thing you're gonna have on by the time this game is through, so you might as well make sure it's comfortable. Ready?"

"I love your confidence," she says with a grin. It's cute on you." She nods and gets into a batter stance. "I'm ready."

I grin and hold a finger up. "Wait... I'm not quite ready yet." Placing the ball under my arm, I slowly undo my shirt and pull it open, making sure she gets a nice view of my chest and abs.

"You play dirty, I see." She shakes her head and puts on a serious face. "Show me what you got, big guy."

"You sure you want me to?" I lift a brow and reach down to unbutton my jeans.

"That's not what I meant!" she yells.

"Oh." I smile. "Just checking..."

I catch her gaze zone in on my chest, watching it flex as I prepare to pitch the ball.

"Hey!" I yell. "Eye on the ball."

"Just throw it," she demands, while looking up and pretending she wasn't just staring at my body. "I'm ready."

Keeping my gaze on her, I throw the ball and smile when she misses.

"That was my warm up swing," she says with a small smile. "Don't judge me just yet."

"I wasn't going to blame it on my body or anything..." I reach up and catch the ball as she tosses it back. "I swear."

"Good. Because you'd be wrong anyway." She smiles and gets back into position, clearing her throat a few times and fighting to keep her eyes off me. It has my confidence spiking.

After Eden takes all her swings, only hitting one out of three balls, I take a swing, hitting the first ball so far that we just let it go.

"I believe that means I'm the winner of round one..." I nod down at her feet. "I'll start out easy so you're not naked within the first two rounds. Lose the sandals."

Surprising me, Eden strips her shirt off with a confidence that has my cock jumping. "I'm not worried, Kash. I won't be naked within two rounds. So don't take it easy on me."

Apparently, she's going to play by her own rules, just not the ones she set for the game.

Holy fuck...

I have no doubt she's doing this as more of a distraction than anything. A way to get back at me for screwing up her first three swings.

And seeing as I can't seem to take my eyes away from her perfect breasts, it might just help her at least get my shirt the rest of the way off.

"I've mastered multitasking pretty damn well. I'll prove it in more ways than one, Eden," I say next to her ear as we pass each other to switch places.

You can tell my words have worked her up a bit, because she doesn't seem quite as confident as she prepares for the second round.

She shakes her head. "No talking... cheater."

I laugh at her calling me a cheater. "You're the one standing across from me topless, when all you had to lose were your shoes. You want to play... so I'm playing."

And apparently, my dick wants to play too, because it's standing at full attention as I take her in, standing across from me in that red, lacy bra.

"Any day now," she taunts. "Who's distracted now?"

I pitch her three easy balls to hit this time, wanting to make sure this game doesn't end too fast. I'm enjoying myself with her way too much to let this game be over soon.

I'm actually surprised when she hits the third ball far enough to just let the ball go and use a new one.

It's pretty fucking hot.

Especially the way her breasts bounced as she swung.

Shit... how can I play this off?

Fuck it. I won't.

I let myself be distracted as I take my swings, not hitting them far for shit.

Truthfully, I want out of these clothes anyway. I want us both naked, our bodies pressed together as I give up my restraint and take her.

I want to feel her warm skin against mine, our sweaty bodies rubbing together as I bury myself deep and make her forget about Knight altogether and how shitty he was to her.

I want to erase her memory with any other man, only allowing her to think about me.

Setting my gaze on hers, I pull my shirt off and toss it, before unzipping my jeans and yanking them off too.

This has her pulling her eyes away from mine to scan over my entire body.

"Your turn," I say, not giving her a chance to ask me why I took off two items of clothing instead of one.

She'll find out soon enough...

CHAPTER THIRTEEN

EDEN

I DON'T KNOW WHAT KASH is *trying* to do to me, but I can tell you what he *is* doing to me.

He's making me want him so badly, that it's making me wish I never suggested playing this game with him.

Now I want to run my hands over every hard inch of his body, feeling him beneath my fingertips.

Every time I even look in his direction or hear the deepness of his sexy voice, I have to clench my thighs and take a deep breath.

I just wanted to have fun with Kash. For us to run around and laugh and just let loose, be free. Something I haven't done in a while.

I didn't mean for it to turn into me wanting his hard body against me.

All I can think about is him kissing me, our half-naked bodies molded together as his tongue runs along my lips, tasting me.

I'm trying so hard not to picture him slamming me against this fence behind me with his body between my legs.

"Any day now..." Kash teases with that sexy little smirk of his. "If you think you can focus on the ball, that is."

I clear my throat and point the bat at him. "That's the only thing I'm focused on," I lie.

"I see." His eyes follow mine down to his package as I lose my battle and look down again. "That's not the *balls* you should be focused on, darlin'."

"I can't help it." I laugh and then quickly gather my composure. "It's the white boxer briefs. They're distracting in the dark."

"I know," he responds, cockily. "Why do you think I took my jeans off too?"

"Oh, you ass!" I hold the bat into position, feeling my pulse racing. "So now what happens if I win this round? You have nothing left to take off." I bite my bottom lip, trying to hold back my smile as I watch him tossing the ball up and down.

He grins and snaps the top of his boxer briefs. "Sure I do. If you win… I lose the briefs."

My eyes widen, not expecting that answer. "Seriously! You're going to get completely naked… out here? What if someone sees you?"

"It wouldn't be the first time I've been nude outside in public, Eden. I've done far worse things than just be *naked* in public. Trust me." He arches a brow, trying to hold back a smile. "Batter up."

He's getting under my skin and he knows it. He's good with that mouth of his, always knowing just what to say to keep my curiosity piqued.

As hard as I try to stay focused on the ball, his confession and those underwear keep pulling my attention away, causing me to hit all three balls like crap.

I toss the bat down and meet up with Kash in the middle, smiling as his hand grips my waist. "I should kick your ass for distracting me. That's not even fair."

He smiles and grabs my chin now, causing me to look up at him. "You should," he whispers against my lips. "But we both know it's making you want to kiss me instead."

With that, he releases my chin and walks away, leaving me standing here, breathing heavily.

He's right. I do want to kiss him, but I want *him* to kiss me even more.

And we both know what this next pitch will lead to… us both in our underwear, out here, alone, in the night.

The thought has my heart fluttering and my skin burning with need.

"Ready?" I watch as he hits the bat against the dirt and then gets into batter position. Holy shit, this is the hottest thing I've ever seen.

A man playing ball in his underwear.

I'm crazy for suggesting this game with Kash. I'm even crazier for thinking it wouldn't make me want him more than I already do.

Taking a deep breath, I slowly release it at the same time I release the ball.

My gaze stays locked on it flying through the air as Kash's bat smashes against it with a loud thud.

I don't even have to look to know I've lost. The look on his face says it all.

"Looks like we'll both be out here in our underwear."

Shaking my head, I undo my jeans and slowly strip them down my legs, feeling excitement course through me at the thought of being out here in just my underwear.

I've never done anything like this before.

"I still say you cheated." I walk over to him and toss my jeans at his face, right as he gets ready to speak.

I can't help but laugh as he just stands there with a surprised look on his face. "It's like that, huh?"

My breath hitches in my throat as he quickly reaches out and pulls me into his arms, our half-naked bodies molding together as he smiles down at me.

"A little distraction never hurt anyone, and I can promise you that you were just as much of a distraction to me as I was to you." He gently rubs his thumb over my bottom lip, before leaning in closer, our lips brushing together. "You've been a distraction since the moment I laid eyes on you, Eden and I've been wanting to do this more than fucking anything."

His lips crash hard against mine, his kiss overpowering and breathtaking, causing me to hold onto his neck for support.

My hands move up to dig into his thick hair, my heart racing fast against his, as his mouth claims mine, tasting and owning me.

I'm so lost in the intensity of our kiss, that I don't even realize I'm off the ground, until my back is slammed against the fence, his hard body pressed between my legs.

It feels exactly how I imagined. Exciting and extremely hot.

I moan out as he bites my bottom lip and grabs both my hands, holding them above my head, pressed against the fence.

"Hold on..." he whispers against my lips.

I grab onto the fence behind me, holding on as tightly as I can, as he lowers his hands down to grip my ass.

The way his hips move against me as he kisses me has me wrapping my legs tighter around him, desperate to feel him hard, against me.

He's so big and so stiff.

Pulling away from his kiss, I slam my head against the fence and bite my bottom lip as I feel Kash's hand running down my stomach, teasing me.

The way my body heats up with excitement once it slides down my panties surprises me. I've honestly never been this turned on in my entire life.

"Yes..." I nod my head, giving him the okay to go further. "Keep going."

"You sure?" He kisses my neck, before nibbling it. "There's a huge fucking chance that if I touch you the way I want to that we'll both end up naked in the dirt."

I swallow, my whole body reacting to his words. If Kash were any other man, I'd be pushing him away right now, but I don't want to.

I need this. I want this.

It's been too long.

"Touch me," I whisper.

As soon as the words leave my lips, Kash's fingers slide between my slick folds, causing me to gasp out.

"Oh shit, Eden." He slams me harder into the fence, his body holding me in place. "You're so damn wet."

His mouth captures mine, hard with desperation, his two fingers pushing into me at the same time.

The feel of him inside of me almost instantly sets me off, so I clench my thighs around him and yank at his hair. "It's been a while, Kash." I pull his hair harder, my body squeezing him tighter as he begins pumping in and out with a sexy little growl. "You're going to make me come..."

"That's my goal, Eden." He moves his thumb up to rub my clit as his two fingers continue to pump in and out of me. "I want to feel your pussy clench my fingers as I make you come. Show me how good it feels."

My breathing picks up, my body now feeling as if it's on fire as he picks up speed, making me feel a sensation I've never felt before.

My body is on the verge of exploding right here in Kash's strong arms and I don't feel one bit of shame or regret.

All I feel is need. A need to let him take care of me.

It's when I feel his thick cock press against my ass as he grinds his hips into me that my orgasm sweeps through me, making me scream out in pleasure as my pussy clamps around Kash's fingers.

"Kash! Oh shit... oh..." I grab onto the back of his neck and hold on tightly as I ride out the intense wave of pleasure.

A smirk takes over Kash's face as he waits for my orgasm to stop, before finally pulling his fingers out and sucking them clean with his mouth.

"Fuck... Eden." He licks his lips as if making sure to get every last drop of my taste from his mouth. "You taste fucking fantastic."

I don't know what to say, so I just bury my face into his neck and smile, while trying to catch my breath.

"I don't think this is the right kind of massage you promised me..."

He cups my face, making me look up at him. "This isn't even half of what I promised you, Eden. I want to give you so much more and I will... soon."

"Hey!"

We both look over at the sound of a male voice. "You guys having sex over there or can we play some baseball?"

"Oh shit." I cover my face and laugh, happy that we didn't end up naked in the dirt. "We should go."

"Give us a minute, man." Kash grins and sets me back down to my feet, doing his best to keep my body covered. "You get dressed first. I couldn't give a shit if they see me in my underwear."

Rushing to reach for my clothes, I cling onto Kash, trying to keep a straight face as I get dressed.

I would think that I'd be embarrassed right now, but surprisingly I'm not.

Knowing that Kash is in this with me and I'm not alone, has me smiling and feeling... free.

Once I get my clothes on, I grab his shirt and jeans and start walking to the truck, looking behind me to see him following me with a huge grin.

There's now a group of six young adults, probably close to eighteen or nineteen years old. Two of them are girls that keep whistling at Kash, showing admiration for his hot body.

Smiling, I toss his clothes into the back of the truck and hop in the passenger seat.

I laugh when Kash leaves his clothes in the back and jumps into the truck in his underwear.

"Good thing I left my keys in the truck." With that he smiles and starts the engine. "And seeing as you like my body so much, I left my clothes in the back where you put them."

"Good." I place my hand on his muscular thigh and squeeze it. "Because I more than like the view next to me right now."

I could stare at this man's body all night...

CHAPTER FOURTEEN

KASH

OH FUCK...

Eden is making it impossible at this point not to pull this truck over and fuck her on the side of the road.

After getting a feel of her tight, wet pussy and how hard it clenched as I made her come, makes me want to pleasure her even more.

I want to feel her clamp hard around my cock as I make her come undone with my body. I want her arousal coating my dick, showing me how good I make her feel.

My muscles flex as Eden moves her hand further up my leg, stopping right next to my hard-on. "Touch it, Eden. It's yours to fucking handle any way you please."

Without a word, she slides her hand where she really wants it. Where we both really want it.

"Mmm fuck..." I let out a growl when Eden's hand grabs my cock and squeezes it through the thin fabric.

The little gasp that leaves her lips tells me that she's surprised at how huge it feels in her hand. I'm used to that reaction.

"Shit, Kash..." She releases my cock and looks at it with wide eyes. "It feels even bigger than it looks. I'm a little intimidated, to be honest."

"Don't be." I release the steering wheel long enough to grab both her hands and place them on my erection. "Use both hands. I promise you can handle it."

She leans over and kisses my neck with confidence, while pulling my cock out of my boxer briefs and grabbing it with both hands.

"Holy fuck, Eden..."

I growl and grip the steering wheel tighter, as she begins stroking my thick shaft with both hands, brushing her thumbs over the head of my cock each time she reaches the top.

I honestly didn't think Eden would let things get as far as they have tonight, which only makes it that much fucking harder not to bust my load all over this truck right now.

She's about to make me lose it with one more damn stroke. I can't handle not being inside her right now.

Fuck...

A small breath escapes her as I pull my truck over on a side road and reach over to undo her seatbelt.

"I can't handle this shit, Eden."

I can see her chest quickly rise and fall as her eyes meet mine, waiting for me to make my next move. "Can't handle what?"

"Not being inside you. Not fucking making you come again. Shit... not giving you what you deserve."

Keeping my eyes on hers, I grip the side of her face and lean in, pressing my lips hard against hers.

A surprised breath escapes her the moment our lips press together, her hands reaching around to grip the back of my hair with desperation.

"Kash..." she whispers, pulling away slightly.

I grip her tighter and rub my thumb over her bottom lip with a smirk. "You want me to make you come again?" I brush my lips over hers, before growling against them. "I'm trying to take it slow for you, but I have a feeling you need me inside you just as much as I need to be."

She sucks in a quick breath right before my lips slam against hers again, my mouth claiming hers, recklessly.

She tries pulling away after a few seconds, but I bite her lip pulling her back to me. Her mouth tastes so fucking good that I'm not ready to stop yet.

Keeping my mouth on hers, I reach down and push her seat back as far as it goes, before spreading her legs and moving in between them. Her body feels so fucking good beneath mine that I can't help but to be rough, my kisses becoming harder and deeper, giving her a glimpse of how I am in the bedroom.

I'm anything but gentle when it comes to being inside a woman. From my experience, they all want it hard and deep, hitting every fucking spot and I more than deliver.

Eden has no idea the things I can do to her.

Both of my hands tangle into the back of her long hair as she moans into my mouth, before speaking. "I do want this... you... but..."

"Tell me, Eden."

"I'm not sure I'm ready," she admits. "But I want you so badly right now. All I can think about is how you'd feel inside me. I haven't wanted a man inside me for a while now but you make me want things, Kash."

I grip the seat around her, trying like hell to keep my cool and prepare to talk my dick down if it comes down to it.

"I'm ready to give you anything you want, Eden. I want you for more than just *this*. But I won't lie when I say I want to fuck you hard and fast right now and show you how a real man takes care of a woman's needs."

She looks down and moans as my cock jerks. "Holy shit..."

That's all it takes for me to know she wants this just as badly as I do.

Locking eyes with hers, I undo her jeans and slide them down her legs.

Then I slide my hands up her stomach and grip her shirt, pulling it over her head, stripping her back down to just her bra and panties once again.

When her lips part and a sexy little breath leaves her lips, I lose it and grip her thighs, bringing the head of my cock to meet her entrance.

It brushes against her warm pussy, causing her to spread her legs for me and bite her bottom lip with need.

Fuck me...

I want to do this. I want to be inside her more than anything, but as soon as her phone vibrates next to us, "*dad*" popping up on the screen, I hesitate, knowing that it's most likely Alec calling her.

If I fuck Eden on our first date, she's going to think I only want her for this reason once it's over. I can't have that shit. I can't have her thinking I don't want to be there in the future for her and her son.

"I'm sorry," I whisper into the side of her hair. "Your son..."

She leans forward with a quickness, once she finally notices her phone going off. "Oh shit!"

I instantly see the guilt take over her face as she turns the phone over and looks me in the eyes. "I should get dressed so I can call Alec back. I never miss his call before bed."

Smiling, I cup her face and press my lips against hers, letting her know I understand. "I agree and you shouldn't start now."

Reaching beside me, I grab her jeans and help her pull them back up her legs.

As she's finishing getting dressed, I run around to the back of my truck and get dressed myself, smiling as a car full of women slowly drive by, honking and whistling at me, while I stand here half-naked on the side of the road.

It's then that I look over to see Eden standing next to my truck, smiling too as I pull my jeans up. "Not sure we would've gotten much privacy here. Those women looked as if they were ready to pull over and join you until they noticed me."

I walk over and grab her waist, pulling her against me to show her I'm focused on her and her alone. "Do you want more privacy next time? I can arrange that."

She leans in and presses her forehead to mine, seeming a bit embarrassed by our situation. "Maybe... I don't know. We were two seconds away from having *sex*, Kash. I don't know what I was thinking. I was too wrapped up in you and that's not something I let happen so easily with anyone." With that she kisses my cheek and pulls away from me. "I need to call my son back before he falls asleep."

Giving her some privacy, I jump back into my truck and turn on the radio, letting the whole night replay in my head.

I never have unprotected sex, yet with her, it didn't even cross my mind to search for a condom. It was as if being with her just felt so natural. Kissing her, touching her and being inside her was all that mattered when it came down to it.

Pulling me from my thoughts, Eden hops into the truck a few minutes later with a huge smile on her face. "Alec just wanted to say goodnight and tell me how much fun he's having beating grandpa at video games. I love that kid so much."

"He sounds like a great kid."

My stomach sinks at the thought of keeping this secret from her, but I need more time to show her who I am.

We need more time before she gets scared and pushes me away.

"It's getting pretty late..." I grab her hand and pull it into my lap. "I should get you home in case Alec calls again because he wakes up."

She squeezes my hand. "Thank you."

I press her hand to my mouth and kiss it. "For what?"

"For understanding... for stopping when you saw my phone go off. Not many guys would give a shit."

"Well I do. I give a shit more than you know." I place her hand on my thigh and squeeze it, keeping my hand on hers the whole way to her house.

Pulling up in the driveway, I quickly undo my seatbelt and run over to open the door for Eden.

She smiles, grabbing my hand as I help her down to her feet. "Don't get me too used to this," she says with a laugh. "Then I'll expect it from every guy in the future."

I reach behind her and shut the truck door, before grabbing her face and speaking next to her ear. "Maybe getting you used to *me* is what I want so there won't be any other guys in the future..."

I hear the slight sound of her swallow, before she lets out a small breath. "Goodnight, Kash. Thank you for a fantastic night."

"Goodnight, Eden." I place a gentle kiss beside her lips, before watching her disappear into the house.

I have no fucking idea how I'm going to get any sleep tonight after watching her walk away, but I know without a doubt that I did the right thing by not fucking her like I wanted to.

Eden isn't like other women and I need to make sure I show her that...

CHAPTER FIFTEEN

EDEN

AFTER KASH DROPPED ME OFF last night, I spent the entire night thinking about him and how good he made me feel, not just physically but emotionally.

He made me smile and laugh harder than I have in a very long time with anyone other than my son.

Kash has a way of making me feel carefree and full of life, allowing me to let loose and just live for the moment.

I don't seem to worry about all the small things when I'm with him and I know more than ever now that I need that in my life.

I *want* that in my life.

The only thing that scares me when it comes to being around Kash is that I want him *physically* more than any man I've ever met.

When I'm with him all I can think about is him touching me. His sexy lips and hands all over my naked body, making me come undone until I'm screaming out his name.

I want to *feel* every inch of Kash. My desire for him almost got me in trouble last night and it was only the first date. I have no idea what I'll allow to happen if I see him again, yet I still *want* to see him again.

I've been awake for almost an hour now, lying in bed, thinking about him and how much I want to spend time with him again.

That says a lot.

"What am I going to do with this man? He's everything... Ugh..."

Rolling over, I smash my face into the pillow, smiling into it as I think about how hard he made me come last night.

Just the memory of him slamming me against the fence with his fingers inside me sets my entire body on fire with this desire I've never felt before.

The way he touched me was unlike anything I'd ever experienced before. It was as if he was taking the time to learn my body and find out exactly what spot would set me off and send my body into an overload of sensations.

It didn't take him long to find what he was looking for and when he found it, he mastered it, completely owning my body until it exploded around his fingers.

Rolling back over, I slide my hand down my panties, needing some kind of release, but nearly jump out of bed when the doorbell goes off.

"Holy fuck!" I throw my hands over my face and shake my head, hoping like hell it's not my father and Alec right now. With the thoughts running through my head, seeing them is the last thing I want. "Please be someone else. Please..."

Sitting up, I adjust my pajama shorts and jump out of bed, rushing into the living room to look out the window.

My heart drops to my stomach so fast that I almost feel sick when I see whose vehicle is parked outside.

My need to be quick suddenly disappears, causing me to hesitate before I undo the chain lock.

Apparently, that was the only thing keeping Knight out, because as soon as I drop the chain, he's pushing the door open with a scowl.

"Really? Since when do you lock that damn thing?"

Rolling my eyes, I make my way into the kitchen to start a pot of coffee.

Seeing *him* right now only guarantees it'll be a crap day. Nothing good ever comes out of his visits.

"Since you decided to keep letting yourself in without my permission.

Dammit, Knight... What do you want? You know Alec is at my father's."

"Some alone time with you." He grips my waist from behind, pulling my ass against his erection. His horny little moan beside my ear has my stomach twisting into knots. "Been thinking about you all morning and how good you feel wrapped around my dick, baby. It's been a while."

"Let go." I punch his hand repeatedly until he eventually lets go, allowing me to walk away. "I don't think so. Nope. Not happening."

"Why the fuck not?" he snaps.

I turn around to look at him, letting him see the hatred in my eyes. He's such an asshole. "Because we're not together anymore, that's why. What the fuck, Knight. This needs to stop."

"That shit doesn't matter, Eden. You belong to me still and we both know it."

"The fuck I do." I slam my fist down onto the counter, causing him to grin like an asshole. "I don't *belong* to you, Knight. Never fucking have, but you were too thickheaded to get that. Just leave. There's no reason for you to be here."

Keeping that stupid, asshole grin on his face, he reaches for his shirt and yanks it over his head as if that's all it'll take for me to change my mind. His eyes meet mine as he comes closer to me, reaching for my waist. "I'm so fucking horny right now, Eden."

Me too, asshole. Just not for you...

"I'm not having sex with you, Knight. What the fuck is wrong with your head?" I roll my eyes at his chest when he flexes it, thinking it'll have me falling all over him. "Put your shirt back on. It's not working." I slap his hand away when he reaches for me again.

He lets out a confused little laugh. "And what... someone else's works better for you?"

"Yes," I say matter-of-factly. "Your chest isn't the best one I've ever laid eyes on so get over yourself and leave."

He grabs for his shirt, and balls up in his fist, pissed off that I find someone else's body more attractive than his. "You talking about that asshole from the club?"

"He's not an asshole," I point out. "But you're being one, as usual. Goodbye, Knight. I don't want you here. Leave. Now."

"Fuck this shit. I have bitches on standby twenty-four seven. You're lucky I'm even here to begin with. Don't you get that? I can do so much better than you."

I laugh at his delusional comment and pour myself a big ass cup of coffee. I need it more now than ever, after dealing with this asshole. "So damn lucky," I say mockingly. "I get to deal with the biggest asshole to walk this earth at..." I look up at the clock. "Seven in the morning. How fucking lucky could I be?"

Before I know it, Knight grabs the entire coffee machine, picks it up and tosses it across the room.

I stand here, sipping on my coffee, trying to give off the impression that he has no effect on me whatsoever.

"You can leave now," I demand.

He growls out and punches the wall, standing in front of it for a few seconds, before speaking. "That little asshole of yours can expect a visit from me at the club. Don't be surprised if he never looks in your direction again. He won't want to after what I plan to do to that pretty little face of his."

This has me losing my composure. Even though I'm sure Kash could handle him, he shouldn't *have* to. "Leave him the hell alone, Knight! Get the fuck out! Now!"

I slam my coffee down next to me and point at the door when he doesn't make a move to leave. "Get. Out." Realizing that he doesn't plan on going, I give him a shove toward the door.

"Get off me, bitch." With one swing, he knocks me down to the ground, before tossing his shirt at my face. "Like I said, we'll see if this asshole still wants you once I'm through with him. I fucking doubt it so don't hold your breath."

With that, he takes off, slamming the door behind him, so hard that the walls shake.

I lay here for a few seconds, fighting to catch my breath from the hard impact of hitting the floor, before I finally sit up.

Carefully, I reach up and touch my face, wincing from the tenderness, before I scramble to my feet and lock the door again, including the chain lock.

This is the last time Knight will be allowed inside. I'm having the locks changed *today*.

This asshole has me worked up completely, feeling shaky and on edge. He's never once laid his hands on me before now. I'm so angry that I could cry, but I won't.

I've cried too many times over the years because of that piece of shit.

An overwhelming feeling to talk to Kash hits me, causing me to make my way to my bedroom and grab for my phone.

I'm not sure why but I feel like I need him right now.

Eden

Are you awake?

Ten minutes go by without a response back from Kash. With his late-night work schedule, I expected Kash to be a late sleeper, so I'm not really surprised.

Just disappointed.

I toss my phone down and run my hands over my face, in an attempt to calm down and forget about Knight.

I'm tired of feeling helpless when it comes to him. I'm tired of him disrespecting me and thinking he can walk all over me, although I know that won't change anytime soon.

I was his first and he was mine. He planted his seed in me and he'll always think he owns me because of that.

Just as I begin to calm down a bit and clean up Knight's mess, the doorbell rings again.

A whole new wave of stress hits me, causing me to feel sick to my stomach.

I can't deal with Knight again. If I see his face again today, it's going to take everything in me not to punch it.

Setting down the dustpan, I walk over to the window and look outside, praying with everything in me that I don't see Knight's car.

The sight in front of me has all my stress melting away and a small smile taking over.

I need this right now. I need *him* right now.

Looks like Kash is awake after all...

CHAPTER SIXTEEN

KASH

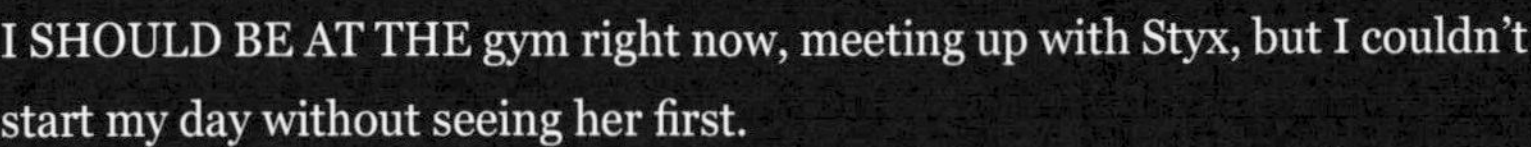

I SHOULD BE AT THE gym right now, meeting up with Styx, but I couldn't start my day without seeing her first.

Eden's been the only thing on my mind since I dropped her off last night and to be honest, I can't even remember a time when a woman has had me all twisted up, needing to see her and talk to her.

My thoughts wouldn't let me sleep for shit, so I jumped out of bed at one and hit the bags at the warehouse, needing some time to myself to relieve some tension.

Even after wearing myself out, I still didn't get but maybe two hours of sleep after that.

All I wanted to do was text Eden or just show up at her house but I didn't want to be that asshole who puts my needs first.

I almost allowed that to happen last night in my truck and I won't do that to her again. Not until I know she's ready.

She's worth too much to me and I plan to do what I can to prove that to her.

Standing on the front porch, I take a deep breath and ring the doorbell, my heart fucking racing with anticipation.

I have no idea how she's going to react to me showing up at her door unannounced, but I hope like hell she wants to see me right now just as much as I want to see her.

If it weren't for the fact that I know Alec is gone, then I wouldn't be here, but he is and I want to do something nice for her.

The door opens and my chest tightens at the sight of her, standing there in a pair of little white cotton shorts and a gray tank top shaking before me.

She's doing her best to hold it together, but there's no mistaking that someone upset her and left her pissed off and shaken up.

I don't wait for her to invite me in. Fuck that. Someone messed with her and I need to know what the hell happened.

Tensing my jaw in anger, I step inside and toss the bag of pancakes down beside me, before reaching out to cup her face in my hands. It's then that I notice her right cheek is red as if someone's just slapped her.

"What the fuck happened? Did Knight hit you?" Rage takes over as I picture him putting his hands on her. "I'll fucking kill him for hurting you, Eden. Where is he?"

She places her hands on mine in an attempt to calm me down. "He stopped by about fifteen minutes ago... he's gone." Her hands squeeze mine as I run my thumbs over her cheek to comfort her. "He said some things that really got to me and made me lose it. I don't get why I still allow him to get me so worked up but I do. He always knows exactly what to say to piss me the hell off. I shoved him to make him leave and he swung out and knocked me down."

I tense my jaw again, knowing that I'll need to take care of him later for placing his hands on her. Right now, I need to take care of her emotionally. "Tell me what that piece of shit said to upset you."

She releases a breath and kisses my arm as if it's so natural to do. I love that she feels comfortable with me right now, even with seeing how pissed off I am. "He threatened to pay you a visit so you'll stop talking to me. The idea made me lose it."

Pissed off, I close the door behind me and turn us around so that her back is now pressed against the door. "He's mistaken if he thinks there's anything he can do to keep me from you, Eden." I lean in and press my forehead against hers. "I'm already in too deep to let anything fuck that up and scare me away."

She smiles and wraps her arms around my neck, gently pressing her lips against mine, before speaking. "I care about you, Kash." The feel of her lips brushing mine as she speaks, instantly has my cock hard, even though sex is the last thing I should be thinking about right now. "Doesn't mean I expect you to stick around and fight my battles. You shouldn't have to."

"Fuck what I shouldn't have to do. What you make me want to do is what matters to me." I suck her bottom lip into my mouth, gently nibbling it, before I release it. "I'm here for as long as you want me to be. That's no fucking lie, Eden. Let your ex try to run me off. That shit ain't happening."

My words have her breathing heavily against lips as if she wasn't expecting that answer. "You're so different than I expected. It scares me."

I press my body into hers, while reaching down to grip her hips, digging my fingers in with need. "Don't let it."

Her heart is beating wildly against my chest, as her fingers dig into my shoulders, letting me know that she's just as desperate to touch me as I am her right now.

As much as it turns me on, I can't stop thinking about what that piece of shit did to her. The things he fucking said... his hands on her.

I need to get to him.

"Fuck..." I bury my face into her neck, before trailing my lips up it, stopping at her ear. "Tell me where I can find Knight."

"Kash, that's not a good idea." She releases my shoulders and grabs my hand pulling me through the house with her, until we're in her bedroom. "He's with a bunch of his friends right now. They're all assholes and won't hesitate to jump on his side."

I stand in the doorway and watch as she changes into a small white sundress, before she walks over and kisses my cheek.

Seeing her dressed like this is making it even more impossible to not want her right now, but I need to keep my head where it belongs.

And that's knocking Knight on his ass just like he did to Eden.

Growling, I cup her face and bend down so our lips are close. "I don't care if he has a fucking army with him. Please... tell me where this piece of shit is."

She lets out a defeated breath as I bury her face into my chest and rub the back of her head. "A warehouse over on Burrow Street."

I kiss the top of her head and turn around to leave. "I'll be back."

Just as I'm about to pull out of the driveway, I look over at the sound of my passenger door opening.

Eden looks up at me and jumps inside, slamming the door behind her. "I'm not letting you go there alone, Kash. The only reason this is happening is because of me. I hate that."

I close my eyes and take a few calming breaths, needing to do something before I lose it. As much as I hate this son of a bitch and want him to hurt, I can't do what I want to him with Eden around.

With a growl, I reach over and grab Eden's waist, pulling her into my lap so that she's straddling me, our faces almost touching. "I want you, Eden. I'm not gonna let some asshole and his douche friends stop me from getting you. They can't keep me away. I want you to know that."

"I do now," she whispers against my lips. "But I don't want you fighting for me."

I wrap my arms around her neck and pull her further down into me, tensing my jaw at the feel of her body against mine. "Fighting for the ones I care about is what I do. Nothing can stop me from doing that."

Her eyes meet mine and the expression in them tells me just how badly she truly needs me right now.

She needs me just as badly as I need her and this time I know she's ready. I can *feel* it.

Tangling my hands in her hair, I lean in and swipe my tongue over her lips, causing her to close her eyes and moan.

"You're so hard, Kash." She digs her nails into my shoulder and leans her head back. "You feel so good beneath me."

I move my hands down her body to grip her waist as I begin grinding my hard cock against her pussy, showing her just how hard I really am. "I'll feel even better inside you."

My words have her body shaking above me as if that's all that's needed in this moment to set her off.

Her lips meet mine, roughly, with a need that has my cock fighting to break free from my denims.

Unable to hold back anymore, I lift her body up and undo my jeans with my free hand, allowing my erection to spring free.

Keeping my mouth on hers, I reach into the glove compartment and pull out a condom, before pulling away and ripping the wrapper open with my teeth.

I keep my right hand wrapped inside Eden's hair as I struggle with rolling the condom on with my left. "Fuck, these things never fit right."

"Forget the condom, Kash," she breathes out in desperation. "I'm on the pill. Shit..." She stills for a second as if she's not sure she said the right thing. "I trust you. You've given me every reason to."

"Fuck... Eden." My heart jumps around in my chest at the idea of being inside Eden bare. And the thought that she's allowing me to, has me already wanting to come.

I trust her too. So...

Digging my teeth into her neck, I push her panties aside with my free hand and slowly push her down onto my cock, us both moaning out as I fill her.

Her wetness coats my dick, letting me know just how turned on she is by me being inside her this way.

"Holy fuck, Eden..." I grip her hips with both hands and squeeze. "You ready for me to move?"

She digs her nails into my shoulders and presses her forehead to mine, taking a few deep breaths. "Yes. I'm ready."

Taking control, I lift her up and push her back down, hard and deep, causing her to scream out and bite my shoulder. I don't move too fast though, not wanting to hurt her too much.

I do this a few more times, getting her used to my size, before I begin moving myself, meeting her body halfway with each thrust.

Our bodies are molded together, sweat coating our skin as I continue to move inside her, being sure to hit deep with each move of my hips.

"Kash..." she moans into my ear, before biting it. "I've fantasized about this moment since the day you showed up at my work. What it would feel like to have you inside of me... filling me."

"Holy fuck, Eden." I grab her shoulders and hold her down on my cock. "Seriously?"

She smiles against my ear before whispering, "Yes. I've touched myself to thoughts of you more times than I can count."

"Fuuuuck." I reach down and push the seat back as far as it can go. "Hold on, baby. It's about to get rough."

I grab the back of her head and slam my mouth against hers, biting her lip to keep her close as I begin bouncing her up and down on my dick so hard that she has to hold onto my shoulders to keep from banging her head on the roof.

Moaning out, I protect her head with my right hand, while holding her hip with my left.

"Kash..." she moans out. "I'm about to come... fuck... ohhhhh... fuck..."

"That's good, baby. Come... come all over my dick for me."

With a few more hard thrusts, I feel myself close to busting, so I slow down, wanting to make sure she comes before me.

I grip her ass with both hands and squeeze, guiding her body, slow and deep, hitting her where it counts. "I'm coming," she moans out as the same time I feel her pussy squeezing my dick.

"Oh fuck..." I feel myself about to lose it from her pussy clenching around me, but throw my head back and tense my jaw, fighting it. "You good?"

She nods her head and presses her lips against mine. "So damn good, Kash. Holy shit..."

"Okay... good. I'm gonna bend you over the seat now." I pick her up and adjust her how I want her, with her elbows on the passenger seat, her ass facing me. "Dig your nails into my leather if you have to. I'll fucking replace it."

Before she can say anything, I wrap an arm around her waist and grip her hair with my other hand, slamming into her so hard and deep that she screams out and buries her face into the seat.

I continue to fuck her hard just like I'm used to, taking her deeper than I hope that motherfucker has ever been.

I want my dick to erase any memories of that asshole ever being inside of her. I *need* it to feel so good that she'll never want anyone other than me again.

Her nails dig into my leather as she screams out my name so loudly that it has me pulling out of her and releasing my load on her ass.

"Fuuuck me..." I rip my shirt off over my head and place it on her ass, while fighting to catch my breath. "Shit, Eden. I'm sorry if I hurt you. I can't control myself when it comes to you."

"Good," she says breathlessly. "I don't want you to."

After cleaning her off and adjusting our clothing, I pull her back into my lap and kiss her. "I'm not going anywhere, Eden. I can promise you that sex isn't what I want from you. I want *you.*"

"I know," she says softly. "If I didn't then what just happened wouldn't have. I need to be careful for my son, but I feel like I can trust you. Please don't let me down."

I kiss the top of her head, before running my hands through her sweaty hair. "I won't."

At least I hope I won't. I still haven't told her about Alec yet, but now isn't the time. Plus, I have no idea where to start.

"I should probably clean up and pick Alec up. It's my only day off this week and I promised him we'd do lots of fun activities." She runs her hands over my facial hair and smiles up at me. "I wish I could spend more time with you today, I really do, but you understand that I can't have you around my son right now, right? It's just too soon."

I smile and lean my forehead against hers. "Yeah. I wish we could spend more time together too, but we have later tonight. I'll come see you after Alec is sleeping. Is that okay?"

"I'd love that." She wraps her arms around my neck, before gently pressing her lips against mine. "I'll text you once he falls asleep."

"I'll be waiting." I open the truck door and help her out to her feet, grabbing her face to kiss her, before she can walk away. "I'll be at the gym with my buddy Styx if you need me. Promise me that you'll call me if that asshole shows up again."

"Kash..."

"Promise me."

"I promise."

I kiss her one last time, before jumping back into my truck. "Good."

I have a feeling I'll be seeing him tonight no matter what...

CHAPTER SEVENTEEN

KASH

BY THE TIME I MEET Styx at the gym, he's looking at me as if I've just lost my mind.

"What?" I question, while tossing my bag down by his desk. "Stop giving me that look."

Lifting a brow, he tosses a stack of folders into the top drawer and leans back in his seat. "Why does it look like you're ready to knock someone's head clear off their fucking shoulders?"

Growling to myself, I run my hands down my face and shake my head. "There's just an asshole I need to take care of later. Someone who's fucking with someone I care about and pissing me the hell off."

This has Styx straightening up, looking as if he's pissed off now. "Yeah..." He cracks his neck, while looking across the desk at me. I've realized that Styx and I are a lot alike. Protective and loyal as shit. "You need me to help out with this little prick?"

I smile and stand up. "Nah. Looks like he plans to come see me tonight.

I'll handle him." I grip the top of the chair. "How's Meadow? She miss seeing me dance yet?"

Styx laughs. "She's good. And not as much as you hope, fucker. She did tell me to tell you that you need to find a girl though so we can do some double dating bullshit."

I look up at him and can't help the smile that takes over. "Maybe I already found one."

"Fuuuck. You're gonna make my ass go on a double date." He smiles and stands up, pushing his chair in. "Meadow is gonna ride my ass now until we set one up. Might as well let your girl know."

"She's got a kid." My smile widens when I think about Alec. "A five-year-old son."

"You ready for that?" he asks, putting all joking aside. "I haven't seen you serious with anyone, brother. Think you can handle having two people not to let down?"

I nod my head. "Hell yeah, I'm ready. I *want* a family to take care of, man. Fuck being a stripper. The life gets lonely and does nothing for me but pass the time. It does nothing for my ass when I'm lying in bed at night, alone, with no one to hold and take care of. I want that special someone in my life. As soon as I get the rest of the money I need scraped up, I'm buying the warehouse I've been renting out and turning it into a training gym. I'm ready for serious shit to happen, Styx. No more stripping or fighting soon."

"That's some deep shit, brother." He grabs his keys from his desk, keeping his gaze on me. "Sounds like she might be good for you then. I've never heard you talk like this. I still remember when you told our asses to stay single for the job."

"Yeah, well I was a dumbass back then. Things have changed since I've been spending time with Alec."

"That's the kid your sister babysits, right?" he asks, before tilting back his bottle of water.

I nod my head and grip the top of the chair tighter, feeling stress and worry kick in. "Yeah... he's also Eden's son." I look up and flex my jaw. "She just doesn't know I've been spending time with him yet. It's too soon to tell her."

"Well fuck..." Styx looks as if he's worried for my ass. I am too, to be honest. "That's not good, man. That shit could blow up in your face and ruin your chances with this girl."

"I know that shit," I say stiffly. "I just need to find the right time to tell her. I'll figure it out."

"Let's hope so," he says. "Come on."

"Where we going?"

"You got the keys to the warehouse with you?"

I nod my head. "I always do."

"We both know there's no way you're making it through the day without letting off some steam." He waits for me to follow him out of his office, before locking it behind him. "Think you can take my ass?"

I stop in front of my truck and smile. "Are you serious?"

"Yup. Is that cool with you?"

"You don't train like I do so don't complain if I mess up your pretty face."

He smirks and straddles his motorcycle. "Reason for my woman to baby and take care of me. Ever dated a nurse before?"

"Nope."

"Then you don't know what it's like to be treated by a naked one. Don't worry about my fucking face."

With that he takes off, speeding out of the parking lot.

This motherfucker...

I jump into my truck and pull out a cigarette, lighting it.

I'm gonna need a couple of these before fighting my best friend. I should've known he'd do this shit for the simple fact he knows I need it right now.

Styx is standing by the door of the warehouse, waiting for me when I arrive a few minutes later.

He watches as I hop out of my truck and toss my cigarette down into the dirt. "Hurry up, asshole. I don't have all day."

I walk past him with a grin and unlock the door. "Don't be in such a hurry to get your ass kicked."

I hear him chuckle behind me as he follows me over to the makeshift ring. "How about we not waste time wrapping our fists and shit and get this over with."

"Seriously?" I turn to face him, watching him as he paces the ring.

"I've never wrapped my fists on the streets. I'm not about to start now just because we're in a ring." He smirks. "Let it out, motherfucker. Show me how pissed this asshole made you. Just don't forget I'm *not* him."

"Alright… you asked for it. But I'm warning you, you're not going to like it."

We circle each other around the ring a few times, stretching and cracking our bones, getting pumped up.

I can't believe I'm about to do this shit. I'll have to remember to make up for it later.

With a small smirk, I come at Styx swinging my left elbow at his jaw. It connects hard, sending him stumbling to the side.

He grins, keeping his eyes on me, making sure he has a good shot before swinging out and connecting his knee to my rib cage. The asshole is quicker than I expected.

"You get into a lot of fights as a kid or some shit?"

He flexes his chest and laughs. "More than I can count. So don't take it easy on me, asshole."

"Don't worry. I won't. Especially not now."

Coming at him, I wrap one arm around his neck and pull him to me, kneeing him in the stomach repeatedly, before releasing him and connecting my fist to his mouth.

He wants me to take this shit out on him. He wants to feel my rage right now. That's what he's going to get.

Spitting out blood, Styx stares me down, before growling out and swinging his fist to my right eye, causing me to lose my footing a little, before regaining composure.

"Who's this asshole?" he questions.

Just the thought of his name fires me up even more, causing me to swing out, connecting my fist to Styx's left side. "Knight fucking Stevens."

Styx pauses for a second. "Seriously? The fighter?" He catches me off guard, his elbow connecting to my chin.

"Yeah…"

"Why didn't you say that shit to begin with?"

"Because I hate to acknowledge the fact that he's known around here. That piece of shit already has a big head, thinking he can have whatever he wants. That shit stops now."

"Well shit…"

I turn around and grab the ropes, squeezing as tightly as I can. "He's never heard of me, but I'm going to make sure it's me he's fighting next week. He's going to feel my fucking wrath and learn that Eden is mine. Not his. I'll take care of her and *his* son. He's going to be hurting by the time I'm done with him. Trust me on that."

"I don't doubt it," Styx says from behind me. "Not one fucking bit. You really care about this Eden and her son. This is the real deal for you?"

I turn around to face Styx, letting him see the truth in my eyes. "I may have only known Eden for eight days, but yeah... what I feel inside is the real deal. The way she makes me feel when I'm around her, is the real fucking deal. I haven't wanted anything this bad in a long time, man. I'm gonna do whatever it takes to keep her and Alec in my life. I'm in too deep to walk away just because someone is threatening to fuck things up. Nah, I'm not going anywhere."

Knight is going to feel what it's like to lose everything he thinks he owns...

MY ENTIRE BODY IS COVERED with sweat, making it almost impossible to see because of it falling into my eyes with each thrust against the chair I'm currently grinding against.

These leather pants are only making me that much hotter, reminding me that I need to get to the part of my routine where these fuckers come off.

Holding onto the top of the chair, I take my other hand and slowly run it down my chest and abs, before undoing my pants and lowering them down my hips a bit.

My head is so far away from where it should be right now that it's making it nearly impossible to get through this night; through this forced act with tons of women breathing down my body, trying their damned hardest to touch me.

To get a feel of my hard body beneath their fingertips. Just that one touch that will get them through the night once they get home to their beds.

I'm a dirty temptation for them to get off to.

I've been so far off my game tonight, my moves not really up to par to my usual nights, but surprisingly none of the women seem to notice.

They just keep grabbing at me with one hand, while tossing me money with their other.

I've been too distracted to really pay attention to any of them tonight, my mind staying on Eden and our earlier conversation about Knight and his threat.

I'm not gonna lie, I've scanned the crowd numerous times tonight looking for that son of a bitch to show up, just to come up empty.

Has me worrying that maybe he's decided to show back up at Eden's place instead, knowing that I'd be here, preoccupied by a bunch of women for a while.

It's been an hour since I've been able to get to my phone and my anxiety is at an all-time high, hoping like hell that I haven't missed a call or text from her, needing me there.

"Damn, take them offffff!"

"Yeeeeees! That's so hot! Work that chair for us, Kash!"

The yells from the crowd pull me back to the moment, reminding me that I need to get my shit together and make it through this song.

I have less than three minutes left on the stage and then I'm free to go. Shouldn't be that hard to handle, but somehow it is. Every song tonight has felt like ten minutes, dragging on.

Standing up, I kick the chair over and pull a random girl onto the stage, allowing her to remove my pants for me.

She takes this as an opportunity to touch my body, running her nails down my thighs and digging them in, seductively. I don't miss the fact that she also makes sure that at least three different parts of her body brush against my cock on her way to stand back up.

It's only slightly hard, but she bites her bottom lip and growls up at me anyway, obviously turned on.

Stepping out of my pants, I grab her hair and wrap it in my hand, before turning her around and bending her over.

I'm probably being a little rougher than usual right now, but fuck, I have a lot of anger built up right now.

Doesn't matter though, she only seems to like my roughness more, popping her ass out further for me to grind on it.

I only allow her the pleasure of feeling my cock against her for a few seconds, before I walk her off the stage and into the crowd where she belongs.

That's when I look up to see Eden lost in the crowd, her eyes locked on me and the girl who is still feeling up my body while she has the chance.

She knows this is only my job, but it's still hard to miss the slight disappointment and jealousy in her eyes.

Fuck, I hate that look.

Removing the girl's hands from my body, I push my way through the crowd, toward Eden.

She just stands there and watches as multiple women reach out to touch me as I walk past them, as if they have a right to feel me up. It's hard to make out the look on her face now, but she almost looks angry and embarrassed.

Her and I both know that as soon as I get to her that every set of eyes in this room will be focused on her and what I'm about to do.

But I don't give a shit. She's my girl and I want her and everyone here to know it.

I finally reach Eden and before she can say anything or walk away, I grab her face with both hands and kiss her so damn hard that she almost falls over, but reaches out to grab me instead.

Her lips feel so fucking good right now. *This* feels so fucking good; her in my arms, everyone here watching as I show her she's mine.

I needed this moment, especially with how much I've been worrying about Eden all night. Her being here has my heart fucking jumping with joy.

"Kash..." she says while fighting to catch her breath as she looks my face over. "What happened to your face?" She looks frightened for me as she runs her fingers over my bruises. "Did Knight do this to you?"

I smile and shake my head. "Nah, this wasn't him, baby. Just a friend helping me release a little steam earlier."

Wanting her as close to me as possible, I slowly back her up against the wall, closing her in with my body. I lift both her hands above her head and run my lips up her neck, before kissing it. "So... Knight didn't show up here?"

"No," I whisper in her ear. "Remember this song?" I lift her up and wrap her legs around my waist, just like the first night we met. "I never did get to finish dancing to it for you."

There's less than a minute left of the song, but I begin grinding and dancing against her anyway, brushing my lips over hers.

Everything about this moment feels so much different than the first time. So intimate and personal as if there shouldn't be a crowd here to watch us.

She's completely relaxed this time, her body naturally moving with mine, our breathing heavy and needy as my hips move her up the wall with each slow thrust.

By the end of the song, her hands are digging into my shoulders, her legs squeezing me so tight that it almost hurts.

"Shit… I missed you today," I say against her lips. "A lot."

She smiles and moves her hands up to tangle in my hair. "Same here, Kash. I got here as soon as I could. Didn't want to wait until you got off."

I close my eyes and lower her legs down to the ground as she runs her fingertips over my face again. "I don't like seeing this. Does it hurt much?"

"No." I lean in and gently kiss her. It hurts, but I'm not gonna let her know just how much. "Can barely even feel it. Who's with Alec?"

"The babysitter. I asked her to come by for an hour as soon as he fell asleep. He exhausted himself today so I'm pretty sure he won't be waking up anytime soon."

I smile and run my hands through her hair. "Good. Still want me to come by when I get out of here?"

"I'd like that. I'll text you when I get home just to make sure he hasn't woken up."

We both look toward the stage when the next song blasts through the speakers, seeming louder than all the rest. "Fucking Colt and his hardcore rock. Scares the crowd every time it starts."

Eden laughs and stands up on her tippytoes to kiss me. "See you soon. And by the way… thanks for breakfast." She smiles, showing her appreciation.

With that she walks away, getting lost in the crowd.

I don't miss the fact that most of the women stop watching the stage to look over at her and give her dirty looks.

Makes me want to protect her, but she just stands up straight and smiles, not letting them get to her.

I wait until she's outside and away from all the dirty looks before I rush over to the bar to get my phone from Sarah.

She grins from ear to ear when she sees me. "Looks like you've found that special someone. Lucky her."

I grab my phone from her and can't help the smile that takes over. "Not as lucky as I am. Clock me out, will ya?"

"Sure thing, babe. Go get that beauty."

"I plan on it."

It takes me a bit to make my way through the crowd and to the locker room, but I quickly shower and get dressed, doing my best to hurry.

As soon as I'm pulling on a fresh pair of jeans, a text comes through from Eden letting me know it's okay to head over.

I smile like a fucking idiot in love. Something I've never done before. Especially over a simple text.

Shoving my phone into my hoodie and grabbing for my keys, I walk out of the locker room, ready to get the hell out of here.

That's when I look up to see Knight sitting up at the bar, watching me with a cocky grin.

Keeping his gaze on me, he stands up and tilts back his glass, emptying it.

Then he winks and walks away, making his way toward the door with a confidence I don't like.

Fucking son of a bitch.

Letting my anger get the best of me, I fight my way through the herd of crazy women, not giving a shit that their hands are grabbing at every one of my body parts at the moment.

The only thing that matters is where that son of a bitch is going right now.

I don't like the look he gave me one bit. It was as if he was letting me know he won.

Once I finally make it to the door, I push past Kass and look around, not finding him anywhere.

"Fuuuck." I run my hands through my wet hair and turn back to face Kass, about to lose my shit. "Where did he go?" I growl.

"If you're looking for the same asshole from before, he jumped into the passenger side of some car and sped out of here."

"Thanks, brother." I slap his chest, before rushing over to my truck and speeding out of here my damn self.

I honestly have no idea what I'll end up doing if that prick is parked outside Eden's, but I know one thing...

I'll kill him if he puts his hands on her again...

CHAPTER EIGHTEEN

EDEN

I STAND IN THE DOORWAY of Alec's room, watching him as he sleeps, looking so peaceful and comfortable.

Hannah said he didn't wake up once when I was gone and that's what I was hoping for.

The idea of him waking to me not being here makes me feel sick to my stomach.

I struggled a while with my decision to leave and check on Kash tonight, but honestly, I *needed* to see that he was okay.

After the promise Knight made, I was almost positive he'd show up like he said and cause trouble for Kash.

I never planned on being gone for longer than I had to and when I called Hannah and told her my plan was to stop by the club to see someone, she sounded more than happy to stop by for a bit.

Even though I should be happy that Knight didn't show up at the club tonight, I can't help but worry still. Knight's an asshole. He'll still do what he said. He always does.

When I hear a vehicle pull up outside, I softly close Alec's door, careful not to wake him, before walking into the living room and looking out the window.

A little black sports car is sitting across the street, so I'm assuming it must be for one of the neighbors.

It hasn't been long since I texted Kash, so I suppose it's a little too soon for him to be outside.

A few minutes later I hear another vehicle pull up, so I look out the window again, hoping it's Kash.

My heart speeds up with excitement at the sight of his truck parked out front.

With a huge smile, I unlock the door and open it, watching as he jumps out of his truck and walks up the sidewalk.

His face looks even more bruised up and swollen when he steps into the porch light. The darkness of the club hid them better.

"Hi," he says with a small smirk.

"Hi back." I smile and step out of the way, allowing him to come inside. "Just be quiet."

As soon as I close the door, I feel Kash come up behind me, his hard body pressing firmly against me. "I'll do my best."

I close my eyes and swallow, when I feel Kash's hands move down my body and grab my hips. "Your hands..."

He kisses my neck, before moving around to whisper in my ear. "What about them?"

"They feel so good." I barely get the words out, because he begins kissing his way around to the front of my neck. "And your lips... shit, Kash."

He spins me around and cups my face with both hands, brushing his thumbs over my lips. "Want me to stop?"

I shake my head and wrap my arms around his neck. "No," I whisper. "But we have to be careful. I can't have... sex. Not with Alec in the next room."

He smiles against my lips. "I'm not here to have sex with you, Eden. I'm here to spend time with you." He grabs my hand. "Come on."

He guides me over to the couch, pulling me into his lap. Then he reaches for the blanket on the back of the couch and covers us up. "I like this," I admit, while snuggling into the warmth of his strong body. "What now?"

He reaches for the remote and places it in my hand. "Pick out a movie." He kisses my neck, before smiling against it. "Now we relax as I massage you. The clean version. You know... since I'm not naked and all."

Chills run over my body as he pulls me against him and begins rubbing my shoulders and arms as I search through movies to watch.

I could seriously get used to this and it's easy to picture the three of us hanging out, watching movies and spending time together. Something Knight was never into.

"This looks good."

"I'm good with whatever," he says into my hair. "Whatever makes you happy."

I smile and kiss his arm. "It's working..."

"What's working?"

"You getting me used to you," I admit. "But I like it."

"How much?"

"A lot more than I ever expected."

He wraps his arms tighter around me, making sure I'm comfortable as the movie starts. "Good. That's what I wanted."

PANIC WASHES OVER ME WHEN I wake up in Kash's arms.

We were both so comfortable on the couch that we fell asleep during the movie.

"Kash," I whisper yell. "Wake up. We fell asleep!"

I feel Kash move beneath me, before he sits up and presses his lips against my neck. "Shit. I'm sorry. What time is it?"

I look up at the clock to see it's just past six.

Luckily Alec never wakes up this early so I begin to calm down a bit and think rationally.

"Don't apologize. I fell asleep too." I remove the blanket from Kash and straddle his lap, pressing a quick kiss to his lips. "He didn't wake up or else he'd still be in here sleeping on the floor next to us. He always does that if he wakes up to me sleeping on the couch. So we're good for a few minutes.

Long enough to say bye at least."

Kash smiles and it instantly melts my heart. It's so beautiful and sincere. "I'm glad I get to see you before work at least."

"Me too..." I lean in and press my forehead against his. "I have a feeling work won't be so bad now."

With a small growl, he grabs my hips and pushes me further down into him. His morning erection has me letting out a small moan as it grinds into me. "Work might be hell for me now. Fuck, Eden." He brushes my hair away from my neck, before kissing it. "I'm gonna need to relieve myself in the shower." I smile when he does, knowing something smartass is most likely coming next. "But I'll be sure to think about you as I'm stroking it slow and hard."

I laugh and slap his chest. "Now I'll be picturing that in my head all day at work, while I'm rubbing down dirty, sweaty men."

He moans and sets me to my feet. "Good."

"Not good!" I stand on my tippytoes and wrap my arms around his neck when he stands. "How am I supposed to focus on work when I'm turned on and thinking about you?"

"How about this..." He lifts a brow. "I'll try to come visit you. Maybe give you that massage I owe you."

"I could like that... maybe."

"Mommy!"

"Shiiiit. You've gotta go, Kash." I push my way out of Kash's arms and rush over to the hallway to poke my head around the corner. "I'll be there in a minute, baby. Just stay there! Don't get out of bed yet."

When I turn back to face Kash, he's got his hood pulled over his head and he's standing by the door with it open and ready for him to make a quick escape. "I'll see you later," he mouths. "Take care of the little guy."

I cover my face, embarrassed that I'm rushing him out like this. Like I'm some kind of teenager. "Thank you," I mouth back. "Bye."

He blows me a kiss that melts my world, before walking outside and gently closing the door behind him.

"Holy shit," I breathe out.

I stand here for a few seconds with my hand over my racing heart, before I make my way to Alec's bedroom.

"Hey, baby boy."

He smiles up at me and stretches. "Hey Mommy. Is it time to go to Hannah's yet?"

I shake my head and walk over to kiss him on the forehead. "Not quite yet, baby. It's a little early. Why don't you lay back down while Mommy takes a shower and gets ready for work, okay."

He yawns and lays back down. "Okay, I'll do that. I'll lay back down and close my eyes. Can you let me know when it's time, Mommy?"

I smile at how sweet my little boy is. This kid truly lights up my life and getting to see Kash this morning on top of it, only makes it feel like today is going to be a good day. I really need one too.

"Sure, baby boy." I rub my hand through his messy hair. "Be back soon."

When we pull up at Hannah's, she's waiting outside like usual, but this time she's smiling at me as if she knows something I don't.

She waits until I say goodbye to Alec, before turning to me and finally speaking. "So… who were you going to see at the club last night? I was too tired to ask before I took off."

My face turns red as I realize I'm about to admit I'm sort of dating one of the strippers. "His name is Kash and that's all I'm saying right now."

Her eyes grow wide and her mouth drops open in surprise. "Whoa."

"What?"

She shakes her head. "Nothing. Cool name, that's all." She lets out a small laugh. "You're going to be late again."

I look down at my watch to see that she's right. "Shit. Gotta go!

"You really need to set your watch like ten minutes ahead. I swear!" she yells to me as I rush to my Jeep.

"Good idea! Thanks again. I don't know what I'd do without you."

"No problem." She smiles and waves me off before disappearing inside.

I spent a little too much time in the shower this morning, apparently.

Guess I have Kash to thank for that…

CHAPTER NINETEEN

KASH

SHIT...

When I heard Alec's tired little voice this morning calling for Eden from his bedroom, I wanted nothing more than for him to come out and see me standing there in his house.

I wanted to see the excitement in his eyes that's always there whenever he sees me show up at my sister's house for him.

It fucking hurt that I couldn't let him know I was there. I threw on my hood as if that would somehow stop him from noticing me if he were to walk into the living room.

Truthfully, I knew Alec would know it was me no matter what. The kid has been around me far too many times to not notice this old hoodie I wear.

But I did it for Eden's sake. I knew how much it would hurt her if she found out that way. Alec rushing over to me, calling me Hunter would fuck with Eden's head, making her lose all trust for me.

That's the last thing I want to happen. I know now more than ever that

I need to have that talk with Eden and soon. If I'm not the one to tell her, it can ruin everything we've built over the last nine days.

The thought causes my chest to ache.

I care about Eden more than I've ever cared about a woman before. Some may say I'm an idiot for falling so quickly, but sometimes the fall happens so fast that you don't even know until you've already fallen.

And after falling asleep with Eden in my arms last night, getting to feel how fucking good it was to have her let go around me and allow her walls to come down, I know without a doubt that I'll never get over that feeling for as long as I live.

The way her small body melted into my arms, tangled up in me as if I was her safe haven had my heart beating, making me feel more alive than ever. I want that feeling every day.

I want to be her safety; the one she can come to when she needs comfort and protection from everything bad in this fucked up world.

I want to be that for her and Alec.

That's exactly why I set up dinner plans for tomorrow with Styx and Meadow. I want her to see what it's like to be a part of my life. I want to know what that feels like before I break the truth to her and possibly push her away.

I'm a selfish asshole for not telling her in the first place. I know that and I hate myself for it.

But when it comes to a woman like Eden, you do stupid things sometimes in fear of losing something that was probably too good for you to hold onto in the first place.

"Fuuuuck!" I run my hands through my sweaty hair and step out of my truck.

That's when I notice the same black car that was parked in front of Eden's house last night, now parked across the street.

Keeping my gaze on the sports car, I pull out a cigarette and lean against my truck, letting it known that I see them.

It's not until I'm halfway through my cigarette that the car finally pulls out of the parking lot across the street and slowly drives past me, giving me a clear view of Knight in the passenger seat.

He flexes his jaw, staring me up and down, making it pretty fucking aware that he's sizing me up.

I take one last drag off my cigarette and smirk, before flicking it toward the street, letting him know he doesn't intimidate me.

Like I told Eden, I'm not going anywhere.

He wants a fight and that's exactly what he's getting in six days. I just have one more fight to get me to that spot.

This shit is happening when we're both prepared and ready to go head to head. He just doesn't know it yet.

Pushing my hood back, I give the little car one last look before heading toward the door. From what Riley told me before, Knight isn't allowed here anymore, due to him making a huge scene once when Eden was working.

Riley had to push him out the door and make it clear he's not to step foot into the parlor again.

Good to know the son of a bitch is staying off the property at least. He's already fucking with the woman I care about. He fucks with family and he's for sure dead.

Riley immediately looks up from the computer and gives me a surprised look when I step inside. "What happened to your face?"

I shrug and walk up to the counter. "I don't know what you're talking about?" I smile when she does. "Styx happened to my face. Him being a good friend and all."

"Alriiiight."

I grab her head and kiss it, before rushing past her and down the hall.

"She has a client in ten minutes, Kash!"

"Good to know!" I yell back.

I catch her shaking her head, right before I reach Eden's room and push the door open.

Before Eden can manage to say anything about me showing up unannounced, I stalk inside and pick her up, setting her on top of the table.

With a small growl, I wrap my hand into the back of her hair and press my lips against hers, kissing her hard and deep.

My heart flutters in my chest the moment her tongue swirls around mine and she moans into my mouth.

Fuck, this woman does things to me I can't explain.

"Kash," she breathes against my lips. "I have a client soon."

I smile against her lips and run my thumbs over her cheekbones. "I know..." I press my body further into hers, making my erection known.

"Cancel it."

She digs her nails into my arms and closes her eyes, most likely fighting her need for me to take her. "I wish it was that easy, Kash."

Pushing her further onto the table, I climb above her and settle my body between her legs. I slowly run my hands up her sides, before reaching up to grab her throat.

I see the excitement in her eyes at the idea of me being rough with her and I love it. She's no longer holding back with me.

Keeping my hand on her throat, I grind my body into hers and lean in to bite her bottom lip. "Are you sure it's too late to cancel? Fuuuuck me, Eden. I want to rip your clothes off and fuck you against the wall."

She lets out another little moan, enjoying the feel of me between her legs, before she finally slaps my chest and smiles. "Dammit, Kash. You're good. Really damn good, but my client is most likely checking in right now. I can't cancel with her right in the lobby."

I growl against her lips, before kissing her one last time and stepping down off the table. "I want to do something with you tomorrow. Can I have you for a few hours?"

She smiles as I help her back down to her feet. "Depends... what do you want me for?"

I grab her waist and pull her against me, wanting to feel her close to me for as long as possible, before I have to leave her until tomorrow. "Styx hates double dates and his woman wants us all to go on one. Help me annoy him and then spend a little alone time with me after. You in?"

"Styx..." She kisses my face. "The one that messed up this handsome face of yours?"

I nod. "Yup."

"I think I'm up for annoying him." She smiles against my lips. "I'll have my father come by for a few hours. Alec's been wanting to show him his new room set up."

"Perfect." I cup her face and kiss her, causing her to moan against my lips and wrap her arms around my neck.

"Kash... you should..." I kiss her again, making it hard for her to get her words out. "Dammit... you're making this hard."

Smirking, I grab her hand and lower it down my body and down to my hard cock. "Like this?"

She nods her head and rubs me through my pants, her breathing picking up. "Mmmhmmm... exactly like this."

Locking eyes with hers, I back her against the wall and pick her up, wrapping her legs around my waist.

"Maybe it's not too late," she breathes. "Maybe they're not here yet..."

I'm just about to reach over and lock the door, when someone knocks on it, scaring the shit out of Eden.

She jumps out of my arms and quickly fixes herself, fighting to catch her breath. "Shit... Shit..."

I push down on my erection and growl under my breath, sexually frustrated. "Fuck. Looks like they're here."

We both smile as she fixes her hair and splashes a little water on her face to cool off.

"I'll text you later with a time for tomorrow." I grab the back of her head and kiss her one last time, hating the fact that I have to leave her now.

"I so hate you right now," she says against my lips.

"But you'll love me later..."

I open the door and smile when some pretty brunette looks me up and down and then shoots her attention over to Eden who is still looking hot and bothered.

"Very nice... talk about being lucky."

I can practically feel her eyes burning into my backside as I walk down the hall.

Riley immediately laughs when she notices the look of disappointment on my face. "Sorry. I held her off for as long as I could. She's annoying so I had to let her go."

"Thanks," I say sarcastically. "Still love you though."

"Love you too, punk." She stands up and fixes my hair. "When is your next fight before the big one?"

"Tomorrow night."

She pushes my shoulder. "Good luck, babe."

"I won't need it." I grin and walk outside, looking to see if Knight is anywhere around.

The asshole's lucky he's not...

CHAPTER TWENTY

EDEN

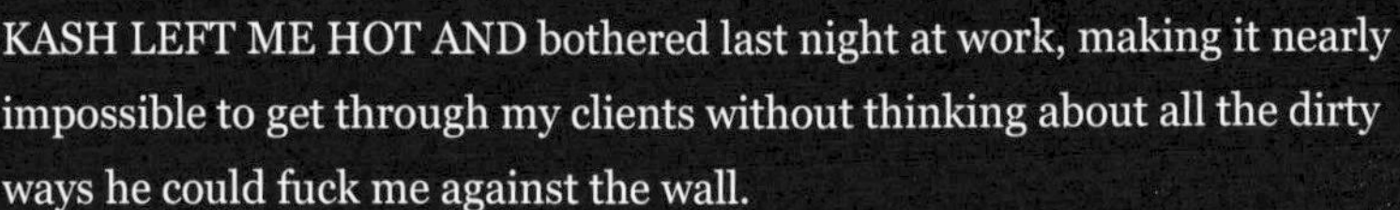

KASH LEFT ME HOT AND bothered last night at work, making it nearly impossible to get through my clients without thinking about all the dirty ways he could fuck me against the wall.

The way his hard body moved between my legs was so hot that it had me sweating every time I thought about it. I swear I even almost passed out at one point from the heat the memory brought.

I can't even count the number of times my clients had to ask me if I was alright before the night was over.

It really makes me believe he did it on purpose just to leave me thinking about him all night. He knew it would only make me crave him more and he was right.

The thought leaves me smiling as I pull out of the driveway and head toward the park. The same one Kash and I played baseball at last week. The same one we *almost* had sex at.

I also think he asked me to meet him there on purpose as well. He and I both know exactly how hot that night was and going there again is only going to bring up memories and leave me on edge with need tonight.

As soon as I told him it wasn't a good idea for him to pick me up at the house, he suggested we meet here.

I swear I could hear the smile in his voice as he spoke, setting the plans in motion.

He wants to play… so I'll play.

We'll just see who gives in first before the night is over.

I asked my father to stay over for a few hours, giving me enough time for dinner and whatever else Kash has planned for after.

As expected he was fine with it and happy to see me out doing something for myself for once. The only thing I feel guilty about is lying to Alec and telling him I was going out with a few friends.

I plan to talk to Alec about Kash soon, but I just don't know how to bring him up. I mean do I call him my guy friend? Or do I just come out and say that mommy has a new boyfriend?

I've never had to do this before and it's not easy. It's really damn hard. He may be only five but he understands that his daddy and I used to love each other very much and that's why he was born. I have no idea how he's going to feel finding out that I'm letting another man into our lives that isn't Knight.

Alec doesn't open up easily and let people in. It scares me that he might not give Kash a chance, but scares me even more that he will and things won't work out in the long run. I don't want to add any stress or heartache to my son's life, when he's already had so much over the years, due to Knight so easily abandoning him.

He's been scarred enough by a man that's supposed to be there for him.

But I feel like Kash is different. He makes me believe he's different and I want nothing more than to believe that with all my heart.

I just need more time before I make such a huge, life-changing decision. I've only known Kash for ten days. It shocks me that I'm even thinking about this so soon, but everything with Kash seems to be different.

I plan to talk to Kash about that tonight and let him know that I'm just not quite ready for them to meet yet, but soon. Maybe another week or so. I don't know for sure but I have a feeling that I'll know when the time is right.

Or maybe it already is and I'm just too scared to see it.

Kash is already parked over by the baseball field, waiting on me, in the same spot he parked the last time.

He immediately smiles and jogs over to my Jeep, opening the door for me. I can't deny how his gorgeous smile has my heart aching in the best way possible.

Without saying anything, he grabs my waist and pulls me into his arms, pressing his lips against mine with a desperation that has my heart going crazy for him.

He makes me feel needed and wanted, a feeling I'm afraid of losing. I hate being afraid, but with Kash it's a good kind of scared that's completely worth it.

We're both breathing heavily, with my arms wrapped around his neck when he pulls away to look me in the eyes. "Fuck, I've been wanting to do that all day." He tangles his hands into the back of my hair and kisses me again, this time much harder and deeper, making it almost impossible to catch my breath.

"Oh yeah..." Smiling, I reach in between us and rub my hand over his erection, before running my tongue over his ear. "I've been wanting to do *this* all day. Too bad your friends are waiting for us to have dinner."

Kash places his hand over mine and lets out a sexy little growl that has my pussy aching for him. "You trying to get me back for yesterday, baby?" He lets go of my hand and reaches around to cup my ass, practically lifting me up off the ground. "I'll fuck you on the dinner table if it comes down to it, baby. Don't test me. The whole restaurant can watch."

I feel him smile against my neck, before he bites it and backs me into his truck. Keeping his body against mine, he reaches for the door and opens it. "You ready?"

I swallow, still trying to compose myself from his words. "I'm a little nervous, but ready."

He pulls me further into his arms and tilts my chin up, until our eyes meet. "You're *my* girl. No need to be nervous, ever. Got it?"

I nod my head and smile. Hearing him call me *his* girl has my heart doing crazy things.

"Good." With that he boosts me up into the truck and shuts the door, before walking over to the other side and getting in himself.

I wait until he takes off, before leaning over and grabbing his thigh. That's when I notice a black and pink baseball mitt in the backseat.

He must notice me looking, because he smirks. "Hope you're up for a little ball after dinner. We have a game to finish."

I laugh and squeeze his thigh. "Is that right? Are we playing with or without clothes this time?"

"We'll definitely start out with clothes." He grabs my hand and places it on his dick, causing chills of excitement to run all throughout my body. It's so hot when he's in control. "I just can't promise we'll end with clothes. Besides..." he nods down at his crotch. "I'm pretty sure you want me naked. I don't blame you."

There he goes again turning me on and making me laugh at the same time. "So does that mean it'll just be the two of us playing ball? Or is there going to be four grown adults running around in their underwear like lunatics? Should I be worried? Is that part of the whole double dating scene?"

A small smile creeps up on his lips. "Definitely just the two of us." He reaches for my hand and holds it now. "It'll always just be the two of us... until it's the three of us."

My heart practically jumps out of my chest from his words.

Why does the idea of that make me feel both happy and scared?

I think I know though. I don't want to lose Kash, that's why. Because deep down inside I want it to be that way too. The three of us...

We sit in silence, my hand still in his, for the rest of the way to the restaurant.

But I can tell by the way he keeps glancing over at me with that little smile of his that he knows his words affected me in a good way.

He's just giving me this moment to prepare before meeting his friends.

"Styx and Meadow are inside already. They saved us a table so there wouldn't be a wait." He shifts the truck into park and reaches over to grab my chin. "They're like family to me. Just be yourself and I promise everything else will just fall into place and they'll fall for you just as I did."

With a small smile, I grab the back of his hair and lean in to press my lips against his. I love how he can manage to make me feel so comfortable with his words. He always seems to know the right things to say. "I'm ready."

KASH

JUST KNOWING THAT EDEN IS less than ten seconds away from meeting two of my best friends has me smiling so big that I can hardly contain it.

The thing about us boys is that we never bring a girl to meet up with our *Walk of Shame* family until we know she's the one we want to be serious with. In all the years I have known them, Eden is the first one I've invited out with us.

Fuck if that doesn't mean something big to me.

Grabbing onto her hand, I pull her against me, keeping her close as I pull the door to the restaurant open and guide her inside.

My eyes immediately seek out Styx and Meadow sitting to the far left, kissing and flirting as if they're the only two in the damn place.

"That's them." I point over to their table. "Think they'll even notice we showed up for dinner? Or should we just leave now and go play some ball?" I wink, causing her to wrap her arm around my neck and kiss my nose.

"I don't know... I guess we'll see. If they don't notice us within the first two minutes then we'll leave and have our own fun."

Her response has me laughing, which has Meadow looking over and waving for us as if we don't notice the two practically fucking on the table.

"Too late now," I mutter. "Story of my life lately. My timing is has been really shitty."

Grabbing Eden's waist, I kiss her on the cheek, before guiding her over to the table, where Styx and Meadow are both standing up now.

"Oh thank goodness." Meadow reaches for Eden's hand and pulls her in for a hug, talking next to her ear. "My date's been working on getting me to *bed* since the moment we walked in the door. Not sure how much longer I could've held him off."

"I have all night, baby. Don't think for one fucking second that I'm going to be tired anytime soon. I have a lot of stamina. Don't you forget it," Styx says with a cocky grin, before looking back at Eden. "Sorry, babe. You'll get used to us."

I wait until Meadow releases her hold on Eden, before I pull her into my arms and whisper against her ear. "You sure you don't want to just escape now? Last chance."

Eden places her hand on my abs and grins. "Nope! A little too late for that." She looks Styx's bruised face over as I pull out a chair for her to sit down. "And I thought his face was a hot mess. You boys really did a number on each other."

I laugh and take my seat next to her, watching as Meadow smiles across the table at Eden.

"Oh this one loves it. A good excuse to keep me being his nurse long after hours. He may look tough but he looks for any excuse to have me make him *feel better*."

Styx grins and nods his head at me. "Told you, brother. All good."

Everyone talks and laughs easily for the next hour as if Eden has known Styx and Meadow for just as long as I have.

Shit, that makes me so damn happy. I love seeing how easily they accept her and she accepts them.

"Oh wow." Meadow's eyes widen as she laughs. "He sounds like a fun kid that keeps you on your toes."

"He's a hyper little guy. Definitely keeps me busy, but I wouldn't have it any other way. He's the best thing to ever happen to me." Eden smiles and leans across the table a bit. "What about you and Styx? Any plans for a kid anytime soon?"

I catch a look in Styx's eyes that tells me maybe he's been thinking about it. Truth is, I could definitely see him having a family with Meadow.

Meadow smiles, before taking a drink of her water. "I don't know. Haven't really talked about it. We'll give it a little more time. I don't think either of us is in a rush."

"It's definitely better to wait until you know for a fact you're both ready. That's something I didn't do."

Growing impatient with the women chatting, while Styx gives me grumpy looks for getting him into this double date, I grab Eden's chair, pulling it closer to me as she continues her conversation with Meadow.

It's when I press my lips against her neck, that she pauses mid-sentence and closes her eyes.

Styx takes this opportunity of distraction to get to Meadow too, because when I look over, Styx is pulling Meadow into his lap, whispering things into her ear.

"I love my friends. I do…" I brush Eden's hair away from her neck, before kissing it again, making my way up to her ear. "But I only get you for a little while longer. Let's get out of here, babe."

Surprising her, I stand up, lifting her up with me, not giving a crap that everyone in the restaurant is watching us. "Kash!" She laughs and grabs onto my back as I lift her higher, so her feet are off the ground.

"Love you both. Let's do this again." I reach into my pocket and throw a pile of money onto the table, not giving a shit how much it is. "Dinner's on me."

"I'll get your number from Kash," Meadow says from Styx's lap as Eden attempts to look back at her. "I'm pretty sure we're out of here too."

Styx growls before biting her bottom lip and grinding beneath her. "We're definitely out of here, babe."

"Sounds good. It was…" I don't even give Eden the chance to finish saying bye, before I'm rushing through the restaurant and setting her down in front of my truck, desperate to get out of here and get her alone. "I didn't even get to say bye."

"My friends love you. You can say bye next time. It's dark. Perfect time to play ball." I wink and open the truck door for her, boosting her ass up and slapping it. "Let's go."

Excitement courses through me as memories of the first time we attempted to play baseball take over, causing my cock to grow hard.

Shit… I hope we get to finish this time…

CHAPTER TWENTY-ONE

EDEN

WE PULL UP AT THE park and my heart immediately begins racing with excitement when I realize we're the only ones here.

I'm not gonna lie, the thought of Kash slamming me against the fence and fucking me right here in the open has my whole body on fire.

If it weren't for the teenagers that showed up last time and interrupted us, I would've let him take me any way he wanted.

That's how excited he gets me and I've never felt this adventurous when it comes to sex. Knight always tried to get me to let him have sex with me in bathrooms at bars or in his training room before fights, but I never wanted to.

All I kept thinking about was someone possibly catching us and Knight getting a big head and gloating about it to his friends.

But with Kash... the thought of him taking me anywhere he wants—even here at a baseball field—is extremely exciting.

"You thinking about me over there?" Kash undoes my seatbelt and reaches in the back for his equipment, handing me the black and pink mitt. "If you're trying to think of ways to get me naked, all you have to do it turn on some music. That usually does the trick."

"Is that all it takes? So when you meet my dad I should make sure there's no music?" I grin and jump out of the truck, shutting the door behind me.

I can't believe I just mentioned him meeting my father, but it came out so naturally as if it's inevitable for it to happen at some point.

A few seconds later, Kash slips in behind me, wrapping his arms around my waist. "So you like me enough to keep my clothes on... fuck, talk about making me one happy guy." He kisses my neck and squeezes me tighter. "I like the idea of meeting your family. But we'll see how you feel *after* I beat you at ball."

With that he laughs and bends down to pick up his equipment, before jogging over to the fence.

I stand here for a few seconds and watch as he strips his shirt off and picks up the bat, flashing me the sexiest smile I've ever seen.

"Any day now," he teases. "Should we start out where we left off or start a new game?"

"Hmmm. Maybe a fresh one." I grab the bat out of his hand and give him a cocky grin. "Well pitcher... any day now."

He lifts a brow and begins backing up as if me teasing him only has him pumped up more and ready to go.

"I think we need to change the rules a bit," he says once he reaches the pitcher's mound.

"Okay." I position my hands on the bat and flash him a smile. "Tell me these new rules and maybe I'll agree on them."

"If you miss this ball." He tosses it up and catches it with confidence. "Then I get to kiss you..." he lowers his eyes toward my pussy. "Right there."

I can practically feel my face turn red as I imagine him between my legs, tasting me. "And what if I hit it?"

"Then I'll take you on another date." He smirks and gets into position, looking so sexy.

"I can agree to those new rules, Mr. Cocky."

He does this little thing to make me believe he's about to pitch the ball, but then stops and changes positions.

"What are you doing over there? Come on!" I yell out.

He cracks his neck and smiles. "Making sure you miss this ball. That's what."

Right when I lower the bat and laugh, he pitches the ball. Excitement and adrenaline courses through me as I quickly swing the bat out, my heart racing with anticipation.

Kash smiles when the crack of the bat hitting the ball rings out through the park.

He runs over and stops in front of me. "I was secretly hoping you'd hit it." He wraps his fist into the back of my hair and leans down to whisper in my ear. "I can always kiss you down there after the date."

I swallow and reach for the extra ball he brought. Keeping a smile on my face, I walk over to the pitcher's mound and run my fingers over the dirt on the ball. "If you miss this ball, then you have to cook me dinner."

"And if I hit it?" He raises the bat and swings out as if he knows there's no way he's missing it.

"Then you get to give me that massage you promised. And I'll let you do it in the nude so you can do it to your full ability."

He bites his bottom lip as if he's picturing it now. "I so fucking agree to these rules."

Putting on a serious face, I pitch the ball and watch as it flies across the park, Kash hitting it further than the last time we were here.

Shaking my head, I walk toward him and stop in front of him. Feeling his breath against my neck as he moves his body up against mine has me wanting him like crazy right now.

I grin and reach for the top of his jeans. "I changed my mind... I say we start out where we left off now. This game didn't count."

With a small smirk, he grabs my waist and slowly backs me against the fence. "That would be with you pinned against this fence with me about to *fuck* you so good that you'll forget any other guys exist."

"Oh yeah?" I whisper, while unbuttoning his jeans. "I definitely want to start there, Kash."

He flexes his jaw and grabs onto the fence, watching me as I lower his jeans. "You sure that's where you want to start? I've been craving to be inside you for days. It's not going to be gentle or sweet."

Wanting nothing more than for him to take me how he wants, I run my hands up his chest, before wrapping my arms around his neck. "I don't want you gentle or sweet. I want you just the way you are."

With a small growl, he pins me against the fence with his body. "Fuuuck. I hope no one interrupts us, because this time I'm not stopping."

Putting all gentleness aside, Kash bites the top of my tank top before ripping it open with his hands. Goosebumps cover my entire body as I grip onto the fence behind me and hold on as he yanks my jeans and panties down my legs.

With this look of need in his eyes I've never seen before, he bites my bottom lip and grabs my ass, lifting me up so that my legs are wrapped around his waist, just like the last time he had me pinned against this fence.

I moan into his mouth and dig my nails into his shoulders when I feel him slam into me, stopping once he fill me completely.

"I need you to tell me something," he breathes against my lips. "And I need you to mean it."

"What?" I dig my fingers deeper into his shoulders and squeeze him with my legs when he begins pumping in and out of me. "Holy... Kash... that feels... good... so damn good."

He pushes deeper inside and stops, leaning in so our mouths are brushing together. "Tell me I'm the only one you want inside of you. That there'll be no one else fucking you the way I do."

The truth is, I can't even imagine another man being inside me the way Kash is right now and feeling as good as it does. I don't want any other men. I want him. So fucking much.

"There'll be only you, Kash. I don't want anyone else. I mean it."

"Good. That's all I needed to hear."

Slamming his lips against mine, he pushes me up the fence with one hard thrust, causing me to grab onto his hair for support.

With each perfect move of his hips, excitement and need overwhelm me, causing a mix of chills and heat to run throughout my entire body.

I close my eyes and lean my head against the fence when Kash's hand moves up to brush over my throat. "It's okay," I breathe. "Don't be scared of hurting me."

"Fuck!" he growls and grabs my throat, gently squeezing it as he continues to thrust in and out of me, his thick dick slamming into me hard and deep.

I open my eyes and look around, a new kind of excitement filling me as I take in the open field around us.

Anyone could show up at any moment and all Kash is thinking about is me and his need to take me.

I find it extremely hot.

My body tenses around his and I moan out the moment I feel his thumb reach in between us to rub my clit.

"Oh fuuuckkk..." I reach behind me and hold onto the fence, breathing heavily as he continues to fuck me and rub me at the same time. "Keep going," I beg. "I'm so close."

He rubs his mouth up my neck, before biting it and thrusting into me at the same time, causing me to clamp around his dick and scream out in pleasure as an orgasm rushes through me.

I can feel him smile against me, before he moves around to kiss my lips. "Hold on for this part. Okay, baby?"

I nod my head and hold onto the fence as tightly as I can.

He grabs my waist with both hands, his fingers digging in as he pounds into me hard and fast.

So hard and fast that I feel as if I'm close to another orgasm.

Holy shit... this feels so damn good. I can't imagine anyone fucking as good as Kash.

He thrusts into me a few more times, before pushing in as deep as he can and growling against my lips as he comes.

Him filling me has another orgasm washing through me, causing me to moan against his mouth and wrap my arms around his neck for support.

As soon as I'm able to catch my breath, Kash kisses me, being gentle and careful as if he wants to take care of me now.

He holds me against the fence for a few minutes, our lips touching as we fight to catch our breath, before he lowers me to the ground.

"You okay?" he questions, while caressing my cheek.

I smile and nod my head. "More than okay, Kash. I told you not to be gentle and I meant it."

He smiles back and helps me get cleaned up, before slipping his shirt over my head and getting dressed himself. "Sorry about the shirt. I'll replace it."

I shake my head and walk into his arms as he holds them out for me.

"This one will do just fine."

He kisses the top of my head and smiles against it. "Then it's yours." He grabs my hand and walks out into the open field, before laying down and pulling me into his arms. "We have a little more time before I have something to take care of tonight. Something important to help me open my training gym. My dad used to train fighters and I always thought we'd open a gym together."

I lay my head on his chest and look up at the stars, wishing that we could stay out here like this all night. Us just talking. "Where's your father now?" I hate to ask this. Worry kicks in that I might get an answer I don't want.

"He passed away three years ago." He holds me tighter. "I'm doing this gym all on my own."

"I'm sorry, Kash. So sorry to hear that." I kiss his arm, wanting to show him I care. "What happens after you open this gym? Will you be working at the club too?"

"Nope. I'm done with the club as soon as I get the cash I need. It's the only reason I really started stripping in the first place." Kash grabs my hand and places it on his chest, holding it over his racing heart. "It feels really nice being here with you, Eden. I know you don't want to rush into anything and I don't blame you. It's not just yourself you have to worry about. But I want you to know I care about you a lot. It's not often that I let women into my life. You're the first since high school."

My heart swells up from Kash's words and I find myself smiling so big that it hurts. First I find out that he won't be staying at the club much longer and now this. I wasn't expecting either. "I care about you, too. You have no idea how much it means to me that you understand my situation and respect it. It's just that... well Alec is still so young. I don't want to confuse him if I don't have to. I need to know one hundred percent that you're in it for the long run before I even think about you two meeting. You understand, right?"

He nods his head and smiles, but I can see the worry in his eyes as if he has something he wants to tell me. "I'm in it for as long as you'll have me, Eden. I'm not going anywhere. I meant what I said. But I know it's still early. I need you to trust me. When the times comes... I have something important to tell you. Promise me you'll let me tell you when you know the time is right."

"I promise, Kash. If that's what you want." I relax into him and close my eyes, getting comfortable as he begins rubbing my head.

We lay this way for close to an hour before I feel my phone go off in my pocket.

It's getting late so I know it's Alec, calling me before he's about ready to fall asleep.

"I've gotta go," I whisper. "I want to be home before Alec goes to bed."

He stands up and helps me to my feet. "I love that about you."

I wrap my arms around his waist and just hold him for a few minutes, not wanting to leave him yet. It only seems to get harder the more we spend time together.

Looking down at me, he grabs my face and kisses me. "Call me when you get off work tomorrow?"

I nod my head and jump inside my Jeep when Kash opens the door for me. "I can do that." I smile and grab his neck, pulling him down so I can kiss him one last time. "Goodnight."

He smiles and shuts the door, before jogging over to his truck and jumping inside.

I get this sinking feeling in my stomach as I drive off, leaving Kash in the parking lot. I hate the feeling of leaving him.

Maybe it's about time I talk to Alec about him. It's too late tonight and I need a little time to clear my head and think it over before I figure out how to explain Kash to him.

I hope tomorrow is the right time and I'm not being stupid by doing this too soon.

But I know without a doubt that I have fallen for Kash. I know that because it hurts right now not being able to be with him.

I've never felt this way. Not even with Knight...

CHAPTER TWENTY-TWO

KASH

FUCK... LAST NIGHT REALLY GOT to me in a way I wasn't expecting it to.

After Eden jumped in her Jeep and took off, I sat in the parking lot for a good twenty minutes trying to get my head straight.

I thought long and hard about showing up at her doorstep and telling her the truth, hoping like hell she didn't slap me and then slam the door in my face, never wanting to see me again.

I'm in too deep with Eden to just let her walk away and forget I ever fucking existed all because I was a selfish prick, afraid of losing her over the truth.

She needs to know that I've been spending time with Alec for over six months and love the kid and care about his safety just as much as she does. I never want to see him hurt. Ever.

I was so damn close to telling her at the park, until she came out and told me she wasn't ready for Alec to know about me yet.

That messed me all up and even my fight wasn't enough to pull my head away from that shit.

My head wasn't into the fight at all last night. Not one bit.

It almost cost me my fight and then I would've been fucked on getting the money I need to buy the warehouse from Don. The big fight—that has now gotten pushed to next weekend—has a prize of ten grand so last night was important. You need to be ready at all times. Locations and dates always change when you least expect it. That's why I was even fighting last night to begin with. But I'll take what I can get.

I only need eight more grand since I've been saving for a while now, but I know it'll take years for me to save that kind of money with helping my sister out with rent and taking care of my place too.

The big fight will get me there next week instead.

But to tell you the truth, I'd give it all up for Eden anyway. But then where would that leave me?

Stripping to get by. I can't do that shit. Not if I want to be in her and Alec's lives.

That's why I need to be on top of my shit next week. There's no way in hell I'm letting Knight win. If anything, wanting to beat his ass for hurting Eden will be all the motivation I need to win.

He may have more experience and training, but I have more heart and I'll put every bit that I have into taking his ass down.

There's no way he's walking out of that ring without getting the fucking message.

Eden is mine and there's no way I'm allowing him to hurt her anymore. Her or Alec.

I just need for Eden to know that too.

And no matter how much it might hurt me in the long run, I'm letting her know tonight. Every little fucking detail. I don't matter. They do. If she leaves me to keep them both from hurting, then I'll take all the pain thrown at me.

I overslept this morning, apparently exhausted from my fight last night so it's now well into the afternoon.

It may be a little too late to bring Alec pancakes, but it's never too late to play with his new ball with him. I missed bringing him yesterday and it fucking hurt my heart. So here I am. And who knows if I'll get to see him again after this.

Without knocking, I walk into my sister's house to see Alec and Hannah coloring at the table. He looks bored and I can tell he's ready to get up move around.

I'm right, because a smile immediately takes over his little face the moment he notices me standing in the doorway. "Hunter!" He jumps up from the kitchen table and runs into my arms. "You made it today. Did you bring pancakes?"

I laugh and set him back down to his feet, feeling bad that I was too late for breakfast. "Not this time, little man. It's a little late for breakfast." I bend down and grab his shoulders. "Did you bring your new ball?"

He nods his head with excitement. "I did! It's in my backpack. I keep it in there."

"Okay good. Why don't you run and grab it and we'll play a little ball."

I stand up and lock eyes with Hannah from across the room after Alec rushes to the spare bedroom, excited to play.

"What the hell, Hunter?" she whisper yells. "You're dating Eden and you didn't tell me?" She rushes over to me and slaps my shoulder. "She doesn't know either, does she? She doesn't know you've been spending time with Alec?"

I shake my head, guilt taking over as I watch Alec drag his backpack over to the couch and begin digging through it. "Don't start, Hannah. I already know I'm a huge jerk for not telling her in the beginning. You think I wanted things to go this way? That I expected to meet Alec's mother and fall for her? It just sort of happened."

She smiles slightly at the fact that I just admitted to falling for someone. Hannah knows more than anyone how hard it's always been for me to find a girl I truly want to be with. "Well when did you find out then?"

"I found out after we were already spending time together. I didn't know how to come out and tell her without scaring her off." I flex my jaw and watch as Alec runs out the door, yelling for me to follow him. "I was going to tell her last night but then she said she wasn't ready for us to meet yet. What the hell was I supposed to say to that?"

"I don't know..." She huffs and shakes her head. "I get it. Eden is tough when it comes to Alec. I know she's been hurt by his father and I know she's overprotective of Alec. But she's going to be really pissed and hurt once you finally tell her. Maybe you shouldn't worry about her not being ready and more worried about how upset and hurt she's going to be that you waited so long."

"Fuuuck." I run my hands through my hair, knowing she's right.

"Fuck is right. You better tell her today, big brother. She may be pissed for a while, but she'll eventually forgive you. I believe that because I've seen how happy she's been lately. It's the happiest I've seen her since I began watching Alec for her."

"I hope so." I push the screen door open and join Alec in the yard, knowing that my sister will most likely join us outside if she still wants to talk.

I just hope she doesn't because I'm already feeling really fucking emotional and I've never done well with my emotions.

Alec looks over as soon as I step outside and barely gives me enough time to stop, before he tosses the ball to me.

"Whoa!" I quickly reach out and catch it, pretending as if I'm about to fall over. "You've got a strong arm there, buddy. How about you be more careful next time so you don't hurt me."

Alec laughs and reaches out to catch the ball when I toss it back. "I don't think so, Hunter. You just need to be as strong as me. Maybe drink more milk?" He shrugs. "That's what mommy makes me drink to be strong."

"I'll try, buddy. I'll try..." I toss the ball back and he jumps into the grass to catch it.

"I almost missed it! Did you see how fast I am?" He jumps to his feet and runs around in a circle yelling about how fast he is.

"Yeah, but you're so fast that I almost missed it." I begin running as if I can't keep up with him and throw my arms up. "Throw it to me, bud. Just not too hard."

He gets ready to throw it to me but stops. "What happened to your face?" He tilts his head up and looks me over, just now noticing the bruises. "Did you get beat up?"

I laugh and shake my head. "Nah, I was stronger than the other guy. So maybe he needs milk too. Now throw me the ball."

"My daddy is strong too. He beats people up." He looks sad for a moment. "It's why he's never around."

My heart fucking breaks for him as he looks down at the ground and drops the ball.

"Hey. Hey." I run over and crouch down in front of him. "I'm here if you need me to be, buddy. Your daddy might be busy but I'll never be too busy for you, alright."

He smiles and looks up at me, his eyes filled with excitement. "For really?""

"For really." I grab the ball and toss it up in the air before catching it. "Maybe I'll come around more often and we can hang out. Would you like that?"

"Yeees!" He jumps up and grabs the ball out of my hand, before running around in a circle again. "Maybe you can come to my mommy's house. She's needs a friend too and we can all play!"

My heart jumps around in my chest at the thought of us all together. "Yes... maybe." I hold my hands out. "Ready?"

"Ready!"

I lose track of time while playing ball with Alec and forget about everything else that's been going on. I'm not sure how much time has gone by, but all that seems to matter right now is the smile on his little face.

That is until I look up to see Eden watching us from the driveway with a look of pure shock on her face. I was so zoned into playing with Alec that I didn't even notice her pull up.

"Eden..."

Holy fuck this is not how I wanted her to find out.

If there was any chance of her forgiving me for not telling her in the beginning, I'm pretty sure her finding out this way has ruined it...

EDEN

I SWEAR I STOP BREATHING the moment I realize who Alec is playing with in Hannah's front yard. I'm not even sure how I missed his truck parked across the street, but I guess it's because I wasn't even thinking for one second that there'd be a possibility I'd see him here.

Not at my babysitter's house of all places.

Seeing Kash here confuses the hell out of me to the point that I find myself just standing here in a state of shock, watching them laugh and play as if they're close and have known each other for Alec's entire life.

The emotions running through me right now are so confusing that I don't know if I want to scream or cry.

I'm angry because Kash clearly knows something he didn't tell me and I'm overwhelmed with happiness at the sight of seeing the two men in my life that I care about the most spending time together.

I've imagined what it would be like when the two finally came face to face and here I am watching them interacting with so much love and happiness as if nothing else in the world matters right now.

My heart can't take the confusion. It hurts so bad.

"Eden..."

My heart drops to my stomach the moment Kash looks up, it clear on his face that he feels guilty, for me catching him here with Alec.

"What is this, Kash?" I take a step closer, trying my best to keep my composure as Alec comes running at me, excited to see me. I pick him up in my arms and force a smile, while glancing over his shoulder at Kash. "What are you doing here with my son?"

"He's my friend!" Alec says while jumping out of my arms. "Hunter. See I told you..." I watch with my teeth clenched as he rushes over and grabs Kash's hand, pulling him over to me. "Now we can all play. Mommy likes to play ball too but she's not as good as you are. We can teach her to be better!"

Kash flexes his jaw as his gaze meets mine. "I was going to tell you last night. I just didn't know how to bring it up."

"How long?" I question through tight lips, feeling as if my heart's about to beat out of my chest. "How long have you known?"

He goes to grab my hand, but I quickly pull it away, unsure of how to act right now. "Don't," I growl out. "Don't touch me."

A part of me wants to yell until he tells me the whole truth, while the other part wants to forgive Kash and believe he had good intentions for keeping this from me.

He looks hurt, but quickly hides it before Alec can catch on to the fact that we're upset with each other. He's still talking about baseball and making sound effects so I know he's not listening to our words, but his eyes catch on to emotions easily. "As soon as you told me your son's name."

I turn away and run my hands over my face, feeling like an idiot. He's been keeping it from me for longer than I thought. "Why didn't you tell me then? Dammit, Kash. I can't believe this right now."

"Alec..." Hannah appears on the front porch. She gives us both a sad look and motions for Alec to join her. "Come inside and pick out a popsicle. I'll even let you choose a flavor for me this time."

"Okay! I'll be back and then we can play." He releases both mine and Kash's hand and rushes up to the door to Hannah.

I wait until he's out of sight before turning back to Kash and losing it. "How the fuck could you do this to me, Kash? Or Hunter... whatever your name is. My son. My fucking son. You've been spending time with him behind my back, knowing that I wasn't ready for this. How could you *keep* this from me?"

His eyes look intense before he closes them and runs his hands down his face. "I was scared of losing you. That's why. Fuck!" He grips his hair in frustration, before attempting to touch me again, but I push him away. "I'm sorry." He throws his arms up, letting me know he won't touch me if I don't want him to. "I knew how much you wanted to protect Alec from getting hurt again and I felt that if you knew I'd been spending time with him for a while now that you'd freak out and push me away." He places his arms back down to his sides. "I'm sorry, Eden. You have no idea how bad it's been hurting me to keep this shit from you. The last thing I want to do is lie to you. I was a dick and there's nothing I wouldn't do to somehow make up for it."

My heart speeds up as I watch the pain and hurt take over Kash's face. I want to forgive him right now. I want to be able to come out and say it's okay, but I can't. It's not. It's far from okay. "I seriously don't know what to say right now. I feel betrayed and that's not something I get over so easily. I need some time, Kash." My voice comes out harsh. "I'm sorry. I just can't think straight right now."

He leans his head back and tightly closes it eyes. "I'm sorry." He reaches out and cups my face, closing the distance between our bodies as if he can't stay away from me right now. "I can't lose you, Eden. Look at me." He tilts my chin up until our eyes lock. "The last thing I ever want to do is hurt you. That was never my intention and it fucking hurts so bad that I did that to you."

"You do realize this is one of the worst possible things you could've lied to me about, right?" I shake my head and attempt to push his hands away, but he just cups my face again, not giving up. "Kash. You fucking have my son playing ball with you. His favorite thing to do. He only ever does that with family. It's a family thing and now he's going to think you'll always be around for him. What am I supposed to do with that? Huh? Tell me!" I yell the last part, my emotions overwhelming me.

"Believe that I will be around. That I'm not fucking going anywhere. See that I'm not like that piece of shit who left you both without so much as thinking about how it would hurt you. That's where we're different. You and Alec are what matters to me. I couldn't give a shit about myself. But I do care about not having you as mine. I do fucking care about not spending time with Alec ever again. I can't let that happen."

I close my eyes, finding it so easy to get lost in his touch. It's almost crazy the way a simple touch from him can unravel me.

"Mommy!"

I open my eyes to the sound of Alec's voice and quickly remove Kash's hands from my face, before he can begin asking me a bunch of questions that I'm not sure I'm able to answer right now.

I'm a fucking mess right now and the last thing I need is for Alec to see it.

"I've gotta go. I just..." I grab Alec's hand and begin walking him toward the Jeep, trying my hardest not to cry.

"Where are we going?" Alec asks in a confused voice, while looking back at Kash. "I thought we were going to play with my new baseball."

It hurts my heart so bad to do this to him. But I need to deal with this situation when I have a clear head.

There's three people here I could hurt if I say the wrong thing. I just can't...

"Mommy took the rest of the day off work so we could visit grandpa at work and he can show you around the houses he's building. Doesn't that sound fun?"

I'm shitty for making this up on the spot, but it's the only thing that I know will make Alec forget about playing ball and leave without too many questions.

"But I want to play with Hunter, Mommy. Can't we stay for a while longer?"

Kash puts on a smile and crouches down in front of him. He's trying his hardest to be strong but I can see the worry in his eyes. "Sorry, "lil man. I have to get going now." He rubs the top of his head, before kissing it. "Be good for Mommy and drink lots of milk so you can continue to be strong. Always be strong, okay?"

Alec nods. "Okay. I can try..."

"I'll see you later, buddy."

"With pancakes?" Alec smiles up at him, waiting for his answer.

"Always..."

The ache I feel in my chest is unlike anything else when Alec throws his arms around Kash's neck and gives him a big hug. He's squeezing him so tightly that he's choking him, but it doesn't seem to bother Kash. "Bye, Hunter!"

"See ya, buddy."

I look back at Kash one last time, because truthfully, I have no idea when I'll be ready to see him again.

"I'm here if you ever need me," he says softly. "And I mean that. Just please don't walk away."

I don't know what to say to that so I don't say anything. I just hop in my Jeep and take off, hoping with everything in me that I don't break down and cry in front of Alec.

That's exactly why I need to get him to my father so I can have a few minutes to myself and let it all out.

Kash kept the biggest secret from me that he ever could. Even his excuses might not be enough to ever fix this.

I have no idea how long it's going to take me to get over it. If I even can at all...

CHAPTER TWENTY-THREE

EDEN

IT'S BEEN TEN DAYS SINCE I discovered Kash had been spending time with Alec behind my back and I have yet to be able to face him or accept his apology.

He's sent me one text message a day every day since then to check on me, but truthfully, I just don't know what to say to him. So I haven't responded to any of them.

I thought Kash was different. The last thing I was expecting was for him to lie to me and hide something so big. Even if it was only because he was afraid of losing me. He should've gave me the chance to figure out how him knowing Alec already would've made me feel.

This is the kind of behavior I'd expect from Knight and I just don't know what to do with that. Makes me wonder what else he could be hiding from me, although my whole body is telling me he would never hurt me on purpose.

What makes the whole situation even worse is that Alec's been asking about Hunter... Kash... I don't know what to call him anymore and I hate that.

After I took some time to calm down last week, I called and talked to Hannah about the situation and she assured me that she just pieced it all together the night I asked her to watch Alec so I could go to the club for a bit. She was just as clueless as I was.

I didn't want to punish Hannah for her brother's mistake so I told her she could continue to watch Alec just as long as Kash doesn't come by and see him anymore. For now at least.

"Hey! Can my right shoulder get a little attention, please?"

I pull out of the zone I'm in and focus my attention on my last client for the day. "Yeah, sorry."

Squirting more oil into my palms, I move over to the guy's right shoulder, just now realizing that I've spent the last fifteen minutes on the other one, while I was zoning out.

This client only has five minutes left and I have a feeling, I'll never see him on my table again after this session.

The timer goes off faster than I expected, causing the elderly man to groan out his displeasure.

"Well at least one shoulder will be nice and relaxed. As if my old ass isn't off balance as it is. Thanks for that."

"Sorry. If you want to lay back down I'll add ten minutes for free. I was zoning out, I admit it, and I apologize."

"Don't have time," he groans, while sitting up and throwing his sheet off, exposing himself. "Gotta pick my wife up from BINGO. I'll get my ass chewed out if I'm late."

"What the hell... thanks for the warning." I cover my face and blindly reach for the door.

"Well I didn't get a warning that this massage would suck as much as it did but sometimes life isn't fair, little girl."

I grip the handle and squeeze it, this old fucker beginning to piss me off. I apologized and offered to make up for it. What more does he want? "Fuck you, old man. Take your wrinkly balls and shit attitude and get the hell out of my room."

This has the old man laughing behind me as if me being an ass to him amuses him.

"Something funny, old man?"

"Yeah... finding out you have more balls than most men I deal with on the daily gives this *old man* something to smile about." He pauses for a second. "Thanks for that."

I feel his hand squeeze my shoulder, before I turn around to see him fully dressed. "See you next week, girl. Leave a spot open for me."

Not sure what to say, I just move out of the way and watch with a smile as he leaves my room.

"Seriously?" I burst into laughter, not sure what the hell just happened.

I can't seem to stop laughing, which only proves that my emotions are all over the place right now.

It takes me about twenty minutes to clean up for the day, before I meet up with Riley at the counter to clock out.

"You okay, babe?"

I nod my head and smile when I see she has Haven with her. "She's getting so big!" Haven laughs and swats my face when I bend down close to her.

"Sorry, she's in that phase where she just swings her arms everywhere."

"I remember those days with Alec. No need to apologize." I grab Haven's little fingers and smile down at her, hoping that something as cute as this little booger will help me forget about Kash for a moment.

It doesn't...

"Still not talking to Kash?" Riley finally comes out and asks.

I know she's been wanting to this entire week but has been trying to spare my feelings by bringing him up. It's not hard to figure out that look of pity in her eyes every time she looks at me.

"No." I stand up and walk behind the desk to clock myself out. "I'm not ready yet. I just... I don't know how to forgive him for something so personal like that. He hurt me, Riley. Really bad."

"I know, babe." She looks away from Haven to look at me. "Look at it from his point of view," she says. "That's how you begin to forgive him and realize that he'd never do anything to hurt you on purpose. I think you'll understand more that way that he was just scared."

I look over at her with wide eyes as if I haven't thought of that myself. Maybe I did but hearing it from someone else just seems to make more sense.

"Kash has never been serious with a woman in the whole time I've known him. I've never seen him so scared to hurt or lose someone before." She stops and picks Haven up, holding her above her as she makes funny faces up at her. "Guys do crazy things when they're in love, Eden."

"In love?" My heart races at just the thought of Kash being in love with me.

"Yeah. In *love*. You don't know?" She smiles over at me. "Kash is in love. It's easy to see. Especially since he's been so miserable without you. He's barely left the house unless he has to and he's called off work at the club almost every night since you guys got into that fight last week. The couple nights he *did* work he refused to do any private dances and only made appearances in the club when it was his time on the stage. He spent the rest of the time in Cale's office talking about how much he misses you and Alec. Cale says it's been pretty painful to be around him. Last night was his last night. He's done with the club now."

There's an ache in my chest that is almost enough to make me burst into tears when I think about how miserable Kash has been.

I honestly didn't think me and Alec not being in his life would affect him the way it apparently has.

"I should go," I whisper, feeling overwhelmed again. "Knight is coming by to see Alec for a bit before his fight tonight. "I... um... I'll see you tomorrow."

I don't even give Riley a chance to speak before I rush out the door and to my Jeep, needing to be alone as quickly as possible.

Finally letting my emotions out, I bury my face in my hands and burst into tears.

Being a mom isn't always easy. I know this. Making decisions for Alec and what's best in his life is so hard.

What if Kash being in it is the best thing for him? The best thing for both of us and I've just ruined it by shutting him out?

I sit here for ten minutes... maybe twenty before I finally compose myself enough to drive myself home.

Knight text me ten minutes ago and said he was at my place with Alec so he told Hannah she could leave.

I hate that Knight is already there. The last thing I need is for him to see how torn up I am over Kash right now.

Just something else for him to rub in my face and try to make me feel horrible about myself over.

When I pull up in the driveway, Knight is sitting on the porch and Alec is playing with the baseball Kash gave me to give to Alec that first night he took me out to the baseball field.

Knight looks up from his phone with a cocky grin when he sees me step out of my Jeep. "Looks like showing my face was enough to show that asshole I wasn't going anywhere."

"What are you talking about?" My heart stops, nervous that Knight did something to Kash that I don't know about.

"I have eyes, Eden. I see that he hasn't been around in days. Do you really fucking think that I haven't been watching him, making my face known to him?"

"You're an asshole." I look across the yard and smile at Alec as he tosses the ball up and down, playing by himself. "Don't cause a scene in front of my son, Knight."

"Don't have to." He stands up and places his hands on my shoulders, rubbing them. "He's out of the picture and that's all I wanted."

Feeling disgusted, I shake his hands from my shoulders and back away from him. "It's not because of you. Your face isn't as intimidating as you think. Trust me on that." I push past him and to the house. "Now go play with your son for once and leave me the fuck alone."

I begin shaking the moment I step inside.

What the hell did he mean by making his face known? Kash never mentioned to me any problems with Knight.

But knowing Kash he was probably just looking out for me.

"Shit." I lean against the wall, everything hitting me all at once.

All Kash wanted to do was protect me from the truth until he knew I was ready. I told him repeatedly how Alec had been hurt by his father and he knew how scared I was to let another man into his life.

I can't really blame him for already knowing Alec ahead of time. He was stuck in a situation that he didn't know how to handle and I'm punishing him for that.

Is this how I should look at it?

Fuck, I don't know...

It's not even five minutes later that Knight barges his way into the house, looking pissed off. "You never gave Alec the gift I left for him?"

"Nope." I stand up and brush my hair out of my face. "You need to give it to him yourself. It's not my fault it's taken this long for you to come spend time with your son."

"Well where the fuck is it?" He rushes into the kitchen and begins pulling out drawers. "When I leave something here for my son you give it to him."

"No," I say firmly. "*You* come around enough to give it to him yourself."

He finally pulls the small box from the kitchen drawer I hid it in. "I'll give it to him myself right now, bitch."

"Fuck you, asshole," I say through clenched teeth. "Give it to him and leave. And by the way... I still need that child support money you promised. This is your last chance or I'm taking your ass to court and letting them deal with you."

He stops at the door and looks back at me. "Like I said before. You want the money you come and get it tonight after the fight."

With that he walks outside and slams the screen door shut.

I jump from the sound, my nerves all messed up right now.

This asshole must be crazy if he thinks I won't show up tonight for the money he owes me. I'm getting every last cent of the two grand he owes me for back child support.

A few minutes later, Knight speeds off and Alec comes rushing into the house, holding up a video game that he already owns.

"Daddy got me this game. I told him I already have it and he got upset." He gives me a sad look and runs into my arms. "I miss Hunter, Mommy. He always played with me and knew all the games I have. Where is Hunter? He hasn't come to Hannah's to bring me pancakes anymore. Did I do something wrong?"

My heart drops to my stomach when I hear the pain in his voice. I hate it so much and I hate that I'm the reason Kash isn't in his life right now.

I'm so scared right now, but I think now is the time I tell him the truth.

"No, baby boy. Never. Don't even think you did something wrong." I crouch down in front of him. "Mommy cares about Hunter in the same way I cared about your father. Something happened and I asked him to stay away for a bit. I'm so sorry, baby."

A tear falls from his eye that he quickly swipes away. "Are you mad at

Hunter, Mommy? Don't be mad at my friend. He's my only friend. I miss him."

His bottom lip begins to quiver so I quickly pull him into my arms, wanting nothing more than to stop the tears from coming.

Kash not being in our lives is hurting the both of us and I hate it. Alec just hasn't been the same since the first day Kash didn't show up at Hannah's when he was expecting him.

"You'll see him soon, baby." I rub the back of his head, before kissing it. "He misses you too. I promise you that. I'll fix it, baby. I'll fix it..."

Alec must be exhausted, because I feel him going slack in my arms the more I rub the back of his head.

Picking him up, I carry him to his room and place him in bed.

I wait until he's asleep, before leaving him alone in his room and shutting the door behind me.

Sitting here alone on the couch, my thoughts go back to Kash and that little ache in my chest returns and this empty feeling fills my stomach.

I find myself staring at my phone for a few minutes, before I pull up his number and type out a message. I need to fix this. To fix us.

Eden

Can we talk tonight?

I just hope I haven't waited too long...

CHAPTER TWENTY-FOUR

KASH

IT'S BEEN DAYS SINCE I'VE seen or spoken to Eden and Alec and it's fucking with me big time, sending me into a depression I haven't felt since losing my father.

I've been doing everything I can to try not to think about how bad it fucking hurts losing them, but it's the only thing that matters to me now.

The only thing that's been slightly distracting is my constant training for the fight that's happening in less than ten minutes.

I don't even give a shit about the money at this point. All I want to do is fuck Knight up for placing his hands on Eden and treating his family like they don't matter.

Family is everything and he has one that means the world to me. I'd give anything to have them as my own.

"Fuuuuck!" I swing out and punch the bag one last time, before grabbing it and fighting to catch my breath.

"You're good, man." Calvin grips my shoulder and hands me a bottle of water. "You're taking this motherfucker down. Don't even sweat it."

"I'm not," I grit out. "I'm just getting my head in the right place and trying to keep it there."

Abe laughs from the doorway. "He's going crazy right now, breaking stuff and shit. He just realized Hunter Knight is *you* because of the poster on the wall. I've never seen him so worked up about a fight before. This is fucking awesome."

I broke down and told the guys *everything* a few days ago. The whole situation. I had no choice. They could tell I was fucked up.

I grin and crack my neck, before pouring water over my head. "Good. I want him worked up for our fight. It'll feel that much better when I take everything from him."

I take a seat on the old worn out couch and close my eyes, getting lost in thought as Calvin re-wraps my hands for me.

I may have been giving Eden space, but doesn't mean for one fucking second that I've given up. That's something I'll never do when it comes to her. When it comes to *them*.

Even if it takes a year, I'm not going anywhere. I already promised her that and I don't break promises.

"Hey, bro. Your bag's vibrating. Want me to get it?"

I open my eyes and look up at Abe, who's holding my gym bag. "Nah. I can't have any kind of distractions right now. It's probably just one of the guys checking on me for the hundredth time this week. Leave it."

Abe shrugs and tosses my bag back down. "Knight may not lose fights but he *is* tonight. Don't let his experience in the ring intimidate you. Fight with your heart. Just like you taught us. From what I can tell, man, he doesn't have much of one."

I nod and jump to my feet, getting myself pumped up as we begin making our way to the main event.

There's people scattered all around this place, in the hallways, in the rooms with other fighters that fought earlier, but the main event is packed full. There's barely even room to stand without being shoulder to shoulder.

This is the craziest shit I've ever seen.

But when you fight without rules, it brings curious people in. Everyone wants to see someone get hurt and everyone wants to bet on who that person is going to be.

I know I should be nervous, because a lot is riding on me winning, but I'm not. I'm pumped up and ready to take this asshole out. He's got me all fired up. Has for a while now.

Flexing my jaw, I make my way to the middle of the room where the ring is. Adrenaline pumps through my veins the moment I look out into the crowd, listening to the cheers of excitement.

I know most of them are here for Knight because he's well-known, but I don't let that mess with my head.

I keep my gaze straight ahead, never taking it off Knight as he pushes his way through the crowd and jumps between the ropes with a cocky grin on his face.

He thinks he has me. That this is the moment he's been waiting for. He's been following me around for days, keeping an eye on me, and now I'm exactly where he wants me: In his territory.

That shit doesn't intimidate me.

My eyes meet his and lock as we both start to circle around each other, waiting for the signal to fight.

I'm so zoned in on Knight, thinking of all the ways I want to make him hurt, that I don't even hear the announcer, until the bell dings, indicating that the fight has started.

Knight cracks his neck and begins hopping in place, showing me how pumped up he is. "Unlike last time, I'm ready motherfucker. This will teach you to stay away from what is mine."

Not letting his little trash talk get to me, I swing out, hitting Knight with a right hook. He stumbles back, not expecting it and spits out blood.

I smirk as he wipes his lip off and growls at me. "Are you sure about that?"

"Fuck you!" he bites out, while swinging out with his right foot, knocking me off balance. He takes this as an opportunity to dig into my ribs, pushing me against the ropes with his body weight.

The crowd begins cheering Knight on, only giving him more confidence that he can take me, but I manage to grab the back of his head and connect my knee to his face, putting all my anger in the blow.

Blood gushes down his face, dripping down my knee, only making the blow feel that much fucking better.

I grab his hair and yank his head back so he's looking at me. "Never fucking hurt the people I care about, motherfucker. Touch her again and you're dead. That's a fucking promise." Rage courses through me as the words leave my mouth. "I keep my promises."

With that I release his hair and swing my fist up, connecting it with his chin. He falls back, but quickly makes his way back to his feet.

The way he's looking at me right now, as if he's got the right to touch Eden any way he pleases, only makes me want to rip his throat out more.

The only reason I didn't come after him the moment I found out about him hurting her, was because I knew this moment would come. There was no way I wasn't letting it be us in this ring tonight.

He takes his eyes off me and turns around to face the crowd. He runs his arm over his face and grabs the ropes, screaming out in anger. Then he comes at me, slamming me against the other set of ropes with his body weight, before punching me in the ribs a few times and then the side of my head.

He continues to take jabs at me, but he's becoming winded. I can feel it, so I push him away, allowing us both to return to the middle of the ring.

We circle around each other a few times before Knight comes at me, diving for my legs, but I grab onto his neck and plow my knee into his head twice, allowing him to fall back.

I stand above him, knowing that I can finish him here and now, but I'm not done with his ass yet. Not until I know he gets the fucking message.

Taking a slow breath, I look away from Knight and into the crowd when a group of women begin screaming my name, cheering me on. Everything around me stops the moment my eyes land on Eden pushing her way toward the ring.

Knight must notice who I'm staring at, because before I know it, he comes at me and captures me in a headlock. "Looks like she came here to see me after all," he growls into my ear, before kneeing me in the stomach and bending down to speak in my ear again. "She'll always be mine. I was her first and I'll be her last." He takes another swing to my ribs, before pushing me over.

I place my hands on the mat and get ready to push myself up, but get lost in Eden the moment our eyes meet.

Her eyes widen as if she's just now noticed me as she continues to push her way through the crowd to get closer to the ring.

Before I know it, Knight kicks me in the face, knocking me back down to my side. It stings like hell, but I push past it and jump to my feet, him not expecting me to recover so quickly.

This is it. I'm done playing this little game with him in the ring. This is the moment he learns not to fuck with what I love.

Grabbing the back of his head with both hands I push his head down and lift my knee, plowing it straight into his face between the eyes. I don't give him a chance to recover, before my fist connects with his face repeatedly, all my rage going into the blows.

As soon as I release his head, he falls back, knocked out cold.

There's a mixture of cheers and boos throughout the crowd, but the only thing I'm focused on is Eden climbing between the ropes and running toward me.

I have no idea what to expect. Especially since I never told her about my fighting, but I can't deny that seeing her is the happiest I've been in over a week.

She stops in front of me and grabs my face, before throwing her arms around my neck and kissing me long and hard as if she's missed me just as much as I've missed her.

Her heavy breathing hits my lips as she pulls away and looks my face over, taking in the blood and bruises. "Shit, Kash! Your face. Are you okay?"

"Don't worry about my face. I'm so fucking sorry, baby." I pull her into my arms and place my forehead to hers, locking my gaze on hers. Looking into her eyes is all it takes to calm me and help me breathe again. "I didn't tell you because I didn't want you to think I was anything like that piece of shit. This was my last fight. I promise. I only needed the money for my gym and—"

"I don't care," she says, cutting me off. Her arms tighten around my neck as if she's desperate to feel me next to her. "I know you're nothing like Knight. That's all I've been thinking about for days. I texted you a bit ago because I miss you. I've missed you so damn much. So has Alec. I don't care anymore. We *need* you."

My heart fucking jumps all over the place with excitement. I smile against her lips, before cupping her face and slamming my lips against hers again, desperate to show her how much I need her.

I don't even notice Knight being helped up by a couple of his guys, until he pushes one of them down and growls out his anger. "Don't fucking touch me. Get off me."

Wanting to protect Eden, I push her behind me and watch as Knight gets up to his feet.

"So that's how it's going to fucking be, Eden?"

I wait until he's steady and looking at us, before I get up in his face. "Never fucking hurt *my* family again. I plan to take care of them in ways you'll never be capable of." I grab the back of his head and growl the last part in his ear. "I'm not going *anywhere*."

Walking away from him before I lose my shit again, I pick Eden up and carry her out of the ring and through the crowd, not setting her down until we're in the hallway.

Then I slowly back her against the wall and pin her body against it with my sweaty one. I just stare into her eyes for a few minutes, letting her see how much I fucking care. "I love you, Eden. You may still be pissed at me for a while but I promise to do everything in my power to make up for it. I'll never lie to you again and that's a promise. You and Alec mean the world to me. I don't need months or years to figure that shit out. I've been a miserable asshole without you two."

She smiles against my lips and grips my face. "Do you mean that?"

I rub my hands over her head and nod. "With everything in me."

"I was scared, Kash. Scared of getting hurt and making it possible for Alec to get her too. It's my job to protect him. When I caught you two playing and having fun together I knew there was *nothing* I could do to protect him at that point if you were to walk out of his life. I freaked, unsure of what to do." She runs her fingertips over my lips, causing me to close my eyes. "I knew at that very moment that Alec and I were both in too deep with you. That we both had fallen. I love you, Kash... Hunter... I don't care. I'll call you anything you want, but I love you. I don't want to feel the pain I've felt for the last week anymore. I've realized that letting you in and risking possibly getting hurt in the long run is far better than not having you in our lives. I want to give us a chance. I want you in our lives. No more secrets."

Fuck, my heart is beating so fast that it hurts right now. I never thought words could be so powerful until this very moment.

I hear footsteps behind us, before Abe speaks. "Holy fuck that was intense!"

"Give us a few," I growl. "Or maybe thirty."

Grabbing Eden's legs, I lift her up and wrap them around my waist.

I desperately need to be alone with her right now. It's been too long since I've been able to touch her.

Making my way down the hall, I quickly push the door open to the room I've been in all day and shut it behind me.

Claiming her mouth with mine, I fall back onto the couch and pull her body up so that she's straddling me.

I growl out in surprise when she bites my lip and reaches in between us to undo my jeans. "I've missed you inside me, Kash. I want to feel you. Only you..."

Letting her pull my cock out, I wrap my hands into the back of her hair and pull back as she pulls her dress up, pushes her panties aside and slides down onto my cock.

We both moan out at the feel of me being inside of her. I hope like hell that I never have to go without this feeling ever again.

It's not just the physical pleasure, it's so much more than that. It's the way I feel inside knowing that she's mine and I'm the only one being inside of her this way.

I fucking love it.

We get lost in each other, her riding me slow and deep, our mouths barely ever separating except for me trailing kisses over her neck and whispering in her ear that she's mine.

We may be in the back of a training gym with a shit ton of people in the building, but none of that matters to us right now.

It feels like it's just the two of us.

I feel her body begin to shake above mine as if she's getting close to reaching orgasm, so I grab her hips and take control, sucking her bottom lip into my mouth as she comes undone above me.

This has me holding her down onto my cock, releasing myself as deep inside her as I can as I look into her eyes.

"Holy shit...Kash." She places her forehead to mine, while fighting to catch her breath. "That was amazing."

"I know, baby." I pull her in for a kiss and she smiles against my lips.

"Are you being cocky?"

I laugh and grab the back of her head. "No. I didn't mean it in that way. Although..."

We both just stay this way for a while, neither one of us wanting to move.

That is until one of my idiot friends knock on the door.

"Fuck me..."

"Already did," Eden says with a grin. "See I can do it too."

I grip her hips and lift her off me, kissing her one last time before standing up and grabbing something to clean her off with. "That's why we're perfect for each other."

Grunting, I open the door to Abe and Calvin pushing their way inside.

Calvin gives me a slap on the back and shakes me with excitement. "Good shit, man. I've never seen that look on Knight's face before." He turns to Eden and smiles. "You came at just the right time."

Abe comes up behind Eden and drapes an arm over her shoulder. "So I heard you're friends with Hannah..."

"Don't even think about it, dick." I grab Eden away from Abe and kiss her. "Don't put in a good word for him. He's an idiot."

Abe shrugs and hands me an envelope. "I collected this for you, man. Congratulations. You've got your own training gym now."

Eden's smile widens as she wraps her arms around my neck. "Congratulations, baby."

"Fuck yes!" I pick her up and kiss her hard. "Let's get you home to Alec."

Eden gives me a confused look when I set her down and grab her hand. "Aren't you staying to celebrate?"

I shake my head and run my thumb over her cheek. "Don't need to. You and Alec are the only ones I need to celebrate with and since Alec is sleeping..." I lean in to speak against her lips. "We can celebrate alone until you kick me out."

"Maybe I won't kick you out this time..."

Those are the exact words I needed to hear tonight after being away from Eden for this long.

"Fuck, baby. Now I'm really ready to get out of here."

Before anyone can stop us, I grab my things and escape out the back door with Eden.

The moment we pull up at her house and she drags me along behind her to her bedroom, I know it's going to be one of the best nights of my life.

Here with her is where I want to be. Nothing else matters but being with her.

From here on out, I'm doing everything in my power to prove to her she's my world. Both her and Alec...

CHAPTER TWENTY-FIVE

EDEN

I WAKE UP AND ROLL over, running my hand over the empty mattress beside me.

Even though Kash is gone, I can't help the smile that takes over at the memory of him sleeping in my bed last night.

Laying in the safety of his strong arms, resting my head on his chest, made me realize I've never really felt as safe and cared for as I do when I'm with Kash.

It was comforting knowing that when I woke up in the middle of the night that I'd feel him against me, our bodies tangled together beneath the sheets.

The fact that he kissed me every chance he got and whispered in my ear how much he loved me and missed made me feel more at ease that I followed my heart and let him back in.

I know without a doubt that Kash is the only man able to break down my walls and make me feel as much as I do.

There's a small ache in my chest that he was gone before I woke, even though I knew to expect it.

Right before we started dozing off, he set his alarm for early this morning, wanting to make sure he took off before Alec woke up.

It's probably better this way so that the first time Alec doesn't see us together is in my bed, wrapped in each other's arms.

I have so much respect for Kash for thinking of Alec over anything else. That's exactly the kind of man he needs in his life. Someone who will put him first even over us.

With a smile on my face, I sit up and grab my phone, checking to see if Kash sent me a message after he left.

Uneasiness fills my stomach when I see ten missed text messages from Knight. I'm sure he spent the night freaking out after we left him in the ring. Probably drinking and complaining to all his little friends how I chose someone else over him for once.

Doesn't bother me one bit. He deserved every bit of what he got.

Knight is no longer my problem. Come Monday I'm looking into lawyers and taking him to court for child support and letting them deal with everything else involving Knight and him being in Alec's life.

I will not allow him to hurt my son anymore. I've given him all the time in the world and he has yet to change. His time is up.

"Mommy..." Alec appears in the doorway with tired eyes and messy hair. "I had a nightmare. I don't want to go back to sleep. Can I lay with you?"

I frown and hold my arms out. "Come here, baby boy. Mommy will keep you safe." I wrap my arms around him and rub the top of his head when he crawls into the bed next to me. "Never forget that."

"Are you strong enough, Mommy? You don't have big muscles like some of the monsters." He looks up at me, waiting for an answer.

I smile and kiss his forehead. "Being strong enough for you is my whole reason for living, baby. That and loving you. I'll take down anyone who hurts you."

"Love you too, Mommy." He sits up on his knees and wraps his arms around my neck, before kissing my forehead just like I just did to him. "Is it because you drink lots of milk like me?"

I laugh and grab his face, kissing his nose. "Yes, baby. That's part of the reason I'm so strong."

Alec and I both look toward the hallway, when the front door opens and someone steps inside.

There's only three people who would be inside my house this early and without knocking. My father, Knight, or Kash, although I'm not sure Kash plans on coming back this morning without talking to me first.

It almost sounds like someone is digging through some kind of plastic bags and pulling things out.

This instantly has Alec's ears perking up, before he jumps out of bed and runs toward the hallway as if he's very familiar with the sounds he's hearing.

I quickly run after him, my heart speeding up when I notice Kash standing in the kitchen, unzipping his hoodie as if it's so natural for him to be here bringing breakfast for me and Alec.

Alec notices him at the same time and his eyes light up. I can't deny that mine do too.

"Hunter!" He rushes through the kitchen with the biggest smile on his face I've seen in a long time. "You came and brought me pancakes?"

Kash reaches out to give Alec a high five, Kash pretending to miss his hand a few times, before they finally connect hands and he pulls him in for a quick hug. "Of course, buddy." He looks over Alec's head and winks at me. "I told you I'd always bring you pancakes. I keep my promises. I'm not going anywhere."

Alec turns to me with excitement and grabs my hand, dragging me over to the table. "Mommy! Hunter came back! He brought pancakes just like at Hannah's. You were right. He's not mad at me."

Kash makes a pained face as if Alec's words just shot him straight through the heart. He quickly turns away as if he's trying to hide his emotions from us.

Shows me right here just how much he truly does love Alec.

I sniff the air, trying to lighten the mood. "I can smell them, baby. Mmmm... Mommy's starving. I'll try to save you one, but I can't make any promises."

Alec's mouth drops open as he looks up at me. "You're not going to save me any!"

Kash laughs and pulls out a kitchen chair for Alec, before setting a plate down in front of him. "I got you, little man. All the pancakes your little heart desires right here on this plate. I'll even get you more if you really want."

Alec looks over and sticks his tongue out at me. "Ha! I don't need to worry. Hunter will get me more. Eat all you want to, Mommy. Doesn't matter."

I stick my tongue back out at him, before tickling him so hard that he almost falls out of his chair with laughter.

When I turn to Kash he's smiling bigger than I've ever seen him smile before.

"Thank you for doing this." I watch as he sets a plate of pancakes in front of me. "You really didn't have to."

"I do this because I want to, Eden. I do it because it makes me happy. It's always made me happy bringing Alec pancakes and spending time with him." He tilts my chin up and kisses me. "You both make me happy and I'd do this every day if it made the two of you happy."

My heart does this little flutter and a smile takes over that I can't hide. I'm pretty sure it's bigger than the one Kash just had on his face.

This man makes me happy and from the look on Alec's face right now and the look I saw on his face last week when they placed together; he makes Alec happy too.

I can't ask for anything more than that.

KASH

SPENDING THE NIGHT WITH EDEN wrapped in my arms last night was far more fulfilling than earning the rest of the money needed for my gym.

Yeah it felt good as hell knowing I have everything I need to get it up and running after all these years, but knowing that I was the man holding Eden in my arms as she curled into my chest made my life feel so damn complete.

It hurt leaving her this morning, but I did it for Alec. I wanted him to see me the right way. The same way he's always seen me.

I knew showing up with pancakes like I do at Hannah's would be a simple way to show him I'm not going anywhere. Just like I haven't for the last six months.

Alec knew he'd see me every week and now I'm hoping he'll get to see me every day.

Once we're all done eating and just playing with Alec at the table, Eden's phone rings, so she grabs it and walks into the living room to answer it.

I sit with Alec and listen to him talk about his video games and how his daddy brought him LEGO Star Wars. Of course that dick wouldn't pay enough attention to him to know he already owned it.

"Well you know what..." I pull Alec's chair out and begin cleaning up the table. "How about sometime this week we go and get LEGO Batman. You still want that, 'lil man?"

He nods his head and begins making sound effects like he's driving the Batmobile.

"Done deal then, buddy."

When I look up, Eden is standing in the doorway watching me with a smile.

"I'm so glad you came back." She walks into the kitchen and wraps her arms around my neck. "I hated waking up to you being gone."

I run my thumb over her bottom lip, before kissing her. "I hated leaving too. I hope with everything in me that I don't have to do that again."

She shakes her head. "I don't want you to have to. I want Alec to know how much I love you."

Alec's head suddenly pops up, between us. "Mommy you said you love Hunter. Does that mean he doesn't have to stay away no more?"

Eden smiles at me, before she rubs the top of Alec's head. "Nope, baby. Kash is welcome to see us anytime he wants."

Alec makes a funny face and looks up at me. "Kash? Who's that?"

I laugh and rub his head. "It's what a lot of people call me. Pretty cool, huh? Like money."

"That is pretty cool. Can I call you that, too?"

"You bet, 'lil man. Whatever makes you happy."

Eden waits until Alec zooms out of the kitchen before she wraps her arms around my neck again and smiles. "That was my dad on the phone. I forgot that I told him that Alec and I were going to visit him today. I'm not sure what your plans are..."

"My plans are whatever you want them to be, Eden." I pull her bottom lip into my mouth, before releasing it with a smile. "I was hoping to take you and Alec to play some ball, but I'm wherever you want to be."

"Would you mind if my dad stops by the park? If not then I can just visit him later. He won't mind—"

"I'm okay with meeting your dad, Eden. Like I said..." I lean in and press my lips below her ear. "I'm not going anywhere."

She laughs as Alec runs past us and I reach out and mess up his hair. "Good. I was hoping you'd say that. And we should probably choose a different park to go to..."

I let out a small growl, thinking about that night. "We'll keep that park to ourselves. I have one in mind for us to take Alec to."

It's the one my father always took me to as a kid. Now I want to take Alec there.

Eden looks at me and stiffens up, immediately looking worried when the front door opens to someone stepping inside.

On instinct, I push Eden behind me and look around the corner to see who's inside the living room.

Rage courses through me when my gaze lands on Knight walking toward Alec, who is now sitting on the couch.

"You really think it's smart to show up here unannounced?" I step into the living room and clench my jaw, not taking my eyes off Knight. "I'm pretty sure you don't live here."

He looks surprised for a second as if he's just now noticed I was here, before his face turns to pure anger. Apparently, he missed a big ass truck parked in front of the house.

"It's none of your concern. I'm here to take my son. I don't want him around another man." He turns back to Alec and holds his arms out. "Come with Daddy. We're leaving."

"You're not taking *my* son." Eden gets ready to push past me, but I place my hand on her arm, letting her know I'll take care of her and Alec. I'll always take care of them.

"The hell you are," I growl out. "Come here, Alec."

Alec stands up and looks back and forth between myself and Knight, as if he doesn't know what to do, before finally running into my arms and burying his face in my shoulder.

"Leave, Knight," Eden says from beside us. "You have no right to be here. I won't tell you again."

"No, fuck that!" He grabs for the coffee table and flips it over, causing Alec to whine and grab onto me tighter. "You're *my* family. Not his. What the fuck, Eden. This is bullshit."

As much as I would like to rip Knight's throat out for acting this way in front of Alec, I know I need to keep my cool. Violence is the last thing I want it to come down to.

"I'm asking you not to do that in front of Alec. If I have to ask you again, then we're going to have to step outside and handle this like men."

"I'm done playing games," Eden adds, while rubbing Alec's back to comfort him. "You've got five seconds to get out of my house or I'm calling the cops."

He looks shocked from Eden's threat. As if he didn't think she'd ever get the law involved. "You know what. Fuck this shit. You can have the two of them. I don't want them anymore."

Eden releases a relieved breath the moment Knight rushes outside and speeds off in his car.

I turn to her and kiss the side of her head. "You okay, babe?"

She nods and grabs both mine and Alec's arm. "Yeah. I'm good." She kisses Alec's arm and then rubs it. "Daddy won't ever act that way around you again. I promise."

I look down at Alec when he raises his head to look up at me. "Was I strong, Kash?"

I smile and push his hair out of his eyes. "Yeah, 'lil man. You were strong." I set Alec down and turn to Eden. "Come on. We need some time to cool off. Leave the table and I'll clean it up when we get back. Okay?"

She nods her head. "Yes. I like that idea."

It took everything in me to keep my composure the way I did, but I can assure you I would've liked to kill him there on the spot.

Now I'm taking Alec and Eden out for a day they both deserve. Knight will be forgotten soon enough...

CHAPTER TWENTY-SIX

EDEN

IT SEEMS ALEC HAS ALREADY forgotten about the huge scene Knight made back at the house.

We've been at the park for an hour, the three of us playing ball as if we're a family. My heart has never been so happy. This is exactly the kind of childhood I wanted Alec to have.

Two people who care about him, playing and spending time with him, like he matters.

Alec deserves a man in his life who wants to do things with him. Seeing Kash and how he treats Alec as if he's his own son has me so happy that it hurts.

Seriously, my face hurts from smiling so much.

I'm just sitting back, taking a break from playing ball when I hear footsteps in the grass beside me.

My heart does a little happy dance when I see my father standing beside me, watching Kash and Alec with a smile on his face.

It's been a while since he's seen Alec so carefree and fun with anyone besides the two of us.

"This is the guy you've been telling me about?"

"Yes. He's so good with Alec that I seriously have no words, Dad. They've been spending time together all morning and afternoon. It makes me so undeniably happy."

"Hey." He reaches for my hand and helps me up to my feet. "Makes your old man happy, too. I knew that piece of shit father of his would never do these types of things with him. I just hope you're sure he's going to stick around and not hurt Alec."

I turn away from my dad and laugh as Kash hits the ball and then picks Alec up and begins running to first base with him.

The look on Alec's face is pure happiness.

"You see that?"

My dad nods. "Yeah, I do."

"That tells me that he's not going anywhere. I have to listen to my heart and that's exactly what I plan to do."

"You love him?"

"I do. A lot more than I ever imagined I could in such a short time. Everything I do is for Alec and I believe he needs Kash just as much as I do." I turn back to face my dad again to see him smiling at me.

"I haven't seen you this happy in a long time, baby girl. So I'm going to trust this Kash guy is going to take care of your heart better than Knight did."

Just then Kash looks up at us. He freezes for a second, before pointing up the hill to show Alec who's just joined us.

I can tell Kash is a little nervous but he waits for Alec to take off running before he walks up the hill, behind him, trying to keep his cool.

He waits for my dad to get done hugging Alec, before he reaches out to shake his hand. "It's good meeting you, sir. I admire how much you love and take care of your daughter and grandson. Reminds me a lot of how my father would be if he were still around."

My chest aches at the reminder of Kash losing his father. I lost my mother too but it was from her running off when I was young. I can't even imagine his loss.

"It's nice to meet you too, young man." My dad gives him a sympathetic look and gives his hand a pat. "I'm sorry to hear you lost your father. He sounds like he was a good man and from what I hear from my daughter... you are too."

"Thank you, sir. I do my best." He smiles. "You here to play some ball? There's always room for one more."

My dad shakes his head and releases Kash's hand finally. "Not today. Just wanted to swing by and meet the guy my daughter's been telling me about for the last couple weeks."

"Okay, I'm ready to play again!"

Kash smiles and tosses the ball up to Alec when he begins bouncing around with energy.

"Looks like I've got a kid to play with." Kash reaches out and grabs my father's shoulder. "I hope to see you again soon. For longer next time."

"Me too," my father says with a sincere smile. "Take care of my daughter and grandson until then. That's all I ask."

"That's all I want," Kash responds. He leans in and kisses me on the forehead. "We'll meet you on the field, babe."

Happiness fills me as I watch Kash run down after Alec, them stopping every so often to toss the ball back and forth to each other.

"I have to say I'm impressed with this young man." He kisses my forehead. "I should get going. My guys are a little behind so I've got to light a fire under their asses to get this job done."

"Alright, Dad." He gets ready to walk away, but I stop him. "Thank you, Dad."

"For what?"

"For always taking care of us. Just like Kash said. I know I haven't really told you how much it means to me."

"You're my baby. Always will be."

I smile and watch him walk away, before I make my way over to where Kash is pitching the ball for Alec.

"Way to go!" I scream when Alec hits the ball across the field. "Wooo!"

Alec gets a big grin on his face as he takes off running to first base.

"Your turn, Momma." Kash winks and tosses the ball up, before catching it. "I'll take it easy on you."

"Yeah!" Alec yells. "Come on, Mommy. You can hit it too."

I narrow my eyes at Kash and pick up the bat, getting into stance. "Oh I know I'll hit it. I'm not worried. Just wanted to let you boys warm up first."

"Is that it?" Kash asks with an amused smile. "Someone being Mrs. Cocky now?"

I lift a brow. "Maybe you rubbed off on me."

"I love that," Kash says with a grin.

"Hurry and throw the ball!" Alec yells. "I'm ready to win!"

"Alright." Kash winds up before pitching the ball.

Both boys look at me with wide eyes when the bat smashes the ball across the park.

This has me doing a little happy dance all the way to first base.

I know this is just the beginning, but I'm hoping with everything in me that things stay this way for as long as possible.

Kash being here makes everything feel so complete. Makes me believe that everything in this world is A-Okay.

I never thought that feeling was possible until him...

EPILOGUE

KASH

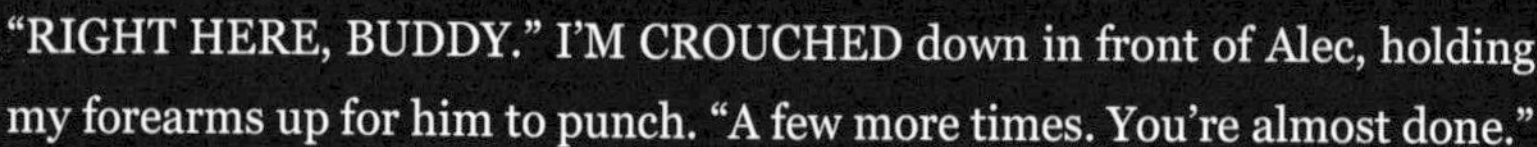

SIX MONTHS LATER . . .

"RIGHT HERE, BUDDY." I'M CROUCHED down in front of Alec, holding my forearms up for him to punch. "A few more times. You're almost done."

Alec does as told, letting out a grunt with each impact. The face he's making is of pure concentration.

"Good. Now elbows."

"I'm so strong, Kash!"

"Yeah you are, 'lil man. Pretty soon you might be able to take me."

I pull the sparring pads off my forearms and grab Alec's head, resting my forehead to his. "I'm proud of you. Love you, bud."

"Love you too, Kash." He smiles when I mess up his hair. "Watch this."

I stand up and watch with a proud smile as Alec begins punching and elbowing the air.

The sound effects only make it that much better to watch. I don't remember ever being as good with that when I was a kid and my father taught me how to fight.

I love knowing that I'm the one who taught Alec everything he knows about fighting and self-defense. Makes me feel like my father. He was the greatest man I ever knew and it's because of him I know how to be a father to Alec right now.

"You two behaving?"

We both look over at the sound of Eden's voice.

My heart still goes crazy at the sight of her even after all these months. I'm pretty positive it's only gotten more intense as time has passed.

Alec runs around in a circle and begins punching the air again. "Watch this, Mommy! Kash says I'll be able to take him soon."

A huge smile spreads over Eden's face as she watches her son go all crazy on the air like nothing in this world can hold him down. "Good job, baby boy. Just remember what you promised me, okay?"

"I know!" He stops punching the air and runs over to give Eden a hug. "I promise not to hit anyone."

She grabs his head and kisses it. "And I know you'll keep that promise. Remember how Kash taught you the importance of keeping promises?"

He nods his head. "Yes, Mommy. Kash is a good teacher. First baseball and now fighting. I'm going to be so cool!"

I laugh and walk over to take Alec's gloves off. "So cool, kid. Now why don't you run over and have a snack before we take off."

As soon as Alec runs out of the room, headed to the snack area, I grab Eden's waist and pull her against me. "Fuck, baby. I've missed you all day."

She grins and wraps her arms around my neck, pulling me down to her. "Looks like you and Alec have been having fun running this place together though. I'm sure you can't miss me that much."

I growl and pull her bottom lip into my mouth. "If Alec weren't here, I'd show you just how much. I'm sure you'd believe me then."

She places her hands to my chest and laughs when I run my short beard over her neck, teasing her. "As much as I wish we had time for this..." She tugs on my beard, pulling me in for a kiss. "The others are waiting on us. Styx has already started the grill and Meadow has sent me three texts telling us to hurry before the guys lose their shit. Apparently, they're starving."

"Fuck me," I growl. "They can start without us. They're not going to miss us if we're twenty or forty minutes late or so. I'll let you choose which room. Alec will be busy with snacks for a while. He won't even notice we're gone."

"And let him empty out the snack stash?" She shakes her head and begins backing away with a grin. "Why don't you get this place closed down and Alec and I will meet you at Cale's. Riley has already text me that she's home."

I grunt and run my hands down my sweaty face. "Alright, babe. But you're mine after this little cookout and Alec falls asleep. We're both turning our phones off and I'm dedicating all my energy into making you scream my name."

She laughs when I lift a brow and slap her ass.

"I'm serious, babe. Our friends barely give us any alone time anymore. I'm desperate to get you to myself. No fucking lie."

I grab her hand, before she can get too far away and pull her back against me. "Kash, we've gotta go!" She closes her eyes and moans when I run my tongue over her lips. "Okay," she breathes. "Our phones are going off after this cookout. I promise."

"I knew you'd say that," I tease. "You never can resist my mouth."

"That's not a lie." She kisses my neck and turns away. "See you there."

I push down on my erection and watch as she walks away, that perfect ass of hers swaying in front of me.

I only seem to want her more with each day we spend together and to be honest, I've never been happier in my life.

Everything is going fucking perfect.

I opened my training gym two months ago. I've been teaching MMA to both kids and adults and I couldn't have asked for a better family of people to have at my gym as both trainers and students.

Eden and I moved in with each other just before I opened my gym and Alec was so excited I was going to be around more that he slept at the foot of our bed for a week straight and followed me around the house every chance he got.

We've been spending all the time in the world together that it honestly feels as if he's my own son. I love him as if he is. That's for sure.

Eden took Knight to court and set up child support arrangements and that's the only involvement he has in Alec's life now.

That's pretty fucking shitty on his part but Alec doesn't seem to mind now that he's with me every day and like I said before... I'm not going anywhere.

After shutting off the lights and closing down for the night, I hop into my truck and head over to Cale's.

Of course the whole crew is already here when I walk through the back fence.

Slade, Aspen, and their newborn son Mason.

Hemy and Onyx with her swollen belly.

Cale, Riley, and baby Haven.

Stone and Sage.

Styx and Meadow.

And *my* family: Eden and Alec.

They're all sitting around the huge table, waiting for my ass to arrive.

There's so much food out that you'd think we're expecting the whole neighborhood to show up.

Slade stands up and tosses a brat at me with a grin. "Sit down so we can eat, dickhead."

"Language!" Aspen scolds him. "You're gonna have to learn to get that in check now."

Slade uncovers Mason's ears. "I covered his ears, babe. I'll take care of this little guy with my life." He kisses his baby on the forehead as if he's the most precious thing in this world. "I love this little guy more than my own life."

"You're a good father," Riley adds. "I'm so happy for the two of you. Even though you didn't tell us right away! But... I guess I forgive you."

Sage reaches over Stone to grab the corn, but he bites her arm and hands it to her instead. "I got you, babe."

"Bite me again and I'll be sure to bite you later."

Onyx laughs and rubs her belly. "You should know by now that threatening to bite any of these men will do nothing but turn them on and excite them."

"I'm always excited," Hemy says with a grin. "Bite me and it's on against every surface in the house. Pregnant or not. You're gonna feel that bite."

I take my seat between Alec and Eden and cover Alec's ears. "Hey now. There's little ears here that understand somewhat. Let's not talk about banging all around the house. Not until we're away from the table at least."

Eden leans in and kisses my neck. "Thank you, babe. I was too far away to protect him from this crazy group."

"Ouch!" Meadow squeals as Styx bites her bottom lip with a growl. "That was really hard!"

Styx rubs his thumb over her lip and then gently kisses it. "Sorry, babe. All this talk about biting has me wanting to be rough."

"Really guys?" Cale says while bouncing Haven up and down on his knee. "Can we ever get through dinner without someone being bitten or fondled? Just remember at some point these babies are growing up." He rubs the top of Alec's head. "And we have this little guy."

Alec laughs and bites into his hotdog as if he's just happy to be here with everyone.

We've been doing this once a month for the last six months and Alec loves being around everyone. He barely wants to leave once we get here so we have to wait for him to fall asleep so we can slip out without him noticing.

We're all a big family here and no one will ever let anyone hurt our family.

Alec jumps up and screams Hannah's name when her and Abe show up.

He somehow managed to weasel his way back into her life. But I'm good with it as long as he doesn't hurt her again. I'd hate to have to kick his ass after he's been working his ass off for me.

I take a bite of my steak, before leaning over to run my lips up Eden's neck, stopping below her ear. "I love you so much, baby. This—us being a family—makes me happier than I've ever been. I'm never going anywhere. You and Alec are my life. Never forget that."

She turns to me and grabs my face, pulling me in close so she can speak against my lips. "I know that, baby... Alec knows that. We love you more than life. We're a family and I wouldn't have it any other way."

Eden and Alec have made my life complete in the last six months and I promise to do everything in my power to keep them safe and protected.

I'd give my life just to keep them happy. This is what life is made of. Love, happiness, and family. And mine is right here next to me...

EDEN

MY HEART SWELLS WITH JOY when I walk into the living room to see

Alec sleeping in Kash's arms, with his little arms wrapped tightly around Kash.

The position Kash is in looks uncomfortable, but he doesn't move anyway.

"Want me to take him to his room?" I get ready to reach for Alec, but Kash shakes his head. "Are you sure? You look uncomfortable."

"I'm good," he whispers. "Come here."

With a smile, I crawl onto the couch next to them and lean into Kash when he reaches one of his arms around to hold me.

"He just fell asleep. I don't want to wake him up." He looks down at Alec when he stirs in his arms. "He had a pretty crazy night."

I laugh quietly and close my eyes. "Yeah. He always does during our family cookouts. I should thank everyone for wearing him down. He's always so quiet after we get home."

Kash leans over and kisses the side of my head. "I'm always worn out after being around them too. I was hoping to spend some alone time with you tonight, but I think I like being right here, where I am. I feel most complete when I'm near the both of you."

My heart practically beats out of my chest from Kash's words. "How do you do it?" I question.

He smiles against the side of my head. "Do what?"

"Manage to make me melt from your words. And make me believe that nothing else in this world matters to you other than us."

"Because it's the truth. You're everything to me, Eden. And I will keep on proving that to you for as long as I live. You and Alec both."

"I love you so much, Kash," I whisper.

"Love you more, baby. Always will."

Kash truly has no idea that there's no possible way he can love me more than I love him.

He came into mine and Alec's lives and made them complete. I honestly can't imagine him not being here. The thought kills me.

He's ours. Kash is everything we need and want and we're never letting him go. We're not going anywhere. That's a promise...

BOOKS BY VICTORIA ASHLEY

Standalone Books

Wake Up Call

This regret

Thrust

Hard & Reckless

Strung

Sex Material

Wreck My World

Steal You Away

Walk of Shame Series

Slade

Hemy

Cale

Stone

Styx

Kash

Savage & Ink Series

Royal Savage

Beautiful Savage

Pain Series

Get Off On the Pain

Something For The Pain

Alphachat Series (Co-written with Hilary Storm)

Pay For Play

Two Can Play

Locke Brother Series (Co-written with Jenika Snow)

Damaged Locke

Savage Locke

Twisted Locke

ACKNOWLEDGMENTS

First and foremost, I'd like to say a big thank you to all my loyal readers that have given me support over the years and have encouraged me to continue with my writing. Your words have all inspired me to do what I enjoy and love. Each and every one of you mean a lot to me and I wouldn't be where I am if it weren't for your support and kind words.

Also, all of my beta readers, both family and friends that have taken the time to read my book and give me pointers throughout this process.

I'd like to thank another friend of mine, Clarise Tan from *CT Cover Creations* for creating my cover. You've been wonderful to work with and have helped me in so many ways.

Thank you to my boyfriend, friends, and family for understanding my busy schedule and being there to support me through the hardest part. I know it's hard on everyone, and everyone's support means the world to me.

Last but not least, I'd like to thank all of the wonderful book bloggers that have taken the time to support my book and help spread the word. You all do so much for us authors and it is greatly appreciated. I have met so many friends on the way and you guys are never forgotten. You guys rock. Thank you!

ABOUT THE AUTHOR

Victoria Ashley grew up in Illinois and has had a passion for reading for as long as she can remember. After finding a reading app where it allowed readers to upload their own stories, she gave it a shot and writing became her passion.

She lives for a good romance book with tattooed bad boys that are just highly misunderstood and is not afraid to be caught crying during a good read. When she's not reading or writing about bad boys, you can find her watching her favorite shows or hanging out with her family and pets.

FOR MORE INFORMATION VISIT:
https://victoriaashleyauthor.com